THE COMPLETE COLLECTION

FIGHTING LOVE

#GETHOOKED

TAPPING OUT

TAPPING OUT

The act of a struggling fighter signaling to the referee, usually by quickly tapping three times on the mat or opponent, that they give up and concede defeat.

ONE

BELLA
PRESENT DAY

TWO LINES MEAN PREGNANT. ONE LINE MEANS NOT.

Two lines. Pregnant.

One line. Not.

I sit on the edge of the tub in the bathroom with the door locked. My head is down as I stare at the tiled floor. There are thirty-four tiles. One is cracked. The grout is dirty. I should buy better cleaning supplies. The test said three minutes. It's probably been closer to ten, but I can't look. Will the test still be accurate if I don't look right away? Maybe I should take another one just in case.

Two lines and my life changes.

One line and nothing changes.

"Bella, you've been in there forever. Are we still going to dinner? The shower isn't even running. Gina is going to be here any minute." When I don't respond, Tristan knocks on the door again. "Bella!"

"I'll be out in a minute," I yell through the door, praying he can't hear the tremble in my voice. If he knows I'm freaking out, he will without a doubt force his way in here to find out what's going on, and right now, Tristan is probably the last person I want knowing what's going on.

Taking a deep breath, I stand and walk slowly toward the counter silently praying for one line—as if praying now is going to make a difference—if I pray right this second, the results will miraculously change in my favor. The second line will just disappear and all will be right with the world. Maybe I don't need a miracle. Maybe there's only one line. Maybe I'm freaking out over nothing. I swear to God if there's only one line, I'm getting on birth control today. Not that I'll need it, because if I'm not pregnant, I'm never having sex again. Okay, maybe not never again, but not anytime in the near future.

Closing my eyes, I take a deep breath to calm my nerves. After holding it in for a few seconds, I let out a slow exhale. Nope, doesn't work, I'm still freaking out. I open my eyes and stare at the test.

TWO

BELLA
FIVE YEARS AGO

I'M SITTING IN MY BEDROOM STARING OUTSIDE AT THE BEAUTIFUL weather. After five days straight of rain, I am sick of being indoors. The sun is shining and there isn't a cloud in sight. I'm dying to go for a run, but I'm not in the mood for another run on the treadmill indoors, so I text my two best friends: Marco and Tristan. Surely, one of them will want to join me for a run.

Group text: (Marco, Tristan, Bella)

Me: What are you guys doing? I'm bored.

Tristan: Mom is making me help clean the house. You?

Me: That sucks. Watching Something About Mary.

Marco: Of course you are...

Me: Oh hush! Wanna go for a run?

Tristan: Can't... cleaning!

Marco: Where?

Me: Red Rock.

Marco: Okay. Pick you up in twenty.

Me: Okay.

Tristan: Have fun

I pause my favorite movie and throw on my athletic shorts, a sports bra, and a tank top. Then I grab my favorite hoodie from over the back of my chair and throw it on over my head. Even though it's April in Vegas, the weather is cooler along the trails. I put on my socks and running shoes then grab my water bottle from my nightstand to fill it up in the kitchen. Once I'm dressed and ready to go, I grab the hair tie from around my wrist and throw my thick mane up into a ponytail.

As I'm leaving my room, I get a text, so I stop and check it.

Lucas: Wanna hang out?

Me: Can't

I stuff my phone into the front pocket of my hoodie then pull it back out.

Me: Sorry. Another time?

Ever since starting high school this year, it feels like everything is changing. For so long, I was just Bella, the MMA fighter. Guys always saw me as one of them. But this year, something shifted.

I look at myself in the mirror to see if anything significant has changed, but I'm still just… me. I have chocolate brown hair that has a natural curl to it and matching brown eyes just like my dad. I am on the skinnier side from years of working out but was blessed with decent cleavage. I take a closer look in the mirror. My lips are naturally full like my mom's, and my skin tone is an olive color like my dad's. Most people say I'm the perfect mixture of both my parents.

While I don't think I'm ugly, I don't think I've suddenly morphed into some hot chick. I don't wear makeup, my hair is almost always up in a ponytail out of my face, and I can usually be found wearing nothing but athletic attire when I'm not in my school uniform, since I pretty much live and breathe fighting.

My phone dings again.

Lucas: Sure. Maybe we can go to the movies?

Not having any idea how I want to respond to his question, I close out the text and put my phone away. I don't think I look any different than I did last year, but for some reason the guys are acting like I'm the new girl in town. I was born in Las Vegas and have lived here my entire life, so I don't get it. I take one last look at myself in the mirror then turn my light off and head downstairs.

"Mom! Dad!" I yell as I walk through the living room. "I'm going running with Marco."

No answer.

I get to the kitchen and see my younger siblings—Nathan and Lilly—sitting at the bar eating a bowl of cereal. Nathan is five years younger than me and Lilly is seven years younger. Long story short, my parents met when they were young, real young. My mom was eighteen and fresh out of high school and my dad was twenty-two. They fell for each other instantly but were both heading in different directions in life. My mom had no idea she was pregnant when they parted ways, and once she knew, she had no way to get ahold of my dad. Five years later, they found each other, and surprise! I was in tow. Once they fell back in love, they got married and then came my brother and sister.

"Hey, where are Mom and Dad?" I grab an apple from the fridge, my go-to fruit in the morning, and take a bite, then fill up my bottle with cold water and ice.

"In their room," Nathan says through a mouthful of cereal. I look at the clock. It reads 8:00. There's only one reason my parents would still be in their room this late and I don't even want to think about that reason. Sure, I'm aware that's how my siblings and I were brought into this world but still…

"Okay, well, let them know I went running with Marco."

"Ugh. Running." Lilly scrunches her little nose in disgust. She clearly takes after our mom when it comes to exercise, which means it doesn't happen. Like at all. Give my mom a book and a comfy couch and she's good to go. My dad, on the other hand, is a retired UFC fighter and owns a couple UFC training facilities, including one here in Las Vegas, called Cooper's Fight Club. While I enjoy curling up with a good book on a rainy day, I've grown up in the gym and will choose anything athletic over lounging around like a couch potato.

"Can I go?" Nathan asks. Like me, Nathan enjoys the more physical activities. He's not really into fighting, but he loves to sweat. He usually spends his days at the recreational center my dad and his friends started years ago. It's a sport's complex for kids and teens to spend their time at as opposed to running the streets. Nathan is really into football and for only being ten years old, he's actually really good at it.

"Not today. I'm hoping to get in at least seven miles. How about we go for a run together around the neighborhood tomorrow after school?"

"Okay, cool," Nathan says, shoving more cereal into his mouth. I finish eating my apple and throw the core in the garbage. I grab a cereal bar and my bottle of water and head toward the front door to wait for Marco as my parents come down the stairs.

"Morning. Just getting up?" I give them a knowing look.

"Actually, we've been up for a couple hours. We just had to go upstairs to…" My mom blushes at the realization she's about to be busted.

So, of course, my dad saves her. "Find something. Where are you going?" *Good change of subject, Dad.*

"I'm going jogging over at Red Rock with Marco."

"Have a good run, honey." My mom gives me a quick kiss on my cheek before going to the kitchen.

"Make sure you warm up good first," my dad says. Always in trainer mode.

"You got it."

Marco pulls up in his black Audi A5, a birthday present from his parents for his eighteenth birthday. I yell bye to my parents and run out the door toward his car. I still have ten months until I turn sixteen, but I'm hoping I get something half as hot as his car.

"Hey!" I say, getting in and putting on my seatbelt.

"Morning Belles," he replies.

Just like I do every time I get in his car, I begin to mess with the music. I grab the auxiliary cord and plug my phone in, clicking play on my playlist.

"Damn, Bella. It's too early in the morning for your girly shit."

"Don't talk trash about Avril. She's badass." I stick my tongue out and Marco rolls his eyes at me but still lets me turn it up.

The ride to Red Rock is about twenty-five minutes and the entire way I sing the lyrics to the songs obnoxiously. Marco shakes his head, but he's smiling. Our friendship has always been easy. Even when he hit high school, and I was much younger, things pretty much stayed the same between us. Sure, he made new friends and would hang out with them occasionally, but he still made fighting and training his number one priority which meant I still saw him daily at my dad's gym. He's never cared that I'm six years younger than him. He's always treated me like his equal.

Then, when he turned eighteen and started fighting professionally, I was a little older, and in the back of my mind I thought for sure he would forget about me and our friendship, but here we are almost three years later and still hanging out like we always have. Marco knows what fighting means to me and he's amazing about encouraging and supporting me.

The only person I'm closer to than Marco is Tristan. Tristan and I have been friends since we were born (okay, not really, but pretty much). But while Tristan loves to fight and enjoys it as a hobby, he doesn't really plan to go professional with it. He has mentioned taking the training route like his dad or even possibly becoming a sports agent one day. Who knows.

Fighting, in some shape or form, has been a part of our lives for as far back as I can remember. Marco's dad, Caleb, is a retired fighter from the UFC just like my dad, and Marco's mom is a doctor who runs a sports medicine clinic. My mom does the accounting at the rec center and at my dad's gym. Tristan's dad, Kaden, is a trainer at the gym, and his mom, Ashley, runs the rec center. My dad's best friend Bentley used to be a UFC fighter but quit to become a stay-at-home dad years ago, and his wife, my aunt Kayla, who pretty much helped raise me for the first four years of my life, works with Marco's mom at the sports clinic as a physical therapist.

See what I mean? Fighting is my life. My dream is to one day become a UFC women's champion. Marco understands where I'm coming from because his goal is just like mine. Since he started fighting, he has been in several fights in the last couple years and is undefeated in his weight class. His most recent fight was a few weeks ago and he was the main card event on Pay-Per-View. It's the first fight he made seriously good money on, especially since he won, but more importantly he has become a household name. He has women showing up to the gym wanting to go out with him, they are stalking his social media, and guys will ask him for his autograph while we're out somewhere.

Watching him fight and win is amazing. If Marco can do it then I know I can as well. He might be older but I've been fighting longer. I can't wait to turn eighteen and join the UFC, and I *will* join the UFC because I am determined.

"You ready to do this?" Marco parks his car in the parking lot and turns to me, his smile making my heart beat just a little out of rhythm. With eyes the color of onyx, raven-colored hair shaved short, and caramel colored skin courtesy of his Hispanic roots, Marco Michaels is a damn good-looking guy. Then you add his carefree attitude and his fit body, and it's no wonder girls swoon over him on a regular basis.

I ignore the way his smile makes me feel and answer him. "Yep!"

We get out of the car and walk to the trail. After warming up and stretching, we start on our run. While Marco could easily outrun me, he always runs next to me, keeping at the same pace. We run side by side in comfortable silence. The only noise is my app letting us know when we hit each mile. After the third mile, Marco slows down.

"Holy shit! I feel like I haven't run in years." Marco comes to a standstill, sitting on a rock on the side of the dirt trail.

"What have you been doing the last few weeks since you won your fight?" I laugh, continuing to jog in place to keep up the momentum.

"Basking in the glory of my win," he jokes.

"Well, you need to bask in the glory of this run. Let's go!" I take off running to get a head start knowing Marco will follow and catch up to me in no time, but when I turn the corner, I don't see the huge ass rock in my way. My foot hits it, and because there's nothing but air around to catch my fall, I fall onto the ground right onto my knees.

"Ow!" I roll over onto my butt, holding onto my legs. My knees hit the hard ground. That shit hurt. Bad.

"You okay?" Marco kneels to check on my knees.

"I'm fine. It just hurts."

"Let me see." He sits next to me and grabs my legs, putting them on top of his. Both my knees are bright red and lightly bleeding.

"We need to clean these up in case there are pieces of rock in your cuts." Marco rubs his hands down my leg causing my stomach to do flip-flops.

"I'm fine," I insist, trying to move my legs out of his reach.

"Stop. Let me clean your knees." He grabs my legs and holds onto them tight. Then he grabs his shirt from the back and lifts it over his head, leaving his sweaty front on display. I divert my attention back to my cuts.

Taking his bottle of water, Marco wets the shirt and gently rubs each of my knees. I flinch when the material hits my cuts.

"Sorry," he says softly. He leans over and gently blows on the cuts, making my stomach clench and my heart go erratic. After both my knees are clean, he stands then reaches down to help me up as well. As I come up onto my feet, my body hits his, not realizing how hard he was tugging me up. Our faces are close, only inches apart. He glances down at me and sighs, his cool breath hitting me. It smells like the peppermints he's always sucking on. Our eyes lock and we kiss.

And holy. Shit. Do we kiss.

His lips start off soft just barely touching mine like he's testing the waters, unsure of himself. Our eyes are still open, neither of us daring to be the first to blink. My heart is pounding, and his breathing is heavy. When my lips move in sync with his, his eyes close, his kiss becoming more aggressive. My head tilts to the side and his tongue finds its way inside. Marco's hands leave mine and land on my butt, pulling me closer to him until our sweaty bodies are lined up with no space between us.

Our kiss goes from sweet and gentle to frantic and desperate within seconds. Our tongues entwining with each other. I finally close my eyes and sink into his hold. Just as I think I'm getting the hang of this, it stops. Marco's lips leave mine and he backs up.

"Shit." His hands come up to his face, his head shaking in disbelief. I don't even know what to say. I would be lying if I said I've never imagined what it would be like to be kissed by Marco. I'm a teenage girl, of course I have. But I never imagined it would be so… Wow! This is my first time being kissed, and if this is what my first kiss feels like… well, I can't even imagine it getting any better than that.

"Shit," Marco hisses again. His head is tilted to the sky now like he's praying to the heavens above. He's breathing like he just ran ten miles and his fists are clenched at his sides.

"Umm…" I start to say having no idea what to continue with. What I want to say is "Let's do that again," but something tells me Marco's "Shit" isn't a good *shit,* more like a *What the hell was I thinking* shit.

"We need to get back," he says, and without waiting for me, he turns around and starts running back to his car. I run after him, but unlike every time we've run together, this time Marco doesn't wait for me.

"Should we… maybe…talk about this?" I finally ask when I catch up to him outside of his car.

"Later," is all he says.

He hits the key fob unlocking the doors and gets in, and without waiting for me to turn on the music like he always does, he turns it on himself. He turns it up loud, making it clear he doesn't want to talk. *Okay, fine*, I think to myself. We will talk later, like he said. It'll give me time to process what happened.

Tomorrow.

We will talk about this tomorrow.

Once we have both processed what just happened, we'll discuss this.

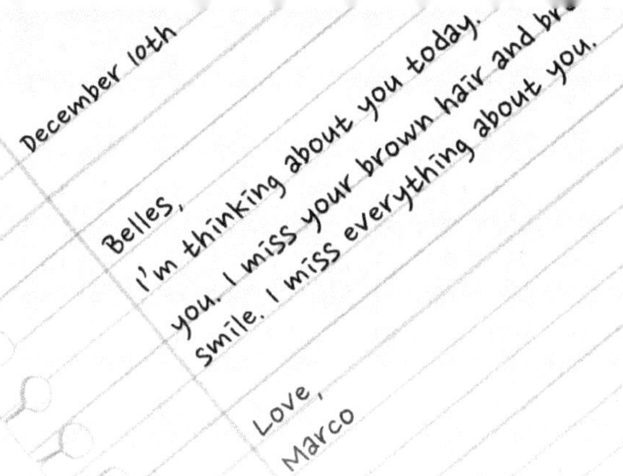

THREE

BELLA
ROUGHLY FOUR YEARS AGO

"BELLA, ARE YOU READY TO GO?"

"Yeah, just give me a minute." I apply a thin coat of clear lip gloss to my lips—just enough to make them shiny—and take one last look at myself in the mirror.

"Bella, let's go!" Tristan yells to me from downstairs. Our parents are out tonight for a fundraiser for the rec center and Lilly is staying at Hayley and Caleb's house along with Tristan's younger twin sisters, Morgan and Emma. Nathan is spending the night at his friend's house, and Tristan and I are going to a bonfire at a friend's house from the gym whose parents are out of town. He lives down the street from Tristan on a bunch of property.

"Coming!" I grab my hoodie off the back of my chair. It's February in Nevada which means the weather can change at any time, so while it's in the seventies right now, the temperature can easily drop where the party is happening. Unlike my neighborhood where houses are no more than a few feet from each other, the houses in Tristan's neighborhood are all on several acres of land in the outskirts, which makes it the perfect place for bonfire parties.

I fly down the stairs and am about to run out the door when Elsa, my dog, comes running toward me, wagging her tail. Bending down, I pet her under her chin just like she likes. My parents bought Elsa for me for Christmas ten years ago. Technically, she's the family pet, but she loves me the most. She follows me around when I'm home and sleeps at the end of my bed every night.

"Bye, Elsa. You be a good dog while I'm gone." Her tail wags harder, hoping I'll say something indicating she can go with me.

"C'mon! When are you getting your car fixed?" Tristan opens the front door for me. I close it behind us and lock it, then follow behind him to his truck. My parents bought me the cutest Volvo SUV for my birthday a couple weeks ago, and of course, my luck, I parked it at the gym and some idiot who wasn't looking where he was going, hit it! So now, I'm carless until it gets fixed.

"It's at the body shop now. My dad said it should be done by the end of next week."

When we drive up to Brandon's house, people are already pulling in and parking. "Hey Brandon!" I wave to him and he comes over and gives me a hug.

"My parents would kill me if anyone goes inside so we need to keep it outside. Can you help me with the drinks?"

"Of course!"

Brandon steers everyone around the side while I go inside to see what he has going on. I find a bunch of drinks and a bag of ice on the counter. After pouring the ice into the cooler, I throw the sodas and waters inside and attempt to pull it out back.

"Jesus, this is heavy," I say out loud.

"Need some help?" I jump at the sound of the deep voice that has ability to make me smile or frown, and turn around.

"What are you doing here?" I ask, hoping my words come across cold to hide the nervousness I'm suddenly feeling.

"I'm in town visiting my parents. I was at the gym visiting my dad when Tristan and Brandon were discussing the party. Tristan invited me."

"Well, it's about time. You really upset your mom leaving for so long." I look down at the cooler and add, "I can handle it myself." Then I silently curse Tristan for inviting Marco even though he doesn't know what happened last year. I turn back around, grabbing the side handle, and lift it up a few inches, willing the heavy ass cooler to drag. Of course it doesn't.

"Here, let me help you." Marco reaches for the handle, his hand grazing mine, and I pull away, the cooler dropping to the floor with a loud thud.

Marco's body is close to mine, too close, so I take a step back, and he frowns.

"Can we talk?"

"I need to get the food and drinks outside."

"Okay… later?"

"Sure, we can have this conversation next year," I say dryly.

Marco frowns. "Don't be like that."

"Don't be like what, Marco?" I ask defensively. "Don't be like you? Choosing to run away to avoid dealing with shit?"

"What we did that day… When we…" Marco closes his eyes like

he's in too much pain to even finish the sentence.

"Kissed." I finish it for him, hoping I'm making him uncomfortable. "We kissed."

"Yeah. It was wrong. You were fifteen years old, Belles. A fucking teenager. I was twenty-one. It never should have happened."

"Oh, give me a damn break. It was a kiss. And then you ran away like a ball-less jerk to another freaking state!" Marco and I are standing less than a foot apart, my hands are on my hips, and his hands are curled into fists by his side. He goes to open his mouth to speak when the back door opens.

"Everything okay in here?" We avert our eyes toward Tristan, his eyebrows dipped in confusion. His gaze bounces from me to Marco and back to me again waiting for one of us to answer.

"Everything's fine," I say. "I can't carry the cooler. I put the ice in it and now it's too heavy."

Tristan studies me for a minute then nods once. "No problem. I'll grab it." He takes the cooler and lifts it like it weighs nothing, carrying it outside.

Just as I'm about to follow him out the door, Marco grabs my hand and pulls me down the hallway. When he turns the knob, it's locked. He goes to the next door and it opens. Tugging me inside the bathroom, he closes the door behind us, caging me in against the door, both hands on either side of me, palms flat against the door.

"I miss you, Belles."

"Could have fooled me." I tilt my chin up in defiance staring straight at Marco. "I'm pretty sure you moved to a whole other state just to get away from me." Even I can hear the hurt in my voice, so I avoid looking at Marco, trying to calm myself down.

With one hand, he grabs my chin, forcing me to look at him. "I'm sorry. You are one of my best friends. I freaked out."

"You don't say?"

Marco smirks at me. "Still a smartass."

"What do you want, Marco?"

"I want our friendship back."

I sigh and shake my head. I want more than that. I want to discuss the kiss and the way it made me feel. I want to kiss him again and see if the butterflies come back. But if all he wants is friendship then it's clear he didn't feel what I felt when we kissed, which means I have no choice but to let it go. Sweep it under the rug just like he's doing. I don't want to lose our friendship. Marco means too much to me.

"Okay."

"Okay?" He looks at me incredulously.

"Okay," I say again. We stand there for a moment and I silently beg him to change his mind, to kiss me, to do something, anything, but instead he simply smiles and backs away from me.

"Good." *Not good.*

We both leave the bathroom and go out back to join everyone around the bonfire. The speakers are blaring country music and people are already drinking and having a good time. Brandon made it clear, if someone drinks they have to give him their keys and spend the night. He has a huge yard, like acres of land, and most people will be pitching tents to spend the night.

Marco finds a seat around the bonfire and sits. I can't be near him right now, so I find a few girls from school and join them.

"Bella!" Joslynn squeals, giving me a hug. "I saw you walk out with that hottie. Anything going on there?" She waggles her eyebrows and the other girls all giggle. Because Marco is so much older, unless someone goes to the gym we go to, they won't know him.

"No, he's just an old friend."

"Would you mind if I go talk to him?" Kimberly asks. An uneasy feeling in my gut washes through me and I feel sick. I want to scream at her and tell her, "*Yes, I mind!*" but instead I grab a beer from a cooler and say, "Go for it." Then give her a fake smile.

Four beers later and I'm feeling tipsy. The amount of cardio I'm going to have to do tomorrow to burn off these wasted calories is going to be ridiculous. This is why I never drink—besides the fact that I'm underage and my parents would kill me if they knew. Having to burn off the calories isn't worth the few hours of drinking. It makes me sluggish the next day and I feel gross when trying to train.

But watching Kimberly shamelessly flirt with Marco the last couple hours is enough to make even the biggest saint drink. It's getting a bit chilly so I walk over closer to the fire. There are no available seats so I just stand a couple feet from the pit, sipping on my beer.

"Bella." I glance over see who's calling my name and spot Marco. He gives me a lazy smile and nods his chin, beckoning me to him. I look around and don't see Kimberly anywhere near him.

"Sit with me." Marco pats his thigh, and I eye him suspiciously.

"Where's Kimberly?"

"Who?" He gives me a confused look.

"The girl you were talking to for practically the entire night."

"Oh… I don't know." He shrugs. "Come here."

I walk closer to him, and before I can decide whether to stay standing or sit down on the ground next to him, Marco grabs my hips, and making the decision for me, pulls me onto his lap.

"Marco." I sigh.

"What?" His lips are right near my face and I can smell the alcohol on his breath mixed with his signature smell of peppermint. I scan the area for Tristan. The last thing I need is him seeing me sitting on Marco's lap.

"You're drunk," I say to him.

"So are you. Just sit with me. Your body is cold. I can warm you up." He twists my body, so I'm sitting across his lap, and rubs his hands over my arms, eliciting a chill down my spine.

We sit like this for who knows how long, staring at the fire crackling and drinking our beers. At first my body is stiff up against Marco's, but after a while my body loosens up and I get comfortable in his arms.

I don't know if it's from the alcohol or Marco's body against mine, but as I cuddle closer to him, my body goes completely lax.

"Bella, are you awake?" Marco whispers in my ear. I can feel his soft breath against me.

"Yes."

He shifts my body a little and I feel something hard against me. Holy shit! Is that his…?

"Do you want me to get off you?" I ask.

Marco doesn't answer but instead lifts me and turns me to face him so I'm straddling his thighs

"Marco," I warn.

"I just want to see your face." He gives me a boyish grin and my belly flip-flops. Before I can think of a valid argument—because apparently when you're drunk your brain works a little slower—his lips are pressing against mine. My head tells me I should pull away and stop him—we've both been drinking, this can't end well—but my heart and hormones win out and I kiss him back. Hard.

My tongue enters his mouth, and he sighs in contentment. It's all it takes to make me forget about every reason we shouldn't be doing this. He tastes like beer and peppermint, and I crave that taste because it's all Marco. His hands go to my butt, massaging me and pulling me closer to him. Shamelessly, I grind against him not evening thinking about the fact we're surrounded by dozens of people.

He must realize where we are because he stands, still holding on to me. "Wrap your legs around me."

I do as he says and he carries me away from the fire. I think he's going to walk us inside, but instead he walks us around to the side of the house. When he gets to a darker area where the music can barely be heard, he pushes me up against the wall and goes back to kissing me. My hands go to his hair, my fingers running up and down the back of his shaved head, then they go to his neck.

Marco ends our kiss abruptly only to move his lips downward. He trails soft, wet kisses down the side of my neck and over my collarbone.

"Bella?" Both our bodies stiffen at my name being called, my eyes shooting open. Standing behind Marco is Mason. Mason is a UFC fighter Tristan's dad trains. Over the last year Tristan and I have started to hang out with him more often, especially since he lives with Tristan. Nobody really knows the entire story, but when Mason showed up here asking to be trained, Ashley found out he was homeless and without any family. She insisted he move in with them and he and Tristan share a room.

Marco's eyes snap to mine, quickly sobering up. He drops his hands from my butt, my body sliding down the wall. I come close to not landing on my feet, but Marco reacts quickly and catches me, making sure I'm steady before he lets go of me and turns around to face Mason.

"Marco?" Mason looks confused. "Sorry… I didn't mean to interrupt. I saw Bella and…"

"No, it's cool man." Marco's body is straight as a board.

"I'm just going to…." Mason tilts his head toward where the party is still going on, then starts to walk away.

"Wait, Mason." Marco calls out and Mason turns around. "Can you do me a favor? Can you not say anything to—"

"Say no more," Mason cuts him off, nodding in agreement before walking away. Marco stands with his back to me for several long seconds, and when he finally speaks, he doesn't even look at me.

"This shouldn't have happened."

"Are you freaking serious right now?" I yell louder than I mean to causing Marco to turn around.

"We've both been drinking. Things got out of hand."

"Nothing even happened."

"Which is for the best. I need to go."

"Of course, walk away… that's what you do best."

"I didn't mean for this to happen. I missed you. I just wanted my best friend back. And there you were, looking like you always do." He nods toward me. "And Damn it, Belles, I couldn't help myself. This is why I moved!" Marco yells, his arms flaring out. "I knew if I stayed here, I wouldn't be able to resist you. Fuck!" He turns and punches the thing closest to him, a ceramic potted planter. It shatters everywhere. He gives me one last look before he walks away, once again.

FOUR

BELLA
TWO YEARS AGO

I CAN'T BELIEVE AFTER TWO YEARS OF AVOIDING HOME, HE picks now to show up. It's like he does this shit on purpose to torment me. He should have stayed away. He should have stayed in California where he lives and given me the five more months I thought I had to come to terms with the fact that I'll be living less than thirty minutes from him.

But no, Marco had to grace everyone with his presence. I mean, sure, I can't really fault him. His dad did fly to San Diego and practically drag him back here to join them on our yearly traditional Christmas trip to Breckenridge Ski Resort. But would it have killed him to shoot me a text and give me some warning so I wouldn't have to find out in the middle of the mall food court in front of his mom, Tristan, and Mason?

I know at some point I'm going to have to deal with all this. I'm moving to San Diego to attend the University of California after all. Sure, it's a big city, but there's only one UFC training facility, which means we will be training in the same building. I know it's my choice to move there. I know the potential situation I'm putting myself into. Don't ask me why I'm doing this to myself. Does a part of me miss Marco? Of course. Do I sometimes hope by moving there we'll rekindle our friendship? Sure. Do I secretly wish that maybe one day we could be something more? Yeah, I do.

But at the same time, I think I want to move there just to stick it to him. Because fuck him for running away from me.

You know what? I don't even know why I'm so stressed over all this. I'm not the one who ran away. Twice. I'm not the one who started shit I couldn't finish. Screw him. He's the one who should feel uncomfortable, not me.

It's Christmas eve, and somehow, I've managed to avoid Marco for the most part, aside from the two-hundred-dollar bet I lost on the slopes when I said I could outboard him… and lost… twice. It hasn't been easy since we're staying on the same property, but luckily, he's sleeping out in the guesthouse of my uncle Bentley's parents' cabin. I've been spending a lot of time reading at the resort, snowboarding, and taking walks. Pretty much doing anything to avoid coming face to face with Marco. Which makes me mad because I don't have any reason to avoid him. I didn't do anything wrong. He did. He chose to walk away, leaving our friendship in limbo over a couple of damn kisses.

It's late, probably almost midnight, and everyone is sleeping. I should be asleep as well, but I can't stop thinking about Marco, wondering if this is my last chance to talk to him before I move to California. I know two people can live and train in the same city and avoid each other, but that's not what I want. Marco has been in my life for so long. The idea of going another year or more without talking makes me sad.

Concluding it's best to stop dwelling and obsessing, and just go to him so we can talk, I grab my cell phone and head out back quietly so I don't wake anyone up.

I get to the guesthouse and knock before I chicken out. About a minute later, Marco answers the door. He's standing there in nothing but his tight grey briefs, his chiseled abs taunting me. He opens his mouth to yell at whoever was banging on his door, but when he sees it's me, his mouth closes momentarily.

"Bella." One word. Just my name. Yet it has so many emotions behind it.

"So, about that bet…" I have no idea where that comes from.

"You here to pay up?" Marco smirks.

"I'm here to discuss payment options. Can I come in?"

Marco studies me for a moment. What he's looking for, I'm not sure, but whatever it is, he must find it, because he opens the door wider allowing me access. And suddenly all the anger I had built up, all the words I had rehearsed to say to him, go straight out the window, lust taking over in its place.

I throw myself at Marco, my arms going around his neck while my legs hop up to wrap around his waist, not even considering he might reject me, that he might push me away. But he doesn't, instead he catches me with one hand, his other hand slamming the door behind us. I assume he's walking us to his bedroom, but I pay no attention, keeping my focus on the man carrying me.

Our mouths collide, and we're all teeth and tongues and hands. Marco lays me on the bed and breaks our kiss. He stares at me for a moment and I hold my breath, afraid he's going to run.

"Fuck it," is all he says before his mouth is back on mine.

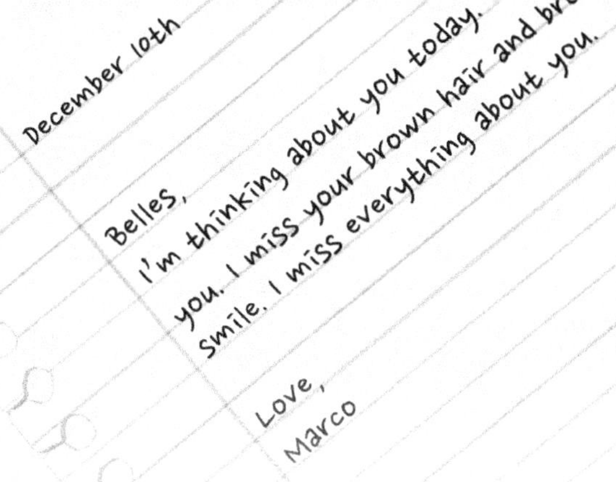

FIVE

MARCO
FOUR MONTHS AGO

"LADIES AND GENTLEMEN, IN ROUND TWO BY WAY OF A chokehold, the new Light Heavyweight champion… Marco 'The Maniac' Michaels!"

The crowds' screams—which were already loud—go deafening. The belt is put on me and it seems in this moment like my life is almost complete. My dad comes running to me from the corner and envelops me in a hug. With the fight being in Vegas, there was no doubt my dad wouldn't be ringside with me.

The rest of my team all come over to give me hugs. I know this is only the beginning of my career as a fighter, but fuck if this doesn't feel damn good. With sixteen wins, I am undefeated and now carry the championship belt for my weight class.

After a couple quick interviews in the octagon, I head to the locker room to get the medical attention I need and take a shower.

"Son, I am so damn proud of you," my dad says again as my mom rubs alcohol over the few cuts on my face. I always insist—even though she isn't the medic for the UFC anymore and is now running her own sports medicine clinic—that she be my medic at any fight she can attend, and she always agrees.

Hayley and Caleb Michaels are the two people who matter the most to me in this world. They saved my life thirteen years ago from my druggy biological mom. Caleb literally saved my life from drug dealers who were going to kill me, and Hayley took me in and adopted me like I was her own. The two of them are the reason my sister was adopted by Bentley and Kayla, and has lived a life most kids only dream of. I owe them everything, and I doubt I will ever be able to pay them back. The fact is, if it wasn't for them, I would either be dead or still on the streets selling drugs to take care of my mom and sister.

"Fuck yes!" My best friend Logan stalks into the locker room and comes at me for a hug. "Fuck yes!" he repeats. I met Logan when he started training at the UFC training center in San Diego about three years ago and we became quick friends.

"You too, man! You rocked your fucking fight!"

"Hell yeah! Let's go! We need to celebrate! And since you're the champion, I'm driving."

We both shower and change clothes to go out. My parents join us, along with some of my parents' friends. Because the fight was in Vegas and not California, only a few other fighters from my training camp are here as well.

We agree on Club Eleven and Logan calls ahead to let them know we're on our way. With the win tonight being on Pay-Per-View, it's going to be crazy no matter where we go. We jump into Logan's rental car, a beautiful Porsche 911. Like me, Logan comes from a family who makes a decent living, but where I prefer to save my money, in fear of one day not having it, Logan likes to spend his anywhere and everywhere he can. When you've never gone without a meal for days at a time, you can't understand what it's like.

I pull my phone out and see a bunch of texts from people congratulating me on my win. I type out a thank you to each one. Then I see one from someone I haven't spoken to in two years: Bella.

Belles: Congratulations

It's only one word, but it weighs down my stomach like lead. For a while I used to see her almost daily at the gym, until I figured out her schedule and since then have gone out of my way to work out and train when she isn't there. She and Tristan moved here to attend college in San Diego about a year and a half ago, and I thought for sure she would push for us to pick up where we left off, but she hasn't so much as spoken a single word to me, and in return I haven't tried to talk to her.

The way I left shit over Christmas break was fucked up, but that seems to be how it goes with me when it comes to Bella. I met her when I was twelve years old. At the time, she was only six, but we quickly became close. While she and Tristan were already friends, Bella and I formed a different kind of friendship. I can't explain it, but she was everything to me.

She never asked questions. She just wanted to fight. She pushed me to my limits and encouraged me. Everything was fan-fucking-tastic until she hit puberty. I don't know when it happened, but I stopped looking at her like one of the guys and saw her for who she was... who she is: a beautiful fucking woman.

The first time I kissed her, I knew I was fucked. I ran like the little bitch I was—well, still am—straight to California. I saw her a year later at a party and, if it wasn't for Mason stopping us, we would have probably fucked right there against the wall.

You would think those two close encounters would be enough for me to stay the hell away from her, but then my dad begged me to join them for Christmas, and there she was looking stunning as always at my door, in her tiny fucking pajamas throwing herself into my arms, and like the dog I am, I thought with the wrong fucking head.

I took her virginity that night. We had sex… no, fuck that, it was more than sex with Bella. We made love a few times that night, but then when I woke up and reality hit me, once again, I ran. Bella is probably the best person I know. She's selfless and giving and she cares about everyone around her. She is genuine and sweet and so damn smart. Any guy would be lucky to have her. But I can't be that guy for multiple reasons:

One: I'm six years older than her. Sure, now it's not really a big deal, but back then we would have gotten major shit for being together; not legally, because it's legal where we lived in Nevada, but her parents would have killed me.

Two: Our parents are best friends and work together. What if we gave it a go and then it didn't work out? And while I'm Caleb and Hayley's kid, I'm still me, which leads me to the next reason.

Three: My bloodline is tainted. My biological mother was a druggie whore. She wasn't always that way but once she met my biological father she fell down the rabbit hole and never came back up. My biological father is Ricardo Sanchez. He's not alive anymore, but when I hired a private investigator to look him up, I found out he had multiple wives illegally, as well as several children. All his wives are druggies just like my mom.

Seeing how much he fucked up each and every one of those women, I made the choice to never settle down. There's no way I'm taking the chance of fucking up another woman, let alone procreating. Fuck that.

So, that's why I had to walk away from Bella. Every day I miss her something fierce. I see her at the gym and want to go to her. I want to hug her and hold her and go back to being best friends again. There's a hole in my heart where she belongs. But we crossed the line and there's just no going back from that.

I'm assuming by the fact that I'm still alive, she never told anybody about us. Because if she had, I'm fairly certain her father would have hunted me down and killed me. Tristan and I still talk and hang out. He asked me once what happened with me and Bella, but when I asked him to drop it, he did.

Tristan is a good guy. I thought for a while, he and Bella might end up together, but it seems they are just good friends. They share an apartment right off campus, which is situated between the college and the gym. I live on the beach in a kickass condo with my cousin, Mathias.

One good thing that came from my mom—other than my sister Chloe—was her sister, my aunt Jenn and her son, Mathias. My dad found them for me and I used the excuse of wanting to get to know them as my reason for leaving for California so suddenly. My aunt had cut all ties with my mom so she had no idea my mom had overdosed all those years ago, but once I contacted her, she welcomed Chloe and me with open arms.

"Bro! Snap out of it!" I look at Logan and see we're parked in front of the club, the Valet guy standing there, waiting for me to get out of the car.

"Sorry. I was just thinking."

"No thinking tonight. Tonight, we celebrate. You drink, and I'll drive. You've earned a night of letting loose."

I glance down at my phone at Bella's text. There are so many ways I could respond to her text. I could reply with a simple thank you, leaving no room to continue the conversation, or I could tack on a 'How are you?' which would mean she would reply.

Knowing it's best not to lead her on, I go with a simple *thank you*, then shove my phone into my front pocket wishing things could be different but knowing they can't be.

IT'S THREE IN THE MORNING. EVEN THOUGH I'VE BEEN DRINKING, I'm not trashed. I've spent most of the night talking with my family and friends, especially those I don't get to see often. My parents and their friends have just left, and I promised Kayla I would be by in the morning to have brunch with them so I can visit with my sister before I head back to California. I can't believe my baby sister is thirteen years old.

"You ready to head out?" I ask Logan. He's been sweet talking some female all night and I wouldn't be surprised if I'm taking a taxi back so he can head out with her.

"Yeah, I'm ready." He stands from the booth and wobbles a little bit. I haven't seen him touch an ounce of alcohol all night, but…

"You good to drive?" I ask. "We can take a taxi back."

"No, I'm good. You know they'll tow my car if we leave it here overnight."

"All right."

We say bye to anybody still here then head to the valet stand to have them bring Logan's car around. Usually I stay with my parents when I come to visit, but with Logan and a couple of the other guys from our gym staying at the MGM Grand where the fight was held, I decided to room with them instead.

The valet opens our doors for us and I throw them a tip. Then Logan takes off back to the hotel. My phone dings with a text, and when I look to see who it is, I find myself disappointed it's not Bella.

Janell: Nice win tonight. See you when you get back <insert winky face>

Attached to her text is a photo of her lying in bed, naked.

Me: Thanks

I don't bother commenting on the photo. She sends them all the time. She already knows she's fucking hot, and she knows when I get back I'll be fucking her. She also knows that's all we'll be doing. Before I put my phone away, another text comes in.

Bella: I miss you

Well, fuck me. I didn't see that coming. I stare at my phone trying to figure out how to respond. It's three in the morning. I'm surprised she's still awake.

Me: Me too

I hover over the send button. Fuck! That sounds douchey. I hit backspace and type out **I miss you too**. Just as I'm about to hit send, the car jerks to the side. My head shoots up to see what's going on and suddenly the car is flipping in the air. I hear glass shattering as the car flips several times, then my head hits the side—or maybe the ceiling—I'm not sure. And everything goes black.

SIX

BELLA
THREE MONTHS AGO

"MARCO IS FINALLY HEALED ENOUGH TO COME HOME AND WILL be arriving this morning. Are you seriously not going to visit him?" Tristan gives me a look that tells me he thinks I'm being a bitch, but I don't give in.

"Marco and I haven't spoken in over two years. I'm not just showing up at his condo."

The truth is I've typed up several text messages to him but chicken out every time I go to hit send. The last text I sent him was me telling him I miss him and he never responded. The message said read so I know he saw it but he didn't reply. It was the night of his accident, the night he won the championship belt. I got emotional and tried to put myself out there. Unfortunately, he didn't reciprocate. I should give him the benefit of the doubt since it's possible the accident happened before he could respond, but I'm too scared to text him and put myself out there, again. What if he saw it and just didn't want to respond? God! I sound like such a wimp right now.

"For reasons nobody will clue me in on. Whatever happened between you two isn't important right now. The guy was in a car accident. He was nearly killed. Shit, Logan is still in a coma. Whatever beef you have with Marco should be put on the back burner. He needs us, Bella."

"Tristan, will you just leave her alone?" Gina, Tristan's bitchy girlfriend, gives me a saccharine smile, but I know it's fake as hell. Everything about her is fake. From her fake hair, to her fake nails, to her fake-ass personality. They met at the bar she works at and hit it off, which completely blows my mind. She's the opposite of everything

Tristan stands for. She smokes weed, dabbles in drugs, and has no goals for her future other than finding out where and when the next party is. To be honest, I don't even know what the hell Tristan sees in her but whatever. She apparently makes him happy and I guess that's all that matters.

"If she wants to visit Marco, she will. Can we just go, please? And we need to stop by Starbucks on the way. I need a coffee so badly. I have the worst hangover." Ugh! Her whiny voice is the equivalent to nails on a chalkboard… No! Worse! The equivalent of a knife scraping a ceramic plate.

"You wouldn't be hungover if you wouldn't have hit the bottle so hard last night." Tristan gives her a look that a parent gives a teenager who has misbehaved, and I have to hold back my eyeroll. I swear he spends ninety percent of their relationship trying to reign her in and change who she is. When will he realize he can't fix her?

"Tristan… can we please not do this? My head is going to explode."

Tristan sighs but nods in agreement grabbing his keys. Before they walk out the door, he gives me a look of disappointment. I grab my phone and pull up my text messages. Scrolling down, I find Marco's name. It still shows the message I sent him that night. I take a deep breath, then type out a text.

Me: I heard you're going home today. I'm glad you're okay.

There! He knows I care, but I'm not opening myself up to be rejected.

I stare at the phone for a few minutes, and when it dings—even though I'm staring at the damn phone!—I jump.

Marco: Thank you

Okay… I guess that's that. Another thank you as a reply pretty much makes it clear how he feels… or doesn't feel, in this case. I click out of the text message and click on YouTube. I have a fight coming up in four months and am determined to learn everything I need to about Shawna Fields. She is originally from Russia and has been fighting her entire life like me. She's currently undefeated just like I am, only she has twice as many wins under her belt as I do. It's not going to be a main fight, but if I can beat her, I'll be on my way to securing something bigger.

I watch three different videos, but I couldn't tell you what happens in any of them. My brain is mush. Ever since I found out Marco was in a horrific car accident, where his best friend Logan swerved to avoid a collision only to cause one of his own, leaving him in a coma and Marco with a broken arm, three broken ribs, and God knows what else, I haven't been able to focus on anything but thinking about Marco and how he's doing.

Because the accident was in Las Vegas, Marco and Logan were brought to the local hospital. After the doctors determined Logan was in a coma, Logan's parents had him moved to a private facility. Marco was in the hospital for about two weeks then he spent another couple weeks recovering at his parents' house. My dad asked if I wanted to fly over to visit Marco, but I told him I couldn't, using school as an excuse. With midterms next month, I need to stay on top of my studies.

The truth is I'm halfway through my sophomore year and surprisingly, I'm enjoying being in college and am on top of all my classes. I could have made a weekend trip to see Marco, but I just couldn't do it. I couldn't walk into his room and see him battered and bruised and broken. I couldn't see him after he almost lost his life. I wouldn't have been able to handle it. I would have lost it in front of everybody, and I can't do that. I have to keep it together because whether I like it or not, Marco doesn't want me the way I want him. I know he loves me in his own way, but it's not the way I love him, and it hurts too damn bad to be around him knowing I will never have his heart the way he has mine. The way he's had my heart for the last several years.

Deciding to get ahead on my homework, I grab my backpack and bring it over to the table. At the end of this year, Tristan and I are going to have to pick a major. Up until this point, we've taken all the same classes since it's just been the general subjects, but now we're almost done with them and will have to figure out what we want to earn a degree in.

Even though fighting is what I want to do with my life, I understand where my dad was coming from. I need to have a backup plan. Look what happened to Marco. Sure, he's expected to make a full recovery, but what if he wasn't? What if he could never fight again? Then what?

The problem is I have no damn clue what I want to do with my life outside of fighting. My mom told me I need to do some soul searching. I'm hoping something will just fall right into my lap.

I pull out my English II reading for the week. We're expected to read the current event article and write an argumentative essay on whether we agree with the topic. I read the article twice and still have no idea what the hell the person is arguing about. So, instead, I run into my room, change my clothes, and head to the gym to get a workout in. At least when I'm working out, I don't have to think.

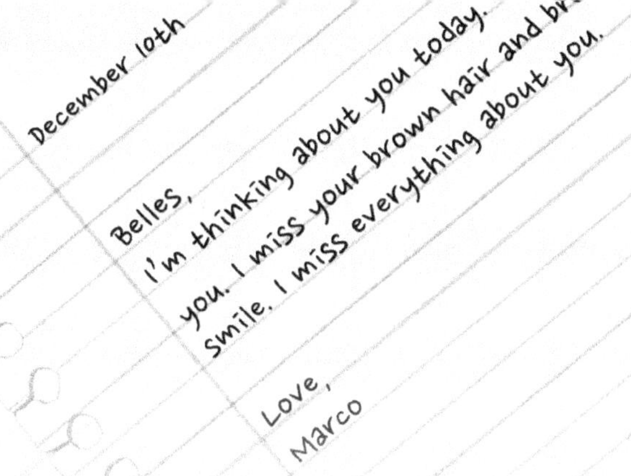

SEVEN

MARCO
TWO MONTHS AGO

FUCK! I AM IN SO MUCH GODDAMN PAIN. THE DOCTORS PREDICT I will make a full recovery but they can't be sure, and right now, I can't imagine ever being fully recovered. My arm is almost healed completely—they took the cast off at the doctor's appointment yesterday. My ribs and shoulder are also close to being healed. I'm still sore where the ribs were broken, but that's not the problem. The problem is my back.

When the Porsche flipped, I wasn't wearing my seatbelt, so I flew out of the vehicle while it was in motion. My back hit the concrete and I now have a herniated disc which is pressing on the nerves causing the pain to run from my ass down my leg.

The doctors are trying to treat the herniated disk with pain meds and chiropractic therapy before they go in to do surgery. Because of this herniated disk, I can't be cleared to workout at all. So, I'm stuck at home, not able to do shit all fucking day long.

When I told the doctor the pain meds weren't working, he upped my dose. The next time I told him, he told me he couldn't up the dose and to try using cold and hot compressions. What I want to do is take the cold and hot compression packs and shove them up his fucking ass.

I know I shouldn't be complaining. It could be worse, especially since I wasn't wearing a seatbelt. I could be in a fucking coma like Logan is. The thought of my best friend stuck in a hospital, unable to wake up, makes me sick. When the car flipped, he wasn't wearing his seatbelt either, and when he got flung from the vehicle, he hit his head hard. There was swelling in his brain and he went into a coma while being operated on. While there's still brain function, the doctors can't say if or when he will wake up.

My phone rings and it's Janell. I might not be in any place to have sex yet, but she sure as fuck gives good head.

"Yeah."

"What's wrong baby?" Her voice is high pitched and gives me a headache. I prefer her not talking, which means her mouth stays around my cock as much as possible.

"I'm in fucking pain, Janell."

"I can bring you something for that..." She's told me this same thing numerous times, and every time so far, I've turned her down. I don't want to become a druggy like my biological mom.

But how the hell am I ever supposed to get back to fighting if I can't get cleared because of the fucking pain I'm in.

"Okay," I tell her, then hang up without waiting for a response.

About thirty minutes later she knocks on my door then lets herself in. Mathias is at work, as usual, so it's just us.

"I brought you a couple different things to try," she says, waggling her eyebrows. Janell has bragged several times that her brother is a huge drug dealer and can get her anything she wants. She doesn't a lot drugs when we hang out, but I know through friends of ours she can party hard.

"I have coke, OxyContin, and Percocet." She hands me three baggies.

"My brother also gave me some heroin." She places a foiled square on the table.

"What the fuck, Janell! I'm not shooting up."

She rolls her eyes at me. "There are other ways to do heroin. It's a powder so you can heat it up in the foil and inhale it, or you can sniff it like you would coke. No needles necessary."

"I'm not doing coke or heroin." I grab the two baggies with pills from the table and decide on the Oxy. It's one step up from the shit my doctor prescribed me. I open the baggy and pop two of the pills into my mouth praying for some relief from this pain.

I close my eyes and let the drugs do their job and soon the numbness begins to take over. Maybe for a little bit all the pain will go away. I'll forget my best friend is in a fucking coma, that I can't fight, that Bella didn't even bother to come see me in the fucking hospital. Maybe for just a little while I can forget it all. I feel Janell's hands wandering up my leg, but I am finally at peace for the moment.

"Go away," I tell her before falling asleep.

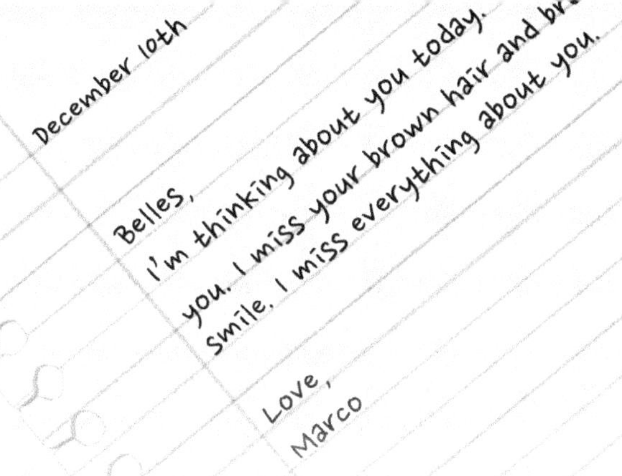

EIGHT

BELLA
FOUR WEEKS AGO

"WHAT DO YOU MEAN THERE'S A PARTY GOING ON AT MARCO'S place?" Tristan asks Gina while they're sitting on the couch watching one of her ridiculous reality shows. I hear Marco's name and instantly my ears perk up. It's been a month since Marco has been back in California and I've heard from my parents he's struggling with the fact that the doctor hasn't cleared him to exercise in any way.

"It's all over Facebook. Janell has invited everyone."

"Who's Janell?" I ask, trying to sound nonchalant while I'm sitting at the table studying for my math test. Tristan should be studying as well, but whenever Gina is around, she gets upset if he doesn't give her all his attention, and since she's not in college, she doesn't understand how much studying is required.

"Marco's girlfriend," Gina says. "She waitresses at Bradley's with me." I knew Tristan met Gina at the bar she waitresses at, but I didn't know she hangs out in the same circle as Marco.

"All right, let's go." Tristan sighs.

"Yes! This party is going to be lit." Gina jumps up, ready to head out the door.

"We're only going there to check on Marco. Caleb just texted me and said Mathias is out of town. He's afraid Marco might be sinking into some kind of depression. No drugs, Gina, please," Tristan pleads, and my heart breaks for my best friend. It's evident he cares about her, but it's also evident she cares more about getting high than taking his feelings into consideration.

"Do you need to get changed before we go?" I think he's still talking to Gina, but when I look up I see they're staring at me.

"Oh no, I'm not going to a party at Marco's. It's like one in the morning." I shake my head to put emphasis on my answer.

"Yeah, you are, because Caleb is worried about Marco and has asked me to go over there and check on him, and Marco hasn't answered any of our calls or texts."

"And how does that translate to me going to Marco's house?"

Tristan stands and walks over to me, leaning over the table with his fists hitting the tabletop. "Because regardless of why you and Marco aren't talking, he's our best goddamn friend. More so yours than mine. And if something is wrong, we're going to be there for him. So, for one fucking minute, put aside your petty bullshit and think about our friend."

Well, shit.

"Fine." I throw on a pair of skinny jeans, a loose tank top, and grab my Cooper's Gym hoodie.

We pile into Tristan's truck, and about twenty-five minutes pull up to what I assume is Marco's condo. Since we stopped talking before he moved, I've never seen the place he shares with his cousin, Mathias. Tristan said it's on the beach, but holy shit, this place is amazing.

Tristan finds a parking spot and we walk up the stairs to the second floor. I know exactly which condo is Marco's as soon as we reach the second-floor landing. There are people standing outside, the music is blaring, and his front door is wide open. There's got to be at least fifty people here.

"Let's split up and look for him," Tristan suggests. Gina sees some girls she knows and starts chatting and laughing with them. When we get inside, I'm shocked at what I see. There are drugs and liquor bottles scattered all over the table and counters. Pills, powder, there's even someone shooting up.

I start searching for Marco in the living room and notice Tristan is heading out to the back patio. So, I head in the opposite direction down the hall. The hallway is filled with people, forcing me to have to push through them. As I'm about to knock on the first door, a guy and girl come out. *Okay... guess he's not in there.* I glance inside and see it's a bathroom.

The second door is locked, so I knock a few times but nobody answers. I spot one more door a little farther down so I go to that door. It's unlocked, so I open it up slowly, afraid of what I might find. The room is pitch black, but I can see the silhouette of a body lying in the bed.

"Marco?" I whisper. Realizing there's no way he can hear me over the music, I say his name louder. "Marco?"

"Bella?" he responds, his voice gruff. When I know it's Marco in the room, I close the door behind me and lock it. It's hard to see and I trip over something on my way to him, but once I'm closer I can confirm it is in fact Marco. Sitting on the edge of the bed, I look around and don't see anyone else in the room.

"I'm not sure if you noticed but you have a party going on outside your room." I try to go for light to break the ice.

I hear him take a deep breath and release it. "Yeah, Janell loves her parties."

"Your girlfriend, right?"

"Janell? No, just a… no, she's not my girlfriend."

"Marco, there's a lot of drugs out there."

"Belles, I can't deal with whatever is going on out there." He sounds completely defeated. I reach into my back pocket and text Tristan, the phone illuminating the room.

Me: I found him in his room. I'm talking to him.

Tristan: I'll work on breaking up this party without causing a scene.

"How are you doing?" I ask, which is so stupid. I mean, really? The guy's best friend is in a coma and he can't train. Of course he's doing shitty.

Marco ignores my question and says, "C'mere, Belles." I scoot a bit closer to him. "Come sit next to me, please. I've missed you." This time I crawl across the bed and sit next to Marco. Now that I'm closer, I can see he isn't lying down—he's slouched but sitting up against his headboard.

Marco turns to face me, the little bit of light peeking through the blinds letting me see his face. "Damn, Belles. You're really here. I've missed you so much."

"It's only been a few months since you've seen me."

"Seeing you at the gym doesn't count. It's not the same." Marco runs his hand up my arm and cups my cheek. "I've missed you so fucking much."

I swallow thickly at his words because I've missed him just as much. It was easier to pretend I didn't miss him when he wasn't this close to me.

"Have you missed me too?" he asks.

I nod slowly, the lump in my throat preventing me from saying the words.

"It was your choice, Marco," I finally say after a few minutes of silence. "You pushed me away."

"I was trying to do the right thing." His fingers trace over my chin then move to my lips, up the curve of my nose, and down my cheek, like he's trying to relearn what I look like. It makes me think of what a blind person might do to learn the facial features of someone they can't see.

"We weren't doing anything wrong, Marco." I take his hand and bring it down to the bed. His touch is driving me insane. When I go to pull my hand away, he grabs it.

"I need you, Belles." Those four words send chills up my spine. He says them with such conviction I almost believe him.

"No, you don't," I whisper.

I feel the bed shift and suddenly Marco is hovering above me. "I need you, Bella. Please." His breath fans across my face and then his mouth is on me. His lips aren't gentle like they were in the past. They're rough and punishing. They don't taste like my Marco, and somehow, I find the strength to push him back a little, breaking our kiss.

"Marco…" I say because I don't know what the hell else to say.

"Please… Please, Bella. I just need to be close to you. I need my best friend back." The vulnerability in his words are my undoing. I know damn well I'm going to regret this tomorrow, but right now all I can think about is how much I love this broken man, and the fact that he needs me.

"Okay," is all I can get out before his lips sear into mine. He's kneeling in front of me, and not wasting any time, he grabs my hoodie and tank top and pulls it over my head, then he grabs his own and throws it all to the ground.

Sitting back, he pulls my body down so I'm lying under him, then he unbuttons my pants and pulls my panties and jeans down. I've imagined every day over the last several years about what it would be like to be with Marco again, but being with him right now…there's no emotion. He says he's seeking comfort yet his moves are all robotic.

Reaching over to his nightstand, I hear him grab a foil packet. He lifts his lower body up, his arms caging me in, and kicks off his shorts. His lips return to mine, his tongue entwining with my own. There's no foreplay, it's nothing like it was the last time. He pushes into me too soon. I'm not wet enough and it hurts. But I don't say anything. I just lie there, letting Marco use me.

He nuzzles his face into my neck as he thrusts in and out of me lazily. My body finally accepts him, my sex getting slicker, and then… it's over. I don't even orgasm. Marco stops thrusting and rolls over to lie next to me.

"Marco?" I move my face closer to his to get a better look and see he's passed out. Sighing heavily, I go to the bathroom to clean up. As I stand, I feel liquid dribble down the side of my leg. It's dark so I can't see what it is. I go into his in-suite bathroom and close the door, turning the light on.

I sit down to pee and grab the toilet paper to wipe myself. I don't remember being this wet the last time we had sex, and last time, Marco made sure to get me off. Using my finger, I swipe the liquid from the inside of my thigh. It's sticky…

Oh no. Oh no. Oh no.

After wiping up my leg, I flush the toilet and wash my hands. Leaving the light on so I can see Marco, I walk up to the side of the bed and shake him. He doesn't move at all.

"Marco," I say not bothering to whisper. Trailing my eyes over his body, I see he's still naked. His dick is now flaccid and there's no condom on it. I know he grabbed a condom…

I start shaking out the sheets not even worrying about waking him up. I mean, really…who the fuck just passes out immediately after sex? As the sheet catches air, I see the foiled packet fly up and then land back on the bed. I reach forward and grab it. *Still wrapped!* What. The. Fuck! He came in me? *Motherfucker!*

"Marco!" I shake him harder. "Marco, wake up!" When he doesn't stir, I place my hand on his chest to make sure his heart is still beating. It is. I leave it there a few seconds to feel his chest rising and falling. Then I glance at the clock seeing it's almost three in the morning. I have a math test in less than five hours.

Throwing the sheet over his naked body, I grab my clothes and quickly get dressed. When I walk out of his room, the house is quiet. Tristan must have gotten rid of everyone. The house isn't spotless and the music is still playing, but it's been turned down. I also notice all the drugs are no longer littering the surface areas.

I see him and Gina sitting out on the back patio having what looks like a heated conversation. I don't want to interrupt them but I need to get out of here. "Hey, sorry to interrupt."

They both turn to face me. Gina's eyes are bloodshot, clearly high. Tristan closes his eyes briefly and takes a deep breath before reopening them. "It's fine. Is Marco okay?"

"He's sleeping. Can we go?"

"Yeah." Tristan's brows furrow, clearly wanting more but I'm not in the mood to give him anything else.

"Might as well…Tristan killed the party." Gina stands, but wobbles shakily. Tristan quickly grabs a hold of her hips to steady her. I can see a myriad of emotions cross his features as he looks at Gina—anger, shame, annoyance, defeat, but most of all sympathy. And it has me wondering if maybe there's more to why Tristan stays with someone like her.

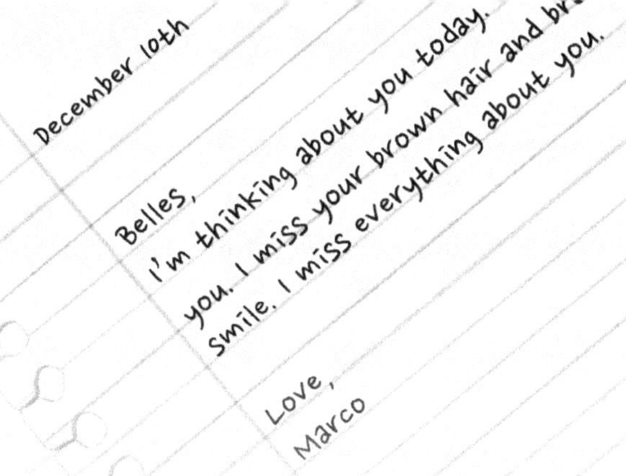

NINE

MARCO
THE NEXT MORNING

HOLY SHIT, MY HEAD IS POUNDING. THE LIGHT IS SEEPING through the windows making me feel like my brain is going to explode. I reach into my drawer and feel around for a baggie. When my fingers touch it, I snatch it, open it, and pour the white powder right onto my nightstand. Grabbing the razor I keep in there, I push it into a straight line then bring my nose down to the wood, inhaling deeply. The coke enters my nostrils and almost seconds later, I feel numb again.

I close the baggie and throw it back into the drawer before shutting it. Lying back against my pillow, my arm comes up over my face to block out the sunlight.

"Marco? Are you awake?" Janell's annoying fucking voice booms through the door.

"Can you shut the fuck up, please?" I yell back. She opens the door and comes inside.

"I just wanted to check on you. Your friend made everyone leave last night. Fucking goodie-goodie. I can't believe Gina is wasting her time with him. Like being with him will suddenly change her circumstances. You can take the girl out of the trailer park but you can't take the trailer park out of the girl. Ugh." I'm trying to process everything she's saying, but I have no clue what the fuck she's talking about.

"What?" I rub my eyes then grab a baggie of pills from the drawer, popping two into my mouth, swallowing them dry.

Janell comes over and sits on the bed next to me. "Are you naked?"

I look down and see the sheets pulled from her sitting onto the bed and sure as shit I'm naked. I slowly sit up and try to think…

"Did we…." I ask slowly.

"Excuse me?" She stands, arms crossed. I sit up and look around the room. My clothes are thrown all over the floor, and on my nightstand, there's a condom wrapper. I swipe it up and see it's unused.

"I'm just asking. I don't know why I'm naked. You said my friend was here last night?"

"Tristan and some other girl showed up with Gina and broke up the party…sent everyone home."

I try to remember last night, but it's just a blur…I remember people coming over, everyone hanging out…but nothing stands out.

"Whose is this?" She throws a grey hoodie at me.

"I don't know, Janell." I just need her to close her mouth and go away. Grabbing the sheets, I pull them back over my body and roll over away from her, hoping she'll get the message.

A few seconds later the door slams shut. *Guess she got the message.*

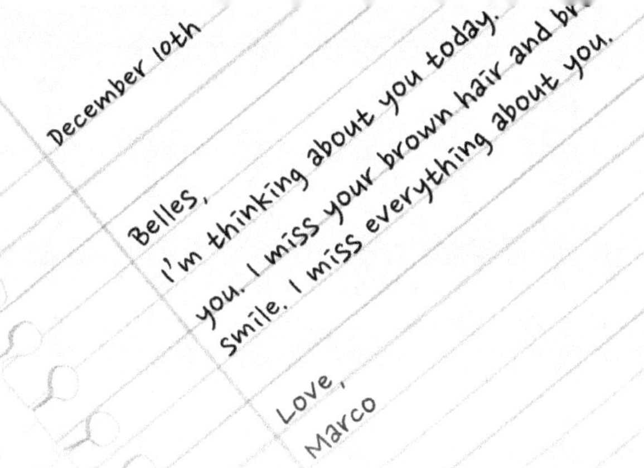

TEN

BELLA
THE NEXT MORNING

GREAT! I'VE MISSED MY MATH TEST AND I'M NEVER GOING TO make it in time for my English Lit. class, either. I got home and started googling pregnancy.

When do women ovulate? Ten days after the first day of her period based on a twenty-eight-day cycle.

I pulled out my calendar and tried to figure out my cycle. After an hour, I gave up.

How many days a month can a woman get pregnant? The average woman ovulates for forty-eight hours a month.

Okay… so, does that mean the other twenty-six days a woman can't get pregnant?

So, then I Googled the morning after pill… and I almost had a heart attack. Sure, most people said it works if taken within twenty-four hours. It has an eighty-nine percent effective rate. But then when I typed in side effects I started to see words like nausea, vomiting, dizziness, fatigue, headache, bleeding, lower abdominal pain, and I started working myself up.

Then I came across an article where a girl died! *DIED!* Now, it can't be proven if it was the pill that killed her, but do I really want to take that chance? My mom always tells me not to Google shit. I do this all the time. Tristan has even forbidden me from using Google because he's so sick of hearing me tell him the stuff I've read on there. But I digress…

Now, look, I'm not judging anyone who chooses to take this pill. To each their own. But if I can only get pregnant two, maybe three, days a month then I'm thinking I might just be better off praying Marco's dumb ass shot his semen in me during one of the other twenty-six days.

I hate pills as it is. I never even take Tylenol because it makes me gag. I still buy the liquid shit when I have a cold.

So, I close my laptop, with it in my head that there's only a ten percent chance that I'm ovulating right now. I would say the odds are in my favor.

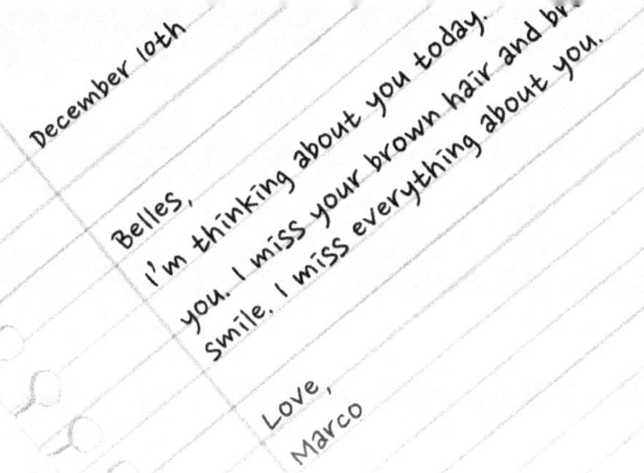

ELEVEN

BELLA
PRESENT DAY

I STARE AT THE STICK WITH TWO PINK LINES, GLARING AT IT, willing one of the lines to disappear. Whelp! I guess I was ovulating during that ten percent chance timeframe. I don't know whether to go play the lottery or never play it again…

I mean. Ten. Percent. Chance. That means I had a ninety percent chance of *not* ovulating on that day.

Some would see this as a miracle. A cancer patient gets told he only has a ten percent chance of beating it. He beats it. *Miracle.*

A woman plays a scratch off with only a ten percent chance of winning the jackpot. She wins. *Miracle.*

Someone is in an accident and is told there's only a ten percent chance of surviving. The person survives. *Goddamn Miracle.*

I had a ten percent chance of getting pregnant. And I'm pregnant. *Miracle?* Some would say so.

Me? Right now? Not so much.

"Bella! Are you coming to lunch or not?" Tristan bangs on the door.

"Umm… just give me a minute." I grab the offensive stick, shove it back into the container, and shove the container into the back of the cabinet under the sink. Since we each have our own bathroom, the chances of him looking under there are…

On second thought, I'll just take that box with me. Because apparently the odds are in my favor, which means Tristan *will* look under the sink and find the box.

I open the door a tad, peeking out to make sure Tristan isn't near it and then make a mad dash to my bedroom to hide the box. After throwing it in the very back of my closet, I get dressed.

"I'm not going to be able to make it to lunch," I say to Tristan and Gina. Tristan gives me a quizzical look. Gina rolls her eyes.

"You sure?"

"Yep, I have something I have to take care of."

"Okay, if you need anything call me." Tristan leans forward and gives me a quick kiss on my cheek.

Before I lose the courage, I drive over to Marco's condo. However, once I arrive, my courage seems to disappear. So, I sit in the parking lot for a good twenty minutes before I build my courage back up enough to knock on his door.

At first, nobody answers, so I knock once more. This time, I hear voices then the door swings open. A bleach-blonde skinny chick wearing a tube top and boy shorts stands in front of me eying me up and down. Her eyes meet mine and they're blood shot.

"Can I help you?" she slurs.

"I need to speak to Marco." She gives me a dirty look that I ignore. "Now."

She swings the door open wider, her one hand flinging out to the side letting me know I can enter. I see Marco sitting on the couch in the living room, his nose about an inch from the coffee table. He inhales loudly then looks up.

"Janell, who the fuck is..." When he sees it's me, his eyes widen a fraction.

"Belles," he says lazily, drawing out each letter. He's high as a kite. This is the point where I should walk away. But I'm pissed. This guy is getting high while I am freaking out about being knocked up because he didn't put the goddamn condom on his dick before he came inside me. "I've missed you..."

I roll my eyes. The last time he said those words, his fuck-ass knocked me up.

"We need to talk." I put my hands on my hips.

"Marco and I are actually busy right now, so..." the bleach blonde bitch says as she sits next to Marco and snorts a line of what I think is coke.

"Marco," I say. "We need to talk."

"Damn, Bella, I haven't seen you in forever and you come in here all red-faced and mad. Why don't you chill out?"

"Chill out?" I repeat his words, nodding my head slowly while willing myself not to murder the father of my unborn child.

"Chill out," I repeat, again. "I'm pregnant, Marco."

His eyes bug out then he looks down at my stomach. "I'm only like a month along."

"Damn, Bella. That shit sucks." He grabs a baggie and dumps some more powder onto the table, leaning over and snorting it again. "If you need money for an abortion, I can give it to you. Fuck, I can't even imagine." Marco shakes his head in disbelief, his words slurred so badly it's hard to even understand what he's saying.

"I don't need money. I'm not having an abortion." I stare at the man in front of me, the man I've loved in some way or another for more than half my life, and I don't recognize him. It's like he's a skeleton of himself. The Marco I know would never offer me money for an abortion. He would comfort me and be there for me. He would tell me we would figure this out together.

"Hey," he says, only he isn't talking to me. He's talking to blondie. "If you get knocked up, you are aborting that shit. There's no way I'm bringing anything with my blood into this world."

Blondie just rolls her eyes and takes another hit.

"Marco," I say. His eyes meet mine and they don't even look like his beautiful onyx eyes. They're hooded over and the little bit that should be white is bright red. This isn't my Marco. I don't even know this man. I walk closer and kneel next to him so we're eye level. "Leave with me. Right now. We'll get you help. I don't know what's happened but we'll figure it out."

"I don't need help."

"What about fighting?"

"That ship has sailed, Belles. And judging by your admission, it's sailed for you as well. I guess life doesn't always turn out as planned."

Not being able to be in the same room as Marco any longer, I turn to walk out. With one last glance over my shoulder, I give him a sad watery smile before I walk out the door.

Once I'm in my car, I dial a number and hit Bluetooth so I can back out.

"Bella? Is everything okay?"

"No, Caleb, it's not."

"What's wrong?"

"It's Marco. He needs help. Help I'm not able to provide."

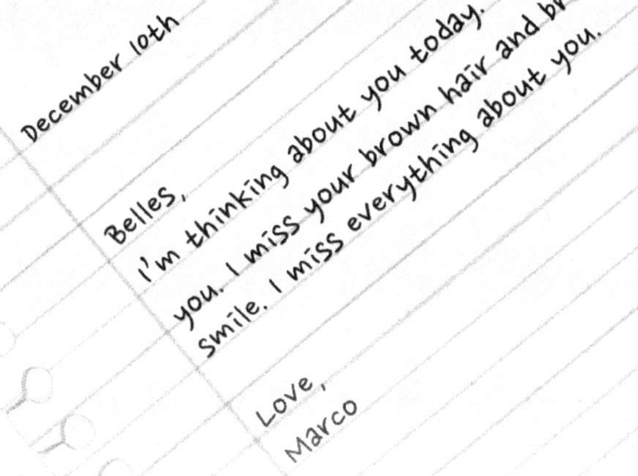

TWELVE

MARCO

I'M SITTING ON THE COUCH GETTING HIGH WITH JANELL WHEN there's a knock on my door. The last person who knocked on my door in the middle of the day was Bella. I know it can't be Mathias because he's once again out of town on business. Janell gets up to answer the door and I put the coke inside the box. I don't need people walking in on my business—like Bella did that day.

The door opens and I hear voices but I can't make out who they are. Then my mom and dad walk in with Janell trailing behind them.

"I've been calling you for two weeks," my dad says, and by the sound of his tone he's more concerned than mad.

"I've been busy." I stand to get some distance, but my dad walks toward me, grabbing my chin in his hand.

"I'm going to ask you this once. Are you high?" Averting my gaze away from his, I shrug and he grips my chin harder. This time I jerk my face out of his clutch.

"It's not your business," I answer, continuing not to make eye contact.

"Sweetie," my mom says only she isn't talking to me. She's talking to Janell who is standing near the wall looking uncomfortable as hell. "Why don't I take you home so my husband and son can talk."

Janell nods in agreement, and after grabbing her purse, they're out the door.

"You're going to rehab," my dad states as soon as the door closes. My eyes shoot up to his. My first thought is if I go to rehab, I'm going to be in pain.

"Fuck no, I'm not," I spit out looking him in the eye, not giving a fuck anymore. There's no damn way I'm going somewhere that requires me to be in pain.

"Marco, Son. Please." He approaches me, but I back up not wanting his comfort. "Your mom and I have been worried about you. When Bella…" He cuts himself off, but it's too late. He tries to recover by saying, "What I mean is, you haven't called or answered any of our calls in weeks," but it's too late.

"Bella called you?" I'm fuming. She has her own shit to deal with, and instead of worrying about herself, she called my damn dad.

"It doesn't matter. What matters is that we're here and we're going to get you help." He moves closer again, his hands up like he's dealing with a wild animal. The look on his face is pained, and even as high as I am, I hate that I'm the one putting it there, but I don't care enough to be in pain for the rest of my life. I need the drugs. They numb me. They numb my mind and my body.

"Marco, we love you. We need you to get help. Please. Your family. Your friends. Bella. Tristan. Your sisters. We're all here for you." I contemplate what he's saying for a moment. When I watched Bella walk out the door, slamming it shut behind her, I considered chasing after her. But I knew she was better off without me in her life. She *needs* someone like Tristan, and she sure as fuck doesn't *need* me. The truth is, none of these people need me.

And then it hits me, I have officially become my mother's son. And no, I'm not referring to the woman who raised me for the last thirteen years. I'm talking about my biological mother, the one who *needed* drugs for most of my life. The woman I swore I would never become.

You always hear the saying, nature over nurture. Guess they were right, because here I am, high as fuck *needing* the drugs. Guess I'm more like my mom than I wanted to admit.

"I want you to get out," I say.

Caleb looks at me with wide eyes. "Marco, don't do this."

"Get out!" I boom. I get up in his face, which is a mistake. We might be built similar, but Caleb isn't high or injured like I am.

"You need help, Son," he begs.

"I'm not your goddamned son! Now get out!" I stalk toward the door and open it for him, but he refuses to leave. So, without saying another word, I walk out the door, slamming it closed behind me. As soon as I'm down the stairs I hit the beach and call Janell's brother, Ivan. He answers on the second ring.

"What's up?"

"I need you to pick me up. Down at Gazpacho's." It's a bit of a walk from my place, but I need to get away from Caleb. He doesn't get it. None of them do. I always knew I was tainted, that blood is thicker than water. But now, it's confirmed. I never stood a fucking chance against biology.

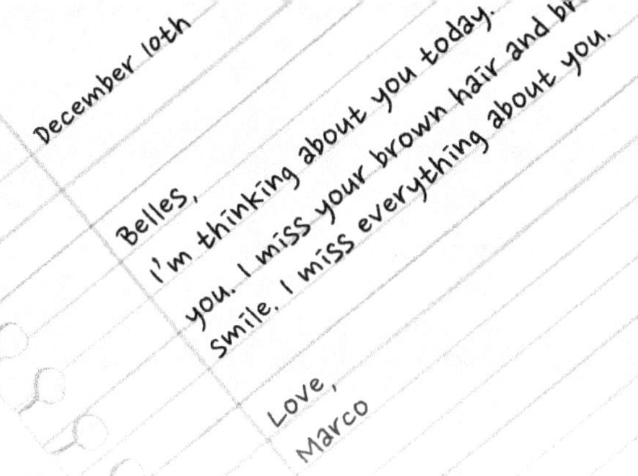

THIRTEEN

BELLA
A FEW MONTHS LATER

"BELLA, IF WE DON'T GET GOING SOON, WE'RE GOING TO BE late."

"I know. I know. I'm sorry! I freaking sneezed too hard and peed my pants. I had to jump back in the shower and change my clothes." I run around my room frantically, making sure I have everything. Cell phone. Pregnancy book. Workout bag for afterward.

We get to the appointment right on time and the nurse brings us back immediately. After doing my monthly weigh-in and bloodwork, she takes me back to a different room.

"Go ahead and take your clothes off from the waist down and use this to cover you." She hands me a paper-looking blanket "The doctor will be in to see you shortly."

After changing and sitting on the medical table, we wait. Not even two minutes later there's a knock on the door and the doctor walks in.

"Good morning, Bella. How are you feeling today?" Dr. Ruben asks.

"I'm doing good." I look down at my protruding belly and rub it. I'm now twenty weeks pregnant which means if all goes well we should be able to find out the sex of the baby. It won't be the first ultrasound I've had but at least this one will be a more positive occasion. It's been a rocky few months, but it feels like lately life has been going a bit smoother.

"And I don't believe we've met before. I'm Dr. Ruben." My obstetrician puts his hand out to shake Tristan's.

"This is Tristan. He's"—I clear my throat—"the father of the baby."

"Nice to meet you. And I see you are now twenty weeks. Are you ready to see your baby?"

"Yes, I am." I hold my breath as Dr. Ruben pulls my cover down and squirts the warmed-up gel onto my belly. When he takes the wand and rubs the gel in, spreading it over my belly, my heartrate picks up like it does every time— praying there will be a heartbeat. When I finally hear the beautiful sound of *whoosh, whoosh, whoosh,* I feel like I can breathe again.

"The baby's heartbeat is running at one hundred and fifty beats per minute right now. Good, strong heartbeat." *Good. Strong. Heartbeat.* I will never tire of hearing those words. Especially, after experiencing the most frightening day of my life a few months ago when I thought I might never get to hear my baby's heartbeat.

"Where the fuck is she?" I'm standing behind the front door where Marco can't see me but my car is in the parking lot so he knows I'm here.

"Marco...you need to calm down, man." Tristan tries to stop Marco from entering our apartment, but it's pointless. Marco is bigger and stronger. He slams his fist against the door and stalks into the apartment looking for me. When his eyes lock with mine, his lip curls with disgust.

"You fucking bitch! What the fuck were you thinking, calling my dad and telling him I'm a fucking druggy? What fucking business is it of yours!"

I back up a little as he comes closer, and luckily Tristan steps in front of me. "Marco!" Tristan booms. "You do have a fucking drug problem. Bella was just trying to help. We're your friends."

Marco glares at Tristan and says, "She's not my friend. She's nothing to me." Then he locks eyes with me. "You have enough problems of your own to be worrying about me. Focus on your fucking self."

"Marco, leave," I say quietly, hoping he won't say what I think he is about to say.

"Why? Afraid pretty boy here will learn the truth? Or wait… did you end up doing what I suggested after all?" His gaze drops to my stomach.

"Bella, what's he talking about?" Tristan turns toward me.

Marco chuckles as he smiles saccharinely. "Oh, this is great! You had time to call Caleb and stir up shit, but you forgot to mention to your best friend here that you're knocked up." Caleb had warned me he accidentally let my name slip out when he tried to get Marco help. He apologized and told me Marco left. He's texted me a few times since then letting me know nobody has heard from Marco. I figured he would be mad I told his dad about his drug problem, but I didn't think he would show up here to confront me.

Tristan whips his head around at me in shock, his eyes going wide. I shake my head softly, silently begging him not to get into this right now. He gives me a look asking if it's true and I close my eyes, giving him a small nod. When I open my eyes back up he gives me a sympathetic smile.

"So, which is it Bella? Did you have an abortion like I suggested, or is your fighting career over before it even started? And while I'm thinking about it, who the fuck is your baby's daddy? Because if the look Tristan just made tells me anything, he's not the one who knocked you up… and I sure as fuck didn't knock you up."

"What do you even care?" Tristan asks, confused. Marco just chuckles and shakes his head.

"So, Bella… tell us. I mean you got in my business, so it's only fair I know yours."

"I'm having the baby," I admit, and Tristan does a good job of keeping his composure.

"And who's the lucky guy? Who's the guy that's fucked for life?"

Hot tears build and I will them away.

As I am about to tell him it's none of his business, Tristan says, "I am. So, worry about yourself."

"I call bullshit."

"You can call whatever the fuck you want. Now get the fuck out. The baby Bella's carrying is mine."

"Oh my God!" a feminine voice screeches. "What did you just say?" Gina steps farther into the room. Of course, at this moment is when she decides to come out of Tristan's room to join the fun.

"Did you just say you're the father of her baby?" Gina shoots daggers my way.

"And the plot thickens." Marco laughs. "I'm out of here."

He reaches the door and glares at me one last time. "You're fucking dead to me." He walks out the door and slams it behind him, causing the picture frame next to the door to fall to the floor, the glass pieces smashing all over the ground.

"Gina, can you go wait in my room for a minute? I'll be right there," Tristan says to Gina.

"No! I want to know what the hell is going on!"

"And I'll explain it to you in a minute. You can either go wait in my room or leave."

"Fine," she huffs, glaring at me and then walking away.

Once we hear the door slam, Tristan says to me, "Is it true?"

"Yes, I'm about eight weeks pregnant."

"Why does Marco know and I don't?"

I give him the half-truth. "When I went to his house to see if I could get him help, I told him."

"Who's the dad?"

I've never lied to Tristan… until this moment, and I feel sick as I do. "It doesn't matter. He doesn't want the baby."

"He knows you're pregnant?"

"Yes, and he made it clear he doesn't want him or her."

"What are you going to do?"

"I don't know yet. I know I'm going to have the baby, but I'm considering giving it up for adoption."

"Shit! Okay, let me go talk to Gina, and then we'll figure this out, okay?" Tristan wraps his arms around me, giving me a hug I didn't realize I needed so badly.

He walks back to his room, and I hear the door close. Before going to lie down, I stop at the bathroom to go pee. After I'm done, I wipe myself, and just before I drop the toilet paper into the water, I spot bright red blood. Grabbing more, I wipe again and see more blood.

"Tristan," I call out. "Tristan!" I pull up my pants, flush the toilet, and run out of the bathroom. He's already in the hallway.

"Did you call me?"

"I'm bleeding. I need to go to the hospital."

"Okay, let's go." He practically pushes Gina out the door, and although she tries to argue, Tristan snaps at her, saying he'll talk to her later.

The ride to the hospital is a blur. We get checked in and I'm given a room and a gown to change into. I answer what feels like a million questions and then blood is taken.

A few minutes later, an ultrasound tech picks me up and rolls my bed to another room, but before we leave, Tristan promises he'll be waiting for me in the room.

The tech tries to do an external ultrasound first, but she can't find a heartbeat.

"Don't worry," she says. "You probably aren't far enough along yet."

Then, using a probe, she tries again. I hold my breath, praying to hear the heartbeat. She clicks a couple buttons and I feel like I'm going to pass out.

"Okay, here we go." She turns a knob and I hear it—my baby's heartbeat—and it's the most amazing sound I've ever heard. "See that little blip?" She points at the screen and I see a small dot with something blinking in the center.

"Oh my god! Is that her heartbeat?"

"It sure is. I will print you out a picture." She clicks a couple more knobs then she grabs something from under her. "Here you go." She hands me a black and phot grainy photo. "Your baby's first photo. According to my measurements, you're eight weeks along. Congratulations. Everything looks good from my end, but the OBGYN on call will come in and double check everything since you had bleeding."

A few minutes later the doctor comes in and checks out the ultrasound images then she does a pelvic exam. "Your uterus and placenta all look perfect. The baby's heartbeat is strong and you're measuring correct according to the first day of your last period. Minor bleeding in the first trimester is common, so I don't want you to be concerned. If you feel any cramping or the bleeding worsens, come back in. Otherwise, make an appointment for your checkup with your preferred obstetrician."

"Okay, thank you."

The nurse comes in and wheels me back to the room where Tristan is waiting for me. "Everything okay?"

I hand him the picture of the most perfect little blob. "She's perfect."

"It's a girl?" He looks at me shocked.

"I don't know. I'm only eight weeks along, but I didn't want to call it an 'it' and she was the sex that came to mind." Giving the baby a gender makes this whole situation feel even more real. I have a baby growing inside of me. A perfect little miracle.

Tristan puts his face in his hands and scrubs up and down. "Do you think it's wise to get attached? You mentioned giving her up for adoption."

"That was before I saw her on the monitor. Before I saw the blood and thought I was going to lose her. I was scared. I still am. But I can't give her up. She's mine and I already love her." I rub my hand over my belly. "My mom did it alone for the first four years."

"Your mom had your aunt Kayla."

"That's true, but she still did it and I will too."

"You aren't going to do this alone. My mom had to do that shit alone and I'm not letting you go through what she did."

"Tristan, I can't let you do this."

"Yes, you can, and you're going to. I want to. Kaden isn't my biological father, but I love him just the same and he loves me as if I were his. We'll do it together. As far as everyone will know, I'm this baby's father."

"No, you can't do that. What about Gina? I can't be the reason you two break up."

"Bella, you're my best friend. You come first. You want to keep this baby then I'll support you one hundred percent and be by your side. We'll do this together."

The following weeks are crazy. Tristan breaks things off with Gina, telling her I'm pregnant. Unfortunately, that also means pretending he cheated on her. Tristan feels it would be best if everyone, including Gina, think he's the biological father, so I go along with it.

After our huge fight with Marco, Tristan spoke with Caleb, who said he's cut Marco off completely. He flew out again and tried to get him help but Marco refused all help, and then Mathias kicked him out. Marco has money from his fights, so I doubt he's homeless, but Tristan and I haven't spoken to him since that day, and I have no desire to ever speak to him again. Do I love Marco? Of course I do. But I have to put my baby first.

Tristan and I have agreed to take things slow. I'm not ready to be in a relationship with him, especially not sexually, and he says he understands. I told him I would understand if he wants to have sex with other women but he said he's fine.

When we told our parents, our moms cried, my dad freaked the hell out, and Kaden said he'll do anything he can to support us. My dad asked if we were going to get married and we both agreed we're taking it one day at a time. It was a shock to everyone that Tristan and I were together. My mom gave me a weird look a few times but didn't call me out on it, thank God.

Because of being pregnant, I had to cancel my UFC fight. I'm still allowed to work out while pregnant, but I can't fight, obviously. Once I'm healed, I fully plan to get right back into training. But for now, my focus is on the baby. I took the summer off school to get situated, but I'm back for the fall semester. With the baby not due until the end of January, I'm taking a full load now and taking next semester and the summer off.

The last two appointments I insisted on going myself since they were just routine visits, but since this one I knew we would get to see the baby, Tristan insisted on coming along, which is why Dr. Ruben is just meeting Tristan for the first time.

Tristan squeezes my hand and I look over at him and then back to the monitor. "Here's your baby's feet and hands. There's the spine. Are you finding out the sex today?" Dr. Ruben asks.

"Yes," I say, staring at my beautiful little alien-looking baby.

"Okay, you see these three lines? Right here?" Dr. Ruben freezes the screen. "These mean you're having a girl, and right now she's measuring perfect." He takes a few more pictures of the baby before he says, "Everything looks great. Go ahead and get dressed and schedule your next appointment up front."

A girl. I'm having a girl. I wonder if she'll have my naturally wavy brown hair or Marco's… No! I am not going there. I am not going to think about whether she will have my olive complexion or take after her father's beautiful caramel skin, or if she'll have his onyx eyes or my light brown ones. There's no point. This is the way it needs to be even if I wish things could have been different. The thought makes my heart hurt, and I feel a small tear escape, but I wipe it away quickly.

"You okay?" Tristan asks.

"Yeah, thank you for being here."

"There's nowhere else I would rather be." He takes my hand and brings it up to his lips, softly giving it a kiss. And I feel like the worst person for wishing for things I shouldn't be wishing for.

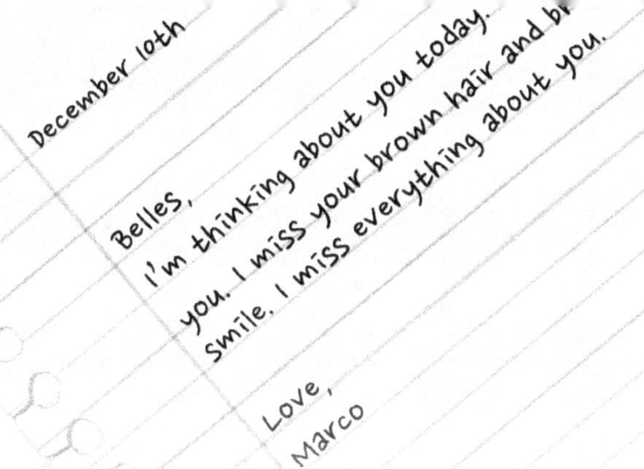

FOURTEEN

MARCO

I'M SITTING ON THE BACK PATIO OF MY NEW CONDO overlooking the water. My head is pounding because Sara is running late. After I made the decision to walk away from Caleb, I stayed with Ivan for a couple weeks. When Caleb returned, trying once again to get me to go to rehab, and I made it clear he has no say in my life, he practically disowned me and told Mathias about me doing drugs.

Mathias, of course, sided with Hayley and Caleb and kicked me out, saying once I'm ready to get help I am more than welcome to move back in. So, I moved into a new condo complex. I met Sara and quickly learned she's into the same recreational activities as I am.

Janell was getting too fucking clingy, so I cut her loose once I found out Sara could score for me. She's running late from work and I just did my last bump a few hours ago so I'm coming down hard. If she doesn't get here soon, I'm going to have to call my dealer. I can't stand dealing with him, especially since he thought he recognized me once. The last thing I need is it getting out who I am.

There's a knock at my door and I jump up to answer it. Usually Sara just comes in, but maybe she forgot her key.

I swing it open and come face to face with… not Sara. "Can I help you?"

"Actually, I can help you."

"Aren't you Tristan's girlfriend…or I guess ex-girlfriend?"

"Yes, Gina. Are you going to invite me in?" I look out the door to see if anybody else is here, not having any clue why the hell she's here.

"Umm…yeah, sure." I let her in and she goes right to the couch to sit down. "You don't by any chance have any powder on you, do you?" She glares are me. "Okay, I take that as a no. Pills?"

"No! My God, you need to get your shit together."

"Oh fuck, did Tristan send you here? Didn't he cheat on you?"

"He didn't send me here, and that's actually why I'm here. Tristan didn't cheat on me."

"Umm…sweetheart, the baby in Bella's belly says otherwise. Look, if you don't have any powder or pills, you're no use to me, so…" I stand to open the door for her in case she doesn't get the hint.

"Actually, that's where you're wrong. I *am* of use to you because I know something you might want to know."

"Doubt it."

"How about the fact that Bella is pregnant…"

"I already know that."

"…with your child. Not Tristan's."

"And you're fucking delusional. Get out."

The door opens and Sara comes in. "Thank God!" I grab the baggies from her hand and ignore Gina still standing in the room, going straight to the table to line up the powder.

"I'm not delusional. I even have proof."

Using my razor, I make a straight line and lean forward.

"Look." She sticks her phone out in the way of my bump.

"Move," I growl.

"No, look." She shoves the phone in my face. At first, I'm not sure what I'm looking at. It looks like a picture of a handwritten letter. I scroll down, but there's no name. The letter is unfinished.

"What's this?" I ask.

"Read it."

My sweet baby girl,

I'm 24 weeks pregnant today and read in my baby book that moms sometimes write notes to their unborn babies. When I thought about writing to you, the first thing that came to mind was telling you the truth. I don't want to begin our mother/daughter relationship with lies, even though we will be, but this letter is in case something happens to me. If you're reading this, it means you know your dad isn't your biological father and you've asked for answers.

First, I want to tell you that I love you more than life itself. You aren't even here yet but my heart beats for you. I hope if I'm no longer with you for whatever reason you know how deep my love runs for you. Every choice I've made was made out of love for you. I can't tell you if I made the right decision, but I will tell you I made what I felt was the best decision at the time.

With that said, the man who you share DNA with is Marco Michaels. He is Caleb and Hayley's son. He doesn't know you are his and he never *denied you. You also need to know that your dad (Tristan) loves you already, but he doesn't know who your real father is either. I chose to keep it a secret because your biological father wasn't in a good place, even though I promise you, you were made from love.*

If you're reading this, something's happened to me, and it will be up to you if you choose to seek him out. I hope and pray he is in a better place, but if he's not, just know that at one time, Marco was my best friend. He was

I reread the unfinished letter three more times. How the fuck is this even possible? How am I that baby's father? It doesn't make sense.

"How is this possible?"

"Well, according to Tristan, the night we came here for the party, he and Bella ended up hooking up, but since I know that isn't true, I'm thinking you and Bella hooked up that night. And I take it, you don't remember that night…"

The party? Fuck, there's been so many parties. How could I have had sex with Bella and not remembered?

"It was like six months ago at your old place. We went over there to break up the party. Bella went into your room with you, and when she came out, she said you were sleeping."

The party.

My bedroom.

The grey hoodie.

Fuck!

The grey hoodie said Cooper's Fight Club, I knew I recognized it. It was Bella's.

If this letter is true, if I'm the father of her kid…

Oh, my God! The shit I said to her.

I told her to have an abortion.

Fuck!

I click on the photo and text it to my phone. "Here, you can go."

"That's it? Aren't you going to go to her? She's carrying your child. Tristan was supposed to be mine and that bitch fucked it all up," Gina snaps. "You need to claim that baby."

"Watch your fucking mouth and get out." I look at Sara. "Both of you." Sara puts her hands up, and both girls leave, Gina continuing to call Bella every name in the book.

I grab my phone and dial the only person in the world who can help me right now.

"Marco? Son?"

"Dad, I need you."

He sighs into the phone. "Marco…"

"I need to go to rehab. I need help. Please."

"I'm on my way. I love you, Son."

I sit in my living room for what feels like hours, staring at the image of the letter supposedly written by Bella. I want to call her and ask her if she really wrote it, but deep down in my gut, I know she did. I think back to the look on her face when she showed up here to tell me she was pregnant. She was so scared and vulnerable, and instead of lashing out, she tried to get me help. I don't even deserve this woman.

Then I think about when I showed up at her place and Tristan said the baby was his. I yelled and screamed at her. I called her names and told her she was dead to me. Maybe I should just pretend I didn't see the letter. Maybe she and our baby are better off with Tristan.

There's a knock on my door and I know it's my dad. I open the door and he comes in and, without saying a word, wraps me up in a hug.

I lose it. I cry until I'm sobbing. But my dad doesn't say anything. He just lets me lose it. Once the tears stop, he says, "I need to know what caused all this, Marco. I need to make sure you get the right help." We have a seat on the couch and I take a deep breath, trying to figure out how to answer that question.

Where do I even start?

"I'm in pain. My back wasn't healing and the pain became too much. I was grieving for Logan and not able to fight, and I lost it. Pills turned to coke and it just all spiraled out of control. I need the drugs, Dad." I look him dead in the eyes. "I need them. I can feel it in me. I am craving them right now."

I stare at my shaky hands and wonder what will happen once the need is too much. Right now, I'm okay, but what will happen when I need the pills and powder in my blood stream? Will I give up and choose the drugs over my baby?

"What if I can't do it? What if I can't get clean? My mom…my biological mom…"

My dad jumps out of his seat, bridging the gap between us. "Don't you fucking finish that goddamn sentence. Don't you dare blame her, and don't you dare believe you can't get better because of her. You are my son. Mine and Hayley's. I don't give a fuck whose blood runs through your veins."

I nod in understanding, choosing not to voice my doubts.

"Let's get you to the facility. I've already called ahead and let them know you're coming in. What you need to understand is that you're an adult. This is one hundred percent voluntary. If you choose to leave, I can't stop you."

"Thank you. I'm not coming out of there until I'm clean."

"I'm going to tell your mom about your pain. She'll know who to contact. We'll get your back fixed. I promise."

We both stand and head to the door. I give him my keys and cell phone, knowing I won't be able to bring them with me. The drive to the rehab facility is about an hour away, and of course it looks like an expensive resort. This is California after all.

My dad stays by my side through the entire check-in process. He doesn't once leave me until the doctor tells him this is where we have to part ways. He envelops me in a hug, his words coming out gritty. "I love you, Marco. You are going to get through this. We'll come and visit as soon as we're allowed."

"There's something you need to know," I whisper. "I think I'm the father of Bella's baby." I feel his body stiffen, but he doesn't say anything, only nods then looks me straight in the eyes.

"You get better for you and only you. You understand me?"

I agree, giving him one last hug before following the doctor into the facility where I'll be spending the next ninety days.

FIFTEEN

BELLA

"SURPRISE!"

After a relaxing morning of reading and writing down my birthing plan at the local coffee shop near campus, I walk into my apartment to find every woman I know standing in my living room. After nearly having a heart attack, I take in the room. There are presents, food, and a huge cake on the table, the entire place looking like it threw up an entire bottle of Pepto Bismol. Pink streamers, pink ribbons, pink balloons. *Yuck!*

But then I see my mom and I smile, knowing she's the reason for all this. So, in the grand scheme of things, pink isn't so bad. I run up to her and wrap my arms around her neck. Some girls can't stand their moms. That's not the case for me. My mom is my best friend in the entire world. Maybe it's because she had me at eighteen so she was a young mother, but we have always had an amazing relationship.

This was the first Christmas Tristan and I didn't get to spend the holidays with everyone in Breckenridge. With me so close to my due date, the doctor said it would be best if I didn't fly. So, our families spent Christmas together, and Tristan and I spent it here in San Diego. We got a small tree and exchanged gifts, but it wasn't the same. I missed my family so much, so getting to see my mom is the best surprise of all.

"Thank you for doing this. But more importantly, thank you for being here."

"You aren't getting rid of me. You only have a couple weeks, so I'll be staying here until this precious little one comes. I'm not chancing being over four hours away when you go into labor."

"Where are you staying? I mean, you can stay here, but with us only having two bedrooms and my room being cramped with the baby's stuff, you'll be stuck on the couch."

"Don't you worry. Your father found a good deal on a hotel downtown so I'll be staying there. I can't deal with trying to get on a plane when my daughter goes into labor. Your dad and siblings will fly out once we let them know."

"Oh, Mom, thank you." I give her another hug.

"What I want to know is, and we can talk about this later, why aren't you and Tristan sharing a room if you are together?" Her one eyebrow goes up and I feel sick. The only lie I have ever told my mom was about the father of my baby and it doesn't surprise me she knows something is up.

"Mom…"

"Not now, let's enjoy this baby shower. We have plenty of time to talk later."

I see some of my friends from school smiling and laughing, so I agree and walk over to my friends. "Happy Baby Shower," Lauren says. I met her in our freshman math class and we quickly became friends. She introduced me to Stephanie, Kristen, and Michelle, who are all in the same sorority as her.

At first, I thought they would be stuck up and full of themselves when I heard they were all in a sorority, but I quickly learned there is a stigma about sororities that just might be wrongfully placed. These women are sweet and smart and have become friends I can lean on.

"Thanks for coming," I tell the four of them, then continue to work my way around the room. Ashley, Tristan's mom, is here, along with Tristan's sisters. My sister, Lilly, is here. I spot Hayley, Marco's mom, with Marco's sister, Mackenzie, and then I spot my aunt Kayla, who is here with her daughters, Faith and Chloe.

While Kayla and Bentley are Chloe's parents in every way that matters, biologically Chloe is Marco's sister. They shared a mom, one who overdosed on drugs when Chloe was only a baby. Hayley and Caleb adopted Marco, and Kayla and Bentley adopted Chloe. I hate that Chloe will never know this baby is her niece. I know she's happy, but I've heard her mention on several occasions she wishes she had more biological family like Marco has with Mathias. I make a mental note to make her feel like an aunt, even if she won't know they are blood.

When I get to Hayley, I give her a hug and I can't help but ask, "How's Marco?" I know she knows I'm the one who called Caleb, I just wish it would have made a difference.

"He's okay," she says. I want to ask her to elaborate but feel like now isn't the right time. The last I heard Marco was on a downward spiral and Caleb and Hayley had cut him off completely after he refused to get help. Ever since Marco came over yelling and telling me I'm dead to him, I didn't have it in me to ask for updates.

The day goes by quickly. Food is eaten, the cake is delicious, and the amount of stuff people bought the baby is ridiculous. I think my mom covered my entire baby registry herself.

As the party winds down, I say bye to my friends and the only people left are my mom and her friends.

"Have you thought about any names yet?" my aunt Kayla asks. I've thought about names, a lot actually, but I don't want to tell anyone what I'm thinking. I'm afraid it will give away who the father is. I know that sounds stupid, but because it makes me think of the dad, I'm afraid someone else will put the pieces together.

"A little. I'm waiting until she's born to decide for sure."

The front door opens, and in walks Tristan and Mason. Mason flew over the day after Christmas and has been hanging out. He mentioned he's thinking about moving out here, something about wanting a change of pace.

"Hell yes, just in time to eat all the leftover food," Mason says, his hands rubbing together like he's preparing for a feast, as he walks straight for the food table.

Tristan sits next to me, placing a kiss on my cheek. "Did you not tell them you hate pink?" he whispers.

I laugh and shake my head. "No, I didn't have the heart to."

"How was the shower?" Tristan asks loud enough for everyone to participate in the conversation.

"It was good. You should see all the cute clothes and toys everyone bought." I turn to everyone sitting with us. "Thank you. This shower means a lot to me."

"Of course, sweetie." My mom leans over and gives me another hug.

"I'm going to head out. Caleb flew in with us and we have to… meet with someone." She gives Mackenzie a hug and kiss. "Be good for Aunt Kayla and I'll see you back at home."

She walks over to me and gives me a hug, "Congratulations, Bella."

One by one everyone leaves. My mom said she needs to check-in to the hotel and Ashley and Kayla are flying back in the morning because school starts back up in a few days. Mason leaves last, saying he's meeting some females for dinner. I tell Tristan he can go but he just gives me a look telling me to shut up.

"Bella, there's a lot of shit in that room. I know you don't want to share a room with me but maybe we need to consider getting a three-bedroom place." Tristan and I have circled around whether to be a couple for the last few months. When he mentioned us sharing a room so we could make the second room a nursery, I gave in. We spent one night in the room together and I told him I couldn't do this.

I know he was disappointed, and I hate that I'm tying him down with a baby and the poor guy isn't even getting laid. He's a twenty-one-year-old man who should be out dating and having fun, not tied down to a woman and some other man's baby. I just don't know what to do. I've considered moving out and doing this on my own, but every time I mention it, Tristan tells me I'm being ridiculous.

"The baby will sleep next to me anyway for the first few months so I can feed her."

"But you'll be pumping so I can help." I went over the pros and cons of breastfeeding and came to the decision I would try to breastfeed and pump. I want to get back into working out and training after she comes as well as having to return to school, so pumping seemed like a good compromise.

"I know, but I want to be close to her. Can we please just take it one step at a time? Once she gets bigger, if we need to, we can move into a bigger place."

"All right."

"I'm really tired. I'm going to go to bed. You should go meet Mason."

"All right… Maybe I will. I kind of hope he decides to move out here. I've enjoyed hanging out with him."

"Good. Go. Goodnight," I say. "Have fun!"

"Night, Bella," Tristan says as he walks out the door.

I lie down in my comfy bed, and not even ten seconds later, I'm out.

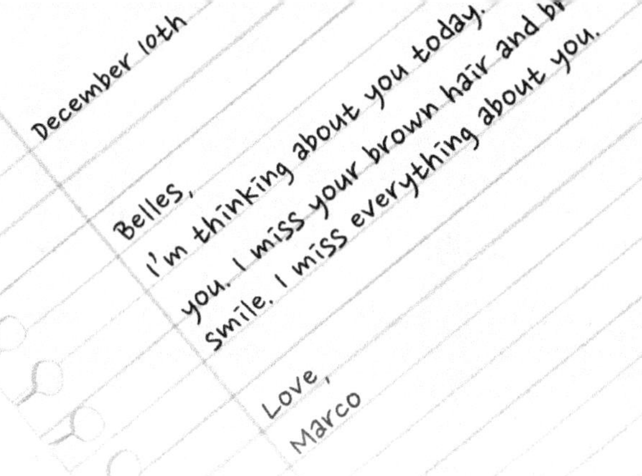

SIXTEEN

MARCO

"THANK YOU FOR PICKING ME UP. SINCE I DIDN'T DRIVE HERE, I would have had to take a cab home, and I have no money on me." I give my dad a hug and we walk out of Sunny Creek rehabilitation center, a place I don't plan to ever need to return to.

"Of course I'm here. You think I would let you get out of this place and not be here?"

I throw the luggage—filled with some clothes and stuff I've accumulated during my three months here—into the back of my car.

"Thanks for letting me take your car, your mom needed to use the rental."

"Seriously? You're thanking me for letting you use my car? I owe you a lot more than the use of my vehicle."

We get in and my dad starts driving to my place. "I made sure all your bills were kept up with like we discussed, and someone came in once a month and cleaned. How are you feeling?"

"I'm feeling damn good. I'm ready to get my life back, but I'm not going to fuck this up. I have my sponsor on speed dial, and I have the locations of the narcotic anonymous meetings in my area."

"That's what I like to hear." He shoots me a smile.

"I know we talked about all this when you guys visited, but I need to say it again. I'm sorry for what I did and said."

"I appreciate it, Marco. You're our son and we'll always be here for you. It killed me having to walk away. Every day I prayed you were alive and would stay alive long enough to get help. Now let's put all this behind us."

"Where's Mom?" I ask. I'm surprised she isn't here, and if I'm honest, a little disappointed.

"She's meeting us for dinner. She wanted to be here, but since you insisted on us not telling anybody about you being in rehab, she couldn't think of an excuse to be in California and not…umm…" My dad trails off unsure of how to finish what he was saying.

"Dad, you know one of the things we talked about in rehab was not coddling me. What's going on? Whatever it is, I can handle it."

"Bella's mom threw her a baby shower today. When Liz invited everyone, she didn't know we were already coming here for you, and since Hayley couldn't say anything, she just acted like we were coming here for the shower."

Bella's baby shower. As much time as I have thought about Bella and our baby the last few months, it still hits me hard hearing her name spoken out loud.

"Have you told mom what I told you?"

My dad shakes his head. "You said you thought she might be. You were high and heading to rehab. I felt it was best to wait until you were sober and ready to deal with this head on. Are you sure you might be the dad?"

"Do I remember having sex with her? No." I hang my head in shame. My counselor and I spoke at great lengths about Bella, the baby, and how she more than likely isn't going to forgive me right away. We talked about being ready to co-parent without being together, and Dr. Wells recommended we consider going to counseling together. But the first step is finding out from Bella if this baby is mine.

"I have a letter I wasn't supposed to see and it states I'm the dad."

"Just remember you're only ninety days sober, and while this baby should be a priority, you also need to put yourself first so you stay sober for the baby."

We arrive at my condo and Dad gives me space to unpack my stuff. I look around and can't believe this is my home. I was so high and fucked up, I never even bothered to do anything with the place. It's a three-bedroom condo on the beach on the first floor. You can literally walk outside and step foot in the sand, but other than the necessities like a bed and dresser, everything in this place is empty. The walls are white and bare, and there's no pictures out. It's the opposite of the home I grew up in with Hayley and Caleb.

I throw my luggage onto the bed and open it up to put my clothes away. As I pick up the pile, the stack of envelopes falls out onto the floor. Picking them up, I put them back in a neat pile and place them into my drawer. Eighty letters. One for every day I was in rehab minus the days I was detoxing and wasn't allowed to have anything dangerous near me such as a writing utensil.

I thought about mailing them so many times but chickened out every time. Something told me I needed to say all the words in person. But I never got rid of a single letter. My counselor said maybe it was cleansing for me to let it all out on paper.

After changing into clean clothes, my dad and I head out to meet Mom for dinner.

"Oh, my baby!" My mom spots me outside the restaurant and runs to me with open arms. "You look so good!" Tears fall down her cheeks, and I hate that there was a time I didn't look good. I hate what I put my parents through. But I can't look back. All I can do is move forward and make things right the best I can.

We hug for a few more minutes, until the hostess lets us know our table is ready. "So, what are your plans?" my dad asks.

"Honey, just let him be. He just got out."

"And he needs to have a plan."

"Dad's right. My plan is to work on making amends with the people I wronged. I want to go visit Logan in the hospital. I found out he was moved to Sharp Hospital here in San Diego into a long-term facility."

"And what about you?" my mom asks.

"My back is still sore, but it's getting better." I put my head down, still feeling shame. "I'm so sorry I didn't come to you guys. I should have told you the pain I felt. I shouldn't have turned to drugs."

"Hey, you did come to us."

"Yeah, too late."

"No, too late would be us burying you. It wasn't too late. You are here, and you are well," Mom says.

"I want to get back to fighting. I know I have a long road ahead of me, but I want to start working out and training again." But even as I say the words, I feel like they're no longer true. Like they're what I'm supposed to say, what people are expecting me to say, what I should be saying. I'm just not sure if I truly mean them anymore.

"And you're sure you don't want to move back home?" Dad asks.

"I have to be here." I hate that I'm keeping this secret from my mom, but what if the letter wasn't true? What if Bella's baby isn't mine. I need to talk to Bella first before I start running my mouth to everyone in sight.

We enjoy the rest of our meal then head back to my place. Mom and Dad insist on spending the night in the guest room, and I welcome the company. I excuse myself to call my sponsor, a man named Jay who has been a recovering addict for thirty years. After going over my plan and when I'll be attending my first meeting, I go to bed, grateful to finally be sleeping in my own bed, in my own home.

I wake up to the smell of bacon. Mom must have gone to the store because there's no way anything from that fridge was still good.

"Morning," I say, giving my mom a kiss on her cheek. Her phone dings, and she looks at it on the counter.

"Oh, no!" My mom says looking at her phone. "Bella had the baby. She was brought in via ambulance last night and they had to do an emergency caesarean."

My heart races at the thought of something happening to Bella and our baby.

"Is she okay? Is the baby okay?" I blurt out. Please let them both be okay. I shoot up a silent prayer to the man upstairs.

"She's okay. They both are."

"We should head over there," my dad tells her, getting up from the couch. My mom flicks the stove off and covers the bacon with foil.

"If you don't want to go, we'll completely understand. I know something happened with you and Bella, but I'm sure she would want you there."

If she knew the way I treated Bella the last time I saw her, she would think otherwise. It's not that I don't want to visit her, to see our baby and apologize to her for everything I did. Beg for forgiveness. But the day after she's given birth isn't the time or place to do that.

"No, that's okay. You guys go. I need to visit Logan."

"Okay, sweetie." She gives me a quick kiss on my cheek then grabs her purse.

My dad murmurs, "I'll let you know how she is."

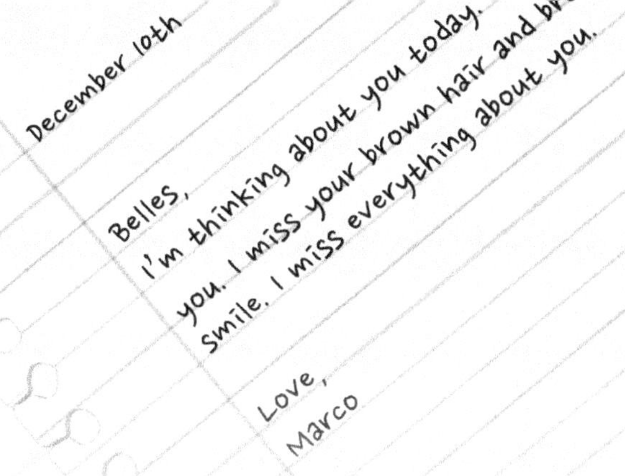

SEVENTEEN

BELLA
TWELVE HOURS EARLIER

MY EYES SHOOT OPEN, FRANTICALLY GLANCING AROUND THE dark room. The clock reads 10:03 p.m. I've only been asleep for a couple hours. My entire pregnancy I have slept like the dead every time my head has hit the pillow so why am I awake? I push my covers off me and throw my legs around to the side of the bed so I can get up to go pee and get a drink.

I feel a strong kick from my little one and smile down at my belly. I can't wait to meet her. As I stand, a huge, sharp pain hits me and I double over, gabbing my belly. *Something's wrong.*

"Tristan!" I shout, then remember I insisted he meet Mason for drinks. I consider driving myself to the hospital when the pain shoots through me again. Instead, I dial 911.

I barely make it to the door to unlock it so the paramedics can get in, when the pain comes at me ten-fold. I stumble to the couch, holding my belly, and pray everything will be okay.

Remembering I need to let my mom and Tristan know I'm going to the hospital, I send a quick text to both of them. Immediately my phone rings, but at the same time, the paramedics come in and my phone is an afterthought.

The minute the paramedics take control, everything happens at lightning speed. I'm put on a gurney and raced to the hospital. On the way, I'm set up with an IV and asked a bunch of questions I have no answers to.

They pull right up to the labor and delivery ward and nurses are there waiting for me. I'm rushed into a room where the on-call doctor assesses me. "We need to prep her for an emergency C-section. The baby is in fetal distress."

Then everything is just a flurry of chaos. A nurse helps strip me of my clothes and puts me in a gown. She covers my hair with a net and then I'm whisked to a freezing cold room.

"Because we didn't have time to give you an epidural, we're going to give you general anesthesia. I want you to count down from twenty for me and you will fall asleep."

The thought of not being awake when my little girl is born causes me to panic and the nurse notices. "It's only going to be for a short time. The baby will be taken to get checked out and before you know it, she will be in your arms."

I nod my understanding, but I can feel the tears dripping down my face, hitting my temple and ears. She places the mask over me and I begin counting. "Twenty… nineteen… eighteen… seventeen… sixt—"

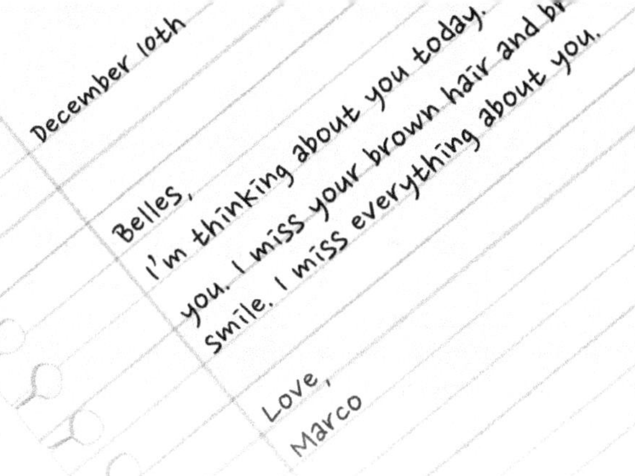

EIGHTEEN

MARCO

"FUCK, MAN! I HATE THIS SHIT SO MUCH! I SHOULDN'T HAVE LET you drive. I should've insisted we take a taxi. I should have been looking at the road instead of down at my cell phone." I'm sitting on the side of my best friend Logan's bed for the first time since he's been moved to San Diego.

"I'm sorry it took me so long to come and visit. I'm a shit friend. I chose drugs and denial over being here. Damn it! You need to wake up. I haven't trained since the accident. I need you to wake up and train with me. I can't do this alone. I don't even think I want to do this anymore. Please. Please wake up." I grab my friend's hand and squeeze it, my head falling to the side railing.

"I'm so sorry, man. I'm so sorry." I start to sob, not being able to control my emotions any longer.

"You have nothing to be sorry about," a soft voice says. I whip my head around to find Logan's sister, Reese, standing in the doorway.

"I didn't mean to overhear. I didn't realize anyone was in here."

"I wipe the tears from my face and stand to give her a hug. "It's good to see you, Reese. I'm so sorry…"

"Stop saying sorry. He tested negative for alcohol. The only thing in his blood were muscle relaxers, which he had a prescription for. He didn't cause that accident and who's to say, had the drugs not been in his system, he still would have reacted the same way. There's no point in thinking about the 'what ifs'."

"I know that, but if I would have insisted…"

Reese cuts me off. "What? The accident never would have happened? You don't know that. The taxi driver could have gotten into an accident and killed you both. Nobody can predict anything."

I know she's right, and I've discussed this at length with my counselor, but sitting in front of Logan makes me question every decision I made leading up to that moment. I want my best friend back.

My phone vibrates in my pocket and I see my mom has sent me a picture text. I click it open and see the most beautiful baby I have ever seen complete with olive skin, black curly locks, and eyes as dark as a midnight sky.

Mom: She looks a lot like Chloe when she was a baby, doesn't she?

She knows. I've seen the looks she's given me and chose to ignore them. And if she knows, who else knows?

Instead of texting her back, something comes over me. I look at Logan and it hits me how unpredictable life is. It can end today. Tomorrow. We never know.

"I need to go." I give Reese a hug and run out the door. I'm on the other side of the hospital, but I make it to the labor and delivery ward in record speed.

"I need to see Bella Cooper," I tell the nurse.

"And you are?"

"I-I'm a friend."

"I will need to approve you." She picks up the phone and dials her room. "I have a…"

"Marco Michaels," I tell her.

"Marco Michaels here to see Bella…Okay…I'll let him up."

"She let me up?" I ask incredulously.

"That was her mother. Bella is signing the birth certificate right now…with the father."

"Not if I can help it."

The nurse tells me the room number, and since I already have a visitor pass from visiting Logan, she presses the button to open the doors. Before they are even fully open, I'm running toward her room, not even thinking about what it is I'm going to say.

I probably should have thought about what I was going to say.

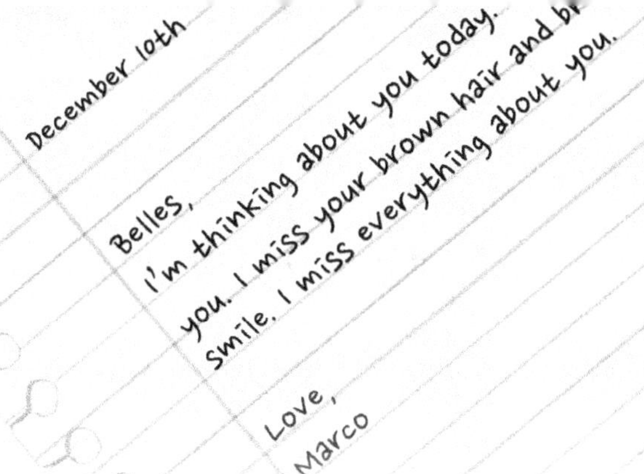

NINETEEN

BELLA

"HERE ARE THE FORMS YOU NEED TO FILL OUT. THIS IS FOR THE birth certificate. This one is for the insurance. This one is for the application for a social security card." I stare at each form and try to remember what each one is for as she continues her list.

"I'm going to go check on a couple other patients while you're filling these out," the nurse says before leaving. The entire staff here have all been wonderful. The data processing woman continues to explain the forms to me when the phone rings next to the bed for the millionth time.

"Mom, can you answer it?"

"Sure, honey."

I take the forms from the woman and hand Tristan the baby so I can fill them out. *The baby.* That's what everyone keeps calling her because I haven't decided on a name yet. Only I have decided, but I'm afraid to say it out loud. The minute I woke up from surgery and they wheeled her into my room, I almost had a nervous breakdown. She's literally a spitting image of Marco. It's almost like I wasn't even a part of conceiving her. I'm sure other people have noticed, how could they not? But nobody has said anything.

"Marco?" Someone says his name and I look up and see Marco standing in the doorway glancing from me to Tristan.

"I need to speak with Bella," Marco says, his eyes locking with mine. He looks good. Nothing like he did the last time I saw him when he told me I was dead to him. He's a bit less built than he used to be. It looks like he's lost some muscle mass, but he looks good nonetheless.

"Son, I don't think right now is the best time." Caleb puts his hand on Marco's shoulder.

"I understand that, but it's important." Marco's eyes plead with me.

"Bella, I think something is wrong with the baby," Tristan says. I drop my pen to take a closer look at her. It looks like she's having a difficult time breathing.

"Mom, get the nurse!"

My mom rushes out, and a few seconds later, she's back in with the nurse.

"It looks like she's have a difficult time breathing," I say, starting to freak out. I attempt to get out of the bed, but my dad stops me. The nurse takes the baby from Tristan, puts her back in her rolling bassinet, and says, "I'm going to get her checked out."

"Can I go with her?" Tristan asks.

"It's best if you stay here. I'll come back in and update you once we know something."

"Oh my God!" I start to breakdown. "What could be wrong with her? She looked perfect."

My mom comes around to the side of the bed and holds me tight. "Don't freak out, Bella. It could be nothing."

The room is silent for what feels like an hour, everyone worrying about the baby. The tension in the room is so palpable that it's beyond uncomfortable. Finally, the nurse and doctor walk back in.

"After running a battery of tests, we have concluded she'll need a blood transfusion," the doctor says.

"What? What's wrong with her?" I cry out.

"It appears she's anemic and the lack of red blood cells are what's causing her to have trouble breathing. The issue is she has a rare blood type. Her blood type is O and only another person with an O blood type can donate. There was an accident a couple days ago, and that patient required the same blood type, so we have put a call to the hospital closest to us for them to send some over; however, if one of the parents or a family member could donate it, it would speed things up."

"Mom, what am I?" I ask.

"You're blood type is B, Bella."

"Okay, then the father has to be O," the nurse states matter-of-factly.

"No, that can't be right," Ashley says. "Tristan is AB."

"Are you sure?" the nurse asks.

Before Ashley can answer, Hayley says, "Marco is O. He got a horrible stomach virus when he was thirteen and was admitted to the hospital. Because I wasn't sure, I asked the nurse when she took blood and she told me."

Everybody's heads swing toward where Marco is standing.

"Fuck," Tristan says. "Bella…"

"Okay, come with me," the nurse says, leading Marco out in a rush.

"Wait!" I shout, Marco and the nurse coming to an abrupt halt.

"He's a drug addict. Can he give blood?"

The nurse looks at Marco then to me. "It will go through a process. If it's not clean, he can't." Then she turns to Marco. "When is the last time you did drugs?"

Marco shakes his head in shame, but I don't give a shit. This is my damn baby and she isn't going to be given blood from a drug addict.

"It's been ninety days since I've touched a drug," he says, causing me to gasp because holy shit, Marco is clean!

"Then we're good, but all blood will get checked before they begin the transfusion. I will keep you updated." Once Marco and the nurse are gone, the room goes silent for a beat and then there's an uproar.

"Bella, what's going on?" my dad asks.

"Bella, tell me this isn't what I think it is," Tristan says softly.

"What's going on?" my brother, Nathan, asks.

Suddenly, it feels like there are way too many people in this small room.

"Okay, everyone needs to calm down," Hayley says over all the questions and accusations. "There's a baby who needs our thoughts and prayers right now. We can deal with this after we know she is okay."

"Why don't we go down to the cafeteria and get a bite to eat?" Ashley suggests to Kaden, taking Nathan and Lilly with her. Mason is at the hotel watching the other kids, but my siblings insisted on coming to see their niece.

"We'll join you," Caleb says, he and Hayley following them out.

"I need to go for a walk," Tristan murmurs and walks out the door without looking at me.

Once it's only my parents left in the room with me, my dad says, "Bella, you gotta talk to us. My imagination is running wild here."

"Cooper, her baby is sick and getting a blood transfusion. This can wait," my mom admonishes.

I close my eyes and think about how I'm going to handle this. I was so stupid to think I would ever get away with nobody finding out Marco is the father of my baby. I don't regret my decision because I did what I felt was best at the time, but now that it's coming to the surface, I need to handle this. I need to woman up and face this head-on. Marco said he didn't want a baby. He recommended I have an abortion. There was no way I was going to tell him I was pregnant with his kid after the things he said.

What I do regret, is lying to Tristan—even if it's only technically by omission. He should have known Marco is the dad. He's been nothing but supportive, and for him to find out I kept this from him is such a slap in his face. I can't even imagine how betrayed he must feel. I need to explain things to him, make him understand why I kept this from him.

I'm not sure how long I lie here thinking about how bad I've fucked up, but when the door opens and I see Tristan and Marco walk in, the blood in my body goes cold.

"I donated the blood. They said once they run it through the tests, as long as it's clean they'll do the transfusion."

"Is it clean?" Tristan sneers.

Marco's nostrils flare and his fists clench as he tries to compose himself. "Yes, it's clean. I've been clean for three months now."

"This is unbelievable," Tristan booms. "I want the truth, Bella."

"Not now," my mom pleads, but Tristan ignores her.

"Is Marco the baby's father?"

"Yes," I say, done with the lies.

My mom covers her mouth, and my dad lets out a loud growl. My mom has hinted to me several times that she knows who the dad really is, so it doesn't surprise me that she isn't shocked. My dad, on the other hand, looks like he's about to murder someone, which means my mom never mentioned her assumptions to him.

"Are you fucking kidding me?" Tristan punches the wall. "Wait a second, you said the father of your baby didn't want the baby." He turns to Marco. "Did you tell Bella you didn't want this kid?" He stalks up to Marco and gets right into his face. "Did you?"

"No, I didn't know…" Marco begins to say, and his lie sets me off.

"You told me to have an abortion. You told me you didn't want a baby."

"You did what?" my dad booms. "You knocked up my fucking daughter then told her to have a goddamn abortion!" My dad grabs Marco by the collar and shoves him against a wall.

"I didn't know she was pregnant with my kid, I swear. I was fucked up. I was on drugs and I didn't know. I don't even remember sleeping with her."

My dad's fist cocks back and it lands straight on Marco's jaw, his face jerking to the side from the impact. At that moment, Caleb and Hayley come in. Caleb rushes over to my dad and Marco to separate them, but then Tristan is in Marco's face.

"I have spent my entire life loving this fucking girl and you had her and can't even remember it. We've been friends for fucking years! How could you do this? Then, because you chose to get high instead of dealing with the accident, you told her to abort her baby. And all of this was before you showed up at our apartment yelling and screaming at her because she tried to get you help!"

Tristan doesn't even cock his hand back when he sucker punches Marco. All the guys grab them, tearing Tristan away from Marco. Once he gets himself somewhat composed, Tristan looks me dead in the eyes and says, "You should have told me, Bella. You should have told me the father of your baby was our best friend. It's one thing to raise a stranger's baby, but you were just going to let me raise our friend's baby without me knowing."

My eyes close as I will the tears to stop. I know I'm wrong here, I don't deserve to cry, but the tears come anyway.

"I'm so sorry," I say. It's not directed at any one person.

"Okay, we need to calm down. Bella just had a baby and that baby is getting a blood transfusion as we speak. All of this can be dealt with later. We need to focus on the baby right now," Hayley begs.

"I gotta get out of here," Tristan huffs and walks out of the room, slamming the door behind him.

"Bella, can I talk to you alone, please?" Marco asks.

"Over my dead fucking body!" my dad roars.

"Cooper, let's give them a few minutes," my mom says, pushing him toward the door.

"What? No! He had sex with my little girl and knocked her up. He's never going to be alone with her again."

"Coop, Bella is almost twenty-one years old. She's not a little girl. Let's go."

"We'll give you guys a few minutes," Caleb says, and a few seconds later the room is empty except for Marco and me.

We both stay silent for a few minutes, neither of us having any idea how to start this conversation. Finally, Marco breaks the silence. "She's beautiful."

"You saw her?" I know he came in just before she was taken out, but I didn't think he was able to get a good look at her.

"My mom sent me a picture. She looks just like Chloe as a baby."

"I was too young to remember what Chloe looked like, but she definitely looks all yours." I shake my head. "Funny how I carried her for nine months and she comes out looking just like you."

Marco chuckles. "What's her name?" I guess we're going to ignore the important shit for right now.

"I haven't named her yet. I was scared to say her name...afraid people would put two and two together."

"What do you mean?" He has a seat in the chair next to my bed.

"I wanted her to have a piece of you. So, I wanted to name her Micaela, after your last name. I remembered one time when we were talking, you said you loved your last name because it represented the best part about you..."

"Hayley and Caleb," Marco finishes, his eyes filled with unshed tears. "Even after everything I said and did, you were still going to name her after me?"

"Of course, she's the best part of the both of us. I wanted to remember the good in you, the you before the drugs."

Marco comes around to the side of the bed and takes my hand in his. "I'm so sorry, Belles. I never should have said the shit I said. I was in a bad place and I wasn't thinking."

"I know, but it still hurt. You broke me, Marco."

"What do we do?"

"What do you mean?"

"I want to be a part of this baby's life. I know you and Tristan are together, but maybe we can work something out, some way I can be there as well. I know it's going to take time to figure it all out, but I'm here now."

"Tristan and I—" The door swings open, cutting me off, and in comes the nurse, the doctor, and the baby.

"Here she is." The nurse wheels the baby in and then hands her to me. "We had to give her a small bottle of sugar water during the transfusion, but you can breastfeed now. The doctor will explain everything to you."

I take my baby in my arms and look her over. Her eyes are open wide, staring at me, her lips making a sucking motion. Not caring about anybody else being in the room, I pull my nursing gown down and latch her on the way the lactation specialist showed me, then pull the light blanket over her so she can eat in peace.

I look up and see Marco staring at me with a look of…awe? I'm not sure.

"The blood transfusion went through without any complications," the doctor says. "Normally the IV is taken out, but because she is a baby, we've taped it up and are keeping it in in case she needs anything. We ran her blood and her red blood cell count is up."

"Is there anything I need to do for her?" I ask.

"You're breastfeeding and that will help with the anemia. We're going to monitor her for the next twenty-four hours. If we need to, we'll put her under the UV lights. To prevent jaundice, you will want to expose her to the sun light. Have her sleep near a window, take her for walks."

"Okay, thank you." I peek inside the blanket to make sure my daughter is breathing and eating okay. I have a feeling I'm going to be hovering over her for the next several weeks—maybe months—making sure she's okay.

"I'll be by later to check on her." The doctor and nurse both excuse themselves and I lift my daughter up over my shoulder to burp her.

"Can I hold her?" Marco asks.

"Not on your damn life." We both look over and see Tristan stalking in. "You think because you suddenly show up, you're just going to have access to her? That's not happening."

Tristan walks over and stands next to me. I latch the baby onto my other breast and cover her with the blanket.

"You can't keep me from my kid," Marco says.

"The kid you told Bella to abort?" Tristan scoffs.

"I didn't know she was mine."

"That may be true," I say, "but you looked right at the blonde you were snorting coke with and told her if she ever got knocked up she better be ready to have an abortion."

I hear a gasp from the door and see Hayley and Caleb as well as my parents all standing in the doorway.

"You did not say that, Marco. Please tell me you didn't." Hayley has her hand over her heart. I didn't mean for them to hear that.

"I was fucked up. I can't take it back, and I'm not trying to make excuses, but I wouldn't have said it if I wasn't high. I know I need to take responsibility for the shit I said and did while high and I have every intention to. But the problem with words is, I can't take them back. I can only try to make it right," Marco pleads.

"You told me plenty of times you didn't want to have kids, Marco. You told me you didn't want kids because according to you, your bloodlines are tainted, and you weren't high when you said that," I point out.

"I know that! I know what I said"–Marco rubs his face with his hands, clearly frustrated–"But that was before we created a baby."

"I need some time," I say. "I need to focus on Micaela. Right now, she's all that matters."

"Micaela?" Tristan questions.

"Yes, her name is Micaela. Spelled M-I-C-A-E-L-A."

"You're naming the baby after the guy who said he didn't want her?" Tristan looks at me incredulously.

"Look, why don't we take a step back?" my mom suggests. "Emotions are running high. We don't want to say things we can't take back. Marco and Tristan, why don't you both go home for a little bit. Let's give Bella some time with Micaela. She'll be discharged in less than forty-eight hours and we'll sort this all out then."

Both guys nod in understanding and walk to the door not daring to argue with my mom. Hayley comes over and gives me a kiss on my forehead. "I think her name is beautiful."

Caleb gives me a small smile before they both leave.

"Bella, for what it's worth, I agree with Hayley. I think it's a beautiful name," my mom says.

"Thank you."

My dad doesn't comment on the name. He simply says, "You're moving home."

"What?" I lift Micaela up and burp her once more.

"You're moving home."

I place Micaela back in her bassinet and make sure she's wrapped up tightly before I say, "That's a decision I'll have to make."

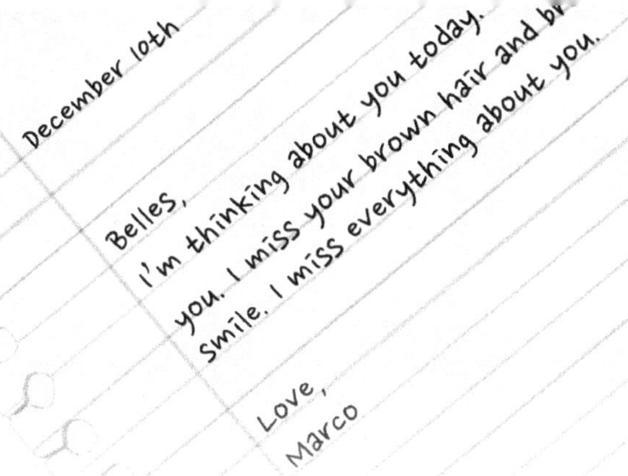

TWENTY

MARCO

MY PARENTS, TRISTAN, AND I STEP ONTO THE ELEVATOR together, the tension in the small enclosed space so thick you could cut it with a knife. Speaking of a knife, it's a damn good thing weapons aren't allowed in the hospital because Tristan is glaring at me like he wants to stab me. When I open my mouth to say something to him, my dad shakes his head, so I close my mouth. I can't even imagine how Tristan is feeling right now, and I don't blame him for being pissed at me for hurting Bella and at Bella for hurting him. This entire situation is a goddamn cluster-fuck of epic proportions.

We get to the first-floor and Tristan walks away without saying a word.

"Now wasn't the time," my dad says. "That man spent the last nine months taking responsibility for a baby he knew wasn't his just for Bella. You need to respect that."

"I do respect it, but I'll be damned if I'm going to have another man raise my baby."

"It was obvious from the get-go Bella and Tristan weren't really together," my mom says. "But one day she will be with someone and you will have to accept that."

The thought of Bella being with someone else, loving someone else, kissing someone else, having sex with someone else, has my fists clenching.

"What's going through that head of yours?" My dad nods toward my tightened fists.

"Bella and Micaela are mine."

My dad laughs. "Well then you better get to groveling because I guaran-fucking-tee she wouldn't agree with that statement."

I know he's right. I have my work cut out for me, but I'm not giving up. I'm the one who fucked this all up and now I'm going to make things right.

"What time is it?" I ask.

My mom looks at her watch. "A little after two. Why?"

"We need to go to the baby store. I need to get my condo baby ready. Then I need to go to a meeting."

My parents give each other a look. "You don't think maybe you're jumping the gun, Son?"

"My goal is to have both those girls under my roof, but regardless, Micaela will eventually be under my roof. I've messed up, but Bella's not the type of person to keep her from me."

And I truly believe that. Bella is one of the best people I know. On top of that, she grew up for the first four years without her dad in her life, and I know she wouldn't purposely do that to the father of her child.

"Okay then, we have some baby stuff to buy, but Marco, you need to give Bella some time. Don't push her, because if you do, you just might push her too hard."

My parents and I spend the afternoon shopping for all things baby. The store says they can have it delivered tomorrow and have it all set up. I never realized all the shit babies need. My mom never had half that shit for my sister Chloe. It makes me sad to think about how much she was truly neglected, and makes me that much more thankful to Kayla and Bentley for adopting her.

Afterward, my parents go back to my place to relax and shower while I attend my first narcotics anonymous meeting. It's held in a church, and I spot my sponsor right away. I met him a few times while at the facility. I'm nervous about being here. I know everyone here has been through their own shit, so they won't be judging me, but sitting here makes it all too real. For the rest of my life, I'll be a recovering addict. I'll have to work every day to make sure drugs are never part of my life again.

Jay tells me I don't have to introduce myself if I don't want to, but I do. I need to take this shit seriously. This isn't just my future at stake if I don't, it's also Bella's and Micaela's. When the gentleman at the front asks if there's anyone new joining who would like to introduce themselves, I stand.

"My name is Marco and I'm a recovering addict," I start. Everyone says hi, then I continue. "I was in an accident with my best friend. He was left in a coma and I was left injured and in pain. I need to be well to work and the pain got to be too much. I turned to drugs… to pills and eventually coke and heroine to numb the pain. My biological mom was a drug addict who overdosed, and I don't want to end up like her." I sit and the gentleman thanks me, and the meeting continues.

A few people go up to receive their different color key tags to celebrate their different lengths of staying clean. My name is called last and I go up to receive a white key tag. Engraved on it is *Welcome*. I thank the gentleman, who I learned is named Brad, and have a seat until the meeting ends.

Once I say goodbye to a couple of people who introduced themselves to me after the meeting concluded, and speak with Jay, I head out to meet my parents for dinner. We spend the time together discussing Bella, my meeting and sponsor, Micaela, and how Mackenzie and Chloe are doing through all this. I make a note to call them both to speak to them about all of this. They're both Micaela's aunts.

After dinner, my parents call it a night. It's around nine o'clock when my phone rings, an unknown number popping up on the caller ID.

"Hello."

"Umm… hey… it's Bella. I wasn't sure if this was still your number, but I figured I would try." She's rambling nervously and it pulls at my heart strings. There was a time when Bella wouldn't have been nervous to call me. God how I've missed this girl. Missed our friendship. "Anyway, I just wanted to thank you—"

"Thank me?" I cut in.

"For giving Micaela your blood. If you wouldn't have, we would have had to wait. I know her anemia wasn't life threatening but still…"

"Belles." I sigh. "You don't have to thank me. She's my daughter too. And even if she wasn't, she's yours. I would do anything for her. I'm just glad I was sober and didn't have any drugs in my system so I could donate. If this were three months ago, I wouldn't have been able to." And fuck if that isn't a shock to my gut, just another reminder what's at stake by me staying clean.

There's a pregnant pause and then Bella says, "So you went to rehab." I think it's meant to be a question but it comes out as more of a thought.

"I did. I'm ninety-two days sober. I got out yesterday actually. I was planning to come by to talk to you, but then everything happened before I could."

"I'm glad you got help, Marco." I can hear the raw emotion in her words and it guts me.

"When I found out the baby was mine, I called my dad."

"Wait, when you found out—" There's a loud wail and the phone gets all muffled. "Hey, Marco, I have to go. Micaela is up and needs to be fed. I sent my parents back to their hotel because they were beyond exhausted and my dad has to head back tomorrow with my brother and sister."

"You're there by yourself?" I don't know much about babies, but I can't imagine just having been sliced open would make it easy to care for a newborn.

"Yeah, the nurses come around." The baby's cries get louder. "I gotta go, but I just wanted to say thank you."

Before I can respond, the line goes dead. I throw on a pair of basketball shorts, a T-shirt, and slip on a pair of slides, grabbing my keys and cell phone. I find a piece of paper to leave a note on the counter, letting my parents know I went to the hospital, in case they wake up and I'm not back yet. Locking the door behind me, I head to the hospital.

As I'm hurrying down the hall, I spot a gift shop and take a detour inside. I noticed when I visited before, all the flowers and balloons filling up her room.

"Can I get a dozen of these balloons blown up?" I ask the lady at the counter.

"Sure."

Then a thought comes to mind. "Wait! Do you have a permanent marker I can use?" She looks at me confused but hands it to me.

After writing what I need to on each of the balloons, I hand the marker and balloons to her. While she's filling them up, I spot Bella's favorite candy on the display rack near the register.

"These too, please."

Once she's done blowing up the balloons and ringing me up, I make my way to the Labor and Delivery ward, to the recovery wing. Because I'm the father, they let me through after I show them my identification. I open the door slowly in case Bella and Micaela are asleep, but when I walk in, the scene in front of me nearly takes my breath away. Bella is talking softly to Micaela. She's holding her close and smiling at her daughter like she hung the moon and if it's not the most beautiful sight I've ever seen, I don't know what is. Without her knowing, I pull out my phone and snap a picture to capture the moment. Only I don't realize my phone is on loud, so when the picture snaps, it makes a shutter sound.

"What are you doing here?" Bella looks up in surprise.

I walk inside, the balloons bobbing everywhere—getting stuck in the doorway—and Bella gives me a *what the fuck* look. After finally getting all the balloons into the room, I place them next to her bed. When they float to the ceiling we both look up.

"I probably should have tied those to something, huh?"

Bella just giggles.

"What do they say?" She tries to read the writing on the balloons, so I grab one and bring it down.

"It's not a boy?" she questions.

"Yeah, because I know you hate pink and they didn't have any blue 'It's a girl' balloons."

She cracks up laughing and fuck if I haven't missed that sound.

"Umm… you know you could have just crossed out the word boy and wrote girl, right?"

I look up at the balloon. "Well, shit. I guess that would've made more sense." I shrug and she laughs some more.

"Well, I love them. All of them."

"Yeah, I got a dozen. Figured it would help even out all the pink. It looks like Barbie's dream prom up in here."

"Ha! Apparently having a girl means dressing her in all pink. I tried to buy a green onesie once and my mom thought I was crazy and made me put it back."

"And I would bet my life, you went back and bought it."

"Hell yes, I did!"

A memory pops into my head and I laugh.

"What?"

"I was just remembering that time you grew out of your MMA gi and your mom ordered you a new one."

"Oh my God! It was magenta! Like, who the hell wears a magenta freaking gi?"

"You did! Until you threw it in the washer with bleach."

"I was hoping to turn it white! My mom said the bleach turned clothes white! How was I supposed to know she didn't mean literally?"

We laugh.

"I also brought you these." I hand her the bag filled with white KitKats.

"Oh, yum! My favorite." She opens one up, taking a bite.

"Yeah, I was shocked to see them at the register because everybody knows white chocolate is gross."

"It is not. They're the best! Better than the milk chocolate."

"I've said this before and I'll say it again. Candy bars are meant to be made of chocolate. That white shit is like eating fake chocolate."

"And I will say it once again, we will just have to agree to disagree because white chocolate is the best chocolate."

We sit there in silence for a few minutes, neither of us knowing what to say next. I breathe a sigh of relief when Bella says something.

"Did you come all this way just to bring me balloons and candy?"

"I'm here to help." I grab a seat and pull it up to her bed then lean over to take a look at our daughter. Her eyes are just barely open.

"She just finished eating so she's going to pass out soon. Want to hand me a diaper and wipes so I can change her?"

"I can do it if you want." I put my hands out to take her but quickly pull them back in. "If that's okay."

"Of course, it is. Do you know how? I can walk you through it."

I put my hands out and Bella hands me my daughter for the first time. I gently cradle her head and hold her tight. For a minute I don't move, I just look at this precious little miracle that I can't even remember creating.

Without realizing I'm doing it, I sniffle back the tears that are trying to seep out and Bella puts her hand on my arm. "Hey, what's wrong?"

"God, Belles, I don't even remember making her. I'm such a piece of shit."

"No, you aren't. You were on drugs. I just didn't realize it."

"That's not a damn excuse." I shake my head and look down at our baby. "She's so tiny. I remember when my mom brought Chloe home, and then when Hayley brought Mackenzie home. I didn't think it was possible to love a baby any more than I loved them, but looking at my daughter, my heart feels like it's going to explode, and because I chose to turn to drugs, I almost never met her."

I glance up at Bella. "Thank you for not aborting her. I can't even imagine how scared you were and then I said all that shit, and I wouldn't have blamed you if you would have had an abortion."

I raise Micaela up to my nose and sniff her. She has that baby scent newborns have. Chloe and Mackenzie both smelled the same way.

I stand and head over to the changing table to change her diaper. "I used to change all of Chloe's diapers. My mom—when she came home from the hospital—sunk right into depression. Chloe's dad had been killed in a drive-by shooting, and my mom, she just couldn't handle it. She would smoke and drink all the time and I would take care of Chloe. I hated when I would have to go to school and Chloe would be left alone with my mom. Or when I would go to the gym, I would feel so guilty, but I was so young and I needed to get away sometimes. The best day of my life was the day Caleb saved us."

I button Micaela's onesie bottom back up then rock her softly until her eyes flutter closed and she's asleep. Wrapping her up gently in a blanket, I lay her down in her bassinet before I go back to sit next to Bella. Grabbing her hand, I thread our fingers, needing the connection to ask the question I've been dreading. Bella flinches at my touch and I hate what's become of us. What I've done to us.

"I need to know…the night we made her"—I take a deep breath—"was I mean or rough with you?" I take another deep breath. "What I mean is, the night we…" I can't even finish. Bella's mouth opens to answer when the door closes shut. We both look at it, waiting to see if someone's coming in, but nobody is there.

"You weren't mean or rough." She looks anywhere but at me, a sign she's lying.

"Belles, you can't sugar coat it. One of the things my counselor said at my sessions in rehab is that I have to face and deal with everything I did while on drugs."

"You weren't mean or rough. You just weren't you. I should have known something was wrong with you. You said you missed me and needed me, but it wasn't like the night we were together in the cabin.

You just got straight to it and then passed out."

"Fuck." I release her hand, resting my elbows on my knees. My hands scrub the sides of my face. "I'm so sorry. Did I force you?"

"No! No, we both wanted it. You reached for a condom and I thought you put it on. It was dark and I couldn't see. It wasn't until afterward I realized you…well you know." She shrugs shyly.

"I came in you." Bella's face and neck turn pink when I say that and I can't help but chuckle. She looks so adorable embarrassed.

"Yeah." She sighs then laughs.

"How did you know I came in you?" I ask just to fuck with her. Her face turns an even darker shade of pink and she grabs a pillow, lightly smacking me with it.

"Shut up, Marco!"

"Okay, okay." I give her back her pillow. The nurse comes in and checks on Bella and Micaela and then another lady comes in.

"Bella, I'm about to leave for the night and was just wondering if you've filled out the paperwork yet. If all goes well you'll be discharged tomorrow."

Bella looks at her sheepishly. "I'm sorry, I haven't. I promise I will tonight."

"Okay, dear. I'll come back tomorrow morning to collect them."

"Thank you."

When the lady leaves, I ask, "What was that about?"

"I have to fill out the paperwork for Micaela. For her birth certificate, social security number, and insurance. I should have filled them out earlier, but I forgot with everything going on."

"Does she have insurance?" I didn't even think about how much a hospital stay for a baby must cost.

"Because I'm in school, I'm on my dad's insurance so I'm covered, but Micaela's hospital stay isn't. I have to fill out the paperwork for her to get insurance."

"Okay, we'll handle it." She looks at me skeptically. "Belles, she's my responsibility as much as she is yours. Please let me help."

Bella averts her gaze and I know she's keeping something from me, but I'm not going to push it tonight.

"How about I help you fill out those forms and then you can get some sleep?"

"The baby might wake up."

"Have you been awake the entire time since she was born?"

"No, I slept a few hours. My mom stayed awake. That's why I sent them to the hotel. She was exhausted."

"Then you'll sleep and I'll keep an eye on her, but Bella, you know it's okay to sleep, right? The baby's cries will wake you."

"I know. I'm just not ready yet." I hold back my laughter. She's already a hundred times better of a mom than my biological mom was.

I grab the papers and ask her each question, writing down the answers she tells me. When we get to the birth certificate form, I know this is going to be a tough one.

"Name."

"Micaela."

I look up and she gives me a look of uncertainty. "Yes, but you need a middle and last name. Well, I guess just the last name. I don't have a middle name."

"I was thinking Micaela Lizbeth after my mom. But if you want to maybe name her after your mom…"

"Fuck no, your mom is amazing. Micaela Lizbeth is great. Now we just need a last name."

Bella doesn't say anything for a minute, so I decide to let her off the hook, tell her the baby should have her last name, but before I can, she surprises me by saying, "Michaels."

"Look, Bella…" I start to give her an out. Twenty-four hours ago, she didn't even plan on me being in the baby's life, let alone giving her my last name.

"You're her father. Unless, I mean…" she backtracks. "I guess we haven't discussed anything really…I don't know if you're planning to be in her life or to what extent."

"Bella, stop," I say gently. "I'm in her life as much as you'll let me. I know this is all a shock, but I want to be her father. I know we have a lot to figure out, but I want to be her dad."

"Are you sure? Because you said your blood was tainted. I don't believe that or agree, but Marco, I can't have you calling yourself her dad then walking away from her down the line."

"I would never ask to be a part of her life and then walk away. Yes, I was afraid of ending up like my biological parents. But one thing I've learned in rehab is that we pave our own paths. I didn't turn to drugs because my mom did them. I turned to them by choice. My father was a piece-of-shit drug dealer who used women, but I am not going to be like him. I have a sponsor and I went to my first meeting today. I'm not saying shit will be perfect, but I'm not going to do drugs again."

"Okay, then I want her to have your last name. Micaela Lizbeth Michaels."

After we finish filling out the paperwork, Micaela wakes up to eat again, and once she's done, she passes right back out. I convince Bella to fall asleep as well and then I spend the night watching them sleep— and thank God for this second chance.

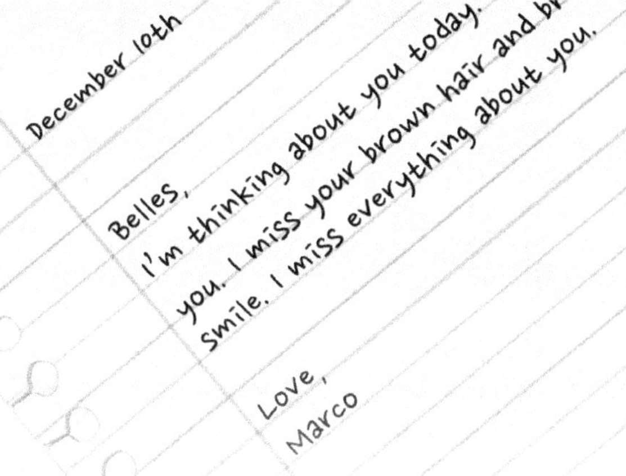

TWENTY-ONE

BELLA

I WAKE UP AND LOOK OVER TO SEE MARCO PASSED OUT IN THE chair. The entire night he was helpful. Every time Micaela would wake up, he would hand her to me and then change her diaper before laying her back down. Surprisingly, I slept well between feedings and feel refreshed. Well, as refreshed as a new mother can feel, anyway. I, at least feel less exhausted than yesterday.

Micaela is still asleep, so I grab my phone from the nightstand to text Tristan since I haven't heard from him, but when I look up, he's standing in the doorway.

"Hey," I say, putting my phone back. "How long have you been here?"

Tristan steps in closer and I notice he has black circles under his eyes. His hair is a bit disheveled, and if I'm not mistaken, he's wearing the same clothes from yesterday.

"Just a few minutes. We need to talk." He walks closer to the bed.

"Okay." I'm not sure what Tristan is going to say but I know whatever's coming my way, I deserve. I put him in a shitty situation. Even though I was always upfront about not wanting to be a couple, he was still one hundred percent committed to being Micaela's father.

"I know there's nothing between us and I finally accept that, and while I'm pissed you kept her paternity from me, I want you to come home. I want you to raise her in our apartment. I don't trust Marco. He just got out of rehab. What if he relapses?"

After my parents left, I weighed all my options and came to a decision. "I'm moving back home."

"Good." He nods.

"No, I don't think you understand. I'm moving back home… to

Las Vegas. My parents are going to help me raise Micaela. I want to finish school. I didn't understand how important it was until I had her. I need to make sure I can provide for her. I want to train as well. I can't move back in with you. It's not fair to you."

"Bella..."

"No, Tristan. You are one of the most selfless people I know. You have been my best friend for as far back as I can remember. You have always put me first, but I'm not going to let you do this. You deserve to be happy, to find love, to have a damn life. I never should have put you in this position. I'm so sorry."

Tristan's head drops and he sighs just as Marco clears his throat. Shit! I am such an idiot! I completely forgot about the guy sitting in the chair next to me, sleeping. I have no idea how much he heard until he says, "You're moving to Las Vegas." It's not a question; he heard me.

"Which is for the best," Tristan adds. Marco stands and I'm scared they're going to get into it again. Marco's jaw and lip are already puffy from being hit by Tristan and my dad yesterday.

"Deciding what's best is between Bella and me."

"Marco," I chide. "Don't act like that." I give him a warning glare and his eyes soften.

"Are you serious right now? I'm pretty sure you lost the right to *decide* what's best for either of them the day you told her she was dead to you."

"Tristan, that's not fair," I say. I'm stuck in the middle of these two guys battling over me and my daughter and I can't help but feel guilty. We were all friends and our friendships have been destroyed.

"I'll give you that," Marco says calmly. "I know I said some fucked up shit that I can't take back, but I'm working on making it right, which starts and ends with being the man Bella and our daughter deserve. Here's the thing, I respect the hell out of you for being protective of and caring for Bella and my daughter, and if you two were in love and wanted to be together, I would suck it up and be happy for you two."

I'm shocked by Marco's admission and maybe even a little hurt that he would be okay with Tristan and me being together. I know Marco doesn't see me the way I see him, but still...

He continues. "I would live with it. I would co-parent the best I can with you, man. But you two aren't together. You said it yourself. So, I don't want to sound like an asshole but Micaela is my daughter and I'm here, and Bella choosing to put my name on her birth certificate gives me the right to make decisions with her."

Tristan's eyes shoot to mine in disbelief and maybe even a little bit of disappointment. Then Marco says, "Look at the bright side. Now you and Gina can be together." Tristan's look turns to confusion.

"What the fuck does Gina have to do with this?"

"She's the one who told me about the baby, that she's mine."

"What did you just say?" Tristan asks slowly.

"She came to me three months ago and said I was the father. She showed me a letter Bella wrote to Micaela and it stated I was the dad. Gina said she knew you didn't cheat on her and she asked me to take responsibility so you two could be together again. Something about you being hers."

Tristan turns to me. "You wrote the baby a letter letting her know who her father was? You were going to let me raise her with every intention of telling her one day Marco was her dad?"

Oh shit. "No, that letter was in case I died. I read moms should write their babies letters, so I wrote one in case I died and Micaela wanted to know the truth. I never planned to just give it to her."

"This is un-fucking-believable. So, you knew you were the dad three months ago, yet you waited until she was born to make it known."

"No, man, I didn't want to go to Bella while I was on drugs. I called my dad and checked into rehab. I knew I needed to be clean when I went to her. She wasn't due for another few weeks. I thought I had time. I didn't know she would give birth early."

"Holy shit." Tristan laughs humorlessly. "I can't even deal with all this. Bella, if you choose to stay in the apartment, you know I won't kick you out. Just let me know. If you're leaving, I need to look for another roommate."

Tristan walks toward Micaela and I hold my breath. "Goodbye, pretty girl." He brings two fingers to his lips and presses them to her forehead. Then he comes to the side of the bed and gives me a chaste kiss on my forehead. "I need some time, Bella." His words sound a lot like goodbye.

"Please tell me I'm not losing you, Tristan."

"Right now, I can't tell you anything."

Hot tears prick my eyes as I nod my understanding. "Okay."

"Let me call you," he says. The tears release and fly down my cheeks as my best friend walks out the door and out of my life.

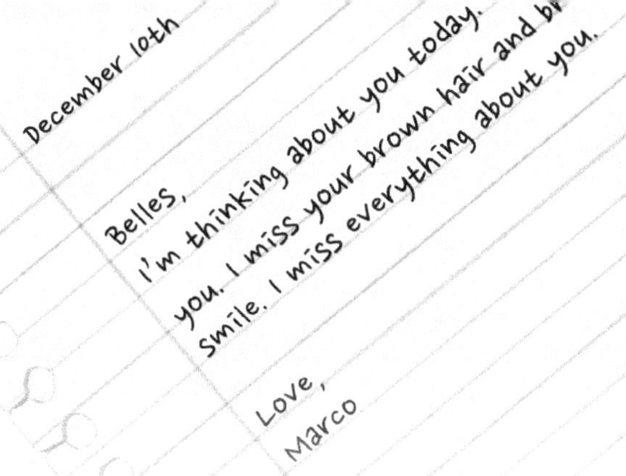

TWENTY-TWO

MARCO

TRISTAN LEAVES, SLAMMING THE DOOR BEHIND HIM, AND THE sound reverberates through the walls waking Micaela. Bella quickly wipes her eyes and stands to grab our crying baby.

"Wait, let me grab her for you," I say as the data specialist walks in. It's like this hospital room has a revolving door.

"No, it's okay. I need to walk around. I appreciate you helping me but you're making me lazy." She gives me a small smile to try to hide the fact that she's heartbroken her best friend just walked out the door—literally and figuratively—and I can't help feeling like it's partially my fault.

"Good morning! I'm here to pick up the forms so we can update the chart," the woman says.

"Yes, I have them here for you." I hand her the packet of papers and she smiles, thanking us before leaves.

As Bella sits on the couch feeding Micaela, I watch her stare out the window for a long time before I ask, "Do you want to talk about it?"

She turns to me and gives me another one of those fake smiles I hate. "No, I deserved it. I should have been honest with everyone from the beginning. I know Tristan needing space is for the best, but it feels like a piece of me just walked out that door with him."

"He's just upset right now and needs time."

"I know," she agrees absentmindedly, focusing on Micaela.

"You did what you felt was best given the circumstances. What I did, what I said, I put you in that position."

"But I chose how to handle it. I'm not some kid anymore. I'm a mother and I need to make better choices. Lying and keeping stuff from my family, from Tristan, is not okay."

We sit in silence for a while, and then I remember what she said to Tristan.

"So… Las Vegas?"

Bella's eyes go wide. "I just think it's for the best. Like I told Tristan, I want to finish school and I still have a few semesters left."

"What are you majoring in?"

"It was a tough decision because as you know I just want to fight."

"And become a UFC champion," I add.

"Yeah." Her lips curl into a real smile. "But since I had to pick a major, I ended up going with business management. I know I can't fight forever, and with the women's division being so small, I wanted to get a degree in something that will give me an opportunity to provide for Micaela."

"That makes sense. What are you planning to do with your degree?"

"I talked to my dad and he said he's planning to step back from the gym sooner rather than later, spend some time with Nathan and Lilly since neither of them are into the gym, and spend more time with my mom."

"Okay…"

"He said while I'm training, he would show me the ropes for me to take over the gym. Since the first time I stepped foot in that gym, it's felt like my home away from home, you know."

"I know exactly what you mean."

"I was thinking I could move back and start learning, and with my degree in business management, I'm hoping it will provide me with ways to successfully run the gym."

"I get that, I do. But what I don't get is why you asked me if I'm going to be in our daughter's life and to what extent if you were just planning on moving to another state with her."

Bella burps Micaela and walks her to the changing table to change her diaper. With her back turned to me, she says, "I never said you couldn't be in her life. I just feel like this is the best option for my daughter and me."

She turns back around and I can see the tears filling her lids as she holds our daughter to her chest, using her as a protective shield. "I can't live with Tristan. I mean, I could. I know he would let me since it's my apartment just as much as it's his, but I need to give him his space. I hurt him so badly. My parents are in Vegas, and so is my aunt Kayla and my brother and sister. Sure, I've made some friends here, but I can't ask them to watch Micaela. I'm taking off the rest of this semester, but I'm hoping to at least take a couple classes online this summer and go back next fall full time. You know you can visit anytime."

"Visit?" I laugh incredulously. "You don't really think I'm going to let you and our daughter move to another state and I'll just simply *visit*? If you're moving back to Vegas then I guess I am as well." I shrug.

"What?" She gasps and places Micaela back in her bassinet. That little girl drinks and then passes out into a drunken milk stupor.

"Marco, your entire life is here in California."

That's where she's wrong, so damn wrong. I get off the couch and close the space between us, pushing a wayward hair that's escaped from her pony tail behind her ear. "No, Bella, my entire life is apparently moving to Las Vegas."

Bella looks at me dumbfounded, but before she can open her mouth, she looks over her shoulder, her eyes widening. She takes a step back from me.

"What are you doing here?" the deep voice booms. Knowing who's voice it is before I even turn around, I take a deep breath preparing for the fight that is going to take place.

"Dad, calm down." Bella walks up to her dad and gives him a hug. "Marco helped me with Micaela last night."

"I told you we could have stayed." Cooper glares at me like I'm the devil, and I don't blame him. While on drugs, I knocked up his little girl.

"It's fine. The registrar says if all goes well I will be released today. You guys needed your sleep."

"And you're moving back with us. Did you ask how soon Micaela can be cleared to fly? Are you staying at your apartment until then?" Cooper speaks like I'm not even in the room, and I know I need to earn back his respect, so I refrain from arguing with him.

"I don't know what I'm doing," Bella says softly, suddenly unsure of herself.

"Yes, you do," I speak up. "We're moving to Las Vegas."

"What the fuck do you mean 'We're'?" Cooper steps into my personal space.

"Marco, you can't do that. You can't just up and move. And I told you, you can visit her any time," Bella insists.

"Where Bella and Micaela go, I go. It's that simple," I say calmly to her dad. Then I turn to Bella and say, "I have absolutely nothing keeping me here. I have a condo I haven't lived in in over three months, which I can cancel the lease on. We can find a three-bedroom place near your parents, near the gym. I know I don't have the right to ask anything of you, but I am asking you anyway for this chance. I don't want to see my daughter on weekends or holidays. Give me a chance. Give us a chance. Please."

"Wait a fucking second. You can't be considering this, Bella. You can't even trust this guy." He turns to me. "You aren't welcome anywhere near my daughter or granddaughter."

Liz, thankfully jumps in. "Liam Cooper." *Oh shit! She used his first name.* "You missed out on four years of raising our daughter and you say all the time it's your biggest regret, and you're going to try to stop another man from taking responsibility. What is wrong with you?"

Cooper sucks in his lip, trying to keep his mouth shut, not wanting to upset his wife further, while Bella comes closer to me. "Giving you a chance as a father and giving us a chance are two completely separate conversations. They can't go hand in hand. We can raise a baby together without being together and we shouldn't be together just because we share a child."

"I want both." And it feels damn good to say that out loud. I have loved this woman for years and my running from her thinking I was doing the right thing only hurt both of us. I'm done running.

Bella looks me right in my eyes, assessing me, maybe trying to see if I mean what I say. "How about we start with the first one and maybe in time we can consider the second one."

"Okay, I'll take it."

"So, that's it?" Cooper asks Bella. "Just like that you're letting him into your daughter's life? Your life?"

"I went four years without you. You didn't get to hold me in the hospital or bring me home. You missed my first steps and my first words."

"Bella…" Cooper chokes out her name.

"No, I know it was out of your control. I know you and Mom regret not exchanging numbers the weekend you met. But the fact is, we missed out on a lot and not by our choice. I'm not going to do that to Marco. Do I trust him? No. Trust is earned, not given." She raises a brow at me. "But if he wants to move back to Vegas with me and be in our daughter's life, I'm not going to stop him."

"It's not the same thing, Bella. He said he didn't want the baby."

"No, he said he didn't want a baby. He didn't know my baby was his, and you might be mad at Marco right now, but you know the person he was before. You loved him like he was your own son. If I messed up, if I turned to drugs and lashed out, would you disown me too?"

Cooper doesn't say anything. He just shakes his head, his eyes bloodshot like he's holding back tears and I know exactly how he feels, because the large lump in my throat tells me I feel pretty much the same thing. Bella is the youngest one here, yet in this moment, she is probably the wisest. She is also the most forgiving. She could easily push me away, make shit hard on me, and I would deserve it. I told her she was dead to me for crying out loud. I told her she should abort her own fucking kid! But instead, she opens her heart up and lets anyone and everyone in, and tries to see the best of everyone in every damn situation.

Cooper gives Bella a hug and tells her he loves her. While they're embracing, the pediatrician comes in. "Good afternoon, I'm Dr. Weisberg. I'm just going to check on baby"—He flips through his chart—"Michaels. And if all is well, you will both be discharged today."

"Baby Michaels?" Cooper asks Bella.

"Yes, I gave her Marco's last name, the same way mom gave me yours once she knew what it was."

"Doctor, how soon can the baby travel via private plane?"

"Normally, the recommendation to fly is two months to give the babies time to build up their immune systems, but by private plane, there's no reason she can't fly immediately. Just make sure to keep her away from others at the airport."

"Thank you," Cooper says, then he pulls out his phone and puts it to his ear. After a few seconds, he says, "I'm going to need the plane in San Diego… Yes, tonight… Thank you."

"Dad, I can't just leave tonight! I still need to get my stuff from the apartment."

"I can take you over there after you get out. We can pack what you need and have the rest shipped. I'm going to do the same for my stuff," I point out.

"I don't think us going to the apartment together is a good idea," Bella says.

"I'll go," her dad says. "While you're waiting to be discharged I'll go by the apartment. Text Tristan and let him know. I'll be back after it's all taken care of and we'll fly out tonight."

"We need to find a place," Bella says, suddenly looking extremely overwhelmed.

"Hey," I murmur. "I'll stay with my parents and you'll stay with yours for the time being, and as soon as we find a place, we'll move in and give Micaela a beautiful home."

Bella nods. "Okay."

Micaela cries out and we all turn to look at her. The doctor is checking her out and Bella rushes over to make sure she's okay.

"Micaela is doing very well. I just want you to make sure you give her exposure to the sunlight and follow up with whichever pediatrician you choose for her. You'll need to make an appointment to get her one week shots done.

"Okay, I'll call the pediatrician my mom used for me and my siblings."

"Very good. The nurse should be in shortly to give you your official discharge paperwork." He shakes Bella's hand then mine. "Congratulations."

"Thank you," we both say and then he's out the door.

December 10th

Belles,

I'm thinking about you today. I miss your brown hair and big you. I miss everything about you.

Love,
Marco

TWENTY-THREE

BELLA

Me: I know you asked for space and I promise I'm giving it to you. My dad needs to come by to get my stuff from the apartment. When would be a good time?

I STARE AT THE SCREEN SCARED TO DEATH OF WHAT TRISTAN'S response will be—if he even responds at all. It's insane how much has changed in the last seventy-two hours. I went in to give birth to my daughter with one guy claiming to be the father, only to have my entire world shaken and knocked around. And when I think of how Tristan must feel—I know in the long run, this is for the best, but that doesn't mean my heart isn't hurting any less for my best friend and what he must be going through.

Tristan: He can come by any time.

Tears prick my eyes when I read his text. I know I shouldn't have expected anything more, but deep down I was hoping he would say something more. What? I have no clue. I just hate that I'm about to move over three hundred miles away and we aren't even on speaking terms.

Me: Okay, thank you. And Tristan, I'm sorry...for everything.

I probably shouldn't have written that second half, but I needed to say it one last time.

Tristan: I know. Just give me time.

Me: Okay

My eyes stay trained on our conversation, hoping to see the bubbles bouncing, indicating he's texting back, until the nurse comes in and hands me Micaela's and my discharge papers. Then I put my phone away, take a deep breath, and prepare to start my new life.

"IT'S A ONE-STORY HOME IN THE SAME NEIGHBORHOOD YOUR parents live in."

The realtor reads off the address and we agree to meet her there in fifteen minutes. At this point, I would agree to sign a lease to live in a cardboard box if it meant moving the heck out of my parents' house. You know the saying, *once you move out of your parents' home you can't ever move back*? Well, it's true. Damn true. Listen to whoever tells it to you.

It's been one week since I've been back in my childhood room under my parents' roof and if I don't get out of here soon, I just might kill my father. His hovering and protectiveness has grown to an entirely new level since he found out Marco is the father of Micaela. Every time I'm texting, he's looking over my shoulder. He's asked— no, *suggested*—on numerous occasions I stay living here. He's even asked me multiple times if I'm planning to have sex with Marco in the future! And when Marco and I decided to have dinner with his parents after Micaela's checkup, he texted me thirty times asking when I would be home.

Oh! And don't get me started on the night Marco came over to visit with our daughter and we fell asleep on the couch…with our clothes on…and our baby between us. You would think we were buck-naked and screwing right there in my parents' living room the way he yelled. He not only woke up Micaela, but he woke up my brother and sister who thought something was wrong.

Like I said, I need to move out. I may have only been out from under his roof for two years, but it was long enough that my wings cannot go back to being clipped. I need to soar on my own, especially if I want to keep the good relationship I have with my father.

Marco insisted on picking me up to check out the house since our cars haven't been shipped back over yet, and I'm not supposed to drive for a couple weeks after having a C-section. He still has his car here for when he visits his parents. Since he said the home we're looking at is close by, I left Micaela with my mom.

"Marco, these homes are expensive. I thought we were looking at apartments."

"Please don't worry about the money." Marco gives me a look. We've argued over several of the apartments we've seen. I insisted on finding the places after Marco took us to see a penthouse condo on the top floor of downtown Vegas. Unfortunately, the ones I have found are so tiny, yet so expensive.

I never realized how much it costs to live in Vegas, and with me going to school full time, no longer on scholarship, there's only so much I can contribute. I have my trust fund my dad set up for me years ago from when my grandfather died, but I'm using it to go to school and would like to save whatever is left of it for the future. I'm planning to speak to my dad about maybe hiring me at the gym during the days and hours I'm not in school or training.

"I need to worry because I'm going to be contributing and I would rather not dip into my trust fund." Marco just shakes his head. We pull up to the house and I see it's only one street over from my parents' house. It's one of the smaller homes in the neighborhood, but it's beautiful. It is all brick and stone and has a huge white privacy fence. There's no way we can afford this place.

Instead of arguing with Marco, I let the realtor show us around. It has three bedrooms, a den, a living room and family room, an off the kitchen dining room, and a huge back patio. The owners even built an outdoor kitchen out there. I can't even imagine how much the rent is for the place.

"What do you think?" Marco asks.

"I think we should discuss this *alone.*" I glance toward the realtor not wanting to have this conversation in front of her.

"How about I let you two speak and I'll wait for you outside?" She smiles brightly, leaving without waiting for an answer.

"Okay, so what do you think?" Marco asks again.

"I think we're both currently unemployed. I think I'm a full time student, no longer on a scholarship. I think there's no way we can afford this place unless I use the money my dad put away for me. Have you spoken to the UFC about your contract?"

Marco's brows furrow. "Bella, you are aware up until last year I spent the last eight years fighting in the UFC, right? I am completely undefeated and currently hold the championship belt. Until I was injured I was making enough from my sponsorships alone to afford this place."

"Thanks for the recap," I say dryly.

Marco chuckles. "I'm not trying to rub it in your face, Belles. One day you will be a fucking champion. You will have sponsors begging you to sign with them. My point is those fights add up, and since I moved to California, I lived with my cousin Mathias who I split the bills with. Then I rented my own place but was in rehab for most of the lease. I have plenty of money saved up and I don't expect you to— or want you to—use the money your dad put away for you. What I need to know is if you like this place. Can you see yourself raising our daughter here?"

"Yes," I blurt out.

"Okay, then." Marco walks out the front door, with me trailing behind him. "We'll take it," he says to the realtor.

"Perfect! Since you're preapproved, we can go over the down payment and all the other specifics. I think we can probably get the closing date set to the end of next month."

Most of what she says goes over my head, but I do understand end of next month, which means six more weeks of living under my dad's roof. *Ugh!*

"What's wrong?" Marco asks, sounding concerned.

"Huh?"

"You made an annoyed sound. Is this house not what you want?" Hmm… I must have said that last part out loud.

"No, it is! It's living under my dad's roof for the next six weeks that I don't want." And even I can hear the whininess in my voice. Marco laughs. *Laughs!* Because he's living with Hayley and Caleb who couldn't care less what their son does, meanwhile my dad thinks in four weeks I'll be turning twelve instead of twenty-one.

"Since I'm planning to pay cash for the house and the pre-walkthrough has been done, can you please ask the owners if they would mind us moving in early, like as soon as possible, since it's empty anyway."

"Cash?" the realtor and I say in unison.

"Wait, Marco! Are we renting or buying this place?"

"Buying. My dad looked at the price and details before we came to check it out. He said it will make a great investment for me."

"I'll call them right now!" The realtor pulls out her phone and walks a few feet away from us to call the owners. After a few minutes, she comes back with a huge smile on her face. "We are good to go." She hands Marco the keys. "Let's go to the office now to sign the appropriate paperwork and do the good faith deposit."

"Sounds perfect." Marco takes the keys from her then leans in close to my ear and says, "Welcome home, Belles," which causes chills to spread throughout my body, making me visually shake. Marco sees my reaction and gives me a knowing smirk.

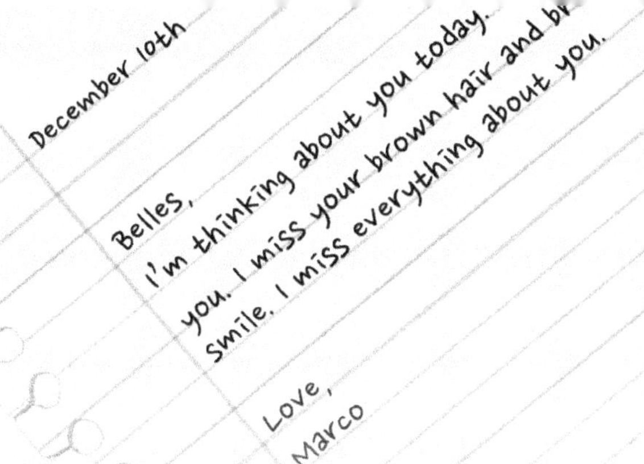

TWENTY-FOUR

MARCO

IT'S BEEN FOUR WEEKS SINCE BELLA, MICAELA, AND I HAVE moved into our new home. Unfortunately, to Bella's dismay, having keys to the place didn't mean moving in immediately. Not unless she wanted to sleep on the floor, and when I pointed that out, I think she almost considered it.

After taking measurements, we went shopping for furniture. My stuff came in and we used what we wanted and got rid of what we didn't want. When Bella saw what I had purchased for Micaela back in San Diego being brought into the house she nearly lost it.

"M-Marco…what is all that stuff?" Bella watched, with eyes as wide as saucers, as the delivery people brought in all the furniture and accessories I purchased the day after Micaela was born.

"I told you I wanted you and Micaela to live with me. I bought it all when she was born."

"Oh my God! Between my stuff and yours—what are we going to do with it all?"

"Well, she'll need stuff at your parents' place as well as my parents' for when they watch her or we visit, so we'll sort it all out and see what can go where."

She followed the guys up the stairs. "This stuff is beautiful. I had no idea." Tears pricked her eyes and she threw herself into my arms. At first, I was shocked to have her in my arms, but I quickly reciprocated and enjoyed the moment. When she realized what she did, she tensed and backed up, the moment quickly coming to an end.

The next day all of Bella's stuff came in, and thankfully Liz and my mom came over to help her go through it all. With her having had surgery only a few short weeks prior, I didn't want her lifting anything.

After many hours, we got it all situated and officially moved in the following week.

Since moving in, Bella and I have fallen into a comfortable routine. She has her own room (she insisted and her dad glared and I gave in) and sleeps in it, but many nights we also fall asleep on the couch. Our days usually consist of spending time with Micaela, taking her for walks, visiting our parents, and occasionally visiting the gym as well as visiting the rec center. I put in for a new sponsor since I would be living here and met with him a few days after we arrived.

His name is Steve and he's a no-bullshit kind of guy. He helped me find a location to attend my meetings and it's only about ten minutes from the house. I received my thirty, sixty, and ninety-day key tags a few days ago. Since I was in rehab during these milestones, Steve wanted me to have them, to remind myself I still chose to stay clean. When I got home, Bella saw them and asked me about them. I tried to play it off like it wasn't a big deal, but she insisted we go out for dinner to celebrate. She also asked if she could attend the next time I receive a key tag. She has no idea how much her support means to me.

My sisters, Chloe and Mackenzie, have spent the night a few times on the weekends. To say they're happy to have me back is an understatement, although they might be happier to have their niece close to them. I think I have officially been thrown to the side and replaced by my daughter, but I'm okay with that. I love watching them spend time with their niece.

Since Bella and I have moved in together, I haven't brought us up once. Not when she walked out of the bathroom in nothing but a towel still dripping wet because she forgot to bring her clothes into the bathroom with her. Not when she insisted we binge watch The O.C. (Because according to her, you can't live that close to Orange County and not experience Ben McKenzie as Ryan Atwood). And not even as I watched her ice cream drip down the center of her luscious tits. I watched her swipe it up and lick it off her finger while wishing it was my tongue licking it up, but I didn't say a damn word. And as hard as it was, I didn't bring us up when we stopped at the ice cream truck while walking around the park where Bella purchased a chocolate covered frozen banana and I was forced to watch her plump lips wrap around the fucking banana like it was a cock. I know she saw me adjusting myself, but what the fuck else was I supposed to do. The woman is sexy as fuck and has no goddamned clue.

Now it's her birthday and she's on her way back from seeing the OBGYN. She had to find a new one for her postpartum visit since we moved. When she called me to let me know her appointment went good, she was rambling off everything she can now do, such as driving and having sex. Yep, she mentioned that, and then right afterward, got awkward and hurried off the phone.

Today, Bella turns the big two-one and I want her to have the perfect night. I've moved the kitchen table to the living room and purchased five pounds of snow crabs, Bella's favorite. I have two potatoes baking and I bought homemade clam chowder from the local seafood market. I even rented her favorite movie, *There's Something about Mary*.

While the fact that she's now cleared to have sex again will be stuck in my mind, my goal is not to get laid tonight. It's to remind Bella of the friendship we used to have before I fucked it all up. I'm not stupid enough to think the way back to Bella's heart is through her pussy.

My cellphone goes off, and I grab it from the end table before it wakes Micaela up. Sure, the little angel can usually sleep through anything, but I'm hoping since Bella pumped so I could feed her, and I kept her awake for a while, she'll sleep for a little bit so we can spend some time together.

Daniel: Doc said he cleared you last week.

Daniel: We need to talk.

Daniel: I have a proposition for you.

My heart literally skips a beat when I read the text messages from Daniel West, the President of the UFC. I had a checkup last week, one I didn't tell anyone about, but should have known the doctor would forward my results to Daniel. It makes sense seeing as he's the doctor the UFC uses, but since I wasn't injured during a fight, I didn't think he would forward my results to them.

Me: Okay

My phone lights up and I quickly swipe my finger across the screen to answer.

"Hey Daniel, how's it going?" I leave Micaela sleeping in her bassinet and walk into the other room.

"Marco! Damn, you answered the phone fast." Daniel laughs.

"Yeah, well, I got a sleeping baby."

"Yeah, man. I heard you've been busy since getting injured. A baby with Bella Cooper, dabbling with a bit of powder, rehab, a move back to Vegas. The gossip rags have been having a field day. It's cost me a damn fortune to remove half that shit off the internet. So, how are you feeling?"

When I don't say anything right away, he repeats his question. "How are you feeling, Marco?" I know where he's going with this. He wants me to fight. The man is all about business. There's a reason the UFC is worth billions. The man knows how to run a business. And normally I would look forward to these calls, but right now I'm dreading it.

I clear my throat. "I'm okay."

"Good, that's what I like to hear. So, how soon can we schedule a fight for you?"

"I'm out of shape. I haven't worked out in over a year. I just don't know how long it's going to take me to get back into shape. Plus, Bella's dad, Cooper, isn't too thrilled about me being back here and living with his daughter. I'm not sure he's even going to let me train at the facility."

"Look, Marco, I'm going to be upfront with you. The fans want to see two fights: you and Bella. Your name was already all over the internet from the accident and you showing up to various parties. I was able to keep most of it under wraps, especially since you were out for an injury. But now, it's gotten out that two fighters—one of which holds a championship belt and is contracted for one more fight—the other had to cancel a huge debut fight because she got pregnant—are living together with a baby. People are gossiping. Women are wondering if you are off the market and they want to see you."

"Great. Just what I need," I mutter. "So people know I was in rehab?" I probably should have paid attention to what was going on around me.

"No, and there's no reason for them to know. I kept that shit under wraps. It would be bad for business, but it's my job to know what's going on with my fighters. They think you've been missing because you are upset over Logan being in a coma, and it will stay that way. One of the paparazzi was around the hospital the day Bella got out and he recognized you. Not sure why it took him so long to sell the photos, but the magazines are going crazy."

Fucking Fabulous. "Who would I be fighting?"

"Antoine Benitez. This past year he's been fighting his way up and winning all his fights. He's gained popularity and we want you to fight him for the belt. A comeback fight of sorts."

"When?"

"Well, we're looking at Bella and you fighting the same night. I need to speak to her and find out how long she thinks she will need to train. I'd like for it to be soon while the hype is there."

"All right, just do me a favor and don't mention anything about me to her. I would like to speak to her about it myself."

"Whatever you say."

I hang up just as I hear the garage door opening and pray she didn't hit anything. Our vehicles arrived a couple days ago, and when I mentioned to Bella I was going to sell both of my sports cars and get an SUV, she laughed and said I should keep one because she thinks it's hot. How could I say no to that?

She also insisted we both park in the two-car garage. She's excited to be able to park inside with the baby to avoid the rain. The problem is, Bella is probably the worst driver ever given a license and she can't park straight for shit. Last night when she pulled in, I thought she was going to take out the side of my car. Thank God for insurance.

I quickly remove the baked potatoes and snow crabs from the oven and place them on the table. Then I pour the soup into the bowls from the stove. I fill our glasses with sweet tea and place the mini bottle of Jack Daniels I bought her as a gift on the table. I know she won't drink while breastfeeding, but I had to get her a bottle of alcohol to celebrate her twenty-first birthday.

Grabbing the flowers and balloons I bought, I go to the kitchen to greet her at the door. She's only been gone for a few hours and I already wished her a Happy Birthday this morning, but I want her to feel special.

"Happy Birthday!" I whisper-yell as she walks through the door. Her face lights up and she gives me a huge smile. Then her dad walks in after her, followed by her mom.

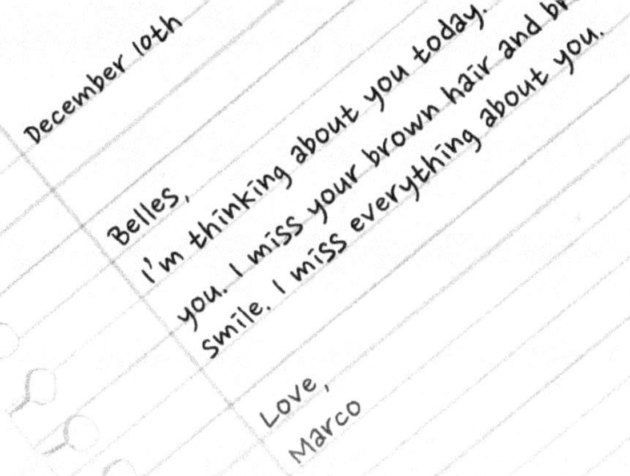

TWENTY-FIVE

BELLA

"YOU DID ALL THIS FOR ME?" I GLANCE AROUND THE ROOM seeing the table set up in front of the television with my favorite foods, complete with two candles lit up in the center. It's been six weeks since Marco confessed to me he wanted to have his daughter and me in his life. I assumed at the time he meant he wanted us to be more, but after all these weeks and not even a mention of us, I was starting to think maybe I misunderstood.

I know I told him we needed to take things slow, that we need to focus on our daughter, but it was easier to say that when I was in the hospital. Living in the same house as Marco is downright torture. The guy hasn't worked out in almost a year and still looks hot as hell. Then add the fact that he cooks for us, helps take care of Micaela, and does laundry. A woman only has so much self-control.

He hasn't left once to hang out with friends, despite me telling him he can go. He attends his meetings a few times a week but always comes right back. And when he's home, his attention is focused entirely on me and our daughter. I couldn't ask for anything more, right? Then why do I feel like there is still this void? When we are watching television and he's sitting close to me, I feel the butterflies deep inside me. When he smiles at me for no reason, my heart skips a beat. I know I shouldn't rush things. I'm the one who said we need to take things slow, but dammit if I don't daydream about this man pushing me onto the couch and making my body feel good.

The truth is, I can count the amount of times I've had sex on one hand and they have all been with him. The only pleasure I've ever known has been at the hand of Marco or my own. But Marco, on the other hand, has been with a whole slew of women. Lots of hot, sexy women. There's a reason why he ran from me all those times. Sure, he said he felt it was wrong, but if I was enough, if I was undeniable, unforgettable, wouldn't he have had no choice but to stay? He was with that blonde bimbo, Janell, more than he was with me. What if I'm just not enough for a man like Marco?

A loud grunt knocks me out of my insecure inner monologue and I remember my parents are here. They pulled up at the same time I did to visit me for my birthday and to see Micaela.

"I didn't realize we were having company," Marco says. "I'm sure there's enough for all of us."

"Oh no! I have an idea," my mom jumps in and says. "Why don't we take Micaela for the night? Do you have some bottles you've pumped?"

"I do, but are you sure? What if she wakes up and is scared I'm not there?" I begin to panic. My baby girl is only six weeks old.

"Bella, honey, I have raised a few kids. I will give her a bottle when she wakes up and you will be over first thing in the morning to pick her up. We can even do breakfast."

"Is that okay with you?" I nervously ask Marco, silently hoping he will be the bad guy and say no.

"I'm sure she'll be okay with your mom, Belles." *Damn traitor!*

"Or we can stay and eat here," my dad says dryly, earning him a smack in the chest from my mom.

Marco secures Micaela into her car seat while I pack up her stuff, packing enough for a week when she will only be with them for roughly twelve hours, most of which she'll be sleeping.

After giving our little girl kisses and reminding my parents of things like making sure her diaper is dry and which cry means what—like they didn't parent three children—they leave out the door, taking my heart with them.

"I don't know if I can do this."

"What?" Marco laughs, earning him a glare. "I'm sorry." He wraps me up in a comforting hug and gives me a chaste kiss on my forehead. "She'll be fine and if you really can't handle it, we'll go get her. But for right now, let's enjoy your birthday. You hungry?"

"I'm starved." After Marco reheats the clam chowder and potatoes, we sit down and eat, watching *There's Something about Mary* in a comfortable silence. After we both finish, he pauses the movie so we can clean up. Then he brings me out a couple of cupcakes, mine with a lit candle in the center.

"Happy Birthday, Belles. Make a wish." The first wish that comes to mind is—well, I can't say it out loud or it won't come true. But let's just say it involves the man standing in front of me smiling.

After we eat the sugary goodness, we move to the couch to continue the movie.

"Oh my God!" My hand comes to my mouth.

"What?"

"I haven't seen this movie in years. I had no idea that stuff she sticks in her hair is… is…" *Oh my God! How did I not know?*

Marco laughs hysterically. "You didn't know she uses his cum to do her hair?"

"I can't believe my mom let me watch this movie! This is so inappropriate! Micaela is never watching this movie."

Marco continues to laugh. "You were so innocent. Shit, you still are." For some reason, his comment rubs me the wrong way, reminding me that I'm nothing like the women he's used to.

He must notice the sudden change in the mood because he says, "Hey, there's nothing wrong with being innocent. It's a good thing."

I know he isn't saying this to hurt me, but I bite out, "Just not what you were looking for, right?"

He looks at me incredulously, the movie suddenly forgotten. "Where is this coming from?"

"Well, it took like three different attempts before you actually had sex with me, then you regretted it afterward, and the only reason why you even had sex with me again was because you were high. I mean, you didn't even remember it. Meanwhile, you were with that blonde model-looking chick for like ever. I was never enough to keep you like she was."

Marco gives me a look indicating his confusion, but I don't care. It feels like a weight has been lifted off my shoulders. I've been carrying those words and feelings around for too damn long. Marco stares at me for a minute, making me uneasy. Did I piss him off? Did I remind him of Janell? Shit! Does he still want Janell?

I open my mouth to say something—what I have no clue—when Marco stands from the couch and then leans over, scooping me up into his arms. My legs instinctively wrap around his back. Without saying a word, he looks at me while walking us to his bedroom. Then he sets me on the bed, sitting in front of me, leaning in so close, his mouth is only inches from mine. I can smell the peppermint he must have popped into his mouth after having dessert. The mint reminds me of the days before everything went to shit. My eyes lock on the wall next to him, afraid of what he's about to say.

"Look at me, Belles." He grabs my chin gently and tugs it so I'm looking at him. "The day I met you I fell in love with you. I might have only been twelve at the time, and it was a different kind of love, but I felt it. You were my best fucking friend. For that first year before Caleb and Hayley saved me, you were the bright part of my dark as fuck days."

"But that's…."

"No, you need to listen. At home, it was drugs and drinking, and fuck, so much bad. Yes, I had Chloe, but she was a baby and she cried and had needs that a twelve-year-old shouldn't have had to take care of. But for those few hours when I was with you at the gym, sparring and laughing, they were everything to me.

"And then one day you grew up. You were still you, but you were more, so much more. And I knew I was well and truly fucked. And then we kissed and I knew it, I knew I could never go back to the way things were before that kiss. I had to leave before I fucked it all up."

Marco leans in closer and gives me a soft kiss, his teeth grazing my bottom lip as he pulls away.

"The night we made love in the cabin, I knew I crossed a line. Your dad has always been so good to me, treated me like his own, and I never should have had sex with his daughter. It was wrong of me and it was a slap in your dad's face."

"We didn't do anything wrong."

"Just because I said it wasn't right, doesn't mean I didn't enjoy it or want it. Wanting you has never been the problem."

"But being with Janell was right?"

"I thought doing the right thing meant staying away from you. And as far as Janell goes, she was my drug connection. I was in a bad place and she had no problem joining me there. I can't take back what I did or how I acted. I hate myself for having sex with you and not being able to remember it, but I've always wanted you. You are all I want."

Marco grabs the curves of my hips and pulls me onto his lap, moving us up against his headboard. Straddling him with one leg on either side of him, I feel his dick twitch from under his shorts and my face heats up.

"See what I mean by innocent? You feel my cock poking you and your face turns the most beautiful shade of pink."

"Yeah, like a little girl."

"That's not what I meant. Have you seen your body?" Marco pulls my shirt over my head then expertly unsnaps my ugly nursing bra, taking it off. "You see these full, perky tits?" He gently holds them in his hands, his tongue darting out to lightly lick my pink nipple. I whimper at his touch. "These are all fucking woman, Belles." He moves to my other one and licks the nipple.

Keeping my breasts in his hands, he places open-mouthed kisses all over them, leading up to my collarbone and neck, eliciting chills all over me. Then cupping my ass with one hand, he pulls me even closer to him, changing our positions so I am lying on my back with Marco hovering above me.

"This neck, all woman." He sucks on the sensitive skin just below my ear for a second, causing me to let out an embarrassingly loud moan, before he works his way over to my face.

"These lips." He sucks on my lower lip first, then my upper lip, and then deepening the kiss, Marco's tongue seeks out mine without needing an invitation, our tongues colliding with such force, it just about takes my breath away. Before I can bring my hands up to touch him, he pulls away. "Fuck, baby. These lips are all woman."

I pout when he backs up farther. "Don't pout, baby." He gives me a quick peck then pulls his shirt over his head. His body is perfection. I can't even imagine how fucking hot he will look once he's working out again. He sees me ogling him and gives me a knowing smirk before moving downward.

He stops at my chest again and I think he's going to give my breasts some more attention, but instead he places a single kiss just above my left breast. "This heart, baby. How selfless you are. How much you give to those around you. The way you love our daughter. It's all woman."

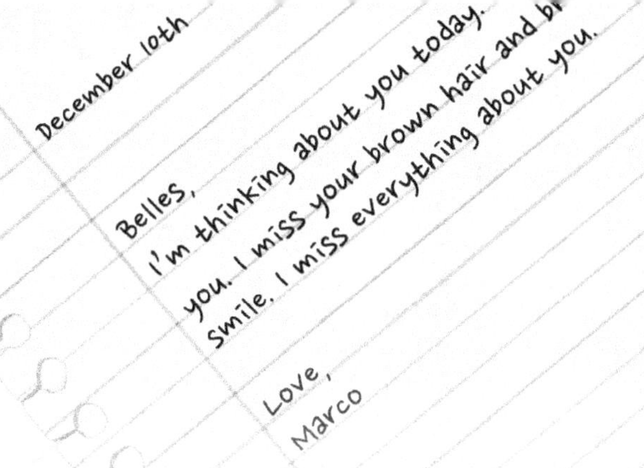

TWENTY-SIX

MARCO

AFTER GIVING BELLA A SOFT KISS OVER HER HEART, I MOVE downward, landing on her soft belly. Her belly button ring is back in and sparkling in the light. She told me she got it with her friends her freshman year in college and fuck if it isn't a turn on. I give it a small kiss. "This belly, that carried our baby, it's one hundred percent woman." She squirms slightly, and I chuckle at how responsive she is. I've barely touched her and she's already completely turned on.

I peel Bella's shorts and panties from her body and swallow thickly at the sight in front of me. How she doesn't get she's all woman, I don't understand, and her thinking she isn't enough for me is ludicrous on so many levels. I'm about to move down her body and devour this woman, but before I do so, I need to make sure we're on the page.

"Belles, tonight wasn't supposed to go like this. I know that sounds cliché as fuck, but it was just supposed to be dinner for your Birthday. Are you all right with this?"

She gives me a small smile and nods.

"Babe, I'm going to need the words. Are you sure you're okay with what's about to happen?"

"I'm definitely okay with it. But Marco…" Bella's eyes cast down like she's nervous.

"Bella, talk to me."

"Please don't leave me, again." Fuck! This woman.

"I promise, Belles. I'm not going anywhere."

"Then yes, I want you, Marco. I want you so damn bad."

My cock twitches at her words as my mouth waters at the thought of licking and sucking and nibbling on every inch of this woman. She attempts to close her legs when I stare too long at her naked body, but

I'm not going to let that happen. She has absolutely nothing to be embarrassed or shy about.

"Fuck, Belles." I spread her legs open. "This bare, perfect cunt, baby. It's all woman." My finger starts at the top and works its way down the middle. She's so soaked, my finger is covered in her juices, and I haven't even stuck it in her yet.

"See how wet you are for me?" I show her my glistening wet finger and she nods slowly. Sticking my finger in my mouth, I suck on it, tasting her essence. "This is definitely all woman." She writhes under my touch, so I swipe up some more of her juices and bring my finger to her mouth.

"Taste yourself, baby." Her eyes go wide, but she opens her mouth for me, allowing me to push my finger into her hot mouth. Her lips close around my finger and my cock jumps as I picture her mouth wrapped around a different part of my body.

Pulling my finger back out, I ask, "Does it taste good?" Her lips twitch unsure of what to say as her cheeks turn a beautiful shade of crimson. She has no idea how much of a turn on her innocence really is.

Without waiting for a verbal answer, I return to her sweet cunt and give it a kiss, my touch causing her to jump. Spreading her wide open, I run my tongue along the middle starting from the top and ending in her pussy hole.

"Oh God," she whimpers.

"No, baby, It's Marco."

She laughs at my playfulness and I can feel her body relaxing.

Sticking one finger inside, then two, I start to fingerfuck her, slowly building the momentum until I'm three fingers deep. Bella's *Oh God's* turn to *Oh, Marco's,* and then as my tongue joins the party, massaging her tight nub, her words turn into incoherent screams.

"That's it baby," I say, sucking on her clit and sending her into an orgasm that has her ass coming off the bed.

When she calms down, I take my fingers out of her then sit up to remove my pants and boxers, kicking them off me and onto the ground. Moving back up her body, I can feel my hard-on pushing against her warmth. "Please Marco," she moans.

Once we're face to face, I bring our lips together for a kiss. Taking possession of her mouth, I thrust my tongue inside, and swirl it around, making sure she can taste herself on me. She sighs loudly, and I know she can.

Only taking my mouth off hers for a second, I ask, "Are you on birth control?"

She nods and that's all I need. My mouth crashes against hers, my tongue dominating hers. With one hand holding me over her, I use my other hand to guide my cock into her hot, soaking wet cunt.

"Fuuuck," I groan into her mouth, taking a deep breath, trying not to come this very second. It's been months since I've been inside a woman, and to top it off, I'm inside the one woman I want more than anyone in the goddamned world. Our lips are still touching, but we aren't moving.

Once the need to come is somewhat tamed, I start to thrust inside her as I go back to kissing her. Our kisses get deeper, turning ravenous, as my thrusts get harder, more out of control. I feel my orgasm building, but I need her to get there first. Finding her clit with my fingers, I stroke her as I thrust into her.

"M-Marco…Oh my God, Marco," Bella yells, her head going back, breaking our kiss. I watch her eyes roll back before her lids close as she comes all over my cock. Her insides tighten, spurring me on, and a few thrusts later, I'm finding my own release.

Her eyes open back up slowly, a small, satiated smile crossing her lips.

"All. Fucking. Woman," I say, giving her one more kiss before pulling out of her.

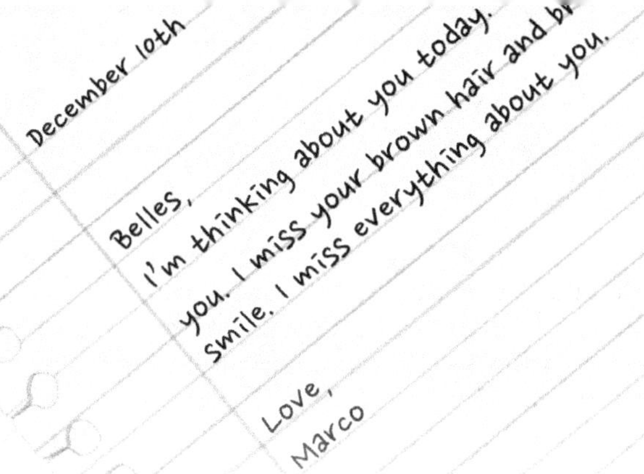

TWENTY-SEVEN

BELLA

I STIR AWAKE, AND FOR A SECOND, FORGETTING MICAELA ISN'T here, I freak out when I can't remember the last time I checked on her. My breasts are sore and need to be relieved. Then I feel a different kind of soreness between my legs and the memories of last night come flooding back to me. After Marco made love to me, he asked if I wanted to shower, but I was too exhausted. Between the two orgasms he gave me and the last six weeks of not getting a full night's sleep, all I wanted to do was cuddle up to Marco and pass out, and that's exactly what we did.

As soon as his arm came out and he pulled me into him, my head hit his chest and I was out. Marco's body might be hard, but it's my new favorite pillow. Speaking of which… I look next to me and see the bed is empty. I listen for a second, and when I don't hear anything, an uneasy feeling washes over me. There's no way after the night we shared, he would leave me.

I look over at the nightstand and see his cell phone is gone. Scooping up the shirt he took off last night from the ground, I throw it on. My mind is racing, and I can feel my body beginning to shake nervously. I tell myself to calm down, he is probably just in the bathroom or kitchen, but I can't stop myself from getting worked up. I grab my phone and see it's only five in the morning.

I start to search the house, the bedrooms, the bathrooms, but there's no Marco. When I get to the kitchen, I check the coffee maker to see if he made himself any coffee, since it's the first thing he does every morning. The pot is still cold. I step out into the garage and switch the light on. My stomach plummets, the blood in my body draining downward. I clutch my chest, suddenly struggling to catch my breath.

Marco's car is gone.

Gone.

He left me. Again.

I turn the light back off and close the door, then I pull up his name in my contacts and hit send. It doesn't even ring before it goes to voicemail. I hit end and then try again. Voicemail again. I do this several more times. Each time it goes directly to his voicemail.

I pull up our messages and send him a text. Waiting for it to go through, I hold my breath.

I am not this girl.

I am not this insecure girl, freaking out over a guy leaving.

But I am this girl. Marco repeatedly leaving has turned me into this girl.

And I hate this girl.

The text message turns green, which tells me his phone is off. Running back to the room, I look for a note. I search behind the bed, under the bed, on the counter in the bathroom. Nothing. He's just fucking gone.

Needing to calm myself down, I jump into the shower. The hot water that would normally calm my nerves, does nothing for me right now. After I'm done rinsing off, I go back to my room to get dressed and head over to my parents' house. Maybe Marco went to see our daughter.

I make it out of the garage when I stop and get out, running back inside to leave him a note in case this is all a misunderstanding and he comes home to find me gone. Then I head to the next street over to my parents. I could have just walked, but it's still dark outside and I want to get there as fast as possible.

When I get to their house and don't see Marco's car, a large lump forms in my throat making it hard to swallow properly. This is not good. I walk up to the front door and it's locked, so I grab my keys, and with shaky hands—after missing the lock twice—unlock my parents' front door, rushing to unarm the alarm. I am immediately greeted by my dog, Elsa. Her moves are slower, but her tail is wagging, ecstatic to see me. I bend down and let her lick my face. She's getting older and I know it's only a matter of time before she'll go to doggy heaven. The thought makes me sad.

"Hey there, girl." I pet her for a minute before heading upstairs to find my baby girl. Before I make it to the stairs, though, I see my dad sitting on the couch with Micaela in his arms. He's holding her in one arm while feeding her with the other.

"Dad." The tears prick my eyes, and all I want in this moment is for my father to hold me. I sit next to him, my head resting on his shoulder, while he feeds my little girl. When she's done, he lifts her over his shoulder and burps her. I put my hands out and he hands her to me. He hasn't said a word to me yet, and I appreciate it.

"Hey, sweet girl." I give her a soft kiss on her cheek, then extending my legs and putting my feet up on the coffee table, I lay her small body vertically on my thighs. She wiggles a little, her arms flaring up, and a small trace of a smile graces us.

"The last few days she's started to smile a little," I say. When my dad doesn't say anything back, I add, "Thank you for taking care of her." The last word comes out higher as the tears begin to fall. My dad puts his arm around me and says, "She reminds me so much of you as a baby. As you know, I didn't get to see you when you were a baby, so when I finally met you, I was upset at having missed out on so much. Your mom gave me a book of photos. I spent months staring at them, trying to memorize every moment, every memory I missed. She has your nose."

Without being able to look at him, I say, "He left."

My dad's arm around me tightens and I know he's trying hard to keep his temper in check. "You're going to have to give me more than that, sweetie."

"I don't know, Dad. We, umm…we…last night." I look at him to make sure he's following along and he gives me a slight nod, his jaw clenching. "And this morning, I woke up and he was gone. His phone, his car. Gone. No note, nothing. I tried calling and texting, but his phone is turned off."

My dad doesn't say anything for a few moments. Then he says, "I'm going to kill him." The words are spoken so soft and cold and without any emotion, they give me goose bumps.

"I thought this time would be different, Dad." The tears are starting to drop faster. I swipe up a few but eventually stop trying. It's pointless. "I thought this time he wouldn't run."

"Bella?" I look up and see my mom at the bottom of the stairs. "What happened, honey?"

"Marco left," my dad answers for me.

"Oh no, did you two get into a fight?" She comes over and sits on the love seat across from my dad and me.

"No, but…" I dread saying the next part. "It's not the first time he's run."

"What do you mean? He's left you and Micaela? Why didn't you tell us?"

"No, when we kissed for the first time, he left for California. Then when we were together the first time, he left again afterward. The night Micaela was created, he passed out afterward because he had been high. I didn't know it at the time. Umm… when I tried to tell him I was pregnant and saw him doing drugs I told Caleb, and when Marco found out, he burst into my apartment and told me I was dead to him. He ran from getting help and from me."

I take a deep breath, trying to get control of my emotions. "It's what he does; he runs." I pick Micaela up and hold her close, inhaling her sweet baby scent.

"I'm going to call Hayley. Maybe something happened." My mom stands and goes in search of her phone. A few minutes later she comes back, shaking her head. "Neither of them have heard from him. They said if they do, they'll let us know."

Seeing that Micaela has fallen asleep, I place her in the rolling bassinet, giving her a soft kiss to her temple. "Could you guys watch her a little longer? I'm going to go for a run."

"Why don't you come to the gym with me after breakfast?" my dad suggests. I told him yesterday I have been cleared to train again.

"Okay."

After breakfast—one that I'm sure tasted delicious but I could barely taste, let alone enjoy—I breastfeed Micaela and pump what's left, bottling it up for later in case I'm not back from the gym in time for her to eat. When I insist on taking my car to the gym, my dad follows me to my house so I can get changed. I think he was hoping to see Marco so he could lay into him for leaving.

I, on the other hand, was hoping to see Marco so I know he's okay and could explain why he left. I change into a pair of yoga pants, a sports bra, and a loose tank top. I'm determined to work off what's left of the baby weight I've put on and more importantly gain my muscle and strength back. I worked out my entire pregnancy, but not like I would have had I not been pregnant.

We walk into the gym at seven and the training center is already hopping. The music is blaring and you can hear the sounds of grunts from the guys. God, I've missed this place. I've only been here once since I've been back to show the guys Micaela. Marco didn't want to come, saying my dad wouldn't be happy with him going into the gym.

"I'm going to warm up and go for a run."

"Okay, sweetie. Then maybe we can get some training in."

"Sounds good, Dad."

I turn the treadmill on and put my headphones in, clicking on my favorite playlist. Eminem's *Till I collapse* fills my ears. It was my dad's intro when he was a fighter and it's one of my favorite songs. Every single time I hear it, I get pumped up. I set the song to repeat and turn the speed up higher and higher until I'm at a steady running speed. Then I get lost in the song, in the moment, in the run, and let everything else fade around me.

"Bella!" I hear my name being called, so I remove an earbud from one of my ears and see my dad standing next to me. When I struggle to catch my breath, I click the down button to slow down. The screen reads five-point-two miles.

"Hey, sorry! I didn't even realize I was running for so long."

"You don't want to overdo it on your first day back. We need to talk. Cool down and meet me in my office."

I do as he says, and after wiping down my face, neck, and the equipment, I walk toward my dad's office. My legs feel like Jell-O, a feeling I haven't felt in a long time. He's right. I do need to take it slow. I say hello to a couple different guys on my way and notice, for the first time, Mason isn't around. "Hey, have you seen Mason lately?" I ask, sitting in one of his office chairs.

"Mason moved to California."

"What? Really? Is he staying near Tristan?"

"He's living with Tristan."

"Oh. Well, that's good. I'm glad Tristan found a roommate. So, what did you want to talk about?"

"Daniel West called."

"The president of the UFC?" I stupidly ask because really…what other Daniel West would he be referring to?

"He said he's planning to call you but wanted to do me the courtesy of letting me know first. He wants you to fight."

"The one that got cancelled when I got pregnant?"

"Yeah, have you kept up with Shawna Fields?"

"Of course, she's kicking ass and taking names."

"Yes, she is. But those girls aren't the same level of competition you would have been. Apparently, there's a title fight coming up in a few months. He wouldn't tell me who, said he couldn't yet. But he wants you and Shawna to open with the first fight. It will be at the MGM. Now, because it's not a main fight, it's not going to pay much, but it can open the doors for you, especially if you win. Maybe get you some sponsorship opportunities. What do you think?"

"Of course I want to do it!" I grab my phone to text Marco and remember he's still MIA. I hit his name to try to call him again and it goes to voicemail.

"Still not answering?"

"His phone is still off."

My dad nods. "Why don't we get a couple of hours of training in before you go pick up Micaela?"

"Sounds good."

It's early afternoon when I pick up Micaela from my mom. She begs me to stay for dinner, but I tell her I need some time alone. I take Micaela to the park to go for a walk, then once we get home, I give her a bath and spend the evening playing peek-a-boo with my baby girl while watching *Gilmore Girls* reruns. I try to call Marco several more times, but it goes to voicemail like always. I send a silent prayer that nothing is wrong. I hate that he ran again, but I would never wish him any harm.

My phone pings with a text and I see it's Gina. Why the hell would she be texting me?

Gina: Just saw Marco drinking at Dexter's. Guess you picked the wrong guy after all.

Dexter's is a local bar we all used to frequent. They have the best wings known to man and have several pool tables set up in the back along with a dart board. I actually ran into Marco there a few times while I was in San Diego when we weren't speaking. Talk about awkward. Why the hell would Marco be drinking at a bar in California? Unless—Oh my God! He left and went back to California. Not wanting to give her the satisfaction, I don't respond, and instead lie down for a few minutes while Micaela is napping.

I WAKE UP FROM WHAT FEELS LIKE A DEEP SLEEP BUT DON'T hear Micaela, so I look over and she's still asleep. I must have dozed off while she was taking a nap. The clock next to my bed reads 4:03 p.m. I was only asleep for two hours. My phone lights up and I'm thinking that's what woke me up. Hoping to see something from Marco, I type in my passcode so my phone comes alive.

There are no missed calls or texts, but I notice a ton of notifications on my social media app, so I open it up and click to see what's going on. Scrolling down, I see Marco has been tagged in a post, so I click on it. It's a photo of Marco sitting with a woman. His arm is around her and their faces are merely inches apart. It's too dark to see his expression, but it's definitely him. The photo caption reads: **Look who's back!**

Back where? Then I see the owner of the post is Jelly Licious. What the hell kind of fake name is that? I click the name and the profile pic is of a marijuana leaf. *Real nice.* Swiping left, I go through the person's pictures until one stops me in my tracks. *It's her.* Janell. The blonde bimbo I last saw Marco snorting coke with almost a year ago.

Clicking back on the picture, I look to see if she checked in when she posted the picture. **Logan Heights** and it was posted an hour ago. *What the hell is Marco doing in California? Did he move back? Just like that?*

Confused as to why I would even get this update since I never added Marco as a friend, I click on my notifications to see I was tagged in a comment. It's from Gina.

Bella Cooper

There's no comment, just my name so she could rub it in my face. Looking closely at the picture, I can see the drugs on the table, and it hits me like a ton of bricks. Once again, Marco has left me. Except this time, he didn't just leave me, he left our daughter as well. Throwing my phone against the wall, I watch it smash as it hits the wood floor, and then I grab my pillow and let the sobs come.

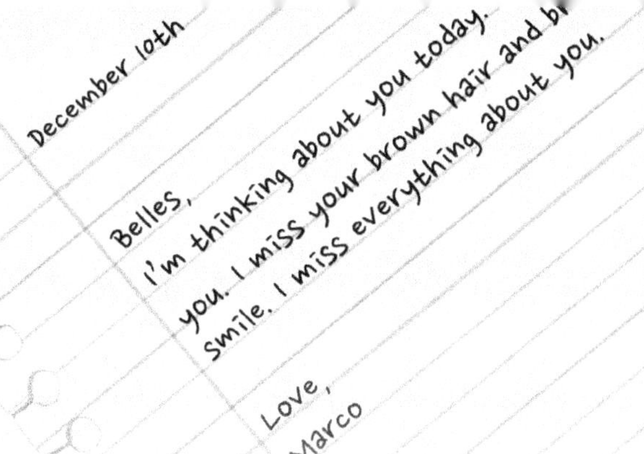

TWENTY-EIGHT

MARCO

FUCK. FUCK. FUCK. FUCK!!!! THIS IS NOT GOOD. I AM SO FUCKING fucked right now! I did it again, only this time I didn't mean to. But it isn't going to matter that it wasn't on purpose. It isn't going to matter that the last eighteen hours have been hell—hours I never want to relive again. There is no way Bella is going to forgive me.

EIGHTEEN HOURS AGO

MY PHONE BUZZES ON THE NIGHTSTAND AND I IGNORE IT. WHEN it buzzes again, I grab it to make sure it isn't Bella's parents since they have Micaela. The caller ID reads Reese, so I slip out of bed, throwing on a clean pair of boxers and shirt, and walk outside the bedroom to answer the phone.

"Hello?"

"Marco! I'm so sorry to have called you so late but something's happened. It's Logan, Marco. He's taken a turn for the worse. It's not good. He may not live through the night."

"What happened?" I'm already grabbing a pair of jeans from the laundry room.

"He went into cardiac arrest. They resuscitated him, but it's not good. They are saying it can happen again."

My phone beeps indicating it's about to die. "I'm on my way," I say quickly before it powers down. Thinking about nothing else other than getting to my best friend, I set my phone on the dryer so I can find some clean socks. Once I find a pair, not giving a shit if they even match, I slip them on along with my shoes. Then grabbing my keys, I get in my car and start driving west. It's a four-hour drive from here to Sharp Hospital and I make it in less than three hours.

Pulling up to the wing he's in, I park and check-in at the front desk. Thankfully visiting hours began a few minutes ago. They let me through and a few minutes later I'm sitting at the side of my friend's bed. My best friend, who barely looks like himself anymore. He's skinnier from the lack of working out and being fed through a feeding tube. His skin is a pasty white and he looks like he's aged years instead of months.

"Hey." I look up and see Reese standing in the doorway. I get a sudden sense of déjà vu like we were in these same positions before.

"Hey," I say back and then turn my attention back to Logan. Reese must get I just need some time with my friend because I hear the door close. Taking Logan's hand in mine, I put my head down against the rail and close my eyes for a few minutes. I've been driving since four in the morning. I'm mentally and physically drained, and on top of that, my heart is hurting for my best friend who I will most likely never have another conversation with.

"Sir! You need to move." I feel a tapping on my shoulder causing me to jolt up. There's a loud beeping sound going off and I realize it's Logan. Something's wrong. I stand to back up, sending the chair toppling over.

"Sir, you need to leave while we assess the patient."

I'm kicked out of the room and feel sick to my stomach. Is he going to die right now? Is this the end? Not being able to be anywhere near the hospital right now, I run out the door and into my car. Before I know it, I'm sitting at the bar I used to frequent with a bottle of Jack in front of me and the first shot already poured.

It's been over a year since I won the title fight. It's been over a year since my best friend was put into a coma after celebrating our wins. Why the hell doesn't it get any easier? Will it ever get easier? And while I'm sitting at this bar, Logan is probably dying, and if I'm honest it's probably for the best because is he even really living? The thought that I just wished my friend dead is what sends me over the edge and, before I can think twice, I'm downing the shot, my body welcoming the liquid burn as it goes down my throat.

"What the hell are you doing here, man?" I look to my left and see Tristan. What are the fucking odds?

"Drowning my sorrows. You?"

"I'm meeting someone here. Is everything okay?"

I chuckle darkly. "Wouldn't you love it if everything wasn't."

"What the hell is that supposed to mean?"

"C'mon, like you didn't call it. You said it yourself. I can't be trusted, and here I am, drinking a bottle of Jack while Bella is at home with our daughter."

"You fucking left her, again?" Tristan sneers, taking the bottle away from me.

"Logan went into cardiac arrest. I drove here and was in there with him when it happened again. He's in that coma because of me."

"Really? Don't be a whiny bitch, Marco. You didn't cause the accident. Don't go playing the whole woe-is me bullshit. Does Bella know you're here?"

I reach for my phone and can't find it. My phone. Fuck! It's not on me. Where the hell is my phone?

I pat my pockets as I try to think about the last time I used it. I was on the phone with Reese and it died. Shit! It's at home. Then I remember the promise I just made last night not to leave her, yet here I am over three hundred miles away.

"No, she doesn't know where I am."

"Look, Marco. You have only had one shot. Have a glass of water, go check on your friend, and go home."

"What if I can't be what she needs? What if I'm too weak? If you wouldn't have showed up here…"

"I watched Bella love you for most of our lives. All she needs from you is for you to love her back. Stop making her be strong enough for the both of you. Man the fuck up and stay clean."

I drink the glass of water, then stand and put my hand out. He stands as well and pulls me into a hug. "You know she misses you, right? It's killing her not to be able to text or call you."

"I know. I just have a lot going on. A lot of shit I need to figure out."

We both hug one more time before I head back to the hospital. As I'm walking down the hall back toward Logan's room I run into a crying Reese.

"Whoa, hey! What's going on? Is he okay?" Please God don't let him have died while I was gone.

"No, I mean, yes, he's okay. Well, he's stable. It's Kaitlyn. She's missing. When they said Logan might not make it, she took off." Kaitlyn is Logan's sister. With only ten months between them, they grew up best friends. When Logan slipped into the coma, Kaitlyn went down a dark path. I'd seen her at several of the parties I was at, but I was too fucked up myself to do anything to help her.

"It's okay." I hug Reese as she cries against my shoulder. "I'll find her."

"You will?"

"Yes, I promise. I will bring her back." It's the least I can do for my best friend since he isn't able to find her himself. Realizing I won't be heading home right away, I figure I should call Bella and let her know I am okay. She's going to be hurt and pissed no matter what but at least she won't be worried.

"Can I borrow your phone?"

"Sure." She hands me her phone after typing in the password. I go to dial Bella's number before I realize I don't fucking know it! Fucking technology. It might be convenient, but it's made us lazy. I've had Bella's number saved for so long, I don't know what the number is. Then I curse myself for not thinking about this earlier when I was sitting in the damn bar with Tristan.

I click on the internet and do a search for Cooper's Gym. When the website pops up, I hit call. It rings a few times before a woman picks up.

"Hi, who's this?"

"This is Carla with Cooper's Fight Club." I have no clue who she is so she must be new.

"Hey Carla. My name is Marco. I'm looking for Cooper or Bella. Are either of them there?"

"Nope, they left a little while ago."

"Okay, how about Caleb or Hayley, or maybe Kaden or Ashley?" It's a long shot since they are rarely there, spending most of their time at their clinic or the rec center.

"Nope, sorry."

"Okay, do you by any chance have any of their numbers?"

"I'm sorry, but I'm not at liberty to give out anybody's numbers. I can take your name and number and have them call you."

I sigh. "Fine, but can you call Cooper and give him the message now?"

"Sure thing."

"Please tell him it's Marco and I'm in California and to let Bella know I left my phone at home. My friend who is in a coma took a turn for the worse."

"Okay, got it. I'll let him know. I hope your friend is doing better. Bye!"

After I hang up, I use Reese's social media account to click on Kaitlyn's name. I see her tagged in a bunch of posts and spot Janell in one.

"Okay, I think I know where she is." I hand her back her phone. "Once I get her, want me to bring her to your place?"

"Yes." She sniffles. "Please. I'm so worried. I can't lose my brother and my sister."

"You haven't lost either one," I say, hoping to comfort her and praying that remains the truth.

"I'll see you in a little while. Stay positive."

Not having any way to get a hold of Bella at the moment, I focus all my efforts on finding Kaitlyn. I drive around checking out all the usual places Janell would be at. Just as I'm about to give up, I remember her brother's place.

It's been awhile since I've been there but I know the area, so I drive up and down the streets looking for a house with cars lining the road. The picture I saw had a bunch of people in the background. I spot the house and park my car at the end of the road.

Without knocking, I walk in, and of course, the first person I see is Janell.

"Marco?" Janell smirks. "Gina mentioned you were back. I knew it was only a matter of time."

Not even bothering to explain myself to her, I ask, "Is Kaitlyn here?"

"Really, Kaitlyn? Her brother is in a coma and you're trying to get with her." I close in on her without laying a hand on her. "Is. She. Here?" My patience is wearing thin. I don't have time to deal with her.

"Whatever." She rolls her eyes. "I saw her around here earlier." I step back from her and start searching the house. It's like three in the afternoon and these people are partying like it's a Friday night. I can't believe this is what I resorted to.

I spot her on the couch taking a bump of coke and I sit down next to her. "Katie," I murmur. She turns to me and throws her arms around me. "It's okay. It's okay. We're going to get out of here."

"He's going to d-die, Marco," she hiccups. I don't respond because the truth is Logan is probably going to die eventually and right now I can't even think about that. I almost got drunk earlier today and now I'm surrounded by every drug known to man and I'm not exactly feeling strong.

"He wouldn't want you doing this to yourself," I say to her but also in a way to myself. "C'mon, let's go." We both stand and, with my arm around her, I guide us out of the house and to my car.

She's quiet the entire drive to her sister's place. There isn't anything to say. That accident changed so many lives and not for the better. We were all affected in some way and it's pointless to discuss it. Logan will most likely never wake up and there isn't anything any of us can do to change that fact.

After getting her inside with Reese, I borrow her phone again and try to contact the gym. It's almost six o'clock and nobody answers. The receptionist is probably gone for the day.

"I'm going to head out. I left without my phone and my girlfriend is most likely freaking out."

"Thank you for bringing her home, Marco."

"Of course. I'll see you both soon." I give them each a hug then I head home.

I pull up to the house roughly four hours later, after stopping by the store to pick up flowers and candy since tomorrow is Valentine's day. Not wanting to wake Bella or Micaela up, I park outside and go through the front door. I check the laundry room, and sure enough my dead cell phone is sitting on top of the damn dryer. I throw it into my pocket and head down the hallway. I check my bedroom first and see it's empty.

I go to Bella's room next and see her curled up in a ball snoring softly with Micaela in her bassinet right next to her sleeping soundly. I place the flowers and candy on her nightstand so she'll see them when she wakes up. Then I kick off my shoes and undress down to my boxers before I pull the blanket back and climb into bed behind Bella. Spooning her from behind, I wrap my arms around her waist and wish that in the morning when we wake up this entire day won't have happened, and it all will have just been a horrible nightmare.

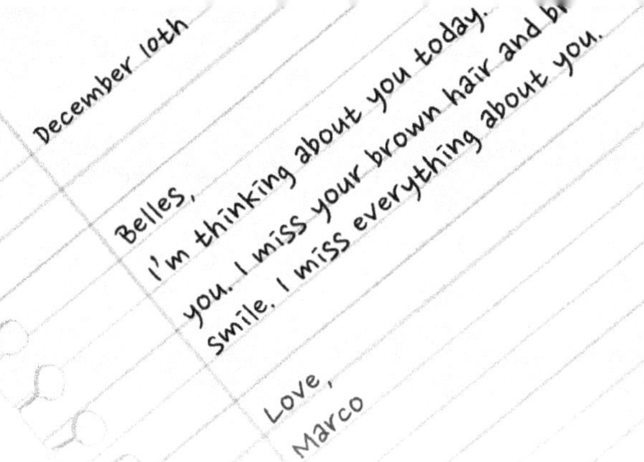

TWENTY-NINE

BELLA

MY EYES OPEN. AND I JERK UPRIGHT WHEN I SEE THE CLOCK reads 9:15. It's Valentine's Day. Yay! Not. Then I notice the beautiful roses and huge box of chocolate on my nightstand. *Marco must be home.* And he's lost his mind if he thinks flowers and chocolate will make me forgive him.

Realizing Micaela should have woken me up by now to eat, I lean over and see she's not in her bassinet. In panic mode, I check the floor because it's not like my six-week-old daughter is getting up and walking around the house. Oh my God! Where is she? I jump out of the bed and run toward the front door only to be stopped in my tracks by Marco sitting on the couch holding our daughter. Duh! He's home! Hence the flowers and candy in my room. He's speaking softly to her and I can see her arms flaring in excitement.

"Seriously?" I bite out.

"I can explain about yesterday."

"I don't give a fuck about yesterday. I do care about the fact that I woke up to find my daughter gone. You want to run away without saying a word? Fine! Run! It's what you do best. But do not take my damn daughter out of her bassinet without letting me know!"

Marco looks at me for a moment in shock. "I'm sorry. She woke up, so I brought her out here to feed her so you could sleep in. Did you see the flowers and candy next to your bed?"

"I did. And coming from a caring, selfless man all of this would be super sweet, but since it's coming from you, it's called guilt. Now please give me back my daughter." I put my hands out, waiting for her because seriously… you don't run and then the next day take my baby without saying a word. I almost had a damn heart attack.

"Bella," Marco says as he hands Micaela to me. "Please give me a chance to explain."

"There's no explanation in the world other than you being kidnapped that would make walking out the door without telling me, okay. Were you? Were you kidnapped?"

Marco sighs and shakes his head.

"Let me ask you one question," I continue. "Did you get drunk or high while you were gone?"

"Why would you ask that?"

"Don't dodge the question. Did you get drunk or high? It's a yes or no question." Knowing a fight is about to ensue, I lay Micaela down in her crib in her nursery and give her her pacifier, knowing she always falls back asleep after her morning feeding.

Then I walk back out to the living room. "Did you get drunk or high?"

"No, I didn't get drunk or high."

"You. Are. A. Fucking. Liar."

"Bella, listen to me, please. Logan went into cardiac arrest. His sister Reese said he might not make it so I drove to the hospital."

"And what? You ended up drinking at Dexter's and getting high with Janell?"

"Tristan fucking texted you?" Marco hisses

"Tristan?" I'm confused, not sure what Tristan has to do with any of this. "I haven't spoken to Tristan in months. Don't bring him into this."

"Who told you about Dexter's?"

"Gina."

"Well, maybe that coke-whore should get her facts straight. Yes, I had a drink. One drink. But then pretty boy showed up and stopped me."

"Really? You're going to call her names when it wasn't too long ago you were hanging out and doing the same drugs she does."

"Yes! Because I know firsthand she doesn't care about anything except her next fix. She's starting shit because Tristan chose you over her. He was supposed to be her meal ticket and you got in her way. So now she's going to cause problems."

"She wouldn't be able to cause problems if you were home where you belonged."

"Bella—"

I cut him off needing to remain in control of this conversation. He's not about to veer it toward Gina and her issues. "So, Gina and Tristan both saw you drinking? And this was before you went to hang out with Janell?"

"I didn't hang out with Janell. I went to a party to—"

"Jesus, Marco! Do you hear yourself? It was posted on social media.

Gina saw you drinking, Tristan knows you left, and Janell was posting goddamn photos of you! You promised! And you still left. How can you say I'm enough and then walk away from me so easily? You put me last. While I was scared and worried, you were putting everyone else first. You didn't stop drinking for me or for your daughter! Tristan stopped you. I can't do this. I have a daughter I have to protect from being hurt." I sigh in defeat, refusing to let any tears come through.

"It's not like that. Please listen to me." Marco stalks up to me. "I get that I fucked up. I should have told you I was leaving. I got the call about Logan and my phone died. I set it on the dryer and left it! I got there and he was in such bad shape. I lost it and went to Dexter's. I shouldn't have had that drink. Tristan stopped me and then I went back to the hospital. I ran into Logan's sister Reese and she said Kaitlyn, their younger sister, was in a bad way so I went to find her to bring her home, and Janell was at the party. But Belles, I swear to you, I didn't touch a single drug."

"I'm sorry about your friend." I can't even imagine having to watch my best friend from the bedside while he remains in a coma, slowly deteriorating.

"Bella, I'm so sorry." Marco places his hands on my arms. "Please forgive me."

"I—I just," I begin, when I hear my phone ring. I run to grab it and see it's a number I don't recognize. "Hello?"

"Bella, this is Daniel West." And just as my dad said would happen, Daniel offers me a chance at another fight, which I accept. When I hang up, I check on Micaela then get dressed because I just can't deal with Marco and his shit right now. If I'm going to win this fight and make a name for myself, I'm going to need to take training seriously and since I've made the decision not to go back to school until next fall, I can give my training one hundred percent.

After Micaela wakes up, I feed her and then put her in her car seat.

"Where are you going?" Marco asks from the kitchen, drinking his coffee.

"I'm going to the gym to train. Daniel West offered me a chance at another fight."

"That's awesome. I can watch Micaela while you go."

"That's okay. I'd rather my mom watch her. I can't risk the chance you just up and leave. I mean, would you leave her here? Or would you take her with you? I could come home and my daughter's photo could be blasted on social media." Realizing how mean that sounds when Marco's face drops in defeat, I add, "Look, I just don't trust you." And without waiting for another excuse or apology, I walk out the door.

I drop Micaela off at my mom's and she asks me to come inside for a few minutes. We sit on the couch together. "I need to talk to you about something, but first, is everything okay with Marco? Have you found him?" my mom asks.

I let out a long sigh, shaking my head. "No, I mean yes, I found him. Marco's home but everything is far from okay. I'm just so upset with him. He left for California and he has all these excuses for not telling me and they sound legit. His friend, the one in the coma, went into cardiac arrest. Marco drove there to be with him and I get that, I do. But there were photos of him at a party and it's all just too much. I can't trust him, and I don't know if I will ever be able to."

"Oh, sweetie." My mom envelops me in a much-needed hug. "Maybe you both need to take a step back. It sounds like it's coming at you guys from all angles."

"I know. That's why I left. I need to just focus on this fight Daniel West offered me, and on Micaela. So, what was it you needed to talk to me about?"

My mom frowns and I mentally prepare myself for bad news. "Elsa is sick. She's getting older and your dad and I think it's time to put her down. Your dad brought her to the Vet this morning and she's in a lot of pain."

I knew this was coming, but my heart still breaks. "I feel like I just keep losing my heart. Tristan, Marco, Elsa. Does it ever stop?"

My mom gives me a sad smile. "No, it doesn't," she says honestly. "Life is full of love and laughter, but it's also full of heartbreak."

"When will they put Elsa down?"

"She's at the Vet now. I thought you would want to say goodbye to her."

"I do. I'm going to go there now. I want to be there when they put her down. I need to be."

I give my mom a hug goodbye then drive over to Elsa's Vet. When I walk through the door, my heart aches knowing this is the last time I'll come here for Elsa. She's been coming here since we got her.

"Oh, Bella!" Peggy, Dr. Rowes' wife and assistant comes around her desk to give me a hug. "She's hanging on, sweetie. Go say your goodbyes."

I'm completely choked up, so I simply nod and follow her to the back. Dr. Rowes is there with Elsa. She's lying on a soft dog pillow, and when she sees me, her tail wags but she doesn't get up. "Oh, puppy," I cry, petting her head softly. "I'm going to miss you so much." Images of all my years with Elsa float to the surface as I sob into her soft fur.

"Can I stay, please?" I ask Dr. Rowes. "I don't want her to be alone." He gives me a sympathetic look and nods. I don't watch anything he does after that. I just lie on the ground next to my dog and pet her face, speaking soft words to her until Dr. Rowes says, "Bella, honey. She's gone." I give her one last kiss, then I stand and lose it. Dr. and Mrs. Rowes hold me while I cry in their arms, mourning my best friend.

After I'm done crying and they assure me they'll have her cremated so I can have her ashes, I drive to the gym. It's already the afternoon but I need to work out. I need to do something to get my mind off everything. I jump onto the treadmill and do five miles before going in search of my dad.

I don't find him right away, but I do see Caleb. "Bella, get over here!" Caleb gives me a hug. "Your dad told me about your upcoming fight. You here to do some training?"

"Yeah, I was just looking for my dad."

"I think he's out back dealing with a delivery. Everything okay?"

"No, I had to put Elsa down this morning." The words come out watery and Caleb pulls me into a hug. "I'm so sorry. I remember when your dad bought her for you. What are you doing here?"

"I just need to keep my mind off it all. The gym is the only place I can take my mind off things."

"All right then. Throw on some gloves and let's spar. Let's take your mind off shit."

"Okay."

After about twenty minutes of sparring, we both stop for a water break. "I didn't realize how badly I'm out of shape."

"Don't be so hard on yourself. You just had a baby. You'll get there. You have months to train and you have Marco to help you." I feel myself flinch at Marco's name and hope Caleb didn't see it. I know he did, though, when he comes and sits in front of me.

"What happened?" I go into the entire story about Logan, Marco leaving, the photos and texts.

"I just can't trust him. I know he was hurting, but…"

"No, fuck that. Don't make excuses for him. Many years ago, I walked away from Hayley because I was too scared to talk to her. It was the day she and Marco were kidnapped. Now it's not the same as what you and Marco are going through, but if I hadn't walked away, they wouldn't have been taken."

I gasp, my hands covering my mouth. I was little when they were taken. I don't know all the specifics other than Marco was selling drugs and his biological mom was spending the money. They got in over their heads and Caleb saved them. Marco's mom had overdosed and died and the men were charged with a bunch of stuff. They kidnapped Hayley and Marco in an effort to get Caleb to drop the charges.

My dad, Bentley, Kaden, and Caleb got there just in time with the police and they were arrested. But I didn't know he left them that day.

"You couldn't have known."

"No, I couldn't have, but it doesn't matter. We all make choices that affect those around us. Marco shouldn't have left without telling you. He's a twenty-six-year-old man. He's had to grow up too fast in some ways, but in other ways, he still hasn't grown up."

"I'm afraid if I forgive him, I'll look like a fool. Especially if he does it again." I'm shocked to admit it out loud, but I feel relief to have said it.

"Love isn't easy, Bella. All you can do is listen to your heart. Every one of us have fucked up and anybody who cares about you isn't going to judge you, but that doesn't mean you should run back to him with open arms. Make him earn that. Because if you let him get away with it, he will continue to do it."

"Thank you, Caleb."

I head to the office to talk to my dad, and as I'm walking over, my mom comes walking in with Micaela, Lilly, and Nathan. "Mom!" I run over to her, pulling her into a hug, Micaela becoming the crème in our Oreo. "She's gone, Mom."

"Who's gone?" My dad comes out of his office and asks.

"Elsa. They put her down."

"I'm so sorry, sweetie. I brought her to Dr. Rowes this morning when she wouldn't walk on her own. I wanted to call you, but you were already dealing with so much."

"It's okay. I got to say goodbye. I loved her so much." Then I turn to Nathan and Lilly. "How are you guys doing?"

Lilly shrugs. "We said goodbye to her this morning. I'm sad to see her gone, but she wasn't doing well."

"I'm sorry you lost your dog, Bella," Nathan adds. "I mean, she was all of ours, but even when you were away at college, she slept in your room."

"Thanks, Nate." I give him a hug.

We all go into dad's office and spend the next hour talking about Elsa and our memories of her. I will miss her so much.

Eventually Mom says she needs to head to the rec center and Lilly and Nathan head out with her. After I feed Micaela, my dad and I go over a schedule, and he sends me some videos of Shawna Fields' previous fights to look over at home, and when I can't avoid my house any longer, I go home.

I walk inside to find the table set similar to the way it was the other night. There's a different array of food this time and the table is where it belongs instead of in the living room, but it has the candles in the center.

"I figured with you training, you would want to eat healthy so I made dinner."

"Hmm… this feels a lot like déjà vu. Oh wait, this did happen. The dinner. The candles. And I don't really like how that all ended. What, with you leaving and all. So, I think I'll just pass on dinner. I've had a long, shitty day, and I can't deal with you right now."

I go to walk away but Marco stops me in my tracks. "Please just eat," he pleads, and of course at the moment, my stomach growls. "What have you eaten all day?"

"I was busy putting my dog down, thank you very much. Then I went to the gym to work out."

"You had to put Elsa down? Why didn't you call me?"

"Marco! Seriously? Why would I call you? You have made it a habit of breaking my heart, not piecing it together, so I'm pretty sure the last person I would call when I need to be comforted is you."

Marco's head hangs, but I don't have the energy to feel bad. "Okay, I get that. I hate that you can't come to me or count on me to be there for you. But you can at least let me feed you."

"I'm not hungry," I say stubbornly.

"Belles, you're breastfeeding and training. You need to work out a food plan. You need high proteins plus you need to eat several small meals to make sure you and Micaela are getting the nutrients you both need." I know he's right. I didn't even think about any of that.

"How about we eat dinner and then we can go over a meal plan?" I want to say no, but he's trying.

"Fine. But only because it will help keep my mind off Elsa and I need a meal plan."

After dinner, we go over a meal plan and Marco says he'll pick up the food tomorrow so we can put them together for the week.

After I get out of the shower, he knocks on my half-open bedroom door. "Can I come in?"

"I guess."

Sitting on the bed next to me, he holds out a box. "I bought this for you for Valentine's Day. You know, before I messed everything up."

Taking it from his hands, I open the teal blue box and inside is beautiful silver charm bracelet with a heart dangling from it, and written on the heart says *Mom.*

"It's a locket," Marco says.

I open it up and nestled inside is a tiny picture of Micaela. "It's beautiful. Thank you." I take it out of the box and hand it to Marco to put on me.

"I know Valentine's Day is supposed to be romantic, but it's also about love. No matter what happens between us you will always be the mother of my child and you are a damn good mom, Bella."

He leans over and gives me a soft kiss on my cheek before standing up. "Goodnight."

"Goodnight, Marco."

The next several days we fall into a routine. I leave to work out for a few hours, my mom watches Micaela, and Marco has dinner waiting when I get home. He always makes sure my meals for the day are packed and he never asks to take Micaela. The food he makes is always healthy and delicious and we always eat in silence. Finally, after a week or so, I decide to ask Marco something that's been on my mind while we're eating dinner.

"Why aren't you at the gym working out?" He looks shocked at my question, which I don't understand. He's been fighting his entire life. Sure, I appreciate that he's doing some laundry while I'm gone and having dinner ready, but what I don't get is why he isn't working out. I know he's been attending more meetings, but those are only like an hour long.

"I can't," he mumbles. I didn't even think about the fact that he hasn't been cleared yet.

"When do you go to the doctor?" He just shrugs and continues to eat.

Several more days pass and our routine continues. Then one day, my dad says, "So I take it Marco found another gym to train at."

"What do you mean?" I huff out, hitting the mat flat on my back as my dad throws me into an arm bar for the takedown. I smack the ground in frustration, tapping out. Every time my dad sweeps my legs, bringing me to the ground, I get even more pissed. Standing up fighting, I got that shit all day, but the minute I hit the ground I'm fucked. I used to be so good at ground fighting, but as I got older, I focused more on stand-up fighting and less on grappling. Now it's become my weakness.

My dad reaches his arm out and I take it, letting him help me up. "Well, he must to be training somewhere. The fight is coming up and he's got to be freaking out."

"My fight?"

"Well, honey, I mean, yes, it's your fight, but Marco is getting paid six figures to defend his belt on top of what he gets paid in his contract."

"What?" I say louder than I mean to. "Marco isn't fighting. He's not even allowed to."

"Unless I misunderstood Daniel, Marco is fighting and he's the main event. It will be announced in a few days. Daniel called to see how Marco is doing, but I told him he's not training here. Marco's got a lot at stake here. If he wins, his bonus is huge, so he has to be training somewhere." He pulls out his phone and shows me the text.

Daniel: Marco is cleared. You training him?

The conversation continues, and everything my dad said is true. Marco is fighting the same night as me as the main event. I am stumped by this. Every day I've left to train, Marco has acted like he's been home or at a meeting. Is it possible he's leaving to go train somewhere else? He's been giving me space since the whole California thing happened. He doesn't go to my parents with me, and he hasn't stepped foot in this gym since we returned, but would he really lie to me about not being able to train? And why? Why hide the fight? It's not like I'm not going to see him at the MGM Grand on fight night.

"None of this makes any sense." I grab my bag and head home to find out what the hell is going on. Before I take off, I text my mom and tell her I'll be by the rec center to pick up Micaela, but she says Marco has her. She dropped her off to him a couple hours ago because she had a meeting she needed to go to.

I send her an angry text because seriously? She knows I don't trust him and she goes and leaves Micaela with him without even letting me know. She texts back she's sorry and that it was an emergency, and I immediately feel bad because she is already doing me a favor by watching my daughter. If she had to drop Micaela off to Marco, it had to be for a good reason. She wouldn't just do that for no reason. I send her back a text apologizing and thank her for watching Micaela.

When I walk through the door Marco stands and looks at me confused. "I didn't expect you home yet."

"Yeah, well, I found something out today and figured I should come home and give you a chance to explain."

"Okay…" Marco takes my hands and pulls me onto the couch next to him. I pull my hands out of his and back up a bit so we aren't touching. He frowns and says, "Talk to me."

"You said you weren't cleared. You lied." He flinches but quickly composes himself.

"No, I said I couldn't fight. You assumed that meant I wasn't cleared. I just didn't correct you." I glare at him because really…lying by omission. Will this man ever learn?

"So, you can fight."

"No, I can't." He shrugs and hits play on the television to continue watching whatever he was watching, trying to end this conversation.

Not happening.

Grabbing the remote, I click pause and toss the control to the other side of the couch. "Don't ignore me, Marco. Why can't you fight?" The look he gives me is one I've never seen before. It looks like he's scared, which is crazy because Marco is one of the strongest people I know, at least physically anyway.

"Marco," I say again.

"Fine! I'm fucking afraid, Belles!" He scrubs the side of his face with his hand and I keep quiet to let him continue. "I'm afraid I'll go back to getting high. I'm afraid of the pain. Then there's the fact that one of my best friends is lying in a coma because of my fighting. I spent the last four years training with him and now he's in a goddamn coma. I'm a dad now and I'm trying to make shit right with you. Look what happened a few weeks ago. I had a shot of liqueur, and yeah, I know I can drink if I want to, but it's not smart. I'm just trying to stay above water right now."

In this moment, my heart breaks for this man. He has been through so much his entire life and the only time he was truly happy was when he was fighting and now the one thing that makes him feel whole is the very thing he's afraid of.

I crawl into his lap to be close to him, suddenly missing Marco and our friendship. We might be living in the same house, but we have been a million miles apart lately. His words of admission remind me how fucking human he is. His entire world imploded the night of that accident. Then there was the pain and drugs and what happened with us.

He turned to the one thing he swore he never would do, the very thing that killed his mom. And now he's associating fighting with everything bad that's happened.

"Hey," I whisper. Marco's hands hold onto my thighs lightly, his face looking down between us. "Hey," I repeat. This time his face lifts and I can see the tears. Wrapping my arms around his neck, I hug him as tight as I can. We sit like this for I don't know how long before I pull back.

"Are you still in pain?"

He shakes his head slowly.

"You'll get through this." I give him a small smile before getting up. As I go to swing my leg over to the other side, Marco's hand grabs my thighs tighter, sending an electrical charge straight to my center.

"Marco…"

"I need you, Bella." He pulls me close to him and nuzzles his face in my hair. "I miss you so damn much. It's like I was given a sample, but when I went to order the full portion, it was sold out."

I roll my eyes and laugh softly but go along with his analogy. "No, it was more like you had the perfect, homemade, cooked to perfection meal right in front of you and you walked out without finishing dinner."

I don't hear Marco, but I feel him shaking with laughter. "I was stupid, Belles. I'm so hungry."

"Yeah, well, maybe next time you won't choose a drive thru over a home-cooked meal." It's meant as a joke but Marco stiffens and I feel bad for throwing that in his face. I know he didn't do anything with Janell or any other woman for that matter. "I'm sorry."

"No, don't apologize. I'm going to earn your trust back, Belles. But not just your trust, I'm going to earn your mind and your body and your heart. One day, you will be completely mine and I will have earned it."

Silly boy…if he only knew—he already owns me, all of me, every piece of me: mind, body, and heart.

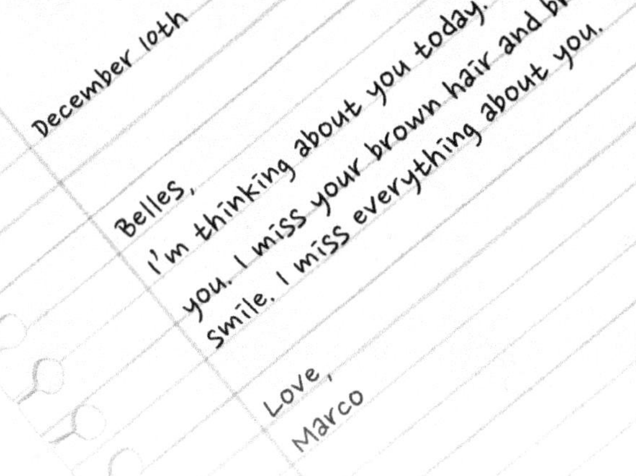

THIRTY

MARCO

EVER SINCE BELLA AND I TALKED THE OTHER NIGHT, IT SEEMS like we've moved into a new type of comfort. We aren't back to where we were before I fucked it all up by leaving, but I'd like to think we're at least back on track and heading in the right direction. We watch TV together at night, converse during dinner more, and we have been to my parents' house to visit several times. It's like we're back to being friends again except we have a baby together. It's been nice.

I do have to say I'm kind of shocked that Bella hasn't pushed me more since I admitted to her my fears about fighting. We haven't even spoken again regarding my admission. So, when she stumbles into the house trying to carry a big box inside, while I'm in the middle of folding clothes, I'm not at all suspicious.

"Whoa, there! Let me help you." I grab the box from her tiny hands and pick it up to bring inside. Once I set it down in the living room, I take a look at the picture and see it's a stroller. "Don't we already have a stroller, Belles?"

She closes the door behind her and smiles. "It's a better stroller. Will you help me set it up?"

I'm not sure why we need a better stroller for a three-month-old baby that weighs like ten pounds dripping wet, but I'm not going to argue. Bella rarely buys anything other than what's needed. She's not your typical female and it's one of the things I love about her.

"Sure." We spend the next hour putting the stroller together. Once we're done, I check it out. Instead of four wheels, it has three huge ones, the front one being able to swivel. It has a couple cup holders, a large area underneath the seat for storage, and the thick handlebar goes across the top. It's a sturdy stroller, but I'm still not sure why we needed another one.

"What do you think?"

Bella jumps up and down squealing, clapping her hands together. "I love it! Let's try it out now."

"Okay…" I'm still confused as to why we can't just take Micaela for a walk in her other stroller. "I'll grab her from her room. She's due to wake up from her nap anyway. Once you feed her, we can head to the park. But afterward I have to go to my meeting. It's important I'm there tonight."

"Oh, Marco! Are you getting your six-month tag tonight?"

"Yeah." I shrug nonchalantly. "Any chance you might want to go?"

"Yes! I am so proud of you. While I get ready, call your mom to see if she wants to spend some time with Micaela and then I can go with you."

"Okay, Belles."

"Oh! And I want to go somewhere else besides the usual park. Make sure you put on comfortable shoes." She gives me a wink then walks away, picking up Micaela to feed her.

After I've gotten dressed and confirmed with my mom she can hang out with Micaela for a little bit, I come out to find Bella putting our daughter into her car seat. We throw the stroller in the back of my SUV, and since Bella insists on driving, I jump into the passenger seat. About twenty-five minutes later, we pull up to Red Rock. I haven't been here since the day I kissed Bella. God, it seems like that was a lifetime ago.

"Wanting to take a walk down memory lane?" I joke.

She frowns but quickly recovers and says, "I was thinking more like a jog." And then it hits me. She's just tricked me into working out. She's fucking slick, I'll give her that much. I should have seen this coming.

"Belles, I don't think…"

"Nope, don't think. We are going for a jog, that's it." She jumps out of the vehicle and grabs the stroller from the back, popping it open. I can't help but stare at the way her spandex pants mold around her tight round ass. She bends over to put the diaper bag underneath and her full tits, which barely fit in her sports bra thanks to her breastfeeding, practically spill out from the top. When she stands back up, her belly ring glitters in the sun. The woman is completely unaware that she's like a walking billboard for MILF porn.

Of course, she catches me staring at her. "What?" She looks down at herself. "Do I have something on me?"

"No, you're just fucking gorgeous."

Her nose scrunches up and she rolls her eyes. "Shut up."

"I'm serious." I grab her hips and pull her over to the side of the vehicle, pressing my body against hers. She blushes the cutest shade of pink when my hard-on makes its presence known against her stomach.

Nuzzling my face into her neck, I murmur softly into her ear, "Your sexy ass, babe. It's on fire." My hands glide over her hips and land on her ass, giving it a squeeze. "And those perky fucking tits are just begging to be sucked." My mouth goes down to her cleavage and I give the top of each tit a soft kiss. "Fuck, and that goddamn belly ring that I want to lick. Belles, you are one hot mom."

"Oh, my God! Marco!" She giggles and swats at my chest. "You are too much."

She grabs Micaela from her car seat and plops her inside the stroller as I attempt to adjust myself.

"Okay, all ready!" Notice she doesn't ask me if I'm ready; she just says she is as she grabs two water bottles from the car and places them in the cup holders while I check out Micaela in her seat all buckled in. She looks adorably tiny in the huge stroller, but she's smiling and ready to rock and roll just like her mom.

I bend down to stretch and make sure my shoe laces are tied tight and notice my hands are shaking. Taking a deep breath, I stand and nod. "Okay, I'm ready."

We start off slow, neither of us saying a word, eventually picking up speed. I focus on the trail in front of me, occasionally stealing a glance at Bella, and she focuses on running. I recognize the area where we kissed when we get to it and smirk before I pretend to trip. I fall to the ground and roll a few feet.

Bella parks the stroller and crouches down next to me. "Oh no! Marco, are you okay?" When she hears my laughter spill out, she slaps me in the chest. "You scared me!"

"Don't you recognize this place?" I look around. "It's where you conned me into kissing you." I laugh harder when she glares at me.

"I didn't con you! I really did fall!"

"And so did I…for you." I waggle my brows and give her a wink. Her face breaks out into a wide grin and she throws her head back in laughter.

"You are so damn cheesy, Marco!" she says once she's caught her breath.

"I think I might need some mouth-to-mouth, Belles. I'm seriously hurt." I roll over dramatically and she giggles.

"And how will giving you mouth-to-mouth help you?" Her one brow quirks up.

"Don't parents say that kisses make the boo-boos all better?"

"Umm… yeah… but I'm pretty sure they mean to kiss the actual boo-boo."

"My mouth is hurting, Belles. It's suffering emotional pain from being neglected. It misses you."

Bella rolls her eyes trying to fight a smile, but when I sit up onto my elbow, her eyes go wide. "Kiss me, Belles," I whisper. And I am shocked as shit when she does.

She leans in and our lips meet. At first, it's a soft kiss as I let Bella guide us, but then she grabs the back of my neck and kisses me with such passion I almost come in my pants. I feel her tongue seek entrance, my lips parting to give her access and that's when things heat up even more. Her tongue swirls around with mine and she tastes so damn good.

I sit up without breaking our kiss, and she climbs up onto my lap. My hand goes to her ponytail, and wrapping my hand around her mane, I pull her face closer to mine. She lets out a soft groan and starts to grind down on my cock. That's when we hear a cooing sound coming from our daughter in her stroller only a couple feet away—snapping us back to where we are. Bella climbs off me, her breathing erratic, and I stand up needing to adjust myself.

Micaela's coos get louder by the second, until she's screeching for attention causing us to laugh.

Once we finish our run, we head home to shower and change before dropping Micaela off with my parents so we can go to my meeting. I'm nervous as hell about Bella attending one of my meetings. What if being there makes her realize she is living with a recovering drug addict? It's one thing to know it, but it's another thing to sit in a meeting, surrounded by other recovering addicts. These meetings will most likely always be a part of my life.

We get to the meeting, arriving only a few minutes before it starts. We have a seat in the back and listen as the speaker talks. Bella moves her hand toward mine, entwining our fingers together and places both of our hands in her lap. When the speaker calls my name to give me my six-month key tag, I stand up and walk over to the podium. I don't usually say much, but with Bella sitting in the back smiling at me, I feel like I need to say something.

"Thank you." I feel myself getting choked up, so I take a calming breath before continuing to speak. "My mother was an addict. I swore I would never become my mother. One day I woke up and realized I had in fact become my mother. Only looking back, I see I never became her. She refused to get help. She refused to get clean. I am not my mother. I am me and every day I will fight to stay clean for my daughter, my family, and most importantly for myself."

After the meeting ends, we pick up Micaela and head home. Other than congratulating me, Bella doesn't bring up the meeting. After putting Micaela to bed, we end up on the couch watching more episodes of *The O.C.*

"So, today's run was good, huh?" She thinks she so damn sly.

"Yeah, it was good."

"And you don't feel any pain?"

"Nope."

"So, you might want to join me at the gym tomorrow?"

"Nope."

She whips her head to me and scowls. "Why not?"

"One, I don't have anyone to train me. Two, your dad isn't going to let me into that gym. And three, your dad isn't going to let me into that gym."

"Really? You had to mention that twice?"

"Hell yes, because it's worth two reasons. I can't believe your father hasn't come here while you aren't home and killed me yet."

"Whatever, Marco." She rolls her eyes. "Sometimes you are such a baby."

"Baby?" I ask as she stands up.

"Yes, baby. I'm going to go take a shower. Feel free to continue your pouting and boo-hoo session while I'm gone. Then maybe once it's out of your system you can go to the gym and talk to my dad. You agreed to that fight. You can't just back out now. That's not who you are. I saw you tonight at that meeting. You are a fighter."

She walks down the hallway toward her bathroom and I can't help but watch as her ass sways. Fuck, what I would give to get a hold of that sweet ass. For a minute, I sit and ponder and then decide to see if she'll let me join her in the shower.

When I get to the shower, I second guess myself. What if she thinks I'm trying to use her? But we did almost fuck right there in Red Rock park today, and I know she was just as into it as I was.

Fuck it. I swing open the door and the visual in front of me has my dick twitching. Bella is naked and sitting on top of the counter next to the sink with the baby monitor next to her. The water is going, but she's making no effort to get in.

"Took you long enough." *What the hell?*

"You were waiting for me?" I smirk, suddenly feeling more confident.

"Well, I was hoping." I close the distance between us, my shirt coming off along the way.

"And what if I didn't come in here?"

Bella shrugs and then smirks. "I guess I would have had to handle it myself."

"Handle what?" I ask slowly. *Please say what I think you're going to say.*

"This..." She makes a show of wetting her pointer and middle finger with her mouth. And then opening her legs wide, she brings her fingers down, spreading the lips of her pussy and visibly massaging her clit. A soft moan comes out of her and I know she's hitting the spot that will have her coming quickly. But there's no way in hell I'm letting her finish without me.

Bridging the gap between us, I grab her hand to still it, and I grip the back of her head as I kiss her hard. She tastes like the tea she drank during dinner, cold and sweet. She lets me kiss her, but as soon as the kiss stops and my mouth starts to work its way down, she grabs my chin gently and says, "Nuh-uh. Not yet." She shakes her head.

"What's wrong?"

"Before anything happens, we need to settle a couple of things first." I stand back up and, with her legs wide open, stand between them, my hands resting on her toned creamy thighs, my eyes meeting hers, giving her my full attention.

"Okay. Lay it on me."

"No more lying about shit. No more hiding shit. No more leaving without telling me. Either Micaela and I come first or I'll be the one leaving. I need to be your partner and that means we handle all this shit together."

"That's a whole lot of shit," I joke, but then I get serious knowing she is being serious. "I know it's going to take some time to prove it to you, but I promise no more lying and hiding shit. You and Micaela will always come first. We're a team." I lean forward and give her a soft kiss on her lips. "I won't take this chance you're giving me for granted."

"You better not," she warns. Her hands go to my chest, rubbing down my torso. "Don't make me regret this, Marco." She leans forward and gives my chest a light kiss before sitting back.

My lips move to the corner of her mouth as I brush my lips across hers. "You won't," I say with conviction, my lips pressing against hers a little harder, before I move down to her jaw, trailing gentle kisses along the way—down her neck toward her collarbone. When my lips move to her luscious tits, Bella shivers as I lick each of her perfect pink nipples.

"Fuck, Bella." I plant one more wet kiss on each of them before I continue my journey downward, kneeling in front of her. With her legs already open and ready, I give the top of her mound an open-mouthed kiss then I move to her clit to give it a kiss as well.

Spreading her pussy lips open, I push my tongue into her tight hole and begin tongue-fucking her. I'm addicted to everything about this woman. Her taste. Her touch. Her mouth. Her mind. There's nothing in the world I wouldn't do to be able to have her for the rest of my life. I can't fuck this up again.

Bella's breathing builds up and soon she's panting. "Marco, please," she begs.

I glide my tongue back up to her clit to give it the attention it needs, getting lost in her pussy until she's moaning my name as she comes all over my tongue.

Without giving herself a chance to come down from her orgasm, she pushes me away and I'm scared she's regretting letting me in. But then she drops to her knees, taking my shorts down with her, and before I can protest, she takes my cock into her mouth completely. It hits the back of her throat and she gags slightly.

"Jesus, Belles." My words coming out like prayer. She grips my shaft tightly in her hand as she sucks and pumps my cock until I'm about to come. "Bella, I'm going to come," I warn her. This is the first time she's ever had her mouth on my cock and I never stood a chance at lasting.

She pulls her mouth off my shaft but continues to stroke it. Her eyes lock with mine, her lips plump and swollen from sucking me off. My orgasm shoots through me as I come all over her tits. The sight of her covered in my seed has my dick pulsing, wanting more. I stand in front of her, entranced. She gives me a small smile then leans forward slightly, giving the head of my dick an open-mouthed kiss. *Holy fucking shit.*

I can't take it anymore. I pull her up and drag us both into the shower. The water is still hot, and as she stands under it, I watch my cum on her tits wash away. But before it all disappears, she swipes some up with her fingers and sticks it in her mouth. "It doesn't taste that bad. Kind of salty." She sucks her fingers for a few more seconds. "Maybe next time I'll get a better taste."

I feel myself smile wide at her antics. I love Bella like this. Bold. Sure of herself. She's a spitfire. I don't ever want to take that away from her again. I don't ever want to be the reason she's not like this.

I pull her close to me and kiss her with purpose. "I love you, Belles. So damn much."

She gasps, her eyes going wide. She opens her mouth, but I cover it with my mouth before she can speak. I kiss her for several long seconds before I break the kiss. "You don't need to say it back. I haven't earned those words from you yet. But I will, baby."

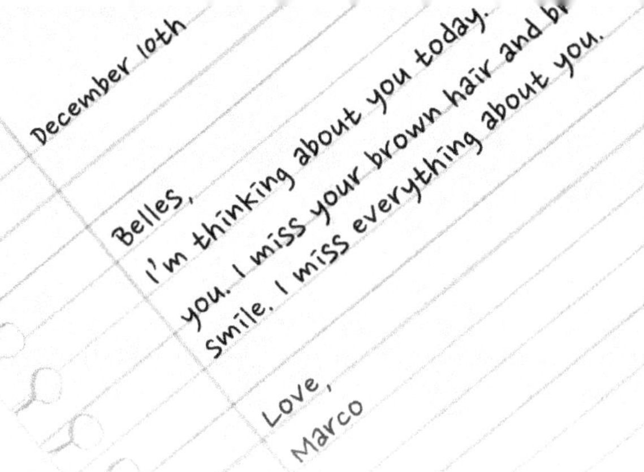

THIRTY-ONE

BELLA

AFTER WE FINISH IN THE SHOWER, MARCO WRAPS A TOWEL around the both of us and guides me into his room, throwing one of his shirts at me.

"Stay the night with me."

I agree and pull his shirt on over my body then crawl into his bed, setting the baby monitor on the nightstand. Marco pulls on a pair of briefs then lies down next to me. He pulls my body slightly onto his, my head resting on his chest and my legs tangled in his. Being in Marco's arms feels good. I lie quietly and think about our past, what we've been through to get to this moment. I think about the promises he made tonight. About his words. *I love you.* I think about the future and find myself praying all those words were the beginning of something special. Maybe this time we'll get it right.

I fall asleep thinking about babies, houses, UFC fights, and I love yous with the hope of forever.

Micaela only wakes up once in the middle of the night to eat. The older she gets, the longer she goes between feedings. I feed her, change her diaper, and rock her back to sleep. I've just stepped out of Micaela's room and am heading back toward my room when I see Marco standing in the doorway. His eyes are hooded, looking only half awake.

"I thought you left."

"I was feeding Micaela." Since I prefer to breastfeed when I'm home, I don't usually wake Marco up when I get up to feed. I only recently moved Micaela to her room and into her crib. Her bassinet was getting to be too small.

Marco grabs my shirt and pulls me to him, kissing me lazily. His lips move from mine and he trails feather-light kisses down my neck, sending shivers down my spine.

"Sleep with me, Belles," he murmurs. "Sleep in my bed. Let's make it ours, please."

"I can't," I blurt out without even thinking. "I can't make anything ours yet." I'm suddenly scared. I went to bed wanting this, hoping for this, but as Marco stands in front of me, asking me in a roundabout way to make us official, I find myself starting to freak out. I want this—him—too badly. What if he leaves again? What if he walks away from Micaela and me. What if he changes his mind? How many times can I pick up the pieces of my broken heart and try to put it back together? I can't chance waking up in his bed and him being gone again.

"Because you don't trust me." He doesn't ask because he already knows.

"I'm sorry. I know you made promises tonight, but those are just words. I need to see the actions. The last time I woke up in your bed, you were gone."

He shakes his head. "No, I get it. We'll take things slow."

I give him an appreciative smile and thank him for understanding before going back to my own room. I lie down on the cold sheets wishing I was lying in another bed wrapped up in the warmth of Marco, but knowing I'm doing the right thing. If Marco is serious about us, he'll be there in the morning and every day following until I am ready to turn whatever is his and mine into ours.

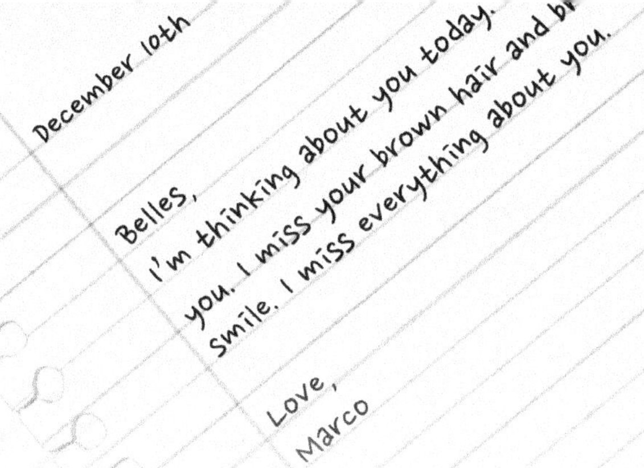

THIRTY-TWO

BELLA

"MORNING!" I YELL TO MY DAD. IT'S BEEN A FEW WEEKS SINCE I tricked Marco into going jogging. I was hoping he would come and talk to my dad about training here again, but it's clear he's going to be stubborn and I'm going to have to take matters into my own hands. I love going jogging with Marco, but there's only a few months until this fight he's in denial of, and I am not about to let him make a fool out of himself.

"Morning, sweetie. Your mom wants to know if you want to come over for dinner tonight." My dad has become an expert at pretending Marco doesn't exist. Marco hasn't stepped foot inside the gym or my parents' place and he usually visits his parents or his sister when I visit mine.

Well, I'm done with all that. They're acting immature and it stops now. "Sure, I'm bringing Marco with me." My dad's smile fades. "And you are going to talk to him." His jaw visibly clenches.

"I have nothing to say to him." My dad says it like a warning, but I ignore him. There was a time Marco was like a son to my dad and I'm not going to let them continue their crap.

"Yes, you do. You are going to forgive him."

"Like hell, I am!"

"You are going to forgive him," I repeat, ignoring his protests. "Because he didn't do anything to you. Everything that has happened between Marco and me, is just that. Between Marco and me."

"He got you pregnant!"

"It takes two. Remember that time you knocked up my mom."

"He left you."

"You left her! You walked away without exchanging numbers! We were never together. As soon as he found out about the baby, he got his shit together." I know it's a low blow, but c'mon. He and my mom's relationship wasn't always perfect.

"He left you, again!"

"His friend had a heart attack. He should have told me he was leaving, but I've forgiven him. I'm giving him another chance."

"Are you back together?"

"Not completely. We are taking things slow." Apparently real slow…like as slow as molasses, so slow we might be going backward. So slow, he hasn't touched me since the night in the bathroom. I just might have to force myself on him soon. Maybe I can explain to him slow means still moving forward.

"Damn it, Bella. He's going to hurt you again."

"Did you hurt mom again?"

He sighs in defeat. "You're my little girl."

"I'm twenty-one and an adult. Please make things right with Marco. He needs a place to train."

"I'm not training him. I'm only here to train you."

"Just make it right. Let him know he can come here to train."

"Fine," he huffs. "I'll talk with him tonight."

"Thank you."

After we're done training for the day, I shoot off a text to Caleb. Our parents have remained friends through all this craziness, keeping it separate from their friendship, but they've made it a point not to discuss fighting or the gym regarding Marco. Caleb has said on several occasions he understands where my dad is coming from and respects how he feels toward Marco.

Me: My dad is going to let Marco train at the gym but he needs a trainer.

Caleb: I'll handle it. Thank you.

I get home from the gym and the house is empty. Marco had texted me earlier letting me know he was meeting his mom for lunch, so he's probably with her. I noticed some clothes he folded still on the coffee table and smile. He has been absolutely amazing since we moved in together. He cooks and cleans and does the laundry. He takes such precious care of Micaela, especially since I started trusting him to keep her while I'm training. He made me promises and I'm giving him the chance to show me he can back them up. The truth is we work well as a team.

I grab a stack of clothes to bring them to his room to put them away while thinking about what will happen once he goes back to training. If all goes well, my dad and him will talk tonight and Marco will begin training. We will need to figure out care for Micaela. On top of that, I go back to school in less than three months.

I make a mental note to speak to my mom tonight. Maybe she has some advice on how to handle this. I always knew from the minute I made the decision to have Micaela this day would come, but I wasn't prepared to feel that ache in my chest at the thought of someone else other than my family caring for my baby girl, but I don't know what else to do. I have to go back to school, right? I know my end goal is to fight and run my dad's gym and there's no way he will let me takeover if I don't finish college. Plus, I need to know I can provide for my daughter. What if Marco up and leaves? Or what if something happens to him? I need to be independent.

I open his drawers one by one shoving his clean clothes into them. When I get to the bottom drawer, where he keeps his socks, I notice a stack of envelopes in the back. Plopping my butt onto the ground, I open the drawer and pull the stack out. There's got to be close to a hundred stuffed envelopes. I consider putting them back, not wanting to invade Marco's privacy, when I catch my name and old address on the front. *What the heck!*

I skim through the front of each envelope and see the same thing. My name and my old California address. There's a stamp in the upper right corner, but they were never mailed. *I should put these back where I got them from.* If he wanted me to have them, he would have mailed them. But maybe I could just open one? I take the rubber band off the stack and hold the front envelope in my hand, ready to open it when the front door slams shut. *Shit!* My guilt takes over and I'm stumbling over my own hands trying to hurry up and put the envelopes back, when Marco enters the room with a smiling Micaela.

My attempt to shove them in the drawer is almost a success until I slam the drawer with my fingers still inside.

"Motherfuckingsonofabitch!" I jump up, holding my fingers and Marco shifts Micaela to his hip, grabbing my hand in his.

"Are you okay? Let's get you some ice." He pulls me into the living room, pointing for me to have a seat on the couch, then he sets Micaela under her play gym, her little feet kicking the piano and making noises.

"Thank you," I say when he hands me the ice. I hold it to my fingers for a few minutes before I blurt out, "I saw the letters."

He looks at me confused for a second, but I can see the moment his mind makes the connection. "Did you read them?"

"No, I was about to, but you came home and I slammed my fingers in the drawer."

Marco laughs. "Such a sneak." He shakes his head.

"When did you write them? Wait, are they letters? Why didn't you send them?"

He gives me a comical look and waits for me to stop throwing questions at him.

"I wrote them while in rehab. I was going to send them, but every time I went to, I felt like a coward. I needed us to talk in person. So, instead of sending them, they kind of became a form of therapy in a way. I would write them and save them. I wrote one every day I was in rehab after my ten days of detox was over."

Eighty letters from Marco. I can't even imagine what they all say. Do I want to know what they say? Those were some seriously dark days for Marco.

"Do you want to read them?"

"Do you want me to?" I volley back, putting the ball in his court.

He gives me a nervous smile and nods. "I do, but you need to understand I was in a weird place. You may not like everything I have to say." He gets up and leaves the living room, coming back a few minutes later with the massive stack of letters. "I'm going to go talk to your dad. He texted me asking to speak to me and I would rather go now. Want to meet at your parents in a little bit for dinner?"

"Sure." I take the letters from him and he gives me a small kiss on my cheek before disappearing out the door. I stare at them for a few moments before Micaela makes herself known. Setting them aside, I lift Micaela from the floor and latch her on to eat.

"Hey, baby girl." I run my fingers through her dark curls. She smiles wide and swings her arm up then goes back to eating. She takes her meals seriously.

Taking a deep breath, I open the first letter.

October 18th

Dear Bella,

Shit, that sounds so formal, like you haven't been my best friend since I was twelve years old. I'm sitting here in rehab and there's so much I need to say to you. So, I decided to write you. First, I know you are pregnant with my kid. Second, I shouldn't have told you to have an abortion when you came to see me that day, but maybe it's for the best I did because it forced you to walk away from me. I spent years saying I would never end up like my mom yet I ended up just like her. High on coke and heroin. Only, I know our stories won't be the same, because you would never let me destroy our child the way my mom did. I know that's why you decided to name Tristan as her dad, to protect her, and I need you to know I don't fault you for that. You're doing something my mom never knew how to do. You're putting your baby first.

when I get out of here, I'll sign whatever papers you need me to sign. I'll sign over my rights. I don't deserve you or that baby. If you would have listened to me, she would've been aborted. I'm glad you didn't listen to me.

Marco

I finish reading the letter and stare at it. If he felt this way, why did he come to the hospital? What made him change his mind? I can't leave it like this. I need to read the next letter. After I finish feeding Micaela, I put her into her swing and grab the next letter hoping to get some type of answer.

October 19th

Dear Bella,

Today has been rough. It's been 11 days since I've had a single drug and while my 10 days of detox ended yesterday and the drugs are technically out of my system, it feels like I'm drugged out. My body is craving the drugs. Do me a favor, please? Never tell your baby about me. Pretend like I don't exist. Don't tell him, he comes from druggie bloodlines. Keep him the fuck away from all temptation. I'm not saying he will go that way and I'm not using the excuse of my genetics as to why I turned to drugs. But just to be on the safe side, make sure he never goes near them. Don't let him ever be a fuck up like me.

Marco

My God! Poor Marco. The struggle and guilt he felt. I almost feel like I'm invading his privacy reading these words, even if they were written and addressed to me and he gave me permission to read them. Not having the patience in the moment to sit through reading the other seventy-eight letters I grab the one in the back and open it up. I need to see how the story ends. Don't judge me! It's not like I'm reading the end of a real story… although, I may have done that a time or two as well. What? I have no patience!

January 5th

Belles,

Today is the last day I will be writing you a letter. It feels like I've been having a one-sided relationship with you, one that you know nothing about. It's been a crazy ninety days, but I'm getting out tomorrow and I'm coming for you, Belles. It may take a few weeks for me to get settled before I come for you, but mark my words, baby, I am coming, and once I have you in my arms, I am never letting you or our baby go.

Love,

Marco

Gah! Now I wish I would have read them all! This letter is literally everything, but I want to know is how he got to this point. Yeah, yeah, I know. It's my fault for skipping to the end.

I tuck the letter back inside and place it in the back again then start from the front working my way back to the end. I read every single letter. I laugh. I cry. I cry a lot. Marco's right. It's like he had a one-way relationship with me for almost three months. He went through so much during his ninety days of rehab. He had so many thoughts and feelings. I wish I could have been there for him. I wish I could have visited him and held him and kissed him.

One of his biggest regrets was not being there for my pregnancy. I hate that he feels this way. We can't go back and we can't live our lives with what ifs.

Deciding I need to see him and give him a hug, I get Micaela ready and run out the door to my parents' place to find Marco. I'm still scared and I still don't completely trust him not to run, but I love this man. The good. The bad. The ugly. And I'm going to make sure he knows it.

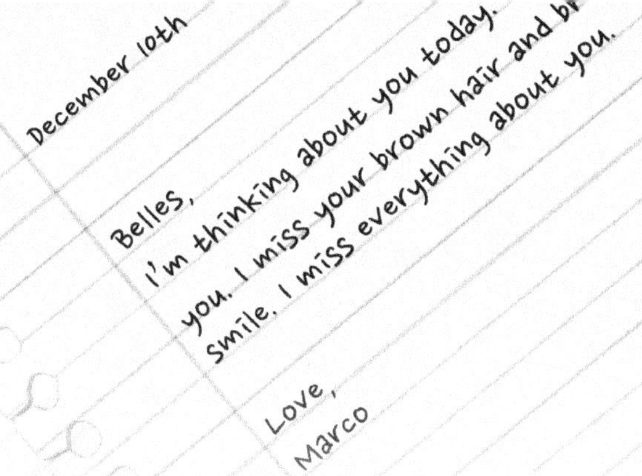

THIRTY-THREE

MARCO

IF YOU ASKED WHAT'S IN ALL THOSE LETTERS I MIGHT BE ABLE TO tell you a few of the topics. I know there are a lot of I miss yous, plenty of I'm sorrys, and quite a few I love yous, but other than that, I couldn't tell you what I wrote in all those letters. Did I mean everything in them? Yeah. But being in rehab was a difficult time. Nobody, who's never been in that situation, can understand what it's like to come off drugs and be isolated from everyone for three months.

I wrote whatever I felt at the time and I didn't second guess it. I also didn't read them after I wrote them. Even being in a high-end rehab center, I still saw some awful shit. I saw a drug addicted pregnant woman lose her baby, a husband trying to deal with physically abusing his wife while high. I listened to people talk their tales of how they got the way they are, and while every story is different, we all ended up in the same place, addicted to shit that hurt us as well as those around us.

When I told Bella that I'm scared to go back to fighting, I wasn't kidding. The very thing I love just about killed me, pretty much killed my best friend, and almost cost me the woman I love and my daughter. When I envisioned making it in the UFC, this was not how I envisioned my life, and if I have to choose one or the other, I'm going to choose Bella and Micaela. I'm not going to talk to her dad about fighting. I'm not going back to fighting. What I am going to talk to him about is something else, though.

I pull up in the driveway and go to type the code in like I've done for half my life but stop myself and press the button. It buzzes, letting me drive through, and when I get to the front of the house Cooper is standing outside waiting for me.

"Let's go for a walk." He nods back down his driveway. We walk for probably a half a mile before he starts talking.

"I've known my daughter was in love with you since she was ten years old." I do the math and that would have made me sixteen. Our age difference now isn't a big deal, but nothing would have happened back then. Before I can respond, he continues. "Not like two adults love each other. But still love. She came home from the gym one day. You had ignored her to practice fighting with some friends. She was upset and crying. She didn't understand the age difference. I don't think she ever has. You've always just been you to her. I held her on the couch and tried to explain you were older and it will happen more because you need to fight people your age. But you know Bella, stubborn as a bull. She shook her head and said she would just learn to fight harder, better, so you would want to train with her. I knew in that moment, she would do anything for you. I watched her grow up, but she never dated. She fought. She fought hard, and every time I saw her struggle and overcome obstacles, I remembered our conversation. I wasn't surprised when she said she wanted to move to California."

"We weren't even on speaking terms."

"It didn't matter. She's always gravitated toward you. Tristan might have been by her side, but you were in her heart. I think it was your strength. Tristan is easy-going, but Bella needs someone to push her and encourage her. And you did. Until you hurt her."

Cooper stops walking and turns to me. "You hurt her, Marco. You used your strength and you made her doubt herself, as a woman, as a soon-to-be mom. Whatever you said to her, she always took like it was gold, and I get that you were high for some of it, but I saw when things started changing. It was long before then."

"She was young. I thought I was doing the right thing pushing her away. I could have handled it differently, though. I know that now."

"And how are you going to handle things now?"

"She wants to trust me, but she's scared. I'm taking it slow. Trying to earn back her trust."

"Do you see a long-term future with Bella?" Cooper locks eyes with me and I see all the love he has for his daughter. He would do anything to protect her.

"I do. I want to spend my life with her. Marry her. Create a family and a life with her. But there's something you should know. I don't want to fight anymore."

"Cooper looks at me incredulously. "Aren't you committed to a fight in a few months?"

"Yeah, but I'm going to announce that win or lose, I'm out."

"Because you're hurt?"

"Because fighting caused too many people too much pain. Logan is in a coma. I turned to drugs. I almost missed out on being a part of Bella's and Micaela's life. My back is okay, but that's because I'm not fighting all the time. Can it handle one more fight? Yeah. But not years of it. And I'm not willing to take the chance. My back injury led me to drugs. It's not worth it to me."

"How are you going to provide for my daughter and yours?" Cooper crosses his arms over his chest in a defensive stance.

"That's actually what I wanted to talk to you about. While Bella is going to school and fighting, because we both know she will be fighting for at least the next ten years, I was thinking about staying home with Micaela."

"Pulling a Bentley?" He raises one brow.

I chuckle. "Kind of. I was thinking I could help you run the gym. Help with the training, the MMA classes."

"You want to be a part of my family business?"

"I want to be a part of your family."

"Are you asking my permission to marry my daughter?"

"No, I'm not."

Cooper tilts his head to the side in a *what the fuck* kind of way. "I'm not ready to ask your permission to marry her. Not yet. But once I've earned her trust and deserve to marry her, I'll be back to ask."

"You're a good man, Marco. You just need to find your way, and you will. You have an amazing support system so lean on us when you need to. Take care of my daughter and granddaughter, and don't fucking run again. We're here for you. Let us be here for you. As far as the gym goes, focus on this fight coming up, and once the fight is over, we'll figure it all out."

I reach my hand out to shake his. "Thank you."

We get back to the house and Bella's vehicle is parked behind mine. She must have gotten to her parents' house while her dad and I were talking. I don't even make it through the doorway and she's flinging herself into my arms. Her arms and legs wrap around my body and if I wasn't standing in her parents' foyer I would be throwing her ass onto the bed.

"I love you," she whispers into my mouth, our lips mere millimeters from touching. The conviction of her words just about brings me to my knees. I have no idea what I ever did to deserve this woman, but I am going to live the rest of my life making sure she never regrets saying those words to me.

"I read all of your letters." Her eyes shine brightly and she gives me a watery smile. I bring my lips to hers, but our kiss is nothing more than a tease. A promise of something more to come later.

A throat clears, reminding us we aren't alone. I reluctantly set Bella back on her feet and that's when I notice it's not just her parents who are here. My parents, my sisters, as well as Kayla and Bentley are all staring at us. And just as I'm about to close the door behind me, in walks Ashley, Kaden, and their daughters. The only people missing are

Tristan and Mason. Liz is holding Micaela, but as soon as she sees me, she starts screeching, her arms reaching out for me. I grab her from Liz and give her a kiss on her cheek. Nothing feels better than having Micaela in my arms and Bella by my side.

Dinner is ready so we all grab a seat outside—while it's still cool enough to eat out here—and dig in. Liz went healthy for Bella since she's training and grilled up some chicken and pork chops. There's salad, sweet potatoes, and tons of fruit and vegetables. It's all delicious.

"Can I sit with you?" Ryan, Bentley and Kayla's adopted son, asks me. He became a part of their family about two years ago when his mom committed suicide and his dad got busted with drugs. When he moved in, he had selective mutism, meaning he could talk but wouldn't. During our Christmas vacation to Breckinridge, Ryan and I bonded. No idea why but he trusted me and spoke to me. Since then, we have weekly video chats. Except for when I was high and didn't give a shit about anyone around me. The first time we video chatted once I was clean, Ryan asked me where I was for so long, and it broke my heart.

Since Bella and I moved back here, I've brought Micaela over to visit with Bentley and Ryan on several occasions. The kid holds a special place in my heart. He reminds me a lot of myself when I was little, only he was fortunate enough to be given a better home at an earlier age.

"Of course you can." I pick him up and swing him over the bench to sit next to me as Kayla brings over his plate of food and juice box.

"So, I'm thinking of joining a mom's group," Bella announces. Bella… in a mom's group? I hold back my laughter. She barely has any girlfriends because she can't handle the drama and cattiness that goes along with befriending most women.

"Mom's groups are the damned devil," Bentley points out seriously. Kayla and Liz laugh.

"That's only because they all wanted themselves some Daddy Bentley," Liz jokes through her laughter. "Bella, I think if you want to join a mom's group, that's great. But are you doing it to meet other moms or to socialize with Micaela?"

"I don't know. I feel like it's something I'm supposed to do." She shrugs. Bella has always been confident in herself, but being a mom is new to her and she questions herself a lot. "And I need to find out about daycare for Micaela. I thought maybe other moms would have ideas or know of good places."

"Why would you put her in daycare?" Liz asks.

"I go back to school in less than three months."

"You have an entire group of people who can help you. You don't need a mom's group to help you figure out childcare for your daughter."

"You guys are all done raising babies. And I don't think any of us were even in daycare." She says the last word softly, like she's embarrassed her baby would have to be put in daycare. Doesn't she realize what an amazing mom she is? To even think about stuff like that, to make sure her baby is taken care of.

"Tristan was," Ashley points out. "There are a lot of nice childcare places in the area."

"She's not going to daycare, Belles. So, it doesn't even matter." I stab a piece of chicken with my fork and throw it into my mouth. I've got nothing against daycare. Shit, for kids with parents like my biological mom, it's probably better than their home life, but there's no reason for our daughter to go to daycare. Not when I have fought for the last eight years and saved my money, and have the means to be home with her.

"I want to finish school, Marco. And I want to fight."

"And you will do both, if that's what you want. I'll be staying home with her."

"Because you're scared to fight! I'm not letting you give up because you have linked every bad thing that's happened to you fighting."

"Maybe we should all go inside and give them space to talk." My mom stands.

"No need." I stop her. "You all should hear this because in some way you all have been affected. Kaden and Ashley, my drug addiction is why your son was going to raise my daughter. You thought you were going to be grandparents and then she was ripped from you."

Ashley gives me a small smile. "We're just glad it all worked out. We aren't going to judge you."

"Maybe not, but I'm going to judge me. I pushed away my parents, Bella, almost didn't get to raise my daughter. Logan is in a goddamned coma from us celebrating."

"Marco." Bella puts her hand on my arm to comfort me.

"No, it's the truth. I'm well aware the fighting isn't to blame, but I was injured in that accident and when I thought I lost fighting for good, I lost it. I turned into someone I never want to be again. I'm going to fight to defend my title, but then I'm retiring. Fighting was my life for a long time, but it's not where I see my future anymore. My future is making sure I'm healthy and clean for my family."

"Who's training you?" Kaden asks.

"I haven't made it that far yet. But I committed to the fight and it's going to be a huge event. The money they're willing to pay me if I win is too much to pass up. I'm contracted for one more fight so I'm going to give it to them. Plus, it will help gain viewers for Bella's first fight."

"I'll train you."

I glance at Kaden, shocked as shit. "After what I did to your son? Why?"

"Like Ashley said, we aren't going to judge you. Tristan knew he wasn't the dad. He made his choices and he's dealing with the fallout the best he can. With Mason moving to California to live with Tristan,

I have time. If you're only going to fight one last time, you need to make that shit count."

"All right. Thanks."

"And Marco and I talked," Cooper adds. "After the fight is over, he's going to start taking on some fighters himself. Helping at the gym. We'll figure out a schedule around your class schedule."

"And I have already hired someone to start learning the ropes of the accounting department at the rec center so I can be home more with Cooper and the kids. She just graduated with her accounting degree, and so far, she seems to be a good fit. I would love to watch my granddaughter," Liz says.

"Hell yeah, and I'm home with Ryan. We would love to hang out with Micaela," Bentley adds.

"And I can watch her if you need me to," Bella's brother points out.

Liz gets up and walks over to Bella. "There is nothing wrong with daycare, Bella, and if you had to put Micaela in daycare, we would find one that works for you and Micaela, and it wouldn't make you any less of a mother. But when you have family that can help, that's what we do. We help each other. When it was just you and me, we had Kayla. But had she not have been there, you would have been in daycare because I would have done whatever I needed to make sure you were taken care of and fed."

Bella's eyes fill with tears. "Thank you, guys. I don't even know what to say. I love you all so much."

"Good! Now let's eat!" Bentley shoves some food into his mouth to make his point.

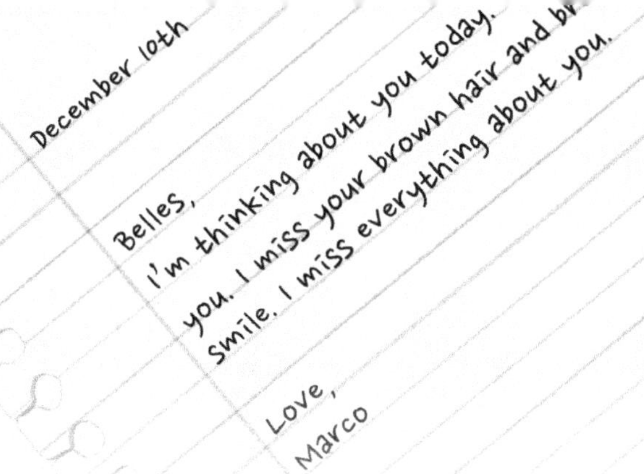

THIRTY-FOUR

BELLA

WITH BOTH OF US TRAINING FOR THE UPCOMING FIGHT, MARCO and I have been busy. I'm still sleeping in my own bed and we haven't been intimate anymore, either. According to Marco, the best way of taking things slow and proving himself is to also take a step back from being sexual. I brought up the subject once and he said he wants to have my trust, and for me to be sure of us before we're together again, sexually.

That doesn't mean we never kiss or touch. We do. We hang out on the couch almost every night talking about our day. We're finding our friendship again and it feels good, like we've started fresh. It's how I imagine a new relationship would go. Slowly learning about each other intimately before taking the next step, sexually. I know it sounds stupid because we've already been together, but I appreciate Marco recognizing we need to connect and get to know each other on a deeper level. It's easy to have sex with someone. It's a lot harder to connect with them on an emotional level. I'm glad we have taken a step back and are trying to do this the right way.

I've signed up for my fall classes, which start in a couple months. After my fall semester, I'll have two more semesters of classes left and then will be able to graduate.

I'm on the couch with my laptop, uploading some new pictures of Micaela when Marco sticks his phone in my face. "Let's go away."

I look at the photo on his phone. "Isn't that in California? Like as in where we just moved from?"

"Yes, but I want you to meet my cousin, Mathias, and I would also like to visit Logan. You never got to meet him. We can fly out for the weekend, just the two of us."

"You mean leave Micaela?" I gasp.

"Belles, she's five months old. Your parents can watch her for the weekend. We'll have fun. I'll rent us a hotel near Mathias."

The thought of being a plane ride away from my daughter is terrifying, but it would be nice to get away with Marco, maybe discuss taking the next step with us. Marco has been proving himself and I'm ready to go all in.

"Okay."

♥♥♥♥♥

FOUR DAYS LATER WE'RE ON A PLANE TO SAN DIEGO. BEING THIS close to Tristan and not seeing him makes me sad, but like he asked of me, I have given him his space.

"What's wrong, Belles?" Marco takes my hand in his, entwining our fingers. He brings our joined hands up to his lips and gives my knuckles soft kisses.

I almost consider lying to him, but instead go with the truth. "I wish Tristan were talking to me. The idea of going to San Diego and not seeing him makes me sad."

Marco lifts the seat divider and pulls me into his side, placing a chaste kiss on my cheek. "He just needs time. If your friendship is as strong as I think it is, he'll come around."

"I'm going to need you to keep me busy this weekend." When I replay how that sounded, my cheeks warm up.

"Oh, baby," Marco murmurs into my ear, placing a kiss to my earlobe then biting down and lightly pulling. "I will gladly keep you busy all weekend."

We get to the hotel and it's late, so Marco says we'll visit Mathias and Logan tomorrow. We're on the first floor with an ocean view and as soon as we drop our luggage down, I open the sliding glass door to feel the breeze.

"Let's go sit on the beach," Marco suggests.

Grabbing a blanket from the linen closet and changing into comfortable clothes, we make our way down and find a secluded spot to sit. The sun has already gone down and the beach around us looks abandoned. Marco drops himself on top of the blanket and pulls me down after. My back is pressed against his front and I'm snuggled between his muscular thighs.

Dusting my hair to the side, Marco kisses down my neck then places several kisses on my shoulder. "I never imagined in a million years we would get to a place in our lives where I could take you away and sit on the beach, kissing you, and it be okay. It's like a dream come true."

"Who said it's okay? Did I give you permission to touch my body?" Marco stiffens, but when I giggle, he relaxes.

"Don't fuck with me, Belles. This body is mine," he growls into my ear, nipping at my lobe. Turning quickly, before he can react, I pounce on him, his back hitting the ground, my legs falling on either side of him. I grab a hold of his hands with both of mine and pin them down like I would do in the octagon.

"Yours, huh?" Taking both of his huge hands into one of mine, I use my other hand to pull up his shirt, exposing his perfectly chiseled abs. Leaning forward, I place open-mouthed kisses down Marco's torso. My arms are too short, so my hand slips from his as I work downward, but he leaves his hands over his head like I'm still holding him down.

"Does that mean *your* body is mine?" I kiss each one of the indentations of his abs until I get to the top of his board shorts.

"I am definitely yours."

"To do with as I please?" I look up through my lashes to see Marco giving me a smoldering look that just about melts my panties off.

"Whatever the fuck you want to do with."

I look around me to make sure we're alone before I pull Marco's already hardened length out of his shorts. Putting my mouth over the mushroom head, I swirl my tongue around tasting the salty precum. He groans and bucks slightly. His hands, no longer pretending to be held above his head, come down as he grips my hair like it's his lifeline.

Starting at the bottom, I glide my wet tongue slowly up his shaft until I get back to the head, licking the droplets of cum he keeps releasing. My eyes connect with his, and keeping my eyes on his, I tilt my head slightly, taking him all the way down my throat. Marco loses the stare down as his eyes roll back and he lets out a guttural moan that has my clit throbbing in anticipation.

I close my eyes and start to work his dick over, giving his dick the attention one would give to their favorite lollipop. Suddenly Marco's grip gets tighter on my mane as he pulls my mouth off him, my lips making a popping sound. I can't help but pout, which causes him to chuckle.

"Get your ass over here, Belles." I'm confused at first as to what he wants, but Marco sits up and, grabbing my thighs, pulls my bottom half toward him showing me what he wants. He pulls my cotton shorts and panties down then places each of my legs on either side of his head. He spreads my pussy open and his mouth is on my clit in two-point-five seconds. I moan in pleasure as his teeth bite down on my clit, his tongue swiping immediately after to soothe it. Still hovering over Marco's dick only in the opposite direction, I go back to sucking him off, only this time with a renewed purpose.

Unable to see what Marco is doing to me, but being able to feel it, is the biggest turn on. I can feel his hands grabbing my ass, feel his tongue all over my folds and clit. I suck, and he licks. I slurp, and he bites. I take his dick all the way down my throat and he… slips a finger into my ass! I gasp at the intrusion, but when his tongue massages harder, I just about lose it.

I continue to suck and pump, as Marco licks me and fingers my ass. It feels amazing, better than I would have thought. I never want this to end. My pussy is throbbing and my clit is pulsing and my ass—fuck! It just all feels so good and I know, as much as I want this feeling to last forever, I'm going to explode. I want so badly to get Marco off first, but as my climax edges closer, I know it's not going to happen.

His tongue presses down on my clit one last time as his finger presses down harder. Heat spreads through my body as my orgasm rips through me, my entire body shaking. I can barely stay up on my knees, my legs weak from the pleasure.

Marco lifts me off him, my limp and relaxed body rolling onto my back and then he's on top of me—his hands palms down on either side of my head. My hands grip his biceps as he enters me with such force that if I wasn't holding onto him, I would be slammed into tomorrow. My legs wrap around his back as he pumps into me almost violently, nearly taking my breath away. I gasp, but before I can make any noise, his mouth crashes onto mine, his tongue entering, the tastes of me mixed with him assaulting my senses.

His thrusts become more frantic and he goes deeper into me, his shaft rubbing against my clit until I'm wound so tight my body has no choice but to let go. And it does, around Marco's dick. My orgasm sets off a domino effect and seconds later, Marco's pulsing inside of me as he fills me up completely.

He thrusts a few more times before coming to a complete standstill, his dick still throbbing inside of me, his mouth still pressed up against mine.

Then he pushes up a little so our mouths are close but not touching. "I know I promised to take things slow, Belles. But you have to know, you're mine, baby. Mine." He growls out the last word then kisses me hard one last time before pulling out of me.

"And you're mine," I reply, earning me a huge smile.

He hands me his shirt so I can clean up, then hands me my shorts and panties to put them back on. We both stand, and he shakes out the blanket. Then, with his hand on my lower back, guides us back up to the hotel room, where we spend the rest of the night proving our statements to be true.

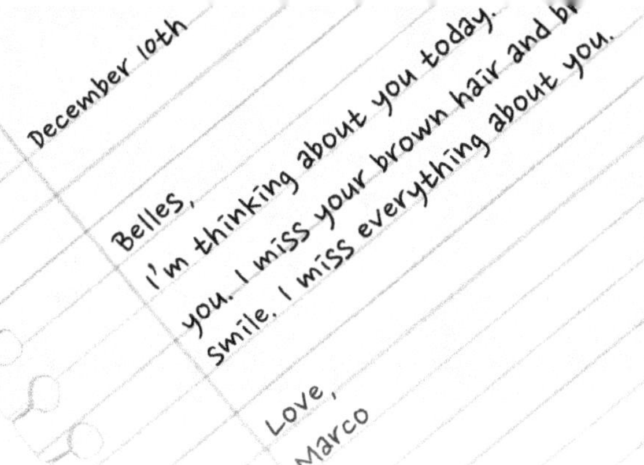

THIRTY-FIVE

MARCO

MY EYES OPEN AND THE FIRST THING I NOTICE IS IT'S STILL DARK out. Thanks to having an infant, my body is used to getting up at the crack of dawn. Thinking about Micaela has me missing the hell out of that little girl. Maybe we should have brought her with us. What if she forgets I'm her dad? I make a mental note to FaceTime Liz later so she can show Micaela my face.

The next thing I notice is I'm freezing my ass off. It's got to be like sixty-five degrees in here, which is the new norm since Bella and I moved in together. She seems to think she's meant to live in Alaska. When I mentioned it to her dad, he laughed his ass off and told me to have fun paying that electric bill. Apparently, he had to threaten her life when she was growing up to stop her from touching the thermostat.

Normally it would be fine. After our first night of living together, I went to the home goods store and purchased the thickest down comforter they sell. Micaela will probably wear winter clothes indoors until she's ten. The problem is, right now I'm lying in bed with no covers and I'm pretty sure my dick has shriveled up inside of me.

I roll over to see where the fuck my covers went and spot the culprit. Bella. Fucking woman is a goddamn blanket stealer. She is curled up facing away from me and has all the sheets wrapped around her. She looks comfy as hell. I bet her ass isn't freezing. As much as I want to be annoyed, having her next to me in bed is worth my balls shriveling up into little corn nuts. I hope she knows when we get home, all her shit is being moved to the master bedroom. Originally, I recommended she take the master and I would take the second bedroom, but she insisted she needed to be in the room directly next to Micaela. There's no way I'm going another night without Bella in bed with me.

Reaching over her, I attempt to grab a little bit of the blanket to cover my lower half at least, when she growls. *Fucking growls!* And wraps herself up tighter in the blankets. Fucking woman. I grab a hold of the edge and tug harder. The blanket comes undone and Bells rolls with it trying to steal back the sheets.

Before she can grab them, I grab her by her hips and pull her to me. Her head lands on my chest and her legs come up around mine. I pull the blanket up and over the both of us. The angle I'm laying at, I'm able to see her portrait. Her eyes are softly closed, her eyelashes thick against the tops of her cheeks. Her cute button nose, just like our daughter's, is scrunched up and the smallest smattering of freckles cover her nose. She's so fucking beautiful.

Looking at her like this, one would never know she could probably kick most grown men's asses. The thought makes me chuckle. She is so tiny, yet strong. She has such a big heart, yet is so stubborn. She knows what she wants and she goes for it. I can't wait to watch her fight in a few months. Win or lose, this fight is huge for her. She's been working her entire life to be in that octagon. I vaguely remember when she told me she was pregnant, I threw it in her face that her UFC career would be over before it even started. But I shouldn't have doubted Bella. She can and will accomplish anything she sets her mind to. My woman is the ultimate badass.

Her legs wrap harder around my thighs, and her warm cunt rubs up against my side. With my cock no longer in hiding from the cold, he stands at attention like he knows she's near. I want so badly to wake her up for some morning sex, but she looks too peaceful asleep, and she deserves to sleep in. It's not often she gets a morning without having to wake up with Micaela or to train.

Carefully, so as not to wake her up, I grab my cell phone from the nightstand and shoot off two text messages. One to Mathias to see what his plans for today are. I also want to bring Bella by the hospital to visit Logan, but after that we have roughly twenty-four hours to have a little bit of fun. The other text goes to her mom to check on Micaela.

Mathias responds immediately, suggesting we meet at Dexter's. Not exactly my first choice, but it's a huge hangout and Bella might want to meet up with some of her friends while we're there. I let him know what time we'll meet him.

Not having heard back from Liz, I text the same message again. This time she responds right away with a video. I click on it and it's a close up of Micaela rocking back and forth on her knees. She wants to crawl, but hasn't done it yet. She's smiling wide, staring at someone, and when the person goes closer and tickles her, she lets out a loud laugh as she moves her knees forward, crawling a few inches before she plops down. Holy shit! My daughter belly laughed and crawled. The laugh rings out though the room and it wakes Bella. The video ends with Nathan giving Micaela a kiss on her cheek, laughing with her.

"Marco?" Bella rubs her eyes and stretches. "Is Micaela here?" She squints, confused.

"Babe, you have to see this. Your brother made Micaela laugh—"

Bella, still half asleep, cuts me off before I can finish. "Marco, she laughs all the time."

"No, like a big laugh, and she crawled. Watch." I hit play on my phone and hold it up so she can see it. The video plays through with Micaela laughing hard again, then her little legs scurrying forward.

"Oh my God! We missed her really laugh! And she crawled!" She jumps out of bed and starts running around the room like a crazy person.

"Belles, what are you doing?"

"I'm packing. We're going home. I missed her laugh! I missed her crawl! What else am I going to miss while we're gone? Her talking? Walking?"

Even though I know she isn't serious, I know she's serious, so I hold back my laughter. "Belles, we aren't leaving." I get up and stop her from shoving everything within her reach back into our suitcases.

"Babe, stop." Caging her between my arms and the dresser, I give her a kiss. "We're staying and enjoying ourselves. You want to video chat? Fine. But then we're going to get breakfast, to visit Logan, and spend some time at the beach because I saw those sexy bikinis you packed, and then we're meeting my cousin for dinner at Dexter's."

I can feel it when Bella relaxes into my arms. "Okay, but if she does any more cute stuff, I'm getting on the next flight back home."

"Deal."

"I slept so good last night." She smiles and gives me a kiss. I almost bitch jokingly about her stealing the covers but don't.

"I did, too."

"So, I didn't steal the covers?" *Huh?*

"Umm. No. Why would you ask that?" If she says she slept with another guy I might be arrested for murdering the motherfucker she slept with.

"I knew he was lying!" Her face contorts into the cutest angry face. "Ow. Marco!"

I look down and see my fingers are digging into her sides and immediately let go. "Sorry, I need to go for a run." I start throwing on my shorts and running shoes to go run off some steam. Without saying another word, I pull open the slider door, almost taking it off the track, and slam it closed.

Without even warming up, I put my earbuds in, turn my playlist to loud, and take off for a run. The whole thing is stupid. Bella and I slept together three years ago. She's a beautiful woman. Of course she's had sex with other guys since we were together. There was a good two years before we hooked back up which landed her pregnant. I know logically I can't be mad. I spent most of my teen years as well as my twenties majoring in fighting and minoring in fucking. I couldn't even begin to count the number of women I've been with.

I'm almost twenty-seven years old. While I haven't dated anyone serious, I've been on my fair share of dates, had plenty of one-night stands. I wish I could say I fell in love with Bella as a kid and waited around for years to be with her—it would definitely make me more likeable. But the truth is, while I have always loved Bella, I never imagined actually being with her. Between our age difference and our families being close, and then add the fact that I had no intention of settling down or getting married let alone procreating, we were on two different paths and I never thought they would collide.

I knew having sex with her at the cabin was wrong, but I couldn't help myself. I was selfish. I wanted her. I had to have her. But I never deserved her. I still don't deserve her.

Bella deserves the fucking world. She should have ended up with a guy with a perfect head on his shoulders. The guy who would graduate from college and provide a stable and loving home for her. He would be sweet and tender and patient. He would come from a good upbringing and bring as much to the table as she does. I know it makes sense she's probably had sex with other guys, guys a hell of a lot worthier than me, but fuck if it doesn't kill me inside. Because her having been with other guys is because I chose to be stupid and ignore the pull between us.

I run harder and faster, my lungs struggling for air, my heart pounding to its max, as I picture everything she's not getting, and it's all because she fell in love with a fuck up. She got knocked up while I was high, was forced to put fighting on hold, had to drop out of college and move home so her family could help her. Fuck! She deserves so much more than a guy whose longest relationship was with the woman who supplied his heroin and coke to him.

I reach the bridge and feel my legs give out. I give in and collapse onto the hard sand, focusing on my breathing, trying to steady it out. Trying to catch my breath, with my knees up, my head falls as I take in huge gulps of air, trying to fill my lungs.

"Hey!" My head shoots up at the sound of Bella's voice. She's out of breath standing above me. Her hands go to her knees as she bends over panting for a minute before she sits next to me.

"What the hell was that for?" I can feel her glare on me, but I stare out at the ocean instead of looking at her.

"You do hog the blankets."

"What? You ran away because you lied about me hogging the blankets?"

"No." I snort. "I ran because I pictured you hogging the blankets with another guy."

This time it's her turn to snort. "Are you jealous?"

"Fuck yeah, I am," I say, owning that shit.

"Should I be jealous of all the women you've slept with?"

"I didn't say it was justified. I just said I was."

This earns me a laugh.

"It was Tristan."

I jerk my head to face her in shock, almost giving myself whiplash. "You and Tristan…" I can't even bring myself to finish the question.

"What? No! I mean, we slept together but only together in the same bed. We didn't have sex. You're the only person I've had sex with."

"Great."

"Now you're upset I haven't slept with anyone else?" she says, incredulously.

"Yes. No. Fuck. No, I don't want you to have sex with anyone else, but I'm already barely worthy of you. Now, add that you waited for me while I whored myself all over town. Why the fuck are you even with me?"

I scrub my hands over my face in frustration.

"Marco Michaels, what the hell are you talking about?" Bella demands.

"You. Me. The fact that I was a male-whore while you were only with me. I don't fucking deserve you. You deserve better."

"Seriously? Just because I chose not to have sex while you chose to doesn't mean shit. Are you still having sex with other women?"

I look at her like she's fucking crazy because she must be to think I would ever choose another woman over her now that I have her. "Of course not, but you belong with a guy who has shit going for him."

"You have had a damn good career as a fighter and you will be running my family's gym soon and training fighters."

"You should be with a guy who has a college degree and a good upbringing," I argue.

"So, you're saying Hayley and Caleb are trash? That's not nice." I hear the humor in her voice.

"You know what I mean."

"You need to stop, Marco. Everybody deserves to be loved. I don't care where you came from, who gave birth to you, who you slept with, or what mistakes you've made. I love you for you."

"Maybe that's because I'm all you know. You haven't experienced anyone else. You don't know if some other guy will make you happy or satisfy you."

"Did you really just go from being jealous of me possibly screwing some other guy to trying to convince me to screw some other guy?"

"Well when you put it like that, it sounds ridiculous."

"Marco, there are no guarantees in life. You could wake up tomorrow and decide I'm not the one for you. The professor in a psychology course I took said seventy percent of marriages end in divorce. I would say the odds are against most people. So what if I didn't sleep with other people, and who gives a shit that you did. And fuck anyone who chooses to judge either of us."

And this right here, ladies and gentlemen, is why I will spend the rest of my life making sure this woman knows how wanted and loved and needed she is. This is why I took her for granted. This is why she was my best friend for half my life. Because she loves unconditionally and without judgement. She is an amazing person who brings out the best in everyone around her.

"Now, you're going to have to carry my ass back because holy shit! I just about died trying to catch up to you."

"Your ass is about to be in your first UFC fight. You better be in better shape than that." I give her a wink and she glares.

"Fine, I'll race you back."

She jumps up and takes off, and of course I run after her, because let's face it, I would follow this woman anywhere, and I fully plan to for the rest of my life.

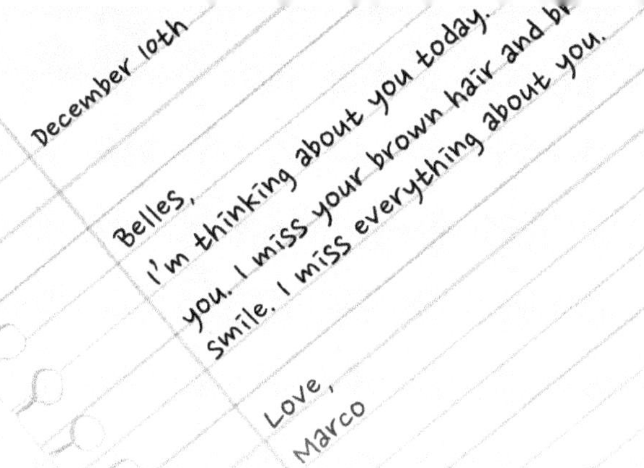

THIRTY-SIX

BELLA

AFTER MARCO BEAT ME BACK TO THE HOTEL, WE TOOK A SHOWER together where he insisted he needed to dirty me up some more before getting me clean. Once I was clean—a second time—we left for breakfast, which was more like brunch. I took him to one of my favorite diners my friends from college and I used to frequent. When I posted a picture of Marco and me on social media, Stephanie immediately recognized the place and commented that we better be getting together while I'm in San Diego. When I mentioned this to Marco, he said we should make it a group thing at Dexter's since Mathias will be there as well.

At first, I was a little reluctant about going to Dexter's. It's a popular bar and pool hall and it's the last place Marco ran into Tristan. Marco told me not to worry about stuff out of my control, so I said okay and invited Stephanie, Lauren, Kristen, and Michelle to join us. Kristen and Michelle have dates but said they would try to meet up later. Stephanie and Lauren said they will be meeting us. I'm excited for them to meet Marco.

We pull up to the hospital in our rental car and Marco turns the car off but doesn't get out. After a minute he says, "Logan was a good-looking guy."

"Okay?" I'm not sure where this is going.

"That came out wrong." I see his Adam's apple bob as he swallows thickly. "From being in a coma, Logan doesn't look the same. He's thinner, paler. His body has softened and lost his muscle."

"Marco, I don't care what Logan looks like."

"I know, but I just wanted to warn you. Every time I see him he looks worse, but I try to picture him pre-coma. You won't have a visual to pretend with."

"I know what Logan looks… looked like. He was… is a UFC fighter. I saw him fight on several occasions. I saw him fight the night—"

"Of the accident," Marco finishes. "That's right. Okay." He opens the door and gets out. When I come around the car, he grabs my hand, and his fingers weave through mine tightly. We check-in with the front desk, get our visitor passes, and head to the elevator, Marco's hand never letting go of mine.

When we get to Logan's room, Marco walks in first. The room smells of antiseptics and the only noise is the constant beeping of the monitor.

"Hey man, I have someone I want you to meet." Marco pulls two chairs over and places them next to each other, his hand still not leaving mine, and motions for me to sit in one of the chairs. He goes on to talk to Logan like he would anyone else. He tells him all about me, Micaela, the upcoming fight. Logan, of course, doesn't respond, but the way Marco talks to his best friend you wouldn't even know the guy was in a coma. I just sit and listen and continue to hold Marco's hand.

When he's done, he grabs Logan's hand with his free one and brings his head down to it like he needs to touch his friend in some way to make it feel like he's here in a bigger way than he really is.

After he's done talking to Logan, he speaks to the nurse who comes in to check on Logan. He asks how he's doing and if there has been any change in his condition. She tells him he's stable and there's hasn't been any changes. We both say goodbye and leave—my heart feeling a lot heavier than before we walked through those doors—heading back to the hotel in silence. There's so much I want to say but hold back, letting Marco work through his feelings. I can't even imagine one of my best friends being in a coma let alone knowing it will most likely end in death and just waiting for it to happen but praying it doesn't.

Once we get back, Marco's mood shifts to playful when he insists on picking out my bikini. It shouldn't surprise me when he picks the all black bikini with the cheeky bottoms. We spend the rest of the day bouncing back and forth between the pool and beach. Since I'm pumping and dumping this weekend, I enjoy being twenty-one and legally order a few fruity drinks. Marco sticks to water.

When we've had enough of the sun, we head back to our room to take a short nap before getting ready to go out for the night. Cuddling with Marco has officially become my new favorite pastime. You would think with all those muscles, he would make for a horrible pillow, but it's like my body fits perfectly against his, and when my head goes into the crook of his shoulder, I fall asleep like I've been drugged. We're going to be sharing a bed from now on, that's for sure.

After our power nap, we get ready to go, then head over to Dexter's.

Before we walk through the doors, Marco stops me, pulling me to the side. "Babe, you realize with that tight dress you're wearing, I'm going to be all over you all damn night, and there's no way in hell you will be leaving my side."

I roll my eyes. Yes, it's true. I am wearing a dress. It's one of the few I own, and even though it's tight and is a dress, because it's a comfortable cotton T-shirt material shaped like a long tight jersey, it doesn't feel like a dress. If you're looking at me from the waist up, it looks like a short sleeve olive green button-down shirt, but as you go lower the shirt continues a few inches above my knees. It's not short in length, but it has wide slits that run high up—which is why it's called a jersey dress—and reveals a hell of a lot of leg.

Because I'm not a dress and heels kind of girl, I'm wearing my favorite taupe-colored Chucks, making my outfit more casual than club.

We walk inside and Marco says Mathias is already here.

"Cuz!" A good looking Hispanic guy comes walking over to Marco and gives him a one-armed hug. While Marco is more of a bad-boy sexy with his tats, ripped jeans, and plain black T-shirt, Mathias is more pretty-boy sexy. He's wearing a mint green button-down shirt and his jeans look like he ironed them before putting them on. His hair has gel in it while Marco keeps his shaved short. But when you see them side by side you can tell they are related. They have a similar jawline and their noses are almost identical. I would bet they both look a lot like their mothers.

"Mathias, I want you to meet Bella. Bella, my cousin, Mathias." Mathias shakes my hand then pulls me into a hug.

"It's nice to meet you," he says, giving me a warm smile that reminds me so much of Marco and Chloe's. We have a seat at the large booth and order drinks. A few minutes later, Lauren and Stephanie show up to join us and I introduce them to Marco and Mathias. We're all joking and laughing and Marco and I are showing everyone at the table pictures and videos of Micaela. Before I know it, I've probably had three mojitos and announce to everyone I need to use the restroom.

"Oh! I need to go as well," Lauren says.

"Me, too," Stephanie adds.

Before I can stand, Marco pulls me in for a quick kiss making me smile. This is what I wanted for so long, to be with Marco in every way. It's finally happening, and it's amazing.

The girls and I each enter a separate stall to go pee, gossiping through the walls. "Mathias is a hottie," Lauren gushes.

"Yeah, he is," Stephanie agrees.

"I'm going to ask him for his number."

"He's moving to San Fran," I jump in.

"Hmm… well, I can enjoy him until then."

We all giggle.

When we exit the stalls, we all crowd around the sinks to wash our hands. Lauren and Stephanie reapply their lipstick while I try to tame down my hair. As we're heading out, the door swings open, causing me to stumble back. Stephanie grabs my arms to hold me in place before I hit the ground on my butt. When I see who has entered, I want to punch someone, preferably one of the two women who just entered.

"Well look who it is." Janell gives Gina a bitchy smirk.

"Pretend like I'm not here." I roll my eyes and attempt to pass by, but before I make it to the door, I notice Gina sporting a small bump. A bump that would indicate she's pregnant. She gives me a knowing smirk when she sees where my eyes landed.

"Yes, I'm pregnant, and to answer the question I know you're dying to ask. It's Tristan's." There's no way in hell Tristan would have slept with her after she threw me under the bus for keeping my baby's paternity a secret. Sure, it worked out in the end, but what she did by taking a picture of my letter was conniving and there's no way Tristan would have forgiven her. Right?

"Bullshit."

Gina shrugs. "You don't have to believe me, but you'll believe it once we're officially back together."

"Good, I don't, and there's no way Tristan would ever get back together with you. Now if you'll excuse us…"

Janell steps in front of me and my fists tighten. I'm not above knocking this bitch out.

"Someone should seriously teach you a lesson in staying away from another woman's man. First you sink your nails into Tristan, then when that doesn't work out, you go after Marco."

Gina steps up next to Janell, and I take a step back. Is she out of her mind? She's fucking pregnant for God's sake. Lauren and Stephanie take a step forward ready to have my back.

"I'm not fighting a pregnant chick, even if you deserve to have the shit knocked out of you, so back the fuck up," I say dryly.

"Oh, that's right. You're the wannabe UFC bitch. The one Marco couldn't stand to be around. He told me all about how you used to follow him around like a puppy dog like you were one of the guys. Too bad you couldn't be more of a woman, then he might actually want you." Janell cackles at her words and I mentally have to remind myself not to knock her out. I need to get the fuck out of here before I do something I'll regret. Marco's entire relationship with her was based on drugs and getting high.

"I heard he didn't even remember knocking your ass up."

"You mean while he was high on the drugs you were giving him? Drugs that ended up putting him in rehab? Are you proud of that? You were nothing more than a fix to him." I look at her with disgust because the thought of her supporting Marco's habit instead of trying to get him help makes me want to throw up all over her.

Once again, I try to leave before shit gets ugly, but Janell grabs hold of my bicep, and when I spin around to knock her hand off me, she sucker-punches me. *Wrong move, bitch.*

I've been fighting with guys twice her size for most of my life. Her punch does nothing more than shock me for a second, and then I'm on her. My body flies into hers, pushing her up against the wall as I grab hold of her chin, forcing her to face me.

"Don't ever fucking touch me again. And while you're at it, stay the fuck away from Marco."

"If he didn't want to keep in touch, why does he have me on Facebook and Snap?" So that's how she knew we'd be here.

"That was an oversight on my part."

I turn my head slightly, my fingers still gripping the bitch's chin, to see Marco and Mathias standing in the women's restroom. Marco and Mathias walk closer, Marco taking my hand off the bitch, and Mathias sandwiching himself between us.

Marco whispers into my ear, "If you fight her, which we both know isn't even a challenge, you will be suspended from the UFC. She's not worth it." I know he's right, but the shit she said stung.

He wraps his arms around my waist and gives me a small kiss on the side of my neck. Then he says to Janell, "I don't know what was said and it doesn't even fucking matter—"

Janell cuts him off. "We were good together until she got herself knocked up! You didn't want her. You wanted me."

"We were never good together," Marco booms and releases me to get closer to her, Mathias moving to the side. "We were high together. That's it. I wanted the drugs so badly, I would have probably fucked your brother instead of you if he would have required it. You were nothing more to me than my drug fix. We spent all day and night getting high. I turned into someone I didn't even know anymore. Stop saying shit you know nothing about. You are only making a fool out of yourself. Fuck, Janell!" He smacks his hand against the wall next to her causing her to flinch. "I can see it in your eyes. You're high now. Get help. Go to rehab and get fucking help. You're better than this shit."

He doesn't wait for her to respond before he turns his back on her. Gripping my hand in his, he walks us out the door. I'm not sure who's following us, my only thought on the man holding my hand like I'm his lifeline. He walks us outside and around the side of the building without saying a word until we're alone and away from all the noise.

He cages me in against the wall, his face mere inches from mine. "I'm sorry. I can't even imagine the shit she said to you."

I place my fingers up to his lips to stop him. "It doesn't matter. If you said it or didn't say it. It doesn't even matter."

"I was in a bad place." His eyes plead with me to understand. "I don't know what I said or didn't say, but…"

"Stop," I insist. "It doesn't matter," I repeat.

"It does, though, because if you leave me because of this…" What the hell is he talking about?

"You think I would leave you over some shit talking by a drugged-up bimbo? You need to have a little faith in us, Marco. A little faith in me. You said a lot of shit to me when you were high and I'm not holding it against you." I wrap my arms around his neck and pull him down to me for a kiss before I pull back a little. "I will always fight for you Marco, for us. I will never fucking tap out when it comes to us. I'm in it for the long haul. I will fight for us as long as you are here to fight alongside me."

He gives me a bright smile that could light up the dark alley. "I love you, Belles."

"I love you, too."

Marco gives me a hard kiss before we go back into the bar to join our friends again. We spend the night playing pool and darts, my friends and I having a few drinks. Everybody is acting like the shit with Gina and Janell never happened, but I can't get it off my mind. Not the part about Janell, but the part about Gina saying she's pregnant with Tristan's baby. I go against my promise to give him space and shoot him a text.

Me: I'm sorry to bother you, but there's something you should know. Gina is pregnant and saying the baby is yours.

I put my phone away and focus on the pool game I'm playing with Lauren, Marco, and Mathias. It's Marco's turn when I feel my phone buzz from inside my purse. I reach in and grab it to quickly check and see who it's from.

Tristan: You are never a bother. Yes, I know she's pregnant. Are you in Los Angeles?

Los Angeles? Why would I be there?

Me: No, San Diego at Dexter's. She's here with Janell. They came in looking for a fight. Why did you ask if I'm in Los Angeles?

Tristan: Great…I'll deal with her. Mason and I moved to Los Angeles. Gina's living here as well. I didn't realize she went down to San Diego. Thank you. Hope all is well with you.

I'm not sure what any of this means. *I'm never a bother.* Does that mean he forgives me? Wants me back in his life? I'm afraid to ask, so I don't. He knows my number and when he's ready, he will text or call me. *They've moved to Los Angeles.* Is he finishing school? Is Mason training over there? Why Los Angeles? *He'll deal with Gina.* Is he really the dad? I have so many questions, but I don't ask any of them. When he's ready he'll tell me. So, I text back a simple **Okay. I'm here if you need anything** and get back an even simpler text from him saying **Thanks.**

"Everything okay?" Marco comes up behind me, his hands gripping my waist. Every time he touches me I want to jump his bones.

"I was texting with Tristan." I place the phone on the table and reach back, my left arm hooking behind Marco's neck as I tilt my face to the side, bringing his face closer to mine for a kiss. It starts off slow but builds up quickly, Marco's tongue finding mine and his dick grinding into my back. He swings me around to face him, his lips finding mine again. We make out until Mathias yells for us to get a room.

"We already have one," he yells back. Then to me says, "Let's go use it."

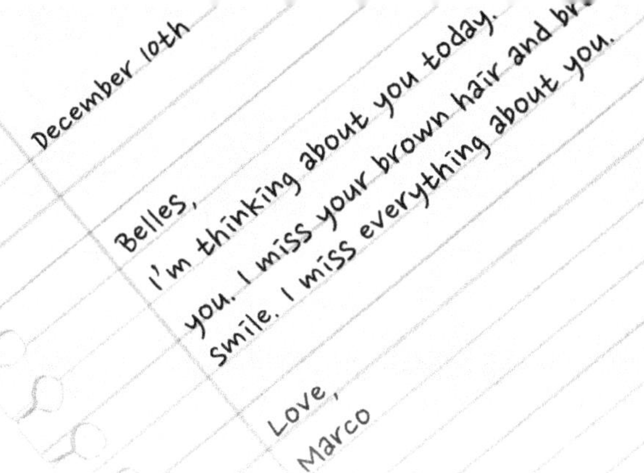

THIRTY-SEVEN

MARCO

IT'S BEEN A LITTLE OVER A MONTH SINCE WE'VE BEEN BACK from San Diego, and to say we've been busy as hell would be putting it mildly. Bella and I spend our days juggling training, spending time with our daughter who is now six months old and sitting up and crawling, finding time for us, and on top of all that, I'm learning the ropes of the gym and Bella is getting ready to go back to school next month.

I'll be glad when this fight is behind us. We had a photo shoot we had to do, and of course, they ended up taking photos of us separate and together. Daniel West knows what he's doing. People are eating this shit up about us being a couple and both fighting. With the fight being promoted like crazy, my fans have come out of the woodwork. Everyone is commenting and posting all over social media. There are the guys who are pumped for me to fight and win, and then there are the guys who make it known Bella can do better and hope I get my ass kicked. The gossip rags that are making accusations about me being hooked on drugs doesn't help.

The women are even worse. There are the women who are pro-Bella and me and post hearts and flowers, and then there's the crazies. The women who call her names and tell her to kick rocks so they can have me to themselves.

Bella's dad hired a PR specialist to handle her social media once she came to the gym pissed off and almost in tears about the mean shit some women were posting about her. He wants her to focus on the fight and ignore the rest.

Bella and I moved all her stuff into the master bedroom and we've slept together every night. But even with us living in the same house and sleeping under the same roof, I'm missing my woman like crazy, which is why I have texted Cooper and told him Bella won't be in today. He threw a fit through text messages, but when I told him I need some time with her and my daughter, he texted back that he understood and said he would see me tonight.

I hear the baby monitor light up and crackle with Micaela's coos so I jump out of bed to grab her. I change her diaper and get her dressed then bring her into our room for Bella to feed her.

"Morning." I give her a kiss before handing our daughter over to her. She stretches her arms, her tiny tank top lifting and exposing her defined torso and shimmering belly ring. Training for this fight has toned her already toned body even more, but the few stretch marks from her pregnancy are still present. Whenever I see them, it reminds me I never got to see her pregnant. I saw several pictures but I didn't get to experience it with her and it was entirely my fault.

She pulls her top up and takes Micaela from me. "What?"

"I want to have another baby."

Bella's eyes go wide and she coughs in shock. "Umm…"

"Not right now." I laugh. "I know you have school and the UFC and you want to make a career out of it, but one day, when we're in a good place to have another baby, I want to give Micaela a brother or sister. I want to go to all your appointments with you. I want us to do it right next time."

Bella gives me a small smile and nods in understanding. "Okay, one day, a *long* time from now, we'll have another baby."

While she feeds Micaela, I jump in the shower and get dressed, and then once she's done, I tell her to get ready. "I'll just shower after I get back from the gym."

"No gym today."

"What? The fight is in like a week!"

"That's very true and tomorrow you can go back to training. But today is a family day. Now go get ready."

She gives me a side-eye glance but doesn't argue.

Once we're all packed up, we head out. About twenty minutes later, we arrive at our destination. Bella grabs Micaela and I grab the diaper bag. When we walk through the front door of the place, music fills our ears. Little kid music. There's a register and café to the right, and to the left are see-through glass walls with a huge indoor playground inside.

"Wow! Marco, this is so cool!" With it being close to a hundred degrees outside, I searched for stuff to do and found this place. It's an indoor playground for toddlers and kids from ages six months to six years old. We pay the lady at the counter, sign the waiver agreeing if Micaela gets hurt we can't sue them, and put the socks on I brought for us, since I read we would need them.

When we enter the glassed-in playground, there are little kids running around everywhere. There are jungle gyms and fake tree houses.

There's a huge rectangular trampoline that's built into the ground and a big pit filled with balls. There's an area for dress up and make believe and a kitchen with tons of fake food. Along the walls is every toddler toy imaginable from puzzles and blocks, to books and light up toys.

Micaela takes it all in for a minute before she wriggles out of Bella's grasp to get down. Bella sets her on the soft foam ground and she starts to crawl away. We both stare at our little girl as she leaves us like she doesn't even know us, until she stops, sits up shakily and checks to make sure we're still here. My heart constricts at the thought of one day my daughter not turning back and looking for me or feeling like she doesn't need me.

We spend the day playing with Micaela. We jump on the trampoline while holding her, slide down the twisty slide into the ball pit, and show her every block and puzzle. We break for lunch and then go back at it again, showing her how to climb up the blow-up slide that she isn't ready for, and play in the kitchen, which her only goal is to shove every fake piece of food into her mouth to taste it. It's a great day that ends with Micaela passed out in the back seat while we go to our next destination.

"Thank you for finding that place. That was so much fun! I saw they do yearly memberships. I think we should get one."

"Sounds good, babe."

"Where are we going now?"

"Dinner."

We pull up to the Rain Forest Café and I let the hostess know we're here for the Michaels' party. When she takes us back, everybody yells out, "Happy Half-Birthday!"

Bella gasps in shock and Micaela squeals seeing all our family here.

"What the heck is this?" Bella laughs, stunned.

"It's Micaela's half birthday. When I moved in with my parents, I had never had a birthday before, so my mom made up a birthday called a half birthday."

"I remember that! Every year you would get a birthday and a half birthday."

"Yep! And I thought it would be cool to continue the tradition with our daughter, so today we're celebrating her half birthday."

"You are such a good daddy," Bella murmurs against my lips, making my cock twitch.

"Woman, you can't do that in public. I might have to resort to taking you in the bathroom."

When she doesn't argue, and her eyebrows go up silently challenging me, I laugh. My girlfriend is always horny and she knows I love it.

Challenge accepted.

♥♥♥♥♥

WE'VE HAD DINNER, SANG HAPPY HALF-BIRTHDAY TO THE birthday girl and everyone is starting to say their goodbyes. It's now or never. "Meet me by the bathroom," I whisper into Bella's ear.

I don't give her a chance to argue before I disappear down the hall to the family bathroom that's situated between the men's and women's restroom. I open the door halfway, then pull Bella inside as she walks by unsure of where to go, locking the door behind us.

She gasps when I push her up against the sink, her hands landing on the porcelain to hold her up. Her eyes lock with mine in the mirror and I don't waste any time tugging her shorts and panties down to her ankles. With my eyes never leaving hers, I push one finger into her tight cunt while my lips press up against her neck, sucking softly on the spot that gets her going every damn time.

With her hands still holding onto the sink, her eyes roll back as I kiss and suck on her skin. When I feel her getting wetter, I add another digit. Her pussy is already tight, and with her shorts wrapped around her ankles, her legs can only open so much.

"Fuck, baby. Your cunt is gripping the fuck out of my fingers." I work her pussy up, getting it wet and loose. While my fingers fuck her, my thumb massages her clit. She lets out breathy moans telling me she's close. A few seconds later, her pussy tightens as she comes all over my fingers.

Not being able to go another second without being inside of her, I unbuckle my pants and shove them, along with my briefs, down just enough to free my cock. One hand grips the curve of her hip and the other pushes her back down. Her ass pops up enough that I can slide my dick into her wet cunt from behind. And holy fuck, it's tight like this.

"Belles, there's no way I'm lasting," I warn. "You're going to have to help me out here." She knows exactly what I mean, her hand going to her pussy as she begins to massage her clit.

Grabbing hold of her hair with one hand and holding onto her hip with the other, I drive in and out of her, our eyes staying trained on each other. Her mouth is parted, and her face is flushed, and fuck if she isn't the most goddamn beautiful sight to be seen. I can feel her fingers graze my cock every so often as she rubs her clit and it only spurs me on. My thrusts get harder—more erratic—then without warning, I'm bottoming out in her, coming so hard my body shakes and my legs almost give out. She moans out my name as she comes with me, her pussy contracting around my cock, milking me until I'm bone dry.

"I think bathroom sex is my new favorite kind of sex." She gives me a wink, and I laugh which causes me to groan because my dick is still buried inside of her.

"I'd have to agree."

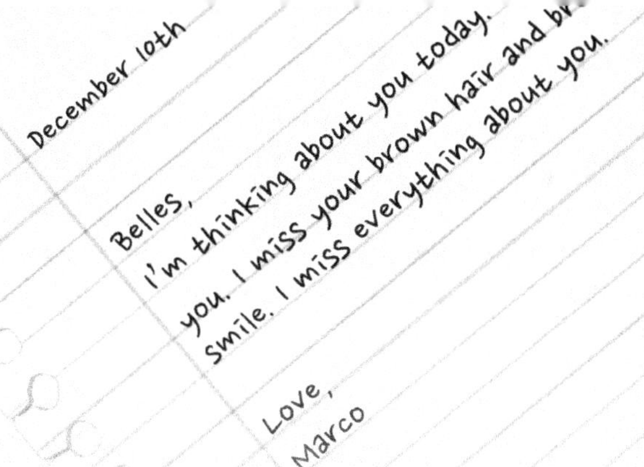

THIRTY-EIGHT

BELLA

IT'S FIGHT NIGHT, OR I GUESS DAY, SINCE IT'S ONLY SIX IN THE morning. I wake up with a mix of emotions: excited to fight, scared I'm going to lose, nervous I won't live up to being publicly known as Marco's girlfriend.

Shawna Fields and I were scheduled to fight eighteen months ago before I got pregnant. Since then she's won two fights. Her record is four-and-oh, while mine hasn't even started. I have several wins under my belt from my amateur fights, but those don't count here. I'm nervous I'll choke. I've been in a million tournaments over the years. I've been in more fights than I can count at the gym, but I feel like nothing I've experienced has prepared me for fighting at the MGM Grand. I'm excited to be given this opportunity, even knowing I'm only getting it because of Marco and the publicity our relationship is getting. Even if I lose, this is my dream. I'm determined. So damn determined. I'm going to give this fight my all. I've trained my entire life for this and I feel ready.

Feeling suddenly pumped and needing to release some of this built-up tension, I decide maybe going for a short jog might help before we head to the arena.

"Hey, Marco." I roll over and find Marco's side of the bed empty. I feel the sheets and they're cold. Grabbing my phone from my nightstand, I check for any texts or phone calls and there aren't any. Throwing the sheets off me, I go pee, then go to Micaela's room. She's still asleep. As she gets older, she sleeps in a little later—seven o'clock being her current wake up time.

I check the kitchen, guest room, laundry room, all while ignoring the pull in my gut that's screaming Déjà-fucking-vu. I open the door to the garage and my heart skips a beat or maybe two. His SUV is gone. *Gone.* I try to think about the last week. Everything has been good, better than good. There's no reason why he would leave. Maybe he's at the gym. But why didn't he text or call me? There's no way he would fucking do this to me again.

I pull up his name and hit send. The phone goes to voicemail. *No fucking way!* I call again and get the voicemail again. I shoot him a text and watch the blue turn to green. His phone is off.

I call Kaden, who has been training him. "Hey, is Marco with you?" I ask without even saying hello.

"No, we agreed to meet at the arena later. Is everything okay?"

"I don't know. He's gone. Did he maybe say something?"

Kaden stays quiet for a moment before he says, "No, he's been training hardcore."

"Okay, if you hear from him…"

"Of course."

We hang up and I call my parents next. "Have you been by the gym yet?"

"Good morning to you, Bella." My dad chuckles.

"Have you?"

"No, what's going on?" His voice turns serious.

"Can you go by there and see if Marco is there."

"Bella…"

I don't want to say the words. If I say them they'll be real and I'll be a fool because my dad warned me about this.

"Just please go check."

"Okay."

I sit on the couch and stare at the black television screen thinking about all the possibilities, but no matter which one I think of, every one of them ends with Marco being able to leave a note or send me a text. It doesn't make sense. He loves me. He said I'm his forever. He wants to make more babies with me. He wouldn't do this to me—to us.

I get on Facebook and search Marco's name. There's nothing new from him. There are tons of posts and tags but none of them from this morning indicating where he might be. I search for any accidents in the area but don't find any, so I jump in the shower since Micaela is still sleeping.

Once I'm done, I make myself a cup of coffee and by the time I've finished drinking it, Micaela is stirring in her crib ready to get up for the day. I go through my routine robotically. I change her, feed her, and get her dressed. I put her in her car seat and bring her to my parents' place. I'm pulling up at the same time my dad is. "He's not there. Now tell me what's going on." I think for a moment how to explain something I don't understand myself, when my phone rings. I look down at it and it's Marco.

"Hello."

"Fuck, Bella."

"Marco, are you okay? Where are you?" Even I can hear the panic in my voice.

"I'm at the airport. They made me turn my phone off to go through the metal detectors." *The airport.* He left me again.

"You left without telling me again." It's not a question. He did. He left without a word. Again.

"No, listen—" I hang up and shove my phone into the diaper bag not wanting to look at it. My dad starts to speak, but I put my hand up.

"I have a fight in a few hours. That is what I'm going to focus on. Unless it's fight related, I don't want to hear it. I'm going to the gym for a little bit. I'll meet you at the arena.

I give Micaela a kiss on her forehead and hand her over to my dad, along with her diaper bag.

With my earbuds in, I have Eminem's *'Till I collapse* on repeat as I beat on the bag like it's personally offended me. Low kick, high kick. Left hook, right hook. Knee strike. Repeat. I'm in the zone, refusing to think about Marco or why he left and is at the airport, or on an airplane at the moment. When a hand comes up and grabs my shoulder, I spin around in shock and almost punch the person.

It's Marco.

Maybe I should still punch him.

Fuck that. He's not worth my time.

I glare and go back to focusing on the bag. His hand grips my shoulder again, his body coming up behind me, his arms encasing me, forcing me to stop my workout. We both stand here together, in silence. My music still on full blast, the words reminding me I am fucking strong.

After a few minutes, Marco's face nuzzles into my sweaty neck. I feel him shaking. I press pause on my music and remove my earbuds but don't say a word.

"Logan died."

Fuck! I knew something must have happened and I was right, but it doesn't change the fact he left.

"He had a heart attack and they couldn't revive him." I hear the tears in his words. "I grabbed my cell phone and left, got to the airport, purchased a ticket, and went through security."

Tears sting my eyes, but I stay quiet. His arms are wrapped around me, and even though the gym is filled with other fighters, it feels like it's only the two of us here right now.

"I went through the metal detectors, which is why my phone was off, but the moment I sat down to wait for my flight to be called, I thought about you. I realized I'm not in this alone anymore. I've spent so many years running. Running from home. From you. From love. From my parents. From the reality of Logan's condition. From my injuries.

"Fuck, Bella. I started to freak out when I realized what I did and I came right back. I swear I did. My phone had no service, and as soon as I got to my car and had service, I called you. I'm so sorry, baby." He didn't leave. I know he almost did, but he didn't leave. He thought about me and came back.

"Please tell me you'll forgive me."

"You came back." The tears fall in relief. To some people, him leaving would be enough to be mad, but to me, him coming back is what I'm going to focus on. His best friend died and in the midst of freaking out, he remembered me and came home. Marco isn't perfect, and expecting him to be is ridiculous.

"I did. I need you so much, Belles." I feel Marco's tears running down my neck as he cries, so I turn around to look at him. His cheeks have tear stains and his eyes are bloodshot. I put my arms around his neck and hug him tight.

"You have me, Marco." His body visibly relaxes at my words. "But you can't keep fighting me, fighting us."

Marco grabs my chin with his thumb and forefinger. "It's why I'm here right now. I promise you, baby, this is me tapping out. I'm done fighting. You have me, all of me."

"Don't let Antoine hear that. He might think you've gone soft."

Marco smiles cockily. "The only person I'll ever be submitting to will be you." His lips crash against mine, his kiss sending shivers down my spine. It ends too quickly, with both of us panting.

"What time does your flight leave for San Diego?"

Marco looks at me confused. "Not for another two hours, but I'm not going."

"Yes, you are. We are."

He envelops me into a tight hug before he pulls back and says, "Baby, I appreciate that so fucking much, but we're going to the MGM Grand for our fights. Once we're both done kicking some ass, we'll book a flight together."

"Are you sure?"

"Fuck yeah, I'm sure. And when I win this fight tonight, I'm dedicating it to Logan."

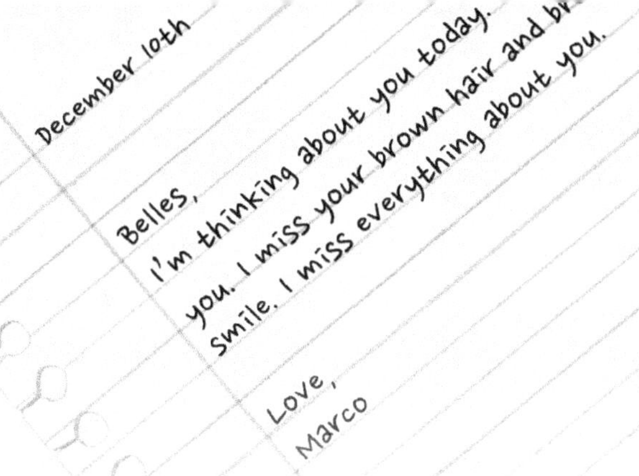

THIRTY-NINE

MARCO

IT'S ROUND THREE—THE FINAL ROUND—WITH ONLY TWO minutes left. Bella has held her own like the damn good fighter she is. Shawna, who has four fights and wins under her belt, has gotten her on the ground several times, but Bella has managed to get out every time. Bella and Shawna are currently going toe-to-toe. Bella's throwing punches, and Shawna is trying to get her onto the ground. If something doesn't happen in the next minute and a half, the decision will go to the judges, and while Bella has fought hard, Shawna will win with the points.

The women circle each other, throwing punches that aren't connecting. Then out of nowhere, Bella comes in for a kick to the back of Shawna's thigh. She connects, but Shawna is quicker and kicks back, only she misses, leaving room for Bella to take a shot. Bella's fist connects with Shawna's face, and Shawna flies backward landing on her back. *Holy shit!*

Bella follows through, and with one more punch to Shawna's face, Bella knocks her the fuck out, the referee grabbing Bella to pull her off and declaring her the winner by knockout. The crowd goes crazy and her dad and I are both running up to her.

I grab her gently by her neck and bring her in for a kiss, ignoring the chants and screams around us. I can taste the blood from her cut lip as I pick her up into my arms, her legs wrapping around my waist, and kiss my woman with everything I have. Too soon, I'm forced to put her down to let my mom clean her up. The commentator asks her a few questions and then we head out of the octagon and back to the locker room so I can warm up for my fight. Since mine is the main card event, I have nine more fights until my own, which can be hours from now.

When my mom insists that she check out Bella completely, they leave to the showers. It's just Cooper and me in the locker room since Kaden is filling out paper work and Liz is at home with Micaela and the other kids.

"I'm ready," I blurt out like an idiot.

"I would hope so. If not, it's too late." Shit, it would help if I explained myself better.

"No, I didn't mean about the fight. I meant I'm ready to ask your permission to marry Bella." Cooper stares at me showing no emotion. "I know it's only been six months since we've been together, but I love her."

"You left her today," he argues.

"I didn't leave. I was in shock that Logan died and I did leave the house, but I came right back. We both know I'm not perfect. I'm pretty fucked up. It's been fifteen years since my mom killed herself, and since then I've lived a life most kids dream of. But for some reason, I just never stopped running. It's how I ended up at your gym when I was eleven years old. I was running from my home, from my life."

"And are you done running?"

"Bella is my safe place. I hate that it took me so long to come to terms with that. But she's it for me."

Cooper looks me dead in the eyes. "I've cared about you like my own son since I met you and I'll give you my permission to marry my daughter, but Marco, if you ever hurt her like you did when you ran, I'll hunt you down myself and kill you." Then he smiles and adds, "Welcome to the family, son."

December 10th

Belles,

I'm thinking about you today. I miss your brown hair and your smile. I miss everything about you.

Love,
Marco

FORTY

BELLA

SHORTLY AFTER I'M CLEANED UP AND CHECKED OUT thoroughly by Hayley, my dad and I make our way to the seats Caleb has reserved for us. Hayley is the medic for Marco's fight so she stays back, and Kaden, since he's Marco's trainer, stays back as well. We watch each fight, cheering for the guys we know and want to win, until the main fight of the night comes on. The music goes silent as the ring announcer announces up next is the main fight.

When Marco's name is called, the crowd goes nuts. He walks out with his mini entourage, but my eyes are only on him. He looks sexy as hell and he's all mine. Once he gets to the ring, Antoine is announced and the crowd cheers *almost* as loud.

The two men are given the rules by the referee and the fight begins. Both guys are throwing punches and kicks, getting hits in. It seems like an even match up. Neither giving in or making any huge moves. Round one ends, and the guys are broken apart and cleaned up.

Round two begins and they both come at each other swinging. They're getting more hits in. Marco's left hook connects with Antoine's face. Antoine's kick connects with Marco's leg causing Marco to almost stumble back. The atmosphere suddenly changes. They both start giving it all they got. Marco's punches get stronger, he connects harder. Antoine's knee connects with Marco's ribs. Marco jumps back, then comes at Antoine with sheer determination and force. He attacks his body over and over again, pinning him up against the cage. Antoine has nowhere to go. He's blocking but isn't fighting back. The horn blows. Round two ends.

Round three begins and Marco doesn't hold back. He charges at Antoine: punching, kicking, kneeing. Antoine swings but misses.

You can tell he's winded. Marco gets Antoine against the fence again, and with an upper cut has Antoine close to giving up. Marco follows through with blow after blow until Antoine goes still and the referee has to pull Marco off him announcing him the winner.

"Ladies and Gentlemen, with a TKO in the third round, the winner and still reigning champ is Marco 'The Maniac' Michaels." The commentator raises Marco's hand as Daniel West comes out with the belt to put it back on Marco for the second time. I'm jumping up and down, screaming. He did it, again! And this time, I'm here to witness it firsthand.

Marco takes the mic from Daniel West. "Thank you," he says, and everyone screams. He waits for the crowd to calm down before he continues. "I would like dedicate this win to Logan. Some of you might know him. He was my best friend, a damn good fighter, and he passed away this morning. So, Logan, this one is for you." He looks toward the ceiling, trying to collect himself.

"I would like to thank my girlfriend, Bella, for standing by my side these last several months. Baby, we have been through so damn much. I love you." At this, there are several *awws* mixed with plenty of *boos* coming from the audience. I shake my head and laugh.

"I have an announcement to make. I'm officially retiring from the UFC. I have made the decision to focus on my family. Thank you to everyone who has supported my career, Kaden, Cooper, and my dad who taught me everything I know, and my mom, who always made sure I was cared for after each fight. To my fans, you guys fucking rock! Thank you!"

Marco hands the mic back to Daniel West, shakes his hand, and then is led back to the locker room to get cleaned up for the post-fight press conferences. A couple hours later and we're heading out of the arena. Marco is quiet and I'm sure it has a lot do with that fact that a year and a half ago, when he won his title fight and became a champion, tragedy followed. Holding Marco's hand, we make our way out of the arena and to the hotel part of the MGM Grand.

He walks up to the front desk. "I need to check in. Last name is Michaels."

"We're staying here?"

He glances my way and nods, then takes the keys from the woman and signs the necessary paperwork.

"Can you please have our luggage brought up?"

"Yes, sir. I'll have valet go out to get it."

I wasn't even aware we had luggage. "Does my mom know we're staying the night? She has Micaela."

"Yeah, she knows. We're going to meet them for breakfast in the morning. It's already after midnight. We wouldn't want to wake her to bring her home anyway."

Marco presses the button for the elevator and once we are inside, inserts a card and hits the button for the penthouse. We take it straight up to the top and get off.

Once he unlocks the door, we don't even make it all the way into the room before he stops short causing me to bump into him from behind. He turns around and says, "I thought about all the places I could take you tonight, but every place meant getting into a car. I know it sounds ridiculous but…"

"No, it doesn't sound ridiculous."

"I booked this room the day I knew we would be fighting, once I made the decision to fight. My first thought was history repeating itself. If something happened to you…"

"Marco, let's sit down. It's been a long ass day. My body is sore as hell."

Taking Marco's hand in mine, I steer us to the couch so we can sit. "I think my body is in shock."

Marco chuckles. "Wait until tomorrow. You won't want to get out of bed."

"It was worth it. I want to fight again." I grin wide and then groan in pain. My busted lip doesn't appreciate me smiling.

"You will fight again. You did great, Belles. I'm proud of you." Pride bursts inside me. Marco is one of the best fighters I know, and while this might only be my first fight, him complimenting me feels good.

"And you won the belt again. I know you mentioned retiring, but I just thought it was because you were scared. I thought once you got in the octagon and fought, you might change your mind."

Marco takes my hands in his, bringing them up to his lips to kiss each of my battered knuckles. "I'm done fighting, Belles. If you would have asked me two years ago, I would have told you I would fight until they scraped my old ass off the mat, but things have changed. Your dad is giving me an opportunity I can't pass up. To run the gym and train others is exactly what I want."

"Are you okay with me fighting?" I don't know what I'll even say if he says no. Fighting is my dream and I've only just begun.

"You don't need my permission to fight. Whatever you do in life, my job is to support you, but I don't want to support you as your boyfriend. I want to support you as your husband. I want to run the gym with you, raise our daughter with you, grow old with you."

Marco pulls a small blue box from his pocket and opens it up. Then he gets down on one knee in front of me. "Baby, I told you this morning, the only person I would submit to is you, and this is me, down on one knee, tapping out and asking you, will you marry me?"

Tears fill my lids, quickly spilling over. My hand goes to my mouth in excitement. I nod yes until I can make the words come out. "Yes. Yes, I will marry you."

Marco takes my left hand and guides the ring up my finger then raises it to give it a kiss. He gets back onto his feet, lifts me into his arms, and takes me to bed, where he very carefully and gently makes love to me for the remainder of the night.

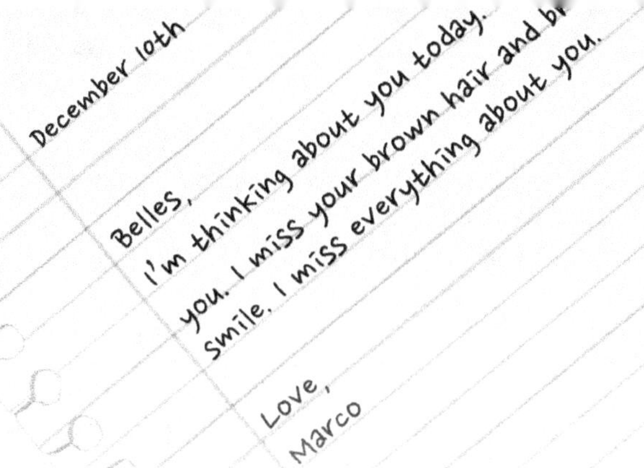

EPILOGUE

MARCO
ROUGHLY FIVE YEARS LATER

I WAKE UP AND PEEK OPEN MY ONE EYE TO CHECK THE TIME. SIX in the morning. That means I have about an hour until Micaela wakes up, maybe a little less because we're in a hotel and she's excited to celebrate her cousin's birthday. Technically, they aren't really cousins but try to tell them that and they might knock your ass out.

Bella is lying on her back sprawled out across the bed, her hair everywhere, legs spread open, leaving me barely any room, and of course, she has all the blankets. *Fucking blanket hogger.*

I scoot down the bed, and once I get to the bottom, pull the sheets off the bed and lay myself between my wife's legs, staring up at the perfect view of her bare cunt. I love it when she falls asleep without panties on.

Starting at her ankle, I trail kisses up her calf, moving up her leg, and ending at the apex of her thighs. She visibly shivers, and when I look up, I see her blinking at me, barely awake. Spreading her pussy lips, I dive right in, my tongue swiping at her clit—not wasting any time, because let's face it, when you're a parent time is limited. I push two fingers in, and Bella's hips buck in pleasure as she releases a soft moan.

"Shh… you have to be quiet. Our daughter is still asleep." She moans out her acknowledgement and then I go back to eating her pussy like it's my breakfast until she comes all over my tongue and fingers.

"Get up here and fuck me," she whines.

At six months pregnant, my wife is even hornier than usual. Without needing to be told twice, I situate myself at her entrance and guide myself into her. With her legs hooked around my arms, I'm in the perfect position to fuck her slow and deep. I feel her orgasm building again, and when she screams in ecstasy, I drive in harder, my orgasm following right behind her.

"Let's shower before Micaela wakes up." I lean down and give her cute as hell pregnant belly a kiss.

"And you know she will be up soon," Bella adds knowingly. "She's been counting down the days until our trip to Los Angeles to celebrate Lexi's birthday. Speaking of which, I should call Tristan and see if he needs any help setting up for the party.

BELLA

MARCO, MICAELA, AND I WALK INTO THE BOWLING ALLEY WHERE we spot Tristan, Mason, and Lexi, along with Tristan's family and a bunch of their friends. Micaela goes running straight for Lexi, who runs toward Micaela meeting her halfway. The two girls hug like they haven't seen each other in years, when the truth is they video chat several times a week.

"Happy Birthday, Lexi!" Micaela hands her the wrapped gift with the big number five on the front.

"Thank you, Micaela! My daddy said you can spend the night tonight after the party! And my grandma is going to watch us!"

I give Tristan a pointed look, but he just shrugs and smirks. Every time we come out to visit him and Lexi, he always insists on taking us out to show us more of Los Angeles. I think he believes if he makes us fall in love with the city, we'll make the move here. We've all begged him to move back home over the last several years, since Lexi was born, but he says he loves where he lives. He loves rooming with Mason, and he loves owning his own gym.

Tristan walks over and gives me a hug. "Thanks for flying out."

"You know we wouldn't miss her birthday. We've been to every single one." Tristan hooks his arm around my neck as we join everyone. "Would be nice if you moved back to Vegas. Then we wouldn't have to fly or drive five hours to get to you." I elbow him playfully and he doubles over pretending I hurt him.

"I have to second that," Ashley says.

"We're not moving to Vegas," Mason says. "The only hot available women in Vegas are prostitutes."

He earns a slap to his gut courtesy of Tristan's sister, Emma. "Don't be a douche."

Mason chuckles. "I said available. You're unavailable until you're thirty. Don't make me and Tristan come to Vegas to whoop some guy's ass."

"You're not going to Vegas to beat up any guys so give it a rest."

"Hell yes, we will. It would be a lot easier if you would just make the move to L.A. like Morgan did. You can go to college here and room with her."

"Can you stop trying to convince my only child who is still living near me to move?" Kaden growls. "If she moves, we're going to have no choice but to move here. Ashley is already bringing it up more and more."

Ignoring their continuing banter back and forth, Tristan quietly asks, "So, is it a boy or a girl?"

"You have to wait to find out like everybody else." I laugh. Marco and I couldn't agree on whether to find out the sex of the baby. I wanted to know, but he wanted to be surprised. So, we compromised and I found out but agreed not to tell anyone else. The nursery door stays closed so Marco won't find out. Micaela knows the sex but hasn't let it slip yet. It's only been a few weeks, though.

"Give me back my wife and stop trying to find out the sex. There's only a few surprises in life and this is one of them."

"Are you hoping for a boy this time?" Tristan asks.

Marco pulls me out of Tristan's arms, plops himself onto a chair, and pulls me onto his lap. He tilts my head back and gives me a hard, wet kiss on my lips. "It doesn't matter what the sex is because we'll be having at least three or four more." He waggles his eyebrows at me and I roll my eyes because he's lost his mind.

"I'm just kidding. All that matters, is that the baby is healthy... and comes out wanting to fight. Because lord knows, that pretty pink princess over there has no desire to fight." We all laugh. Marco might be joking about the baby coming out wanting to fight, but he is dead serious about the pretty pink princess part.

As soon as Micaela was old enough to pick out anything for herself, it had to be pink. Pink dolls, pink babies, pink clothes, pink shoes, pink leotards. Yep, that's right, our daughter, who is being raised in a family of fighters, does gymnastics and dance, and you better believe Marco is right there at every recital cheering her on like she's going for a UFC championship, and we wouldn't have it any other way.

MARCO'S LETTERS TO BELLA

October 18th

Dear Bella,

Shit, that sounds so formal, like you haven't been my best friend since I was twelve years old. I'm sitting here in rehab and there's so much I need to say to you. So, I decided to write you. First of all, I know you're pregnant with my kid. I shouldn't have told you to have an abortion when you came to see me that day, but maybe it's for the best I did because it forced you to walk away from me. I spent years saying I would never end up like my mom, yet I ended up just like her. High on coke and heroin. Only, I know our stories won't be the same, because you would never let me destroy our child the way my mom did. I know that's why you decided to name Tristan as her dad, to protect her, and I need you to know I don't fault you for that. You're doing something my mom never knew how to do. You're putting your baby first.

When I get out of here, I'll sign whatever papers you need me to sign. I'll sign over my rights. I don't deserve you or that baby. If you would have listened to me, she would've been aborted. I'm glad you didn't listen to me.

Marco

♥♥♥♥♥

October 19th

Dear Bella,

Today has been rough. It's been 11 days since I've had a single drug and while my 10 days of detox ended yesterday and the drugs are technically out of my system, it feels like I'm drugged out. My body is craving the drugs. Do me a favor, please? Never tell your baby about me. Pretend like I don't exist. Don't tell him, he comes from druggie bloodlines. Keep him the fuck away from all temptation. I'm not saying he will go that way and I'm not using the excuse of my genetics as to why I turned to drugs. But just to be on the safe side, make sure he never goes near them. Don't let him ever be a fuck up like me.

Marco

♥♥♥♥♥

October 20th

Dear Bella,

I hope your pregnancy is going good. I noticed in my previous letters I referred to the baby as a "he". Now that I'm thinking about it, I don't want to know the sex. I think it will hurt too much to know. It must be how a woman feels when giving her baby up for adoption. The less she knows, the less it will hurt. Even though nothing will stop the pain.

Marco

♥♥♥♥♥

October 21st

Dear Bella,

I want drugs. My back hurts and my head hurts and everything just fucking hurts. I want the fuck out of here. I came here to get better when I found out you were carrying my baby, but what for? It's not like I'm ever going to see him. Maybe I did it so I can say my blood running through his veins isn't tainted, but I was wrong. It is. It's tainted. Just make sure whatever you do, you keep him away from me.

Marco

♥♥♥♥♥

October 22nd

Dear Bella,

I got into a fight with the doctor today. I considered leaving. They can't keep me here. But something in me is keeping me from leaving. Maybe it was the look of disappointment in your face when you saw me taking a bump of heroin. Or the sadness in your eyes when I told you to have an abortion, but it's those looks that are keeping me here.

Marco

♥♥♥♥♥

October 23rd

Dear Bella,

I miss you. That's all.

Marco

♥♥♥♥♥

October 24th

Dear Bella,

I met with my counselor today. Her name is Ingrid and she's like a therapist. She asked me about my life, but I left you out. I told her about my mom, my life growing up, Caleb and Hayley, Chloe and Mackenzie. I even told her about fighting. But I didn't mention you. Maybe I'm just not ready to share you with her… or maybe it's time I let you go.

Marco

♥♥♥♥♥

October 25th

Dear Bella,

I met a man name David today in group therapy. He confessed to hitting his wife while high and it made me think of how I treated you the last time I saw you. The fear in your eyes when I yelled at you and told you you were dead to me. I'm glad Tristan was there. I'm glad he's there for you. Watching David talk about how he treated his wife before she filed for divorce, I'm glad you walked away. Fuck! That's a lot of "glads".

Marco

♥♥♥♥♥

October 26th

Dear Bella,

I miss you. So damn much.

Marco

♥♥♥♥♥

October 27th

Dear Bella,

Today sucked. I met with the doctor and we discussed treatment for my back. I told him I'm done fighting so it doesn't matter but he insisted. I guess I'm going to see a chiropractor since drugs are not an option. It made me think about you fighting... or not. Don't give up fighting, Bella. Once you have the baby, go back to it. Me, getting a championship and you not getting one isn't right. You deserve it more than me. But when you win, don't celebrate. Go home and be with your family. Celebrating cost me my best friend... hell, in a way it cost me a few. Logan, you, Tristan. Okay, this is getting depressing now.

Marco

❤❤❤❤❤

October 28ᵗʰ

Dear Bella,

I take back what I said yesterday. Celebrate! You aren't tainted like I am. When you win that championship, celebrate the fuck out of that win. You deserve to celebrate all of your hard work.

Marco

❤❤❤❤❤

October 29ᵗʰ

Dear Bella,

I can't stop thinking about you winning and celebrating and me not being there. I know it's for the best, but fuck, I miss you. Damn, I sound like a baby right now. You haven't even fought or won...

Marco

❤❤❤❤❤

October 30ᵗʰ

Dear Bella,

I met a woman in group therapy today who is pregnant. She came in so she can get better for her baby. She cried and said she's scared her baby will be affected by the drugs she already did. I wonder if my mom would've gone to rehab, if she would still be alive. Thank you for taking care of the baby. Thank you for not putting him in harm's way.

Marco

October 31st

Dear Bella,

Happy Halloween! My mom called me today (My first call I accepted since being in here). Mackenzie and Chloe wanted to say hi and tell me about their Halloween party they're having. When the hell did my sisters grow up? Chloe is a witch and Mackenzie is a bottle of ketchup. It reminded me of the year you wanted to fit in and decided to be a cheerleader for Halloween. Your mom must have yelled at you a hundred times to close your legs because you kept forgetting you had a skirt on. And of course, the costume was bright pink and white. By the end of the night, you were going through your gym bag and putting on your workout outfit and saying you were a fighter. Good times.

Marco

November 1st

Dear Bella,

I met with Ingrid again today. We were supposed to meet yesterday but she was off to take her son trick-or-treating. She showed me a picture of him. He was Buzz Lightyear from Toy Story. It made me think about what our your child will be for Halloween. Make sure you take lots of pictures. I don't have any pictures from my childhood. What am I saying? Of course, you will. With you and Tristan as his parents, the kid will never lack for anything.

Marco

November 2nd

Dear Bella,

I hope wherever you are and whatever you are doing, you

are happy.
    Marco

♥♥♥♥♥

November 3rd
Dear Bella,
    Today was rough and it had me thinking about you a lot. Group therapy sucked. I didn't feel like talking, but I did anyway because I'm lonely. I know I did this to myself, but it's still hard. I'll never take my family and friends for granted again.
    Marco

♥♥♥♥♥

November 4th
Dear Bella,
I miss you. Always.
Marco

♥♥♥♥♥

November 5th
Deal Bella,
    I'm pretty sure I miss you more today than I did yesterday and I have a feeling I will miss you even more tomorrow.
    Marco

♥♥♥♥♥

November 6th
Dear Bella,
    I was right. I'm missing you more today. I think I'm going to

tell Ingrid about you tomorrow at my appointment.

Marco

♥♥♥♥♥

November 7th

Dear Bella,

I didn't tell Ingrid about you. I wanted to, but then I would have had to tell her everything. The good. The bad. The fucking ugly. But if I don't tell her, I can just pretend it was all good. Only, it doesn't really work that way. Because even if the words aren't spoken, I still know them to be true. I fucked us up. The bad and the ugly overpowered the good.

Marco

♥♥♥♥♥

November 8th

Dear Bella,

I called the hospital today to check on Logan and he's still in the same condition he's been in. I hate that. I hate that he's in a coma. I wish it were me in the coma. I would trade places with him in a heartbeat. I swear I would. If he wasn't in a coma he wouldn't be fucking up like I am. He deserves to be healthy. I deserve to be in the coma.

Marco

♥♥♥♥♥

November 9th

Dear Bella,

It's been 33 days since I've been in here. I'm 33 days drug free. I guess that's a huge accomplishment. But it doesn't feel like it. It feels like I fucked up and I'm only thirty-three days drug free. I have a long way to go.

Marco

♥♥♥♥♥

November 10th

Dear Bella,

I spoke to my parents and they said they are coming to visit. They didn't bring you up and I didn't want to ask. I often think about what will happen when I get out of here. How will we deal with family functions? I don't want you to feel uncomfortable. Maybe I'll leave. Move across the country and start over. You deserve to be free of me.

Marco

♥♥♥♥♥

November 11th

Dear Bella,

My heart hurts when I think about never seeing you again. But I know it's all my fault. I did this to myself. I hope one day you can forgive me.

Marco

♥♥♥♥♥

November 12th

Dear Bella,

I was thinking a lot about you today. I'm eating the food here and while it isn't too bad, it isn't really good either. It made me think about the time you made us dinner. You must have been what? 14, I think. And I had told you I never had snow crabs before. You couldn't believe it, so you made your mom go to the store and pick us up snow crabs, baked potatoes, and clam chowder. She helped you cook it all. It was the first time someone did something for me just because. Hayley and Caleb have always done for me and I'm not devaluing that, but they also took on being my parents. You are the first person who did it, just because. That was probably my favorite meal and not just because it tasted good but because it came from you.

    Marco

♥♥♥♥♥

November 13th

Dear Bella,

    I hate Tristan. Okay, maybe I don't, but I really, really want to. My dad called to confirm their trip today and he mentioned Tristan taking responsibility for his baby. I wanted to yell and scream and say it's not his. It's my baby! But then I thought about what he's doing, what he's giving up. Does he know I'm the dad? I think back to the day I came into your apartment pissed and high. He didn't look like he knew. Everyone seems to think you guys are together. I hope you're not.

    Marco

♥♥♥♥♥

November 14th

Dear Bella,

    I'm sorry for yesterday. Fuck! This is what my life has come to. Apologizing in letters, for a letter I wrote and didn't send. I know I have no right to be mad at Tristan, but I hate the thought of you two together. Fuck, there I go again. Never mind, I'm sticking to my original letter. I hope you aren't together.

    Marco

PS. I didn't tell Ingrid about you.

November 15ᵗʰ

Dear Bella,

I miss you so damn much. Today I played cards with this guy who is back in rehab for the third time. I don't think I could handle coming back here again. All I want is to be out of here. I fucked up so damn bad.

Marco

November 16ᵗʰ

Dear Bella,

How are you doing? If my calculations are correct, you are roughly 6 1/2 months pregnant. I wonder if you know the sex of the baby. If she's a girl, I hope she looks just like you. Your wavy brown hair and button nose. I hope she has your soft brown eyes. I hope she has nothing of me. She should be all you. Your warm and selfless heart. I took your heart for granted, Belles. I'm sorry. I hope she has your strength. You are one of the strongest people I know. I just really hope she's all you.

Marco

November 17ᵗʰ

Dear Bella,

Today I woke up and ate breakfast and thought about your obsession with eating apples for breakfast. I wondered if you still love apples or if you have moved on to another food. I read a romance novel from the bookshelf because I couldn't find anything else to read. Is this the crap you woman all read? Because I have to tell you, those sex scenes... well Belles, they aren't exactly realistic. I think you should put down the romance novels and switch to mystery. But that's just my opinion. After reading the book, I had dinner and now I'm writing you. I wonder what you're doing right now. who you're with. If you're happy. I hope you're happy, Belles.

Marco

November 18th

Dear Bella,

My dad called today and while we were talking he let it slip you are having a little girl. I guess I better stop referring to her as a he. Damn, a little mini-you. I hope she has your brown eyes and soft brown hair. I hope she has your sass and attitude and determination. I hope she's all you and none of me. I can picture her now, running around your dad's gym and thinking she's one of the guys.

Marco

November 19th

Dear Bella,

I hate this place! I hate being here. I hate talking to the counselors and sitting in these groups. I want to get out of here. Fuck! I just hate this.

Marco

November 20ᵗʰ

Dear Bella,

In case you didn't notice from the letter yesterday, it was a bad day. I'm going to tell Ingrid about you tomorrow. I need someone to talk to and I can't put my parents in that situation. It's not fair to them.

Marco

♥♥♥♥♥

November 21ˢᵗ

Bella,

So, I did it. I told Ingrid everything. I told her about our first kiss at Red Rock. I told her how I moved to get away from you. I told her about our second kiss at Brandon's party. The night I made love to you in Colorado. I told her about our friendship and how I pushed you away. I told her I'm the baby's father, and I told her all the horrible shit I said to you. She said I need to think about where I want to go from here. Can I live with this secret? I need to think on it.

Marco

♥♥♥♥♥

November 22ⁿᵈ

Bella,

My parents, Chloe, and Mackenzie are here for Thanksgiving. Those of us allowed to have visitors, attend a dinner with our family or whoever shows up. I hate that my family has to be here, at a fucking rehab facility for Thanksgiving because of me. It makes me see how bad I fucked up and how my actions affect others. I asked how you were doing and my mom gave me a side-eye. I think she has her suspicions. I didn't confirm or deny. I need to think about this.

Marco

November 23rd

Bella,

I hope you are having a good Thanksgiving. I imagine you with our family and friends. Our moms cooking a feast and our dads watching sports, trying to steal bites of food. I wish I were there... I hate that I'm not there because I know how much it hurts my mom when I miss holidays like today. Hopefully next year will be different.

Marco

November 24th

Bella,

I had a dream about you last night. You were lying in bed and holding our daughter. You were smiling and as I watched as an outsider, I saw Tristan walk into the room and lie next you and our little girl. Maybe it's a sign I need to let you be happy.

Marco

November 25th

Bella,

I meet with Ingrid in 2 days and while I have thought about us, I haven't thought about it the way she wants me to. So, I'm going to make a pro/con list to decide if I should tell the truth about being the dad.

Be back tomorrow.

Marco

♥♥♥♥♥

November 26ᵗʰ

Bella,

The pro/con list isn't going as planned. I feel like I need several lists.

Would I make a good dad?

Would Tristan make a better dad?

Should I make it known I'm the dad?

Should I insist we raise the baby together?

Should we be together?

Then I feel like I'm making a lot of decisions that are out of my control. Decisions we should be making together. But that leads back to the questions above. It's like a never-ending cycle of questions.

Marco

♥♥♥♥♥

November 27ᵗʰ

Bella,

I thought about calling you today. I picked up the phone and went to dial your number and then realized I don't know it by heart. It's probably for the best. What would I say? "Hey Bella. I know I'm the dad. Oh and btw I'm in rehab. Sorry about telling you, that you're dead to me. Can I be the dad?"

Okay, now I need to think about that last part.

Marco

♥♥♥♥♥

November 28th

Bella,

So, I met with Ingrid and told her about my questions. She gave me a list of questions to consider. The first thing I need to think about is if I want to be this baby's father. And it kind of made me feel like a piece-of-shit. I knocked you up and while you are dealing with it, I'm getting to decide if I want to be this kid's father. Meanwhile, Tristan stepped up and took responsibility. I shouldn't have a choice. You and I created this baby. She is my responsibility. So, I've decided I am going to take responsibility once I get out of here.

Marco

♥♥♥♥♥

November 29th

Bella,

Next question: Once I make it known I am the biological father, the next question is, do I want to be the dad. I've been thinking about this question. At first, I thought I shouldn't have a choice, but the truth is, I do have a choice. People give their children up for adoption all the time. I used to wish my mom would have given Chloe and me up for adoption. I hate that she had to overdose before we were adopted. My answer to this question is that I want to be her dad. I know I fucked up, but I'm clean and I want to be in her life.

Marco

♥♥♥♥♥

November 30th

Bella,

Next question: What do I want from you? This is one of those questions I feel like needs to be your decision as well, but when I went by Ingrid's office to talk to her quickly about it, she said it's important I make my decision based on how I feel and what I want. You might disagree and there's a good chance I won't get the outcome I want, but it's important that I know what I want and feel and it isn't based off what you want or feel. I need to think about this.

Marco

December 1st

Bella,

What I want. I want to be our daughter's father. No matter what happens between you and me, I want to be a part of her life. If you want Tristan to be her dad, it will be hard, but I won't argue. But I would like to be her dad as well. I can't take back what I did or said, but once I get out of here, I am going to claim my daughter. I still kinda feel like my blood is tainted, but I'm working on that. Ingrid is working on it with me. What she's helped me realize is, we are given choices and I made mine and they led to shitty consequences. Even if I believe addiction is in my genes, I made the choice to turn to them. Now I have the choice to make it right and I am going to.

Marco

December 2nd

Bella,

Next question: You and me. I need to think about this.

Marco

December 3rd

Bella,

I'm still thinking. Please know it's not about figuring out whether I love you or want you. It's me figuring out whether I deserve you and should pursue you.

Marco

♥♥♥♥♥

December 4th

Bella,

I met with Ingrid today and we discussed you some more. She asked me to talk about why I left... all 3 times. Fuck, Belles. Talking about it with her, I just want to say I'm sorry. I was such a fucking coward. I should have manned up. I should have talked to you. So, I guess now I will explain myself the best I can.

First kiss, you scared the shit out of me. You were only 15 and I know age shouldn't matter but it does. In today's society, it does matter. Before we kissed, I knew I had feelings for you and the kiss sealed my fate. I knew I was in love with you but I also knew I was older than you and didn't want to mess up things with our families.

Second kiss, it wasn't planned, but I'm not going to lie. I went there hoping to see you. Then when that girl was flirting with me, I knew it was hurting you. I did it to hurt you. I wanted to push you away. I know that sounds fucked up but it's the truth. Only instead I fucked with you by kissing you and almost taking you against the wall of the house.

Sex in the cabin. Fuck, Belles! Best experience of my life. It was everything I could have ever asked for. You were amazing.

So why did I run OVER AND OVER again? Because I was scared. I was scared I wouldn't be good enough. I was scared your dad wouldn't approve. I was scared I would fuck up our family dynamic. I was scared to lose you. The problem is I lost you anyway.

Marco

♥ ♥ ♥ ♥ ♥

December 5th

Bella,

Happy Birthday to me...This isn't how I ever imagined I would be spending my birthday. Alone. Without family. Without friends. It makes me realize how badly I've messed up. How much time I've wasted. They celebrate birthdays in here by singing during lunch. There's no cake or dessert, though. Fuck, is it weird how much I wish there was cake? Something to make me feel normal again. I didn't even have a cake until I was 12. But then Hayley spoiled me with her made up half year birthdays, and I was given a cake twice a year. I would give anything to have a cake right now.

Marco

♥ ♥ ♥ ♥ ♥

December 6th

Bella,

Today I'm thinking about Logan. As I think about all my woe-is-me problems, like the fact I couldn't have cake for my birthday, he is lying in a coma. Maybe my problems aren't so bad after all.

Marco

♥ ♥ ♥ ♥ ♥

December 7th

Bella,

I've decided that I'm going to try. I'm going to tell you how I feel, how much you mean to me, how much I need and want you in my life. I am going to apologize to you for everything I've said and done. I hope it's not too late and you will give me a chance.

Marco

December 8th

Belles,

Ingrid just popped my bubble. She asked me a question I didn't want to think about but she's making me. What if I come to you and it's too late? What if you don't want me or need me? What if you are in love with Tristan? Okay, maybe that's more than one question. First, if it's too late… no, I'm not going to go there. I refuse to believe it's too late. I don't believe feelings just turn on and off so I don't believe you would just stop caring about me. Now, if you are in love with Tristan… well that's different. If I get out of here and you are happy, I promise you I won't fuck it up. If I'm too late because you are in love with somebody else then I will live my life with regret but I will be happy for you because you deserve to be happy. But if you aren't in love with someone else, I am going to do everything in my power to earn your love.

Love,

Marco

December 9th

Belles,

Remember I told you about that guy David. The one who is here because he was high and abused his wife? She came to visit him today. He came in the same day as me. It's 60 days. I've been clean for 60 days and so has he. Today was family day. Since my parents visited for Thanksgiving, I didn't tell them about today. Anyway, I was sitting outside when David's wife came in. I watched her hug him and cry. I watched them talk and smile and laugh, but the whole time I kept wondering if they will really be okay. Will he stay off drugs? Will she really be able to forgive him? Will he ever hit her again? It made me think about us. I didn't physically abuse you, but while I was high I yelled at you. I told you you were dead to me. I hope you will forgive me. I promise you, Belles. I am going to do everything in my power to never get high again. I don't want to be David and his wife.

Love,
Marco

♥♥♥♥♥

December 10th
Belles,

I'm thinking about you today. I love you and miss you. I miss your brown hair and brown eyes, and your smile. I miss everything about you.

Love,
Marco

♥♥♥♥♥

December 11th
Belles,

Today has been a rough day. I am missing my family, you, hating that I'm in here instead of making things right with you. The woman, the pregnant one I told you about a while ago. She's 25 weeks and during lunch her baby kicked. It made me think about you (seems like most things these day make me think of you). I will never get to feel our daughter kick inside you. I wasn't there when you found out the sex. I wasn't there to get you ice cream like my dad did when my mom was pregnant with Mackenzie. I am missing out on everything! Fuck! I'm so mad right now. I did this shit! I DID THIS! You came to me and I pushed you away! I want to leave right now. I want to get the fuck out of here and find you.

♥♥♥♥♥

December 12th

Belles,

I didn't finishing writing the letter yesterday, but I sealed it as is. Today is a new day. As much as I want to leave, I'm not. I'm going to finish these 90 days and find you.

Marco

♥♥♥♥♥

December 13th

Belles,

I talked to my dad about leaving early. I couldn't tell him why I want to leave so he didn't understand. He told me I can leave whenever I want and he can't make me stay. I knew that already. I'm here by choice. Of course, I'm staying, but fuck do I want to leave.

Love,

Marco

♥♥♥♥♥

December 14th

Belles,

Ingrid can tell I'm getting antsy. She told me to make a list of everything I want to say to you once I get out. So here goes.

I'm sorry for running.

I'm sorry for running

I'm sorry for running.

I'm sorry for having sex with you and not remembering.

I'm sorry for doing drugs.

I'm sorry for telling you to get an abortion.

I'm sorry for yelling at you and telling you you're dead to me.

I'm sorry for getting you pregnant.

Actually, I'm not sorry for that. I'm sorry for not being there while you're pregnant and all the pain I've caused you.

I'm sorry,

Marco

♥♥♥♥♥

December 15th

Belles,

Ingrid said there's more to be said than just saying sorry. So, I've been thinking about what else I would say to you once I have you in front of me but I'm not sure. What I really want to do is kiss you. You are an amazing kisser. I miss how soft your lips are and the way you grip the back of my neck. I don't think I would want to talk. I would just want to kiss you. Who needs words? I would probably just fuck up whatever it is I would want to say anyway.

Love,

Marco

♥♥♥♥♥

December 16th

Belles,

I spoke with Mathias today. He accepted a job in San Francisco and will be moving in about six months. It's through his dad's architecture firm and he's going to run the office up there. I hate that the last time he saw me I was high. I hate that he's one of the few relatives I have left and I fucked it up. I apologized and he accepted. We made plans for me to visit one day. I was thinking maybe we could go together. I would love for you to meet Mathias. I've lived in California for almost 5 years and haven't gone any further North than Los Angeles. I want to go away with you. I went to the Bahamas a few years ago with friends and it was beautiful. I know you went to New York with Tristan and that guy Mason. Maybe you can show me around? And we can go on new trips together. Like to Paris or Italy... I've never gone anywhere. Let's go somewhere, anywhere, everywhere together.

Love you,
Marco

December 17th
Belles,

I have less than 3 weeks until I get out of here. That's less than 21 days. I can't believe I've made it this long. I hope these next 3 weeks fly by.

Love,
Marco

December 18th
Belles,

The pregnant woman, her name is Heather. She went into

labor today. It's not good. It's too early, I think. I don't know how far you have to be for the baby to be okay but 26 weeks can't be good. My mom said you are due January 30th so that would make you roughly 33 weeks. When I get out of here you will be 36 weeks. I hope I can make it right so I can see our daughter being born. But if not, I am praying everything goes okay. That she is born and you are both healthy. And happy.

Love,

Marco

♥♥♥♥♥

December 19th

Belles,

Ingrid asked me about fighting today. I've spent almost seventy days in here and haven't thought once about fighting. All my thoughts have been about you. There's something you should know. I am never going to fight again. Fighting is what lead to the accident. It's why Logan ended up in a coma. It's what lead to my back being hurt and turning to drugs. It's what kept me away from you while you're pregnant. I loved fighting, Belles. But now it's tainted.

Marco

♥♥♥♥♥

December 20th

Belles,

Now that I'm not going back to fighting, I'm starting to freak out. What will I do once I'm out of here? I have some money saved from the UFC but it's not enough to live on forever. Now I know why your parents are making you go to college. What if I can't find a job? How will I provide for you and our daughter? I don't even know who I am without fighting.

Marco

♥♥♥♥♥

December 21st

Belles,

I'm not going to stress over the whole job thing right now. If I've learned one thing in here it's to take it all one step at a time. One day at a time and that's what I'm going to do.

Love,

Marco

♥♥♥♥♥

December 22nd

Belles,

Maybe I could be a stay-at-home dad like Bentley. His ass loves being home. You could fight in the UFC and I could stay home. Unless you're with Tristan. Let's just pretend there's no possibility of that.

Love,

Marco

♥♥♥♥♥

December 23rd

Belles,

So, I spoke with my mom today and she mentioned you… She didn't actually say it, but I don't think she thinks you and Tristan are together. I've always known my mom is smart, but I think she's got super mom powers or some shit because I swear she knows something is going on. I guess we will find out in a couple weeks.

Love,

Marco

♥♥♥♥♥

December 24th

Belles,

3 years ago today we made love for the first time. It was the best night of my life. I can still remember the way you felt under me. The softness of your skin and the way we kissed for hours. I want to kiss you and feel you. If I have it my way, we will have a million more of those nights in the future. Happy Christmas Eve, baby.

Love,

Marco

♥♥♥♥♥

December 25th

Belles,

Merry Christmas! My mom said they are in Colorado but you aren't there. I guess you can't fly because you are due soon. It made me think of the night we had sex. You still owe me $200.00. We never did discuss those payment options. I hope wherever you are and whatever you are doing, you are having a good Christmas. I am making this promise right here and now. I will never go another holiday without my family and that includes you and our daughter.

Love,

Marco

December 26th

Belles,

Heather is back. Her baby didn't make it. Something about him going into distress. I don't really know all the details. I hate to even write to you and tell you this but I had to tell someone. She's so sad but she came back to keep getting better. I hope she gets better. I wish I was with you right now making sure you're okay. I'm glad Tristan is with you, though.

Love,

Marco

♥♥♥♥♥

December 27th

Belles,

In group today, the counselor said the relapse percentage rate for people who complete the program is 60%. That means I have a 60% chance of relapsing sometime in my life. I don't like those statistics. I have lived in vegas long enough to know the odds are against me. I need to be the 40%. I need to be it for you and especially for our daughter.

Love,

Marco

♥♥♥♥♥

December 28th

Belles,

Thinking about you today. I often wonder what you're doing on a random day. If you're getting coffee with friends or shopping for the baby. Maybe you're sitting on the couch looking at baby names. christmas is over, so I imagine you're taking the tree down while listening to christmas music because you love hearing it even when it's not christmas.

Love,

Marco

♥♥♥♥♥

December 29th

Belles,

I hate that in two days it will be New Year's eve and we won't be starting it together. I try to think back to the past, conjure up memories that will fill the void I feel until I can see you. I don't think we have any significant New Year's memories. I do remember one year, your mom had hidden the candy from you from Halloween and on New Year's when all the adults were drunk, you found it and ate every single Reeses in the bag. You spent hours throwing up and your mom thought you were drunk. Good times.

Love,

Marco

♥♥♥♥♥

December 30th

Belles,

Today I have been thinking a lot about us (I know, what's new?). Remember when you were younger and all the boys wouldn't fight you? They were afraid they were going to hurt you. So, I stepped up and fought you, and even though you didn't stand a chance against me, you fought like hell, giving it all you had. You were so strong back then… You are still so strong, Belles, and our daughter will be just as strong. Never lose that strength.

Love,

Marco

♥♥♥♥♥

December 31st
Belles,
Holidays suck in rehab. The food sucks. The company sucks. There's no music or countdown. It all just sucks. I hope you're having a good night… BUT not too good of a night.
Love,
Marco

♥♥♥♥♥

January 1st
Belles,
Happy New Year. I've been in here for almost 90 days. I've missed Thanksgiving, Christmas, and New Year's. And all because I chose to do drugs. I'm never making that choice again. I have started to put it in my head, there's a chance you and Tristan are together. I know I need to think about the worst-case scenario so I'm not disappointed, but no matter what, I will never miss a holiday with our daughter. This year I'm making one resolution. To stay clean. If I can do that, I believe everything else will fall into place.
Love,
Marco

♥♥♥♥♥

January 2nd
Belles,
I'm ready to get the fuck out of here. Like right this second. I'm sick of the uncomfortable fucking bed and the lack of privacy. I'm sick of missing you. I know I did this shit to

myself. I KNOW this is my own fault. But I'm ready to get out of here.

    Love,

Marco

♥♥♥♥♥

January 3rd

Belles,

I haven't mentioned it in a while but while being here I have been seeing a chiropractor. The pain is gone. When I walk out of here, I will never touch another drug again. Not even Tylenol. I'm never taking that chance again.

    Love,

Marco

♥♥♥♥♥

January 4th

Belles,

    My parents are flying in to pick me up from rehab in two days. I'm going to go home, take a shower, put on some fresh clothes and then I am coming to find you. We are going to figure this out. I promise you that.

    Love,

Marco

♥♥♥♥♥

January 5th

Belles,

    Today is the last day I will be writing you a letter. It feels like I've been having a one-sided relationship with you, one that you know nothing about. It's been a crazy ninety days but I'm getting out tomorrow and I'm coming for you, Belles. It may take a few weeks for me to get settled before I come for you, but mark my words baby, I'm coming and once I have you in my arms, I'm never letting you or our daughter go.

Love,

Marco

CLINCHED

CLINCHED

Definition: A position where two people try to control each other's bodies by wrapping their arms around one another while fighting for the upper hand, right before the takedown.

ONE

TRISTAN
PRESENT DAY

"HAPPY BIRTHDAY TO YOU! HAPPY BIRTHDAY TO YOU! HAPPY Birthday, dear Lexi! Happy Birthday to you!"

Lexi smiles wide, her big blue eyes looking around at all of our family and friends who are here, joining us to celebrate her fifth birthday. When the singing stops, she glances my way and I give her a nod.

"Go ahead, Lex. Blow out the candles and make a wish."

She nods back then closes her eyes hard, her cute little nose scrunching up in concentration. She leans forward, and with all her might, my little girl blows the candles out. Everyone cheers and claps and snaps photos. She opens her eyes and jumps off the chair, running toward me.

"Wanna know my wish?" She's so excited that I don't have the heart to tell her what parents always tell their kids: *If you tell anyone it won't come true.*

Bending, so I'm level with her, I pull my daughter into my arms. "Absolutely."

She cups her hands to cover her mouth then brings them to my ear and whispers, "I wished to buy all the paint in the world and color the bestest picture ever." She says it in such a serious tone, I know she means business.

I'm not sure where it came from, but my daughter, Alexandria Scott, has the creativity gene running through her veins. She lives and breathes art in every way possible. From crayons and markers, to chalk and paint, she could spend her entire day simply creating.

"That's a good wish. How about we open up your presents after we have cake? There might be a present or two on the table that can help make your wish come true." Lexi jumps up and down and then runs over to my mom, who is passing out pieces of cake to everyone.

"Damn, Tristan, remember the day that little girl was born?" Mason plops his ass into a chair, cake in hand, and goes to take a bite, ignoring the fact he has a huge fight coming up in a few months.

"Bro, you can't be eating that shit while you're training." I snag the plate of cake out of his hands and sit next to him, successfully taking a huge bite of his cake. "And of course I remember when my daughter was born. How could I forget? It was the best day of my life."

"Hey, she might be your daughter, but she's my goddaughter, and that counts twice as much because it's from God. You just screwed *SheWhoShallNotBeNamed*. That's not godly. As a matter of fact, that's the opposite of godly. Plus, I pretty much named her."

"You did not name her." I shake my head, ignoring his comment regarding Lexi's surrogate, and take another bite of the delicious cake.

"Did so," Mason argues.

"Did not." Don't ask me why I'm even arguing with this guy. He's a twenty-nine-year-old toddler and I always fall for his shit.

"Did so."

I watch my daughter, with her face covered in frosting, talking and laughing with her best friend, Micaela. They may live several hours from each other and be nine months apart in age, but since the day they met during our Christmas vacation to Breckenridge, they've become best friends, always begging to see each other.

My gaze goes to Bella, Micaela's mom and one of my oldest and closest friends. She gives me a small smile as she sits on her husband's lap, a little over six months pregnant with their second child. There was a time when I would have bet my life Bella and I would've ended up together, the two of us raising her daughter as a family, but life has a way of working things out the way they should be.

In the end, Bella ended up marrying Micaela's father, our longtime friend, Marco, and I was blessed with Lexi. The day Micaela was born, I thought my world had come crashing down. Only, I didn't realize at the time, God had a different plan for me. Lexi was meant to come into my life and I can't imagine a world without her in it.

TWO

TRISTAN
ROUGHLY SIX YEARS AGO

I'M LYING IN MY ROOM WITH MY GIRLFRIEND, GINA. SHE'S PASSED out and I'm watching reruns of *That 70's Show*. I watch her chest rise and fall and wonder if maybe I'm in over my head with this girl, if maybe it would be best to accept she isn't going to change, and walk away. When I first met her at the bar, she was so carefree, and I was immediately drawn to her. She appeared to be completely immune to the world around her, only living in the moment. What I didn't know at the time was that her carefree attitude was due to the excessive drinking and drug use. She hid both from me at first, but slowly she started showing her true colors. We got into a huge fight about it, and she promised she would slow it down, but that was a lie. It has only gotten worse the last couple months.

I've asked her to get help, but she tells me she has it under control, says she's just going through some shit at home. It's obvious she's turning to drugs and alcohol as an escape, but she needs help—help I'm not in a place to give her. I don't know what she's been through because she won't open up to me, but when she gets high enough or drunk enough, she'll let little pieces slip out. I'm worried about her, but I don't know what to do. I'm a twenty-year-old college student living off a trust fund for God's sake. I'm watching one of my good friends Marco go through something similar, and I feel helpless.

There's a knock on the door and Gina stirs, the blanket dragging down enough to reveal her bare ass. I rush out of the room to answer it, so she doesn't wake up. Last night was rough. She said she was visiting her mom, and then a few hours later, she showed up at my apartment drunk and high and crying. I held her hair back as she threw up until she finally passed out. I don't know if her issue is with her mom, so I'm hesitant to reach out to her for help, but I'm going to have to do something soon.

I open the door and Marco comes storming inside. "Where the fuck is she?" he booms. His eyes are bloodshot and glossy, and it's clear he's high as a kite. I see Bella hiding behind the door, looking terrified, so I try to stop him from coming in.

"Marco, you need to calm down, man." While I'm built from years of working out, Marco is a UFC fighter. He slams his fist into the door—pushing it open—then stalks inside looking for Bella. When their eyes meet, he starts spewing out insults, calling her a bitch, and accusing her of ratting him and his drug problem out to his dad.

We've all known for some time he has a drug problem, but because of how it started—his best friend driving them home from the club after Marco won his title fight, wrecking the car, and being put into a coma, while Marco was injured so badly he couldn't fight—we've made excuses for him, hoping he would get it together. Judging by the shit he's saying, Bella must've told his parents what's going on.

I cut him off before he says anything else to Bella. "You do have a fucking drug problem. Bella was just trying to help. We're your friends."

Marco barks, "She's not my friend. She's nothing to me." Then he looks at Bella. "You have enough problems of your own to be worrying about me. Focus on your fucking self."

Bella's eyes go wide and she begs him to leave.

"Why? Afraid pretty boy here will learn the truth? Or wait…did you end up doing what I suggested after all?" His eyes drop down to Bella's stomach and a horrible feeling comes over me.

"Bella, what's he talking about?"

Marco laughs. "Oh, this is great! You had time to call my fucking dad and stir up shit, but you forgot to mention to your best friend here that you're knocked up."

I'm shocked as shit because I didn't even know Bella was having sex. Sure, she's my best friend, but we don't exactly do girl talk. I'm trying to get my head wrapped around the fact Bella is pregnant while Marco continues to spit shit out about her having an abortion.

"So, Bella"—Marco laughs humorlessly—"tell us. I mean you got in my business, so it's only fair I know yours."

Bella's head drops slightly. "I'm having the baby." I have no idea what's going on, but it's obvious Bella doesn't want to say who the father is—or maybe she doesn't know or he doesn't want the baby.

"And who's the lucky guy? Who's the guy who's fucked for life?" Marco questions.

I see the tears streaming down Bella's face and the words come out before I can stop them. "I am, so worry about yourself."

"I call bullshit," Marco hisses

"You can call whatever the fuck you want. I was just shocked you knew. Now get the fuck out. Bella's baby is mine."

Of course this is the moment when Gina decides to come out of the room. Her hands go to her mouth and tears well up in her eyes. I have two options: save Bella or save my relationship with Gina. I choose Bella and I continue to choose Bella for the next seven months.

THREE

TRISTAN
MICAELA'S BIRTH

FOR THE LAST SEVEN MONTHS, I'VE BEEN THERE FOR BELLA AND the baby she's carrying. I never asked questions. She needed me, and like I've done our entire lives, I stood by her side, because even though she only sees me as a friend, I love Bella. Am I in love with her? I'm not sure.

The thing about Bella is she's easy to love. When you're in her circle, she'll give you all of her, and that's why, when she needed me, I chose to give her all of me. I know, without a doubt, Bella would have done the same thing for me, no questions asked.

But as I stood there, after having *our* daughter ripped from my arms because she needed a blood transfusion due to severe anemia, I realized maybe I should have asked questions. When she told me the father didn't want the baby, I left it at that. Did she technically lie to me? No. But she kept a huge detail from me. When I lied to everyone, saying the baby was mine, I had no idea who the real father was.

Marco.

Marco is the father of Bella's baby.

The guy who I almost beat the shit out of for turning his back on his baby and Bella.

The guy who just spent ninety days in rehab getting clean so he could be a good dad.

The guy who was rushed somewhere in the hospital to donate blood to save *his* daughter's life, and he could do that because his blood type is the same. And like a punch straight to my face, it hit me, *I'm not the father*. As much as I love Bella and this baby girl who I watched grow in her mother's belly for the last seven months, I am not the father. Marco is.

And fuck if that didn't change everything.

I screamed.

Marco yelled.

Bella cried.

Our parents begged us all to calm down.

I left.

Marco stayed. Because Marco is the dad.

When I went back to talk to Bella, I found her and Marco holding their baby like a happy fucking family. Like he didn't tell her she was dead to him. Like she didn't keep the fact he was the father from him. Like he didn't tell her she should abort her baby. Like she didn't lie to everyone and say I was the father.

And the visual of the three of them is what led me to the bar where I am currently getting shitfaced, hoping to forget everything that has happened in the last seven months.

"You planning to drive?" the bartender inquires as he hands me my sixth, maybe seventh, double shot of Johnnie Walker Black.

"Nah, I'll get a cab," I slur, and even I can hear the drunkenness in my voice.

"You want some company?" I glance to the left of me to see none other than my ex-girlfriend, Gina. I don't bother to acknowledge her. It's not that I'm mad at her. I'm just mad at the world and she's part of the world.

She doesn't say anything else, just sits next to me and orders herself a Coke.

For the next few hours, I get drunk while Gina keeps me company. She doesn't say a word and neither do I. I don't even know what I would say. When the bartender makes the *ten minutes until closing* call, I take a good look at Gina, her jet-black hair and banging fucking body, and think about what it would be like to get lost in her. It's been seven months since I've been with a woman. Seven months of stroking my dick in the shower.

"What?" she asks, giving me a shy smile.

"I want you." I'm drunk as fuck and the words come out slurred, but I think she gets the idea because she smirks and stands, throwing a couple bills onto the bar.

I stand as well, my head fuzzy, and reach into my pocket to pay my tab. I have no clue how much it is or how much I have, so I throw a bunch of bills on the bar.

I follow Gina into the bathroom, and before she can even lock the door, I'm on her. I have her body pressed up against the sink with my dick pushing against her.

"Tristan, fuck me now," she begs, and I don't question it. Grabbing her hips, I lift her, her skirt scrunching up to her waist. I push her panties to the side, and then unbuckling my pants just enough to pull my dick out, I thrust into Gina over and over again, not sure if she's getting off, not sure if I'm getting off, just focusing on one thing: Getting Lost.

I WAKE UP, AND WITH ONE EYE, I CHECK OUT MY SURROUNDINGS. My head is pounding and I feel drunk. *Drunk?* And it all comes flooding back to me.

Bella.
The baby.
Marco.
The bar.
Johnnie Walker.
Gina.
More Johnnie Walker.
Fucking Gina.
Fuck! I fucked Gina. In the bathroom of the bar. In her kitchen. In the shower. In her bed. I look at the bed and her side is empty, but on the nightstand there are empty drug baggies and a pipe. *Guess she's still the same woman she was seven months ago…*

Grabbing my cell phone from the nightstand, I see it's only seven in the morning. No clue how I woke up this early, but knowing I need to talk to Bella, I make my way to Gina's kitchen and take a couple Advil to help my hangover. I wash my face and teeth the best I can, and call a cab to take me to the hospital.

I get there and Bella is awake with Marco sleeping next to her. The anger that I've been keeping at bay hits me. This guy chose drugs over her, over their baby. I was there for her. I chose her. And what does she do? She lets him back into her life without giving it a second thought. Doesn't she realize he's going to hurt her? And when he does, does she expect me to be there to pick up the pieces?

And what about the innocent baby stuck in the middle of all this?

"Hey," she whispers. "How long have you been here?"

I walk farther into the room, the door shutting behind me. "Just a few minutes. We need to talk."

She says okay and allows me to say what I need to say.

"I know there's nothing between us and I finally accept that, and while I am pissed you kept her paternity from me, I want you to come home. I want you to raise her in our apartment. I don't trust Marco. He just got out of rehab. What if he relapses?"

"I'm moving back home," she says, and I sigh in relief.

"Good," I reply, relieved we're in agreement.

"No, I don't think you understand. I am moving back home…to Las Vegas. My parents are going to help me raise Micaela. I want to finish school. I didn't understand how important it was until I had her. I need to make sure I can provide for her. I want to train as well. I can't move back in with you. It's not fair to you."

"Bella…"

"No, Tristan. You are one of the most selfless people I know. You've been my best friend for as far back as I can remember. You have always put me first but I'm not going to let you do this. You deserve to be happy, to find love, to have a damn life. I never should've put you in this position. I'm so sorry."

I drop my head, sadness engulfing me over the sobering realization I'm about to lose my best friend.

Marco wakes up and hears all of this. We get into an argument over Bella's wellbeing, but in the end Bella makes it clear she'll decide her future.

Then Marco says something that has the room feeling like it's spinning around me. "Look at the bright side. Now you and Gina can be together." I look at him with confusion. *Does he know we hooked up last night?*

"What the fuck does Gina have to do with this?"

"She's the one who told me about the baby, that she's mine."

"What did you just say?" I ask slowly, trying to wrap my still half-drunken head around what he's implying.

"She came to me three months ago and said I was the father. She showed me a letter Bella wrote to Micaela and it stated I was the dad. Gina said she knew you didn't cheat on her, and she asked me to take responsibility so you two could be together again."

Bella tries to explain and Marco gives me his bullshit excuses of why it's taken him so long to come forward, but I can't deal with any of this. I need to get out of here—away from Bella and Marco. Away from Gina and her meddling fucking ass. I need to just get away.

But before I leave, I take one last look at the sweet little girl who's innocent in all of this. "Goodbye pretty girl." I bring two fingers to my lips and press them to her forehead. Then I walk over to Bella and give her a kiss on her forehead as well. "I need some time, Bella."

"Please tell me I'm not losing you, Tristan," she pleads.

"Right now, I can't tell you anything." And it's the truth. I need time to figure out where my life goes from here. Her eyes well with tears, but I ignore them.

"Okay."

"Let me call you," I insist before I walk out the door and out of my best friend's life

FOUR

TRISTAN
THE NEXT NIGHT

I'M LOST AND CONFUSED AND ALONE. MASON IS IN TOWN AND staying with me, but when he asked me to join him at the club with some friends from the gym, I declined, needing some time to figure out where to go from here. I don't know how to handle my anger and resentment. I don't know who it should be aimed at: Bella. Marco. Gina. Myself.

Deciding I need some answers from Gina—needing to hear her side of the story—I head over to her apartment to see if she's home so I can confront her. I park in the guest parking spot and make my way up to her apartment. There's loud music playing inside, and when I knock, the door opens up on its own.

"Hello?" I yell over the music. Dozens of people fill the smoky apartment, the smell of weed permeating my nostrils. As I make my way through the swarm of high and drunk people, who are laughing and dancing, I almost consider joining them. Maybe Gina has the right idea, trying to escape reality. Maybe all of these people are onto something.

"Hey, have you seen Gina?" I ask a random guy who's snorting coke off the table.

"Probably in her room." He nods toward the hallway.

When I get to her room, the door is partly open, so I open it the rest of the way. There's a guy I recognize from the parties she's dragged me to—her friend Janell's brother, I think—the drug dealer—sitting on the edge of her bed. His pants are down and his dick is out. Only I can't see his dick because Gina's entire mouth is covering it as he presses his hand to her head, pushing her head down farther until she gags, her throat making a convulsing noise.

"Hey!" I shout, and his eyes dart up to me, his hand not leaving her head. "Get your hands off her." At my words, Gina looks up at me and stumbles back onto her ass. I rush over to help her up, but the guy stands, blocking me from getting to her.

"Mind your own business," the guy says, smirking. "She's working off the shit she bought from me tonight." Fuck! I had assumed he was forcing himself on her, but I was wrong.

"Gina." I sigh. "Is this guy serious?"

"Oh, come on, Tristan, don't start with your judgements. You were drunk and fucking me last night." She stands and stumbles around the guy. The front of her shirt is down, her tits hanging out.

"Yeah, I had a bad fucking day! I got drunk and had sex with my ex-girlfriend. You're whoring yourself out for drugs. Don't do this shit. Get help."

"Screw you, Tristan," Gina sneers. "You don't know shit." I look into her glossy eyes and have no idea why I even bothered to come here. She's so high, there's no pulling her down, and it's obvious I'm not going to get answers from her.

"You need to go," the guy hisses. He sits back on the bed, his dick now flaccid, and guides Gina back onto her knees. She doesn't even bother acknowledging me again.

I shake my head and walk out the door without looking back. I'm done trying to play hero, when the truth is, I'm having a hard enough time trying to save myself.

FIVE

TRISTAN
TWO MONTHS LATER

Gina: We need to talk.

Me: There's nothing to talk about.

Gina: I'm pregnant.

"FUCK! THIS SHIT CAN'T SERIOUSLY BE HAPPENING RIGHT NOW." I throw my phone at Mason, shaking my head. I should've known better than to think moving to Los Angeles would mean a fresh start. One thing about your past, that bitch follows you everywhere you go.

"Shit," Mason curses under his breath. "Maybe it isn't yours." He stands from the couch and tosses the phone back to me. "There's only one way to find out. Get a paternity test."

Me: I'm living in LA now. I can meet you in a few hours.

Gina: I just need money for an abortion. Don't make this more than it needs to be.

As sick as the thought of Gina being pregnant makes me, the idea of her aborting something that could be a part of me makes me even sicker.

Me: Please don't do that. That baby is half mine.

Gina: Could be...

Of course this is how she wants to play it.

Gina: I lost my apartment and I have nowhere to go. I need to have an abortion.

Me: I'll come get you. Please don't do anything until we talk.

"I have to go get her. She's threatening to have an abortion." I look at Mason and he glances back at me.

"I'm not saying I'm in favor of aborting a baby, but would that be such a bad idea in this situation? Do you really want to be stuck raising a child with that drug whore for the rest of your life?"

"It's a baby…possibly my baby."

"Okay, yeah, I get it. Go get her."

SIX

TRISTAN
THREE MONTHS LATER

AS IF THINGS COULDN'T GET ANY WORSE…THE POSSIBLE MOTHER of my baby is shacking up with her drug dealer, who also might be the father. Fucking fabulous!

SEVEN

TRISTAN
FOUR MONTHS LATER

IT'S BEEN NINE MONTHS SINCE THE LAST TIME I SAT IN THE hospital, in the labor and delivery unit. Granted, this time I'm in a hospital in Los Angeles, whereas last time I was in San Diego. This time, I'm waiting to find out if I'm the father, whereas last time I knew without a shadow of a doubt I wasn't the dad. This time, I'm praying I'm not the father, whereas last time I was praying by some miracle I could've been the dad.

Last time, Bella gave birth. This time, Gina did. Bella held her baby and doted on her. Gina is refusing to hold her daughter and asking when she can get up and go outside to smoke a cigarette.

It's been four months since I've seen Gina. Since she slipped out in the middle of the night and left with Ivan. Four months since Bella texted me Gina was partying it up back in San Diego. Four months since I begged Gina to come back, so I could try to protect the baby from her mother. I even tried to lie and say I would be with her. She called bullshit and refused to come back. So for the last four months I've hoped and prayed the baby is okay, having no clue about anything and feeling helpless as fuck.

When I got the call this morning after she had the baby, I thought I would be making a trip down to San Diego, only to learn she's here in LA, still with the drug dealing loser.

"I'm pretty sure she's yours," Gina whispered into the phone.

"I'm on my way."

"Hollywood Presbyterian."

What the hell! She's in Los Angeles.

Since I've arrived, the baby has been in the nursery. They're running routine tests to make sure she's healthy and doesn't have any issues from the drugs Gina admitted to doing in the beginning of her pregnancy. They tested Gina's blood when she was admitted, and they couldn't find anything in her system. But that doesn't mean she wasn't doing shit that's untraceable.

"Have you done any drugs?"

She rolls her eyes at me and looks away.

"Have you?" I ask louder.

"No, Tristan, I haven't. I smoked cigarettes, but that's it. Speaking of which, I need to go smoke one now."

She stands and puts her sweatpants on she brought with her to the hospital. Without saying a word, she grabs her cell phone from the table and walks out the door.

After about ten minutes, the nurse wheels the baby in.

"Oh, where's the mom?" Her eyes dart around the room looking for Gina who still hasn't returned.

"She's taking a cigarette break."

The nurse, whose name tag reads Mila, scrunches up her nose but doesn't comment. "Want to hold the baby?" Since there's a chance I'm the father, I've been given a matching bracelet allowing me access to the maternity ward and to Gina's baby.

"Umm…" I begin to tell her I would rather wait until I know for sure she's mine, but before I can answer her, she places the tiny baby into my arms. And in that moment, I know what true love feels like. Don't ask me how I know, but she's mine. She doesn't really look like me or Gina. She's just a tiny little thing wrapped up like a tight little burrito. She has a pink, blue, and white striped beany on her head, and the only part of her you can see is her face.

Her nose is small and her eyes are fluttering open, trying to adjust to the lights in here. My heart begins to palpitate as she tries to zero in on me. She can't, though. She's only a day old. Her eyes can't focus no matter how hard she tries. But mine can and I'm one hundred percent focused on this precious little girl.

"She won't hold her." I look up at the nurse. I completely forgot she was still in the room. "She won't hold her or even acknowledge her. I just thought you should know."

I nod slowly and look back down at this perfect little creature and wonder how in the world anybody could not want to hold her. Then it hits me, I didn't want to hold her. But I also wasn't sure if I'm the father. Gina knows damn well she's the mother.

With one hand cradling the baby, I use the other hand to call my mom to bring her up to speed. After Gina ran into Bella one night at a local bar and told her she's pregnant, I told my parents there's a chance I might be the dad. However, I made it clear until I knew for sure, I didn't want to discuss it. I spent the next several months in denial, refusing to buy anything or get anything ready for a baby. My mom tried to bring it up a few times, but I wasn't having it. I didn't want to be in the same position I was in nine months ago. Shit, I could still be in that position. What if she isn't mine? But as I stare at her, something in me keeps insisting she is. I take a picture of her and send it to my mom and Mason. Then I call my mom.

"Tristan, is that who I think it is?"

"She had the baby."

We talk for a good thirty minutes, and she tells me she's going to fly out to help me if the baby's mine. When the nurse comes back in along with the doctor, I tell my mom I have to call her back.

"We're ready to do the paternity test," the doctor says. "Is the mom here? She needs to sign off on it." That's when it dawns on me that Gina never came back up.

"She went outside to smoke a cigarette and hasn't come back."

The doctor calls security to check the cameras. Meanwhile, the nurse gives me a bottle to feed the fussy little girl in my arms. We wait to hear back from security and when we do, the next words he says change the course of my life. "She got into a car and left." He shows me the stilled image of Gina getting into a beat-up Camaro and you can see it's her drug dealer boyfriend, Ivan, driving. She must have looked at the baby and known it wasn't his.

"What do I do?"

The doctor says he'll call a police officer to come speak to me. When the officer arrives, he tells me the best option is to file for emergency custody. Everything following is a blur. They put a rush on the paternity test to prove I'm the dad. They come back positive. I'm the dad.

I call my parents, and my mom says she's going to be here in a couple of days. She just needs to make sure the recreational center she runs is all sorted and under control since she plans to stay here until we get this all figured out. I call an attorney and he files for emergency custody. Within a few hours, it's granted.

The attorney lets me know it's for thirty days, during which time, he'll file for full custody on my behalf. If Gina doesn't respond within those thirty days, I'll be granted full custody.

As the attorney is leaving, Mason shows up with a ton of crap in his hands.

"What's all this?" I ask, grabbing some boxes from him.

"A car seat to bring your daughter home in. Figured you didn't have one." He shrugs. "The woman in the baby department said it's rated the best." He grins wide and I know she most likely informed him of that *after* he screwed her somewhere in the store.

"I also bought some clothes and bottles and stuff." Then he surprises the hell out of me when he asks to hold her. "So, I take it this is her?" I hand her over to him and he sits down, cradling her head. "And what's your name, little cutie?" He speaks to my daughter in a soft voice.

"I haven't named her yet, but I need to. The attorney needs a legal name to add to the petition for custody." On top of that, the data processor left the paperwork to fill out so I can bring her home tomorrow.

"What do you think I should name her?" I ask Mason. I have no clue about naming a little girl. To be completely honest, I think I'm still in shock over this entire situation. I woke up this morning planning to go to class, and instead found out I'm a dad.

Mason thinks for a moment before he says, "Shelly! No, wait. I slept with a Shelly once and she stalked me for months. How about Anastasia? Fuck! I slept with one of those too and she sucked in bed. I got it. You should name her Trina."

"And where did you come up with that name?" I ask, scared of what he's going to say. The nurse walks in, but she's standing behind him, and before I can warn him, he says, "She gave me the best goddamn road head of my life."

"Jesus, Mason! I'm not naming my daughter after one of your conquests. Think of a name of a woman you haven't slept with."

The nurse makes herself known, taking the baby's temperature, cleaning up the bassinet area, and preparing a bottle for the baby to eat, but Mason ignores her, holding my daughter and trying to think of a name.

"Okay, let me think. Jessica… Melissa… Heather…" Mason continues to spit out name after name, shaking his head as he remembers he has had sexual relations with each and every one of them.

"Okay! I got it… no, wait never mind." He shakes his head, a tinge of sadness marring his features.

"What?" I ask, exasperated. "Just tell me the name."

"Renee."

"And have you slept with her?"

"Fuck no! That was my birth mother's middle name and I can most definitely assure you I didn't sleep with her." It's the first time Mason has ever mentioned someone from his past.

"So why did you say no to naming her that?"

"Because it's my birth mother's middle name…You don't want this sweet little girl being tainted by that name." He leans over and gives my daughter a kiss on her forehead.

The nurse comes over and hands Mason the bottle, and he looks up at her for the first time. I notice once again her name tag reads Mila. She's been here on and off since my daughter was born and she's been an absolute godsend. I know a nurse's job can't be to help change diapers, make bottles, and clean up, but she's done it all for me.

"Have you slept with a Mila?" I ask, and she rolls her eyes at me.

Mason runs his eyes up and down her body. "Not yet."

The nurse snorts and throws her head back in mock laughter. "And you won't, ever."

"Perfect! I'll name her Mila!"

"I wouldn't do that if I were you," Mason warns, continuing to eye-fuck the damn nurse. "I can promise you, one day she will most definitely be under me."

The nurse's eyes widen, her brows shooting up, and if Mason wasn't holding the newborn, I can almost guarantee he would be a dead man. "And I can promise you, I will never be *under* him." She emphasizes the word under. I cover my mouth and fake cough to hide my laughter because really, she has no idea she's only making this more fun for Mason. And I must admit, in the last several years we've lived together, back in Vegas and now here, he usually gets whatever woman he wants.

"Just to be on the safe side," I say, "do you have a middle name?"

"Yes, but I am telling you, your friend here"—she gives Mason a harsh glare—"is never going to sleep with me."

"Who said anything about sleeping?" Mason scoffs, and Mila groans.

"You are safe naming your daughter Mila. Although, it might be awkward to name her after the woman who murdered your friend." Her voice raises and her cheeks go pink, and I have to wonder if the tension she's feeling is pissed off or sexual. They say there's a thin line between love and hate…well in this case, it would be lust and hate.

"I understand where you're coming from, but I'm just thinking it would be better to be on the safe side," I admit.

Mason nods in agreement as he lifts my daughter up and gently pats her back to burp her.

"Fine! My middle name is Alexandria."

I look to Mason and he says, "Nope! You're good."

"Great! Alexandria, it is," I announce, happy my little girl has a name.

Mila shakes her head and takes my daughter from Mason. Once she's placed her in the bassinet, she says, "I'm afraid to ask if you're giving her a middle name."

Fuck! "You know what, I think Alexandria is long enough to cover both."

Mason agrees and Mila hands me the paperwork. "Now that you have her name, fill this out, so you can bring her home."

I grab the pen and write down under name: Alexandria Scott

I look toward my now sleeping daughter, and vow, in this moment, to be the best goddamned father *and mother* this little girl could ever ask for.

EIGHT

TRISTAN
PRESENT DAY

I WAKE UP AND SCRUB MY EYES, THEN LOOK TO THE CLOCK: 7:15 a.m. Lexi should be awake by now. It's possible she's so exhausted from her birthday weekend with our family and friends she's still sleeping, but it would be a first. My parents are still in town at a hotel downtown. My mom wanted to stay a few extra days to spend time with us and Morgan—my younger sister, who is going to school here and living in an apartment near campus. Emma is going to school in Las Vegas, so she flew home last night not wanting to miss any of her classes. She's majoring in education, and planning to become a math teacher.

Throwing my sheets off me, I take a quick piss before I head out to search for my five-year-old daughter. Holy shit! I can't believe I have a five-year-old. Where the hell did the time go?

I walk down the hallway of our condo, passing Mason's closed door and head straight to Lexi's room. Her room is empty and so is her bathroom. I hear voices coming from the living room or maybe the kitchen. *Maybe Mason is up or my parents came over?*

"Are you here for my uncle Mason?" I hear Lexi ask.

"I am," a woman replies.

"Did you go fishing with him last night?"

I turn the corner to see Lexi and a barely dressed woman sitting at the kitchen table. Lexi is coloring a picture and the woman is drinking a cup of coffee. *Damn it, Mason!* I rush back to Mason's room and swing the door open without knocking.

"Get up! Your damn *fish* is in our kitchen with Lexi."

He looks around groggily, then bolts out of his bed, throwing his sweats on and hauling ass out the door toward the kitchen. I follow behind him, listening to Lexi and the woman still conversing.

"Uncle Mason says he likes to go fishing a lot." I can hear the disgust in Lexi's voice.

"I've never been fishing," Mason's *fish* says.

"Me neither. I think fishing is gross! It's good that he catches them and then lets them go back into the water. I don't want a fishy to die."

I stifle my laugh as Mason groans. One day when Lexi was younger, Mason used the term fish when referring to one of his many conquests. Looks like it's about to bite him in the ass.

"Lexi girl," Mason says, trying to end the conversation. "What are you drawing here?"

"A fish!" Lexi lifts the paper up and sure enough, there is a huge multicolored fish covering most of her paper, complete with a dark blue ocean and a bright yellow sun. "Did you catch a bunch of fish last night when you went fishing?"

"Umm…" Mason looks from Lexi to his one-night stand. "No, I didn't."

"Good! Fishing is so gross." Lexi scrunches her nose up in disgust. Once, at the beach she saw a real fish firsthand. One touch of its slimy body and Lexi wanted nothing to do with fish or fishing.

"Britney, I need to get going. Why don't you go back to my room and get your stuff?" He nods toward the hallway and the woman glares at him. I'm almost positive she's caught on to the fake fishing scenario. She huffs, and taking my coffee mug with her, goes to his room.

"Mason, kitchen," I demand.

Once we're far enough away so Lexi can't hear, I say, "Things are going to have to change. The whole fishing term was fine when Lexi was little, but now she's old enough to ask questions. If you want to get your own place, I—"

Mason cuts me off. "No, don't even say that shit. You're right. I'm sorry. I thought she had left. I didn't realize she was still hanging around. From now on, if Lexi is home, I'll go back to their place or make sure they're gone the same night. I would never want her waking up to different women here."

"Thanks, man. But you know if you ever want to get your own place, I would understand. I imagine Lexi and I are cramping your style."

"Tristan, we've been living together for the last six years. While my game of catch and release is strong, no woman is coming before our friendship or Lexi. I'll fish elsewhere." He winks jokingly.

"You are *such* a pig!" We both turn to see Britney—I think that's her name—with her hands on her hips. "Really? Catch and release?"

Before Mason can respond, Lexi pops her head in the kitchen. "Yeah! You catch the fish and then throw it back in the water so the poor fishy doesn't die!"

Britney huffs, slamming the coffee mug down, and storms out the front door, slamming it behind her. Lexi looks completely confused. "Uncle Mason, I don't think she likes fishing, just like me." She shakes her head back and forth and then goes back to the table to continue her drawing.

"No more calling women fish," I say, pointing at him so he knows I'm serious. "And no more women around Lexi."

"You got it," Mason agrees. He might be the biggest manwhore I know, but for the last six years—since even before Lexi was born—he has proven to be a great friend to me, and since the day she was born, he has taken his role as godfather to Lexi seriously. Mason never talks about his past but something tells me his commitment issues go deep.

And really, who am I to judge? I do plenty of fishing myself, just in other women's oceans. There's no way I'm bringing anyone back here for my daughter to see. The last thing I need is Lexi getting attached to a woman who won't be around for the long haul.

We both go back into the dining room to find Lexi coloring. "Here you go, Uncle Mason!" She hands him a colored picture and he laughs as he turns the paper around so I can see. It's a picture of a bright pink pig.

Mason takes off for the gym, and Lexi and I meet my parents for breakfast. We spend the day at their hotel lounging by the pool while Lexi and Morgan swim. Mason ends up joining us for dinner at the restaurant in the hotel.

"When do you guys leave?" Mason asks, shoving a bite of steak into his mouth.

"Tuesday afternoon," my mom answers him. "We wanted a couple extra days with our kids and granddaughter without everyone here." She smiles warmly at Lexi and gives her a kiss on her forehead. Lexi pays her no attention, completely caught up in whatever picture she's coloring.

"How would you guys feel about watching Lexi tonight?" Mason asks.

"For what?" I question.

"We would love to!" my mom gushes.

"You, me, and the guys from the gym. We're going out tonight. It's been too long since you"—he looks at Lexi—"went fishing."

Lexi looks up. "Eww! Daddy! Don't go fishing!"

Kaden laughs and my mom shakes her head.

"We agreed no more fishing," I remind Mason.

"I know, but I don't have another way of saying what I need to say." He shrugs.

Morgan looks up from her phone, finally catching on. "Oh my God! Mason, you are such a pig!"

Lexi laughs. "That's what that woman called you this morning! I

drew the best pig, Auntie Morgan! Want me to draw another one?"
We all laugh.

♥♥♥♥♥

WE GET TO THE CLUB AND IT'S ONE WE'VE BEEN TO SEVERAL times. Plush. Mason and several of our friends are members. I'm here as a guest, but because I've filled out the paperwork and had the background check done, I'm able to go anywhere in the club when I come with Mason. We walk in and on the first floor it looks like a typical dance club. The walls and floors are matted black. To the left is a wall-to-wall bar with mirror shelving along the back holding all the liquor bottles. A row of silver and black stools run along the bar while several tables surround the outside area of the room. In the four corners of the club, there are silver cages elevated in the air. Each of them containing a man and a woman dancing to the music—grinding against one another. The men are wearing silver briefs and the women are topless, only wearing silver cheeky shorts, which reveal more than they cover.

"Second floor," Mason yells over the music as I follow him over to the grand staircase, which is being blocked by a black velvet rope and a bouncer. Mason hands the guy our cards to scan and he lets us through.

The second floor is VIP only. It's all black and silver and pretty much identical to the first floor with only a couple of differences. First, it's only one-fourth the size. The other difference is, along one of the walls where there are tables downstairs, there are doors.

We arrive to the third door and the bouncer scans our cards once again before letting us through. Already sitting inside the private room on the circular black and silver sofas are our friends: Brent, Troy, Jake, and Tommy. Brent and Troy stand to greet us before sitting back down. The flat screen television is on in the corner and turned to the Monday night football game. In the center of the room, there are a couple of topless women on the stage dancing together. There are two more women straddling Jake and Tommy. They're dancing to the music— the one straddling Tommy is topless. His attention shifting back and forth between the woman and the game.

Mason and I have a seat, and a woman comes over to take our order. The first thing I notice about this woman is she's wearing more clothing than the others. While her shorts are still tiny, they actually cover her entire ass. Her top is more of an actual top and less of a bra, and it's not see-through like the other women's clothes are. I can see the swell of her breasts but she still leaves plenty to the imagination.

Her name tag reads Charlie. "What can I get you, gentlemen?" Her voice is soft, almost shy, and when she looks down at us, her seafoam green eyes don't make eye contact. They're like nothing I've ever seen before. Bright green on the inside with a pinch of blue and brown swirled on the outside—they're mesmerizing. Around the outside of her eyes is matching green makeup making them pop even more.

Mason pays her no mind, ordering a beer and watching the screen for an updated score on the game, but when she turns back to me, I forget what I'm supposed to be ordering. Her hair is up in a tight ponytail. It's light brown with hints of red shining through from the spotlights. Her skin is naturally tanned, unlike the fake tan you usually see on women in LA.

"Tristan! Order your fucking drink!" Mason laughs.

"Sorry, I'll have a Sam Adams Octoberfest, if you have it." She nods and walks out of the room, the door closing behind her.

We spend the next few hours drinking, watching the game, and shooting the shit. Mason has one of the women give me a lap dance, but my eyes can't seem to leave Charlie the entire time. There's just something about her. She leaves the room and I make the decision to ask for her number the next time she comes back in, only she never does. We stay for another hour, but Charlie never returns. It's probably for the best. Only I would fall for a damn stripper. First Bella, then Gina, now my eyes are on a damn stripper. And the winner of the worst judge of character goes to… me!

Okay, fine. Maybe that's not fair to say since Bella is a great person, but fuck if I'm not a magnet for the wrong damn woman.

We leave close to three in the morning, and a few short hours later, my alarm is going off, letting me know I need to get my ass up to meet my parents, Morgan, and Lexi for breakfast before they leave back to Las Vegas. I hear Mason's shower running and about twenty minutes later we're on our way back to the hotel.

My dad sends me a text letting me know they're at the restaurant so we go straight there. After ordering a cup of coffee and an omelet, I ask Lexi how her night was. She goes on and on about my parents taking her for dessert, buying her more art stuff, and about Morgan taking her night swimming.

"How was your night?" my mom asks.

"Fine," I reply, not giving anything away.

"Fine? Your son spent the night drooling over one of the waitresses. Of course, he didn't ask for her number. He's a puss—" Mason cuts himself off, remembering Lexi's here, but still punches me in the arm.

"Which is for the best," I add. "The last thing I need is to bring a strip—" I cut myself off. "Dancer into my life."

My dad spits out his drink and my mom glares at me.

"I want to dance!" Lexi announces.

"Morgan, can you take Lexi to go see the aquarium for a few

minutes?" my mom suggests. "I need to speak to your brother."

Morgan grabs Lexi's hand and takes off toward the large indoor aquarium that's filled with all types of different colored fish.

"What?" I ask, once Lexi is out of earshot. "I'm adult enough to recognize I suck at picking out women. The first woman I liked was in love with another man. The second woman was a drug addict who left her daughter. And after several one-night stands the last few years, it doesn't surprise me the one woman who catches my attention… dances for a living."

I notice my dad shaking his head, but I don't catch on quick enough to stop what I'm saying.

"You're old enough now that I'm going to tell you something," my mom says, her voice shaky. "When you were little I got in over my head. The details aren't important, but I owed some dangerous people a lot of money." I look at my dad, and his arm comes around my mom's shoulders in support. "At the time, I was a teacher, and for reasons that don't matter now, I lost my job. I ended up working as a stripper."

"What?" I yell louder than intended at the same time Mason says, "Nice!" My dad reaches over and smacks Mason across the back of his head.

"Yes, I was a stripper. At two different clubs. One of which Caleb owned." She tries to keep her head held high, but I can hear the vulnerability in her voice, the shame seeping through her words at having to admit something so personal to her son. I knew once upon a time, my parents' friend Caleb—Marco's dad, who's also a retired fighter my dad used to train—briefly owned a club. I remember them all discussing it when I was younger. What I didn't know was that it was a strip club or that my mom worked there.

"First off," my dad says to my mom. "Don't you ever feel shame for what you did. I might've hated it, but I respect the hell out of you for what you did." Then he turns his head toward me. "Your mom would've done anything to make sure you had a roof over your head and food in your stomach. She didn't think twice about taking her clothes off to make sure you were taken care of. So before you judge a woman, think about that. You don't know this woman's situation, and just because you have bad luck with women doesn't mean every woman is going to have something wrong with her. Not every woman will be a druggie. Not every woman will choose another man over you, and not every stripper is a bad person."

Well fuck, now I feel like a judgmental asshole. I had no clue what my mom went through when I was younger. I knew my deadbeat biological father left when I was little. She met Kaden, and once they were married, he adopted me. He's been the only dad I've known my entire life.

"Plus, those women aren't even strippers," Mason adds. "They're just topless dancers." He shrugs, earning himself another smack to his head by Kaden.

NINE

TRISTAN

"WHAT DO YOU MEAN THE WEBSITE IS DOWN?" I GLIDE MY fingers across the trackpad on my laptop to wake the screen up, then type in the web address for the gym I own here in Los Angeles: Scott's Gym. Sure enough, the damn site is down.

"Okay, let me get back to you." I hang up my cell phone and throw it down onto the desk, taking a minute to calm down. I knew the site was due to renew. Instead of trusting someone else, I should've handled it myself. After Stacy, my last web designer, quit to become a stay-at-home mom, she recommended a friend of hers. I thought for sure I could trust her recommendation.

Obviously, I was wrong. I told the guy the site needed to be renewed before the end of September and he assured me it wouldn't be a problem. Well, it seems like it was a damn problem as my site has been taken down due to nonpayment. I had no clue until a member went to check the schedule and couldn't find the site and called me.

There's a quick knock on my open door and a "Hey Tristan" that follows. I look up to see Brent standing in the doorway. Not only is he a good friend of mine and Mason's, but he's also the gym manager.

"What's up?"

"Lexi's coloring all over the gym equipment again. Just thought you'd like to know." I glance at the clock and see it's already noon. Four hours have flown by since we got here.

"Thanks," I say, standing. "I'm going to head out. The site is down. Do me a favor and print out the schedules of the classes and put them on the front desk until I get it back up and running."

Locking my office door behind me, I head out to the main floor to find my daughter. I spot her sitting on a mat in one of the octagons, coloring with markers. "Hey, Picasso!" She turns to me, her eyes going wide. She knows better than to do this shit.

"Get the cleaner and clean your picture up. You know there's no coloring on the equipment." I point to where the cleaner and rags are.

She pouts, her bottom lip jutting out.

"Don't give me that. You know better. Want to have your coloring stuff taken away?"

She glares as she stands and stomps over to grab the spray and rag. "It's not my fault. I need to get ready for the painting contest at the library, and the poster board is going to be so, so big! I don't have any paper that big, and this place is boring!"

I hold back my smile. Lexi's entire world revolves around art and she hates the gym. Because of her birthday being in October, she doesn't start kindergarten until next August. I've considered putting her in preschool a few days a week, but because I own the gym and can work my own hours, I've never had to depend on anyone but family to occasionally watch my daughter. Between Mason, my sister Morgan, and me, we've been able to take care of Lexi. She's so close to starting school, I had planned to spend these next ten months with her. Once she's in school, I'll have no choice but to let her go. I know she would love going to preschool, but selfishly, I'm not ready to let my little girl go just yet.

As she gets older, we spend a lot of time at the library. She loves reading the big books of art and they do a lot of arts and crafts there, which she enjoys. Currently, she is excited about the upcoming painting contest. It's supposed to be for only school-age kids, but the librarian is letting Lexi join in since she knows how much she loves art. She's five years old, which meets the age requirement, but she's not in school.

"I don't care how bored you are," I say in my dad voice that tells her I'm serious. "You don't color on anything besides paper. You aren't a baby anymore, Lex. Finish cleaning up the drawing and then we'll go to Jumpin' Java to get lunch."

"But—"

"Lex," I say, stopping her from arguing. I swear this child is five going on fifteen.

"Okay." She drags the word out in defeat then starts cleaning up the massive-size rainbow on the mat.

When we get to Jumpin' Java, the local coffee shop and bakery Lexi loves, she runs right up to the counter to place her order. Shawna, the owner, is standing in front of the register and spots Lexi immediately. Since Jumpin' Java is only around the corner from the gym, we've been coming here since it opened two years ago.

"Miss Shawna!" Lexi yells way too loud in the quiet shop, practically bouncing in place. Shawna smiles, not caring how loud my daughter is, and bends over the counter to speak to her.

"Lexi, what would you like today?"

Lexi puts her finger to her chin like she's thinking, which has us both laughing. She always wants the same thing. "Chocolate chip muffin and chocolate milk, please."

"Lex," I say, not having to explain myself because she knows the rules.

"Fine," she huffs. "Fruit and yogurt, please… with a chocolate chip muffin and chocolate milk." Not exactly what I had in mind, but I'll take it. At least she's attempting something healthy. You would think being raised in a home where both adults eat healthy, she would accept it. But no, Lexi is one hundred percent a sweet eater. Getting her to eat fruit and vegetables is an everyday battle.

"Coming right up," Shawna says to Lexi then looks up at me. "Your usual?"

"Yes, please." I pay Shawna then have a seat in a corner booth. Lexi has already grabbed the paper and crayons Shawna keeps here for the kids and is coloring her little heart out.

"I'm so excited for the contest," Lexi says while drawing. "I can't wait to paint on that big poster," she adds, and I smile. It won't even matter if she wins or loses—Lexi is simply happy when she's creating.

Shawna sets our food and drinks down, and I pull my laptop out of my bag and open it up so I can try to get some work done while Lexi is busy. I call Stacy and let her know her recommendation completely flaked and I won't be using him in the future. Good thing I didn't pay him yet. Then I look up web designers in the area, emailing each one, asking about pricing and timeline.

I find out because my domain lapsed, I'll have to have a new site created, which is fine since the old one was looking outdated. When I bought the gym after I graduated from college, I made a lot of renovations. I've added a variety of classes for adults as well as teens and kids. In addition, I added a new weightlifting room and redid the three octagons. Even though the majority of my members are part of the UFC, I've branched out and welcome anyone to workout at my gym. The old website didn't feature any of that.

I'm about to email another web designer when my phone rings. The name *Bella* flashes across my screen and I smile. There's only one reason she would be calling.

"Did she tell him yet?"

"Ha ha! No, not yet," she says in response. It's a running joke when her daughter, Micaela, will spill the beans to her dad the sex of the baby Bella's carrying.

"Who's that," Lexi asks, looking up from her picture.

"Your aunt Bella."

"Hi, Aunt Bella!" Lexi yells then goes back to coloring.

"Tell her I said hello," Bella says.

"Aunt Bella says hello," I repeat to Lexi, then to Bella I say, "And to what do I owe this call? Are you already missing LA? It's only been a couple days since you left."

"Very funny, Scott. No, we just got home. I was calling to find out if you guys are coming home for the holidays. With me due in January, we won't be able to go to the cabin for Christmas, so we're thinking about doing Thanksgiving in Breckenridge." Breckenridge is where our families have been traveling for vacation since we were little. My parents own a cabin there and we try to visit at least once a year.

"I haven't thought about it, but the gym will be closed for the holiday so that could be fun." Bella and I continue talking. The talk of the holidays and closing the gym leads to the website debacle.

"I need to find someone who knows what they're doing. I need fresh pictures of the gym and a new site."

"Well if you were here, you could use Sheila, who manages our site."

"But I'm not there nor will I be." We discuss the gym, Marco, her parents, and when she plans to go back to fighting after she has the baby. She sends over a couple web designers she found online in my area while we were talking and I pull them up on my computer.

The table shakes a little so I look up and see Lexi getting off her chair and walking over to the table next to me. It's occupied by a woman who appears to be close to my age, and when Lexi hands her the picture, she smiles but it looks forced. *Where have I seen this woman before?*

She takes the picture from my daughter and Lexi begins to point out all the parts of her drawing, and then I remember. It's the woman from the club—Charlie. I watch the interaction between them while talking with Bella for a few more minutes, but my attention is no longer with Bella and whatever it is we're discussing, instead on Lexi and Charlie.

When Lexi puts her hand out to introduce herself, Charlie almost looks like she's going to cry.

"Bella, let me call you back. Lexi is sharing her drawings with the customers at Jumpin' Java."

Bella laughs. "A true artist must share their masterpieces. Call me later." We hang up and I watch Lexi and Charlie continue to discuss her drawing. I don't know what it is about this woman but she looks so disheartened. Even when she laughs at something Lexi says, her laugh is all wrong, like she's trying too hard.

She makes eye contact with me for a second and my stomach knots. She's just as beautiful as she was the other night but so damn sad. Her bright green eyes now look glossy like she's a step away from losing her cool. Unlike the other night, her face is free of makeup except for what I think is lip gloss, making her slightly pouty lips look shiny. She breaks the contact, her eyes going back to my daughter, and something in me wants to know what's happened to her to make her so unhappy.

TEN

CHARLIE

AS I'M TAKING A SIP OF MY PUMPKIN SPICE LATTE, A LOUD NOISE rings through the coffee shop. Realizing it's my phone, I grab it and see it's an amber alert. Seven-year-old female last seen in Los Angeles in a silver Ford Focus. The license plate number is given along with her height, weight, hair and eye color. She's missing. I would imagine a missing child is almost as bad as one that's dead. Or is it worse? Death is so absolute. *Final.* Whereas a child missing leaves the parents in limbo, constantly wondering. Where is she? Is she being harmed? Will they ever see her again? A child who is dead, well, there's no wondering about the unknown. She's gone and never coming back.

I click to acknowledge I've seen the alert, the buzzing noise immediately stopping. That's when I notice the date. *October 5th.* A lump forms in my throat. *Five days.* My heart clenches, and I bring my hand up to my chest to soothe the pain, only to stop myself. I don't deserve any reprieve from the pain I feel. It's a much-needed reminder of what I did and what I will have to live with for the rest of my life.

Picking up my book from the table, I open it up to where the bookmark is. It's my day off from Plush, and I'm enjoying doing nothing. Because Veronica, an acquaintance of mine from Plush, needed to leave for San Francisco to visit her sick mom suddenly, I agreed to take on a couple of her shifts. Not only did that mean more hours, but it meant waitressing instead of my usual job of bartending. Luckily, the women I work with were okay with me only waitressing and not entertaining. "More money for us," they insisted since the lap dances and private shows earn good money in tips.

I take another sip of my coffee as I turn the page of my book. I found this coffee shop a few months back when I finally got enough guts to venture out of my loft and do some exploring. It's walking distance from the apartment I moved into eight months ago. The owner of my loft, Mr. Hinton, is an older gentleman who has retired to Florida to be closer to his children. At first, he was hesitant to accept cash, but he gave in when I agreed to pay the one year lease up front. He also agreed once the lease is up, to continue our arrangement on a month-to-month basis. I'm not sure if I will be forced to move... or run, so I don't want to commit to another year. I never planned on staying here this long.

Up until a few months ago, I'd been nervous about leaving, only venturing out for the necessities such as getting groceries and going to the book store around the corner to pick up some reading material. Because I can't use any credit cards that can be traced back to me, I need to stick to paperbacks I can pay for with cash. It has been eight months of finding myself. The problem is, it's hard to find yourself when you're still locked in the dark, so I finally gave in and started exploring the area, and that's when I met Bianca. She was having coffee here at the shop and mentioned they were hiring at Plush when she saw I was looking in the newspaper for a job. Luckily, Tyler—the owner of the club—is Bianca's brother, which meant at her recommendation, he hired me on the spot.

After speaking with Tyler, and explaining I need to work under the table because of my need to remain hidden, he made an exception for me. I think he could see it in my eyes how desperate I was. I couldn't explain why and he didn't ask, and for that I'm thankful. While I might have enough money for the time being, I know it will eventually run out. Bringing in a steady income makes me feel better.

I look out the window of the coffee shop. Growing up in a small town in Georgia, Los Angeles can be quite overwhelming. Even where I lived in Texas, it wasn't as fast paced and chaotic as it is here. I was lucky to find a small community in Los Angeles, which seems to be a bit slower. More mom and pop stores and restaurants. Less glam and more down to earth. The only time I leave my little area of comfort is to go to work. The club is located downtown, so it's a quick cab ride there and back. On my days off, I spend most of my time at this coffee shop. It reminds me of one I used to frequent when I lived in Georgia.

When I think about my hometown, my heart aches. Growing up, my parents didn't have much money, but what they couldn't give me in materialistic possessions, they gave me in love. When I was offered a full scholarship to study art at A&M, they insisted I take it. We didn't have the money for me to visit often, but I did get to visit them during spring break my freshman year, which I'll always be grateful for since it was the last time I saw them.

They were killed in a fire when a line ruptured down in the boiler room in their apartment building causing a fire from the ground up. By the time people realized what was happening, many of them couldn't get out in time. Everything my parents owned burned to the ground, leaving me with nothing more than a small life insurance policy, a few pieces of jewelry, and only the memories to look back on.

Suddenly feeling the need to be creative, I set my book aside, and take my sketchbook out of my bag along with my pencil. I look around for something to sketch, my gaze stopping on a beautiful shade tree on the sidewalk right outside the window. For a few minutes, I get lost in the lines of the thick trunk, the delicacy of the leaves, and the shade the branches and leaves combined create on the sidewalk.

The door opens, the bells chiming, and in walks a little girl who looks like she dressed herself with her pink long sleeve shirt, purple ruffled skirt, and tie-dye colored Chucks. Right behind her is a man who I assume is her father. Even with only seeing a side profile of him, I can tell he's gorgeous. The side of his face is covered in light scruff, and I imagine what it would feel like to rub my hands up and down it. He's wearing a simple navy blue T-shirt with jeans that fit him just right. He's donning a perfect LA tan, and he's wearing Chuck Taylors just like the little girl, only his are white.

He laughs at his daughter who's running toward the counter, clearly excited to be here, and holy moly does his laugh do something to me. It's a foreign feeling to think about a man in this way, but it gives me hope that maybe I'm finally healing. When I took the job at the club, my therapist told me it would be good for me to be in a safe environment with men, to help me remember not all men are violent. But up until the other night, I never felt anything remotely sexual toward a man.

The woman at the counter greets the little girl and the man, and they talk for a few minutes. It's obvious this isn't their first time eating here. When the little girl is done ordering, she runs by me toward the corner booth next to me to set her purse and doll down. Then she runs to the counter to grab paper and crayons. She looks to be five maybe six years old with brown curly hair that is up in uneven pigtails only making her look even more adorable. My throat tightens and my eyes burn as I watch her sit and begin to color. She's completely focused, concentrating hard on whatever it is she's coloring.

The man leaves the counter and I'm able to get a better view of him from the front. Holy shit! It's the man from the club the other night. I believe his name is Tristan. He sits across from the little girl and I will myself to stop staring. Closing my eyes, I count to ten, trying to shake off my thoughts the best I can. I take another sip of my coffee then attempt to get lost in my drawing once again. It's afternoon here in LA, which means the streets are crowded, but what's nice is here in Larchmont Village, the streets are lined with fall decorations, giving the area an autumn feel to it. Fake leaves wrap around the street poles with fake pumpkins placed on top of signs. Orange and white lights cover several awnings. The trees are even a beautiful mixture of green, brown, and red. You almost wouldn't even know Larchmont Village is a part of Los Angeles, only five miles away from Downtown LA.

I was lucky enough to find a loft here in Larchmont at a decent price because there's no way I would be able to afford anything in the heart of Los Angeles, and as luck would have it, Jumpin' Java is walking distance from my loft.

I'm drawing the street pole along with the fall decorations when a voice startles me, causing me to jump.

"Wow! Your picture is so good! Look what I drew." It's the little girl from the booth next to me and she's holding up a picture of a pumpkin, the mouth drawn to appear scary. She pushes the picture toward me, so I take it in my hands, admiring it for a moment. I force myself to keep the memories at bay of the last time I looked at a colored picture.

"This is very cool. Did you make this up or draw it from something you saw?" The little girl grants me a toothy grin at my compliment and points to something in the distance. I turn my head to see a pumpkin on the counter. It's almost identical to the drawing and it's obvious, especially for her age, she is artistically advanced.

"You drew and colored this all by yourself?"

"Yep!" She nods in confirmation. "I'm going to enter a painting contest at the library and the paper they give you is way bigger!" Her hands fly outward to show me how big, her smile never leaving her face. I look around her and notice that even though her dad is on the phone, his gaze is trained on us—his love and protectiveness for his daughter evident in his eyes.

"My name is Lexi." She holds out her hand and I have no choice but to take her tiny hand in mine. It's warm and soft, reminding me of… *No!* I stop myself from going there and close my eyes for a second to stop the tears that are threatening to break free from behind my eyelids. When I open my eyes, I look up to see her dad staring at me, no longer on the phone. Even with a small frown marring his face, the man is stunning. His blue eyes match the little girl's, both dark like the deep part of the ocean. She's sporting the cutest dimple on her left cheek that only seems to appear when she smiles extra wide, and it has me wanting to make him smile to see if he has the same one.

Looking back at Lexi, I say, "My name is Charlie. It's nice to meet you."

"Are you an artist?" she asks.

"Lexi," Tristan calls to her. "Leave her alone."

She turns around to face him, holding up her tiny index, finger indicating to give her a minute. "Dad, one minute." Her hand is on her hip and I can't help but laugh at her sass. *Yep, he's her dad.* He raises an eyebrow, but she's already turned back around looking at me.

"Are you?" she asks again.

"I would like to think so," I choke out the words. "I think anybody who loves to color or paint or draw is an artist in some way."

"I love to color and paint and draw! Does that mean I'm an artist?"

"Absolutely." The lump in my throat gets bigger, making it harder to speak.

"But you didn't color this." She points to my drawing. And she's right, it's not colored nor will it ever be. Drawing I can handle. It's my outlet. But coloring, that won't be happening. I just can't bring myself to use color. Ten months ago, my world lost all its color, becoming nothing more than swirls and shades of black, white, and grey. I swallow thickly but quickly gather myself together. "Would you like to color this picture for me?" I hand her my black and white drawing and her eyes go wide in excitement.

"Really? I would love to." She squeals and turns to her dad. "Look! My new friend, Charlie, said I can color her picture!"

"That's very nice of her, Lex. Did you say thank you?"

"Thank you!"

"You're very welcome, sweet girl."

She puts the paper down on the table then turns back to me. "Saturday is the contest at the library. Since we're friends now, will you come?"

Her request shocks me. I don't want to say no when it's clear she wants me there, but at the same time, I can't imagine her dad being okay with a stranger showing up to the library to watch her paint. Then there's the fact I shouldn't allow myself to infiltrate their life in any way when nothing good can come of me being around them. I know my therapist insists what happened all those months ago was an accident, but to me, it wasn't, nor will I ever consider it to be an accident.

"Lexi, you can't ask someone you don't know to go to your painting contest. She could have plans that day."

"We shook hands and she gave me her drawing to color. We're friends, Dad. Do you have plans?" she asks me, her dark blue eyes pleading. I barely even know this little girl, but something tells me people have a hard time saying no to anything she asks for.

"If it's okay with your dad, I'm sure I can stop by to check it out." I glance toward her dad and catch a hint of a frown before he plasters on a smile.

"Of course, it's fine. It's at the downtown public library on Saturday from noon to four."

"Yep!" she adds. "I have four hours to draw and paint the bestest picture there!"

Her dad stands, takes their garbage to the trash can, and then walks over to his daughter. "C'mon, Lex. We need to get going. Why don't you go say bye to Shawna?" Lexi takes off to the counter to say goodbye to the owner, and once she's out of earshot, he turns to me. "You work at Plush."

Unsure where he's going with this, I confirm, "I do. You were there with your friends the other night."

He looks back to Lexi to check on her before he says, "I judged you when I saw you the other night. I'm not gonna lie. I was attracted to you and I couldn't take my eyes off you, but I still judged you because of your job." I open my mouth in confusion when it hits me, he thinks I'm one of the dancers. He thinks I take my clothes off and give lap dances for money. I close my mouth because well… fuck him for judging me regardless. "Anyway, it's not my business what you do for a living, but I have to ask that while you're around my daughter, you keep that part of your life separate."

Oh my God! What the hell does he think I'm going to do? Show up in a stripper outfit? Take her to the club? I'm so pissed off I want to yell at this judgmental asshole, but my gut tells me to keep quiet. The last thing I need is to get into a heated argument with a man. But then my anger wins out. "So, no pole dancing lessons…got it." I raise one challenging brow up, and Tristan flinches.

He opens his mouth to say something but then closes it quickly, staring at me for several seconds before he says, "Maybe we'll see you Saturday." He gives me what looks like an apologetic smile. Then he walks over to his daughter, puts his hand out for her to take, and then pulls her along.

"Bye, Charlie! See you Saturday!" She waves as they exit. My eyes follow them as they walk down the street until they disappear out of sight. Grabbing my cup, I take a sip of my now cold coffee and notice Lexi left her pumpkin drawing on my table. It's been almost a year since I've seen a child's drawing. My fingers trace the black lines of the pumpkin then move to the inside, the waxy feel of the crayon on the paper making my heart pump a little faster. Bringing the paper up to my nose, I inhale deeply, the distinct crayon smell almost calming me, until I have a flashback of the last time I smelled crayons on paper.

A LITTLE OVER A YEAR AGO

"MOMMY! LOOK WHAT I DREW!" GEORGIA, MY THREE-YEAR-OLD daughter, comes running into the kitchen waving her picture in the air. Turning off the sink, I wipe my hands on the dish towel before taking it from her. There's color all over the paper, messy lines drawn every which way and I have no idea what she's drawn, but it doesn't matter because the smile on her face tells me she's proud of this picture and that's the only thing that's important.

"Tell me about your picture." We sit at the table and Georgia excitedly explains it to me.

"It's a rainbow! But not just any rainbow. The biggest, brightest rainbow." She names each color she's used and then moves on to explain the sun in the upper right corner. When she gets to the birds, the sound of the garage door going up halts her words.

"Mommy," she whispers, fear evident in her voice, but I'm already out of my seat, grabbing the crayons as fast as I can, and shoving them into the container.

"Georgia, go to your room until I come and get you." Georgia listens, knowing the routine, and runs off to her room, closing the door behind her. Just as I think I have all the crayons and paper gathered up, I spot one on the ground. Quickly, I reach down to grab it, but it's too late. The door opens and in walks my husband.

"What the fuck is that shit in your hands?" He towers over me and there's no point in arguing. Anything I say will be used against me. "Answer me!" His hand comes up and backhands me. I try to hold on to the crayons and paper, but they fall from my hands, landing all over the ground.

"What have I told you about this?" He grabs my chin, his cold black eyes staring through me.

"I'm sorry. It won't happen again."

Justin shoves me up against the wall, one hand wrapping around my throat. "Don't say sorry when you don't mean it. You're only sorry I came home early and you got caught."

He's so close to me I can smell the woman's perfume lingering on him. It's the same scent as the last time he stayed away for the entire weekend, so he must be screwing the same woman. You would think after getting laid all weekend he would come home satisfied and happy. Instead he comes home angry and bitter. Sometimes I wonder if that's why he's so mad all the time. Maybe wishes he could stay with her instead of having to come home to us.

But at the end of every weekend or business trip, he always returns home, and he always takes his anger out on me. Then after he treats me like shit, he insists we have sex. He couldn't care less if I get off and there's never any foreplay involved. I'm almost positive it's only in hope of getting me pregnant again, especially since he makes sure to tell me daily how broken I am. Every day I pray he'll leave me for whoever it is he's having an affair with. but I know it will never happen. He's too wrapped up in appearances to divorce his wife for his mistress.

What he doesn't know is that I'm on birth control. I have to drive out of town every three months and pay cash for the shot to ensure he doesn't find out. If he knew, he would probably kill me, but there's no way I'm having another child with this monster. It's bad enough I have to subject Georgia to this life until I can get us out.

"We did a lot of school work today. It was only a few minutes of coloring." Justin was homeschooled by his mother growing up and says it's why he received such a good education. He doesn't want Georgia going to school, so it's up to me to homeschool her. She's only three and isn't due to start kindergarten for another few years, but he requires her to do daily bookwork.

He backhands me once more to the same cheek and my hand instinctively comes up to rub the stinging sensation, but he smacks my hand away, his fingers tightening around my throat.

"The last thing we need is Georgia ending up anything like you. A flaky, worthless, wannabe artist. Now clean this mess up." He lets go of my throat and I stumble to the floor to clean up the crayons, throwing it all in the trash. Before I can grab Georgia's rainbow, he picks it up from the ground and crumples it up, throwing it into the garbage himself.

ELEVEN

TRISTAN

I'M PUTTING AWAY SOME OF LEXI'S LAUNDRY WHEN I NOTICE the giant tree covering her wall, and next to it, the dining room chair. *Little sneak!* "Alexandria Scott!" I yell at the top of my lungs, something I don't usually do, but damn it, this child! I'm all for her being creative, but she's not a baby anymore, and if I'm forced to repaint another wall because of her painting, I'm going to lose my mind.

"Yes?" She slowly walks into her room, her blue eyes meeting mine nervously, making me feel guilty for yelling.

I take a deep breath to collect myself before I say, "Lexi, we've talked about this. You can't keep coloring on the walls and the gym equipment."

"I'm sorry. I was just practicing for the contest tomorrow. Charlie drew the tree and I want to draw one too, but I don't have big enough paper." *Charlie.* For the last few days, my daughter has talked about nothing other than Charlie.

"Charlie is such a good drawer."

"Charlie said I'm an artist."

"Charlie will be there to watch me at the contest."

Unfortunately, my daughter isn't the only one with Charlie on her mind. Several times, I've considered asking Morgan to babysit, so I can drag Mason to Plush to see Charlie. I've replayed my conversation with her a million times. I never should have said what I said. I saw how quickly Lexi latched onto her and I freaked out. I told her I wasn't judging her then completely judged her all in the same breath.

"You need to get a sponge and wash this wall off, Lex."

"Fine." She huffs and heads to the kitchen to grab one of the special sponges I've purchased in bulk that take pen and markers off the walls.

As she's leaving, Mason walks in, still in his workout gear from the gym.

"Lexi girl!" He picks her up and flips her over his shoulder, tickling her. She starts screeching and screaming, but Mason ignores her until she threatens to pee in her pants. She's never done it, but the threat alone always has Mason dropping her back to the ground.

"You stink! Go shower!" She pinches her nose in exaggeration. Mason laughs and then notices the tree on the wall.

"Wow, Lexi girl! Look at that beautiful tree. Is that what you're going to draw tomorrow?" He strolls over to the wall, appraising it like one would do when checking out a picture at an art gallery—his head tilting to the left and then to the right. I stifle my laugh because I'm supposed to be mad.

"It is! I'm going to draw it just like Charlie did!"

Mason turns to me, giving me a knowing smirk. "Charlie again, huh? I still can't believe you ran into her and didn't get her number. What's it been like a year since you've"—I give him a look, and he glances toward Lexi—"gone fishing," he finishes, and I groan because he's still using that damn analogy.

"Ewww! Daddy! You go fishing? Do you throw them back in the water? I hope you don't kill the fishies!"

"Of course your dad throws them back, Lexi girl. No fish are harmed in catch and release." Mason laughs then goes back to appraising the tree. "Great leaves, Lexi! I love the greens and browns."

"Really? Me, too! Daddy said I have to clean the wall." She pouts and glares my way.

"Go, Lex," I say and she stalks off out of the room.

"Really? No fish are harmed in catch and release?" I punch Mason in the arm and he chuckles.

"It's better than saying you need to go get your dick wet."

I shake my head because he's right and I can't think of a legitimate argument.

"Why don't you let her color on the walls? It's not like anybody sees her room besides us."

"Because coloring on walls isn't how we treat a home. It's call learning responsibility."

Mason scoffs. "Responsibility is paying bills, or in Lexi's case, one day going to school and maybe making her bed when company is coming over. Responsibility is taking care of your kid and putting her first, which you do."

"Did your parents let you color on walls when you were a kid?" I ask, but immediately regret it when Mason flinches and walks out of the room. He doesn't talk about his family or his past. A little over ten years ago when Mason showed up in Vegas, at Bella's dad's gym—eighteen and homeless—my parents took him in. My dad was a UFC trainer and took Mason on, starting him on the road which has led to him becoming the successful fighter he is today. Mason has never mentioned his life prior to the day he showed up and it's like an unwritten rule not to bring it up.

Six years ago, Mason visited California and ended up never leaving. When Bella moved out of the apartment we used to share, Mason moved in, and shortly after, we moved to LA so I could get a fresh start. I transferred to the University here and Mason switched to the local UFC gym. After I graduated from college, I had no clue what I wanted to do. I majored in business management with a minor in athletic training. For about a year I dabbled with teaching some classes at the UFC gym as well as training a few new fighters. Then one day the owner approached me. He informed me he was looking to retire, which meant selling the gym. After going over the numbers with my dad, using my trust fund, I bought the place from him.

This was about three years ago. The gym is thriving and Mason is one of the top UFC fighters right now, holding the title in his weight class. He lives and breathes fighting. When he's not fighting, he's fucking. And when he's not doing one of those, he's hanging out with Lexi and me. Mason is a good guy, but he doesn't take anything seriously except for fighting, and even that to him is one big game he's damn good at.

Lexi comes back in and starts scrubbing the wall. She huffs and puffs, but she scrubs it down. I'm sure I should probably ground her for disobeying me, but scrubbing the wall seems to be punishment enough.

"Hey Lex, when you're done we need to go by the gym."

"Ugh! I hate the gym, Dad. Can I stay home with Uncle Mason?" The older she gets, the more my daughter makes it known how much she hates the gym. As much as I love her being home with me, I think it's time we find a compromise.

"How would you feel about going to preschool a couple days a week?"

She drops her sponge and turns to face me. "Yeah! That will be so fun. Micaela said she's in school and loves it! She gets to color a whole lot." Lexi's eyes light up and I make a mental note to look up different preschools in the area, and make sure they allow coloring. I have no clue what going to preschool entails these days.

"Okay, I'll look some up. But Lexi, no more coloring on anything that isn't paper. Got it?"

"Got it."

I GET BACK FROM THE GYM AND FIND MASON WATCHING A basketball game. Lexi isn't anywhere around so I'm assuming she's asleep. I can't get Charlie off my damn mind and before I can give it any more thought, I say, "If I can get Morgan to watch Lexi, will you come to Plush with me?"

"Hell yes! That's what I'm talking about."

"Whatever it is you're thinking, isn't going to happen. I only want to go so I can find Charlie. I said something to her… something kind of rude, and I want to apologize."

"The other night at the club?"

"No. You know how I mentioned Lexi and I ran into her the other day at Jumpin' Java?"

"Yeah, she and Lexi talked about art, and then you left without getting her number."

"Right…well, Lexi invited her to the library on Saturday for her contest and I made a stupid comment about making sure she doesn't bring her job around my daughter."

Mason whistles, shaking his head. "And how did she react to that?"

"She promised not to teach Lexi how to pole dance," I say dryly, which has Mason cracking up.

"I like this woman already." Mason heads to his room to shower and change while I text Morgan. She texts back she's home studying and can be here in twenty minutes.

We get to the club and head right up to the second floor. When I don't spot her anywhere, I find a bouncer who's standing guard and ask for Charlie.

"Sorry man, she's not here tonight. Called out last minute. Is there something I can help you with?"

Damn it. "No, that's okay, but thanks."

I start heading back downstairs when Mason stops me. "While we're out, let's at least have a beer. It's not often your ass actually gets out of the house."

I agree, and we head downstairs to have a beer at the bar. We bullshit over sports, UFC, and the upcoming holidays. Mason is going to Breckenridge with us for Thanksgiving. When we're done with our second beer, we agree to call it a night and head home. Hopefully Charlie will show up tomorrow and I can apologize to her then.

♥♥♥♥♥

WE GET TO THE LIBRARY AT A QUARTER 'TIL NOON. MASON IS with us, and Lexi is bouncing off the walls with excitement. We find Lexi's station and wait for further instructions. I notice Lexi keeps looking around, a frown replacing her usual smile.

"What's wrong, Lex?"

"Charlie said she would be here, but I don't see her yet." I let out a frustrated sigh and hope this woman shows up for my daughter's sake. Then I mentally kick myself because if she doesn't show up, I only have myself to blame for the stupid comment I made. I haven't seen anyone leave an impression on Lexi the way Charlie has, and it will break her heart if she's stood up. Lexi has been raised by two men, and while I would like to think we're enough, I know she craves a woman's presence and approval.

Ever since my sister moved here a couple months ago for school, Lexi has latched on to her. Morgan is an art and fashion major so she can relate to Lexi, but she's still an eighteen-year-old in college, so she's busy finding her place in this world, which means her time with us is limited.

While at Lexi's young age, her happiness is dependent upon those I allow into our life, I learned a long time ago not to depend on anyone else for my happiness. I'm not going to pretend Lexi's mom and I were some great love story that ended with hearts broken. She was nothing more than a blip on my radar. We dated briefly, during which time she was usually drunk or high whenever we hung out. We broke up when I chose Bella, and then we had a one-night stand during a low point in my life. She got pregnant and tried to convince me to take her back. I tried to fix her. I tried to help her. Unfortunately, she only wanted me if I was going to be with her, and when she realized it wasn't going to happen and that Lexi wasn't the other guy's, she took off with her druggie boyfriend never looking back.

The day she left, I vowed to always protect my little girl. Do I think Gina is a piece of shit for leaving her daughter? Hell yeah, I do. But I would rather she have walked away than stuck around only to break my daughter's heart later. My biological father was an abusive asshole and luckily my mom got out before he could do any permanent damage. I'm not saying Gina would have been abusive, but you shouldn't force someone to be a parent who doesn't want to be one. I don't even remember my father, and to be honest, I prefer it that way. Kaden Scott is my dad in every way that matters.

I'm also not going to pretend to be some jaded man who has trust issues with women because the one woman I loved didn't love me back. Did I love Bella? Yeah, I did, and for most of my life, but I know our story wasn't meant to have a happily-ever-after. We were meant to be best friends and I accepted that years ago. One day I will find a woman who is meant for me and Lexi, but at only twenty-seven years old, I have plenty of time.

With that said, I'm extremely cautious of who I let into our circle. I have seen too many parents walk away from their kids. My biological father, Lexi's mom, Mason won't even discuss his parents. Marco was raised by a druggie mom who overdosed. As Lexi's only parent, I need to keep my guard up when it comes to my daughter. I might have been wrong in what I said the other day to Charlie, but I'll be damned if I'm letting just any woman into my life, let alone my daughter's. Trust is earned, not given, and I'm not going to give my trust away. I have to be twice as cautious. Once for me, and again for my little girl.

I look around for Charlie but don't see her anywhere. I hope she shows up, but I feel like I need to prepare my daughter in case she doesn't. She called out from work last night so maybe she's home sick.

"Lexi, listen. I know Charlie told you she would be here, but I don't want you to be upset if she doesn't show up. Something could've come up, and because she doesn't know our phone number, she couldn't call. I want you to have fun. Focus on painting. Okay?"

Lexi nods her understanding, but I can tell she's disappointed. Thankfully the woman in charge steps up to the microphone to go over the contest. She introduces herself as Heather Young and tells everyone she is the gallery coordinator. She explains that all the contestants must be between five and ten years old. They each are given one large canvas and several painting tools and paints. They can only use what's given to them and they only have four hours. The contest is being run by a local art gallery to promote art for kids. The top three winners will get their work displayed in the gallery for a month and the first-place winner will get into the gallery's winter break camp for free. Lexi doesn't seem to care about any of that. My little girl simply wants to paint.

The woman announces everyone may begin and Lexi picks up her pencil to begin drawing. For the next four hours, I sit and watch my daughter draw and color and paint her little heart out. She stops once to use the bathroom and another time to get one of the snacks and drinks they're selling. Her drawing is similar to the one Charlie drew the other day, but Lexi has added her own personal touches to the scene.

Mason stays the entire time and my sister shows up with her boyfriend for a little while to show their support. I send tons of picture texts to my mom and post a few on social media. Every now and then I notice Lexi stops and looks around, and I know she's hoping Charlie will show up. My guilt starts to set in as I wonder if it really is possible Charlie didn't show up because of what I said to her the other day. Regardless, my daughter is about to get her first experience with being letdown and there's nothing I can do to stop it.

Life is messy and full of letdowns, and I know I can't keep my daughter in a bubble, hidden away from all disappointment. But in the future, I won't make the mistake of allowing a woman into our circle so easily.

TWELVE

CHARLIE

WHEN I AGREED TO GO TO THE LIBRARY ON SATURDAY, I DIDN'T realize it would fall on October 10th. Had I known this, I never would've agreed. Yesterday before I left for work I noticed the date and had a full-blown panic attack. After calling out of work, I called my therapist. She talked me down, but when I woke up this morning, it hit me even harder.

I didn't even want to get out of bed. *October 10th*. My daughter's birthday. Only she isn't here with me to celebrate. There will be no cake or presents. She won't be blowing out any candles. My hands go to my stomach, remembering the day she was born. The excitement and love that filled the room. When the doctor took her out of me and settled my little girl onto my chest, my heart felt so full. I didn't think it was possible to love another person as much as I loved Georgia in that moment. As the good memories fill my head, my heart drums so hard it feels like my chest is going to crack.

My therapist, Dr. Monroe, told me last night how I handle today is up to me. I could celebrate on my own—focusing on the positive memories I have accumulated over the years with my daughter—or I could mourn the fact my daughter isn't here with me to celebrate. The choice is ultimately up to me.

I know Dr. Monroe means well, but fuck that. There's nothing good about today. I don't care how much of an optimist you are, there's no way to spin today into something positive. I think back to my daughter's last birthday and how looking back it was the day that set everything in motion.

♥♥♥♥♥

ONE YEAR AGO TODAY

THE COMMUNITY CLUBHOUSE IS FILLED TO THE HILT WITH people. Socialites, politicians, there's even a few celebrities here. Everybody is laughing and socializing, celebrating Georgia's third birthday. Professionals have been brought in to decorate. The balloons and streamers are pink and white, and the cake is a three-tier triple berry. The tables are covered with the finest of linens. Everything about this party screams elegance and wealth. But do you know what it doesn't scream? A child's birthday party.

Georgia is escorted from guest to guest by my mother-in-law, Hilda Reynolds, thanking everybody for coming. There are a few children present, but mostly the guests in attendance are here to mingle with my husband, who is one of the wealthiest oil tycoons in the United States. He privately owns and runs a large oil company out of Texas, where we live. It was passed down to him from his father, who died a few years back of a heart attack.

Georgia wanted a princess party. She wanted Princess Aurora and Cinderella, and her favorite, Jasmine, to all be on the cake. She wanted to invite her friends from the mom's group we're in, and she wanted it to be a tea party. Unfortunately, what Georgia wants doesn't matter. Her father grimaced when she explained what she wanted. Afterward, he told me I needed to stop poisoning her mind with Disney shit and forbade me from attending any more mom's group meetings.

After cake is served, Hilda thanks everyone for coming, and Justin escorts Georgia and me to the town car to take us home. "I'll see you later," he says, giving me a soft kiss on my cheek. He's great at putting on a show in front of others. Georgia and I arrive at home, and since I know Justin won't be home for a couple days, I crawl into Georgia's bed with her and give her my gift.

She smiles sweetly and opens it. It's the only gift she will be given that isn't clothes or money. "Mom!" She squeals. It's a Disney princess tea set—made of ceramic instead of plastic. "Thank you, Mommy! I love it."

"I love you, Georgia." I give her a kiss on her forehead and play with her hair until she falls asleep, clutching the tea set to her chest.

I wake up to being dragged out of bed, pain radiating from my scalp. That's when I realize I fell asleep in Georgia's bed. And the pain is from Justin, who is dragging me out of her bed by my mane. My body hits the hard ground and Georgia wakes up screaming. "Daddy, stop! You're hurting mommy!" It's the first time he's hurt me in front of our daughter and she's scared. Up until now, she has only witnessed him yelling.

"Justin, please stop," I beg. "Not in front of our daughter." But he doesn't listen. He drags me a bit farther then leans over me—the stench of alcohol on his breath making me gag—slapping me in the face the same way he always does. Georgia screams and jumps out of bed.

"No, Georgia!" I yell. "Stay back." But she doesn't listen, and when she grabs Justin's arm to stop him from hitting me, he flings her off him, her head hitting the ground, screams of pain wailing from her.

It's in this moment, I make the conscious decision to leave him as soon as possible. It's one thing to hurt me, it's another to hurt my daughter. He gets off me and picks her up. "See what you did, Charlotte?" He glares my way, then stalks out of the room with Georgia. I follow behind him to the kitchen where he makes an ice pack and places it on the back of her head.

He starts off sweet, apologizing to her, saying he didn't realize she was that close to him. When she continues to cry, he gets agitated and snaps at her. "Stop crying. It's enough." Then he turns toward me. "I only came home to grab a file and I find you sleeping in our daughter's bed. Stop treating her like a damn baby. This is why she cries over everything."

He stalks out of the room, and a few minutes later the door slams behind him. I run to Georgia and hold her close, apologizing for not being able to protect her. She cries that her daddy is mean and I vow to get us away, sooner rather than later.

❤❤❤❤❤

I LOOK AT THE CLOCK AND SEE IT'S ALREADY THREE IN THE afternoon. I have spent the entire day crying instead of going to the library to see Lexi. Then a thought occurs to me—while I can't be with Georgia, I can be with Lexi. I might have let one little girl down, but there's no reason to let another one down. She's expecting me at the library and I'm going to be there. It's not like her father would leave me in charge of her. He pretty much made it clear how little he thinks of me when he commented on me being a stripper. As long as I keep my distance I can't hurt her, right?

I jump out of bed, take a quick shower, then try my best to cover my red streaked and puffy face with makeup—the result from the hours I've spent crying. Once I accept that's the best I'm going to get, I get dressed and grab my purse, lock the door behind me, and grab a cab downtown. I get there at ten 'til four and run through the doors, following the arrow up the stairs to the children's floor of the library.

The place is quiet and it doesn't look like a painting contest is going on. "Excuse me," I say to the librarian, "Do you know where the painting contest is being held?"

"Downstairs in community meeting room A."

Shit! I thank her and run back downstairs. I find room A, but when I do, the place is almost empty. Canvases and easels are spread out through the room, all covered in completed art. The smell of fresh paint permeating in the air. I'm too late, but I try to see if maybe Lexi is still here. Chances are she probably forgot about me by now, but I still feel the need to find her, or at least her finished painting.

"You're late," a voice behind me says causing me to turn around. It's Lexi's dad and if looks could kill I would be a dead woman—his voice is cold and his face is devoid of all emotion. My mind goes back to Justin and the way he would speak to me. Instinctively, I avert my eyes, not wanting to look at him.

"I know. I'm sorry. It's been a rough day. I'm assuming she's still here?" My eyes dart around the room trying to find her.

He doesn't answer me, but instead says, "Her uncle and aunt both came to watch her. I'm here watching her, supporting her. But the entire time, she kept looking for you. You shouldn't have said you would be here if you couldn't make it. I went by your work last night and the bouncer said you called in sick. Are you sick?"

I want so badly to explain why I'm late, but it would mean talking about my past. It would mean having to explain the significance of October 10th, and I'm not ready to speak about today or any other day regarding my daughter for that matter. Speaking to the therapist is hard enough. Most days we focus on me. On me healing and moving forward from an abusive relationship as well as moving forward from—

"Hello?" Tristan waves his hand in the air, clearly annoyed with me. I must've gotten lost in my thoughts. It's been a long time since I've conversed with others—almost a year since I moved here, and before that, my entire world revolved around Georgia. Other than the few mom group gatherings we attended, I lived a lonely life for many years. I may be a bartender at Plush, but with the loud music, and people coming there with the purpose of drinking, dancing, and hopefully getting laid, most pay me no mind. And those who do, generally do all the talking. While I'm friendly with the women I work with, I don't hang out with them. We don't converse. Everybody is busy living their life.

"No, I'm not sick," I say, answering his question. "I'm sorry I'm late, but may I please see her?"

He lets out a sigh and swipes his hand to the left, indicating where I can find her, then leads the way. Lexi is sitting on the stool in front of her canvas. She's done with her painting and my goodness, it's beautiful. This little girl can paint better than most adults.

She looks up, and when she spots me, she smiles wide, but it quickly morphs into a frown when she remembers I'm late. "You came," she says softly, and my heart cracks. All I want to do is rewind the time and get my head out of my ass so I could be here at noon.

I kneel in front of her so we're eye level. "I am so sorry, sweet girl. I should have been here sooner." Tears prick my eyes as I imagine how many times my daughter felt let down by her dad. I don't blame Lexi's father for being upset with me. He's doing what a good parent does—he's protecting his daughter.

"Why were you late?" she asks, and I feel myself losing my resolve. I owe her the truth, but I don't want to lose it in front of her and scare her, so I go with a partial truth.

"Today is an important day for someone I love, and because I couldn't share the day with her, I was very sad."

Lexi places her hands on my cheeks to make sure she has my attention, and the last of my resolve breaks. Tears stream down my face and she wipes them away. "It's okay. I forgive you. I don't want you to be sad." Then she looks to her dad. "Can we take Charlie for ice cream? That's what you do when I'm sad."

"I think that's a great idea, Lexi girl."

Not recognizing the answering voice, I turn around to see who spoke. Standing there next to Tristan is a man I recognize from the other night at the club. He's almost as good looking as Tristan with messy black hair and blue eyes. Only his are a bright baby blue like a cloudless sky, whereas Lexi and her dad's eyes are more of a cobalt blue almost indigo. He's in a grey hoodie and jeans and sporting a huge smirk on his face, unlike the man next to him, who is still giving me the death glare.

"Mason Street." He puts his hand out to shake mine, ignoring the fact I'm practically in tears. After swiping away any leftover tears, I wipe my hands on my jeans to dry my hands before putting my hand in his. "Charlie Pratt," I say, giving him my maiden name. When I left from Texas to LA, I made the decision to revert back to my maiden name. While most people won't know who Justin Reynolds is, I would rather be on the safe side.

"So, ice cream?" Lexi asks, batting her eyelashes at her father.

"Sure," he says to her. Then to me he says, "I'm Tristan."

"Yes, I know. I heard your friends using your name the other night," I point out. Mason chuckles at my response, but Tristan only gives me a small smile and a quick nod.

Lexi spends the next fifteen minutes showing me her painting, explaining in detail each part of the picture, why she chose each color, and she even complains about the lack of choices, saying if she would have been allowed to bring her own paints it would have been even better.

"Lexi, how old are you?"

"I'm five! My birthday was October first."

"You did such an amazing job. Even if you don't win, you should be so proud of yourself."

"Thank you," she says shyly.

"All right. Ice cream," Tristan speaks up. "There's Moo's Creamery over in Larchmont and it's only about a mile from our home. Where do you live?"

"I actually live in a loft apartment on Larchmont Boulevard above the hardware store."

"Perfect. Did you drive?"

"I took a cab."

"You can ride back with us. Mason brought his own car in case he had to leave."

We walk out of the library and into the parking garage. The lights beep on a gorgeous four-door truck. When we get closer, I see it's a Ford Raptor. The truck is midnight blue with black trim. The windows are tinted dark and the tires are black on black. You don't normally see this type of vehicle in LA—usually it's Porsches and Ferraris, cars that draw attention and scream wealth.

"Wow! Your tires are almost up to my chest," I say, making Tristan and Mason laugh. Mason's smaller vehicle beeps and it's more of the type of car I'm expecting. A BMW of some sort but still a four-door like Tristan's truck.

Tristan opens the driver door and turns the truck on. Then he walks around to the passenger side and opens the back door, lifting Lexi up into her booster seat. He opens the passenger side door for me and I stare up for a second wondering how in the world I'm going to get into this truck without making a fool out of myself. I look down and notice the only step is coming out from under the door Tristan put Lexi into.

"How about I ride with Mason?" I glance back at his low to the ground car.

Mason throws his head back with a laugh, and Tristan shakes his head.

"Tristan, be a gentleman and help the lady in. It's not her fault you're trying to overcompensate with your tall as hell truck."

"I don't need to overcompensate for shit," Tristan argues. "I'm not the one buying a fancy foreign car to impress women."

"You know what they say… big truck, small dick." When Mason says this, I turn around to hide my smile and make sure Lexi didn't just hear that—luckily the door is closed.

"You're just mad because my truck will run the hell over your little car."

"When it works! What does Ford stand for? Fix or repair daily." Mason chortles and Tristan rolls his eyes.

"Well, you better hope your car never breaks down because you know what BMW stands for… breaks my wallet!"

I listen to the two grown men throw digs back and forth about each other's vehicles for a couple minutes until there's a knock on the window followed by it rolling down.

"Hello! Ice cream is waiting!" Lexi doesn't wait for an answer before she presses the button to roll the window back up.

Both guys smile, shaking their heads, then Mason says, "You heard the princess. Ice cream is waiting."

I'm about to head over to Mason's car, hoping he'll give me a ride, when strong hands grab hold of my waist. I jump forward in shock, screeching a little, and turn around defensively.

Tristan throws his hands up in the air. "I'm sorry. I was just going to help you up."

I take a few breaths in and out to calm myself while Tristan eyes me curiously, waiting for me to say something, to give an explanation as to why I just freaked out over his simple touch.

"Sorry, I wasn't expecting that."

He quirks up a brow in a way that tells me he thinks my answer is utter bullshit, but I don't give him anything else, so he lets it go.

"Come here and I'll help you up," he says softly.

I walk in front of him, face the passenger seat, and wait for him to hoist me up. This time, when his hands find my waist, I'm prepared for his touch. He leans in and I can smell his cologne. He doesn't smell like a woman. No, he smells like a mixture of sandalwood and citrus, and for some reason it reminds me of winter in Georgia when I was growing up.

"Are you sniffing me?" he asks, amusement in his voice. I turn to look at him only to find his face is less than six inches from mine. His hands grip my waist a little tighter and I can feel his hard front against my back.

"No," I blurt out.

"Yes, you were. I heard you inhale."

Feeling my cheeks heat up, I try to pull away from him so he doesn't see the evidence of my embarrassment. "That's it! I'm going with Mason."

I try to get out of his hold, but before I can, Tristan lifts me up by my hips and plops me onto the seat before slamming the door closed.

THIRTEEN

TRISTAN

CHARLIE SHOWED UP LATE TO THE LIBRARY AND I ALMOST BIT her head off. I was so focused on her hurting my daughter, I didn't even notice her puffy eyes and tearstained cheeks, the telltale signs she's been crying. She gave me some bullshit excuse about having a rough day when it was clear whatever is going on is more than simply having a shitty day. I know she called in sick to work, but she doesn't look sick—she looks sad as fuck.

While she was talking to Lexi, I heard her voice breaking, heard her choking up, despite trying to remain strong for my daughter. I saw the tears silently falling and her trying to hide them. I watched my daughter wipe them away and offer her ice cream to make her feel better. I don't know what's wrong with Charlie, but it's obvious, whatever it is, it's something huge, and it appears she's dealing with it by herself.

Not to mention the way she freaked out when I grabbed her waist to stop her from going to Mason's car. Something tells me this woman has an invisible sign dangling from her neck that reads *handle with care*.

The five-minute drive to Moo's Creamery is filled with Lexi telling us what kind of ice cream she wants and which mix-ins she plans to get. After she lists ten different items, we negotiate she can have three. She then asks Charlie how many she plans to get. When Charlie tells her she's a plain vanilla kind of girl, my daughter asks if she can use Charlie's mix-ins.

Charlie cracks up, and the sound of her laughter has me smiling. It's the first time I've seen her genuinely laugh. I sneak a glance at her sitting next to me and notice she's back to wearing a bit more makeup like the night at the club. While I prefer her more natural, the woman is beautiful. Luscious breasts with an ample amount of cleavage peeking out of her low-cut sweater, a curvy ass I want to grab a hold of, and fuck, those thick thighs men dream about holding onto during sex. Add in her rain forest-colored eyes, that whether she's laughing or crying hit straight to your soul, and her thick wavy hair that would wrap nicely around my fist. And don't even get me started on her pouty lips I want to nibble on. This woman has me imagining shit I have no business imagining.

And all that is just on the outside. I don't know her well enough to speak as to what type of person she is on the inside. However, the patience she's already shown for my daughter, as well as the way she praised her artwork and told her she's an artist, speaks volumes. For the first time in a long time, I find myself wanting to get to know a woman. Wanting to know more than just her body.

"What?" she asks when she notices me glancing at her.

"You're beautiful," I tell her honestly.

She grants me a smile, and I find myself grinning back, but then the next words out of her mouth have me barking out a laugh. "Too bad you can't afford me."

"We'll see about that," I challenge through my laughter, and she rolls her eyes at me.

We pull up to Moo's but the place is closed. There's a sign on the door that reads they're closed while at a family reunion.

"Well damn," I say.

"Oh no! How are we going to make Charlie happy?" Lexi asks.

"Oh, it's okay." Charlie laughs, but it comes out forced. She turns in her seat to face Lexi. "You forgiving me for being late makes me happier than any amount of ice cream ever could, sweet girl." Then she turns back to me. "Thank you for letting me see Lexi. It made my day so much better." Tears well up in her eyes, but she turns away from me before they spill over. She opens her door, and after a second of staring down, she jumps out onto the ground and looks up at me, smiling triumphantly.

"Wait! Where are you going?" Lexi asks. Charlie opens Lexi's door, and using the step I installed for my daughter, steps up so she can talk to her.

"I live on this street. I just wanted to tell you again how beautiful your picture is, Lexi, and I want to thank you for sharing it with me." She reaches over and gives Lexi a kiss on her cheek. "It was really nice to meet you."

Lexi pouts, realizing this is goodbye, but her manners quickly win over. "It was nice meeting you, too."

Charlie closes the door and steps onto the sidewalk, waving at me before walking away. I watch as she walks farther and farther away—stunned at how quickly we went from spending more time with Charlie to her saying goodbye.

There's a knock on my window and then my door swings open. "Tell me you didn't just let that woman walk away, again," Mason accuses.

"The ice cream place is closed and she lives on this street," I say as way of explanation.

"What the hell does that mean? We can go somewhere else, get ice cream from the store. Tell me you at least got her number this time," he says incredulously.

"No, when she saw the place was closed, she practically bolted."

"So, go chase her."

"Yeah! Go get her, Daddy!" Lexi agrees.

I rip my seat belt off and hop out of my truck, running after Charlie, but she's already gone. I walk past several stores, trying to remember which store she said she lived above. When I get to the hardware store, I'm almost positive I remember her telling me she lives here. I press the button on the intercom to be buzzed up several times, but there's no answer. Maybe she said she lived near it? I step back out onto the sidewalk and look around. Almost every business in Larchmont has an apartment over it. She has to be somewhere around here, but as I walk by the surrounding places of business I don't see her anywhere.

Turning around, I walk back to my truck. Mason is standing next to Lexi's door and both of them are watching me. I shake my head. I can't believe I just froze. I let her run away without even attempting to stop her. It's been so long since I've dealt with a woman on a more personal level, I didn't even think. The goodbye just happened so quickly.

"She's gone," I say, jumping back into my truck.

"I knew you were out of the game, but damn, man." Mason shakes his head incredulously.

"I just froze. One minute I was saying the place is closed and then next she was saying goodbye to Lex and walking away."

Mason chuckles. "That sounds like the making of a chick flick. The woman who got away."

Just as I'm about to push Mason out of the way to close my door, Lexi yells, "She's over there!"

I look over to where Lexi is pointing and see Charlie walking out of the corner store.

Shoving Mason out of my way, I jog toward Charlie, calling her name. She stops in her tracks, and I almost run into her from behind. She twirls around to face me, her brows furrowing and her nose scrunching up in confusion.

"Hey, is everything okay?" That's when I notice her nose is red again from crying, her checks are shiny from the fresh tears, and the eye makeup she was wearing is now smudged.

"You were crying again."

She averts her gaze, but I step closer, gently taking her chin between my fingers and forcing her to look at me. There are so many questions I want to ask. So many thoughts running through my head. I want to know what has this woman so sad, why she's so often in tears, but right now on the street corner isn't the time. The way she practically ran tells me she's closed off. So instead of saying what's on my mind, I say, "We're going to get ice cream from the store. C'mon."

Without giving her a chance to argue or come up with an excuse to tell me no, I take her hand in mine and pull her toward my truck. Opening the passenger door for her, I lift her into the seat and close the door. Mason is standing there with a knowing smirk on his lips.

"Shut up."

"I didn't say shit." He lifts his hands in surrender.

"You're thinking it."

"I was just thinking I have a date tonight, so you're on your own after all. Don't fuck it up."

Mason walks over to his car and gets in, revving his engine and peeling out. I get into my truck, and Charlie and Lexi are chatting about art.

"Ice cream party at our place?" I ask, and both girls agree.

FOURTEEN

CHARLIE

WE STOP BY THE GROCERY STORE TO GRAB ICE CREAM AND ALL
the fixings Lexi insists we need then head to their house. When Tristan
found me, I was coming out of the store with a bottle of vodka hidden
in a brown bag, planning to drink my sorrows of today away. Because I
left with him, the bottle is still in the bag on the floor of the truck. I'm
not entirely sure spending the evening with Tristan and his daughter is
the better choice, but it's probably the healthier one.

We pull up to a gated community which can't be more than a mile
from where I live. The gate opens, letting us through. Tristan pulls into
a parking spot and turns the truck off. Whereas Larchmont Village
gives off the feel of homely with a quaint country chic vibe, allowing
people to stay in LA without the hustle and bustle feel of LA; Tristan's
condo development screams wealth and sophistication. Even the name
of the community reads, *Luxury condominiums.* The buildings are
painted a harsh white with dark red doors. The grass and palm trees are
cut neatly, and the luxurious fountains stationed in the entry way of
each building look like they cost more than the entire worth of the loft
I'm renting. I lived many years surrounded by extravagance so I know
without a doubt this condo is worth millions.

Tristan grabs the bags and we head up the sidewalk. Lexi runs
ahead and stops at the door. "This is where we live." She points to the
numbers on the door.

Tristan unlocks the door and motions for me to enter first. I walk
into the foyer and take my boots off, then assess the area. I'm shocked
when I see their home is nothing like the outside. Just as beautiful for
sure, but in a completely different way. The walls are a soft cream and
the furniture is all dark wood and microfiber. There's a huge flat screen

television with a gaming console, and Lexi's dolls and other toys are strewn throughout the living room. The place isn't messy—it's lived in. My eyes go to the walls where I see several framed drawings hung up one after the next.

My heart feels like it's being split open. This is what a home is supposed to look like when a child is loved, yet it's nothing like the home my daughter was being raised in.

♥♥♥♥♥

ROUGHLY ELEVEN MONTHS AGO

"CHARLOTTE, I'M HOME."

I glance at the clock and see once again Justin's home early. For the last several years he has come home at six o'clock on the dot, and now for the last several weeks he's been coming home at all different times. My body and mind go into survival mode as I rush over to greet him. He's standing in the foyer staring down at his cell phone. He's in his usual three-piece suit, tie undone, and shoes that cost more than most people spend on their monthly mortgage. The first time I met him, he looked nothing like this. He was in a plain white T-shirt and cargo shorts. Nike sneakers, dirty from playing football in the grass. He was laughing and looked so carefree. When he asked me out I couldn't help but say yes. His charisma sucked me in. I often wonder which man is the real Justin. If he even knows who he is.

Over the years, I have begged him to take us away, to get away from reality for a bit in hope of the man I fell in love with reappearing. I used to blame the stress of the business on why he treats me the way he does. It started off small. He would snap at me then apologize. At first, he would promise not to do it again. Eventually he stopped making empty promises. Over the years, the abuse increased slowly. A push here, a slap there, until one day when Georgia was almost two, I woke up and realized I was in a physically and emotionally abusive marriage. The last year I have spent every day planning our escape. I know most people would judge me, saying I should have run the minute I snapped out of denial, but when you're married to a man like Justin Reynolds, you don't just walk away. You plan and then you run. Far. Because if he catches you, you're fucking dead. There are no do-overs.

"Hey, you're home early," I mention nonchalantly.

"Is that a problem?" He looks up from his phone and glares at me.

"Of course not. It's just that dinner isn't ready yet."

Justin bridges the gap between us and I flinch, afraid he's going to hurt me. "I'm not going to hurt you, Charlotte," he says incredulously. "Is there a reason I need to?" So, he's in one of those moods, where he pretends he's the perfect, caring husband.

"No." I smile meekly. Justin leans into me and gives me a soft kiss on my lips, and for a moment, I get sucked up in his gentleness until the woman's perfume hits my nose and I step back remembering who it is I'm married to.

"I'm going to finish dinner." I turn to walk away and my head is yanked back, my scalp burning as my hair is tugged violently.

"Do not walk away from me," Justin growls.

"I'm sorry," I cry out, praying he doesn't turn this into another beating. Two nights ago, when he came home mad about work—some business deal not turning out the way he wanted it to—he hit a couple of my ribs and they haven't had enough time to properly heal yet.

He pulls me toward the couch but stops when he almost trips over a couple of toys on the ground.

"This fucking house is a mess." He grips my hair harder then uses it to push me to the ground. I land on the toys, one of them digging into the swell of my back.

"Georgia just fell asleep for her nap. I was about to pick them up. You got home early."

"What the fuck do you even do all day while I'm out making a living so you can live a cozy life of luxury? I took your poor ass out of the trailer park and this is how you act? By being a lazy ass all day!" Justin has never seen where I lived, but I made the mistake of telling him about my childhood. He ignored the parts of my parents loving me and focused on how poor we were, and he makes sure to throw it in my face every chance he gets.

He leans down, gripping my hair once again, and pulls my head back to look at me, then spits in my face. "Are you cheating on me? Is that why this house is a mess?" I shake my head even though it's obviously a rhetorical question. Several times a year Justin accuses me of cheating. It's his guilt eating away at him from being the cheater. Maybe he thinks if he can catch me cheating as well, he'll feel justified in his years of infidelity.

"Nobody will want your broken ass! You know that, right? You're a woman and your body doesn't even work properly. Maybe I should replace you with a woman who can actually get pregnant." The comment would hurt if I didn't know the truth.

"Let's go to the room. I think I need to remind you who your husband is." Pulling me by my mane, he drags me to the room, slamming the door behind us, reminding me exactly who my husband is, and the entire time the same mantra runs through my head: Soon Georgia and I will get out of here.

"CHARLIE… EARTH TO CHARLIE." I LOOK AWAY FROM THE paintings to find Tristan staring at me. He takes a step toward me and I back up, my flashback still fresh in my mind. My back hits the framed picture, knocking it from the wall and sending it crashing to the ground, glass shattering around us.

"Oh my God! I'm so sorry."

Tristan takes another step forward and I duck and flinch out of habit. If he didn't already know I'm damaged goods, he sure as hell knows it now.

"Whoa! It's okay. I'm just going to lift you up away from the glass. You have no shoes on." He reaches down and picks me up just enough so my feet aren't touching the ground then sets me on the carpet.

"Hey Lexi, why don't you put the groceries away in the kitchen while I clean this up?" Tristan says, his eyes never leaving mine. I can't even imagine all the scenarios he has running through his head. This man is the opposite of everything I am. He's stable and put together, and he's successfully protecting his daughter from the cruelties of the world. Does he realize by letting me into their lives, he's putting her at risk?

Lexi grabs the bags and runs into the kitchen. Tristan looks back to make sure Lexi is gone before he says, "You thought I was going to hit you." It's not a question. He's observant, smart, and shrewd. He's onto me and I should speed this story up, tell him everything, so we can flip to the end of the book, and he and his daughter can move onto the next story. One where they get a happily ever after. Because that's what they deserve, and there's no story I'm a part of that will end in any way other than tragedy.

"I'll clean up the glass." I step to the left, but Tristan blocks me in, shaking his head slowly.

"Don't do that. Don't run from me. I know we barely know each other, but did you really think I was going to hit you over a picture falling off the wall?" His tone tells me he's offended that I could think for even a second he's capable of doing such a thing. And for most, that reaction makes sense. But when you've lived a life with a man who is capable of doing just that, the norm becomes all you know, and the reality is, that's all I know.

Hot tears fill my lids, my vision becoming blurry, and I'm forced to blink in order to see in front of me.

"Jesus, Charlie." Tristan's strong arms come around my shoulders and he envelops me in a hug. My body stiffens at first, but all too quickly I allow myself to relax in Tristan's arms, enjoying a man's touch that isn't motivated by hate or spite or cruelty. Keeping my arms by my sides, unable to hug him back, my head tilts down, landing on his hard chest as I close my eyes and bask in the safeness of this moment.

"Daddy! Charlie!" We separate as Lexi comes out of the kitchen, my head snapping back up.

"Don't move, Lex. There's still glass. Why don't you guys go find a takeout place to order from and we'll order in and have a movie night with our ice cream?"

"Yes!" Lexi squeals and then she grabs my hand and pulls me into the kitchen, opening the drawer filled with several dozen takeout menus.

We agree on Japanese, Lexi wanting shrimp tempura, and Tristan and I splitting a sushi boat. While we wait for the food to get here, Lexi insists on showing me her room.

"This is my easel." She points to the wooden stand in the corner of her adorable room. Pinks and blues and yellows make up the color pallet. Her bedding is pink and blue polka dotted, her curtains yellow like the sunshine on a cloudless day. Her walls are covered with tons of her paintings and drawings, and her multicolored bins are filled with every type of drawing and coloring tool. It's what I imagined my daughter's room would look like had I been given the choice.

"This is the wall I drew a big tree on just like yours, just like the one I did at the library, but Daddy made me erase it."

I stifle a giggle when she rolls her eyes. Looking at her wall, I can see where she's coming from. As a lover of art and a creator, her wall looks like one giant canvas. An idea comes to mind, but I quickly shoot it down. This isn't my daughter and it's not my place. She has a father, one who knows what's best for her.

"Ladies! Food is here!" Tristan yells, and we head back out to the living room. When we get there, I notice he's moved the coffee table out of the way and is placing all the food on a blanket, which is spread out across the living room floor.

"Yay!" Lexi cheers. "Indoor picnic!" She plops herself onto the floor and sits with her legs crisscrossed waiting patiently for her food. Tristan dishes out the food and we all eat while watching the movie *Romona and Beezus.* Half my focus is on the movie while the other half is on the two people I'm sitting here with—wishing this could be my life, wishing all those years ago I would have opened my eyes and stopped living in denial just a little sooner.

I'm not damaged enough to believe every man is an abuser. I grew up in a loving household. I know there are men who don't hit or abuse. But it doesn't stop me from wondering if what I see with Tristan is what I really get. Sure, he gave me attitude over my so-called job and got upset when I showed up late today, but both instances were due to him protecting his daughter—something Justin never did. This makes me think about the Justin I first met. I thought he was a good guy until I learned he wasn't. Looking back, the signs were always there but I didn't pay attention to them until I was in too deep. How do I know I'm not doing the same thing with Tristan? How do I know I'm not missing the signs?

I watch Tristan with all the patience in the world and wonder if it's all an act. To an outsider, Georgia looked happy but she wasn't. And for Tristan to trust me in his home, with him and his daughter, how good can his judgment be? He doesn't even realize the kind of person he's invited into his life. For the second time tonight, I consider telling him, but selfishly I want to stay here, in this moment. Once he finds out who I really am…what I'm capable of…what I've done…if he's as good of a dad as he acts like, he won't think twice before banishing me from their life.

Eventually we clean up the leftover food and trash, and move to the couch to finish the movie. Lexi lies between us, and at some point, she lays her head down on my thigh. I run my fingers through her hair, not paying attention to the movie but remembering the last time my daughter and I were in the same position.

❤❤❤❤❤

"MOMMY," GEORGIA LAYS HER HEAD ON MY LAP AND FLIPS HER hair across my legs so I can play with it.

"Yes, baby girl?"

"I don't like Daddy being mean."

My hands still for a beat before I continue running my fingers through her silky curls. I want to tell her she doesn't have to worry because in a couple weeks we'll be gone. I've almost gotten all the pieces of the puzzle put together for Georgia and me to disappear, but I can't tell her that. She's only three years old and if she lets it slip to her father, the consequences could be deadly.

As much as I wish we could leave now, I need to stick to my plan. The calendar says Justin will be gone for a few days leading up to Thanksgiving, and then we're meeting the night before the holiday in Virginia, which means he won't know we're gone until we don't show up at the airport in Virginia.

It also gives me a couple more weeks to gather a little more money and triple check the plans I've made. I've been taking small amounts from the safe for the past year and putting it into a safety deposit box I took out years ago after my parents passed away. With me being young and in college when my parents died, I didn't want to keep the few pieces of jewelry my mom had put into a safety deposit box, in my dorm. So when I closed hers back in Georgia, I took another one out in my maiden name to keep it all safe.

Not wanting to touch the little bit of money left over after paying to have them buried, I left it all in there and luckily, I never mentioned it to Justin. It worked out in my favor because he has no way of knowing I have thousands of dollars hidden away.

I never imagined my life would come to this, but looking back I can see the red flags. The way Justin was jealous and possessive yet secretive. He wanted me to bare myself to him while he kept everything about himself clandestine. I heard rumors he was cheating on me, but whenever I confronted him, he would tell me the women were jealous. I was so desperate for companionship since my parents died, I lived with blinders on. How many times do we wish we can turn back time? If only life worked that way.

I look down at my daughter whose eyes are now closed, and scooping her up into my arms, I lay her down in her bed for a nap. "Don't worry, baby girl, Mommy will get us out of here. Soon...very soon."

"WHERE'D YOU GO?" TRISTAN'S KNUCKLES GENTLY BRUSH DOWN my cheek. I look down at Lexi and she's sleeping. I'm not sure where her mother is or what their relationship consists of, but she deserves more than I can give her. I never should've allowed this attachment to happen.

"I should probably get going." He must be so sick of me ignoring his questions, but he's only known me for a minute. He doesn't understand the simple questions he's asking have such complicated answers. Answers that will inevitably change everything.

"Give me a minute. Let me put her to bed."

He picks up Lexi and carries her to her room, and I start picking up the mess, moving the coffee table back to where it goes, and gathering up the empty bags of popcorn and other trash.

I'm in the kitchen, wiping down the counters when I feel Tristan come up behind me. His hands come down on top of mine, bringing my cleaning to a halt. His simple touch shouldn't feel this good but it does.

I can feel his cool breath against my ear as he whispers, "You're a guest here. It's not your job to clean."

I swallow thickly, confused as to how a simple touch—a single sentence—can bring out so many foreign emotions in me. My heart is racing, my head is foggy, and holy shit, between my legs is buzzing with the possibility of getting attention. It's been almost a year since I've been this close to a man, and almost four years since I've actually *wanted* to be this close to a man. My brain is screaming *abort* while my vagina is screaming *yes, please!*

"It's okay. It was a mess. I don't mind." I go for nonchalant, but my words come out winded like I've just run a mile. Tristan's hands go to the curves of my hips, spinning me around to face him so my back is against the cool, granite countertop, our fronts touching, and his face only inches from mine. His knee parts my thighs and my body gets far too excited. I have to stop myself from dry humping this man's leg like a damn dog in heat. It would be far too easy to just rub my body up and down until I—

"I know you aren't ready to open up to me yet, but when you are, I'll be here. I saw it in your eyes from the moment I watched you talking to my daughter, the haunted look. I felt the sadness right here." His hand moves to my heart, laying his palm flat against my chest.

I shake my head in a futile attempt to deny his accusations, but he ignores me.

"My daughter is an excellent judge of character and she is smitten with you, which means you're now a part of our lives. If you need a friend, someone to talk to, I'm here. Okay?"

I nod in understanding and he grants me a small smile. "Good. Now let's watch a movie, one with actual adults in it. I can't take you home because I can't leave Lexi here, and I don't want to wake her up. And before you say a word, even though it's only a mile from me, you aren't taking a taxi this late at night. Mason should be home later, so I can have him watch Lexi while I take you home after the movie."

FIFTEEN

TRISTAN

AS MY KNEE PARTED HER LEGS, I FELT HER TIGHTEN AROUND ME. She wants me. But I'm not going to take her, at least not yet. A woman like Charlie would be too easy to get lost in. I need to know what she's hiding. I need to find out what makes her eyes well up with tears, what makes her space out at any given moment. It's obvious Charlie is broken, and fuck, if I don't want to be the one who puts her back together.

The woman I first saw that night at Plush was only one layer of the woman standing in front of me right now. There's no doubt in my mind, Charlie has several layers to her. She's complicated, and God knows the amount of baggage she's carrying, but none of that is going to stop me from slowly peeling back each layer of this woman until I get to the core.

Backing up, I let her walk past me as I follow her out to the living room. She walks over to the case where we keep the DVDs but pulls out a video game instead then puts it back. She pulls another one out and frowns.

"Looking for something in particular?"

"Mario Cart. I used to play it when I was younger."

"That would be the Wii U. Those are PlayStation games. But you're in luck, I have a Wii in the cabinet. I bought it for Lexi for Christmas, but she never uses it."

Charlie's eyes light up in excitement. "How about you set it up and I'll grab the Vodka I bought out of your truck?"

Chuckling, I agree, throwing her the keys. "Go for it. Nothing like some drunken Mario Cart."

I get the gaming system set up while Charlie gets the liquor from my truck. She brings it to the kitchen and calls out, "Orange juice or lemonade?"

I reply with a "Don't care" because I don't. Liquor is liquor. I'm not a big drinker and I'm okay with really anything.

She comes back in with two screwdrivers and sets them on the table. I notice her sweater has been removed and she's only wearing a tank top which must have been underneath. Without the sweater covering her upper half, I'm able to see all the curves it was hiding. Her ample breasts are even more voluptuous than I thought. Her tight tank shows the outline of her soft tummy, which has ridden up slightly, revealing just a hint of skin.

I take the drink closest to me and guzzle down half the glass. She frowns and lifts hers up to take a small sip.

"You're not an alcoholic, are you?" she asks hesitantly. I open my mouth to make a smart-ass comment, but her eyes tell me she's being serious.

"No, I barely drink."

She eyes my half-empty glass, her one brow going up.

"You took your sweater off," I grunt and she looks at me confused. *You and me both, sweetheart.*

"Okay," she says slowly looking down at herself, completely unaware how damn hot she looks. "Ready to get your ass handed to you in Mario Cart?"

It's the first time I've heard her come close to being silly, but even as she says it, the words come out serious like it's hard for her to joke around.

"You're crazy! I'm a guy."

"What the hell is that supposed to mean?"

"I'm a ten-year-old boy in a twenty-seven-year-old man's body." I shrug because it's the truth, and any guy who tries to deny it is full of shit.

"So, you think because you're a man-child you'll beat me?" She looks at me incredulously.

"Pretty much."

Her head tilts to the side slightly. "How much are you willing to bet on that?"

"What are we talking here?"

"If I win, you have to let me paint Lexi's room." Her bet confuses the hell out of me, but I don't ask questions right now. I'm more concerned with what I will get *when* I win.

"Okay. And if I win, you kiss me," I blurt out and then wait for her reaction. It'll tell me if the chemistry I felt in the kitchen is one-sided or if she wants me the same way I want her.

Her eyes practically pop out of her head, her brows lifting in shock. Her mouth twitches like she's unsure whether to frown or smile, but she quickly composes herself refusing to give anything more away.

"Fine," is all she says.

I nod. *Game on.*

We sit on the couch next to each other, close but not close enough to touch. I start the game and we pick out players. Most women would pick one of the more girly players like Toadette or the princess, but not Charlie, she picks ugly as fuck Bowser. I pick the toad and hit start.

Charlie leans forward, completely focused, and when the screen blinks *start* her character peels out. I press the button for the gas and my character follows hers, quickly catching up. With one eye on the screen and the other on Charlie, I chuckle when her nose scrunches up and her eyes turn into nothing more than slits out of anger as my guy flings green turtle shells at hers. I'm not sure if she's determined to win for the sake of winning or if she wants to ensure I don't kiss her. I doubt painting my daughter's room is that big of a deal.

"Seriously?" she groans. "They keep giving me crappy banana peels! What am I supposed to do with that behind you?"

When I shoot a path of banana peels at her, Bowser goes flying all over and Charlie huffs in annoyance. It's adorable how serious she's taking this game. With only one lap to go, I know I have her beat, and she must know it too, because she leans over and tries to swipe the controller out of my hand. I'm too quick, though, and she falls to the side, her controller dropping to the ground. I let go of mine and, grabbing her by the waist, start tickling her ribs.

"Tristan, stop!" she tries to say, but it comes out muffled from her laughing so hard. I continue tickling her. Her laughter is loud and melodic and it has me grinning at how fucking beautiful she looks right now—happy and carefree as if she doesn't have a single worry in the world.

"Oh my God! Please!" Her laughter continues, and I finally stop.

"You're a damn cheater." I chuckle while she struggles to catch her breath. I quickly grab my controller to finish the race and she does the same.

We get to the finish line and I consider slowing down to let her win, but my competitive side wins out and I cross the line slightly before her. Charlie dramatically drops her head in defeat and says, "Damn it. I was so close." I glance over at her and she looks genuinely upset, and the kiss I was excited for minutes ago doesn't feel much like a prize anymore. It does, however, answer my question as to whether she feels the way I do, which is clearly a big fat no.

"Um, I need some more to drink." She grabs her glass and hightails it out of the room before I can even tell her I'm not about to make her pay up. I shouldn't have made that bet in the first place. I should only want Charlie to kiss me because she wants to, not because of some elementary school style bet we made.

While she's in there, my mind shifts to the last woman I wanted who didn't want me back. I never pushed Bella to be with me, but she knew how I felt. She knew I wanted more, but she didn't reciprocate those feelings. Then thoughts of Gina pop into my head. The way she begged and pleaded for something I wanted no part of. I have learned over the years you can't make someone want you. There's nothing Gina could've done that would've changed my mind. And as far as Bella goes, I never begged her to be with me and I'm sure as hell not going to beg this woman for anything. She's already all over the place as it is. The last thing I need is to get involved with someone who isn't all in, and in the end, hurting my daughter.

When Charlie returns a few minutes later, her glass is filled back up. She doesn't make eye contact with me and it confirms my decision to let the bet go. I shoot a text to Mason asking him how late he'll be so I can get Charlie home. His response is immediate.

Mason: I know it's been awhile but don't worry, your dick will come back up soon and you'll last longer the next time.

Fucking asshole.

Me: It's not like that. Lexi fell asleep and I don't want Charlie taking a cab back to her place.

Mason: I'll try to make it quick, but I can't make any promises. Great stamina and all that.

"Mason said he should be home in a little bit. Want to watch something on the television?" I'm already grabbing the remote and flipping through the channels before Charlie answers.

"Sure." She takes another sip of her drink and then gets situated on the couch. Note to self: This is why I don't bring women here around Lexi. Because it's awkward as fuck when I can't take them home.

It's Saturday night so of course there's nothing on but reruns of crap television. I find an old episode of Vampire Diaries on, and leave it there. My sisters love this stupid show. Charlie drinks some more of her screwdriver while silently watching the show for a few minutes, when I feel the couch sink next to me, Charlie scooting closer.

"Did I do something wrong, Tristan?" she whispers. I turn to face her, and she has a look of dejection in her eyes I want to take away. I want to worship her body until she knows just how wanted she is. How could she even think that? She was the one upset about the prospect of having to kiss me. Jesus, I sound like a fucking whiny kid right now.

"No." I shake my head. "You didn't do anything. I shouldn't have made that bet."

Charlie frowns then shocks the shit out of me when she slowly climbs into my lap. Her thick lashes hide her gorgeous eyes as she looks down shyly. "Because you don't really want to kiss me?"

Has she lost her fucking mind? Who the fuck wouldn't want to kiss her? My eyes dart to her plump lips wondering how delicious they would taste. Maybe I had it all wrong. Maybe she does want me.

"I didn't think you wanted me to kiss you." My thumb rubs across her bottom lip feeling the softness. I haven't even touched her and my dick is already hard. She parts her lips and darts her tongue out to lick my thumb, taking it into her mouth and sucking on it softly before releasing it. I smell the alcohol on her breath, sweet and cold like lemonade on a hot summer day. It would be so easy to drink her up, savoring every last drop, but no matter how badly I want this woman to hydrate me, nothing can happen. The alcohol on her breath confirms that. It's more than likely giving her false confidence she wouldn't have if she were sober.

"I wanted to paint Lexi's room for her." She pouts. I'm not sure why the hell she wants to paint my daughter's room so badly but with the look she's giving me right now, she can paint this whole damn house if it means she'll never have that look of disappointment on her face again.

"Kiss me, Tristan," she murmurs. "Please." Her tongue darts out to wet her lips, forcing me to lose all resolve.

Pulling her close, my lips brush against hers. They're soft and sugary just like I knew they would be. She sighs in contentment, her lips parting just enough for my tongue to push into her open mouth. My tongue swirling with hers, sending me on a sugar high from her taste alone. Her hands come up to my neck and she breaks the kiss, her lips moving to place open-mouthed kisses along my jawline and down my neck. My hands move down, squeezing the globes of her ass through her denim and pulling her in closer. Needing more contact. One damn taste and this woman already has me addicted.

The door swings open and Charlie jumps—my hands holding her in place.

"Did I misunderstand the text? Was it an invitation? If you wanted to have a threesome you should've told me. I would have come back a hell of a lot sooner."

Groaning, I drop my head to Charlie's chest. I can't see her, but I can feel her silent laughter shaking throughout her body. "Let's get you home."

Charlie climbs off me—her cheeks tinted pink from the embarrassment of Mason walking in on us—and grabs her sweater from the chair, throwing it back on.

"I'll be back," I tell Mason, closing the door behind us, thankful I stopped drinking after my first large sip. Otherwise, Mason would have to take her home for me.

The quick drive to Charlie's apartment is silent. The sexual tension palpable. It would be so easy to get wrapped up in this woman—in her warmth. But then what? She has secrets she doesn't trust me with yet. Now that she's no longer in my house, on my lap, I'm able to think with the right head, and I can't let a woman in my life—into my daughter's life—who isn't all in. But at the same time, I can't be with her with no strings attached. Most red-blooded males would throw caution to the wind, but that's not who I am. It's not how I was raised, and I can't in good conscience allow this woman to become some notch on my belt, no matter how much I want her. I meant it when I said she needs to be handled with care. I don't care what her occupation is, I'm not about to treat her like a piece of ass. I need to proceed slowly and hope over time she'll trust me enough to let me in.

I pull up to her loft and she gives me a quick smile then opens the door. This time I grab her hand, not letting her get away. "Can I walk you up?"

"I don't think that's a good idea." She frowns slightly and I want to argue as the image of her in my lap, us kissing, then her kissing down my face and neck, runs on replay. And fuck, do I want her. Now that I've had a preview of what it could be between us, I need the full-length version.

"Okay." I nod in understanding. Then I add, "Go out with me."

She looks at me incredulously. "Are you serious?" She's asking me a question but the way she asks feels like she's not really asking.

"Umm… yeah?"

"Are you not sure?"

"No… I mean…yes. I'm sure. Fuck, you're driving me crazy." I shake my head completely lost in this conversation, chuckling under my breath.

"Go out with me," I say again. "I want to get to know you. Please. One date."

She takes a deep breath, looking torn.

"What's going on?"

"You asked me to keep my *occupation* away from Lexi. Then you invite me over. You bet me for a kiss. And when we pulled up here you asked to walk me up. Now you're asking me out. If you're hoping for a quick lay, I'm not that woman, Tristan. I can't be that woman, but at the same time I can't be anything more." The last part comes out in a whisper. This woman isn't making any sense. She doesn't want to be a quick lay, yet she can't be more?

"I never should've said what I said to you. I told you I wasn't judging you while I was judging you. I'm sorry. I don't care that you're a stripper. I know there's more to you than that, and I don't want you for a quick fuck." She flinches at the word fuck. "I know we just met, but I want to get to know you."

Charlie bites down on her bottom lip, slowly releasing it. "You would seriously be okay with dating a woman who takes her clothes off"—I'm liking that visual—"and gives guys lap dances for money?" Jesus! Now I have a visual of her dancing topless for other men. And then a sobering thought hits me... how would I ever compete with all of those guys she meets every night? I can't... I won't... and I'll just end up in the same situation I was in with Bella and Gina.

She doesn't even let me answer before she says, "It was really great hanging out with you and Lexi today, but I don't think us taking this... whatever this is... any further is a good idea." She leans over and gives me a chaste kiss on my cheek before jumping out of my truck and running up to her loft, not once looking back, and I think to myself that maybe it's for the best. But somewhere deep inside of me, thinks the opposite, like I just missed out on something that could've been amazing.

I get back to the apartment and Mason is in the living room playing Mario Cart. "I forgot all about this game. I used to play this when I was little, but when it was on the Super Nintendo. Remember that one?"

"Yeah, I do. I used to go over to Bella's and play." I grab the controller and Mason starts the game over again.

"How'd it go? You two looked hot and heavy when I walked in. Your text made it sound like it was a dud." Instead of playing the racing game, he chooses battle mode and selects the course.

"She's all over the place, man. Hot and cold. I don't know. Maybe it's me." I shoot off a red turtle and it pops one of Mason's balloons.

"How would you even know it's you? You've never given a woman the time of day. Every few months, you meet a woman, fuck her, then never call her again. The only women you talk to on a regular basis are Bella, your sisters, and your mom." Mason's guy shoots three green turtles at me and my balloon pops.

"Coming from the ultimate manwhore himself." I pop another one of his balloons.

"I didn't say you were a manwhore. I know what I am and I own up to that shit. I don't want to settle down. I don't want a family." He pops another one of my balloons. "I don't want kids or the white picket fence or any of that bullshit. But that's me. You, on the other hand—" My last balloon pops and my guy wipes out in defeat. I chuck the controller to the floor, suddenly feeling way too annoyed over a stupid video game. Mason turns to face me and he looks more serious than I've ever seen him. "You want that shit. You wanted it with Bella, and you wanted it with Gina."

"What the fuck are you talking about?" I stand and Mason does as well.

"Before you made the decision to play hero with Bella, you were dating Gina. The words 'I love you' were used. The only reason why you pushed her away was because she was heavy into drugs and then she got caught on her knees giving her dealer a blow job. Everyone has a hard limit and yours is betrayal. She betrayed you."

"What's your point?"

"My point is, you love with all your goddamned heart. You loved Gina and you loved Bella, both of which didn't deserve you. You moved me in with you even though I'm a pain in your ass, and you give Lexi every part of you. You love with every piece of you and you got fucked. Bella fucked you over and so did Gina. It's easy to love Lexi because she can't hurt you, and me, I'm just your best friend. We're safe."

Mason stares at me and I don't know what to say. He's right. I've spent the last five years acting like I don't care but I do. Bella apologized and I took her back as my friend, but I never really got over how deep her betrayal cut me. Gina walked away from Lexi and I pretended to shake it off, all the while hating her for hurting my daughter. I never imagined this is how my life would end up. I want everything Mason says he doesn't. I want the family and the kids and the white picket fucking fence. I want what my parents have, but both women I gave my heart to didn't give a fuck about anyone but their damn selves.

I don't blame Bella. She never asked for my heart. But it still fucking hurt. And Gina… fuck! I would've forgiven her for running to Marco, telling him he was the father of Bella's baby, but then she had to go and fuck her dealer. After not being enough for Bella, Gina choosing her drug dealer over me was just too much. I thought maybe she would get it together once she found out she was pregnant, but in the end she chose drugs over her own kid. What mother does that? A selfish one who doesn't deserve to have her daughter in her life. And I got my wish, her the fuck out of Lexi's life, but at what cost? What happens one day when Lexi asks about her mom? How do I explain the woman who gave birth to her didn't love her enough to stick around?

"I don't want Gina or Bella."

Mason chuckles, shaking his head. "Thank fuck because that's not where I was going with this. My point is, you keeping women at arm's length at the chance it could be more will never get you and Lexi that family you want. You're so scared you guys will get hurt, you don't even give a woman a chance to show you she won't hurt you. You're always one step ahead waiting for it to happen."

"Because it did happen!"

"Yeah, it did. About time you admit it."

"I let Charlie in today."

"Yeah, after you treated her like shit because she's a dancer and giving her crap for showing up late. Then you let her run away when the ice cream place was closed. I bet you didn't even get her number when you dropped her off." Mason lifts a knowing brow.

Fuck, he's right. "No, I didn't. And you know why? I wasn't enough for Bella. I wasn't enough for Gina. Both of them turned to someone else. And Charlie spends every day entertaining a variety of men. I would never be enough for her. She'll eventually turn to someone else as well. And on top of that, she's hiding shit. I can't fucking deal with another woman fucking me over!"

"You've known the woman for like a minute. And instead of giving her a chance to open up to you, you'd rather condemn her now. Stick her into the box with Bella and Gina. And who the fuck cares if she's a stripper! Everyone needs to pay their bills. Stop making excuses. She could be the one and you aren't even giving her a chance. Give her a fucking chance."

"So, does all this advice mean you're considering settling down?" I laugh, dropping onto the couch and scrubbing my hands over my face. Mason drops down next to me.

"Nah, it's not for me, man. Relationships mean trusting someone else to make you happy. You have to compromise and sacrifice a piece of yourself to give to someone else in order for them to be happy. I just don't have it in me." Mason shrugs. "I can't be in charge of someone else's happiness."

He stands and heads down the hallway. As I watch him walk away, I wonder if he has any idea how many times he's taken from himself to give to Lexi and me. How many days he's made plans but changed them because of me and my daughter. I wonder if he has any idea how much he's contributed to my daughter's and my happiness. I consider pointing it out to him but don't. One day the right woman will come along and he will give himself to her freely and it won't be called compromise or sacrifice… it'll be called love.

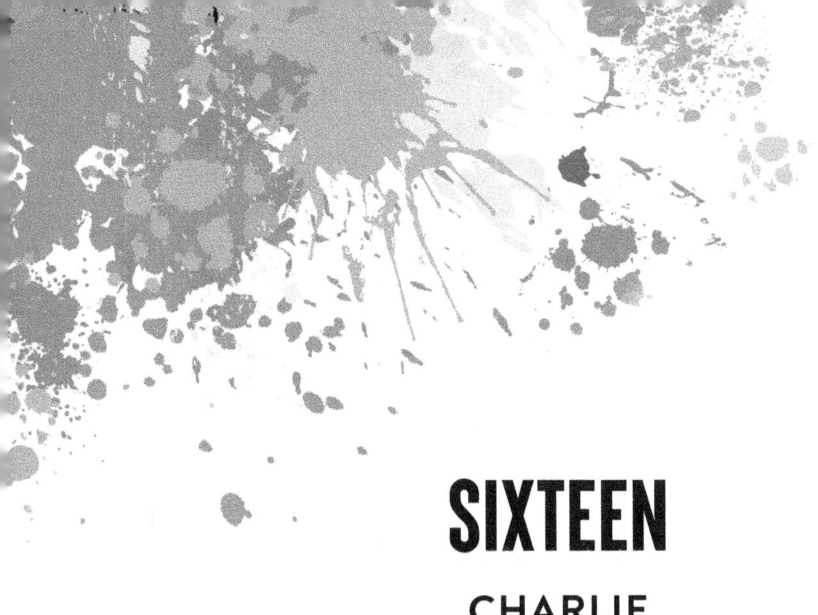

SIXTEEN

CHARLIE

IT'S BEEN THREE DAYS SINCE I DROWNED MY SORROWS IN alcohol at Tristan's house, tried to jump his bones, and then told him us going on a date wouldn't be a good idea. The man probably thinks I'm freaking nuts, and I wouldn't blame him in the slightest. I'm off Sundays and Mondays from the club so I've had plenty of time on my hands to fantasize about the man. Only in every fantasy, I give us the ending I wish we would've had. The one where Mason doesn't walk in and Tristan takes me right there on the couch. Okay, if I'm honest, I might have had one… maybe two fantasies where Mason walks in and they both take me. What? I'm a woman who has had subpar sex my entire life. Let me live through my fantasies at least.

I spoke to my therapist about what happened during our session yesterday and she seems pleased with my progress. Eight months ago, I sat in her office swearing I would never be sexual with a man ever again. I couldn't imagine ever wanting sex. Justin was the second guy I was with. The first was the cliché prom night hook up with my boyfriend of three months. He had no idea what he was doing and neither did I. He took my virginity, the entire exchange lasting five minutes at most, and two weeks later we parted ways to go off to college.

My senior year of college I met Justin. Six months later, we had sex and it was okay but not something a girl would write home about… if her parents were alive… and wanted to hear about her sex life. I've never orgasmed during sex, but I read that's normal. I looked it up and several articles state over seventy percent of women don't orgasm through penetration alone. I know I can orgasm through masturbation since I've done it myself, but Justin never cared enough to bring me to an orgasm. Sex with my husband went from okay to robotic and eventually it was so bad, I would just tune it out completely. Most of the time we had sex, he would finish in mere minutes not even caring if I came.

I'm curious to find out if most men are selfish in bed like Justin, or if they're more like the men in the romance books I've been binge reading the last several months. I'm not getting my hopes up, but it would be nice to experience an orgasm at the hands of someone other than myself. I don't, however, think that will be happening any time soon and most likely not by the hands of Tristan.

"Charlie! I need a White Russian and a Manhattan," Bianca says, giving me a small smile and a wink. Bianca is a waitress here at Plush and one of the sweetest women I've ever met. She helped train me when I first started here a few months ago and was so patient with me. When I told her I had no experience, she insisted everyone has to start somewhere.

I finish making the Manhattan and pour it into its glass, then hand them both to Bianca. She places them on her tray and sashays over to the table to serve the men sitting in her section. It's Tuesday night and the club is busy. I'm working the downstairs bar with another bartender, Nick, and by the time I'm able to take my first break it's already after eleven p.m.

"Hey Nick! I'm going to take a quick fifteen." He looks my way and shoots me a smile to acknowledge he heard me. I use the restroom quickly, wash my hands, and run my fingers through my hair before sticking it up in a high ponytail. Then I grab a granola bar from my purse and scarf it down.

As I'm walking down the hallway back toward the bar, I see Tyler walking my way. He gives me a chin raise and stops in front of me. "A guy came in here looking for you." The blood flowing through my veins drains downward, my body suddenly turning cold. Please God, there's no way Justin could've found me. I've done everything right. I haven't left a single bread crumb for him to follow.

"W-what did he want?" Tyler gives me a look of concern. He doesn't know anything about my past. While I told him and Bianca a little—keeping it simple and only giving them just enough so they understood I needed to lay low because of an ex—I didn't give them any specifics.

"Hey now. It's okay." He places his hand on my shoulder and I flinch. "Sorry." He removes his hand from my body, having figured it out months ago, I don't do touching well. "It was a member… actually, a guest of a member. He came in and requested you, but I told him you aren't available."

"Oh," I say in relief.

"I know your stance on entertaining and working private parties, but you could make a killing." He waggles his eyebrows comically.

"I know, but I love bartending and suck at seduction." I laugh. "I'll leave that to the experts. I wouldn't want to give your club a bad name." I pat him on his shoulder playfully and head back to the bar wondering who came in here to request me. Could it have been Tristan? My heart picks up slightly at the thought of him coming in here looking for me.

When I get back to the bar, I see things have picked back up again, so I jump right in taking and making orders alongside Nick. Once the rush has slowed down, Bianca plops onto a stool and I pour her an ice water.

"Thank you! It's busy tonight." I nod in agreement. "We should go out one night this week. I could've sworn I saw you're off Friday night." She grins mischievously. She knows I'm off because she's the one who makes the schedule. I roll my eyes and then notice a guy sit down a couple stools over. Grabbing a menu, I place it in front of him.

"What can I get you this evening?" When I look up, sky blue eyes are dancing with laughter.

"You work here," Tristan's friend Mason states knowingly, a slight smirk quirking up on one side of his mouth.

"You know I work here. I helped host your private party the other night."

He shakes his head. "You know what I mean. You work down *here* at the bar. That's why you weren't dressed like the other women." Ahh… so he's catching on.

"And?" I challenge.

"And my boy was here requesting you… because he thinks you're an entertainer. But you aren't, are you?"

"I can't help what your *boy* assumed." I shrug and Mason throws his head back in laughter. "What can I get you to drink?"

"I'll take a Heineken." I grab a chilled glass and tip it slightly, pulling the lever up so the beer pours into the glass without all of the foam. Once it's filled to the brim, I flip the lever back down and place the glass on a coaster on the bar top.

"So, do you strip at all?" Mason asks, but before I can answer, Bianca butts in laughing.

"That's funny! Charlie taking her clothes off?" I glare her way and she laughs harder before changing the direction of the conversation. "I don't usually strip or entertain either, but for you"—she checks Mason out from head to toe, lust shining in her eyes—"I might be willing to make an exception."

"That's good to know." Mason smiles wide at Bianca's flirting. "But I'm here for my boy. I'm thinking I should shoot him a quick text and let him know I've found his alcohol-slinging Cinderella."

"Cinderella?" Bianca questions, and I groan, walking away from them to refill another member's drink. When I return Bianca is laughing.

"Charlie! You let the poor guy believe you're a stripper?"

I shrug. "He assumed… and you know what they say about people who assume." Bianca cackles and downs the rest of her water before getting back up to go check on her tables. Once she's gone, I turn to Mason. "Trust me when I tell you it's for the best. If Tristan was smart, he would forget about me and go in search of a woman who isn't as fucked up as I am." It's the first time I've acknowledged just how broken I am, but he needs to know what his friend is trying to get himself into.

Mason shakes his head and takes a sip of his beer. "You sound like Tristan."

"So, he does know how messed up I am."

"No." Mason laughs humorlessly. "He believes he's just as fucked up." Somehow, I can't imagine Tristan's issues measuring anywhere near the magnitude of mine on the Richter scale of fuckedupness, but it makes me wonder about him. I haven't seen Lexi's mom around, nor have either of them mentioned her. Just as Tristan doesn't know anything about my past, the truth is I don't really know anything about his either. He appears put together. He has a nice home, a nice car, a beautiful daughter. Apparently, I'm just as guilty at assuming as Tristan is.

I leave Mason to enjoy his drink in peace while I tend to other members. Another hour goes by and Bianca is back at the bar. "So… Friday night… you, me, Club Hectic." I groan, handing her another water. "Please, Charlie, I need you as my wing woman. Please, please, please, pl—"

"Okay!" I cut her off. "Okay, fine! But only for a couple of hours."

"Yes! I will get a car service and pick you up at eight o'clock. We're going to have so much fun!"

SEVENTEEN

TRISTAN

LEXI'S ASLEEP, AND MORGAN HAS JUST LEFT WITH HER boyfriend, Adam. I had her come by to keep an eye on my daughter while I went to Plush with Mason *again* in an attempt to find Charlie. After the owner told me Charlie wasn't available, Mason suggested we stay and have a drink, but I wasn't feeling it. The last few days I've had Charlie on my brain, but it's obvious it's not going anywhere. Hell, I can't even reserve time with her. I came home and hung out with my sister until her boyfriend came to pick her up to go out for dinner. With a beer in my hand, I sulk in front of the TV watching stupid late-night shows.

The door swings open and closed, Mason entering our condo like a damn tornado. "You. Me. Club Hectic Friday night."

"Lexi," is all I say.

"Have your sister come back over. Trust me." His arms cross over his chest and he gives me a knowing smirk.

"Fine." I sigh, taking another pull of my beer, and go back to watching whatever crap is on the television.

IT'S FRIDAY NIGHT AND MY SISTER IS AT MY PLACE BABYSITTING Lexi. I'm nursing my third beer at the bar of the newest club in the area: Club Hectic. Mason's sitting next to me with a beer in his hand as well, but he keeps surveying the area like he's waiting on someone.

"You ready to tell me why we're here? Why we've been sitting here for the last hour like we're waiting on someone." Mason's about to say something when he looks over my shoulder, his smile widening.

"Because we are and she just got here." He nods so his chin juts out indicating someone is behind me. When I turn around to see who he's referring to, the sight in front of me has me cursing under my breath.

Charlie is walking toward the dance floor with another woman. She's wearing a light blue skintight dress that hugs her curves in all the right places. The dress isn't short by any means which makes it that much sexier. The front is shaped like a V showing her ample cleavage. Her hair is down in thick waves framing her face, and her makeup is done natural—a smidge of blue around her eyes to accent her dress. She smiles at whatever her friend is saying and then throws her head back in laughter. When she gets to the center of the dance floor and turns around to face her friend, I notice the back of her dress is practically missing, revealing her entire sexy back. Holy shit, this woman is fucking stunning.

"You're welcome," Mason says with a laugh before he gets up and heads toward the women. I drop my beer onto the bar top and follow him over. He must know the woman Charlie is with because he doesn't even introduce himself before joining her.

Before Charlie can turn around, I come up behind her, our bodies almost touching. I know she can be skittish, so before I pull her body against mine, I lean close to her ear and whisper, "You look stunning tonight." She jumps slightly, but once she tilts her head to the side and sees it's me, a ghost of a smile splays across her lips, her body visibly relaxing. I take that as my cue to touch her. Wrapping my arms around her waist from behind, I lean down and rest my chin on her shoulder. Her body sinks into mine.

"I should've known Mason would find us." She laughs, shaking her head. At first thought, I'm not sure what she means by that, but suddenly it all clicks. Somehow Mason knew she would be here tonight. Mason glances over at me and gives me a knowing nod.

There's a remix of throwbacks booming through the speakers in the club. The song switches to Bow Wow's *You can get it all*, and Charlie's ass sways to the music. Gliding my hands down her waist and over her hips, I stop at the sides of her thighs, our bodies dancing in sync against each other to the beat of the music. Charlie's arm comes up and her fingers wrap around my nape as she sways seductively against me.

The songs bleed together one after another until the deejay changes it up and a slower song fills the speakers. Charlie turns around, both her arms wrapping around my neck as she continues dancing, her moves slowing down to match the rhythm of the song. My hands go to her ass and I'm surprised when she doesn't stop me. I pull her close until my knee is situated between her thighs, and leaning into her, my mouth grazes her earlobe so she can hear me over the music. "I looked for you at Plush the other night but you were all booked up. You're a busy woman."

I can feel Charlie shaking with laughter at my words before she says, "I must be in high demand."

My hands tighten on her, my body almost one with hers. The thought of her being in demand for anyone other than me has me seeing red. I kiss the shell of her ear and she shivers.

"What if I want to demand your attention?"

She backs up slightly, her eyes meeting mine, and a sad smile mars her face. "I need to get a drink." The warmth of her body leaves mine, but I'm not letting her go that easily. I follow behind her to the bar. She orders a water and I order another beer then insist we take our drinks to an available table.

"How do I get on the approved list?" I ask once we're seated. She gives me a look I can't decipher then shrugs. Knowing I'm not going to get a straight answer out of her, I change the subject. "Tell me about you."

Her eyes widen for a second before she smiles softly. "What do you want to know?"

"Everything… anything. Give me something." I take a long pull of my beer.

"I was born and raised in Georgia. I went to college and graduated with a degree in art and digital design. I live in LA now and work at Plush." She shrugs. "What about you?" Her response is generic. It gives me information about her without really telling me anything about *her*. I go for the same type of answer in return.

"I was born and raised in Las Vegas. Moved to San Diego to go to college, then moved to Los Angeles to finish my degree. I own a gym and you already know I have a daughter. Why do you strip if you have a degree?"

She flinches at my question and takes a sip of her water before answering. "You do a lot of assuming, Tristan." It doesn't surprise me she's giving me another generic response.

I take her hand in mine. "Are you in trouble?"

"And the assuming continues…" she smarts.

"My mom was a stripper once. She was in financial trouble. If you're in trouble I just want to help you."

She takes her hand out of mine. "Even if I was in financial trouble, I would never depend on another person again…especially a man." Her eyes widen when she realizes that while giving me her cryptic answer, she actually gave something away. And judging by the shock in her eyes, it's something big.

"Who hurt you?"

EIGHTEEN

CHARLIE

"THE TOTAL COMES TO $238.27." I HAND THE CASHIER MY CREDIT card and she swipes it. *"I'm sorry, but it's been declined."* She hands the card back to me.

"That's weird. Okay, try this one." I hand her another card. She swipes it again but gives me the same answer. Completely embarrassed and confused, I ask her if she can please hold onto the clothes while I figure it out. She agrees.

Taking Georgia's hand, I walk us to a bench outside of the store and call Justin. *"What?"* Ever since he came home early to find the house a mess and accused me of cheating, he's been even more of a monster, not even caring who is in front of him when his true colors come out.

"My card was declined."

"Yep." That's all he says.

"I was buying Georgia some winter clothes for our upcoming trip."

"I canceled all your cards. Your job is to take care of the house and Georgia, and you aren't even doing that. For all I know you're fucking some other guy instead of taking care of my daughter. And on top of that, my mom is giving me shit about wanting another grandchild. If Georgia needs something, let me know and I'll have my assistant purchase it. Maybe once you start pulling your weight around here, you'll get your cards reactivated." He doesn't even wait for a response before he hangs up.

Having no clue how I would even explain my situation to the cashier, I leave without letting her know I won't be back for the clothes.

"Mommy, what about my new dollie?" Georgia asks as I place her into her car seat.

"Another day, baby girl." I give her a sad smile, and like the beautiful little girl she is, she just nods in understanding.

Two more weeks, I tell myself. Two more weeks, and I will never have to depend on another person again.

"Charlie," Tristan says again. "Who hurt you?"

I hold back the hot tears brewing. I need to get out of here. I need some space. "It doesn't matter. I need to go." I jump out of my seat to go in search of Bianca to let her know I'm going to head out.

"Charlie! Wait!" Tristan yells behind me. He catches up to me and goes to grab my arm but stops right before making contact, unsure of how I will react. *God, I'm so fucked up!* "Charlie, please!" I stop and turn around. "Can I at least get your number?"

Closing my eyes for a long beat, I internally debate whether this is a good idea. When I open them, Tristan is still standing there, his beautiful dark blue eyes pleading. "Please."

And in a moment of weakness, I give in. "Okay." He looks shocked I have actually agreed, but he quickly pulls his phone out—I'm sure before I can change my mind—and has me put my number in his contacts. When I'm done, I find Bianca. She's still dancing with Mason, the two of them looking like they're about to get it on right there on the dance floor.

"I'm gonna go!" I yell over the music. She frowns but nods, backing up from Mason.

"Okay, playboy, I gotta go." She reaches up and gives him a kiss on his cheek.

"You don't have to leave. I can grab a car," I insist. "It's only a few miles away."

"Nope, not happening. You go, I go." She links her arm with mine as we walk out of the club and into the chilly night. Mason and Tristan follow us out and refuse to leave until we're in a car and on our way home.

"Did you have a good time?" Bianca asks. "Mason said that guy is really into you. What's his name?"

"Tristan. I did have a good time. Thank you for dragging me out."

"Any time, sweets. That's what friends are for."

The car drops me off first and Bianca gives me a hug good night, telling me she'll see me at work. Once I'm inside my home, I take a quick shower to rinse off, change into my pajamas, then lie down in bed. As I'm putting my phone to charge, a text comes through. I told Bianca to text me once she gets home so I'm not surprised when I see her name pop up letting me know she's made it to her place. I type out a quick response saying good night. A few seconds later my phone chimes again and I assume it's Bianca, so I'm shocked when I see an unknown number.

Unknown: I can't get the image of you dancing against me in that sexy as hell blue dress out of my head.

Playing coy, I respond with: **Who's this?**

Unknown: Damn, woman, I'm wounded.

Unknown: It's Tristan

Unknown: <Insert selfie>

The image of Tristan is dark and it looks like he's lying in bed, a bunch of pillows behind his head. The image shows his entire face including his lopsided grin along with part of his chest. He's wearing no shirt. He mentioned he owns a gym, one it's obvious he takes advantage of—and I haven't even seen a full body shot of him.

I save the image to my phone and make it my contact image for him.

Tristan: You there? Did I scare you away with my ugly mug?

I laugh at this. Surely, this man knows how hot he is.

Me: Yes! You look frightful. I thought it was a pic for Halloween.

Tristan: Ha... ha... send me one back. <Insert winky face>

I've never sent a picture to a man before. Until I was with Justin, I never even owned a cell phone, never having had the money, and once I did own one, Justin wasn't the kind of guy to send playful pics. At least not with me.

Tristan: You don't have to if you don't want to. I just wanted to say good night.

Before I lose my courage, I snap a picture of me lying in bed and hit send. I cringe at the picture when I see how plain I look, but it's too late. I wait a few minutes to see if Tristan will respond and when he doesn't, I switch my volume setting to silent and set my phone down. Within minutes I'm asleep.

When I wake up, I see several texts on my phone from Tristan:

Sorry, Lexi woke up needing some water.

You look beautiful like that. Even more beautiful than you did tonight.

You must have fallen asleep... I hope you have sweet dreams, Charlie.

IT'S MONDAY MORNING AND MY DAY OFF, AND I'VE DECIDED TO enjoy my day at the coffee shop. I stopped off at the book store and picked up a new romance novel, but I'm currently regretting it. It's the second book in a trilogy and I'm ninety percent in, and it's clear the author will be leaving us with a cliffhanger. I put my book down to prolong getting to the end, and take a sip of my caramel mocha latte. Just as I'm about to pick my book back up—accepting the fact that I'm going to be waiting until the next book comes out to find out what happens with the heroine—the door chimes and in walks Tristan minus his cute mini-sidekick. I take advantage of the fact he hasn't noticed me sitting here yet…you know, to ogle him. He's wearing a white hat, that against his tanned skin makes him look even sexier—there's just something about a man in a hat. A plain white T-shirt which is stretched oh-so-perfectly against his fit body, and a pair of jeans that mold his ass just right. With his laptop bag over his shoulder, he orders at the counter then heads to the booth. As he's passing my table, he stops, looks my way then does a double take, his gorgeous lips upturning into a small, playful smile that has my belly in knots.

After I woke up Saturday morning to his messages, I got nervous and didn't end up texting him back. But I can't even tell you how many times I've pulled the shirtless image up of him on my phone.

"Fancy meeting you here," I say, trying to sound cool as a cucumber while my palms are sweating like I just ate a handful of jalapeño peppers, as I recall the picture of Tristan lying in bed with no shirt on.

Tristan pulls out the chair in front of me but stops before sitting, silently asking if it's okay.

"Please…you can be my distraction."

"And what am I supposed to be distracting you from?"

I'm about to answer when his name is called. "Hold that thought." He gets up and grabs his coffee and sandwich from the counter then sits back down.

"Okay, so back to your distraction." He grins and butterflies attack my belly.

"Cliffhanger." I hold the book up as proof before taking a sip of my coffee.

"And what kind of cliffhanger are we talking here?" Tristan takes the book from my hands, and turning to a random page starts reading.

"Grabbing me by my legs, he pulls me down the bed, and spreading my legs wide open, dives right into my pussy like I'm a feast he's devouring on Thanksgiving. His tongue hits my clit and I—"

I choke on my coffee realizing he's reading a freaking sex scene! "Oh! Okay! That's enough! Thanks!" I grab the book from him.

"And where does this cliffhanger come in? Unsure if she's going to…finish?" His eyes dance with amusement.

"No. She finishes," I answer too quickly without thinking. When I realize what I just said, I let out a groan that has him laughing in delight at my embarrassment. I'm pretty sure I'll never be able to look him in the eyes again.

"That's like the shit my mom and her friends read. My dad calls it mom-porn." The term grips at my heart.

"It's called romance," I correct him, trying and failing to keep the raw emotion out of my voice. "So, what are you doing here?" I ask, changing the subject.

He sits back against his chair assessing me. I can tell he wants to ask why the topic of romance books would cause me to get choked up, but he chooses to go with the flow. "Well, as I told you the other night, I own a gym…" I can't help but check him out some more at the mention of the gym. The image of him the other night was nothing more than a tease. It just left me parched, only giving me a mere droplet of water, when what I really need is a tall glass of this man to quench my thirst. *What the heck am I saying?*

Tristan gives me a knowing smirk and when I look away, my eyes fall downward, settling on his shirt…on his short sleeve shirt… and hello! Can you say arm-porn? Those romance novels have nothing on this man. He clears his throat and I force myself to look at his face. His eyes are laughing at me and his smile is so big there's a tiny dimple sticking out of his left cheek. It confirms my suspicions about whether he has one like Lexi.

"…and I'm here to meet with a web designer to have the website redone."

"And where's your sidekick today?"

His mouth forms into the cutest pout. "Preschool. She started last week."

"Wow! That's a big step. How are you handling it?"

He sighs and averts his eyes, staring outside for a moment. "Lexi's mom left when she was born." Whoa! Whiplash. I remain silent, letting him explain.

"Ever since Lexi was born, it's just been me and her…and Mason." He rolls his eyes when he says Mason's name, but it's obvious he cares about him like family. "I know every kid has to go to school, but I already miss her like crazy. For the last five years, she's been by my side. For the sake of not sounding like a pussy, I won't tell you how I cried for like twenty minutes after I dropped her off."

I let out a quick laugh, dabbing my eyes from the raw emotion seeping through his words. "That doesn't make you a pussy… it makes you a damn good dad. I'm sure she's having a blast."

He nods and takes another sip of his coffee. "Yeah, so far so good. She's only going two days a week right now. We'll work on adding more days if she can handle it."

"You mean if you can handle it?"

"Ha! Very funny."

His phone dings, and when he checks it, his easy-going smile quickly transforms into a look of annoyance.

"So, the other night at the club you said you majored in art and digital design? Like websites?"

"Yeah. My dream is to spend my days being creative with actual paint, but I knew I would need a degree and skills to make a living, so I got certified in digital design as well. Painting won't pay the bills." I cringe at my last sentence, remembering how many times Justin had thrown my degree in my face.

"Well, it just so happens I'm in need of a web designer. Any chance you're looking for a side job?" Tristan grins, wagging his eyebrows.

"Seriously?" I get giddy at the idea of doing something creative.

"Look." He presses a few buttons on his phone and turns it around. It's a conversation between him and *Web designer #3*.

"Number three?" I question while reading the texts. The last message is timestamped two minutes ago and the designer apologized for canceling again.

"Yeah, three people have now canceled on me. My web designer quit to go on maternity leave. She was about to revamp my page. Number two forgot to pay the renewal fee and I lost my domain and page. I got the domain back, but the page was wiped out. Number three—well, as you just read, canceled on me. So, what do you say?"

He takes a bite of his sandwich, and my eyes zero in on the strength of his jaw as he chews. Then as he swallows, my eyes move down to his sexy throat.

"Charlie?"

Holy shit! What is wrong with me? I can't stop staring at this man. "Yeah," I choke out then clear my throat. "Yeah, I can do that for you."

Tristan's face brightens. "Seriously?"

"Yeah, I can design a website in my sleep."

"Thank you."

"No problem."

We spend the next hour going over the details. I argue that I don't want to get paid, but he insists. He wants an entirely new, fresh look with up-to-date images. I let him know I can come by during the day and take pictures of the people working out, of the new rooms, et cetera. I remember I no longer have my camera, but he assures me he has one that will work. Apparently, his mom bought him an expensive camera after Lexi was born but he has no idea how to use it, so he sticks to his cell phone. After going through his calendar, we solidify a day and time.

"Well, I should probably get going. I have an appointment in a little while." And it's not a lie—I have my therapy appointment in less than an hour.

"Okay, I'll see you in a couple days."

"Definitely." I wave and make it a point to walk out the door before he does, all while chanting to myself, "Don't look back."

NINETEEN

CHARLIE

IT'S A BEAUTIFUL DAY IN LA, SO I ENJOY THE STROLL DOWN Larchmont Boulevard as I head to Tristan's gym. Fall is in full swing, the leaves are falling, and kids are already running around in their costumes even though Halloween isn't for a few more days. I see a mom and her daughters walking out of a cute children's boutique, the little girls dressed like pink princesses. A flashback hits me in full force, forcing me to sit down on the bench to catch my breath.

HALLOWEEN (LAST YEAR)

"MOM! CAN WE GO PLEASE?"

"Let me just set your dad's dinner in the microwave and then we'll go."

After putting foil over the plate of food, I grab my purse and keys. It's the weekend and it's doubtful Justin will be home, but I left food for him just in case. The last thing I need is for him to come home and not have dinner waiting for him. I remind myself we have less than three weeks until we run. I just need to get through these next couple weeks and once we leave, we'll never be found, and we will finally be free of the abuse, free to live as we want.

I find Georgia dressed and standing in the foyer, ready to go trick-or-treating. "You are the most beautiful princess, ever!" I gush.

She gives me the most adorable toothy grin. "I'm not a princess yet! Belle isn't a princess until after she meets the beast!" Only my daughter would insist on being Belle pre-princess. She said everyone always wants to be the princess at the end. She wants to be the real Belle. We couldn't find a pre-princess costume, so I ended up finding her a cute blue dress and purchasing a white apron. I hemmed the apron to fit her, and got her adorable black flats. With a big blue ribbon in place, her hair is tied back in a low ponytail.

I tap her on her nose. "That's where you're wrong. Belle was always a princess, even before she found the beast. Every girl is a princess."

"Are mommies princesses, too?"

"Umm..." I think for a moment. The short answer should be yes, but we're in the twenty-first century. Is it wrong to teach her we're all princesses? Would that be degrading to women? My answer is no, it wouldn't be. Even a working woman can be a princess. It's simply a mindset, not a career.

"Yes, every woman is a princess."

"Does that mean Daddy is a prince?" She frowns. "I think he's mean like Gaston." She scrunches up her nose and my heart breaks. This is why in a couple weeks I'm going to get my baby girl out of here. She's getting too old and too smart, and I'll be damned if she's going to grow up believing all dads are Gastons when she should be thinking of her father as a prince. Not wanting to put her father down and risk her saying anything to him, I change the subject.

"Oh no! It's already six o'clock! We better get going."

Thankfully, she lets it go, grabbing her candy bag, and we head out for some trick-or-treating. For the next two hours, we walk up and down the street. Georgia knocks on each door saying, "Trick-or-treat," and after getting candy, she says, "Thank you." Once she's exhausted, we drive back home. I put her to bed and place the candy in the fridge for tomorrow.

Justin walks through the door the next morning while I'm making breakfast and I'm shocked to see him. The first thing he does when he reaches into the fridge to get a bottle of water is throw the candy into the garbage. "Wouldn't want her to end up a fat cow like you," is all he says before he walks into his office, closing the door behind him.

TWENTY

TRISTAN

I'VE SPENT THE LAST FEW HOURS PICKING UP THE GYM TO MAKE sure it's picture perfect before Charlie gets here. I've let the guys know if they see her taking photos to keep doing what they're doing. The janitor service I use was here last night but I still wanted to double check everything.

"Hey, Scott! Want to ref for us?"

I check the clock and it shows it's ten 'til eleven. Charlie should be here soon, but I have enough time to referee a few rounds with Mason and Isaac. They're in different but close weight classes and both of them are fighting in the upcoming UFC fight in a few months. Fighting in the gym is similar to an actual fight but gloves and head gear are used. It's mostly practicing the moves and skills along with the follow through but without shedding blood.

"Sure." I step into the octagon and they meet me in the middle. After bumping fists, I move out of the way and they start circling each other. Mason throws a punch and Isaac blocks it, then he wraps his arms around Mason effectively taking him to the ground. Of course this pisses Mason off because Isaac is new and Mason is one cocky son of a bitch. He's out of the hold in seconds and throws another punch to Isaac's jaw, connecting way too hard. I'm about to call it when Isaac comes at Mason and decks him straight in the face. Mason stumbles back a couple steps before he springs forward with a round house kick to Isaac's temple, knocking him on his ass.

What the fuck?

Just as I'm about to break them up because this has obviously turned personal, I hear a blood curdling scream. My eyes dart up from the guys now rolling on the ground beating the shit out of each other, to Charlie. Her hands are over her mouth, her eyes wide as saucers, and she looks about ten shades paler than usual. Her gaze goes from Mason and Isaac still fighting to me before she turns around and runs, swinging the door open and not looking back.

What the hell?

"Hey!" I shout. The guys ignore me, so I jump in the middle, throwing Mason off Isaac. They fall onto their asses, panting. "What the hell!" I don't wait for either of them to answer before I jump down, out of the octagon, to run after Charlie. "Brent!" I yell as I'm running out the door. "Make sure the two children stay away from each other."

I get outside and look to my left and then my right. I spot her sitting on a bench, her head hanging down. Her hands are covering her face and I can see even from a distance her breathing is labored. Sprinting over to her, I sit next to her on the bench.

"Charlie." My voice is soft. She doesn't say anything at first, her head remaining down. Her breathing is loud and her sobs are even louder. I'm about to put my arm around her but think better of it, pieces of the puzzle coming together.

Charlie getting upset when she knocked the picture down.

Flinching when I approached her.

Thinking I might hit her.

Screaming at the sight of Mason and Isaac fighting.

I would bet in some way Charlie has suffered some type of physical or emotional abuse. By the way she shrank back the night in my house when she thought I was going to strike her, and how upset she got over seeing the guys fighting, I'm leaning toward physical.

Her sobs turn to hiccups and it sounds like she's having trouble breathing. Getting down on my knees, I kneel in front of her, gently framing her face between my hands.

"Charlie, look at me." She looks up with red-rimmed eyes as a new wave of tears race down her already stained cheeks soaking her shirt, and I release her face. "Talk to me, please."

Her bottom lip quivers and her shoulders sag in defeat. She shakes her head slowly as her gaze darts to the sky, her shaky fingers wiping her cheeks every few seconds. Sucking in a loud sniffle, she attempts to collect herself.

"I didn't know it was a fighting gym." She nervously glances down at her hands, and using my thumb and forefinger, I gently tilt her chin back up so she's forced to look at me.

"And that shocked you?" I ask, not making my assumptions known.

"I thought it was a gym where people work out."

"I'm sorry… I didn't even think to mention what kind of gym it is. Charlie, you need to tell me what's going on."

Letting out a long sigh, she says, "I can't go back in there." Her breathing picks up.

"Whoa, breathe. Don't work yourself up, please." Still on my knees, I take her delicate hands in mine. "Why can't you go in there?" I need her to say the words. Until she does, we can't move forward.

"I—I have a bad past."

"Okay. Why don't you come with me to pick up Lexi from school? We can grab a bite to eat and we can talk more after I lay her down for a nap. School's kicking her butt. Not enough coloring and too much math and writing. She swears her brain needs to sleep when she gets home." My last line is meant to lighten the mood and it works. Charlie grants me a beautiful watery smile.

"Poor thing. Doesn't the teacher understand a creative mind can't be tied down with numbers and letters?"

"My daughter just might be the first preschool dropout."

She giggles and the sound does shit to my insides.

We walk back to the gym and I have Charlie wait for me by my truck while I let Brent know I won't be back today. On my way out, I spot Mason heading toward the locker room. "You and me…we're chatting later." He nods in understanding.

Charlie is quiet on the way to Lexi's preschool. It's a small private school near Koreatown, so it only takes a few minutes to get there. When I pull up, Charlie asks me to go in by myself so she can have a few minutes to pull herself together before Lexi sees her.

Lexi's in class playing with a couple of kids whose parents haven't picked them up yet. When I walk in, she spots me immediately, dropping whatever toy she was holding, and running over to me. "Daddy!" she shrieks in excitement. I bend down to give her a hug, her little arms wrapping around my neck as I pull her into my arms, taking her up with me as I stand.

"My brain hurts, Daddy! I did a whole big page of counting a million numbers and shapes and colors! I had to count all the pretzels and candies before I could eat them." She huffs and I stifle my laugh.

"Sounds like a busy day."

We say goodbye to her teacher, and when we get to the truck, I open the back door so she can climb into her booster seat. I know the minute she notices Charlie in the truck, because even with the door closed, I can hear the excited sound of Lexi shrieking.

When I get around to my side, I open the door and Lexi is already telling Charlie all about her being forced to count before being allowed to eat. This time, though, her story is played out even more dramatic and Charlie is a good sport, going along with it. Her eyes widen at the right times and when Lexi's hands come up to her head to emphasize her brain hurting, Charlie covers her mouth with her hand.

"Oh no! Then I guess we can't go where I was thinking of going." Charlie pouts. I have no idea what she's talking about or where she was planning on going.

I quirk a brow up and she winks.

"Well… maybe my brain doesn't hurt so much," Lexi says slowly.

"No? Oh, thank goodness. Because I saw this flyer"—she pulls a piece of paper out of her purse—"and it says today until five o'clock there's a huge art show at the museum."

"Nope! My brain doesn't hurt anymore!" Lexi shakes her head. "Can we go, Daddy? Please?"

Charlie hands me the flyer. "It was on the bulletin board in the neighborhood. I thought maybe we can go and then get something to eat." She pauses suddenly and I look up from reading the flyer to look at her. Her teeth are nervously worrying her bottom lip and I don't like it. It's one thing to be shy or nervous because you don't know someone, but if my suspicions are correct, Charlie's nervousness is due to abuse. She's unsure of whether I'll get upset at her suggestion. "I'm so sorry! I should've asked you first…"

"Stop. It's a great idea. Let's go."

"Okay, but I really am sorry. I wasn't thinking. I know better than that…"

It sounds like she's going to say more, but she doesn't.

"Hey." I turn toward her. "In a way, you're right. It's always best to talk about plans with each other before mentioning it to the kid in case it can't happen, but you wouldn't know that. You don't have kids. And you were obviously excited to share this with her. It's all good."

Charlie frowns but nods. She buckles in and looks out the window not saying anything more the entire drive to the art museum in Pasadena. The woman is way too hard on herself and it needs to stop. Sometimes her actions show her strength, like the night she came over, when she drank and climbed onto my lap. I know she was drunk, but you know what they say: *The drunk mind speaks a sober heart.*

Or when she looks so sad but holds it together for my daughter. Some might think the tears are a sign of weakness but the way she holds them back, refusing to let them fall and show her sadness, it's a strength. Other times, she wears her weaknesses on her sleeve. Running from the gym is the perfect example. I don't know what has her afraid, but I'm going to make it my mission to take those weaknesses and turn them all into strengths. My mom was abused by my biological father when I was a baby but she refused to be weak. However, she had her friends and family, and then Kaden came into the picture. Charlie doesn't seem to have anybody. But she does now. She has me and Lexi, and if she lets us in, we'll be there for her. Which reminds me…

"Charlie." She turns toward me. "Don't think I forgot about us needing to talk later." She nods in understanding.

We spend the afternoon at the museum and both girls are in art heaven. There's painting and coloring. They have games and takeaways—arts and crafts the kids can make and take home. Lexi paints a ceramic unicorn and Charlie paints a candy corn. They're laughing and having a blast. I spot an art book I'd like to get for Lexi, so I lean down to Charlie and whisper into her ear, making sure Lexi can't hear me, "I'm going to go to the bookstore real quick."

Her head pops up, a frown quickly forming. "No!" she shouts loud enough that everyone sitting at the table, painting, looks over.

"No, you need to stay here." She speaks softer this time but her voice is wobbly, almost fearful. Not wanting to make a scene, I nod in understanding and stay seated.

After the girls are done painting, their pieces are sprayed with a sealant and we make our way out. I stop by the bookstore as I had planned, but instead of surprising Lexi, I show it to her. She loves it and the entire drive home she shows the pages to Charlie.

"Dinner?" I ask to make sure we're still on the same page, and Charlie smiles in agreement. During the week, I usually cook, so once we're inside I go about making dinner as I normally would. When I come out to check on them, after throwing the stuffed peppers into the oven, I spot Lexi and Charlie on the couch watching television. Lexi is fast asleep, her little legs sprawled out over Charlie's thighs. Her arms are over her head and she's snoring softly.

"She fell asleep a few minutes ago."

Picking her up, I bring her to her room and lay her down under the blankets. It's already almost seven so more than likely she'll be out for the night. Luckily, she ate a ton of snacks at the museum so she won't wake up too hungry in the morning.

Once I'm done putting Lexi to bed, I set out a couple of plates and silverware, then check the fridge to see what I can offer Charlie to drink. "We have beer, juice, milk, or water."

"A beer actually sounds good. It's been years since I've had one." I grab two beers from the fridge, handing one to Charlie, who is still sitting on the couch watching a kid show.

"The peppers have about thirty minutes. Can we talk now?" I turn the television off and sit next to Charlie. She takes a long sip of her beer and nods. "You mentioned you have a bad past. Can you elaborate?"

Charlie chugs half the beer, closes her eyes, and then after taking a deep breath, reopens them. Her words come out robotic, but at least I've finally got her talking. "I was in an abusive relationship for several years. I left him almost ten months ago."

"Emotionally or physically?"

"Both. Most days I feel like I'm healing, finally getting over the way he treated me, but I guess seeing two people fighting, purposely hurting each other, triggered memories I've been trying to leave in the past."

"I know the fighting looks bad, but I can assure you Mason isn't a violent man. He would never hurt someone outside of the gym."

"Do you fight?"

"No. I train the fighters occasionally. Mostly Mason. I grew up in a gym, but I don't fight anymore."

"I think the fighting just caught me off guard," she admits. "I walked in and they were beating the crap out of each other. Flashbacks of being hit came back in full force."

Taking her small hands in mine, I edge closer. "Thank you for opening up to me. For telling me." Charlie nods silently. "I want to help you." When she doesn't say anything, I continue. "Come in to the gym after hours and I'll give you self-defense lessons. Just you and me. I read that many women in abusive relationships learn to defend themselves. It helps to make them feel stronger. And while you're there, you can do the pictures for the website."

"You read about abusive women?" Shit! I shouldn't have added that part. I might as well come clean.

"You showed some signs… flinching when the picture fell…I didn't want to assume, but I had a feeling. I was hoping I was wrong, but I did some research just in case I was right."

"Why would you do that?" She doesn't sound mad, more like in awe, which confuses me. Needing her closer to me, I pick her up and place her onto my lap, her legs straddling me.

"Because I want you in my life. I don't care if it's as a friend or something more." *Please, let it one day be something more…*

"There's…things in my past. I'm not good for you and I'm definitely not good for Lexi." Her head drops and I pick it up, forcing her to look at me.

"Let me be the judge of that."

Charlie moves slightly against me and my dick twitches at the friction between our bodies, not getting the memo this isn't meant to be a sexually intimate moment. I inwardly groan and move Charlie back onto the couch so I can take the peppers out of the oven. She needs me to go slow. She's only been away from the abuse for less than a year and I need to remember that.

As I'm standing up, her hand grips my arm. "Thank you." She leans in and places a kiss on my cheek. "Thank you for caring enough to look into it."

As we're sitting down to eat, Mason comes strolling in. "Honey buns! I'm home and I smell something delicious!" He enters the dining room and grins when he spots Charlie. "Oh…am I interrupting something?"

Rolling my eyes, I say, "Yeah, a peaceful dinner. Peppers are on the stove. Grab some and join us."

Sitting down with a plate of stuffed peppers, Mason asks the obvious. "Where's my Lexi girl?"

"She had a big day. School and the art museum. She's asleep."

"I'm sure she'll be sad she missed your stuffed peppers," Mason jokes because Lexi hates all things healthy.

"You care to explain what happened at the gym today?" I take a bite of my food.

Mason waves it off. "Isaac was just pissed I—" He looks over to Charlie, smirks, and he says, "caught his fish."

I groan. "Bro, stop using that damn term."

"Oh my God!" Charlie laughs. "I haven't heard that in years. Catch and release, right?"

"See! Even your woman thinks it's clever."

Since Charlie doesn't look uncomfortable at the assumption she's my woman, I don't comment on it.

"When I was in college at A&M, guys would say that, or some of the cowboys would refer to it as steer roping."

Mason laughs. "That's a good one! I like you." He points to Charlie. "What are you doing with this serious guy? You should let me take you out and show you a good time." He winks, and if I thought he was serious, I'd reach over and punch him.

"Ha! I think I'm good. I prefer the dry land if you catch my drift." She winks back at Mason and it's fucking adorable.

"Oh, but I can assure you, the wetter the better," Mason volleys back. They playfully shoot fishing innuendos back and forth while we finish dinner. Charlie's personality is coming out more and more and it's definitely a sight to behold.

"I'm in for the night. Why don't I watch Lexi while you bring Charlie home?"

I look at Charlie and she's suddenly shy. Not wanting her to feel obligated to invite me up, I say, "All right. If I end up staying out later, I'll let you know."

As we're bringing the dishes to the sink, out walks a sleepy Lexi. "Daddy... my tummy is growling so loudly."

"Okay, sweetie. I'll get you something to eat."

"Thank you." She looks around and adds, "But my tummy isn't growling for peppers."

Charlie giggles. "What is your belly growling for, silly girl?" she asks.

Realizing for the first time, Charlie's still here, Lexi smiles. "Charlie! You're here. Did my daddy make you eat peppers?" Her nose scrunches up.

"I am and he did. But they were so delicious."

Lifting her onto the counter, I set her down then set out to make her a sandwich.

"My belly doesn't like peppers. It likes... peanut butter and fluff!" She smiles brightly. My daughter thinks she's so slick, and if she hadn't been sleeping through dinner, I would've made her eat them, but it's already after eight and I'm not about to fight that battle.

"It does, does it?" Charlie giggles some more at Lexi's antics.

"Lexi girl! What are you doing awake?" Mason walks into the kitchen, giving Lexi a kiss on her forehead.

"My belly was screaming so loudly, Uncle Mason."

"What was it screaming?"

"Peanut butter and fluff!" She says it in a squeaky voice, pretending it's her belly doing the talking.

Mason chuckles, handing me the marshmallow fluff. I make her a sandwich and pour her a glass of milk.

"Go ahead and take off, man. I'll wait for her to eat then put her back to bed."

"You sure?"

"Yeah, go." He turns to Lexi. "Look what came in the mail today." He holds up the package we've been waiting on from Amazon.

"Yes! Is that my costume? Gimme!" She puts her hands out, her tiny fingers wiggling in excitement. Mason stretches his arm out before pulling it back quickly.

"What's the magic word?"

"Please!" she shrieks and he hands the bag over.

Lexi rips the bag open. "Look!" she squeals, holding out her costume. She changed her mind over a dozen times, and by the time she finally knew what she wanted to be, the costume store was sold out. Thank fuck for Amazon's next day shipping.

"Wow! Lexi, that costume is awesome." Charlie takes it from Lexi and assesses it. It's a painter's cap, an apron covered in splattered paint, and to finish the costume, there's a paintbrush and an artist palette.

"It's an artist!" Lexi says through mouthfuls of sandwich she's scarfing down. She swallows another bite and then says, "Charlie! Can you go trick or treating with us?"

Charlie sets Lexi's costume down slowly. "Umm...well..."

"Lexi," I say, cutting off Charlie because this is starting to sound a lot like the last time Lexi invited her somewhere, and it's not fair to put her in that position again. I imagine she likes kids well enough because she wouldn't have recommended we take Lexi to the art museum if she didn't, but for some reason, she seems to get uncomfortable when we invite her places. "Charlie doesn't have kids, so she probably doesn't want to spend her night trick-or-treating." Lexi pouts but doesn't argue.

"I need to bring Charlie home. Mason's going to stay with you. Finish your sandwich and then it's bedtime."

"Thank you, Daddy, for the costume!" She gives me a hug before pulling me down by my shirt so she can kiss my cheek.

"You're welcome, Lex. Love you."

"Love you, too."

I set her on the ground and she runs over to Charlie, wrapping her arms around her waist.

"Bye, Charlie. See you soon! And I hope you come with me trick-or-treating."

"Bye, sweet girl."

I pull up in front of where Charlie lives and I can see how nervous she looks so I don't ask to come up. Instead I ask, "When's your next day off?"

"Umm… Sunday."

"How about Sunday afternoon I'll make sure the gym is cleared out and you can take your pictures then, and I can teach you a couple moves?"

Charlie nods in agreement, giving me a small smile. "Okay, sounds good."

TWENTY-ONE

CHARLIE

right?"

It's Sunday afternoon and I'm standing in the middle of Tristan's gym. It's the first time I've ever seen a gym where people go to practice fighting. When I walked into the gym last week and saw the two guys fighting, I freaked out and ran before getting a good look at the place. For some reason when I imagined the gym, I pictured some dingy warehouse looking area with concrete floors and punching bags. But the gym I'm standing in looks nothing like that.

"Yeah. I bought it a few years ago and had it all renovated." Tristan smiles proudly.

In one area, there's a beautiful drink bar where the fighters can order several types of smoothies and shakes. Using the camera Tristan lent me, I snap a bunch of photos.

"I think I should come back and take some photos of the fighters ordering and drinking. It will look more real. But for now, I can use these."

I walk over to another area that contains what looks like state of the art work out equipment and continue to take picture after picture. Then I move over to the big roped-in area where I saw the two guys fighting the other day, and take some more. Tristan continues to show me around as I snap way more pictures than I will need for the website, to be on the safe side. We go through each locker room, the bathrooms, the physical therapy room, and then head to an area in the back.

"This is where our classes are held. We have classes for all ages including little kids." I snap a few pictures. Tristan moves to a small octagon shaped area and steps in. "I was thinking we could practice some moves in here. As you can feel"—he bounces on the balls of his feet—"the floors are soft so you can't get hurt." I'm suddenly nervous. I haven't had a chance to speak to my therapist about this yet, but I'm almost positive she'd tell me this is a good idea. For one, I'll feel prepared if I'm ever in a situation where a man tries to hurt or overpower me, and two, I'll feel stronger and more confident knowing I can at least attempt to defend myself.

"Okay." I set the camera down on the floor, then empty my pockets, placing my keys, cash, and cell phone on the floor before removing my flip-flops. When I turn to Tristan, he's doing the same. Today he's in a pair of basketball shorts, a UFC shirt, and his usual white hat. Tristan makes casual look downright sexy.

We meet in the middle of the fighting ring, and since I'm not sure what to do, I stand in place and wait for Tristan's guidance. He closes the gap between us and slowly places his hand on my shoulder. With only about six inches between us, I can smell the faint scent of his cologne and for some reason it comforts me. He gives me a soft smile. "Breathe, Charlie."

I release the breath I had no idea I was holding and he chuckles softly. "There you go. Just breathe. We'll start off slow and work our way to more difficult positions."

I nod in agreement, waiting for his instruction. "The first move I'm going to show you is an open hand strike." He takes my hand in his, and with his other hand he rubs his fingers along the heel of my hand down to my wrist.

"This move is a good one because you don't need any training. With the heel of your hand all you need to do is strike upward, downward, or to the side. The best areas are to the neck or jawline." With his hand still holding mine, he runs his fingers along my arm until he gets to my elbow.

"Keep your hand open and firm." I tighten my hand, keeping it open as he brings my arm around, softly hitting the side of his neck. "Right here." He locks eyes with me. "When you hit this area hard, it will hurt whoever is attacking you enough that you will have a chance to run." We go over the motion I should use a few times before Tristan releases my arm and hand.

"Okay, now you try. I'm going to approach you and I want you to hit me right where I showed you." He steps back and then walks toward me. When he gets close to me, I bring my hand up, wincing as it connects with his neck, and he chuckles. "Charlie, you need to pretend like I'm the enemy. I want you to try to hurt me. Nothing you do to me will kill me." I think about what he says. If Justin were standing in front of me, I would have connected a lot harder, but Tristan isn't somebody I want to hurt.

"I don't want to hurt you," I whisper, hating violence. Tears spring from my eyes and Tristan closes the space between us.

"Hey, hey, you aren't going to hurt me. But sweetheart, how can you feel prepared if you don't practice?"

"I know," I say, sniffling. "But I don't like violence. Like at all."

"It's just you and me." Tristan bends slightly, so we're eye level. "I hope you never have to use any of these moves, but I think you'll feel a lot better once you have them to use if need be. You may not like violence, but you can't stop other people from being violent. All you can do is be prepared."

He's right. I have to accept the world can be a violent, shitty place. Justin is proof of that. And if I can be prepared, maybe I can stop it from happening in the future. Maybe if I were prepared before and fought back, Justin would've stopped. I'm done being weak. I said I was ready to take my life back, ready to move forward, and in order to do that I need to be strong.

"Okay, I'm ready," I say with renewed confidence.

Tristan smiles. "All right."

He comes toward me again, and this time I bring my hand up and strike the side of his neck with more force. He stumbles to the side and I immediately feel bad.

"Oh my God! Did I hurt you?" I reach for his face, but when I look at him, he's grinning, that one stubborn dimple peeking out slightly.

"That was awesome!" Tristan beams with pride.

We spend the next hour or so going over different moves: a kick to the groin in case I'm grabbed from the front, and a bear hug and a 360 defense in case I'm being attacked from behind. Tristan is a patient instructor the entire time, telling me with every new move how good I'm doing, and showing me each move however many times I need him to.

"Okay, the last move I'm going to show you is if you're attacked while on the ground. Go ahead and lie down in the middle of the mat." I walk to the center and lie on my back, my knees slightly bent. Tristan walks over to me and positions himself above me, his legs caging me in. He bends slightly, his hands on either side of my shoulders. There's nothing sexual in what he's doing, yet I feel my legs tightening and the area between throbbing in need of something more. Tristan situates himself and then locks eyes with me. He licks his lips, about to speak—probably to give me direction—and I have no idea what the heck comes over me, but all of a sudden I'm grabbing him by his shirt, pulling him the rest of the way toward me, and kissing him with everything I have.

TWENTY-TWO

TRISTAN

I'M LEANING OVER CHARLIE, PRAYING MY DICK DOESN'T GET hard in this position, when her hand comes up and fists my shirt, pulling me down. For a second, I'm frozen in place thinking maybe she's trying out a move on me. Only I realize all too quickly, she's actually making a move on me. The woman under me is kissing me and I'm just sitting here like a damn idiot, doing nothing. Her lips are warm and soft, and a beat later mine are curving around hers, my tongue seeking entrance, hers granting access. Our tongues dance around one another and fuck if she doesn't taste sweet. Her hips come up and grind my erection as she lets out a soft moan.

Our kiss deepens, my hands moving to her hair, needing to grip something on her, but I stop short, afraid she'll cower at my touch. Instead, I let her lead as I follow. And let's be real… I'd follow Charlie any fucking where she goes. Her hand lets go of my shirt and both hands come up to my head, her fingers running through my short hair.

"Look, Uncle Mason! Daddy is loving on Charlie." The sound of my daughter's voice is like a bucket of ice water being poured right over my dick. I can feel it visibly shrinking. Charlie's eyes shoot open and she pushes on my chest. I fall to the side of her and she's standing up before I can even get up.

"Looks like Daddy is doing some fishing of his own." Mason laughs, and I let out a groan.

"Ewww! No, he's not! Charlie, do you like fishing? It's super gross and the fish are smelly and slimy." She scrunches her nose up and walks toward Charlie waiting for an answer.

"Nope, Lexi, I most definitely don't like fishing." Her voice is breathless and the knowledge that kissing me did that to her has me wanting to beat on my chest like a goddamn caveman.

"Good!" Lexi nods her approval. "But Charlie, why were you loving on my daddy?" Charlie's head swings to mine, her eyes pleading for me to help her.

"Umm…well…" Charlie stumbles on her words and I almost want to stand back and wait to hear what she says, but I don't. Instead, I come to the rescue. "I was teaching Charlie some fighting moves and she was thanking me." Okay, that probably wasn't the best explanation, but cut me some slack here. I'm improvising.

Mason cracks up laughing. "Really? Charlie, I don't know if you know this, but I'm the real fighter in this room. I can show you moves for days. Tristan here just owns the place… I'm the expert." He smiles wide and I shoot him the finger behind Lexi's back. *Fucker!* I look over to Charlie, and luckily she's silently laughing.

"I thought you were watching Lexi… at home," I say, changing the subject.

"Yeah, but you also said you would be home by seven. I have a date tonight and it's almost eight." Holy shit, I had no idea we were at this for so long.

"Damn, sorry about that. Go ahead and take off. Thanks for watching her."

"No worries. See ya, Lexi girl," Mason calls out. Before he leaves, he adds, "See ya, Charlie. No more fishing tonight you two." He gives Charlie a wink and she giggles, shaking her head.

"Ugh! I love Uncle Mason, but I really hate fishing." Lexi huffs.

"Did Uncle Mason feed you dinner?" Lexi darts her eyes to the side, which tells me he gave her junk food and she doesn't want to snitch on him. "I'm going to go use the bathroom and shut the gym down. Then we can go grab a bite to eat. Meet me in the front."

As I reach the doorway, Charlie yells, "No!" I turn around and she's walking toward me. "Take Lexi with you, please."

I give her a look of confusion. "I'll only be a minute. Just walk up to the front with her and I'll meet you both by the front door."

Lexi is already running out the door toward the front and Charlie's eyes dart toward her. "Okay," she says, her voice shaky as she follows Lexi out of the room. It takes me a second, but I realize this isn't the first time she's tried to stop me from leaving Lexi with her. I didn't think much of it before, but now it definitely has me thinking.

TWENTY-THREE

CHARLIE

"SCOTCH ON THE ROCKS, A DIRTY MARTINI, AND A WHITE Russian." Veronica recites the drinks she needs and I go about making them. It's Thursday night at Plush, and usually the club is crazy busy, but tonight it's practically dead. Tyler said it's because most people are attending Halloween parties. The club's party is Saturday night and we'll most likely be slammed. I hand Veronica the three drinks and she sighs.

"What?" I look up and she's staring at the drinks.

"I asked for a scotch on the rocks, a dirty martini, and a White Russian. You gave me a scotch without the rocks, a Lemon Drop, and a beer."

Huh? I look over at the drinks. Shit! She's right. "What's going on with you? You never mess up on orders, and we aren't even that busy." My thoughts go back to the other night in Tristan's gym, on the mat, where we made out and I pretty much dry humped him like a dog in heat. I've never reacted that way to a man before. I can't imagine how far we would've went had Lexi and Mason not walked in and interrupted us when they did. Actually, I can imagine, which is precisely why I can't focus.

I feel my cheeks heat up as my mind conjures up all the sexual thoughts and fantasies that have been plaguing me these last few days, and Veronica gives me a knowing look. "Ohh…I know that look. Charlie! You have a man on your mind!"

Of course Bianca walks over while Veronica is saying this. "What? You have a boyfriend? How did we not know this? Who is he? Is he hot? Is he good in bed?"

Before I can answer, I hear laughter from behind me. I would recognize that sound anywhere. Turning around slowly, my suspicions are confirmed when I see Tristan sitting on a stool only a couple feet away, and judging by the smirk on his face, he heard everything.

"Please don't go speechless on my account. I would love to know the answers to those questions myself." His grin grows wider, and I glare his way. Needing a moment to gather myself, I make the three drinks—correct this time—and hand them off to Veronica.

Then I take the order from Bianca and make her drinks. Once I hand them off to her, I check on every customer at the bar before making my way back to Tristan.

"Is it my turn yet?" he asks. "If not, I can wait. Lexi is sleeping over at my sister's, so I have all night."

"It's your turn," I choke out. "What can I get for you?"

"An Octoberfest." I grab the beer from the cooler, twist the top, and pour the drink into a chilled glass before handing it to him. Bianca comes over and places another order, so I start working on it.

"So you're a dancer and a bartender?" he asks, taking a sip of his beer. Bianca chokes out a laugh and I stifle mine. Tristan looks from me to Bianca confused but continues. "How many other jobs do you have?"

"Charlie, I didn't know you were working as a dancer. Will you still be working the bar?" Nick asks. I didn't realize he was back from his break yet.

"Charlie?" Tristan says my name in confusion. "You're not a dancer?"

"Nope," I state matter-of-factly.

"Why did you lie to me?"

"I never said I was," I point out, handing Bianca her drink order. Tristan's head tilts to the side giving my words some thought. "You assumed. I simply didn't correct you." He shakes his head and grins.

"You work the bar here?"

"Yep, four nights a week."

"Come home with me."

"Why? Because now you know I'm not a stripper?"

He frowns. "Don't be like that. We have hung out plenty, and the entire time I thought you were one. I apologized for my initial reaction. I'm sorry, Charlie. For assuming. For my harsh words. Please forgive me." He gives me the cutest puppy dog pout, his bottom lip playfully jutting out, and I give in.

"I work until three."

"Actually, I was just about to tell you, you can leave early," Nick says. "It's dead in here tonight. Tomorrow will be busy and Saturday will be crazy with the Halloween party. You can cut out early."

Before I can respond, Tristan says, "Great!" He downs the last of his beer and throws a couple bills on the counter.

I pick them up to cash him out. "Okay, I just need to count my till and then we can go." Tristan nods. I grab my till and walk it to the back room to count my money. After verifying that my receipts and cash match the computer's totals, I clock-out and head to the front.

"You ready?" he asks.

"Yeah."

He drove here, so we jump into his truck. "Mason has a girl over, so I was thinking we could go somewhere."

"Sounds good."

"You hungry?"

"I could eat."

Tristan doesn't tell me where we're going and I don't ask. We listen to music in comfortable silence, and about thirty minutes later we pull up to Santa Monica beach. The pinks and purples of the Ferris wheel light up the surrounding area.

Tristan comes around to my side of the truck, and being a gentleman, helps me down. Holding my hand, he guides me to a café on the pier. "Let's order it to go and eat on the beach." After we get our food, he runs into a touristy shop and comes back out with a large blanket.

We make our way down to the beach and pick a spot close enough that we can hear the music and see all the beautiful lights, but far enough away that we can talk without yelling. After handing me my food and drink, Tristan gets comfortable next to me.

"My name is Tristan Scott. My biological father abused my mom and left us. He was killed in a gambling incident. I have two sisters: Emma and Morgan. They're twins and a pain in my ass. Morgan is going to fashion school here in LA. Emma is going to college back in Las Vegas for education. I'm twenty-seven years old and my birthday is January 28th. I have a degree in business management with a minor in fitness training.

"I thought I was in love with my best friend, Bella, but when she chose our friend Marco over me—after she got pregnant with his baby but didn't tell him, and I agreed to raise the baby with her—I realized it wasn't meant to be. I had a one night stand with my ex-girlfriend, Gina, but Mason calls her *shewhoshallnotbenamed* because he's a closet diehard Harry Potter fan, and because he hates Gina for walking out of the hospital and leaving Lexi—for choosing a life of drugs over her daughter. But I don't hate her."

He shakes his head, pausing for a second, and trying to come up with the right words. "I pity her. Because even a single day without Lexi in my life would be a cold, lonely day, so I can't even imagine how she feels going day after day without her. But then again, maybe she doesn't know what she's missing because she never got to experience the sunshine and brightness that is Lexi."

Tristan smiles, probably thinking of one of the many memories with his daughter.

"My dad, the one who raised me, Kaden, is wealthy, like really wealthy. He created a trust fund for me and my sisters, which is how I went to college with no debt and then purchased the gym. I'm really lucky. Not because of his money, but because he thinks of me as his own and loves me like I'm really his son."

He takes a bite of his food, but I don't begin to eat yet. I'm too busy trying to wrap my head around all the information he's feeding me. When he finishes chewing, he takes a sip of his drink, and then goes back to his story.

"I own the gym, as you know, and Mason is a fighter there along with several other UFC fighters. I own the condo we live in. Mason and I lived together for two years back in Las Vegas, and for the last six years in California. I lived in San Diego but transferred to LA to get a fresh start.

"My favorite color is blue, I love BBQ chicken, and Key Lime pie is my favorite dessert." He smirks, but isn't done. "I've been in one relationship my entire life. I want the family, the kids, the white picket fence, and that might make me sound like a pussy, but it's the truth. I want what my parents have. But until I get that, I'm content with my life with my daughter and Mason. My biggest fear is that something will happen to my daughter and I won't be able to fix it."

A huge knot forms in my stomach at his final words. Those words right there are exactly why I have to keep him and his daughter at arm's length. I can feel myself falling for the both of them. I can see myself falling in love, but is it fair to them if I can never give them all of me? If I'll always feel it's necessary to keep them at a safe distance to keep them safe from me?

"Why are you telling me all this?" I choke out. He sets his food and drink down and pulls me onto his lap, so I'm straddling him. His hands frame my face so I have no choice but to look him in the eyes. His dark blue to my muddy green. It's fitting, really. His world is filled with brightness like the clear skies and deep oceans with only just a hint of darkness to remind us he isn't perfect, while my world is dirty and messy. The dirtiness muddying up the cleanliness I crave.

"Because I know you have a past, but so do I. Nobody's life is perfect. I know you have shit you're hiding, shit you're either afraid to share or are ashamed of, but I want you to trust me enough to open up to me. By nature, I'm a fixer. I always have been. But for the first time in my life, I don't want to fix someone. I don't want to fix you. I like you just the way you are, but I want to understand... No, I *need* to understand why you are the way you are. I need to know why the tears pop up out of nowhere. Why your smiles are always marred with a hint of sadness, and I'm hoping by me telling you about myself, you'll do the same."

The knot in my stomach has moved upward and is now lodged in my throat. Tristan might think his life isn't perfect, but it's pretty damn close compared to the fuckedupness that makes up my life.

He lets go of my face, and it's only then I realize I'm crying. He wipes the tear from my cheek then moves his hands down my arms, landing on my hips. He squeezes my sides tightly. He doesn't say anything, though. I know it's because he's waiting for me to speak. Waiting to see if I'll reciprocate and let him into my life, shine light on the parts I've kept hidden. But I can't do that. So instead I give him what I can.

"My name is Charlie Pratt. As I mentioned before, I was born and raised in Georgia. My parents loved me and gave me all they could, but we were poor. I moved to Texas and went to A&M. I majored in art and digital design, as you also know. My parents were killed in a fire before I graduated. I met a guy and we dated for a short time before getting married." I stop and take a deep breath, shocked I just opened that can of worms. I need to backtrack…

But just as I'm about to steer the story in a different direction, Tristan looks me in the eye and says, "C'mon, Charlie, you can do it. I can feel the tension in your body, you're at the hard part. Don't stop, please. You're right there. At the part that hurts deep down inside of you. The reason for your tears and sadness. Please, tell me."

And I can no longer keep my dark truth from this man. "I killed my daughter."

The way his hands deathly grip my hips is the only indication he heard my admission of guilt.

TWENTY-FOUR

TRISTAN

I knew she was hiding something dark. I saw it in the way she spoke, the way her eyes filled with tears when Lexi would speak to her. I saw the way she would keep us at arm's length. But I never imagined those would be the words that would come out of her mouth.

I realize my hands have tightened on her hips when she flinches. We're both sitting here, her on my lap, not saying a word. It takes me a minute to wrap my head around her words.

I killed my daughter.

There has to be more to this. If she had killed her daughter she would be in jail, and I see the way she is with Lexi. There isn't a mean bone in this woman's body. She ran from a couple of guys fighting in the gym for crying out loud.

"Charlie, you're going to have to explain, sweetheart," I say softly. I don't want her to clam up on me. She swallows thickly and tries to climb off my lap, but I'm not having it. I'm not letting her push me away again.

"I killed my daughter," she repeats. "I was responsible for her and she died."

I hold her tighter, my eyes never leaving hers.

"Talk to me, Charlie. Tell me what happened."

"It was three days before Thanksgiving…last year." I can see it in her eyes as she talks, she's no longer with me. She's stuck in the past with her daughter and the tragedy of what happened.

"I wasn't watching Georgia and she ran outside. She was hit by a car. I don't really remember it all."

"How do you not remember it?" I ask carefully.

She takes a deep breath. "According to the doctor at the hospital, I had blacked out and hit my head on the coffee table. During that time, my daughter ran outside and was hit by a car."

Holy shit! I can't imagine waking up and finding out my daughter was dead. She keeps talking, so I don't say anything.

"Tristan, I can't remember anything from around that time. I've tried to remember so many times, but I can't. It doesn't matter, though. My beautiful, innocent, precious Georgia Rae was killed that day while in my care. She ran outside and a car hit her. I was responsible for her and she's dead because of me."

Jesus, the guilt that must be consuming her, I don't even know where to start, what to say. I've only known this woman for a short time, but I can't see her doing anything that would intentionally harm someone else, especially someone she loves.

"I won't blame you for walking away, Tristan. For not wanting me around Lexi and you." Her eyes fall, no longer looking at me.

"Were you charged with something?"

"No." She shakes her head. "I was told it was ruled an accident. There were no drugs or alcohol in my system. I have never blacked out or fainted from what I can remember, so I don't get it. The doctor didn't have any answers. There was a funeral for her, but I was so grief-stricken I didn't attend. Two months later I moved here needing to get away from everything that reminded me of what I did, and I've been living here for the last nine months."

I wrap my arms around her waist and pull her closer to me. "Hey, look at me." She looks up and I spot the unshed tears about to spill over her lids. "You didn't do anything wrong. What happened to your daughter is a fucking tragedy. But you didn't set out to have her killed. You weren't neglecting her, and you didn't throw her into the road. I trust you one hundred percent with Lexi. Are you seeing a therapist? Someone you can talk to about all this guilt you feel?"

She nods. "Yes, I've been seeing a therapist since shortly after I moved here. It started off as several times a week, but now I see her every Monday."

"And what about Georgia's father?" I ask, and Charlie stills.

"I left him two months after she died, and I haven't seen him since."

I know there's more to this story. She admitted to being in an abusive relationship before. But I don't push her. Having to tell the story of her daughter dying is enough. I don't want to tip her over the edge. She's here in California and no longer with the guy, and that's all that matters. When she's ready, she'll give me more.

"Thank you for sharing your past with me." I give her a kiss on her nose then one on each of her now tear-stained cheeks. "I am so sorry for your loss. Can you tell me about her? I don't want this conversation to end like this," I admit. "She was a part of you and I want to know about her."

Charlie nods emphatically, tears now streaming down her face as she gives me a small smile. "Yeah, I can do that." She climbs off my lap and I let her. "Let's eat, and I'll tell you about her."

She unwraps her tuna salad sandwich and takes a small bite, then she takes a sip of her drink. "Georgia Rae was the light of my life," she begins, and while 1we both eat our sandwiches, she tells me all about her daughter, who—it is evident in every word and story she shares— was her entire world until the day she tragically died.

TWENTY-FIVE

CHARLIE

WHEN I TOLD TRISTAN ABOUT GEORGIA, HE HANDLED IT WITH such grace and compassion. I shouldn't be surprised, though. That's the kind of guy he is. He assured me, just as my therapist has done, it was an accident, but he didn't try to belittle my feelings of guilt. He allowed me to feel what I feel, understanding I will always in some way feel responsible for the death of my baby girl.

And then when he asked about her, wanting to know the good, I knew in that moment one day I would love this man—I was already halfway there. We spent the rest of the night getting to know one another. I kept it positive, only sharing stories of Georgia and me, keeping Justin out of it completely. To get into the physical and emotional abuse he put me through…I just couldn't handle it. Telling him about Georgia had already taken so much out of me.

When I started to fall asleep in Tristan's arms, listening to the waves crash, we reluctantly called it a night. The last couple days he's sent me several text messages asking how I'm doing, how my day is going, and sending me funny as well as sexy pictures of him. I think he's trying to give me some space after the emotionally draining night we had, while still letting me know he's here. Once again, he knows exactly what I need.

It's now Sunday and my phone is ringing. I grab it and see it's Tristan, only he's facetiming me. I also see that it's already the afternoon. The Halloween party was crazy busy last night and I didn't stumble in until almost five o'clock this morning.

"Hello," I say, rolling over to my side. The video connects and Lexi's bright smile graces the screen. I pull my blanket up making sure I'm appropriate.

"Charlie! You're awake!" She giggles. I hear Tristan yelling something in the background and Lexi rolls her eyes.

"I am, sweet girl. Does your dad know you're calling me?"

"Nope! But I was videoing with my best friend and cousin, Micaela, so we could show each other our costumes and then I saw your picture! Are you coming trick-or-treating with me?" Her big blue eyes plead and I'm a goner.

"Lexi! Tell Micaela you'll call her later. We need to go pick up your bag for candy and get dinner." Tristan steps into view, looking confused when he sees it's me on the phone and not his daughter's cousin. "Go get your shoes on."

There's shuffling with the phone and then it's only Tristan on the screen. "Charlie?"

"Hello." I smile at him.

"Are you in bed?" he whispers, his eyes darting around him to make sure Lexi can't hear.

"I am." I shift my body, the blanket falling slightly to reveal my tiny tank top.

He groans. "Jesus, woman. I'm taking Lexi trick-or-treating. How about I pick you up afterward and we can hang out at my place once she goes to bed?" He waggles his eyebrows and I giggle at his playfulness, but then when I realize what he means, that he doesn't want me going trick-or-treating with them, my heart sinks. Maybe he's concerned about the welfare of his daughter after all, and who can blame him? Accident or not, my daughter was killed under my supervision.

"Hey," he says, snapping me from my thoughts. "What's wrong?"

"Nothing." I shake my head. "That sounds good. Just text me when you're on your way." Just then Lexi comes running back into view.

"Is she coming, Daddy? Is Charlie coming with us?" I see Tristan's brows furrow before he turns away from the camera.

"No, sweetie. It's going to be you and me. Mason is out of town for press stuff for his upcoming fight, and Morgan is out of town for the weekend for a fashion show."

"But what about Charlie?" she asks when he doesn't give an excuse for me.

Not wanting to listen to whatever excuse he's going to make up, I speak up. "Tristan, I have to go, I have a call coming in." I hit the end button and throw my phone down. It lands on the end of the bed, and I snuggle back up in my blankets and close my eyes, hoping to fall back asleep.

My heart feels like it's being squeezed and my mind can't stop thinking about Tristan pushing me away. I know he said he trusts me around her. He insisted what happened to Georgia was an accident. He was so sweet and sympathetic the entire time I told him the little bit of details I knew. I just don't get why all of a sudden he seems to be having a change of heart.

"Isn't this what I wanted?" I think to myself. Since the day I met the two of them I pushed them away, so shouldn't I be relieved at this turn of events? No, I decide, I'm not. Because the second Tristan knew the truth about my daughter and didn't judge or blame me, I felt like a bit of weight was lifted off of me. I felt hopeful we could have a real chance at something good, something real. I wouldn't have to hide my sadness when memories surfaced regarding Georgia. I could be open and honest and Tristan would be understanding.

My phone rings and I ignore it. When it rings a second time, I throw my blanket off me and grab the phone. It stops ringing but immediately picks back up again. Tristan. Knowing he'll keep calling until I pick up, I answer, making sure to sound cheerful. Since we aren't video chatting, it makes it easier to hide my disappointment about him not wanting me to join them.

"Hello."

"I'm sorry." Tristan sighs.

"For what?" I ask, unsure what exactly he's apologizing for.

"For Lexi calling and asking you to go trick-or-treating." He's apologizing for her inviting me? What the heck?

"Why would you apologize for that?" I ask, confused.

His voice lowers several octaves. "Now that I know about your loss… about Georgia… I understand why you didn't want to join us at the painting contest."

"That was only because that day was Georgia's birthday. Do you not want me to join you guys? If you've changed your mind about wanting me in Lexi's life, I completely understand—"

"Whoa! Stop. Of course I want you in our life. I meant what I said the other night. I trust you one hundred percent with my daughter. I just figured it would be hard on you. Your first Halloween without her…"

Oh my goodness. This man. I don't deserve his compassion. He wasn't trying to protect his daughter from me. He was trying to protect my heart. "I thought you didn't want me to go," I murmur.

"Of course, I want you to go. Do you have any idea how hard it's been staying away from you these last couple days? I was trying to give you some breathing room. I know shit got heavy. I was afraid too much too soon would have you running."

"I don't want breathing room," I blurt out. "I love being around you and Lexi. When I thought you didn't want me to go with you guys, I could feel my heart starting to break. Yes, it's hard knowing I'll never see my daughter experiencing these moments, but knowing you get it, makes it that much easier."

I hear Tristan release a deep breath. "We'll be to your place in thirty minutes to pick you up…and Charlie…"

"Yeah?"

"Your heart is safe with me. Never doubt that again."

TRISTAN AND LEXI PICK ME UP AND WE HEAD TO THE STORE TO pick her up a bag to hold her candy. Then we go to a local pizza parlor for an early dinner. After we've successfully devoured an entire pie, Tristan hands Lexi a bag. "Okay, let's go to the bathroom so you can get changed."

"Can Charlie take me into the girls' bathroom?"

Tristan gives me a look asking if I'm okay with that. "Of course, I can," I say, not wanting to say no to Lexi. She's too young to understand why I'm so reluctant to be alone with her. "Please stay right outside," I whisper to Tristan and he nods knowingly. I know if I want to be a part of their life long-term there are going to be times I'm alone with Lexi, but for now I need to take it one day at a time. Knowing Tristan is right outside, God forbid something happens, is comforting.

"Okay, sweet girl. Let's do this." Lexi closes the stall door behind her, leaving me in the main area while she takes off her clothes, and my heart picks up over the fact I can no longer see her. I know it's ridiculous. She's in a stall, two feet away, with walls on both sides, but those facts don't stop my brain from conjuring up worst case scenarios.

"Lexi, you okay?"

"Yep! I'm going to the bathroom so I don't have to go while we're trick-or-treating." Smart girl. I hear the toilet flush and then she says, "Can you throw me over my costume?" I take deep breaths in and out once I hear her voice. I pull her costume out of the bag and throw it over the top, holding onto it until I feel her tug on it. A minute later, the lock clicks and she steps out, looking like the cute little artist she is.

"Ta-da!" She raises her left arm striking a pose.

"Beautiful!" I gush, pushing back the memories of the last time I was with Georgia on Halloween. I would never consider Lexi a replacement or a fill-in for Georgia, but standing here, staring at this sweet girl, I feel like maybe she was brought into my life for a reason. For the last several months I've felt like I was stuck frozen in place, not living, and then Tristan and Lexi entered my world, and it's as if they breathed life back into my lungs.

I grab her clothes, fold them, and put them into the bag while Lexi washes and dries her hands. When we exit the bathroom, Tristan is standing against the wall in the hallway messing with his phone. When he hears the door open, he looks up, smiling. "There's my little artist. You ready to rock-n-roll?"

"Yep!" Lexi skips toward the front of the restaurant and we follow behind her. Tristan puts Lexi into her seat in his truck and shuts the door. Just as I'm about to get in, he stops me, his hands holding my shoulders back, his front so close to my back I can feel his cool breath.

"I'm proud of you, Charlie. I know going in there with her was hard, but you did it, and nothing happened." He leans in closer and gives me a kiss on my cheek. "If, at any time, you need me today, just let me know. We'll get through this together. Okay?" I simply nod, the lump in my throat preventing me from speaking. He has no idea how much those words mean to me…or maybe he does.

We pull up to a neighborhood that looks familiar and Tristan parks along the grass where other cars are parking. "Are we near Larchmont?" I ask.

"Yeah, only a couple neighborhoods over. A lot of parents take their kids trick-or-treating here because the homes are close together and the owners all sit outside so the kids don't have to go all the way up to their door. Plus, they always go all out decorating for the different holidays. You should see the place during Christmas."

Lexi joins the conversation. "Daddy and I walk around to see all the lights!" I look around and notice all the houses are decorated for Halloween. Orange, black, and white lights. Blown-up Halloween-themed characters littering the lawns. There's music playing and tons of people are already walking from house to house while others are sitting in chairs giving out candy.

We get out of the truck and head toward the street closest to us. It's just hitting six o'clock and starting to get dark. Kids are everywhere in costumes with their parents following them. When we get to the first house, Tristan stops Lexi and kneels so he's at her level. "Make sure you say thank you even if they give you something you don't like, like raisins, and come back to me after every house. Got it?" Lexi nods then skips over to the first house, Tristan and me trailing closely behind her.

"Trick-or-Treat!" she exclaims, holding her bag out, and the woman holding the candy, drops a few pieces in.

"Look at you!" she gushes. "Aren't you just the cutest little artist!"

"Thank you," Lexi says. "And thank you for the candy!" She closes her bag and runs back over to us. "I got a Hershey bar! And a KitKat!" Her excitement is infectious.

"Score!" Tristan says. "Now, you know half of whatever you get is mine, right?" he adds seriously.

Lexi's head pops up. "What? Why?"

"It's called parent tax, kid. I brought you here, I get half." He shrugs, holding back his grin.

"I don't know what tax is, but I don't think I like it very much." Lexi pulls her bag close to her chest, and I laugh.

"Oh my God, Tristan. Tell her you're joking!" I push his shoulder and he finally laughs. He grabs my hand and pulls me toward him, spinning me around in front of him, my back hitting his front. He wraps his arms around my torso, and whispers, "Quiet. I'm trying to snag us some candy." He gives me a soft kiss on my neck, his lips warm against my chilled skin. I sink back into him, loving the feel of him touching me. A woman could get used to this kind of attention.

Tristan releases me but grabs my hand pulling me along. "C'mon, Lex. Let's go get *us* some candy." He winks at her and she rolls her eyes.

We walk up and down each street as Lexi gets candy from each person sitting at the end of their driveway. She says thank you each time, then runs up to us letting us know what she got.

"That scary man with the mask gave me a Butterfinger!" Lexi's face lights up.

"Yum!" Tristan replies before Lexi takes off in front of us heading toward the next house. Tristan yells to slow down, but Lexi either ignores him or doesn't hear him because she keeps going. It all happens so quickly. One second Lexi is skipping down the sidewalk, her bag swinging back and forth, and the next second a car is backing out of the driveway. Lexi stops, frozen in shock.

"Lexi!" I scream, letting go of Tristan's hand. We're only a couple feet behind her, and I reach her within seconds, pushing her out of the way just as the car's back bumper hits the side of my body.

ELEVEN MONTHS AGO

BEEP.

Beep.

Beep.

Beep.

I hear the noise before my eyes open. What is that beeping noise? I open my eyes and a migraine immediately hits me. My head is pounding and my eyes squeeze shut in an attempt to block out the pain.

Beep.

Beep.

Beep.

"Oh dear, I'll dispense some more pain medication." Slowly, I pry my lids open so I can see who's speaking to me. It's a woman with silver hair pulled up into a high bun, most likely in her sixties. She's wearing scrubs, so she must be a nurse.

I try to speak but my throat is too dry. "Water, please," I choke out. She gives me a kind smile and pours me a small cup of water. She presses the button on the wall and the top half of the bed moves upward until I'm in a full-sitting position. I take the cup from her and close my eyes once more, needing some relief from the pounding in my head.

"Your headache should be improving shortly. If you feel any pain in the future you can press the button right here"—I open one eye to see where she's pointing to—"and it will push some more medication through your IV."

"Thank you."

She smiles. "The doctor will be in to see you shortly."

I nod my understanding, but really, I don't understand anything. I have no clue why I'm here. Then it hits me… where's Georgia?

"Charlotte." Justin walks through the door with another gentleman who's in a suit with a white coat. "This is Dr. Hutchins. How are you feeling?"

"Where's Georgia?" I ask in panic.

Justin glares at me, but it quickly morphs into a sympathetic frown. When the hell has he ever had sympathy?

"Charlotte, it seems you blacked out and took a nasty fall, hitting the table. You have a pretty bad black eye, and you were brought in here for a concussion. What can you remember?" the doctor asks. I try to recall what he's talking about, but everything is fuzzy.

"What's today?" I ask, trying to put the pieces together.

"Wednesday, November 24th," Justin answers. This doesn't make any sense. The last day I remember is Friday. I was making dinner for Georgia and me. I was going through all of our stuff in preparation to leave…

"Where's Georgia?" I demand. Justin glances at the doctor who appears to be uncomfortable.

"Mike, why don't you give me some time alone with my wife?" The doctor—who Justin is apparently on a first name basis with—nods and walks out without saying another word. Once the door closes, Justin comes over and sits on the edge of the bed.

"What do you remember?" Justin asks slowly.

"Nothing! I don't remember anything!" I start to panic while he almost looks…relieved?

"When you blacked out, Georgia wandered out and was hit by a car. I shouldn't have left her with you…" He shakes his head. "I knew you were unstable." Unstable? What the hell is he talking about?

"What do you mean she was hit by a car?" I need to get out of this bed. I need to go to my daughter! "Where is she?" I throw the sheets off me and start pulling at the IV in my arm.

"Charlotte, calm down," Justin demands.

"Calm down? Calm down? My baby was hit by a car! I need to get to her!" I stand, ignoring the searing pain radiating through my brain that feels like nails stabbing me in the forehead and in my eyes.

Justin beats me to the door and calls out, "Mike." The doctor walks back in and Justin says, "She needs to be sedated." The doctor nods, and I back up. What the hell is going on here?

"I don't need anything! I need to get to my daughter!"

"Charlotte." Justin says my name and I want to punch him in the face. I attempt to step around him but I'm stopped by the two men. They grab my arms and the doctor injects something into my neck.

"Charlotte," Justin repeats, his voice devoid of all emotion. "You can't go to Georgia because she's dead. You killed our daughter."

TWENTY-SIX

TRISTAN

IT ALL HAPPENED IN SLOW MOTION YET SO DAMN FAST. ONE minute, Charlie's hand is in mine as Lexi skips along the sidewalk in front of us. The next minute, Charlie is pushing my daughter out of the way from the car backing up. Lexi falls onto her knees on the sidewalk as Charlie's body gets pushed sideways by the car, her body falling limp, half on the driveway and half in the grass. I make it to the car only seconds after Charlie, pounding on the trunk to get the driver's attention. It works and the car comes to an abrupt stop. I grab hold of Lexi and sit her down in the grass, and then lift Charlie up carefully and bring her into the grass, sitting us down with her in my lap.

"Lex, are you okay?" I ask my daughter to confirm she isn't hurt.

"Yes, but my knees are bleeding," Lexi says. "Is Charlie okay?"

Charlie's eyes are fluttering open and closed, but she's not with us. The car was going slow, so I don't think it hurt her physically, but mentally I think my girl has checked out.

"Is she all right?" The elderly gentleman who was backing out comes running over.

"What do you think?" I shout. "It's Halloween! There's a million kids around and you're backing out without looking!"

"I'm so sorry! Should I call an ambulance?"

Before I can answer him, Charlie says, "No, I'm okay." She sits up, her eyes darting to my daughter. I can see it in her eyes, in her face, she's imagining what could've happened. The situation ending like it did for her daughter.

"Hey." I grab Charlie and pull her into me then grab Lexi for a group hug. "She's okay, Charlie. You got to her in time."

"I'm so sorry, Daddy." Lexi sobs, suddenly understanding the seriousness of this situation.

"You always have to look before you walk across someone's driveway." I should have explained that to her. This is her first year trick-or-treating while not sitting in a wagon or stroller. She knows not to cross the road, but we live in a condominium development. I never went over the rules for looking before crossing a driveway.

"Sir, should I call an ambulance?" the man asks again.

"Are you hurt?" I ask Charlie, and she shakes her head.

"No, I imagine my hip will be sore tomorrow, but I'm okay." She's still looking at Lexi. "Are you okay?" she asks my daughter.

"My knees are bleeding." Lexi pulls her legs out to show us her scraped knees, and I thank God that's the extent of her injuries. Had the car hit Lexi, who knows what would've happened. She's one-fourth the size of Charlie.

"Here." The man who was asking about the ambulance hands me a couple napkins.

"Thanks." I blot Lexi's knees, but they really need to be cleaned properly and ointment needs to be put on them. Charlie stands, and Lexi and I follow.

"I'm ready to go home, Daddy." Lexi frowns, tears filling her lids.

"Okay, how about we go home, clean up your knees, and then we can figure out which half of the candy you're sharing with us," I say to lighten the mood.

Lexi groans. "I'm not giving you any. But I'll give some to Charlie." She attaches herself to Charlie's side. "I'm sorry, Charlie."

"It's okay, sweet girl. I'm just—" Charlie clears her throat, trying to tame down her emotions enough to speak. "I'm just glad you're safe." She peers down at my daughter and gives her a small watery smile.

We get back to the condo and Lexi immediately dumps all her candy on the coffee table to check it out while I grab the first-aid kit to clean up her knees. Charlie sits on the couch, still quiet, but no longer as subdued as she was earlier. She's interacting with Lexi. Smiling at all the right times and accepting the candy Lexi is dishing out.

"Two pieces and then it's bath time and then bed," I say to my daughter. She pouts but nods. She picks out her two pieces, then grabbing the bag, runs off to her room. I'll have to find the bag after she's asleep to put it up high. Otherwise, she'll finish off that entire bag of candy in twenty-four hours.

Once Lexi has had her bath—and I've bandaged her scraped knees—and is in her pajamas, she calls for Charlie to say good night. "Good night, Charlie. Thank you for going trick-or-treating with us! And thank you for saving me from the car."

Charlie sits on the edge of Lexi's bed and leans over, giving her a kiss on her forehead. "Thank you for including me, and you're welcome. Sweet dreams."

I give Lexi a kiss, then turn off her light, the nightlight switching on and illuminating the room. I close her door behind us and follow Charlie back out to the living room. She sits on the couch next to me, but I'm not having that. Reaching over, I grip her by her hips and pull her onto my lap.

"Talk to me." Charlie's eyes close and her head falls onto my shoulder. Her arms wrap around me, and her hands hold on to my back.

"I had a flashback from when I woke up in the hospital. From when I found out Georgia was dead." Her breathing is heavy at first, but I can feel it slowing down.

"Thank you for saving my little girl." Her face is buried in my neck, but I can feel her nod her head.

We sit here for a few minutes and I think maybe she's fallen asleep right here on my lap when I feel her lips press up against my neck. I sit motionless, waiting to see what she will do next. A few seconds later, she's kissing my neck again. She sits up slightly, her body rubbing against mine, and I internally groan. This time when her lips go to my neck, she sucks on my skin for a few seconds and my cock stirs.

"Charlie…"

She looks up at me, and her shy, almost nervous smile about kills me. "I want you," is all she says and I lose it. My hands go to her ass, pulling her toward me. My lips crash into hers, my tongue plunging into her mouth. She tastes sweet like chocolate. Her hands go to my head as she runs her fingers roughly through the ends of my hair until she gets enough to grab a hold of.

Without stopping our kiss, Charlie starts to grind against me, her pussy rubbing on my cock. "Oh, God," she breathes, her mouth still on mine. Her tongue swirls around chasing mine and once it's caught it, she sucks on it.

Lifting her off me, I drop her onto the couch and kneel between her legs above her. Her hands move to my stubble as she holds my face to hers, kissing me like her life depends on it.

Starting at her knee, I run my hand up her thigh slowly, her leg coming around and wrapping around me. Goose bumps prickle her skin and I chuckle softly against her mouth. Continuing upward, I stop when I get to her cotton shorts, and pull my head back slightly. My eyes lock with hers seeking permission. Charlie averts her eyes, and I move my hand from her leg to her face, my fingers gently tilting her face back to meet mine.

"We can slow down. Just tell me what you want."

"It's not that." She frowns.

"What is it, baby? Talk to me." I'm in uncharted territory with this woman. The women I'm usually with are one-night stands. They come to me willing and ready and know exactly what they want.

"It's just that I've never had an orgasm…by a man. I can do it myself, but with guys…well, the two guys I've been with, I used to fake it. I don't want to fake it with you. Let's just focus on you." What the fuck? Who the hell has this woman been with? And how did the men she was with not notice she was faking it?

"Oh, baby." I kiss her lips roughly before I stand. "Challenge accepted." She looks up at me confused. "We need to move this to my bedroom. Because when I make you come, you're going to scream, and I can't take a chance of Lex walking out and seeing us." Charlie's eyes go wide.

"Let's go." I pull her up into a standing position. Then grabbing her hand, I guide her into my room. Closing my door behind us, the only light is the outside street lamps casting a faint yellow glow through the blinds. I walk us to the edge of the bed until the backs of her legs hit the mattress.

"Arms up." She lifts her arms and I pull her shirt up and over her head. She is wearing a bright orange lacy bra. I bend down slightly and tug her shorts off her, revealing matching orange panties. They're not a thong, but still sexy. "Get on the bed, baby." She bites her lip nervously but obeys, crawling up the middle of the bed, her ass on display.

She's wearing tiny cheeky style panties with black glittery writing across her ass that reads: I'm not your BOO!

I bark out a laugh. "Nice panties."

"Shut up," she groans, turning over onto her back. "I forgot about them." She shrugs. "I like to buy holiday-themed pajamas and underwear."

I take a moment to look at her. Her hair is splayed out across my pillow, her lips are swollen from our kissing, and her skin is slightly flushed.

"You're beautiful." I crawl up the middle of the bed until I'm hovering above her. "And you look sexy as hell," I add as I lean over her. One of my hands settles next to her head while the other pulls her bra cups down, her perky pink nipples now on display and begging to be sucked. Dropping my head to her breast, I take one of her nipples between my teeth and bite down softly at first then a bit harder. Charlie's back arches slightly.

"Ohhh, Tristan," she moans. My teeth let go of her nipple and my tongue comes out to swirl around the hardened tip before I close my lips around it and suck. "Oh my God, please," she begs. I'm tempted to make her come from nipple stimulation alone just to show her how responsive her body actually is, but the need to taste her pussy wins out, and I release her nipples and move downward. When I get to her adorable orange panties, I pull them off her, tossing them to the ground and spreading her legs.

Lying down between her thighs, I press my nose into the small patch of neatly trimmed curls she has and inhale deeply.

"Tristan!" she shrieks, trying to push my head away, and I chuckle.

"Stop, baby." I grab her hands and pin them by her sides. "Your pussy smells good. I need to taste it. If you want to do something with your hands, play with those nipples." She looks at her hands and then at her nipples. "Go ahead, Charlie. Pinch those nipples, baby."

She nibbles her bottom lip, unsure. But then slowly, both her hands come up to her breasts and she pinches them. *Fuck, yes.* Knowing her hands are otherwise occupied, I spread her legs a little more and bring her knees up toward her chest. Her pussy is glistening with arousal and I need to taste her right this second. Pushing her thighs back a little more so her cunt is completely exposed, I lick up her slit slowly, savoring the smell and taste of this woman. When my tongue hits her clit, I stop and suck on the swollen nub. Charlie's body shakes with need as she lets out a soft moan.

TWENTY-SEVEN

CHARLIE

TRISTAN BITES DOWN ON MY CLITORIS AND THE PLEASURE I FEEL is like nothing I've ever experienced before. He bites again, a bit harder, then massages my clit with his tongue. It begins soft with light circles, then it gets rougher, and for the first time in my life, I feel something building within me... a sensation deep inside me trying to come to the surface.

And then... Tristan's mouth is off my body and my legs are hitting the bed. Is that it? Should I have screamed? Damn it! I knew I should've faked it. But before I can decide how to handle this situation, I glance up and see Tristan is kneeling in front of me, his piercing blue eyes locked with mine. His arm comes up behind him as he pulls his shirt up over his head and shucks it to the side. He backs up and gets off the bed, his eyes never leaving mine, as he unbuckles his belt, undoes the button, and unzips his pants, then pushes his jeans down so he's in only a white pair of briefs.

And holy mother of God! The man is ripped. His chest is rock solid, his abs... there has got to be eight of them! I don't think there's a single ounce of fat on him. On one of his biceps, there's a simple barbwire tattoo and down his side is the name Alexandria with a date. It must be Lexi's full name and her birthday.

He climbs back onto the bed, his lips trailing kisses up the inside of my thigh as he goes. The stubble from his face tickles my skin, causing me to giggle. I throw my hand over my mouth not wanting him to think I'm laughing at him, but instead of him getting mad, he looks up and smirks, laughter evident in his eyes.

"You like the feel of my scruff between your legs?" I nod and he softly laughs before dipping back down and dragging his face up my leg until he gets back to where he was a few minutes ago. He pushes my legs back up and his tongue swipes back up my seam. Only this time, he doesn't stop. He strokes his tongue savagely along my slit as my body begins to buck, my center grinding against his face.

"That's it, baby," Tristan groans. "Come for me." I'm afraid it won't happen and he'll find me to be defective, but I push the thought away as I get lost in the pleasure of his tongue, my hands going back to my breasts—pinching and pulling. My body is wound so tightly, it's begging to let go. I feel like I'm close, and then his tongue pushes down. My head goes back, my eyes closing as my body comes completely unhinged and I come all over his tongue. My entire body shakes and I'm pretty sure I feel liquid gushing out of me. While I should be praying I'm not soaking his sheets, it all feels too good to really give a damn.

"Fuck yes," Tristan murmurs as I start to come down from my sexual bliss. Just as I start to peel my eyes open, I feel Tristan's large hands push the back of my thighs up against my belly and then he's driving into me. I gasp loudly as he stretches me. Holy shit! He's so deep. I look up and his face is only inches from mine. He leans down and kisses me passionately, his thrusts never stopping.

His mouth moves downward as he rains kisses all over my breasts, stopping briefly to suck on my nipples. My hands go to his hair, needing to touch him. My fingers running up and down the back of his head.

There's something happening… something different… deep inside of me. "Tristan," I whisper, and he looks down at me with his lust-filled eyes, silently telling me he completely understands. Whatever is happening isn't just sexual. It's so much more. The connection, the closeness. I've never felt like this. Sex has never felt like this.

"I know, baby. Just feel it," he murmurs as if he can read my mind. He's so in tune with my body, my mind, my needs. His hands are flat on the bed on either side of me, his arms hooked under my knees. His face finds the crook of my neck as he fucks me deep—so, so deep. My vaginal walls begin to tighten and then I'm coming again. My insides are pulsating, my legs are shaking as a massive orgasm overtakes me. I let out an uncontrollable moan and then Tristan's mouth is on mine, silencing my cries. His thrusts turn frantic almost punishing as he hits a spot deep inside me, and my orgasm rolls from one into another, my body going limp beneath him.

Tristan's thrusts slow down and I feel his cock throbbing inside of me as he stills. He lifts his face up and kisses me one last time before he pulls out, his arms letting go of my legs. I have never in my life felt this satisfied and relaxed after sex. And simply calling it sex doesn't feel like I'm giving what we just did justice. It was so much more. It was… everything.

Unsure of how Tristan will react, I lie quietly, waiting to see what he does. After Justin would get off, he would roll off me, take a shower, and then spend the rest of the night in his office—that was if he stayed home afterward.

"Stay right here, I need to throw the condom out," Tristan murmurs into my ear before kissing my temple. Condom? How did I not see him put one on? And why didn't I even think to make sure he was using one? Oh, that's right! Because I was high from the amazing orgasms he was giving me.

He lifts off me, and it's then I notice his condom-covered dick, and even now only semi-hard, it's impressive. He follows my gaze and shoots me a knowing grin before getting off the bed and sauntering to the bathroom, his tight, muscular ass on display. Feeling exposed, I pull one of his sheets over to cover me while I wait for him to return.

A couple minutes later he comes out of the bathroom. Pulling the sheet back off me, he separates my thighs, and using a warm washcloth, wipes between my legs before throwing it into his hamper. He drops onto his side and pulls me into him, so our fronts are touching. I'm so shocked by his display of affection, I don't even know what to say.

"Two or three?" he asks as his hands run down my side, landing on the swell of my butt.

"What?" I'm confused and it's hard to focus with his hands on my body.

"I know for sure you had two orgasms. One by my tongue and another during sex, but that one felt like it might have turned into two."

My cheeks burn with embarrassment as I try to push his chest away so I can get up or hide under a blanket, but Tristan isn't having it. "Don't be embarrassed, baby." He leans down and gives me a soft kiss on my forehead. It's such a small show of affection, but it means so much. It's the first time I've ever cuddled in bed with a man after sex.

Laying my head against the curve of his bicep, I snuggle closer to Tristan. His thighs part, and one of mine fits perfectly between his legs before he closes them. With his one usable arm, he runs his fingertips up and down my back. I should probably go. Lexi will be up in a few hours and I don't want to overstay my welcome, but the comfort of Tristan's fingers lulls me to sleep.

Just a few minutes, I tell myself. Before my eyes completely close, I whisper, "Three."

I think I hear him laugh, but I'm too far gone to know for sure.

I WAKE UP WITH THE URGE TO GO PEE. SITTING UP, I REACH

toward my nightstand to grab my phone to see what time it is, but all I get is bed. What the heck? I pry my eyes open and look around. This isn't my bed and this isn't my room. Then I remember I'm at Tristan's place.

Reaching across the bed, I snag my phone and see it's only eight in the morning. Did Tristan leave me here? It's then I hear a little girl's voice asking if breakfast is almost ready. Oh jeez! I fell asleep and ended up spending the night, and Tristan's five-year-old very impressionable daughter is right outside making breakfast with her father. I wonder if I can sneak out the bedroom window. We're on the first floor.

Getting up quietly, I grab my clothes, which are scattered across the room. I go to the bathroom and go pee, and after washing my hands, I attempt to run my fingers through my hair, then use my finger to brush my teeth—I'm not sure one night of the most amazing sex of my life means I'm permitted to use Tristan's toothbrush. After I'm dressed, I push my phone into my back pocket, go to the bedroom window, and after unlocking it, push it open. I look down and realize my shoes are still by the front door. *Oh well...* I push the screen out and set it on the ground then climb out, close the window, and place the screen back on.

Looking around, I see the front of the building is just around the corner, so I head in that direction. Tristan doesn't live far from me, so instead of calling for a car, I make the decision to walk home. It's a cloudy day and looks like it will rain soon, but I think I can make it back before it does. As I walk down the sidewalk, I think about how much my life has changed. I would give anything for Georgia to be alive and with me. I would trade every ounce of happiness I feel right now to have her back in my arms, but I know no amount of wishing or begging will bring her back. I wonder, had she still been alive and we would've run like I planned, if we would've ended up here. Would we have met Tristan and Lexi in the coffee shop? Would Lexi have still approached me? *Us?*

I would like to think so. I would like to think had Georgia still been alive, we would've still met Tristan and his little girl, and they would've become friends. I would also like to think my daughter is looking down on me and forgives me for not saving her, forgives me for whatever happened on that foggy day. That she knows I love her with all my heart and I live every day wishing she were still alive. I get choked up as I pray she's looking down on me and in her own, now four-year-old, way approves of me finally moving forward and finding a tiny piece of happiness. I hope she knows this isn't me forgetting her. I could never do that. She will forever be in every thought and memory. This is me finally admitting what happened to my precious baby girl was a horrible, tragic accident, and living my life alone won't bring her back. I let the tears fall, but instead of feeling like I'm broken, the tears feel almost therapeutic, like I'm finally being put back together again.

I look up and the sky above me opens, rain falling in buckets, drops pelting my face. My tears mix with the raindrops as I stand frozen in place on the sidewalk feeling like every raindrop is cleansing me of my past.

"Charlie!" I look through the pouring rain at the huge dark blue truck stopped in the road, the window rolled down.

"Tristan?"

"Charlie! Get your butt in this truck now!" he shouts over the rain, which is coming down harder now. It takes me a second, but I shake myself out of my thoughts and run toward his truck. I'm about to jump in when I realize I'm soaking wet. I look down at my clothes then up at him.

"Just get in!" he yells, so I do, closing the door behind me. Once I'm situated, I notice Lexi is in the backseat looking at me confused.

"Charlie! It's raining so bad. Why were you in the rain, silly?" I glance from her to Tristan and back to her again.

"It wasn't raining when I started walking," I say to Lexi but also to Tristan who is side-eyeing me as he drives.

"Then you should have run so fast!" Lexi points out, and I have to stifle a laugh because she's being serious. "Daddy and I were making special pancakes for us." I turn to Tristan silently asking if Lexi knows I spent the night, but he doesn't give anything away one way or another.

We pull up to his condo and Lexi jumps out of the truck before Tristan can get out to help her down. I drop to the ground at the same time—I'm getting good at getting in and out of this monster-sized vehicle—and Lexi comes up to me. The raining has stopped and the blue skies are back in full force.

"Charlie," Lexi says softly. I bend so I'm at her level. "My daddy told me you had a little girl like me." My throat clogs at her words so I simply nod. "He said she was in an accident and now she's in heaven."

"Yes," I say, my voice rough.

"I painted this picture for you." She hands me a beautifully colored picture. "It's of her in heaven." She points to the angel above the clouds sitting on top of a rainbow. "My grandpa had a baby and he went to heaven. He told me every time he sees a rainbow it's the baby. So, I put your baby on a rainbow."

Needing to hold this little girl, who has come to mean so much to me in such a short amount of time, I drop to my knees and wrap her up in a tight hug. "Thank you, sweet girl. This means so much to me."

"Charlie, look!" Lexi shrieks, and I back up slightly to see what she's looking at. "It's a rainbow, Charlie! She's there! You see!" Her tiny finger is pointing up toward the sky and sure enough, there's a picturesque rainbow shooting up from one end of the building to another. "It's like she's sitting over us! Like in my picture!"

TWENTY-EIGHT

TRISTAN
EARLIER

FOR THE FIRST TIME IN OVER SIX YEARS I WAKE UP NEXT TO A woman, and fuck if it doesn't feel right. And not just because it's next to a woman but because it's next to Charlie. I watch her for a few minutes sleeping soundly as I remember the night before and how she saved my daughter from being hit by a car. I was already falling for her, but that act of selflessness has me falling even harder to the point of no return. I take in the sight of her in my bed, her messy hair covering half her face, and it has me wanting things it's too early in this relationship to want. My thoughts go back to my conversation with Mason. I want it all. I want the kids and the dog and the love and the marriage and the white picket fence. But more importantly I want it all with the woman who is currently snoring softly in my bed, in nothing but the sheets that are wrapped around her soft and curvy body that was so fucking responsive last night. My dick twitches at the memory of her screaming out her orgasms, of my mouth covering hers to muffle those same screams. And I know I want to spend the rest of my life making her scream like last night.

There's a knock on my door, alerting me to the present. Lexi. Getting up quickly but quietly—so as not to wake Charlie—I throw on a pair of sweat pants and a shirt to start breakfast. It's Monday morning so Lexi has no school. She greets me happily and we set out to make pancakes. As we gather all the ingredients and Lexi starts to mix them all together, I think about how I'm going to approach the subject of Charlie being in my room. I don't want her to think it's okay for a man and a woman to be sleeping together without being married, but at the same time I want Charlie in my bed in the future.

After giving it some thought, I decide I'm going to be honest with her. She's only five, but I was only a year or so older when Kaden came into my life. My mom didn't have guys in and out of our home. She had Kaden. And I have Charlie. And if I have any say, she will be the only woman coming in and out of my room.

"Hey Lex, can I talk to you for a minute?"

"I'll erase the turkey, I promise!" Lexi's eyes go wide and I stifle a laugh as my adorably bad daughter throws herself under the bus. "It was for thanksgiving! Today is November! I just wanted to make a turkey to show Charlie when she wakes up."

Wait…what? How the heck does she know Charlie is here? My door was closed. "How did you know Charlie is here?"

"Her boots." She points toward the front door where Charlie left her boots last night. "She's here, right?" Her eyes light up.

"Yes, she is, but she's sleeping. That's actually what I wanted to talk to you about. Sometimes Daddy might have Charlie over for sleepovers. Is that okay with you?"

Lexi smiles. "Yes, but do you think maybe I can have Charlie over for a sleepover too?"

Jesus, my daughter is too damn cute and innocent. "I'm sure she would love that."

"Yay!"

"There's something else I need to tell you." I want Lexi to know about Charlie's daughter. She's too young to fully comprehend it all, but I'm hoping it will help her to understand why Charlie gets upset sometimes.

"You know Grandpa Kaden's picture of the baby on the fridge you always ask about?"

"Yes, it's his baby who went to heaven."

"That's right. Well Charlie had a baby too. Her baby was a little girl, and she went to heaven when she was three years old."

"She's with Grandpa's baby?" Lexi asks.

"Yes, I think she is."

"She must be so sad! I'm going to draw her a picture and you make her the special pancakes." She runs out of the kitchen to grab her art stuff then sits at the table, drawing a picture while I make breakfast.

"Daddy, is breakfast ready yet?" Lexi yells from the table.

"Almost."

A few minutes later, I finish the pancakes, eggs, and bacon.

"Breakfast is ready, Lex. Put your stuff away."

"I'll go get Charlie!" Lexi yells, and before I can stop her, she runs down the hall toward my bedroom. Shit! Charlie is naked!

"Lexi! Wait!" But I'm too late. She's already opened the door and is in my room. "Lex, let's give Charlie a minute to wake up."

"She's not here, Daddy." Lexi pouts, and after I assess the situation in front of me, I see she's right. Charlie is gone. The only way she could have left is out the window.

"Let's go see where she is," I say to my daughter as I grab my keys. It's sunny with a few clouds outside, but it's pouring down rain—typical California weather—so we run to the truck and jump in. Not even a mile down the road, we spot Charlie and she's standing in the rain. Not moving. Her face tilted up to the sky.

"Daddy! She's getting all wet!"

After we pull over and Charlie gets in, we make our way back to the house. I am beyond frustrated that she would choose to crawl out of my window and walk home in the pouring rain instead of talking to me. When we get out, the rain has stopped and I hear Lexi say to Charlie, "My daddy told me this morning you had a little girl like me."

I wanted to warn Charlie I told Lexi about her daughter, but it's too late now. Just as I'm about to intervene, I see them talking, and instead of cutting in, I decide it's best to let them develop their own relationship. Wanting to give them privacy, I walk toward my front door. My phone goes off, indicating I have a text, and when I check it, I see it's from Mason letting me know his photo shoot and interview went well in Las Vegas.

A few minutes later, Lexi and Charlie come walking up, both smiling. "Are you okay?" I whisper into Charlie's ear before we walk inside.

"Yeah, I am. I'm sorry about leaving. I didn't want to put you in a bad position with Lexi."

"I was going to warn you I told Lexi about your daughter, but you had jumped out the window before I could. In the future, talk to me, don't run. Got it?"

"Got it."

"Good. Now let's eat. I made pancakes."

TWENTY-NINE

TRISTAN

THE LAST COUPLE WEEKS WITH CHARLIE AND LEXI HAVE BEEN nothing short of amazing. Mason had decided to spend some time in Las Vegas to train with the guys over at Cooper's Fight Club—a UFC gym owned by Bella's dad, Cooper, but is now run by Bella and Marco—after his UFC business wrapped up. This isn't the first time he's done this. He loves the change of pace and environment. He wasn't sure exactly when, but he said he would be back before we leave for Breckenridge for Thanksgiving. We'll be meeting my family over there along with both Bella and Marco's families.

Every night Charlie has slept over. On the nights she works, she takes a cab here. On the nights she's off, she hangs out here more than at her place. Sometimes she sleeps in my bed—those nights are filled with me inside her and then her falling asleep in my arms. Other nights Lexi claims her for herself—those nights are filled with Disney movies and cushion forts. I've been neglecting the gym big time, but luckily Brent has it all under control. One of the important parts of running a successful business is being able to delegate, right?

It's Monday and Charlie's off work tonight. She texted me earlier she'll be over after her therapy session. She also said the website is done and she's dying to show it to me. I have a surprise for her as well. I just hope she'll be as excited about it as I am. The door opens and when I look to see who it is, it's not Charlie.

"Honey, I'm home!" Mason yells out, throwing his duffle bag onto the ground.

"Shh! Lexi's napping." Mason plops onto the couch just as the door opens again. This time it's Charlie.

"Hey baby." She closes the door behind her and throws her arms around my neck for a hug. I glance at Mason over her shoulder to see he's grinning. His brow is quirked up and all I can do is smile. I've texted with him several times about me and Charlie getting more serious, but I don't think he fully grasped it until now. He nods in understanding and I know I have my best friend's support.

"I can't wait to show you the website! I finished it this morning—" Charlie stops talking and glances around. "Where's Lexi?"

"Napping," Mason says, and Charlie jumps.

"Oh! I didn't realize you were here," Charlie says, turning around to face Mason, her hands flying up to her chest. Wrapping my arms around her waist from behind, I rest my chin on her shoulder, breathing in her scent. She's wearing that pink perfume that's currently sitting on my bathroom counter. Coco something or some shit. All I know is it smells sweet and sexy, and almost as good as the scent between my woman's legs. Fuck! Now I'm hard.

Charlie feels my cock poke her back and she lets out a soft moan before turning to face me—pink tinting her cheeks. "What are you doing?" she whispers, and Mason cackles.

"Sorry." I laugh. "I can't help it. I want you all the time." I give her a kiss on her lips, and I'm about to pull her into my room for some afternoon sex—not giving a shit that Mason is home—when Lexi comes walking out.

"Uncle Mason!" Lexi squeals, running over to Mason to give him a hug. "I missed you so, so much! Did you see my grandma and grandpa?"

"I did! They said to give you this…" Mason grabs Lexi and throws her on to the couch, tickling her.

"Uncle… Mason!" Lexi shouts, out of breath. "I'm going to pee my pants!" Of course he stops immediately, laughing as he gets up.

"I need to head to the gym to get a workout in. I'll catch you guys later." He smirks at Charlie. "And I'm assuming that means I'll see you later as well."

"Charlie's living here!" Lexi gushes.

"Lex," I say, "you know she isn't living here. She's just spends the night sometimes."

"But she's here like every day! She should live here!"

Mason laughs as he grabs his keys from the table. "See ya!"

"Daddy, can I watch TV?" Lexi asks.

"Sure." She runs over to the couch, plops her little butt down, and starts switching through the channels on the remote.

Grabbing her laptop, Charlie sets it down on the dining room table. "Come check out your website!" I sit in a chair and pull her onto my lap, craving her body. It's insane how drawn I am to her. If she's in the same room as me, I need to be touching her in some way. I can't get enough of her and I don't think I ever will. No, I know I never will. "If there's anything you don't like, we can change it. Don't say you like it to be nice." She turns her body slightly to face me. "Okay?"

"Okay," I agree, then I give her a quick kiss. She turns back around and starts typing on the keyboard. Once she pulls up the site, she starts going over the details, telling me about the easy navigation and some other details I should be paying attention to, instead of focusing on the feel of her silky-smooth skin under my fingertips. As I run my hands up and down her thighs I wonder if she used the matching pink lotion that's sitting next to the perfume. If I were to splay her out on my bed and run my nose along the insides of her thighs, would it smell as sexy and sweet as her neck does? I bet it would smell even better—

"Tristan?" Charlie glares back at me and I can't help but wrap my arms tighter around her waist, my nose nestling into the bend of her neck. "Are you sniffing me?"

I chuckle into her hair remembering not too long ago when I asked her the same question. "Sorry, babe. I can't help it. I'll focus, I promise." Charlie shakes her head and then returns to showing me the site. Now that I'm paying attention, I'm in awe at the work she has done. "Damn, Charlie. This site looks good."

She turns her face, granting me a thousand mega-watt smile. "Thank you. I think so too. I love being creative."

"Speaking of being creative, I have a little surprise for you. And before you go shooting it down, remember the other night when we were talking about your dreams?"

Charlie's brows come together. "My idea about the painting studio with wine?"

Just then my phone rings and I see it's an unknown number. "Yeah, hold that thought." I hit answer on the call. "Hello?"

"Hey, Tristan. It's Adam." Unsure why my sister's boyfriend would call me, I'm immediately on alert.

"Everything okay?"

"Umm…no…your sister needs you to come over here. Well, actually I do. She's locked herself in the bathroom and I can't get her out." *What the hell?*

"Okay, I'm on my way."

"Thank you. You might want to find someone to watch Lexi. Your sister is kind of in a bad place."

"Do you need to call an ambulance?" I ask, starting to freaking out.

"No, no, nothing like that. Just get here soon, please."

"All right, I'll be there shortly." I hang up the phone and notice Charlie is nervously nibbling on her bottom lip. With her still sitting on my lap, she must've heard our conversation.

"I'm going to call Mason to come watch Lexi." I tap the side of her hip, indicating I need her to get up, and she stands. I pull up my contacts to call Mason thinking I can drop Lexi off to him at the gym on my way. My heart is pounding in my chest not knowing what's going on with my little sister.

The phone rings and rings and eventually goes to voicemail. *Shit!*

I dial again, and it does it again. I dial the gym's number. Holly, the front desk receptionist, answers. "Hey Holly, it's Tristan. Is Mason there?"

"Hey Tristan! He just ran out for a jog with Tommy."

Damn it. "Okay, can you have him call me as soon as he gets back?"

"Sure thing."

I hang up the phone, unsure of what to do, when Charlie says, "I can watch her." I shoot a glance at her and she's now biting down on her bottom lip. Hard.

"That's okay. I'm just going to bring her with me. I don't know what's going on, so I'm just not sure if there should be an audience. Maybe you could stay in the car with Lexi?"

"Tristan," Charlie replies. "I can watch her here."

"Are you sure?" I assess her face for any indication she isn't really sure.

"I'm sure." Her voice comes out confident.

"Okay, thank you." I pull her in for a quick kiss. "I'll call you once I know something." I walk over to Lexi. "I need to go see Auntie Morgan. Charlie is going to watch you. Be good for her. Okay?"

Lexi smiles and nods, and then goes back to watching the television.

I jump in my truck and haul ass over to Morgan's apartment. I park and jog to the door. Without knocking, I use my key and let myself in. Adam is sitting against the bathroom door.

"She in there?" I ask. He looks up and nods.

"What's going on?"

"We messed up." He swallows thickly. "We used protection every single time but once." *Oh, shit.*

"She's pregnant," I state, and he nods. "Morgan, open up." I knock on the bathroom door. I can hear her sniffling, and a few seconds later, the door swings open, and my sister is in my arms. My barely twenty-year-old little sister.

"It's okay," I murmur, rubbing her back. "It's going to be okay."

THIRTY

CHARLIE

TRISTAN WALKS OUT THE DOOR AND IT TAKES EVERYTHING IN me not to freak the hell out. The first thing I do is double check all the doors to make sure they're locked. There's a chain on the front door, so I slide it in place. It's high, so if something happens Lexi won't be able to get out…but then what if something happens and she needs to get out?

"Hey Lexi, do you know what to do if there's an emergency?"

Lexi's eyes move from the television to me. "Like stop, drop, and roll?" Her adorable little button nose scrunches up.

"Umm…yeah, like that, but also like if something happens to me." This gets me Lexi's undivided attention. She sits up, crossing her legs Indian style, the show she was watching no longer on her mind.

"What's going to happen to you?" She frowns and I hate that I'm probably scaring her, but I'm not taking a chance. I've already lost one little girl, I'm not going to let history repeat itself.

"Well, hopefully nothing," I say calmly, sitting next to Lexi on the couch. "But if something did happen, like if I passed out or hit my head." When I say this my brain struggles to conjure up a memory. I push against my temples trying to let it come forth but too quickly it's gone.

"Are you okay, Charlie?" Lexi asks.

"Yes, sweet girl. Sorry. What I mean is if something were to happen, do you know how to call 911?"

"Oh yeah! Daddy showed me a long time ago. He showed me that if I forget his code I can press the red button and it will call the police and fireman and ambulance." It never ceases to amaze me how wonderful of a father Tristan is.

"Yep! Just like that. I have a cell phone as well." I take it out to show her. "If there's an emergency you just press this circle here and the word emergency will come up."

"That's like my daddy's phone!" Lexi says excitedly.

"Good. So I was thinking maybe we can do some coloring while your dad is gone?"

Lexi perks up. "Come see my turkey! Daddy forgot to make me take it down, but I'll show you because when he remembers, I'll have to." She scowls, and grabbing my hand pulls me into her room. On the same wall as before, where she drew the tree, there's a massive turkey with colored feathers. It reminds me I should ask Tristan about painting the wall with chalkboard paint.

"It's beautiful!" Lexi beams then goes to her bins to grab her coloring stuff. We spend the rest of the time Tristan is gone coloring, and it feels really good to be able to experience this with Lexi without the fear of getting caught.

THIRTY-ONE

CHARLIE

"IS A BLINDFOLD REALLY NECESSARY?" I ASK AS TRISTAN GUIDES me blindly out of the truck. I have no clue where we are or what we're doing but Tristan insisted I need to keep an open mind and not say no right away.

"Yes, it is." We come to a stop and I hear keys jingling and then cold air whooshing. We start walking again and the change in temperature tells me we're now inside somewhere. I feel Tristan's body come up behind mine, his arms enveloping me, and his gruff voice hitting my ear. "Remember, I need you to be open minded." I nod in agreement and he unties the blindfold.

As I glance around the empty open space, I'm puzzled. The walls are bare and the floor is dark hardwood. There is a counter near the front, but other than that, there's nothing—it's completely bare. Then I notice a blanket laid out on the floor in the corner, two champagne flutes, and a bottle of some type of alcohol.

Taking me by my hand, Tristan pulls me toward the center of the room. "Imagine this. Dark wood tables lined up with painting easels. Matching comfortable seats for the women—or kids—to sit on." He points to the wall to the left. "You can have all the different canvases displayed. One for every theme." He points to the other wall. "Over here is where you can have your bar for the food and drinks for the parties." He points to the door on the back wall. "And through there are two areas. One for the kids' room you talked about, and the other is a huge storage area to store all the paints and materials. There's even a bathroom. All we would need is an extra sink for the customers to wash their hands."

My mind is racing as he describes every detail of the dream I told him about while we were lying in bed. Not only did he listen, but he remembered.

"…and this place is available. I found a contractor who assured me he could have this place ready for you to open in January."

"Whoa…stop," I say, moving toward him. Taking his hands in mine, I lift up on my tiptoes to give him a kiss. "You, believing in my dream means the world to me, but it was just that…a dream."

"And now it can come true," he says nonchalantly.

"No, it can't." I shake my head. "My credit…it's not good. And…" I swallow thickly. "I can't have my name on anything. I work under the table at Plush."

Tristan eyes me warily. "Charlie, I asked you this before. Are you in trouble?"

"No, I'm not in trouble. I just…I just need to keep a low profile." I advert my eyes, feeling like shit for all the half-truths I'm spewing out.

Tristan lets out a frustrated sigh and I'm shocked when, instead of him asking me to explain, he asks, "Do you want this?"

My eyes dart back to his, and I nod, tears welling up in my lids. "Yeah, but some dreams aren't meant to come true. They're simply there to keep us wishing and hoping and believing." I glance around the room. I can picture it all. The tables, the easels, the color of the walls, the women coming in to drink and paint. The children's birthday parties.

Tristan's arms are around me, his hands gripping my butt as he pulls me into him. "I can make yours come true. Please let me. No strings. I own this building outright. We're standing in a storefront right next to my gym. The studio can be in my name and we'll have an attorney write up a contract for a five, ten, or twenty-year rental agreement. Whatever you want. It will stay between you and me."

Oh, this man. I don't deserve him in the slightest. I never fully understood what I was missing when I was with Justin until Tristan came into my life. "Okay," I breathe. Pulling his face down to mine, my mouth covers his as I try to convey every emotion I'm feeling right now thanks to him.

Soon our kiss turns hungry, greedy, our tongues colliding with one another. Tristan picks me up and my legs wrap around his waist, my ankles locking behind his back as he walks us to the lone counter in the corner. He places me on the cool surface and backs up slightly. His eyes rake down my body, his tongue darting out to wet his lips.

Not able to wait any longer, I pull my shirt over my head and unclasp my bra. My breasts are heavy with want, my nipples rock hard with need. Tristan follows my lead and removes his shirt while kicking off his shoes. He pushes down his pants, and like always, the sight of this delicious man in front of me has my head spinning. But tonight, it's more than the want—or even the need—to be sexual with him. What he's done for me, his blind belief in me…he will never understand what it means to me. He gives and gives without question, without expecting anything in return, and I wish there was something I could give him. Something to put us on equal footing. Because he deserves everything.

In a few minutes, Tristan will be buried inside of me physically, but what he doesn't realize is that he's already inside of me—every second of every day. He has buried himself deep inside my chest, in my heart. He's flowing through my veins and there's no getting him out.

Suddenly needing to show him how much he means to me, I jump off the counter and drop to my knees. I pull his briefs down and his cock springs free. All of the sex we've had these last few weeks, and I haven't yet had the pleasure of tasting this man. He always insists on making it about me. But tonight I want to make it about him.

My eyes lock with Tristan's as my fingers lift his cock, the flat of my tongue running up the underside of his shaft. It's smooth and thick and all mine. When my tongue gets to the mushroom head, my lips wrap around it, giving it a wet, open-mouthed kiss. Tristan's eyes close as he lets out a deep groan. The wetness between my legs pools and my muscles tighten needing relief. His eyelids pull apart, lust and need shining through. My eyes never leaving his, my mouth opens, and I take in his entire length until his shaft hits the back of my throat.

"Jesus, woman," he groans, his hands coming down to my hair, his fingers entwining in the strands. I pull back slightly and then take him in completely, the head of his cock hitting my throat once again. As I pull back for the second time, I go slowly, my saliva wetting his entire shaft. When I release his dick from my mouth, a milky white bead of precum surfaces, and I dart my tongue out to lick it clean. "You taste good. Will you… fuck my mouth?" Tristan has made me tell him what I want several times while in bed, and each time it gets easier, making me feel like I'm in charge of my pleasure even when he's the one giving it to me.

"Is that what you want? You want me to fist your hair and fuck your wet mouth until I come?" His dirty talk has me dripping and I nod emphatically, the thought of his cock driving in and out of my mouth, turning me on. I've learned the last few weeks how amazing sex can be. How passionate and raw and mesmerizing intimacy can be with a man you truly care about and trust. At first, Tristan was gentle with me, but each time he asked me to tell him what I wanted, I found myself begging him to take things a bit further. A bit rougher. A bit rawer. There doesn't seem to be a limit as to how much I want this man. It never feels like it's enough. I'm always left wanting and needing and craving more. More of him. More of his touch. More of…everything that is Tristan.

My hands go to his muscular thighs to steady myself as his fingers grasp my hair tightly, pulling my face toward him. My mouth stays open as he begins to gently make love to my mouth. But I need more—I need to be fucked. I'm like a caged animal being let out into the wild each time we're together. I want to explore and experience everything with Tristan knowing I'm safe with him.

Grabbing his butt cheeks, I pull his lower body toward me, his dick hitting my throat once again, showing him what I need, and like always, he gets it. He pulls back slightly then pushes back into my mouth a little harder as he bottoms out in my throat. My moans of pleasure reverberate around his cock, his thrusts turning savage as he fucks my face. My mouth is so wet, drool drips down my chin. I gag and feel the tears dripping down my face, but I don't care. Because I am with a man who wants me and cherishes me. I am with a man who adores me, who cares about me, who would never hurt me, not physically or emotionally. I am safe with him. My pussy is tingling at this thought, needing more, needing it all.

I consider bringing my fingers to my pussy when Tristan says, "Charlie...fuck, baby...I'm going to come." He tries to pull back, but I'm not having it. I need to taste him, swallow him. I need everything from him. Every last damn drop. My lips tighten around him, my tongue stroking his shaft as he pumps into me. His head goes back, and the look of pleasure on his face has me wanting to please him for the rest of my life. I feel his cock getting harder, the sperm traveling up his shaft, and then it's shooting into my mouth and coating my tongue before it travels down my throat. I swallow his seed until his dick begins to deflate. Once I know he's finished, I gently swipe my tongue across his head, swirling around the crown until there isn't a single drop of cum left.

Pulling back, I stand, suddenly shy. Tristan's hands come up to my face, and he wipes the tears from my cheeks, eliciting a smile from me. He bends slightly, pushing my shorts and panties down, and then I'm in the air and being placed back onto the counter, the cool granite sending shivers up my spine. My legs are spread and Tristan's fingers are pulling my pussy lips apart, his tongue darting across my clit.

I'm wet and horny and so goddamned turned on that when Tristan adds his fingers to the mix, my orgasm hits almost instantly. My butt threatens to bow off the counter, but Tristan's hand holds me down as he licks and sucks and fingers me through my climax.

Once I've come down from my orgasmic high, Tristan leans over me and gives me a soft kiss. "I made us a picnic. There's champagne and food over there on the floor. Let's celebrate."

"Only if you agree to let me lick the champagne off your body."

"That can definitely be arranged."

THIRTY-TWO

CHARLIE

I'M SITTING ON A CHARTERED PLANE WITH LEXI, MASON, TRISTAN, Morgan, and her boyfriend Adam, heading to Breckenridge, Colorado where Tristan's family has a vacation home near a ski resort. The doctor confirmed Morgan is in fact pregnant, almost three months along to be exact, and she's planning to tell her parents when we arrive. That's probably for the best since anybody who has ever been pregnant can tell she's carrying a baby. She's slightly pale yet she has that pregnancy glow going on. She isn't quite showing, but her body is already changing, and unfortunately, she is still throwing up even though she's close to being out of her first trimester.

It's three days before Thanksgiving and exactly one year since my entire world came crashing down—since I woke up and found out my daughter was dead and I wished to God my life would end as well. If you would've asked me a year ago, I would've told you I would never step foot on another private plane again. Leaving Justin meant leaving behind the wealth and accommodations. But I guess it's a good thing Tristan has the money and means to charter a plane. I was able to get on using the fake ID I had created with the name Charlie Pratt. I never would have gotten away with that on a commercial flight.

Tristan takes my hand in his, bringing it up for a kiss. I told him last night the significance of today's date. But the truth is, just like the day Georgia died, the days following were just as foggy. I spent a few days in the hospital, heavily medicated, and it wasn't until I returned home that things started to finally become clear.

♥♥♥♥♥

ONE MONTH AFTER GEORGIA'S DEATH

I'M LYING IN BED PRETENDING TO BE ASLEEP WHEN I HEAR THE door shut loudly and Justin talking on the phone. He stops whatever he's saying when he gets to our room, and when he thinks I'm asleep he continues his call. "I want her admitted. It's obvious she's suffering from depression and is suicidal…I don't care…She shouldn't have tried to leave me…Just tell them she's abusing drugs and her husband is committing her…" His voice trails off the farther away he gets from the room.

I hear his office door shut and my eyes snap open in shock. What a lying bastard! How dare he say I'm abusing drugs. He's the one who has tried to shove pills down my throat every day since I got home from the hospital. At first, I did what he said. I took the pills he insisted I take—the pills he said the doctor insisted I take. But when I woke up one afternoon and he told me I slept through Georgia's funeral, a funeral I didn't even remember him telling me about, I stopped taking the pills. I asked him to take me to see her, but he said I wasn't up for it and handed me more pills. I pretended to take them, but as soon as he turned his back, I spit them out and shoved them under the mattress. Once I heard him leave, I got up and flushed the pills down the toilet.

And for the last couple weeks I've continued to do the same thing while I formulate a new plan to escape. With Georgia gone, I have absolutely no reason to stay here. I have the money I put away, and with our daughter dead, I doubt Justin will even care if I leave.

I replay his conversation in my head. He mentioned me trying to leave him. He must be referring to before Georgia died, but how did he know I was planning to leave him? And he's going to have me committed? To where? A mental institution? None of this makes any sense, but there's no way in hell I'm going to stay here to find out.

"WE'RE HERE, BABE." USING HIS CHIN, TRISTAN NUDGES MY head, which is resting on his shoulder, waking me up from my memories. When my head comes up slightly, he meets me halfway, giving me a soft kiss. "You good?" he asks when he breaks the kiss. I take a deep, calming breath, thankful that last memory was the final one with Justin in it. The day I found out what he was planning was the day I ran, only that time I was successful.

"Yeah," I say. "I'm good." I give Tristan a small smile before standing up and making my way to the front to deplane.

After picking up our rental SUV, we make the drive to the cabin in

Breckenridge. The adults are quiet. Adam and Morgan worrying about how the family will take their news, Mason texting god knows who, Tristan driving, and me lost in my thoughts about meeting Tristan's family.

Lexi fills the silence with her excitement. She can't wait to see her cousin Micaela, build a snowman, go snow tubing, and drink hot chocolate. When we pull into the driveway, the cabin is gorgeous. On our way here, Tristan mentioned we'll be staying in the cabin his family owns, and Bella and Marco's families will be sharing a separate one they rent every year. I know Tristan is good friends with Bella, but I'm not sure how I'm supposed to feel about a woman who strung Tristan along and took advantage of his selflessness only to throw him to the side when the father of her baby decided to man up. Tristan assures me it was for the best, and if he can let it go and not be bitter about it, then I guess I need to do the same. After all, her loss is my gain.

"Yess! We're here!" Lexi squeals as she quickly undoes her seatbelt. I jump out of the vehicle to help get the bags, but Lexi has other plans. Grabbing my hand, she pulls me up the driveway toward the front door. The door swings open and out walks a man and a woman, who I recognize from the pictures as Tristan's parents. His mom smiles wide as she opens her arms for Lexi, and without letting go of my hand, Lexi engulfs her grandma in a hug.

"Oh, Lexi! I missed you so much!" Mrs. Scott gushes over her granddaughter before putting her down as I force back the memories of Justin's cold, heartless parents.

"Grandma! This is Charlie. I told you about her on the phone. She is mine and Daddy's friend. You know, the one Daddy loves on, and she lives with us but still in her own house, and she's building a painting place!"

And now…I die of embarrassment.

Mr. and Mrs. Scott look from their granddaughter to me, and then to each other, both smiling and trying to refrain from laughing. If Lexi wasn't holding my hand hostage, I can almost guarantee I would be running away. Of course, Tristan joins the fun, his arm swinging around my shoulders and tugging my body into his. And does he save me? Nope!

"Lexi, what have I told you? Charlie isn't living with us…at least not yet." He gives me a panty-dropping wink followed by a wet smack of his lips to my cheek, and I wish for the ground to swallow me up.

"Oh my God," I groan, trying to hide my face in his neck.

"Oh! Don't be embarrassed," his mom coos. "I'm Ashley and this is Kaden. We've heard so much about you." She grabs me out of Tristan's hold and pulls me into a hug—Lexi still holding my hand. "Thank you for making my son and granddaughter happy," she whispers so only I can hear. I instantly get choked up at her kind words. I've only been in the presence of this family for a total of two minutes and I can already tell they're nothing like Justin's stuffy, stuck up, cold-hearted parents.

Ashley pulls back from our hug, her eyes zeroing in on something or someone behind me, and when I turn, I see Morgan standing a few feet back, Adam by her side. The look on Ashley's face confirms my earlier thoughts. She already knows her daughter is pregnant. Morgan looks so young in this moment as she waits to see how her mom and dad will react to the news, and suddenly, I feel nervous for her.

But then Ashley closes the gap between her and her daughter, wrapping her arms around her in a motherly hug, and I know everything will be okay. I imagine how I would react if Lexi came home pregnant. After losing Georgia, I don't think there's anything Lexi could do that would have me upset. I learned the hard way that life is too short. Clutching my chest, wishing my little girl was here, I feel the hot tears trickling down my cheeks.

"I need a moment," I whisper to Tristan, and without waiting for a response, I let go of Lexi's hand and take off toward… I have no clue where. My mind flitters through memory after memory of my little girl growing up. I only got three goddamned years with her! It's so unfair! The tears are racing down in bucketfuls when I hear a voice behind me.

"Are you okay?" I turn around, my breathing labored, as I fight off a panic attack. It's Tristan's dad.

"Oh…um, yeah." I attempt to swipe the still falling tears. "I'm sorry," I huff out. "I'm just having a bad moment."

"Tristan told me," he says, "about you losing your daughter." I nod, the lump in my throat preventing me from speaking.

"I went through something similar." He gives me a sad smile and motions for me to sit on the swinging wooden bench. I must have ended up in the back of their house. We sit next to each other and he gives me a second to catch my breath before he continues. "I lost my wife and my son. I was driving the car on our way to the hospital when she was in labor. A truck ran a red light and hit us, and they both died."

"I'm so sorry," I choke out, the tears falling once again. "My daughter was hit by a car, only I can't remember any of it. I blacked out and when I woke up she was gone."

Kaden nods in understanding. "It's hard… to balance what we lost with what's in front of us. To try to love those alive without the guilt of leaving the ones we lost behind."

I glance toward him and take a deep breath at the comfort of someone else understanding. "That's exactly how I feel. When I watched Ashley and Morgan, I imagined how I would feel if Lexi came home pregnant. I felt so guilty that I thought of her and not of Georgia."

"I went almost ten years before I allowed myself to move on. It wasn't until Ashley and Tristan came into my life—and knocked me on my ass—that I considered opening my heart up again."

"It's only been a year since I lost my daughter," I say softly.

"The timing doesn't matter," Kaden says. "Whether it's six weeks, six months, or six years…" He shakes his head. "It doesn't matter. I was waiting for Ashley and Tristan. My heart knew I belonged to that woman before I did. I can't change what happened to Gabby. If I could, I would. I'm sure you know the inner battle… begging God to take away any happiness you feel to have them back."

"I do."

"Unfortunately, life doesn't work that way. The moment I accepted I can still love Gabby and our baby, and move forward with Ashley, was the day I was finally set free." He gives me a warm smile that reminds me of my father.

"Thank you," I say. "I needed to hear that today."

"What do you say we go join everyone inside? I hear my daughter is pregnant."

"I'll be inside in a minute." Kaden pats my knee in a fatherly way before getting up and walking inside, leaving me to my thoughts.

I'm not even out here for five minutes when a little girl comes barreling up the snow-covered ground and onto the porch steps. "Hi! Is Lexi here yet?"

A couple, who I assume are her parents come walking up after her, and my suspicions are confirmed when I see the woman is pregnant.

"She is," I tell her, and she runs past me into the house, the door slamming shut behind her.

"Sorry about her manners. She's excited to see Lexi. You would think she hasn't seen her in a year when it's really only been less than two months." Her hands go to her belly as she waddles up the steps. "My name is Bella." She gives me a sweet smile. "And this is my husband, Marco."

I put my hand out to shake hers and then her husband's. "I'm Charlie," I say, not giving her anything more. Bella's eyes widen at the mention of my name, but she quickly hides her reaction.

"It's nice to meet you," Marco says before going inside, leaving Bella and me alone. She sits down next to me and I'm not sure where this is going to go, so I wait for her to lead.

"I'm really glad to meet you." My head whips around to face her with what I'm sure is a look of confusion marring my features. Bella laughs softly. "I was so nervous about meeting you… Shit, I guess I still am."

"What? Why?" I ask incredulously.

"Umm…hello…I'm the best friend who hurt him. Sure, Tristan forgave me, but that's only because he's Tristan. He's like the nicest guy in the world." She laughs softly. "And I know if a woman hurt my husband, the man I love, I probably wouldn't be too nice to her." She shrugs and we both laugh.

"I don't really know what happened," I admit. "But you're right, I do love Tristan and Lexi…" I pause as the words I just said sink in. *I love Tristan and Lexi.* "And… I probably should be telling him that before you." We both giggle. "I wasn't around when it all went down, so I'm not going to judge. I've messed up so many times in my life." I shake my head. "I've made horrible decisions that ended in tragedy, and lord knows I don't deserve that man."

"Yes, you do." I jump at the sound of Tristan's voice. "I don't know what's going on out here, but I hope you aren't giving Charlie a hard time. Today is hard enough for her." Tristan's jaw is clenched and he's practically shooting daggers at Bella, who suddenly looks nervous.

"Hey," I say softly, standing up to join his side. "She was just introducing herself to me." I reach up and give Tristan a kiss on his cheek, but he isn't having it. Not caring that we're in front of Bella, he turns his face to kiss me on my lips.

Once he releases me, he says, "I don't want to hear you saying some bullshit about not deserving me again. It's me who doesn't deserve you." He pulls me into his arms and kisses my forehead.

"I'm pretty sure you both deserve each other," Bella says sweetly as she slowly stands. "Happy looks good on you, Tristan." She pats his shoulder then turns to me. "Thank you… for what you said about not judging. I'm going to go inside and go pee. This damn baby has been pressing on my bladder for the last month." And with that, she excuses herself inside, leaving Tristan and me alone.

"You didn't need to bite her head off," I murmur, rising on my tiptoes to give Tristan a kiss. He sighs into my mouth as he deepens the kiss before ending it way too quickly.

"I'll apologize to her later. I just want to make sure you're comfortable here and everyone is nice to you. I can't even imagine how hard today is for you, yet you're here because Lexi and I want you to be."

"I want to be here." I wrap my arms around his neck. "There's nowhere else I would rather be than here with you and Lexi."

"Good," Tristan says, his voice suddenly full of emotion. "Because I *really* want you here." His tongue darts out to wet his lips and my body hums, craving his touch. Without even saying a word, I know we're on the same page.

My legs come up at the same time his hands move down to catch me, my ankles locking together as he pushes me against the wall of the house. Our mouths crash into each other, the kiss quickly deepening as our tongues dart in and out of each other's mouths. I let out a moan as I take in the taste of Tristan—peppermint with a hint of something that is uniquely him.

My fingers pull at the tips of his hair as his lips break from mine and move to my neck, trailing soft kisses downward. Needing more, I grind my pelvis against his hard body as his lips go to the swell of my breasts.

"Daddy! Charlie!" Lexi yells, the door swinging opening. Tristan quickly releases me, my body sliding down the cabin wall. I flinch as my back hits the curves of the logs and Tristan curses under his breath, trying to catch me.

"Yeah, Lex?" Tristan asks, his voice rough.

"Uncle Mason and Uncle Nathan said they're going fishing tonight! Are you going fishing with them, Daddy? I don't wanna go fishing." Lexi's hands go to her hips.

"Who's Nathan?" I ask.

"Bella's younger brother," Tristan says, wrapping his arm around my waist. "No, Lex. I'm not going fishing. I've already caught my fish and I have no intention of ever releasing her." He shoots me a wink and I laugh.

"Ewww, Daddy!" Lexi yells before stomping back inside, Tristan and me following behind. She gets to Mason and a guy that looks to be in his early twenties. "Daddy said he caught his fish and he's not going fishing!"

THIRTY-THREE

TRISTAN

THE NEXT COUPLE DAYS GO BY WAY TOO QUICKLY. THE DAYS ARE spent with my family—sometimes Bella's and Marco's families joining in—skiing, snowboarding, snow tubing, and building snowmen at the request of Lexi and Micaela. The nights are spent with bonfires and family dinners, and conclude with me deep inside Charlie. Thanks to my sister Emma for offering to bunk with Lexi, Charlie and I have a room to ourselves. I'll be buying Emma an extra special gift for Christmas this year.

It's Thanksgiving day and the women have been cooking and baking in the kitchen all day. I was worried about Charlie being comfortable but she fits in perfectly with us. The guys are all watching football, but I couldn't even tell you who's playing. My eyes can't seem to veer away from Charlie. In California, she's almost always in shorts, but here she's wearing some tight spandex looking pants which mold to her ass, paired with an adorable Texas A&M hoodie that looks like it's been put through the wash a thousand times. Her hair is up in a high ponytail and she's makeup free. She's setting the table and every time she leans over I'm checking the clock, counting down the minutes until I can peel off those—

My view is cut off when a pillow from the couch hits me right in my face before I can dodge it. "Hey!" I glare over at the guys, trying to figure out who threw it. Caleb is smirking and Marco is laughing. My dad is grinning ear-to-ear, and Mason's face is completely void of all emotion minus the laughter in his eyes. *Fucker!*

"What the hell was that for?"

"I didn't throw the pillow," my dad says, "but I'm pretty sure it was because I called your name several times."

"And your pussy whipped ass was too busy staring at your woman to hear." Mason chuckles. I throw the pillow back at Mason as Cooper and Nathan come walking out of the kitchen, their mouths filled with food.

Not able to go another minute without touching my woman, I use the excuse of wanting some food. The guys all laugh, but I ignore them. When I enter the kitchen, it's filled with women. Bella—and her huge belly—is chopping something, my mom is pulling something out of the oven, Hayley, Marco's mom, is filling a bowl full of bread, but the only person I care about is the woman who is reaching up on her tiptoes.

I come up behind her, my front pushing right up against her spandex covered ass. One of my hands rests on her sexy hips while my other one extends up toward her hand, which is currently trying to reach the good plates. My fingers trail a line up her tricep and forearm, ending at her fingers. Charlie shivers lightly at my touch. "Your ass in these pants are going to have me coming in mine," I murmur into her ear.

She shakes with silent laughter as she comes down from her tiptoes, her ass purposely rubbing up against my crotch, and turns around to face me. "Are you in here to help me or to distract me?" She tries to sound firm, but her lips twitch, a smile breaking free.

"I'm here to help you in *any* way you need." I waggle my eyebrows as my hands go around her back, gliding down to that ass I can't get enough of. I lean in for a kiss when my mom slaps my shoulder, reminding me we aren't alone.

"Tristan Scott, take it to the bedroom," she scolds with zero seriousness in her tone. Charlie's cheeks turn pink and I chuckle, not giving a shit.

"I agree!" I exclaim, grabbing Charlie's hand playfully and pretending to pull her toward the bedroom. "Let's take this to the bedroom!"

"Oh my God! Tristan, stop!" Charlie squeals, pulling her hand out of mine. "Grab the plates, please."

I do as she requests and then head out back to check on Lexi, who is sipping on her hot chocolate while swinging on the bench, watching everyone play. I sit next to her and steal a sip of her hot chocolate.

"Why aren't you playing?" I nod toward the others.

"I'm mad at Micaela," she states matter-of-factly.

"Oh yeah…why?"

"She said she's getting a baby sister and that I can't have one because I don't have a mommy." I store the fact that Micaela let it slip the sex of the baby—I'll definitely be fucking with Marco about that one later—and focus on the issue at hand. I always knew the day would come when Lexi would ask about her mom. I just never knew what I would say. The truth is, I still don't. It's a shitty situation. I think a small part of me—the part that knows what it's like to be without a parent—was hoping Gina would come to her senses one day and show up...or that she would die and I could say she's dead and that's why she isn't around. I know that sounds horrible, but at least it would mean not having to tell Lexi her mom is alive and chooses not to be in her life.

Unfortunately, neither of those scenarios have happened. "Well, Micaela was right, only mommies can have babies." Lexi sets her cup down on the arm of the seat, crosses her arms over her chest, and lets out an annoyed huff. "But that doesn't mean you can't have a brother or sister one day."

Lexi looks at me, her eyes asking for further explanation. "One day I hope to get married, and when I do, you'll maybe get a brother or sister."

"Can you marry Charlie?" Lexi asks.

"I would like to," I answer honestly.

"Could she be my mommy then?" Lexi's voice is now a whisper, and her words going straight to my heart.

"I think that's something we'd have to ask Charlie, but for now, she might not be your mom, but she's your friend, and I know she loves you very much. Plus, Auntie Morgan is having a baby and we'll get to see him or her a lot."

Lexi nods then picks up her mug to take another sip of her hot chocolate. She doesn't ask about her birth mother, and I don't mention her. One day she'll ask and hopefully by then I'll have come up with the perfect answer that won't break my daughter's heart.

"I KNOW THIS ISN'T HOW YOU PLANNED YOUR FUTURE. YOU have everything outlined and in lists and you check them off as you go, but I'm a firm believer that everything happens for a reason. I love you and I'm asking that maybe we can start a new list, one that includes a future with us together as a family. Will you marry me?"

Everyone sits at the dining room table shocked as Adam gets down on one knee next to Morgan's chair—a jewelry box open with a shiny diamond sparkling inside. I glance from my mom, who has her hands over her mouth—she's such a romantic—to my dad, who looks like he's holding back from knocking this guy out. The little kids have no clue what is happening other than the fact that the food isn't being served. The other adults are waiting for Morgan to answer, but then my eyes land on Charlie. Her expression is mournful. She's mentioned before that she was married, and I'm assuming the guy she was with is the one that physically and emotionally abused her. She never brings him up. Any memories shared are only about her daughter.

I haven't wanted to push her, ask her questions she isn't ready to answer, but that doesn't mean I'm not curious. The more time we spend together, the more I notice. For instance, she said her credit is bad and she can't have her name on anything. All signs point to her hiding out, which leads me to believe she's hiding from Georgia's father. In order for Charlie to move forward, at some point we're going to have to face whatever she's dealing with head on, and she's going to have to trust me enough to fully let me in.

Morgan sniffles. "I'll never know if it's just because of the baby." Adam shakes his head. Poor guy, he's proposing to a hormonal pregnant woman.

"I loved you before the baby," he insists. "You know that." Morgan nods knowingly and takes a deep breath.

"Okay, yes, I'll marry you." Everyone sighs in relief and says their congratulations, and then it's finally time to eat some damn food. Lexi is sitting between Charlie and me, and since Charlie goes about making Lexi a plate of food before I can, I focus on piling my plate high: potatoes, stuffing, turkey, cranberry sauce, corn, rolls, and some good old green bean casserole.

"We have an announcement to make," my dad says once everyone is done stuffing their faces with food. Everyone quiets down and he continues. "After discussing this with Emma, who has agreed, we've decided to move to California. With Tristan and Mason over there and now Morgan, who will be starting a family soon. Ashley and I don't want to miss out on the important events taking place, and it's clear our kids aren't planning to move back any time soon. We're planning to put the house up for sale when we get back. Ashley would like to be moved before Morgan has the baby."

"Grandpa and Grandma!" Lexi squeals. "You're moving to me?"

"Yes, we are," my mom gushes as Lexi jumps out of her seat and runs over to my mom, hopping up into her lap.

THIRTY-FOUR

CHARLIE

"QUIT YOUR JOB."

"No."

"Please, baby. You spend all day at the studio and all night working your ass off. I miss you."

Tristan and I are lying in his bed. It's three in the morning and I just got to his place from work. I'm exhausted and I know he's right, but I'm afraid if the studio doesn't bring in a profit, I won't have anything to fall back on. While I gave in on renting the place from Tristan, I insisted I pay him a monthly fee, and I'm covering all the renovation costs that are being done to the studio. It's expected to open right after the first of the year and I am beyond excited. I've finally decided on a name—You Paint Art Studio—and I need to create a website. I even came up with a cute tagline—paint to unwind—and had some cards made up. I need to look into advertising, but I want to wait until most of the work is done so I can take some pictures.

"I'll think about it," I say, then change the subject. "I was thinking maybe we could take Lexi to go get a tree this weekend. Christmas is only a few weeks away."

Tristan wraps me up in his arms, his legs caging mine in. "That sounds perfect, babe." He pulls my face up to his and kisses me before we both fall asleep.

♥♥♥♥♥

"LEXI, GO PUT YOUR CLOTHES AWAY IN YOUR DRAWERS, PLEASE." I hand Lexi a stack of her tiny clothes and she takes them to her room.

Tristan was doing the laundry and making dinner when Brent called him to let him know the kids' mixed-martial-arts class was going to have to be canceled because the instructor called out sick. I told Tristan I didn't mind watching Lexi while he goes over to teach the class, and since he had to leave in a rush, I figured I would finish up his laundry and dinner for him.

As I'm taking the pan of baked chicken parmesan out of the oven, the door slams shut and Mason yells out his usual, "Honey, I'm home."

"Wrong honey," I shout back, placing the pan on the stove and meeting him in the living room.

"Or the right one," he jokes. "Where's Tristan?"

"Teaching the kids MMA class. Evan called out sick. He just left a few minutes ago."

Mason drops his bag to the floor and tosses his keys onto the counter. "I must've just missed him." He plops onto the couch.

"Uncle Mason!" Lexi comes running over to Mason and jumps into his lap. I head back into the kitchen to check on the vegetables and start the potatoes. I'm almost through peeling and cutting the entire bag of potatoes when I hear a Lexi scream. Forgetting the food, I run into the living room to find Lexi in tears, holding her arm, and Mason nowhere to be seen.

I drop to my knees next to Lexi just as Mason comes running out of his room and kneels next to her. Not sure what's wrong, I don't pick her up.

"Lexi, what happened?" I ask, panicking. Tears are flying down her face and she's grabbing her arm, and that's when I notice her wrist is dangling in the wrong direction with what looks like a bone popping out under her skin.

"My-my hand," she hiccups.

"Mason, we need to get her to the hospital. I think her wrist is broken." Mason, who is acting a lot calmer than I am, agrees.

"Okay, I'll pick her up. Go make sure the oven and stove are off and call Tristan to let him know to meet us at the hospital." I jump up and rush over to the kitchen, shut off the oven and stove, and throw the hot pots into the sink. Then I pull on my boots and meet Mason at the door. Lexi is in his arms and is now sobbing uncontrollably.

Mason sets Lexi into the back of his vehicle and I slide in next to her. The ride feels like it takes forever as I comfort Lexi the best I can while texting and calling Tristan. When he doesn't answer, I call the gym and ask that he call me immediately. We get to the emergency room, and after Mason sets Lexi down on my lap, he checks her in.

"It's okay, sweet girl," I coo. "The doctor is going to make it all better." Lexi's tear-stricken face glances up at me, her chest bouncing up and down. "Shh…it's okay," I say as I hold her close, careful not to jostle her arm or hand. Pulling her now wet hair—from all the tears—

away from her face, I grab my ponytail holder from my wrist and tie her hair up in a messy bun.

"Alexandria Scott," a nurse calls out, and Mason gently takes Lexi from my arms, carrying her back as I follow behind. We're brought back to the pediatric unit and another nurse appears.

"Good evening, my name is Mila Sterling and I'll be looking after Alexandria today. It says here you might have..." The nurse stops reading what's on her clipboard and looks up. She takes one look at Mason and starts stuttering. "Umm..." She clears her throat and focuses her attention on Lexi. "It says here you might have broken your wrist?" She keeps her eyes trained on Lexi. "Why don't you set her down on the bed and I'll get the paperwork started before the doctor comes in." Her voice is now all squeaky as she tries to look everywhere but at Mason.

One glance in his direction and I see why. He's smirking. And I'm not talking about his usual *I'm Mason and I know the ladies love me* smirk. I'm talking about the *go ahead and eat your heart out baby because I'm about to take you on the ride of your life* kind of smirk.

Mila quickly composes herself, though, and her face goes from looking shocked to looking...pissed? Disgusted? Oh no! Please don't tell me... "Mason," I whisper. "Did you and her..." I nod toward the nurse—who is now taking Lexi's vitals—and Mason plays dumb. "Did you and her"—He tilts his head. Asshole is going to make me say it— "go fishing?"

Mason throws his head back in laughter and I groan. "Don't tell me you're jealous, Charlie. I don't think Tristan would appreciate that."

I smack him on his arm and the nurse looks back and forth between the two of us. I lean in closer to Mason so she can't hear. "I just want to make sure she won't try to take her anger out on Lexi." And this, of course, earns me another laugh. Shoving Mason to the side, I get up and stand next to Lexi.

"Is my daddy on his way?" Lexi asks, tears welling up in her eyes again. Grabbing my phone out of my pocket, I notice I have no service. Shit! Good thing I texted Tristan what happened and where we are.

"He should be here soon, sweet girl." I grab the chair I was just sitting in and drag it over to her bed. Taking the hand that isn't in pain, I lace our fingers together. "Just let me know if you need anything at all. Okay?" Lexi nods.

Just as the nurse is finishing up taking her temperature, Tristan comes crashing into the room. He's still wearing his MMA gi and he looks like he's died a thousand deaths on his way over here.

"Lexi!" He leans over her bed and kisses her on her forehead. "What the heck happened?" His gaze darts from Lexi, to me, to Mason, and the reality of the situation hits me like a ton of bricks. I'm sitting in a hospital room with Lexi because I was watching her and she more than likely broke her wrist, and I was so worried about getting her here, I don't even know what happened.

"I-I'm sorry, Daddy." Lexi lets out another sob. "I was playing with Uncle Mason and when he left to take a shower, I jumped off the couch. My hand…it hurts so, so bad." Her cries come harder and my heart shatters. I should've been watching her. My eyes should've never left her. If I wouldn't have been trying to play house by cooking and doing the laundry, she'd still be at home safe and sound instead of in a hospital bed. What if she had fallen differently and broken her neck? Oh my God! I could've been responsible for two children's deaths!

"I'm so sorry," I choke out, tears stinging my eyes. But I refuse to let them fall. I don't deserve to cry. I stand up, unsure of where to go or what to do. I don't want to leave Lexi's side, but I shouldn't be here. I don't deserve to be here. Tristan steps away from the side of the bed and is in front of me before I can make it out of the room.

"No…no…don't you dare do this." He grabs my chin and looks me dead in the eyes. "This is *not* your fault and don't you dare try to blame yourself." I shake my head needing him to stop trying to comfort me when he should be comforting his daughter.

"He's right, Charlie," Mason says. "If anyone is to blame it's me. Lexi was jumping off the couch and I was catching her. I didn't think she'd try to jump off the couch when I left the room."

"I was supposed to be watching her," I point out, shaking my head, and suddenly the nurse is by my side.

"Hey, kids get hurt. I've been working in this hospital for the last six years and I've seen a million accidents."

"Wait a second." Tristan stares at the nurse. "Don't I know you? What's your name?" He looks down at her badge. "I do know you! You probably don't even remember me, but my daughter—"

Mila cuts him off. "Yes, I remember you. And I'm assuming the little girl with the broken wrist is your daughter, the one you named after me." *What the heck?*

Mason cackles. "Of course she remembers us. It's me we're talking about here." Mila rolls her eyes and Tristan groans.

"I'm going to go let Dr. Matthews know I'm requesting an x-ray so we can see if the bone is broken, but my guess is, it is." She opens the door to walk away, but before she leaves, she says, "And I told you, you were safe naming your daughter after me."

Mason laughs, nodding in amusement. "Oh, nurse Mila…game on."

LEXI'S WRIST IS IN FACT BROKEN. WHILE WAITING TO BE BROUGHT back for x-rays, Mila came back in to give Lexi some pain medication. It helped her to relax and soon she was in and out of sleep. I was back at her side along with Tristan and Mason. After they wheeled her in to get x-rays—and confirmed the break—the doctor came in and set her wrist. Thanks to the pain meds, Lexi wasn't in too much pain. She picked out a blue cast, and Mila came back in to plaster it on.

"Did you know I was one of the first people to hold you?" Mila says to Lexi while wrapping her arm.

"You were?" Lexi asks, intrigued.

"I was. You're even named after me." Mila gazes over at Mason who rolls his eyes. "My middle name is Alexandria."

"Does your daddy call you Lexi, too?" Lexi asks, and Mila laughs.

"No, since it's my middle name, it stays as Alexandria."

"I don't think I have a middle name," Lexi says, confused.

"Nope, you sure don't. Your daddy said Alexandria was long enough to count as both. He had a hard enough time picking out your first name. He wanted it to be perfect." She laughs and looks over at Tristan who smiles warmly.

"Charlie, do you have a middle name?" Lexi asks.

"Nope, I don't," I admit. "I guess my parents thought my name was long enough for both as well." I give Lexi a wink.

Tristan glances my way. "Charlie isn't that long. Is it short for another name?"

"Umm…yeah," I say, not able to lie to him. Up until this point I've left details out, but I haven't blatantly lied, and for some reason I can't do it now, even if it means he knows my real name. "It's Charlotte," I say softly.

I see his mouth open to respond, but before he can, Mila says, "Okay! There you go. Make sure you make an appointment with your doctor for a follow up. You should be able to get the cast removed in about six weeks as long as it heals properly. No getting it wet, and make sure you have everyone sign it." She smiles at Lexi and hands her a lollipop. She has been so sweet to Lexi the entire time we've been here.

"I know this is totally random," I say, pulling a card to the art studio out of my purse. "I have this art studio opening up soon and I would love to offer you a free session. You've been so kind to Lexi, and I just want to say thank you."

"Oh! I love to paint, even if I stink at it." Mila giggles. "Is this one of those *bring your own wine* places?"

"Yep! It sure is! I'm also going to offer kids classes as well as birthday parties. My cell phone number is on the card since I don't have a phone in the studio yet."

"Cool! Do you live around here? Maybe we can meet up some time for coffee." Other than Bianca, who I have only hung out with a few times, and the occasional conversation with Veronica, I haven't made any girlfriends since I moved here. When I hesitate, she adds, "I'm sorry. That was really forward. I've been divorced for a few years now, and well…most of my friends were from my ex-husband's friends, and while he and I are still friends…" She trails off looking embarrassed at her rambling.

"Divorced?" Mason chokes out.

"I totally get it," I say to Mila, both of us ignoring him. "I've only been living here a short time and I don't really have any friends either."

"Hey!" Mason shouts. "What are we? Chopped liver?" he jokes, and I roll my eyes.

"Anyway, I would love to meet for coffee," I tell her. "When you get a chance, text me your number."

"Sounds good," she says.

"And since we're all exchanging numbers, why don't I give you mine as well?" Mason joins in, and now it's Mila's turn to roll her eyes.

"In your dreams, playboy."

THIRTY-FIVE

TRISTAN

"LEXI! GUESS WHAT? I HAVE SOME AWESOME NEWS!" I SHOUT down the hall, and when Lexi doesn't answer, I head to her room. There's only one reason why Lexi is quiet—she's up to no good. When I get to her room, she's sitting in her bed, reading a book. Okay…at least she isn't drawing all over her walls. Then I look over and see a huge fireplace drawn across her wall complete with stockings hung—one for each of us including Charlie.

I sit down on her bed next to her and notice she's reading one of her Christmas stories. "Lex," I groan, and she glances up from her book.

"Yes, Daddy?"

"We've talked about this." I point to the wall as Charlie comes strolling into the room. Her hair is wet from the shower and she's dressed in a pair of ripped jeans and an off the shoulder sweater that reads 'Let's get lit' with an image of a Christmas tree in the background.

"Oh my goodness! Lexi! Did you draw this yourself?" Really? Like she doesn't already know she drew it? Who the hell else would have drawn it? She's just as bad as Mason!

Of course, Lexi's face lights up. "I did! I read in this book that Santa needs a chimney to come down, so since we don't have one, I drew one!"

"It's beautiful and that's so smart! You ready to go get the Christmas tree?"

"Yes!" Lexi cheers, fist pumping with her one good hand. Of course, her broken one is the left, so she's perfectly capable of drawing…all over her wall.

"Wait! Before we go." I remember why I came in here looking for her. "You won third place in the painting contest. Your drawing will be displayed in the art gallery for the entire month of January."

"Wow! I got third place! Yay!"

"I think this calls for a special present," Charlie says.

"Like what?" Lexi replies loudly, excitement pouring out of her.

"It's going to be a surprise!" Lexi squeals and jumps out of bed. "Go get your shoes on so we can go!" Charlie calls after her.

"Surprise?" I raise my eyebrows.

"Yep! You and Mason are going to paint this wall." She points to the wall currently holding Lexi's fake Christmas display.

"So she can color over it?" I point to the Christmas display.

"It's special paint. You'll see. We can pick it up on our way to get the Christmas tree." Charlie leans in and gives me a quick kiss, leaving me wanting more…so much more.

We went by the home improvement store and picked up the paint Charlie insisted on buying, then we went to the tree lot and picked out a tree. Lexi wanted a small tree for her room and of course Charlie offered to buy it. Afterward, we stopped by another store to get some ornaments and now we're heading home.

"Tonight was supposed to be my last night working at Plush," Charlie says once we're back in the truck, "But Bianca just texted me and said they're slow and I don't need to come in. So, I was thinking…" She gives me a shy look, which is so ridiculous because I would give this woman anything she asked for. "There's a tree lighting ceremony happening tonight. Mila texted me an invite and I was wondering if we could bring Lexi. It turns out Mila has an eight-year-old son, and is bringing him as well."

I choke out a laugh at that, and Charlie frowns. "I'm sorry," I say through my laughter. "Yes, we can go. Lexi will love it. I'm laughing at Mila having a kid. Mason has a strict rule against hooking up with moms."

"He's prejudice against moms?"

"He won't go anywhere near them. Wait until he finds out Mila is a mom. We need to invite him tonight. It's going to be great."

After getting the tree set up and Charlie insisting we need to wait until tomorrow to decorate it so the branches can come down or some shit, we get dressed for the tree lighting.

"Can we stop by my place?" Charlie asks as Lexi pulls on her cute new boots Charlie bought her the other day. "My fluffy boots are there."

"Like mine?" Lexi asks.

"Yep! Like yours," Charlie confirms. I grab her by her waist, and brushing her hair to the side, I give her a soft kiss on her neck, on her cheek, and lastly on her lips. I want so badly to tell her to move in with us. Then she wouldn't have to go anywhere to get her stuff, but I don't. Standing by the front door isn't the place to bring it up.

"Sure, Mason is meeting us at the tree lighting." Charlie shakes her head at how excited I am to see Mason's reaction. I can't help it, though. "The guy has been talking nonstop about Mila since we ran into her at the hospital. When he finds out she's got a kid, it's going to be the equivalent of blowing a big wad of gum into the biggest bubble only to have it pop all over your face!" Lexi laughs at my analogy and Charlie groans.

"I don't think it's going to stop him."

"Ha! We'll see."

The parking garage is jam packed, but after circling around a few times, I snag a parking spot. As soon as we hop out of the truck, Lexi and Charlie join hands and we head toward the event. The temperature tonight is in the sixties, which makes it the perfect evening for an event outside. Lexi is snuggled up in her cute Christmas sweater and ripped jeans which are identical to Charlie's. I never imagined what it would be like for Lexi to have a woman in her life. It was always just us, but watching them walk ahead of me, I know without a shadow of a doubt, Charlie was meant to be in our lives permanently. Now I just need for her to agree.

We stop at a coffee shop and order a couple of coffees and hot chocolates while we wait for everyone else to arrive. The huge Christmas tree is dark, waiting to be lit. The performers are dancing on the stage to Christmas music and fake snow is flying out of snow blowers. Charlie and Lexi talk nonstop about how Christmasy it all feels, and I think about how hilarious it's going to be when Mason finds out Mila has a kid.

"There you guys are!" Mason drops into a chair at our table. "So, when does this lighting take place?"

"Uncle Mason!" Lexi squeals and jumps into Mason's lap. "The big tree over there is going to light up with lots and lots of lights! And guess what?" She doesn't wait for him to answer. "Daddy and Charlie and I got a big Christmas tree today! And I got a small one for my room."

"That's awesome, Lexi girl!" Mason takes a sip of her hot chocolate, which judging by his face is no longer hot. "I'm going to go grab something warm." He lifts Lexi up and places her back in her seat before heading into the coffee shop.

"Hey!" Mila comes walking up. Charlie gets up to greet her, giving her a quick hug. "I'm so glad you guys could make it. Unfortunately, Alec ended up staying with his dad tonight so it's just me." She shrugs.

"Oh no! Is everything okay?" Charlie asks, concern evident in her voice.

"Oh, yeah! Gavin's grandparents are in town for a few days, so Alec wanted to spend time with them. Just means some adult time for myself." Mila winks. "I'm going to run in and grab a coffee. Anyone want anything?" We all shake our heads and watch her go in.

A few minutes later, Mila comes out, her coffee in her hand with

Mason following her. "I'm the one who invited them," she says. "So that means you're following me, not the other way around."

Mason sits in the only seat left and Mila stays standing. "Wow! Such a gentleman."

"You're more than welcome to sit on my lap." Mason's brows lift up and down and Mila makes a noise of disgust.

When she doesn't sit on his lap but instead stays standing, sipping her coffee, Mason stands. "Here you go, Madam." He bows dramatically, which earns him a giggle from Lexi and a glare from Mila.

"Thank you." She sits and dhe and Charlie begin talking about the studio opening up in the next month or so.

"Hey," Mason says to me. "Kenny needs me to confirm the hotel reservations for the fight in Vegas. I had originally put us down for two rooms. Is that still okay?"

"What fight?" Charlie chimes in.

"I have a fight in Vegas next week. We're going to drive there and visit with the family. Some of the guys from Cooper's gym will be there as well."

"I don't wanna go." Lexi pouts and Charlie giggles. Then it hits me I'm going to be away from Charlie for at least four days. Jesus, when did I get so dependent on this woman?

"The UFC fight at the MGM Grand?" Mila questions.

"Yeah, and you're looking at the main card event." Mason smiles cockily and Mila's eyes light up.

"Oh my God! You're a UFC fighter! I knew it! I knew I recognized you."

"I sure am."

"I tried to get tickets for Alec and me, but they were so expensive! He absolutely loves you. We'll definitely be watching the fight on pay-per-view."

At the mention of Alec, Mason's ego deflates slightly, but too quickly he's back to his typical Mason flirting. "How about you drop this Alec guy and I'll make sure you're front and center?"

Mila snorts, quickly realizing what Charlie and I already know. Mason has no clue Alec is her son. "I couldn't possibly go without him. That would be cruel." She glares at Mason, but it quickly turns into a frown. "Do you think maybe you could sign something for him? He's a huge fan of yours. He was supposed to come today but couldn't make it." Charlie and I make eye contact, both silently laughing over the fact that Mila is purposely not telling Mason who Alec is.

"Yeah, sure, whatever," Mason says, then leans into Mila. "But if you ever ditch that guy and want the real deal, I'm right here."

"Sorry, but Alec is the most important guy in my life, and he's not going anywhere."

"I have some tickets," I say to Mila. My mom was a single parent at one time and she would've given anything to get me to one of those fights when I was growing up. Fortunately for her, she had Kaden. But not everyone has a Kaden. "You and Alec are more than welcome to come. As you can see, my darling daughter won't be attending." Then I say to Mason, "Book one additional room for Mila and Alec."

He rolls his eyes but agrees.

"Are you serious?" Mila asks. "I don't think I can let you do that! Maybe I can pay for some of it… or maybe I can—"

"No way," I cut her off. "The tickets don't cost me anything and the room is discounted for fighters."

"Thank you, Tristan! You have no idea how much this is going to mean to Alec."

"You're welcome."

For a brief moment, the Christmas music goes silent while someone comes over the PA system to announce there are five minutes remaining until the tree lighting. Lexi jumps out of her seat ready to go and Charlie and Mila follow. After throwing away all their garbage, Mason and I join them.

The two women and Lexi are dancing to *Rockin' Around the Christmas Tree*. I come up behind Charlie and, taking her in my arms, give her exposed shoulder a soft kiss. She continues to dance but her moves become slower, slightly more seductive as her jean-clad ass rubs up against me. I could hold this woman in my arms for the rest of my life. Screw being away from her for four days.

"Come to Vegas with us," I murmur into her ear. "I don't want to be without you for that long." My lips brush her earlobe and then I place my lips on the soft spot behind her ear, eliciting a chill from her.

Tilting her head slightly, she says, "I would love to go…as long as I can stay back with Lexi."

"That's perfect, babe. We can visit my parents and I can show you around Vegas. Have you ever been?"

She shakes her head. "That sounds like a good time." She turns around and, wrapping her arms around my neck, kisses me as the announcer gives a one minute warning.

Charlie turns back around and pulls Lexi into her front. Encircling my arms around Charlie, my chin rests on her shoulder. The countdown gets down to ten seconds and everyone shouts each number until one. The snow comes falling down and the tree lights up the entire area.

"Charlie! Daddy!" Lexi shrieks in excitement, pointing at the tree. "It's so pretty!"

"I see! It's so beautiful!" Charlie purrs.

The music starts back up as the snow continues to fall. I weave Charlie's fingers in mine, but when I go to weave the other hand, I notice her hand is already taken by Lexi.

"You guys!" Mila yells over the music, "Say 'Merry Christmas!'"

The three of us repeat her words as she snaps a picture of us. If I could freeze any moment in time it would be right here and now. I know firsthand life isn't always perfect, but right now, in this moment, it's pretty damn close.

THIRTY-SIX

CHARLIE

"CHARLIE! THIS IS COMING OUT AMAZING!" MILA TWIRLS around the studio. It's nowhere near close to being done but the cabinets have been installed and the new front desk has been put in.

"I know, right? I'm so excited! They'll be sealing the floors next week and then painting. I'm going to be doing the mural on the wall myself."

"Charlie! Alec called me a klutz and he won't tell me what it means!" Lexi comes stomping out of the backroom, paint covering her from head to toe. Mila's son, Alec, is following behind, a smirk on his face. He is three years older than Lexi and loves to mess with her. I imagine this is what flirting looks like when you're a child.

"Alec, be nice," Mila scolds, and Alec laughs.

"I am! It's not my fault she doesn't know what the word means. And it's the truth."

Lexi glares at Alec and I hold back my laughter. It is the truth. The girl makes messes without even trying to. She spills her drink at almost every meal, and spills the paint every time she's painting. She even trips over her own shoes several times a day. "What's a klutz?" Lexi asks me softly, her cute mouth turned down into a pout.

"It's someone who is kind of clumsy. Like they spill stuff by mistake or trip a lot."

Lexi lets out a huff. "Well I'm not a klutz." She rolls her eyes, and with her hands on her hips, stomps away.

"Start to clean up, Lex! We need to get you home to your surprise."

"Okay!" Lexi runs to the back. After Tristan picked up Lexi from school, he brought her over to the gym to get some stuff done. Since I was next door going over a couple things with the contractors, I insisted on taking her for the afternoon and even got Tristan to agree to paint her wall.

After Lexi and Alec clean up their artwork, we say our goodbyes.

"See you in a few days." I give Mila a hug. We've been meeting for coffee while the kids are in school. It's nice to be able to sit down with another woman and chat.

When I asked Tristan if he minded, he looked at me like I was insane, but then he frowned and said, "Charlie, you never have to ask permission to do anything. Whether it's hanging out with a friend or going out. You are a grown woman." I realized I was so used to having to ask permission from Justin, I asked out of habit.

♥♥♥♥♥

"THIS IS SO COOL!" LEXI SQUEALS, JUMPING UP AND DOWN. HER cast-less hand reaches out to touch the wet paint and I stop her.

"Don't touch." I give her a grin. "It will be good to go when we get back from Vegas."

"And I can draw on the entire wall?" Lexi's arms flail out.

"Yep! It's chalkboard paint. We'll have to buy you some chalk. You can color on it all you want and it will erase with a wet sponge."

Mason and Tristan are standing there admiring their work when Tristan's phone rings. "Hey Lex, it's Micaela. You want to show her your wall?"

"Yes!" Lexi grabs the phone and answers the call.

Leaving her to talk to her friend, I head out of her room to the living room. I have laundry to do and I need to pack for the trip, so I slide on my boots to head out.

"Where are you going?" Tristan asks, sliding his arms around me and pulling me down with him onto the couch.

"I was going to head home to get some laundry and packing done. We leave in a few days."

"I'll take you to get your stuff and you can do it here. You don't even have a washer and dryer." Tristan situates me across his lap, bridal style, and nestles his face into my neck. "Move in with me," he whispers and I still.

"What?" I ask to make sure I've heard him correctly.

"Move in here. You're never home anyway. Lexi would be thrilled and you get along with Mason." He looks up and over my shoulder to his best friend who is smiling.

"Especially when you do my laundry." Mason grins.

"See? You don't need to be paying rent on a place you're never at. This condo is plenty big enough for all of us." He gives me a kiss.

"What do you say?" I don't stand a chance against his adorable puppy dog eyes and my favorite dimple peeking out because he's smiling so hard he's practically cheesing.

"Okay," I agree.

"Yeah?"

"Yeah, I'll move in."

"Fuck yeah, let's do it now." Tristan pulls me up and off his lap and stands, grabbing his keys.

"What? Like right now?"

"I'm not giving you a chance to change your mind. I've been in your place. It has like four pieces of furniture, which we'll put into my garage, and your clothes, which will go in here. Mason, let's go."

"I have to pack!" I laugh at how fast this is happening.

"So let's go!" he says to me. "Lexi! Say bye to Micaela! We need to go to Charlie's old place."

I crack up laughing, shaking my head. "You're crazy!"

"Crazy about you! Now let's go." Tristan slaps my butt as I run past him toward the front door.

I get outside and Mason is standing against the truck. I join him, standing only a couple feet away and lean against the side as well. "Are you sure you're okay with this?" I ask. "I don't want you to feel railroaded."

Mason puts his arm around me and pulls me into his side. "I'm more than okay with this. You're making Tristan fucking happy. How could I not be?"

"He makes me happy," I say, looking up at him. "Him and Lexi… and you. All of you make me happy." Mason nods in understanding. One day I told Tristan he could tell Mason about my past so he didn't feel left out if it was ever mentioned. The next day I walked into the condo and was met by Mason. He hugged me for a long time and told me he's here if I ever need anything. Nothing else needed to be said.

We get to my place and pack up my clothes and toiletries. The truth is most of my stuff is at Tristan's place. Most of the furniture came with the place. I only have a couple pieces I bought myself, which Tristan and Mason load into the truck while I speak to Mr. Hinton. Since I'm paid up until January, he assures me the last-minute notice is fine. When I tell him he can rent it out immediately, he tells me it actually works out good because his granddaughter is coming to California and needs a place to stay. He thanks me for being a great tenant and we say goodbye.

After unloading the truck, Tristan makes a quick dinner while I put my clothes into the closet and then give Lexi a bath. Her cast can't get wet so we have to help her wash her hair and body. Once we eat dinner, Mason takes off with some friends and Lexi goes to bed. Tristan says he's exhausted, so we relax in bed watching television until he passes out.

I pull out my paperback—the second book in the series that had the horrible cliffhanger—and read for a little bit before I snuggle up next to Tristan. "Night, baby," I whisper as he wraps me up in his arms. I look around the room for the first time finally feeling *at home.*

THIRTY-SEVEN

TRISTAN

"ALL RIGHT! EVERYONE HOP IN AND FIND A SEAT. LEXI, I PUT your booster seat in the middle. Buckle in." I throw the last of our luggage into the trunk of the SUV I rented but leave it open. Mason hasn't come out yet and he'll need to throw his stuff in.

"Hey Lexi, can I sit next to you?" Alec asks, and we all wait for Lexi's answer.

"Fine," she huffs out. "But you better be nice, and no calling me names." Her voice is stern and Alec nods in understanding.

"I guess I'm in the back," Mila points out sounding annoyed. I give Charlie a questioning look as we jump into the front seats.

"She's going to be in the back...with Mason for four hours." Charlie giggles and I join in, laughing.

"I'm here!" Mason announces as he throws his baggage into the back and slams the trunk shut.

"Maybe I should sit in the back," Charlie suggests, but I'm already shaking my head.

"No way. I get four hours of my hand on this leg." I squeeze her thigh making her laugh.

"Oh man! Are you Mason Street?" Alec whisper-shouts, completely in a trance at Mason standing in front of him, the SUV door open.

"I am...who are you, kid?" Mason looks around confused like he's standing in front of the wrong vehicle, until he spots Lexi. "He a friend of yours?" Then he looks toward me. "You aren't letting her hang out with boys, are you?"

I hear Charlie snort out a laugh as I say, "No...that's Alec."

We all watch as Mason puts the pieces together. His head swings from me to Alec then to the back where Mila is sitting in the third row with a playful smirk resting on her lips.

"You're Alec?" Mason questions.

"I am! And I'm your biggest fan! I love the UFC. Your record is fifteen and two! And that one fight you lost against Fredrick Ricardo was bullshit!"

"Alec!" Mila scolds. "Don't you use that word."

"Sorry Mom, but it's the truth! I added up the points. Mason should've won that fight!"

Mason is cackling at Alec's antics. "I agree."

"But the other one you lost. I know it was in the beginning of your career, but you deserved that one."

"Were you even alive for that fight?" Mason asks, incredulously.

Alec gives him a look. "I know you're getting old, but haven't you ever heard of YouTube?"

"Alec," Mila chides, and Mason is speechless.

"Is he…yours?" Mason points to Alec.

"Yes, he is. Mason, this is my son, Alec. As you can see, he's a huge fan of yours, and the *only* guy in my life."

"Dammit," Mason curses under his breath. "A man I stood a chance against. A kid…" he shakes his head slowly, then looks to me. "You knew?" I laugh, nodding my head. Next he looks to Charlie. "And you knew?" Charlie cracks up, the smile bright on her face as she nods knowingly.

"Well shit…game over." Mason climbs into the back seat next to Mila, buckles in, and pouts like a two-year old who was just told no to having dessert before dinner.

"What game are you playing, Uncle Mason?" Lexi asks.

"One where I lost, Lexi girl. One where I lost."

♥♥♥♥♥

IT'S BEEN TWO DAYS OF FUN IN VEGAS. WE'VE HUNG OUT IN THE pool, had lunch at the Rainforest Café. We've visited with my parents at the resort since their house is under contract and full of boxes. Mason has been busy working out and preparing with his trainer, and Marco, who is training an up and coming fighter, has been helping him to prepare for his fight. Mila and Alec have been hanging out with us, along with Bella—who's ready to pop any day now—and Micaela.

Now it's Saturday morning and I have to head over to where the event is taking place. Mason has just finished showering and we've all congregated into my room.

"Okay, Mason and I have to go check-in, and he needs to warm up. Mila, here are your tickets and VIP passes. Bring these with you."

I hand her the tickets and the passes hanging on a lanyard. "You'll be seated with my parents and Bella, so if you need anything just ask." Then I turn to my daughter. "Lexi, please behave for Charlie. I won't be back until later. Probably close to four in the morning."

Everybody nods, and I give my girls a kiss before heading out with Mason.

"So…tomorrow?" he asks once we're alone. I nod wordlessly. We're staying one more night and leaving Monday morning. Since winter break has started, the kids don't have school, so technically we can stay as long as we want to, but Charlie wants to be home for Christmas next week, and Mila has to get back to work.

"Yeah, tomorrow night. My parents are watching Lexi at their place, and I made reservations."

"Any doubts?" I think about this for a minute as we walk through the lobby toward the stadium.

"No, I know she has a past, and while I wish she would let me in when it comes to the asshole who hurt her, it doesn't change anything. I know everything I need to know about Charlie. There's no doubt in my mind I want to spend the rest of my life with her."

After I few minutes I ask, "What about Mila?"

"What about her?"

"You know…now that you know she isn't taken."

"Nope. Not happening. You know I don't fuck with moms."

"Yeah, you might've mentioned that once or twice, but you never explained why."

Mason gives me a side-eye. "My mom…fuck…I don't want to talk about it. It doesn't even matter. The point is, moms are a no-go."

We get to the stadium and time flies by. Mason is the main card event and we don't have time to watch any of the other fights. I go out with Steven, a new fighter at my gym who has proven himself in the UFC and earned himself a spot in the lineup. Hours later, Mason is up. He, of course, kicks ass and wins his fight. The crowd goes crazy as the ring announcer announces Mason the defending champion.

We go to the club to celebrate his win along with several other fighters, and around three in the morning, after checking on Lexi who is asleep in her own room, I crawl into bed with Charlie. She's snuggled under the covers and snoring softly, and I take a minute to watch her. If everything goes as planned, tomorrow Charlie will agree to spend her life with me. I think back on everything I've been through the last several years: Bella, the baby, Gina. And the truth is, I don't regret a single moment or decision, because every choice and every heartbreak led me to Lexi and then to Charlie, and I can't imagine my life without either of them in it.

"Hey," she says sleepily, "I missed you." She brings her lips up to mine, and lazily kisses me.

"I missed you too," I murmur against her lips. "More than you know."

"Make love to me, Tristan," Charlie whispers, and my woman doesn't have to tell me twice. If I have it my way, I'll be making love to her every damn day for the rest of our lives.

THIRTY-EIGHT

CHARLIE

AFTER SPENDING THE DAY AT TRISTAN'S PARENTS' HOUSE—technically it was out back because the inside was torn apart in preparation for their move—they grilled and we rode their four wheelers—Tristan and I made our way back to the resort to get changed. He's taking me to dinner, just the two of us. I told him I was more than okay with Lexi joining us, but he insisted he wanted a romantic night out, which means Lexi is staying with his parents.

I get out of the shower—Tristan is getting ready in the other bathroom—and find a box on my bed. The tag reads: **Wear me.** Opening it up, I find a simple yet gorgeous black dress. I step into it and zip it up from the side. It's tight up top with a low V cut and flares out at the bottom, ending just above my knees. Also in the box is a pair of beautiful Christian Louboutin lady peep patent red sole pumps. It's been a long time since I've touched something this expensive, but it feels different coming from Tristan. It's a gift from his heart, no strings attached, and I know he won't throw it back in my face later on.

I'm putting each heel on as Tristan walks out of the bathroom dressed to the nines. I've never seen him in a suit before, but damn does it look good on him. Black slacks, black jacket, and a white button-down shirt underneath. Collar is open, no tie.

"You look beautiful," he says, pulling me into his arms and giving me a gentle kiss on the corner of my mouth so as not to ruin my lipstick. I let out a soft moan wanting more and he chuckles softly. "Later."

"Thank you for the dress and heels."

"You're welcome. But I must admit, they were purchased with purely selfish motives. I get the pleasure of staring at you from across the table all night in that sexy dress."

"And the heels?"

"I'm hoping later tonight they'll be digging into my back while I'm inside of you." I feel my face heat up as Tristan lowers his head down and places a soft lingering kiss on my neck. "You ready to go?"

I nod, and he takes my hand in his, walking us out of the room and to the elevator. When we get down to the lobby, there's a car service waiting for us. We don't even drive a mile down the street when we pull up to the Bellagio. Tristan tips the driver and guides us through the lobby and to an escalator, which leads up to at a restaurant called Picasso.

Tristan flashes me his panty melting grin, his dimple on full display. "I figured it was only fitting." He shrugs. He gives the hostess his name and we're guided back to a balcony overlooking the fountains. The hostess hands us menus and says our server will be right with us.

"Tristan! This view is breathtaking," I say, looking out at the dancing water.

"I agree completely," he replies. My eyes are trained on the show which is taking place, but when I glance to Tristan, he's staring at me.

"My dad brought my mom on a date to watch the fountains, so I figured it was good luck because they have the kind of relationship… the kind of marriage I hope to have one day."

Tristan backs his seat up and gets down on one knee, and I hear myself gasp. "When I made the reservations, they asked me when I planned to propose. I know most people wait until the end of the meal, but I told them in the beginning. There was no way I would be able to sit here across from you with this ring in my pocket and focus on anything other than begging you to become my wife."

He pulls out a small box and opens it. Nestled inside is an exquisite heart-shaped diamond surrounded by several tiny diamonds in what looks to be a platinum setting. My hands go to my mouth in shock and I can feel my body trembling.

"I looked at so many rings." He lets out a quick laugh. "So many… and then I saw this one and I knew this was it. Charlie Pratt, you stole my heart the first night I saw you, and soon after you stole my daughter's." I shake my head, tears burning my lids at his words. "I know some people might think this is too soon, but I believe when you know, you know, and I know without a doubt I love you and want to spend the rest of my life with you. This is me willingly giving you my heart and asking you to never give it back. Will you marry me?"

The tears release and fall down my cheeks as I nod my head yes because it's the only answer I can give him. "Yes! Yes, I will marry you." Tristan grins a boyish smile and plucks the ring from the box, sliding it onto my ring finger. I stare down at the ring and realize I'm going to have to leave the present and head back to my past in order to clear the way for my future, and that thought scares the ever-loving shit out of me.

We enjoy a delicious meal while chatting about our future. I tell Tristan I would love to get married here and he agrees. We discuss purchasing a bigger home and one day growing our family. All of it feels tainted because of what I'm hiding, and I vow to myself to make things right as soon as possible.

After we finish eating, we head back to the hotel room. Awaiting us are several candles placed all over the room and rose petals covering the bed and floor.

"I can't believe you planned all this," I say in complete awe. Tristan comes up behind me, and after gently tugging the side zipper down, removes my dress so I'm in only heels and a black lace matching bra and panty set. Dusting my hair to the side, he kisses right below my ear, and then trails open-mouthed kisses down my neck and over my shoulder.

"Let's take this to the bathroom," he murmurs, taking my hand in his, and guiding us to the bathroom. When we get inside, I notice the bathtub is already filled with water. Tristan lifts me up and places me onto the expansive counter before stepping back and stripping off his clothes. First is his jacket. It falls onto the floor. Next, he unbuttons his pants and pulls his shirt out. After pushing his slacks down, he's in only his briefs and a shirt.

"Come here." I reach out my hand and he steps between my legs. I undo each button of his shirt until his hard chest and abs are on display for me. Leaning down, I kiss his left pec over his heart. He shrugs out of his shirt and is left standing in only his briefs.

I give his pec another kiss, this time my lips lingering on his nipple and he lets out a groan. Reciprocating, Tristan pulls both my bra cups down, my heavy breasts jutting out. He takes both breasts into his large hands, and bringing them together, wraps his lips around both of my nipples and sucks. I let out a moan as the pleasure shoots straight to my core, my thighs tightening around his legs.

My hands move to his freshly shaven head, my fingers caressing the back of his neck. "Lift up, baby," he demands, and I lift my butt up so he can remove my panties. As he pulls them down my thighs, I reach back and remove my bra so I'm completely naked.

Tristan's body moves down with my panties, and once they're off, he spreads my legs, my body on display for his taking. "Put your thighs on my shoulders." I do as he says, my heels digging into his back just like he said they would be doing. He wastes no time, delving into my pussy like he's a starved man and I'm his long-awaited meal. With languid strokes up my seam and ending on my clit, his tongue has me coming apart in what feels like seconds. My body convulses and my legs shake uncontrollably as I scream out in orgasmic bliss.

Of course, Tristan doesn't stop until he's pulled out every last drop of my orgasm. Once I've come down enough, I'm forcing him to stand and pulling him closer to me, our mouths colliding. His tongue swirls around with mine and I taste my essence on his lips and tongue. With the heel of my pump, I hook the band of his briefs and push them down until I feel his hard length spring free, hitting my leg.

Needing him inside me right this second, I push him back slightly, my Louboutin pumps making a clacking sound as they hit the floor. I turn around and lean over the counter. "Fuck me, please," I beg, and seconds later, in one fluid motion, Tristan is entering me from behind. With one hand gripping my hip and the other encircling my hair around his wrist, he begins to thrust in and out of me with such force my head is jerked back, my scalp tingling in the most delicious kind of pain. My breasts are heavy, my nipples are hard, and as they slide against the counter, I reach up to pinch them, the stimulation causing me to squirm in pleasure.

I can feel another orgasm building. My vaginal walls clenching around Tristan's cock as he continues to mercilessly pump in and out of me. "Fuck, baby. I'm going to come. Tell me it's okay to come inside you."

"Come in me," I moan. With my words, his movements turn frantic, savage even. His dick hits that spot deep within me over and over again. His balls slapping my clit. And seconds later we're both falling apart. Tristan lets out a guttural groan and then stills inside me, his shaft thickening as he releases everything he has into me. A few seconds later, his warm seed is dripping down the inside of my thigh as my pussy pulsates from my own orgasm.

Before pulling out, Tristan leans over—releasing my hair—and trails a line of kisses down my back.

"I can't wait to marry you. If it were up to me we would get married right now…tonight." My body freezes at his words, a chill rising up my spine. I can't postpone this. I can't move forward with the man I love until I have dealt with the man I hate.

THIRTY-NINE

TRISTAN

I WAKE UP TO MY CELL PHONE RINGING. REACHING OVER, I notice the bed is empty and the sheets are cool like it's been empty for a while. The phone stops ringing then picks up again. Without looking at the name, I answer while standing up to find my fiancée.

"Hello?"

The voice on the other end hesitates. "H-hey Tristan, it's Bella." I can tell by the sound of her tone something is wrong. I pick up my pace, looking around the suite for Charlie.

"Hey Bella, everything okay?" When she doesn't say anything, I start to panic. "Is everything okay? The baby…"

"Yeah, yeah, everything is okay. The baby is still cooking in my oven."

"Fuck, Bella. What's wrong?" There's no way she would know if something was wrong with Charlie, but between her missing and Bella not saying what she called for, I'm about ready to lose my shit. "Bella! What's up?"

"It's Gina…she's dead. She died a few days ago." My body comes to a stop. My heart hesitating for a brief moment. I'm not sure how to feel about this. Do I mourn? Do I cheer? Isn't this what I wished for? So why does the reality that the biological mother of my daughter is dead make me feel sick inside? "She overdosed. I saw a post from an old acquaintance on social media. There's going to be a funeral. Tomorrow. I just thought you should know."

"Thanks," is all I say before I hang up. Gina is dead and Charlie is gone. I search the rooms again before I call down to the lobby.

"My fiancée isn't in our room. Has anyone come down recently and requested a cab?" I don't even know why I'm asking, it's not like they'll remember every guest that comes down to the desk. I glance at the clock and it's seven o'clock.

"I'm sorry, sir. Quite a few people have requested cabs."

"Okay, thanks."

I sit on the bed and that's when I hear a crinkling sound. Lifting up the sheet, I find a piece of paper with Charlie's handwriting.

> Tristan,
> I have to take care of my past so we can have a future. I'll see you back at home. I'm leaving my heart with you.
> Love you, <3
> Xo Charlie

What the fuck! I unlock my cell phone and hit her name. It goes to voicemail. I hit end and try again. Voicemail.

Again.

Voicemail.

Again.

Voicemail.

"Fuck!" I pull up my contacts and it hits me. I don't know anything about her past! She mentioned Texas once, and Georgia, but I have absolutely nothing else to go on.

Suddenly feeling like it's all too goddamned much, I grab the closest item to me—a lamp—and chuck it across the room. It smashes against the wall, pieces falling to the ground. But it's not enough. I grab something else and throw it, then grab something else. And I have no clue how long I'm destroying everything in my wake when Mason comes in and finds me. I drop to the ground, my best friend wrapping his arms around me, and I sob. "She's gone."

"I heard," he says, and my head shoots up.

"You heard from Charlie?"

Mason gives me a confused look. "No…I was with Marco and Bella when they found out that Gina died. Wait a second." His eyes dart around the room. "Where the fuck is Charlie?"

"She left."

❤❤❤❤❤

IT'S BEEN TWENTY-FOUR HOURS SINCE I'VE SEEN OR HEARD from Charlie. I've looked up every listing with the last name Pratt, but I haven't gotten anything. I've searched every social media outlet for her using Charlie as well as Charlotte. I knew she was hiding, but I didn't fully grasp the reality of it until I wasn't able to find her.

I didn't want to leave the hotel without her, but her note said she would see me at home, so after speaking with Mason and my parents, I made the decision to head back to California. Now I'm standing in front of Gina's grave with Lexi next to me, holding my hand, and Mason holding her other hand…well, her fingers since she's still in a cast for a couple more weeks. The funeral was earlier this morning, but I couldn't bring myself to show up while everyone was here. I almost didn't come at all, and I'll never know if bringing Lexi here was the right decision, but I guess that's part of parenting. Making tough fucking choices and praying I don't fuck my kid up as much as possible.

So, here we are, staring at a simple grey headstone with Gina's name, date of birth, and date of death written across it. There's no quote, nothing but the facts. The grass hasn't been laid yet, so it's dirt surrounding the stone.

"Lexi," I say, bending down, my knees sinking into the dirt. "This place is called a cemetery. It's where they bury people who die and go to heaven."

"Like Grandpa's baby and Charlie's baby?" Lexi asks.

"Yes." Lexi nods in understanding, so I continue. "This one here says Gina Turro. She died a couple days ago."

"How did she die?"

I glance up at Mason and he nods encouragingly. "She was sick. She needed help, but she didn't get it, and she had to go to heaven." Some day when Lexi is older, when she asks, I will explain Gina's drug problem, but today isn't the day.

"She should have gone to the doctor," my daughter answers innocently.

"Yeah, she should have. This woman, Gina, who died, she was… she was…" I choke up at the words. I can't say them. I can't tell my daughter this woman who gave birth to her and left her was her mom. She wasn't! She doesn't even deserve the title. I can't do it. Fuck! I can't.

I wrap my arms around my daughter and hug her tightly, all the events of the last couple days crashing down on me. Standing here, in this cemetery, it hits me that my life has come around in full circle and it's just the three of us, once again.

Mason's hand lands on my shoulder and he gives it a squeeze. I look up at him and say, "I can't do it. One day, but I can't yet." He nods in understanding, and I stand up, picking my daughter up with me.

"It's cold out here, Daddy. Can we go home? Maybe Charlie will be home when we get there."

I give her a squeeze. "Yeah, Lex, we can go home." She squirms her way out of my hold and I drop her to the ground. She takes off running back to the truck and Mason takes off after her.

Before I walk away, I turn to the grave, feeling the need to say something…anything. "I hope you're in heaven and looking down on us. I hope you're finally rid of the drugs and you can watch Lexi grow up. I hope you're finally free."

As I turn to walk back to my truck, my cell phone rings. Charlie's name appears on the screen and I rush to answer it. "Charlie?" I breathe.

"Tristan! I need you." Her voice is pleading and I freeze in place.

FORTY

CHARLIE
TWENTY-FOUR HOURS AGO

TRISTAN FALLS ASLEEP AND I KNOW WHAT I NEED TO DO. I CAN'T bring my past into my future, so I'm going to have to pull up my big girl pants and handle my past. I watch him sleep for a few minutes, his arms securely wrapped around me. One of the things I love most about Tristan is how protective he is of those he loves. Even in his sleep, he makes sure I feel safe.

Carefully, I move out of his hold, not wanting to wake him up. I dress quickly—not bothering with a shower—and grab my luggage. I find a hotel notepad and write him a note. I know he's going to worry, but I can't have him coming after me. This is something I need to do on my own, something I should have done a long time ago. I never imagined I would fall in love and become engaged. Not that it's an excuse, but it's the truth. Had I known Tristan and Lexi would be brought into my life, I would've made sure the door to my past was padlocked shut.

I get down to the lobby, and instead of asking them to call me a cab, I make my way out front and snag one. "To the airport, please."

The taxi driver gets me there quickly, but once I'm at the airport I find out the next flight out isn't for several hours. Using the emergency credit card I've had for years in my name, I book the flight. At this point it won't matter if my purchase gets flagged by Justin.

When I finally arrive in Houston, it's after midnight. I pick up my rental car and check in to the hotel I made a reservation at. Needing to eat something, I order room service, but once the food arrives, my nerves are so fried, I barely touch a bite. I take a much-needed shower, and before I know it, it's morning.

Getting into my vehicle, my first stop is the cemetery. I feel absolutely sick that this is my first time coming to visit my daughter, but I would like to believe what Lexi said is true. Georgia is in heaven looking down on me. And if she is, she knows I think about her often. I don't need to be standing at her grave for her to be close to my heart.

I pull up through the gates and park in the visitor parking. Not knowing where my baby girl is located, I need to have someone look her up.

"Good morning," I say to the gentleman at the desk. "My daughter was buried here a little over a year ago, and I need to know where she's located."

"Sure thing, ma'am. What's her name?"

"Georgia Rae Reynolds."

The gentleman gives me a quick once over. The last name Reynolds holds significant weight in this town as well as the surrounding city. He doesn't comment, though. Only types away on the computer. After several long minutes, he looks up and with a perplexed look on his face, says, "I'm sorry, but I don't have anyone here by that name. Could it have been under a different name?"

After spelling the name out for him several times, he comes to the same conclusion—my daughter wasn't buried here. It doesn't make any sense. This is where Justin's dad was buried. This is where they own several plots. This is the only place she would've been buried. After asking for Justin's father's information as it's been several years since I've been to his grave—and we only visited it once—I take a drive over. I find his headstone immediately, and next to him are Justin's grandparents. But nowhere is my daughter.

Jumping back into my car, I take off needing answers. My first instinct is to go to the source himself, but something steers me in a different direction, and about twenty minutes later, I'm parking in front of my mother-in-law's home. Her car is parked out front so I knock on the front door. Surely, she will be able to explain to me why my daughter isn't buried where she should be. And once I get that sorted, I'll be able to focus on the reason I'm here.

The door opens and Frederick, the butler, is standing in front of me. His eyes go wide and he looks nervous. "Mrs. Reynolds, what are you doing here?" he whispers, blocking the doorway.

"I'm here to speak to Hilda. May I come in?"

"Ma'am, should you be by yourself? I think I should call your husband. He'll want to know you're here."

Before I can tell him not to call Justin, I hear a child's laughter ring through the house and seconds later my entire world tilts on its axis. Two things happen at once: My daughter, my beautiful Georgia Rae, comes running down the hallway, my mother-in-law following close behind, and my mother-in-law locks eyes with me, her face showing one of fear.

What the hell is going on? "Georgia," I try to shout, but the lump in my throat prevents me from even speaking her name out loud. Clearing my throat, I try again, and this time I get her attention. She stops in place, her eyes meeting mine. "Baby girl," I whisper at the same time she yells, "Mommy!"

Hilda cuts her off before she can run to me, and pushing Frederick out of the way, steps outside, closing the door behind her. "What are you doing here, Charlotte? Does Justin know you're here?" My mind is racing. My daughter is alive! She's alive and breathing and smiling.

"She's alive," I say. "I need to see her! Let me through." I push her out of the way, but the door is locked.

"Charlotte, Frederick is calling Justin. We will get this all sorted. Are you hallucinating?"

I shake my head. "I'm not hallucinating! I know what I saw! Georgia is alive."

Hilda gives me an incredulous look. "Of course she's alive, dear, but you shouldn't be here. You should be getting better."

"Excuse me?" I take a step back.

"Don't worry, Frederick knows to call Justin if you show up here. You can't be around Georgia until you are better. I'm sure he's on his way. Please just stay calm."

"What are you talking about?" I'm completely lost and confused. My daughter is alive and they won't let me see her. *I need to get better first?* What the hell is going on?

"Hilda, what did Justin tell you about me? Where I've been this past year?"

She gives me a sympathetic smile. "You suffered a breakdown. You tried to take Georgia's life, but Justin found you in time. It's okay. He'll be here shortly and you'll continue to get the best care, and once you're better you will see Georgia again."

Oh my God! That motherfucker kept my daughter from me! He staged her death and lied to me about her funeral. That's why he wouldn't let me go! And he's on his way here! What will he do when he gets here? What if he really does have me committed?

Needing to figure this entire situation out, I do the hardest thing I've ever done. I walk away from my daughter. Hilda is screaming my name, but I don't stop. I get into my car and head back to the hotel. Tears are pouring down my face, and I call the one person I should have let in. The one person who would have been by my side through all of this, had I let him in.

"Charlie?" he answers on the first ring.

"Tristan! I need you." My voice breaks.

"Charlie, talk to me. Where are you? Wherever you are I will come to you."

"She's alive, Tristan! My daughter, she's alive!"

"Okay, baby. Where are you? I'm on my way. We'll get through this together."

"Tristan…there's something you need to know."

"It's okay. Whatever it is, we'll handle it."

"I'm married."

The line goes quiet and I think maybe he's hung up. But a second later, he says, "Okay, I'm coming to you. Just tell me where I need to go." I give him the details of the hotel I'm staying at and he makes me promise not to do anything until he gets there.

I valet-park my car and rush up to the hotel room. It will be at least three hours until Tristan gets here. While I'm waiting, I try to remember the day Georgia was pronounced dead. My brain is still so fuzzy. I blacked out—although I don't remember it. I woke up in the hospital. Justin told me she died. I was given medication to calm down. The doctor…it was always the same doctor who gave me the medication. Nobody else saw me but him. And Justin didn't call him 'doctor.' He called him by his first name. Why would Justin be on a first name basis with a doctor he just met?

Pulling up the internet on my phone, I search the hospital directory. His name was Mike. After several minutes, I find a Michael Shelby, director of cardiology. Why would a heart doctor have seen me? I click on his profile and see his picture. Oh my God! I was too out of it to recognize him at the time. This is the doctor who operated on Justin's dad years ago. The Reynolds family donated a significant amount of money to this department after his dad passed away. They wanted to thank them for all they did over the years to help his father live longer than anyone thought he would with his bad heart.

I locate the number and call him. The secretary answers and says he's in surgery but she can have him call me when he gets out. I leave my name and number and hang up. Then I start to search the online newspapers for my daughter's name. The Reynolds family would have placed a huge obituary in the paper if they wanted to make it look like she died. I find nothing. Apparently, the cruel joke is on me.

There's a knock on my door, and when I look in the peep hole, I see it's Justin. I back away slowly, not wanting him to hear me, and call Tristan.

"Charlie," Tristan says when he answers the phone. "I'm on my way. The plane just landed, so I'm only about twenty minutes away."

"How did you get here so quickly?" I ask confused.

"My dad chartered a plane."

"Tristan, Justin is here! I don't know what to do."

"Do not answer that door, Charlie. I want you to hang up with me and call 911, okay?"

"Okay." As I'm about to hang up, the door swings opens, the

security latch ripping out of the wall, and Justin walks in, glaring at me, with a gun in his hand.

"No!" I scream. "Please don't do this!"

I know Tristan's speaking on the other end, but I can't hear anything. "Justin," I say out loud so Tristan knows he's in here with me. "We need to talk, please."

"There's nothing to talk about! You tried to run off with my daughter, then you took off on me. I saw you with him. I saw you in California living your new life. I saw your slutty fucking mouth on his. Does he know you're my wife?"

Justin's hands grip my neck as he pushes me against the wall. With one hand holding me in place, blocking my airway, his other hand lets go and smacks me across the face. My face swings to the side at the impact and it all comes back to me.

That day.

Me packing up to leave.

Justin coming home early and finding us running.

Him attacking me.

Georgia running outside scared.

Me trying to tell Justin, but him blocking my wind pipe.

Him punching me in the stomach repeatedly.

One hard hit to my temple.

My head hitting the table.

Everything going black.

I didn't just black out! I was attacked by my husband. Georgia ran outside because he was attacking me. Only she didn't die! She's alive and he made me believe she was dead to punish me. Only I ran.

Looking Justin in the eyes, I remember the moves Tristan taught me. The moves he insisted we practice each week. It may not stop Justin, but I have to do something. I have to fight for my life. Somehow he knows about me and Tristan. He will never let me walk out alive. It's him or me, and there's no way I'm going down without a fight. I spent too many years taking it without fighting back.

I see him lift his gun and I make my move. My hand comes up slicing the side of his neck. It's not enough to knock him out, but it's enough that he loses his balance. He wasn't expecting me to fight back. But I don't stop there. I reach up and, grabbing his shoulders, kick him in the balls.

"Fuck!" he screams, the gun falling from his hand. It fumbles to the ground and we both eye it. I pounce on it at the same time he does, but I get to it first, and without hesitating, I switch the safety off and pull the trigger. He falls back, his cries for help garbled as I drop the gun.

Stunned at what I just did, I start to hyperventilate. I'm not Justin. Who am I to play God with someone's life like he did with mine and my daughter's? I crawl over to my cell phone and dial 911. The operator answers, asking what my emergency is.

"I shot...a man. He's bleeding," I say. "I need an ambulance." I rattle off the hotel information and the room number. The blood is everywhere. I need to save him. He might deserve it, but I'm not a murderer. She tells me help is on the way and to stay on the line, but I drop the phone.

Grabbing a towel, I locate the entry point. It's on his chest, right on top of his heart. I press down on it to stop the bleeding. He's shaking. His eyes are closed.

A few minutes later, the police enter. Then the paramedics. They ask me to release Justin and I do. They put him on a gurney and suddenly Tristan has me wrapped up in his arms. Safe. Secure.

"I—I didn't mean to," I cry out, but Tristan just shushes me while he rocks me gently.

"It's okay, baby," he coos into my ear. "It's all over."

FORTY-ONE

CHARLIE

THE POLICE OFFICER TELLS TRISTAN HE NEEDS TO STEP OUTSIDE. I'm to remain inside because I'm part of the investigation. The investigator takes my fingerprints, dusts my hands for residue, and takes pictures of my neck. Once they're done with me, I'm put into the back of a police car. The officer tries to explain it's just proper protocol, but Tristan isn't having it. He tells me not to say a word until he arrives with my attorney. When we arrive at the police station, I'm brought to a room where I let the officer know I have to wait for my attorney. Once Tristan arrives with him, he requests to speak to me alone. I tell him everything. From the verbal and physical abuse to Georgia being made to appear dead.

Once the detective comes in, questions are asked and answered. It feels like it goes on for hours. Eventually a gentleman in a suit with a badge attached to his belt comes in and informs us Justin has been declared dead. The sense of relief that courses through my body almost has me feeling guilty, but then I stop myself because he did this to himself. He made his own choices. He chose to abuse me for years. He chose to lie to me about our daughter. And he chose to come to my hotel room with a loaded gun with the intent to end my life.

I'm brought into an interrogation room and asked several questions by a few different detectives with my attorney by my side the entire time. Once they're done interviewing me, I'm asked to wait while they look over my case. After what feels like several more hours, I'm told I won't be charged. All the evidence, including the hotel footage of Justin breaking in, proves I shot him in self-defense. Once I'm finally released, the only place I want to go is to my daughter, but I'm covered in blood.

"Can you take me to my car?" I ask Tristan. "I need to go buy some new clothes. I can't go back to the hotel room yet and my clothes have blood stains on them. I need to go to Justin's mom's house so I can get Georgia. I'm not even sure—"

"Hey, stop," Tristan says calmly. "You just went through something life altering. Take a second to breathe."

"I can't stop. I can't breathe!" I exclaim. "My daughter is alive and God knows what she thinks about me! She probably thinks I abandoned her."

"Okay, your car is safe at the hotel. I'll drive you to get clothes and then we'll head over to Georgia. Okay? Just...please, breathe. You've been through a lot."

I inhale deeply and let out a ragged breath, the reality of today's events hitting me like a punch to my gut. I killed my husband. My daughter is alive. Grabbing Tristan's shirt, I pull myself toward him, my head going to his chest as I let out one of the most therapeutic cries of my life. He holds me while I let it all out, running his hands up and down my back in a soothing motion until my tears finally dry up. When I lift my head up, I notice his shirt is covered in my tears. Tristan has always been my strength. Even right now, he's able to take all my tears and remain strong for the both of us.

"You ready to go get your little girl?" he asks.

"Yes, I am."

FORTY-TWO

TRISTAN

I HAVE NEVER BEEN SO SCARED IN MY ENTIRE LIFE THAN I WAS when I heard Charlie scream. When I walked in and saw her trying to save that motherfucker's life, I knew without a doubt, Charlie is the best woman I have ever met. If I had had the pleasure of shooting that piece-of-shit, I would have stuck a couple extra bullets in him just to make sure he was dead. But not Charlie—she tried to keep that sorry excuse for a man alive. The man who put his hands on her over and over again, kept her daughter from her, and tried to kill her. It only makes me love her even more.

We pull up to a beautiful home that screams wealth, and the attorney pulls up behind us. I don't know what will go down when Charlie tries to get her daughter and I'm not taking any chances. We knock and a butler looking guy answers the door. Charlie remains calm and asks to please let us come in and see Georgia, and that's when a woman appears.

"Is it true?" she cries out. "Did you kill my boy?"

Charlie steps closer to me, clearly afraid of what this woman will do.

"Ma'am, we're sorry for your loss," I say, not meaning it in the slightest but trying to calm her down. "We're here to see Georgia."

"She's crazy!" the woman screams out, pointing to Charlie.

"Devon, can you help me out here?" I call the attorney over. He nods and approaches the situation.

"Mrs. Reynolds, I have an emergency court order requesting you to hand Georgia Reynolds over to her mother. If you can't hand her over civilly, I am going to have to ask the police to become involved." That's when I look back and see two police officers standing at the end of the driveway.

"I don't understand!" she cries.

"Hilda," Charlie says softly. "Justin—he had an abusive side to him. I tried to run with Georgia to get away, and to punish me, he made me believe she was dead. When I took off, he told you I was put into a mental institute. I was in California this entire time grieving over the death of my daughter."

The woman—Hilda, as Charlie calls her—brings her hands to her mouth, and begins to cry. "I didn't know, Charlotte. I swear I didn't know."

"It's okay," Charlie assures her. "I would just really like to see my daughter." Hilda moves to the side and lets us in. Once inside, Hilda calls Georgia's name, and several seconds later, a tiny little mini-Charlie comes running into the room.

"Mommy!" she shrieks and jumps into Charlie's arms. "Where were you, Mommy? I missed you so much. You left me."

Charlie tries so hard to remain composed but at those last words, she breaks down. "I'm so sorry, baby girl. There was a big misunderstanding, but I'm here now and I promise you no one will ever keep me away again."

"Can we go home now?" Georgia asks, and my stomach clenches with the realization that Texas is her home. Will Charlie want to stay here? Now that Justin is dead she has no reason to run anymore.

"We sure can, baby girl." Charlie picks her daughter up and carries her to the door. "Hilda, I just want you to know I don't want anything of Justin's. Because of his death, I don't have to file for a divorce, but you can have any papers drawn up you like and I will sign it all over to you including the house if he still owns it."

"But where will you live?" Hilda asks. "Surely, you need a place for Georgia and you to live in. We can figure it all out."

"My home isn't here anymore." Charlie gives me a small smile. "My home is in California. You're welcome to visit Georgia any time you like, but that's where we'll be."

Hilda nods in understanding then gives Georgia a kiss on her cheek. "She was homeschooled by the best tutor, so make sure you continue her education. While Justin was working, she stayed here with her nanny—"

"I appreciate that," Charlie says cutting her off, "but Georgia will be going to school. Call if you would like to visit." She gives Hilda her number and with that, Charlie walks out the door, her head held high, with her daughter's arms wrapped tightly around her neck.

Because it's so late, we have to wait until tomorrow to fly out. Georgia insists we stop at her house to pick up her toys and clothes. Charlie, not wanting to upset her daughter, agrees. While they're inside grabbing the items important to Georgia, I contact the rental car company and let them know where to pick up the vehicle and give them my billing information. Then I book a hotel room for the night for the three of us.

Once we get to the hotel, Charlie gives Georgia a bath. I can see her eyes glassy with emotion in everything she does, and I can't blame her. She thought her daughter was dead, and now to find out she's alive… She never thought she would get to do something as simple as giving her daughter a bath again.

Once Georgia is dressed and fed, Charlie holds her daughter on the couch while they talk. Georgia is only four, so she doesn't really understand it all. It's a good thing because she'll get over it all quickly. When she asks about her dad, Charlie tells her he was hurt and went to heaven. Georgia barely even shows any emotion. I stand by the theory that kids are a good judge of character. They know who is good and who is bad.

Once Georgia falls asleep—still in Charlie's arms—Charlie finally looks my way. "Thank you for coming. For hiring that attorney and for being so amazing through all of this. I'm sorry for lying to you."

"You didn't lie."

"No, don't do that. I should have told you I was still married. I should have trusted you enough to know you would stand by my side and help me through it."

"All that is true. I'm just ready to move forward and make you my wife." I give her a small smile, but she frowns.

"I'm going to need some time, Tristan. I'm moving Georgia to a new state, to a new city, to a new home. I can't just move her into your home."

"It's your home too."

"And I love you so much for that," she says, tears building up in her eyes. I want to shake her, beg her not to do this, but I know she's only doing this because that's what a good mother does.

"I think it's time I tell you about my life in Texas." Reluctantly, Charlie puts Georgia into her bed, not wanting her daughter to overhear anything she's saying. She joins me on the couch but won't let me hold her while she tells me about her old life. She tells me about how she met Justin, her parents having died and her feeling alone. I listen as she tells me how it started with him putting down her degree, calling her love of art, silly, then it moved on to him putting her down as a parent. He would question every decision she made, making her feel like a bad mother. She tells me about the verbal and emotional abuse. Him not allowing her daughter to color. His cheating habits. How she felt trapped in her home and was trying to escape. She tells me about her plan. The money she was stashing away. Finally, she tells me about the day she thought her daughter died. How she couldn't remember what happened until Justin hit her at the hotel. My fists clench at the thought of that guy laying his hands on my fiancée. Needing to touch her, I reach for her hand at the same time the phone rings.

"It's Mila," she says.

She answers the phone and tells Mila about finding her daughter alive. She laughs and cries and then she says, "Actually, I'm going to find a place of my own. My landlord mentioned his granddaughter staying at the loft and I would feel bad asking him if I could stay after all." She glances at me, her eyes pleading for me to understand. "Really? Are you sure?" She pauses while Mila says something. "That would be great. It's only temporary…Okay, thank you. We'll see you tomorrow."

She hangs up the phone. "I'm thinking a June wedding." She slides closer to me, her arms going around my neck.

"But you just said…"

"I said I need some time, and now you know why. I need to make sure Georgia is comfortable with this transition. I've been without my baby girl for a year, and she doesn't know you. Mila is in search of a new roommate. She has a three-bedroom home she wanted to keep after the divorce, but she has been struggling to keep up with payments since her roommate moved out after getting engaged. While she continues to look for a new roommate, Georgia and I will stay with her while we all get to know each other."

"Let's buy a house," I insist. "A fresh start for all of us. Once we're married we can all move into the house together."

Charlie's face lights up. "I like the sound of that…so six months?"

"It will be the longest damn six months of my life."

"I want to get married in Vegas."

"Anything you want."

"I want to honeymoon with both our girls," she chokes out, another sob coming out. "I can't believe it. Both girls," she cries. "I have my daughter back."

"She looks just like you."

"I can't wait for Lexi to meet her," Charlie gushes.

"They'll be best friends. So, where do you want to honeymoon?"

"I always wanted to take Georgia to Disney but Justin wouldn't allow it. I'm thinking a Disney trip or a Disney cruise." She beams.

"I say we do both."

FORTY-THREE

CHARLIE
CHRISTMAS MORNING

"MOMMY! WAKE UP! I WANT TO GO SEE LEXI PLEEEEAAASSSEEE."

I stretch my arms and legs as my beautiful baby girl jumps onto the bed we share, her loose curls bouncing in the air as she jumps up and down next to me in excitement. Watching her face light up will never get old. When you find out you've been given a second chance, you suddenly view the world and your priorities in a whole new light.

"Mommmmmy! Please!" Georgia squeals. "I wanna go see Lexi." She jumps onto my belly, her tiny hands smashing either side of my face in an attempt to make sure she has my undivided attention.

"Did you check to see if Santa came?" I ask, and Georgia freezes.

"No! I'll go now! Get up, Mommy!" she yells as she jumps off the bed and runs out the door, the sound of her tiny feet pitter-pattering down the stairs. A sound I will never tire of hearing.

I've only had Georgia back with me for a little over a week, but she and Lexi have already made the decision to be best friends. When Tristan and I brought Georgia back with us, our first stop was to Lexi. I felt it was important for her to be a part of Georgia's homecoming, and Tristan agreed. What I didn't know was that Tristan had already contacted Mason and Mila, and with the help of Alec and Lexi, they had a mini-surprise homecoming party waiting for us. Takeout food, a cake, balloons, and a huge 'Welcome Home' sign.

We had to explain to Lexi, Georgia didn't in fact go to heaven— we didn't want her thinking people can just rise from the grave and return—and like the sweet girl she is, she welcomed Georgia with open arms.

The days are spent at the studio getting ready for the grand opening—which will take place at the end of January—with Georgia by my side. On the days Lexi has school, I spend that time with Georgia attempting to make up for lost time. The great thing about kids is that they tend to bounce back easily. I am taking her to see my therapist on Mondays with me, and we've discussed her dad going to heaven. He might be an evil bastard, but he was still her father.

"Okay! Okay! I'm up!" I pull the blankets off my body, and as I'm about to stand, when my cell phone rings. I see Tristan's name on the caller ID. "Merry Christmas."

"Merry Christmas, baby," he says. "I wish you were in my bed right now."

"Only a few more months."

"Few? More like five. I think we need to move the date up. The girls adore each other, and they can't wait to live under the same roof."

"We still need to find a house," I argue.

"So, what you're saying is once I find the perfect house for us, you'll move in with me?"

"After we get married," I add.

"I already found it."

"What?" I laugh. "You found us a house?"

"I did! It's perfect and you're going to love it. We're going to look at it next weekend. So...I'm thinking a January wedding."

The fact is, I would love to marry Tristan right this second, but I want to make sure I'm making the decision that is best for my daughter as well as Lexi. I've spoken to Dr. Monroe about this and she says there is no set timeline. However, the statistics for divorce in blended families is high and that scares me.

"How about May?" I counter, and Tristan groans not liking my answer. I laugh.

"February," he argues.

"April," I volley.

"March."

"Sold!" I yell and he chuckles.

"I'll take it."

"Mommy!" Georgia screeches, running back into our room. "Santa brought me so many presents! Can we bring them to Lexi?"

"My daughter wants yours," I inform Tristan, who is laughing over the phone.

"Lexi wants to open her presents with you guys as well. Why don't I pack up her presents and come over with Mason and Lex?"

"Sounds good! See you soon."

We hang up, and I grab Georgia by her tiny waist and pull her into my lap. "They're on their way over. Merry Christmas, baby girl." I give her a kiss on her cheek and hug her tightly, thankful for the priceless gift I've been given this year.

FORTY-FOUR

TRISTAN

WE GET OVER TO MILA'S HOUSE AND THE KIDS ARE ALL chomping at the bit to open their gifts. My mom and dad have made the move to LA, not wanting to miss any more time with their kids. They pull up at the same time Morgan and her fiancé pull up. Emma is in the car with them because she's living with Morgan and Adam temporarily to help out with the baby which is due in June.

"Grandma! Grandpa! Hurry!" Lexi yells from the front door. "We're waiting for you! Santa came and I was such a good girl! Alec got a lot of presents too, but I don't know why." She rolls her eyes. "He wasn't that good."

"Lexi, be nice," I scold her and she just shrugs.

"I was good!" Alec argues.

We all pile into Mila's house and watch the kids open their gifts. A couple days ago we went to see Santa at the mall. When Georgia said what she would like, Charlie freaked out realizing that she completely forgot she would need to buy her daughter presents. We've been so busy getting her situated, it slipped our minds.

I went out that night and bought several gifts for her knowing Charlie wouldn't want to leave her side any time soon. I did it without expecting anything in return, but I will tell you, the reward I was granted by my woman was well worth it.

"Should we tell everyone?" Charlie whispers into my ear. She's tucked perfectly into my arm right where she belongs.

I lean over and give her a kiss on her cheek before pulling her to stand next to me. "We have an announcement to make." Everyone stops talking and turns toward us. "As you guys know I asked Charlie to marry me in Vegas after the fight and we originally decided to put it off until June—"

"But there was no way Tristan was going to wait that long," Charlie says and everyone laughs. "So, we have set a date for March 14th. We're going to get married in Las Vegas at the Bellagio and then we're honeymooning with the girls."

"Which is a surprise," I add, and Charlie gives me a look of confusion. She mentioned wanting to go to Disney for the honeymoon, so she knows that's going to happen, but the little girls don't know, and Charlie doesn't know that I'm booking a two week trip to all of the parks and a weeklong Disney cruise.

"Mason, I would love for you to be my best man."

Mason gives me a chin lift. "For sure."

"And Mila, I would love for you to be my maid of honor," Charlie adds.

Mila glances over at Mason, who looks almost scared at the idea of walking down the aisle with Mila, before rolling her eyes. Then she smiles. "I would be honored."

Everybody gets up to give us a hug and congratulate us. Once Mila announces she's going to start breakfast, Lexi and Georgia come over holding hands.

"Daddy, Charlie, I have a question," Lexi says before glancing over at Georgia who tilts her head slightly. She's been fine around me so far, but it's only been a week. However, if she's anything like her mother, I'll win her over in no time. "Well, me and Georgia have a question."

"Okay. What can we do for you ladies?" I ask, pulling Charlie into my side.

"We were wondering…well…Georgia doesn't have a daddy anymore, and I don't have a mommy. So, I told Georgia I will share my daddy if she shares her mommy."

Charlie stiffens next to me, and when I look over at her, her eyes are already watering. "And what did you guys decide?" I ask.

"We want to share. Is that okay?" Lexi looks back and forth between Charlie and me.

"It is more than okay," Charlie says. Kneeling down, she takes both girls into her arms. "I would be so, so, so happy to be both your mommy's."

"I agree. I'm completely shareable." I give Georgia a wink and she grants me a shy smile that mimics the way her mother looked at me the first time she noticed me in the coffee shop, and I know I'll definitely be winning her over.

EPILOGUE

TRISTAN
WEDDING DAY

I'M STANDING ON THE VERANDA AT THE BELLAGIO SURROUNDED by our family and friends waiting with little patience for the ceremony to begin. It's just me and the pastor up here at the moment. My mom is sitting in the front row, and when our eyes meet, she shoots me a wink. She told me last night at the rehearsal dinner she couldn't imagine me ending up with anyone besides Charlie. For years, she thought Bella and I would end up together, and when that didn't happen, I think she was worried I might've given up on love. And if I'm honest, I think for a little while I did. What I didn't know at the time was that I was waiting for Charlie.

The music begins and out walk my beautiful daughters. Lexi and Georgia are dressed in light pink frilly dresses, their hair and makeup done up to make them look like the most adorable princesses. They both smile up at me as they enter. It's not really a walkway—more like an entrance. They giggle as they throw rose petals from their baskets onto the ground, making sure to throw every last one before they meet me at the front.

"They're all gone, Daddy," Lexi says, showing me her basket. Georgia giggles in agreement.

"Do you like my dress?" Georgia asks.

"I do. You both are the most pretty pink princesses I've ever seen." Both girls giggle again. They sit down next to my mom like they were told to do as we watch Mason and Mila make their way down the aisle. Mason's grinning way too wide and Mila is trying to smile through her scowl, which means Mason probably said or did something to piss her off. It wouldn't surprise me in the slightest. While he might consider

Mila to be off-limits, it hasn't stopped him from driving her nuts the last couple months. If I didn't know better, I would almost think her being off-limits actually has him wanting her more, especially since their living situations have changed. When they get to the front, they separate, Mason standing on my left and Mila standing on the bride's side.

The music changes into the wedding march, and a few seconds later, Charlie and my father appear. Charlie had planned to walk down the aisle by herself, but when my dad heard, he wasn't letting that happen. He offered to walk her down the aisle, and after Charlie cried for a good five minutes, she accepted.

I watch as they walk closer, and I try to absorb every feature of her as quick as possible. The only downside to getting married on the veranda means the walk is short. Charlie's in a simple floor length white gown. There are beads shimmering in the light and while I have no clue the style or name of the dress, she's the most beautiful woman I've ever seen in my life. Her hair is down in loose waves, and her makeup is done naturally. But what makes her breathtaking is none of that, it's the smile on her face. I've seen Charlie smile a thousand times, but I never realized until she was reunited with her daughter, how half-ass her smile really was. Not that she wasn't happy with just Lexi and me, but there was a piece of her missing. A piece I imagine nobody can replace when you lose your child. I don't know about that missing piece and I thank god every day Charlie is no longer missing that piece of her heart.

Now, as I take her hand in mine, and kiss her cheek, I see the difference in her smile. It's bigger, brighter. It tells me her heart is whole. We turn to face the pastor and he begins speaking.

We decided to do the traditional repeat after me vows for our ceremony. The pastor starts with Charlie first, and she repeats after him. To be honest, the best part—and the only part I even care about—of the entire speech is when she says, "I do" and slides my ring onto my finger. I go next, and when I say the same words, I see a single tear fall down her cheek. I know it's a happy tear, but I still catch it. I don't like my woman crying whether it be because she's happy or sad.

"And now can we please have Georgia and Alexandria join us?" the pastor says. The two girls jump up from their seats and join us in the front.

"While today is about Tristan and Charlie coming together, in this case, it's not just about two people merging their lives—it's about four people. I have here the adoption paperwork to make Charlie and Tristan the legal guardians to Georgia and Alexandria. But first, both parents would like to say something. Tristan, go ahead."

I turn toward my two girls, both of them so little and innocent. Georgia has no idea the type of person her dad was or why he died.

Lexi doesn't even know her biological mother is dead. But one day they'll ask, and my goal in life is to make sure when they do, it isn't because they feel I've failed them in some way. Knowing I'm speaking to little girls, I attempt to keep what I need to say short and simple.

"There are three days in my life that I will always remember. The first one is the day my dad, Kaden, came into my life." I look to my dad and he smiles warmly at me. "The next was the day Lexi was born." Lexi grins happily. "The third was the day I met Georgia." I glance Charlie's way quickly and see her single tear is now multiplying by the second. Georgia smiles sweetly. "When I was a little older than you two, I met my dad, Kaden. He loved me and my mom more than anything in the world. He showed me what it means for a dad to love his child, to love his wife, and to be the man his family needs. My promise today is to spend the rest of my life loving the three of you, being the best dad and husband I can be, and supporting you in any way I can. Being there for every stage of your life and making sure you know you are always loved." Taking the box Mason was holding for me, I open it up and hand Charlie, Lexi, and Georgia each a necklace. They are identical—all three having one large diamond heart with each of our birthstones. Lexi's and Georgia's will be put away until they're older, but I figured they could wear it today.

"These necklaces symbolize the four of us coming together, becoming one family."

The two little girls giggle as they put the necklace over their heads. "I love you, Daddy!" Lexi hugs me.

"I love you too, Lex."

Georgia smiles shyly. While she's coming around, she rarely shows any emotion toward me until I do it first. From the stories Charlie has shared, I would bet Georgia is scared because I'm a dad and a man like her father was, and he was a piece of shit. But that won't ever stop me from trying to earn her affection.

"I love you, Georgia," I say, kneeling down so I'm at her level. I put my arms out and she wraps her tiny arms around my neck.

"I love you too," she whispers into my neck. When I go to stand up, she doesn't let go, so I pick her up and hold her.

I look at Charlie and she's crying hard. Mila hands her a Kleenex and she wipes her eyes. Good thing she's not wearing too much makeup.

"My turn?" She laughs through her sobs.

♥♥♥♥♥

CHARLIE

"I WAS SITTING IN A COFFEE SHOP DRAWING THE DAY I MET LEXI."
I look down at Lexi, remembering the first day I saw her. Tristan said
one of the most memorable days of his life was when he met Georgia,
and I know exactly what he means because one of mine was the day I
met Lexi. The fact is, our children are the best part of both of us.

"You painted the big tree," Lexi acknowledges.

"I did. And you're too little to understand this, but that day…" I
take a deep breath. "That day you saved me, Lexi. You gave me your
picture of the pumpkin and it made me so happy. I was missing my
baby girl so much, and you invited me to your contest. It was so, so
nice of you." I'm speaking simplistically hoping Lexi will understand,
but my words aren't telling the entire story. The one Lexi isn't old
enough to understand. The one where I thought my daughter was gone
forever and then Lexi came into my life and reminded me it's okay to
love again. The one where she and her father gave me their hearts so
willingly and trustingly.

"I love you girls so much." I look from Lexi to Georgia, "And my
promise to you both is to be the best mom I can be. To listen to you
and love you and be there for you." My eyes meet Tristan's. "And my
promise to you, as your wife, as Lexi's mom, is to always treat her like
she's my own. Thank you for letting me love your daughter. Thank you
for letting me in."

Tristan nods and smiles, my daughter still in his arms. "I love all
three of you so much." I pull Lexi into a hug and bring her up into my
arms. The four of us hug and everyone claps. Once we're done, we set
both girls down and the pastor says, " I now pronounce you husband
and wife and a family. You may kiss the bride."

Tristan's arms wrap around my waist as mine wrap around his neck,
and we kiss.

"My daddy is always loving on my mommy!" Lexi announce,
making everyone laugh.

TRISTAN
ONE WEEK LATER

"MY FAVORITE PART OF DISNEY WAS SEEING ALL OF THE
princesses!" Georgia gushes.

"Oh! Me too! Me too!" Lexi agrees. "When we get home, can we
paint my room like the princesses?"

"Sure, Lex. I told you, you can pick what you want," I say.

"Me too?" Georgia asks.

"Yep! You too."

"When you said we could go to Disney *and* on a Disney cruise, I thought you were joking," Charlie says as we board the ship. "This has already been the best week of Georgia's and my life. You didn't have to book a cruise as well. This is too much."

"Shh…no more saying anything is too much. Disney parks and a cruise is what you wanted, and it's what you get." I stop and kiss her on her lips.

"And what do you get? I feel so bad that you're stuck with three girls and surrounded by Disney."

I look at Charlie incredulously. She has no idea… "Babe, being here with my three girls is all I need. I don't care where we are or what we're doing. I wouldn't have it any other way. Plus…" I lean in close to her to whisper in her ear. "You thanking me every night is the best wedding gift a man could get." I waggle my eyebrows and she giggles.

My phone dings with a text from Emma, and I read it twice over to make sure I read it right. Then I click on my social media app and do a search. When I see it for myself, I'm shocked. I rarely go on social media except to post upcoming fights and to advertise the gym. There's no way this is real. When he was named Bachelor of the year two years ago, the paparazzi would always spot him with a new woman and make a big deal out of it. Now that it's hardly news that the famous UFC fighter, Mason Street, will probably never settle down, they rarely post about him anymore. Mason is good about keeping out of trouble, and since he doesn't ever do anything news worthy, they usually leave him alone.

"Tristan?" Charlie says my name and then looks over my shoulder before I can close the app. "Oh my God! Does that say Mason and Mila are married?" she screeches. "That has to be wrong. That better be wrong! Tristan… It *is* wrong, right?"

"I'm not sure, but I'll find out. Until I do, please don't say anything to anyone."

"I need to call Mila! How could Mason do this to her? How could he hurt her like this? You said she was safe. You said he wouldn't touch her because she's a mom. She's my best friend, Tristan!"

Charlie pulls her phone out of her pocket, and before she can call or text Mila, I snatch it out of her hands.

"Hey!"

"Let me talk to Mason, first, please."

"Fine," she huffs, "but he better have a damn good explanation for this. I love him, Tristan, but if he hurt Mila, I'll kill him."

TAKEDOWN

TAKEDOWN

Definition: a technique that involves gaining control and off-balancing an opponent, then bringing him or her to the ground.

PROLOGUE

MASON
SIXTEEN YEARS AGO

I SIT ON MY BED, STARING AT THE DOOR. MOM TOLD ME TO STAY in my room until she's done working, but that was a long time ago. Usually, she leaves for work after I get home from school and comes home after I'm already in bed, but sometimes her work comes here. I hate those nights. I hate having to stay in my room and listen to them screw her, and if it's not them screwing her, it's her pimp. She says she hates him but needs him to get her work so she can make money to take care of me. I can't stand the guy. Every time he comes over, he sends me to my room, and my mom lets him, not even caring about the fact that he's not my dad. My dad is dead.

A little while ago when I heard the moaning and grunting of the guy getting off, I thought she was almost done. But then there was screaming and shouting, and shortly after, a door slamming before everything went quiet. I thought my mom would come and get me at that point, but she didn't. So now I'm sitting here, waiting for her, but I don't hear anything, not a single sound. Maybe she forgot about me.

Maybe I should go out there and make sure she's okay. She might think she can take care of herself, but she's delusional. She sees what she wants to see and believes what she wants to believe to convince herself that working for her asshole pimp and having sex with those piece-of-shit guys is what's best for us, but it's not. She blames my dad, says if he wouldn't have screwed her over, she wouldn't be in this position, and that might be true, but it doesn't do any good to blame someone who's dead.

She cries every day, apologizing for not being able to take care of me—of us. She rarely has any money to buy us food or clothes or anything, really. Our electric and water are shut off more than they're on. I hear her every night when she comes home, crying herself to sleep. I hate when she cries. I wish I could make her happy again. I remember when I was little and she would smile and laugh. I want her to smile and laugh again.

I'm considering going against my mom's wishes for me to stay in my room, so I can check on her, when sirens fill the silence. I go to the window, and drawing the curtains back, I pull down the blinds a little bit to peek outside. I count the police cars—six in total—surrounding our house. The house I've lived in my entire life. The same house that has notices on the door to let us know we need to move out soon because we can no longer afford it.

My room is on the second floor, and I can see everything down below. My mom promised me that we wouldn't have to move out. That she would take care of it. But it's a lie. It's always a lie. I don't even think she realizes every single word out of her mouth is a lie. I'm not mad at her, though. I'm sad. I'm sad that my mom doesn't make enough money and that food and clothes cost too much. I'm especially sad that she has to have sex with those nasty guys in order to take care of me.

I watch as my mom is dragged forcibly by her elbow to the police car. When the car door is opened and her head is pushed down for her to get in, I notice her hands are behind her back. It's then I realize my mom is being arrested, and she's not the only one. Her pimp is taken in cuffs, as well as the guy who came over for sex. She doesn't think I know what she does in order to take care of me, but I do. I hear her and her pimp arguing all the time. She's always begging him for more money, telling him she needs to take care of me, and he's always saying she's lucky she gets anything at all. I hate that my mom is in this position. That I'm such a hassle.

My hand comes up to the window and my palm slaps against the glass several times, trying to get her attention. It doesn't work though, and seconds later, the door is closed. I shouldn't have listened to her. I should've known something was wrong. I should've gone out there to help her. Then again, it probably wouldn't have mattered because she doesn't want my help. Every time I ask her if there's anything I can do, she cries. So, I no longer ask. I hate when I'm the reason she cries. I hate that I'm only thirteen years old and I can't get a job. That I can't take care of my mom.

In an attempt to get to her before the police car drives away, I run out of my bedroom and down the stairs. "Mom!" I scream as my feet hit the front porch, but all that's left are the taillights of the car. I'm too late.

A police officer approaches me. "What's your name?"

"Mason Street. My mom was just taken." I point to the police car driving away.

"How old are you?"

"Thirteen."

The police officer nods. "Okay, let's sit out here on the porch. The officers are still investigating inside. We're going to get this figured out."

"Is my mom—" I start to ask but stop, scared of what the answer will be. I'm old enough to know that my mom being arrested isn't a good sign. "Is my mom in trouble?"

The officer gives me a sympathetic smile to hide his quick flinch. "Unfortunately she is, but we'll find someone to take care of you."

His words stop me in my tracks. If my mom can't even take care of me, does he really think he'll find someone else who would be able to take care of me, who would *want* to take care of me? And even if they're willing, I wouldn't want to be a burden to someone else. I know we have no family. My parents are only children. My dad's parents aren't alive anymore, and my mom's want nothing to do with us.

"I don't want to be taken care of," I tell the officer as I back away. He looks confused, but I don't care. If being taken care of means forcing another person to have to do horrible things like my mom has had to do, I don't want to be responsible for that. I don't want to be responsible for another person struggling and crying every day.

I turn to run, but the officer grabs hold of my body, holding me in place. "You can't run. I promise you, you're safe." He brings me to the swinging bench and sits me down. "Someone is on their way. We'll get this figured out. I won't leave until I know you have somewhere to go."

A little while later, a woman shows up. Her name is Michelle Calhoun, and she tells me she's here to help me. "Have you lived in this home long?"

"Yes, my whole life," I tell her. "But there are notes on the door that say we have to move out because my mom doesn't have enough money to pay for the house."

Mrs. Calhoun gives me a small smile and nods in understanding. She takes me away from my home and brings me to her office. She searches for relatives, and just like I already knew, they're all dead, and my mom's parents don't want me. For the last few years—since my dad died when he was hit by a car while walking home from the dog tracks—it's only been my mom and me. She calls several more people before she finally says she's found a place for me. When we get to the house, I'm introduced to Paul and Iris Deluca. When I ask when I'll be able to see my mom, I'm told they aren't sure, but they'll take good care of me until my mom is able to come back and get me.

I live with Paul and Iris for a little over a year. Paul works for the bank, and Iris is a teacher. She doesn't have sex with anyone for money, and neither of them cry or complain I cost too much. Everything is going okay until Paul gets sick and has to quit his job. Iris tells the state they can't take care of me anymore, and I'm picked up.

For the next few years I'm moved from home to home. I learn quickly that most people are in it for the money I come with. They get paid to take care of me. It's too bad my mom couldn't get paid to take care of me. Maybe then she wouldn't have needed to prostitute herself out for money, and she wouldn't have cried every night because she couldn't pay the bills. Maybe if she got paid to take care of me, she wouldn't be in jail, and we'd still be living in our home.

The last house I move into is filled with three other boys. Walter and Janice Saulsberry are nice people. They tell me the boys have been living here awhile, and because one of the teenagers turned eighteen and moved out, there's an opening for me. Apparently, the state stops paying once you turn eighteen, which means you gotta figure shit out for yourself.

I only have six months until I graduate, less than that until I turn eighteen, then I'll have to find a way to take care of myself. I've moved so many times, I'm barely going to graduate high school, and I definitely don't have any money for college. I used to want to be a paramedic, but without the grades and money, there's no way I'm furthering my education. To be completely honest, I have no clue what I'm going to do with my life. My mom was sentenced to jail for five years. Some shit about prostitution and drug possession. I don't know all the details, but from what I overheard, my mom's pimp was using our basement to cook and sell his drugs on top of prostituting my mom out.

"We're heading to the gym," Travis, one of the guys I live with, mentions one day after school. "Wanna go?"

Not having anything better to do, I figure why not? "Sure."

Turns out it's a mixed-martial-arts training facility where the owner lets teens workout and train for free to blow off some steam a few hours every day after school. The first few days I don't work out or train, choosing to watch everyone instead. I watch them spar with each other and practice the moves they've been taught. I pay attention to the moves they make. I've spent most of my life watching and listening. I'm good at blending in… trying not to be a burden. I pick up on the moves that work and the ones that don't.

Then one day Travis is fighting—and losing—against a guy named Cedrick. Without thinking, I yell, "Watch out for the arm bar." Just as I finish my sentence, the other guy pulls him into an arm bar, and Travis is forced to tap out. They both stop and turn toward me.

"How did you know that?" Cedrick asks.

"Know what?"

"How did you know the move I was going to pull?" He walks over to me.

"I watched you," I admit.

He nods slowly like he's impressed. "Wanna spar?"

I shrug my shoulders, not sure if it's really a good idea, but still step into the octagon with him. The owner who plays as a referee starts the fight, and we begin circling each other. My brain plays through his moves like a compilation video as I consider all the ways he might come at me. When he steps forward, coming in for a jab, my brain flashes back to him using this move before, and I know what's coming next. I sidestep his move and, grabbing him by his legs, pull him into a double leg takedown, his back hitting the mat with a loud thud. From there, I put him into a heel hook, forcing him to tap out.

"Holy shit!" he yells as he gets up. I back up slightly, stunned at how easily taking him down came to me. My heart is racing, my blood is pumping, and the adrenaline is coursing through my veins. I'm shocked at how good it felt to make him submit. It was such an unexpected rush, like every broken piece of me came together during those few seconds. Every ounce of pent up frustration left my body during that short time, and all I can think about is doing it again. *I need to do it again.*

"Did you see that?" he asks Carl, the owner.

"Yeah, I saw that. You're a natural, kid. You find the right trainer, and you could be the next big thing."

"As a UFC fighter?" I ask. I don't know what happened in the octagon, but I'm already itching to go again. Those few seconds weren't nearly enough. I've only had a sliver of that pie, and now I'm craving the whole damn thing.

"Hell yes as a UFC fighter. It's not often we come across someone like you."

"Do they make money?"

He chuckles at my question. "Eventually. *If* you hit it big."

"Can you train me?" If I could spend my days doing what I just did and make money doing it, when my mom gets out of jail, she won't have to struggle anymore. She won't have to resort to having some piece of shit pimp prostituting her out. Instead of her not being able to take care of me, I could take care of her.

"I could, but to be honest, this is a small gym. It's not my specialty." My hopes crumble as quickly as they were built up. But then he says, "One town over in Las Vegas, there's a UFC training facility called Cooper's Fight Club. He knows what he's doing and could help you. But it's an exclusive gym, so it's expensive."

"I don't have any money," I admit.

"You could always get a job, and once you save up, join that gym. Until then, you can train here every day after school. It's always free here from three to five o'clock."

"Thank you, sir."

I go home that night, and when it's my turn to use the computer, I search the UFC. I find all types of information about the business. How often they fight, the contracts, the benefits. I find articles on how much they can make per fight. I look up Cooper's Fight Club and find out he's a retired fighter. There's a trainer there, Kaden Scott. Another guy, Caleb Michaels, is retired as well and does some training. His son, Marco, is in the UFC. I write down the phone number, so tomorrow I can call and find out how much it'll cost to be trained there.

The next morning I wake up and overhear Janice on the phone. She's speaking softly but loud enough that I can hear her from around the corner. "He only has six months until he graduates. I'm okay with him staying here." Pause. "I understand, I'll speak to him when he wakes up." Pause. "Okay, thank you for calling. Goodbye." She hangs up, and I walk out to join her.

"Is everything okay?" I ask, knowing the conversation had to have been about me since I'm the only one in the house who's graduating in six months.

"Your mom is out of jail." She gives me a soft, sympathetic smile, one I've learned means something bad is about to come out of her mouth. "She was given the option for you to move in with her, but—"

"She doesn't want me?" I ask, cutting her off.

"No, no, sweetie. It's not that. She just doesn't feel she can take care of you." *Take care of me...* in other words, once again, I'm a fucking burden. I'm an extra mouth to feed, an extra body to clothe. I nod in understanding then excuse myself to get ready for school.

Six months later, I graduate, and two days after that, I'm standing on the doorstep of Cooper's Fight Club vowing that one day I'll be able to provide for my mom and me. I will find her and take care of her, and I will make her happy again. And when that day comes, she will no longer consider me to be a burden.

PROLOGUE

MILA
FIVE YEARS AGO

ONE OF THE MAIN REASONS WHY I LOVE WORKING ON THE maternity floor is because I get to see so many precious babies being brought into this world. While the ER keeps me busy and the surgical unit is interesting, my favorite rotation is maternity. I was extremely lucky when I graduated there was an opening at this hospital. The truth is with money being so tight these last couple of years, I would've had to accept any job that was offered to me. But getting to work with pregnant women and their babies is truly my passion, and I love that I get to do that several times a week. Especially since it feels like I'm at work more than I'm at home these days. With my husband, Gavin, opening up his own real estate agency, we can use every dime we can get. He assures me it will be worth it one day, but right now we're struggling, and not just moneywise, but also with our marriage.

My phone dings, and when I pull the text message up, I see a picture of my adorable three-year-old son, Aleczander. His face is covered in spaghetti sauce, and he's smiling wide. I'm coming off a double shift and missing him like crazy. Seeing his beautiful face is exactly what I needed right now. Noticing the text is from Gavin's mom, Vicki, I call her, wondering why she has my son instead of his father.

"Did Gavin have an emergency?"

"No, dear. He's working late tonight so I offered to pick up Alec from daycare."

"Okay, thank you. I should be off in a few hours. I can come by and—"

Vicky cuts me off. "Just pick him up in the morning. He'll probably be asleep by the time you get off anyway."

"All right, thank you again." I hang up and call Gavin's number, but he doesn't answer. I try once more but still nothing.

I put my phone into my pocket and head to check on my patients. When I get to room 2C, I walk in quietly so I won't disturb the father or baby if they're finally getting some rest. I commend him for stepping up. I know it should be a given that a man takes responsibility for his child, but that's not always the case. In this particular situation, the mom gave birth and took off on her baby. Like left! She went outside for a cigarette and never returned. I've heard bits and pieces, and it seems she took off with her boyfriend who isn't the father of the precious little girl. The father of the baby took complete responsibility and is in the process of filing for emergency custody.

I've been on shift since the little girl was born, so I've gotten to know the father a bit. His name is Tristan, and so far he's been dealing with this all alone.

I notice for the first time that Tristan isn't alone. He's sitting at the table with another guy who is holding the baby. I catch the tail end of what the guy is saying. Something about naming Tristan's daughter, Trina.

Without interrupting them, I walk over to check on her and see that she's sleeping soundly in the man's arms.

I'm about to let Tristan know I need to take her temperature and vitals when Tristan says, "And where did you come up with that name, Mason?" I stop to wait for Mason to answer so I don't interrupt their conversation.

Mason replies, "She gave me the best goddamn road head of my life," and I about choke.

"Jesus, Mason!" Tristan says. "I'm not naming my daughter after one of your conquests. Think of a name of a woman you haven't slept with." Before Mason can answer, I clear my throat to let them know I'm in the room.

Tristan smiles at me, but the other guy ignores me as I go about my business: cleaning up the room, changing the bassinet sheets, and then taking the baby's temperature while she's still in Mason's arms. While I'm checking her out, this Mason guy continues to spit out name after name of women he's slept with. My God! Can you say manwhore?

When I'm done writing down the notes for the baby, I pick up some more of the area to help Tristan out. I notice she's beginning to get cranky so I go about making her a bottle. When I hand it to Mason, he looks up at me for the first time. The man is gorgeous. Inky black hair, short on the sides and messy on the top. His eyes lock with mine and he has the most beautiful crystal clear blue eyes. They are electrifying and mesmerizing. He smiles, and I almost stumble back at how enraptured I am by him.

Quickly, I regain my composure as Tristan asks Mason about my name. "Have you ever slept with a Mila?"

"Not yet," Mason says to Tristan while his spellbinding eyes stay trained on me. Starting from my face and slowly dragging those baby blues down my body, I feel like I'm being undressed right here.

"And you won't ever," I snap, feeling like a horrible person for being turned on right now. I'm married, and this man is a damn whore. What the hell is wrong with me?

"Perfect! I'll name her Mila!"

"I wouldn't do that if I were you," Mason warns as he continues to eye-fuck me. "I can promise you, one day she will most definitely be under me."

My eyes widen in shock. I've never been spoken to like this before, yet he's not even speaking to me. He's speaking about me like I'm not even in the damn room. "And I can promise you, I will *never* be *under* him." I don't know who I'm more annoyed with: Mason, for turning me on with only a look and a few words, or myself, for being turned on.

"Just to be on the safe side," Tristan says, "do you have a middle name?"

Reluctantly, I break the stare down between Mason and me. "Yes, but I am telling you, your friend here"—I glare at Mason, pissed off that he has my heart pumping and my panties wet—"is never going to sleep with me."

"Who said anything about sleeping?" Mason scoffs, and I groan. Of course he would say something like that. It's obvious from the mere five minutes I've spent with him that he's all about sex, and sleeping isn't sex.

"You're safe naming your daughter Mila. Although, it might be awkward to name her after the woman who murdered your friend." That might be the only way to get his magnetic blue eyes out of my head.

"I understand where you're coming from, but I'm just thinking it would be better to be on the safe side," Tristan insists.

Mason nods in agreement as he lifts the baby up to burp her, and my mind goes to Gavin and how hands-on he used to be as a father. How he used to be all about our son and me. Sure, Alec was a surprise to both of us, and he's the reason we got married, but Gavin didn't make me feel like we were ever a mistake—at least not until recently. Now it's like we aren't enough for him. His mother spends more time with our son than Gavin does these days.

I shake myself out of my thoughts. Things may not be perfect, but he's still my husband and I love him.

"Fine! My middle name is Alexandria."

Tristan looks at Mason. "Nope! You're good."

"Great! Alexandria it is," Tristan announces happily, and I shake my head in frustration. I've come across plenty of hot guys since I started working at this hospital, and not one of them has ever had this effect on my libido.

Taking the baby from Mason, I lay Alexandria down in her bassinet. "I'm afraid to ask if you're giving her a middle name."

Tristan thinks for a moment before he says, "You know what, I think Alexandria is long enough to cover both."

Mason agrees, and I grab the paperwork for Tristan he needs to complete. "Now that you have her name, fill these out so you can bring her home."

My shift ends, but I can't get Mason off my mind. I could be wrong but I'm almost positive the man looked at me like he wanted to devour me. The way his eyes screamed lust and want, and in return my traitorous vagina screamed *yes, please!* It's been quite a few weeks since Gavin and I have had sex. I think back to the last time... Jeez! I think it's actually been months instead of weeks. That must be why I'm so turned on. It's not because of that man and his magnetic blue eyes and devastatingly good looks. It's just because he *actually* looked at me.

I get home and see Gavin's car out front. We bought our first home last year, here in Los Angeles. After my grandmother passed away, leaving each of her grandchildren a little bit of money, I used what she left me to put a down payment on a home. It's nothing huge. It's a three-bedroom, three-bath townhome, with a small porch and no backyard...but it's ours. It's only fifteen minutes from the hospital I work at and only a bit farther from Gavin's office.

I unlock the door and find that the place is quiet. "Gavin?" I call out. It's only eight o'clock so I doubt he's asleep. When I get to our room, he's awake and playing a game on the computer. I come up behind him and run my hands down his front and over his stomach.

He grabs my hands, and without even looking at me, says, "Mila, stop. I'm in the middle of a tournament." His voice is full of frustration and annoyance.

Pushing his rolling chair back, I stand in front of the computer. "I was thinking we could..." I waggle my eyebrows up and down, and he looks at me confused. "Have sex," I huff out.

"Okay, just give me a few minutes." He moves me to the side and continues his game.

Feeling defeated, I grab an already opened bottle of wine from the fridge and a wineglass, and go out onto the back porch to call my mom. She recently moved from California and is living in Oklahoma with her husband. They lost their jobs when the company they worked for filed for bankruptcy. When my stepdad was able to find a job there, near his family, working at a large factory, they decided to make the move. I miss my mom every day, but I know they had to do what they felt was best.

"Mila, how are you?" My mom's voice sounds rough, her breathing heavy and ragged. She was diagnosed with lung cancer right after they moved and is currently going through chemotherapy. I wish I could be there with her, but I'm thankful that her husband is taking care of her. She's mentioned wanting to move back here one day, but I know that financially they still aren't in a good place.

"Mom." I sigh.

"Talk to me, sweetie." I could already feel the tears welling up from deep inside and at her words, they course down my cheeks. I tell her about my lack of sex life, the guy hitting on me at the hospital, and how good it felt to be looked at—even if he's someone I would never date. I tell her how stupid I feel for trying to initiate sex with my husband, only to have him turn me down.

"Oh, Mila. You know I hate to talk bad about your dad—God rest his soul—but you know we divorced shortly after you started middle school. I loved your father, and I believe in his own way he loved me too, but we weren't in love with each other. One day I woke up and decided I no longer wanted to settle, so we got divorced."

My parents' divorce was anything but amicable. My mom chose to divorce my dad, leaving him bitter and mad, which led to my parents arguing all the time, to the point they couldn't even stand being in the same room with each other. It's a lot of the reason why I married Gavin when we found out I was pregnant. I wanted my son to grow up in a two-parent loving household.

"Mom, are you telling me to divorce Gavin?" I'm shocked she would tell me this. She knows how hard the divorce was on me. As an only child, I was torn between my parents from the day my mom kicked my dad out, until the day he died from a stroke a year ago.

"No, that's not what I'm saying. I know the divorce was hard on you, and I wish we could've gotten along better for your sake. But even knowing how hard it was on everyone, I would've still made the same choice I did, because in the end I met Greg and I learned the difference between loving someone and *being* in love with someone."

I understand what she means, because while my parents didn't get along, my mom was a much happier person once my dad moved out. She became the life of the party, wanting to go away and go out more often. She made new friends and really started to enjoy and live her life. Then she met Greg, and I could see how different their relationship was—still is—in comparison to her marriage with my father. The giggles and smiles and way too much public displays of affection.

"Oh, and the sex!" she adds, and I cringe.

"Oh my God, Mom!" I screech, but inside I'm happy for her. "I don't want to know about your sex life."

"Okay, okay. My point is, I know you love Alec, and you're an amazing mom, but being Mila, the mom, doesn't mean you stop being

Mila, the woman. You need to put yourself first. You have needs and wants, and life is too short to simply settle, sweetie pie." She lets out a loud cough, which reminds me that our conversation needs to end soon. Her cancer has caused emphysema, and she has to be on oxygen to help with her breathing.

We sit in silence for a few minutes as I think about what she said. Gavin and I have tried counseling, and he's promised repeatedly to try harder, but he never does. And I know it's not just him; it's me too… I've changed. I've grown up. I'm not the same person at twenty-two as I was at sixteen when we met, or at eighteen when I got pregnant.

"Oh, Mom." I sniffle, the reality hitting me smack in the face. The tears are racing down my cheeks, and I would give anything to be with my mom right now so she could hold me.

"He's a good man, Mila," she says. "He provides for you. The two of you are giving Alec a wonderful home. Maybe Gavin is the one for you, but maybe he's not. Just take some time to think about what will make *Mila* happy. Don't stay in a marriage you aren't happy in just for your son. It may not be the popular answer, but it's mine. One day your son will look to you to provide an example of what love looks like. What type of example do you want to set for him?"

There's shuffling and then my mom says, "Oh, sweetie, Greg's niece just got here to visit. Can I call you back later?"

"Sure, Mom," I choke out. "I love you."

"I love you too, sweetie pie."

We hang up, and I head back upstairs to say good night to Gavin, who is still playing his computer game. He doesn't notice my puffy eyes or red nose from crying. He barely even acknowledges me—his full focus on his game. I head back downstairs and lie down in our room, in our bed, where I fall asleep alone once again.

Three days later, I get a call from my stepdad hysterically crying. He tells me my mom passed away in his arms. "She couldn't breathe," he says. He tells me the ambulance came and took her to the hospital where she was declared dead. It turns out she had an undetected blood clot. Three hours later, I'm flying to Oklahoma to attend her funeral. Six months later, I'm filing for divorce, and six months after that, I'm a single mom. *"Life is too short to simply settle,"* my mom said, and in memory of my mom, I refuse to ever settle again.

ONE

MILA
PRESENT DAY

"HAVE YOU GOTTEN ANY NEW BITES?" MY BEST FRIEND AND roommate Charlie asks, causing me to flush with embarrassment at her question. I know she doesn't mean any harm by it, but admitting I'm on a dating site when I'm surrounded by hot guys who can get any woman they want is embarrassing.

"Bites?" Mason asks, and I roll my eyes. Yep! I'm talking about *that* Mason. The one who eye-fucked me in the hospital five years ago, who made me question my marriage and appeared in several of my fantasies over the years, and in case you're wondering…because I know you are—no, we've never slept together nor will we ever. He's just as much of a manwhore as I knew he was all those years ago, maybe even worse.

He's also the best friend of my best friend's fiancé. I met Charlie when she came into the hospital with Mason and Lexi. Lexi is short for Alexandria. Are you putting the pieces together yet? It's a small damn world. Charlie and Tristan were dating—now engaged—and Lexi broke her wrist, and through the ordeal Charlie and I became fast friends.

The only problem is, Mason lives with Tristan, and Charlie lives with me. Well, until March when they get married, then they'll be living together, and I'll need to find a new roommate.

"Yes, bites!" I say, a few octaves too high. Mason throws his hands up in surrender, and I grab a chip to stuff in my mouth before I say something that is so not kid-friendly.

Charlie's daughter, Georgia, and Tristan's daughter, Lexi, come running down the hall with Alec chasing them. "Daddy! Save me!" Lexi yells, grabbing her dad by his waist. "Alec has the cooties and is trying to give it to Georgia and me!”

“I don't have the cooties!” Alec yells.

“Do so!” Georgia chimes in.

With Charlie and her daughter living with us while she and Tristan plan their wedding, it's never a dull moment in this house. Between my eight-year-old and her four-year-old plus Tristan's five-year-old, the place is always loud and crazy, but I wouldn't have it any other way.

I glance over at Tristan and Charlie. They're sitting close to each other, his arm is around her, love evident in both their eyes. Almost four years ago my divorce went through. Gavin and I sat down and discussed it, and thankfully, our divorce was nothing like my parents. He agreed to everything I asked for. We decided, since it was my grandmother's money that made it possible for us to purchase this home, I would get it. He moved into a condo down the street, and we split the custody of Alec, fifty-fifty. We settled on child support—enough to keep me afloat, but not too much that it would pull him under. He's actually become a more hands-on father with Alec as well. On the couple nights during the week and on the weekends he has him, for the most part, he gives him his attention.

While I don't regret the divorce and know it was for the best, my fairy tale that I thought would occur—like my mom's—has yet to happen. At first, I focused my energy on work and Alec. I told myself when the right guy came along I would know it. But life got busy and prince charming never showed up on my doorstep, so here I am, twenty-seven, single, and on a dating site called Plenty of Fish.

“Kids, go play nicely. The pizza will be here soon,” Tristan says with the patience of a damn saint. The kids run back down the hall to Alec's room.

“So, have you gotten any bites?” Charlie asks again, and I swear to all that's holy she and I are going to have a conversation once Tristan and Mason leave.

“What are ‘bites?’” Tristan inquires.

“A dating site,” Charlie informs him. “Plenty of Fish. I helped Mila fill out her profile information.”

“Wait a second!” Mason throws his head back in laughter. “You're on a dating site called Plenty of Fish?”

Tristan chuckles, and I glare at Charlie, who slaps Tristan on his chest. “Sorry, but c'mon, the name…”

“Yeah, yeah.” Charlie rolls her eyes. “Mason uses the analogy that he's going fishing when he's going out with a woman so Lexi doesn't know what they're talking about.”

“Of course he does,” I mutter, silently noting to cancel my membership tonight.

“This is awesome.” Mason laughs, looking at his phone. “An entire dating site dedicated to fishing for women. I'm signing up.”

I groan, my face dropping into my hands.

"Okay, let's see here. My criteria. Hmm…" He looks at me. "What's your criteria?"

"Don't worry about it," I snap, which of course, only causes him to grin.

"I'll just look you up." He shrugs.

I jump out of my seat to grab the phone from his hand, but he senses that I'm moving in and jumps out of his seat as well.

"Let's see here," he starts.

"Get out of my profile!" I yell, but Mason ignores me.

"Twenty-seven-year-old single mom looking for forever. I am not interested in one-night stands or sex before marriage, so please don't message me if you are." He puts his phone down, his one brow quirked up. "Damn, Mila, and that's just the beginning. When was the last time you even got laid? You might as well have a *Don't touch me, I'm off limits* sign attached to your forehead."

Completely mortified, I give up trying to grab his phone. "I need to go to the bathroom." I haul ass to my bedroom and close the door. I should know by now the way Mason is. He says whatever he wants and doesn't care what people think. He's a jokester and takes nothing seriously.

The fact is, even though Mason is a complete ass, he's not off-base. I haven't had sex since Gavin and I split up over four years ago. We separated because I didn't want to settle and wanted what my mom and stepdad had. The problem was, in order to have that, I actually had to meet the one, and so far he hasn't crossed my path. I refuse to have sex with just any guy. I'm not knocking those who choose to, but I'm afraid a one-night stand will turn into two, then three, and before I know it, I'll be giving my goods away with no promise of forever. Sex is okay… but if it's always like it was with my ex-husband, it's not worth sleeping around instead of finding the guy I can spend my life with.

"Mila," Charlie says through the door. "Can I come in?"

I unlock the door, and she enters the bathroom, closing the door behind her. "I'm so sorry. I shouldn't have brought it up in front of Mason. I wasn't thinking." She gives me a hug. I know she would never do something to hurt me on purpose. Charlie spent many years in a marriage where she was physically and emotionally abused. She is one of the sweetest, most kind-hearted women I have ever met.

"It's okay. I shouldn't let Mason get to me."

"Well, just so you know, Mason is gone." She rolls her eyes. "He said something about catching his own fish and left."

"Ladies, pizza is here," Tristan calls out, and we join him for dinner.

TWO

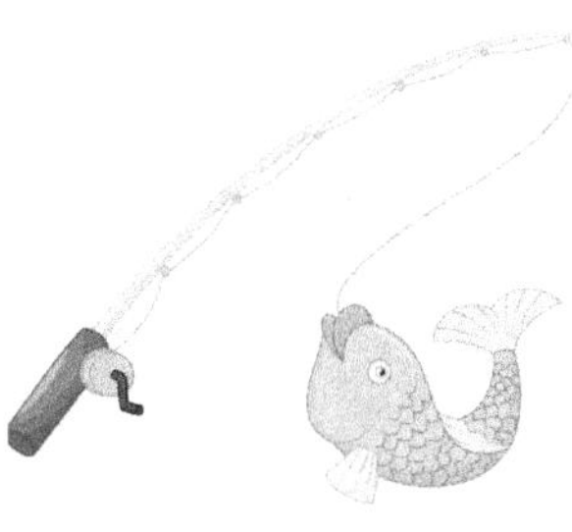

MASON

I'm sitting at dinner with Rochelle…or is it Raquel? Maybe Rachel? Fuck, I'm not sure. It's something with an R. But to be on the safe side, I make a mental note not to attempt to say her name. I would rather be anywhere but here, but she insisted on dinner before bed, so here I am, listening to her drone on about her sorority. I really need to double check age in the future. Sure, she's a senior in college so she's definitely of legal age, but the younger ones seem to be clingier.

"Yeah," is all I need to say for her to continue talking. My brain drowns out her voice when my phone goes off indicating I have a notification. When I check it, not even caring what *she* is saying, I notice it's from Plenty of Fish. Earlier, when we were all at Mila's house, she mentioned being on the dating site. I shouldn't have made fun of her, but I couldn't help it. What almost thirty-year old refuses to have sex before marriage? What if she never gets married again? She's already had one failed marriage. Maybe that's why it failed…because he sucked in bed and she didn't know it until they were married.

I click the notification and see Mila has updated her profile. There's a new picture on it and she looks fucking gorgeous. After I messed with her and she got upset and ran away, I finished the sign-up process. I'm all about getting some fishing in. Catch and release is my motto, and I'm not the least bit ashamed. After all, no fish are hurt in the process. They want to be caught, and they understand I'm not fishing for keeps. They'll be thrown back once we've had our fun.

"Mason!" *she* yells, getting my attention. I really need to figure out what *her* name is.

"Yeah, I agree," I say, because nine times out of ten, agreeing with a woman is all you need to do.

"You agree?" *She* huffs. Shit! This was probably a time when I should've disagreed.

"Maybe…" I draw the word out, unsure.

"Ugh! Can you please pay attention to me instead of to your phone?" I glance back down at my phone, the app still up, at Mila's beautiful face. I can tell it was taken tonight. Her chocolate brown hair is down around her shoulders and her face only has a minimal amount of makeup, making her hazel eyes shine even brighter. I can see the pale-yellow top she was wearing earlier that hugged her curves just right.

My eyes go back to—fuck! What is her damn name?—and I'm no longer feeling it. Pulling a hundred-dollar bill out, I drop it onto the table. "I'm not feeling well. I'll take you home."

She huffs. "Seriously? But we haven't even had sex yet." *And we won't be…*

I shrug and stand. "Sorry, sweetheart, but I need to get going. Grab your jacket and I'll drop you back off at school." She pouts, but it does nothing to me.

After I drop her off at her sorority house, I go home. Tristan and Lexi are both there as well. She's sleeping, and he's watching television.

"You're home early," he says, no judgment in his tone. That's why he's my best friend. Tristan just gets me. He accepts me the way I am and lets me be me. I met Tristan almost twelve years ago when I was homeless and looking for a trainer. His dad, Kaden Scott, took me on, and Tristan's mom, Ashley, welcomed me into their home. Actually, 'welcomed' isn't the right term. When I refused to move in with them, not wanting to be a burden, she forced me to move in by threatening to not allow Kaden to train me for free unless I did. A few years later, Tristan moved to California to go to college, and shortly after I made the move out here as well. He was living in San Diego but needed a fresh start. We moved to Los Angeles together, and six years and one Lexi girl later, we're still living together.

Only, in a couple months everything will be changing. Tristan met Charlie and they fell in love. I'm happy for him. He deserves happiness after what he's been through. In March, they'll be getting married and moving into a new home. They both asked me to move with them, but they need their space. So, in a few months, I'll be in need of a new place to live.

I plop down on the couch next to Tristan. "The woman wasn't my type, so I let her go." Tristan chuckles, shaking his head.

"You upset Mila." In other words, 'Charlie is making me talk to you. You need to apologize.'

"She's always upset with me." I shrug. "Nothing new." In other words, *'I'll apologize when I see her so you're not in the doghouse.'*

"True." '*Thanks.*' And the conversation is over. Because we're men. We say what we need to say and move forward.

After watching crappy television for a little while, Tristan's phone rings and he excuses himself. Not being able to help myself—call it morbid curiosity—I open the dating app and click on my profile. I type in some bullshit description about wanting to take long walks on the beach and that I'm looking for someone to talk to, in order to complete my sign up. Then I click on Mila's name and read through her entire profile.

Twenty-seven-year-old single mom looking for forever. I am not interested in one-night stands or sex before marriage, so please don't message me if you are. I am looking for a man who would like to one day settle down. I am a full-time nurse and I love my job. I want someone to go to the beach with. Someone who will enjoy relaxing in the sand next to me while I read. Someone who will enjoy hanging out with me and my son, and not just because he thinks it will make me happy. My favorite food is fondue. I want someone to watch cheesy movies with and who will take me on picnics in the park. I am looking for a man who is employed but not married to his job. No smokers, please. I was married once and we grew apart. I won't settle ever again. I am looking for romance (romance is not dead and I refuse to believe it is). I'm looking for a man to share my life with. If you are interested, please message me.

Edited to add: No d*ck pics please. I am NOT looking for sex.

Her bio is so open and out there. She lays herself out on the line, completely bare for the world to see. It's obvious she thinks she knows what she wants, but does she even realize, with criteria like that, she's never going to find anyone? Who the hell could ever live up to all of those expectations?

And what the fuck is fondue?

I lift my shirt up and snap a picture of my abs then upload it to my profile. Then I click on Mila's name and shoot her a message.

GetHooked: Hey there, I saw your picture and want to tell you that you're gorgeous.

I look up fondue and find out it's some type of food, like melted cheese or some shit.

GetHooked: I would love to take you out for fondue.

I refresh the screen a few times and the third time it shows she's on. A few minutes later I get a reply.

Looking4Love: Thank you. Your pic is very nice as well. Is that really your body? I didn't see one of your face.

I notice she ignored my offer to take her out.

GetHooked: It is my body. Maybe once you've earned it, I'll send you a picture of my face ;) So, it says you enjoy going to the beach. Do you live near one?

Looking4Love: I do enjoy the beach! I live in LA, so not too far of a drive. I try to go with my son whenever I'm off work. Sometimes I go when he's with his dad and I lay out and read. What do you do for a living?

I chuckle over the fact that she has now ignored my comment about her earning the right to see my face. She seems to pick and choose what she wants to respond to. I go to type back, almost forgetting she doesn't know me. I can't say I'm a UFC fighter. She'll know right away who I am. Instead, I take a page from her book and ignore her question.

GetHooked: Nice! I enjoy the beach as well. I love anything athletic or outdoors: surfing, running, biking, hiking, boating...I must admit I haven't read anything since high school. Do you enjoy those romance novels?

Charlie loves them, and I've seen them laying around the condo on several occasions. The covers are usually some shirtless guy or a couple about to fuck. Tristan is constantly making jabs at her, telling her to put the books down so he can give her the real thing.

Mila responds.

Looking4Love: Ugh! Just reading that list was exhausting. I think we're going to have to end this conversation right now so I can go take a nap. LOL j/k kind of...Yes, I love a good romance book. What do you do for fun when you're not hiking and biking or doing something athletic?

Ha! Who would've known… Mila Sterling actually has a sense of humor.

GetHooked: I hang out with friends, go to clubs...just the usual single guy stuff. Have you ever met anybody on here?

Looking4Love: Not yet, but I did from another site. Mostly, guys just want sex. They ignore my profile description and then they're disappointed when I don't put out.

Damn! She doesn't beat around the bush.

GetHooked: Saving yourself for someone special?

Looking4Love: Yes.

GetHooked: What if he sucks in bed and you don't know it until it's too late? Wouldn't it be best to try out the goods before you purchase the product?

When the circle that indicates she's typing doesn't appear I mentally kick myself in the ass for my response. I shouldn't have been that forward. She doesn't know it's me, so it looks like I'm just a creepy fucker trying to get laid. Then I see the circle appear.

Looking4Love: I'm not going to give my goods away for free. I'm okay not knowing how the guy is in bed. If he's the one for me, it won't matter.

I chuckle at her response. There are so many ways I can respond to that but for some reason I don't want to piss her off. I'm enjoying our conversation.

GetHooked: Understandable. So how will you know the guy is the one?

She responds, saying she will just know, and for the next few hours we converse back and forth. We keep it light, sticking to topics such as our favorite shows, music, and foods.

When my phone beeps with an email, I click out of the app to check it. Shit, it's already after eight in the morning. We've been messaging back and forth all night. I click on my inbox and see it's an email from my attorney, asking me to call him when I get a chance.

"Mr. Street," he says by way of greeting.

"Mr. Lopez."

"I just thought you should know your mom has been released this morning." The first time she was released from jail, I was seventeen and she didn't want me—said she couldn't take care of me. After I won my first big fight, I searched for her only to find out she was back in jail once again for prostitution.

I hired a criminal defense attorney, and he was able to get the illegal solicitation charges dropped. She was released with a few hundred hours of community service. I begged her to let me take care of her but she wasn't having it. She wouldn't even let me speak. She asked me not to help her anymore, some bullshit about not wanting me to take care of her. I tried to argue with her, insisted she let me help her, but she hung up on me and disappeared.

After that, I told the attorney I would pay any time she called him for help. She might not have wanted me to be in her life, but she's my mom, and there was no way I wouldn't help her in any way I could. A few years ago, she was put back in jail, but her offence was more serious than the previous ones: drug and weapon trafficking charges. Mr. Lopez couldn't get her to agree to a plea deal, so she was charged and given a four-year sentence.

"I appreciate you letting me know. Hopefully she stays out of jail this time."

He agrees, then says, "There's something you should know."

"Okay."

"She asked for your number." Well, this is news. I told him he could give it to her if she ever asks for it, but until today she never has.

"Thank you for letting me know. I appreciate you keeping me updated." He tells me if anything changes or occurs he'll let me know. We hang up, and my phone lights up with a message notification from Mila. When I didn't respond, she wished me a good night/morning. I close out of the app without replying. It was nice to talk with someone for a few hours, but nothing has changed. I refuse to be in a relationship. I have absolutely no desire to get married and be responsible for taking care of someone else. It's a huge commitment, one that most people take too lightly, and oftentimes ends with them failing the person they love.

My mom struggled every day to take care of me, and she failed miserably. When she was married to my dad, he had a gambling addiction that cost him his job and eventually his life. One night when he was drunk and walking home from the dog tracks, he stumbled off the sidewalk and was hit by a car. It was an accident, and he died instantly. My mom didn't ask for my dad to die, but he did, and even from his grave, he failed at taking care of us. He was selfish, probably choosing to spend his money on booze or the slots, and allowed his life insurance policy to lapse.

As a result, my mom not only lost my dad, but she didn't get a dime from the policy, and too quickly I became nothing more than a burden to her. I'm not saying people shouldn't get married or have kids. I'm just saying it's not for everyone. I don't want that responsibility. I remember being a kid and wishing for food and clothes that fit me while my mom sold herself to take care of us. She would cry every damn night wishing for a way out, wishing for someone to help her up. Instead, it was as if she was kicked while she was down, over and over again. My dad gave the initial kick and her piece of shit pimp gave the final one.

When you refuse to let someone take care of you, you can never be kicked, and when you refuse to take care of someone else, you never have to do any of the kicking. And in my opinion, that's the only way to live. If my own mother, during her lowest point, doesn't trust me to take care of her, then that should tell you something.

THREE

MILA

"HAPPY BIRTHDAY TO YOU! HAPPY BIRTHDAY TO YOU! HAPPY Birthday, dear Tristan! Happy Birthday to you!" Charlie pushes the Key Lime pie toward Tristan so he can blow out the candle sitting in the middle of the pie. According to Charlie, Tristan loves Key Lime pie more than birthday cake, so that's what she bought him.

"Blow out the candle and make a wish, Daddy!" Lexi yells. He does as she says and blows out the candle, and everyone claps.

"What did you wish for?" Lexi asks.

"I wished for an extra big piece of pie," Tristan jokes, and Lexi's eyes bug out.

"I bet it will come true! But you should've wished for something better, like more crayons for me! My birthday is so far away, and I need more crayons."

Everyone laughs as Tristan says, "Okay, let's do it again." He relights the candle and Lexi gasps.

"You can do it again and make more wishes? Can we do it a million times?"

Tristan's eyes widen, realizing what he's just done. "Um…no, you only get one do over."

"Darn it!" Lexi pouts. "Okay, this time wish for crayons, okay?"

"Okay," he agrees then turns to Georgia. "I can make more than one wish at the same time. What do you want me to wish for?"

Georgia gives him a small, shy smile. She's been through a lot in her short life, but luckily kids bounce back, and with the help and love of Charlie and Tristan, she'll bounce back completely.

"Coloring book," she whispers, and Tristan smiles warmly at her.

"And what about you?" he asks Alec. Not expecting to get a wish, he shrugs at first. "C'mon, there's got to be something you want me to wish for."

Alec glances at Mason who is standing against the wall of the dining room in their condo. "I want to be a UFC fighter," he says softly.

Mason hears Alec and grins at him. "That's a good wish, kid," he says, and Alec beams.

Tristan blows out the candle and everyone claps again.

After the pie is cut and eaten, Mason walks over and sits beside me on the couch. His leg bumps against mine and my traitorous body buzzes at his touch.

"I just wanted to say I'm sorry for the other day." When I look at him confused, he adds, "For making fun of you for being on that dating site."

"Oh, no worries." My eyes dart anywhere but at him, afraid if I look into those crystal blue eyes, my body will betray me some more.

"So, we're good?" he asks.

"Yep."

"All right, cool." As he stands, he pats my leg and my eyes fall to his large, warm, masculine hand. I let out a shiver before I can stop it, and of course Mason notices. He lets out a soft chuckle, but thankfully doesn't comment.

"Happy Birthday, bro." Mason pulls Tristan into a side hug. "I'm off to the gym."

Once he's gone, Charlie joins me on the couch. "Are those…hearts I see in your eyes…or maybe lust?"

"What?" I screech. "Stop!" Changing the subject I say, "So, I did something…"

"What did you do?"

"I applied for a nursing position at a private OB/GYN practice. It would mean no more working weekends, having set hours, and could possibly mean more money." I should've applied sooner, but just like I did with my marriage, I settled. I enjoyed working at the hospital, so I didn't strive for anything more. Lately, for some reason, I've been thinking about my mom and her last words to me. My promise to myself after her death, not to settle. I might not be able to find a guy, but I can take control of my life in other ways, starting with my job.

"That's awesome!" Charlie gushes. "I'm sure you'll get it. And when you do, we'll be celebrating."

♥♥♥♥♥

"I DID IT!" I SQUEAL, WALKING INTO *YOU PAINT ART STUDIO*. Charlie turns around, her smile bright and knowing.

"You did?" She runs toward me, and we meet halfway, hugging each other.

"I did! I got the job. The doctor hired me right there on the spot. I'll be working Monday through Friday, eight to four. No more nights or weekends, and I'll be making more money!"

"Oh, Mila! I'm so happy for you." Charlie hugs me tighter. "This weekend, we're all going to dinner to celebrate your new job. "

"And your grand opening," I add as I pull away from her and glance around the studio. The place looks amazing. For the last three months, Charlie and the contractors have been working around the clock to get this place ready for the grand opening, which will be taking place tomorrow. It's an art studio where kids can have birthday parties and adults can bring their own wine to drink, while they paint and have a good time.

"This place is incredible!" And it really is. Hardwood floors run throughout the entire studio. The most adorable picnic tables run parallel from front to back with individual easels sitting on top of each table. Matching bench seats with comfy cushions are in front of each easel. The walls are filled with art that Charlie, Lexi, and Georgia drew and painted themselves. On the back wall, the shelves are filled with charming wine glasses for the adult guests. The studio is stylish, yet gives off the feeling of comfort, making even a terrible artist such as myself want to spend a few hours here, drinking and painting.

"Thank you! I can't believe the opening is tomorrow. I feel like everything I've ever wanted and dreamt of is coming true." Tears fill her eyes and I pull her into another hug. Charlie has been through so much, more than anyone should ever have to go through, and it's about damn time her dreams are turned into a reality.

"Because they are, and you deserve every bit of happiness life has to offer."

"That she does." Tristan comes out from the back of the studio where the children's birthday party room is, and Charlie and I separate. "And so do you, Mila." He gives me a soft smile.

"Yeah, yeah." I wave him off. "So, do you need any help before tomorrow?"

Charlie twirls around the studio. "Nope. Tristan's sisters have been a godsend. Everything is ready to go for the grand opening and I'm completely booked." When Charlie was looking to hire help, Emma and Morgan, Tristan's younger twin sisters, both volunteered. They're both in college and Morgan is pregnant, due in June, so they'll be working part-time.

"Completely booked?"

"Yep! Actually, the studio is completely booked for the next several weeks. I'm doing kids classes during the day a few days a week, and Emma and Morgan are running the adult parties in the evenings. I'm going to be working Saturdays and Emma will be working Sundays."

"That's amazing. Will they be running the place while you're gone on your honeymoon?" Charlie and Tristan have picked March to get married and will be gone for close to two weeks on their honeymoon afterward. Charlie doesn't know it yet, but Tristan booked them several days at Disney, followed by a week-long Disney cruise. It's what she said she wanted, but I don't think she really believed he would actually book both.

"Yes, thank goodness. I was worried about having to close so soon after opening, but they'll be keeping it open for me while we're gone." Charlie's smile fades. "Wait! Will you still be able to attend the wedding?" I frown and Charlie's eyes go wide. "Mila…"

I grin. "Of course! I told HR I would need that Thursday and Friday off and they agreed."

Charlie sighs in relief. "You scared me! Don't do that again! I was already figuring out how to steal you away!"

"MOM! THIS IS SO BORING! THE GIRLS ARE ANNOYING AND I hate painting," Alec whines, and I shoot him the mom look. You know the one—it silently screams, *"Complain one more damn time and I'm going to take everything humanly possible away from you for a long ass time."* Alec retreats, closing his mouth and sighing, and I immediately feel bad. His father was supposed to take him this weekend but canceled last minute, needing to meet with some big deal client, which means Alec is stuck with me at the paint studio for its grand opening.

"Mmhmm." I turn toward the noise and see Mason standing there with a coffee in his hand and his eyes trained on…my butt? He's in his signature short sleeve grey hoodie that he puts on to cover his body when he's done working out and black workout shorts. His hair is tousled like it always is when he's been sweating.

I clear my throat, and his mischievous blue eyes finally make their way up to my face. He shakes his head slowly. "Were you staring at my butt?" I whisper so only he can hear, calling him out.

He smirks then leans into me, his lips only a breath away from my ear. "I can't help it… I'm an ass man, and you, my off-limits MILF, have a nice ass." I roll my eyes. When Mason hit on me all those years ago, he had no clue I was a mom. When we reconnected a few months ago and he found out I have a son, he pulled back. Something about all moms being a no-go. I should be grateful he's no longer hitting on me, especially since we have nothing in common and want completely different things in a relationship—I want one and he wants to get laid.

And on top of that, him not wanting me because I have a child should be a huge red flag. My son and I are a package deal. But, the insecure woman in me kind of misses Mason hitting on me. It made me feel…I don't know…sexy…un-mom-like.

"Brought you coffee." He backs up and hands me my much-needed caffeine fix. I bring it up to my nose, smelling the aroma and wishing I could inhale it like a drug.

"Thank you." My words come out in a moan and he chuckles.

"My pleasure." Mason's gaze darts around the studio at all of the people who are painting and chatting and laughing with each other. "This place is hopping."

"Yeah, I'm really happy for Charlie."

"Me too," he agrees.

"Me too," Alec joins in. "I just wish I could be happy away from these girls." He glares at Georgia and Lexi, who both ignore his attitude and giggle. "Painting is boring and for girls."

Mason laughs. "Hey now, painting can be fun and manly."

"Really? Prove it," Alec says, challenging Mason. I cover my mouth to hide my laughter.

"Game on." Mason grabs two blank canvases from the storage closet and sets one on an empty easel then hands Alec the other one.

"Now, the key to painting is to become one with the canvas." Alec tilts his head in confusion, and Mason grins mischievously. His eyes lock on mine, and he shoots me a flirtatious wink, causing the spot directly between my legs, which has been dormant for years, to awaken. It's yawning and stretching, and I'm begging it to go back to sleep. Mason is not the guy I want my body to react to.

"If you want to be a painter, you have to look like a painter," Mason says seriously. Grabbing a paintbrush, he dips it into the black paint and brings the paint-covered brush to Alec's face. "Don't move, kid, or you will literally become the canvas." He draws a mustache across the top of Alec's lip, and when he's done, Alec turns to look in the mirror and laughs.

"Okay, now do me." Mason hands Alec the paint brush and he draws a mustache across Mason's upper lip. They both look ridiculous and completely adorable. Pulling out my phone, I take a picture of the two of them. A few months ago, Alec met Mason for the first time, and it was probably one of the best moments of his life. Mason is a huge UFC fighter, and Alec is his biggest fan. Mason walks on water as far as Alec is concerned.

"All right, now your mom." Mason grins wide as I glare.

"No, I don't think…"

"Yes, Mom! You need to look like a painter too."

"Fine," I relent, then bend down slightly so Alec can draw a fake mustache across my upper lip. Mason shakes with laughter, and I vow to get revenge.

"Take a picture of all of us!" Alec exclaims once he's done and, because I can't say no to him, I do. The three of us squeeze in close, and I snap a picture, quickly putting my phone back in my pocket without looking at it.

"All right, now that we look like painters, we have to pick what we're going to paint," Mason points out.

"The girls are painting hearts for Valentine's Day." Alec gags.

"Oh no." Mason shakes his head dramatically. "That won't do." He leans into Alec. "Unless you're painting a heart for your mom, that is." He winks at me again, and I plead with my girly parts to ignore him. It's no wonder he has women eating out of his hand.

"What's the theme in your room?" Mason asks Alec.

"UFC! I have posters of you and George St Pierre!" Yep, that's right. I have to stare at half-naked pictures of Mason on my son's walls.

"Nice!" Mason fist bumps Alec. "What's your favorite part of fighting?"

"When I watch the Ultimate Fighter, I think hitting the bag looks cool."

"All right, then that's what we'll paint: the punching bag." He pulls his phone out and a few seconds later, he pulls up an image of a punching bag. "Ready?"

"Yes!"

They spend the next thirty minutes painting their red and black punching bags. Mason suggests they add the UFC logo to their painting and Alec agrees. When they're done, Alec calls me over to show me his painting. "Can I hang this on my wall?" he asks, pride evident in his voice.

"Of course you can. You did an amazing job."

"See, kid. Painting isn't just for girls."

"I guess it was cool," Alec admits. "But I'd still rather be fighting." Mason chuckles and agrees.

"I can take him to the gym," he says to me.

"Really?" Alex jumps out of his seat. "Yes! Can he? Please, Mom."

"I don't think…" I start to say, but Alec cuts me off, his begging becoming even more dramatic as if being here any longer just might kill him.

Mason laughs at my son's theatrics. "I'll be next door working out. He can hang out and spar with me."

"Are you sure?"

Mason nods. "Yeah. No reason to force him to be here." He leans into Alec. "The only guy that has to be here is Tristan because he's pu—" My eyes bug out, but he quickly corrects himself. "Because he's whipped."

"What do you mean he's whipped?" Alec asks curiously, and I

smirk. *Get yourself out of this one…*

"You know…in love." Mason scrunches up his nose in mock disgust, and Alec giggles. "So, he's stuck hanging out here instead of at the gym." He shrugs.

"Ewww! I'm never gonna be whipped or in love!"

"That's what I'm talking about." Mason high-fives him, and they both head to the door. Before they leave, Mason turns around and says, "Just come by and get him when you're done."

"Okay, thank you."

Several hours and too many parties to count later, and Charlie says goodbye to the last customer, closing the door behind her. Emma, Morgan, and I all drop onto the bench seats at the same time.

"I owe you guys forever."

My phone goes off in my pocket and I pull it out. It's Gavin letting me know he'll pick Alec up from me tomorrow to spend time with him. I text him back that's fine and then panic.

"Where's Alec?" I stand, my eyes darting all over the studio.

"At the gym with Mason." Charlie laughs. "Tristan took the girls home a couple hours ago." I glance at my phone. Holy shit! It's been like eight hours since Mason took Alec next door.

"I better go get him." I head for the door. "Poor Mason has been babysitting all day."

Charlie laughs some more. "Don't be fooled. It was probably Alec who was babysitting Mason."

"Yeah, somehow that doesn't make me feel any better." Emma and Morgan snort-laugh.

"Congratulations on your grand opening." I give Charlie a hug. "I'll see you tomorrow for lunch," I call out as I rush out of the studio.

I arrive next door and the gym is still open. Since it's technically after hours, there's nobody manning the front desk. I glance around the gym and spot Mason in the center of the octagon. There are several guys standing along the ropes, but I don't see Alec anywhere. I walk a little closer as Mason and whoever he's fighting turn slightly, and that's when I realize my son is in the center with Mason.

He's wearing head gear and gloves, striking Mason as he dodges each punch while the guys clap and shout moves at him. When Mason turns, I see the most taunting, sexy, cocky-as-hell grin directed at my son. I've seen Mason fight too many times to count, including in Vegas a few months ago in person, but watching him up close in his element is different.

Alec throws a left hook and Mason weaves out of the way. Alec huffs in annoyance and Mason laughs.

"C'mon, kid…loosen up," Mason taunts him some more. Alec spins with a round house kick, and Mason moves out of the way just before he can connect. I pull my phone out of my back pocket and snap a couple photos. When the heck did my little boy grow up?

Mason stops blocking and quickly takes over the fight. When I briefly stop watching Alec to focus on Mason, I realize he's shirtless. As Alec backs up, Mason's wrapped hand comes up quickly and he runs his fingers through his hair, smirking at Alec, taunting him to not run. I approach even closer and am able to get a better view of Mason. I watch the beads of sweat trickle down his muscular pecs, continuing down the ridges of his abs and ending where that sexy as hell V meets his shorts. They're hanging low on his waist, unlike the ones he's required to wear during a real fight.

Almost as if he can feel me gawking over him like a horny freaking teenager, his eyes dart away from my son and land on me. His brows lift in that smug way that remind me why I stay away from him. The side of his lip curls up into a knowing grin, and I roll my eyes. And then…he's on his ass.

FOUR

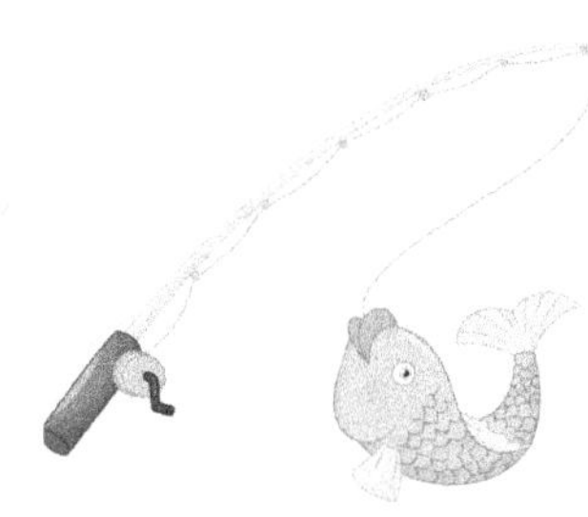

MASON

hanging out with her at home or at the gym, watching her for Tristan, or hanging out with the two of them. We color and paint and watch her girly shows. We play dress up and play with her dolls, and sometimes she even convinces me to bake with her. But spending the day with Alec is different. He's all boy: rough and rowdy and energetic. He's obsessed with the UFC and fighting. Unlike Lexi, who hates the gym with a passion, Alec is enamored with everything associated with it. We spent most of the day with Alec shadowing me. We went for a short run—very short. The kid is only eight years old after all. We worked out using weights, had lunch with some of the guys at a restaurant down the street, where Alec fanboyed like crazy over some of the well-known guys he's seen in fights, and then we came back to the gym so I could get some sparring in.

When I asked him if he's ever fought, he shook his head, and it boggled my mind that someone could love something so much and never have even experienced it firsthand. So, after having Alec watch some of my friends, Troy Declan and Jake Finning—who are also UFC fighters—spar against me, I told him it was his turn. The passion and love for the sport shines so brightly in his eyes, it's almost blinding. I was older than Alec when I was introduced to the UFC, but I remember everything I felt the first time I was brought into the octagon: the fear, nervousness, and excitement all mixed together. It was like a natural high, a rush that's impossible to fully understand until you're in that position.

Alec and I are circling each other. Of course I'm taking it easy on the kid, but at the same time I'm not letting him catch me. He's giving it all he's got. Punching and kicking, trying every move he's seen on TV. The guys are rooting for him and it's spurring him on. He throws another left hook and I jump out of the way. I can see it in his face, he's getting more and more frustrated and it has me laughing. I can't help it. To me, fighting is one big game of cat and mouse. Sure, it's about strength and follow through, but it's more than that. It's about learning the opponent. Watching their every move and learning how they tick. It's about being patient and never getting frustrated. You have to be smart. Memorize their moves. And when the time is right, you go in for the kill.

I feel someone watching me from the sidelines, and when I turn to see who it is, I spot Mila checking me out. Her eyes are dragging down my body, and she's practically eye-fucking me right here in front of her son. Unlike this morning when I saw her at the art studio with her hair down in waves, it's now up in a messy bun. She's still dressed the same, though, in a plain black V-neck tee that shows off her perky tits, and a pair of tight jeans, ripped down her legs. To complete her outfit, she's wearing a pair of black Nike's, unlike most of the women I know who wear high heels everywhere they go. She's the perfect mix of girly and sexy, and I need to stop looking at her... but I can't.

When my eyes meet hers, I give her a knowing smirk—the one that says she's been busted checking me out. Her beautiful green-brown eyes roll in mock annoyance, and I chuckle, completely forgetting that I'm in the middle of sparring with her son. But guess who doesn't forget? Alec. He takes advantage of my momentary distraction, and before I know it's coming, he delivers a successful punch to my jaw, hitting just right. Because I don't have a mouth guard in since I was *only* sparring with an eight-year-old, my lip clashes against my teeth when his fist connects. Losing my balance, I stumble back and land on my ass. I run my tongue over my busted lip and feel the open cut.

Glancing up, I see Alec standing over me, worry evident in his features. I shake my head, laughing that I was just taken down by a damn kid, and he visibly sighs.

"That was badass! I'm thinking your new name around here should be Bruiser." I feel my bruised lip again, the metallic taste of blood trickling into my mouth and hitting my taste buds. Then I dart my eyes toward Mila, who is standing there in shock, her hands covering her mouth. "Please tell me you're going to sign him up for classes."

Jake and Troy crack up laughing, and Brent, the gym manager, brings me over a wet washcloth to press on my bleeding mouth.

"Can I, Mom?" Alec runs toward his mom to beg her. "Please, can I?"

She looks torn when she says, "We'll see, sweetie. I'll speak to your dad about it when he picks you up tomorrow night." Alec's shoulders slump, but he doesn't argue. "Go grab your stuff. We need to get home."

He jumps out of the octagon and heads back toward the front where I had him put his electronics earlier. I stand and cut across the octagon until I'm right in front of Mila, only the ropes separating us.

"Let me see." Her fingers wrap around mine as she moves the washcloth from my lip. "I don't think it will need stitches." She gives me a small smile. "Thank you for hanging out with Alec today."

"No problem." I shrug. "He's a good kid, and as you can see, he's good at MMA. Lessons would be good for him, especially since he loves the sport."

"Yeah, I know. He's been asking more and more lately to sign up. I need to go over my bills, though, before I can say yes. I got a new job yesterday, which will help, but Charlie has been paying half the bills. I need to find a new roommate before I can commit to spending money like that."

"What about his dad?" I have no clue why I ask that. This isn't my business. Mila and her son aren't my business.

"We pay for half of all Alec's extracurricular activities. He'll agree. I just need to make sure I can cover my half." My heart squeezes as I remember how many times I wanted to play a sport when I was younger but my mom couldn't afford it. She would cry for hours after she told me no. Eventually I stopped asking, not wanting to upset her and knowing the answer would always be no.

"I'm ready to go, Mom!" Alec runs back over to us.

"Did you thank Mason for taking care of you today?"

"Thank you, Mason! Today was awesome!" Alec puts his fist out to bump mine like I taught him earlier, and I reciprocate robotically—I'm smiling outwardly, but on the inside I'm freaking the fuck out.

"Anytime, Bruiser." I watch Alec as he runs over to the other guys to say goodbye, Mila's words on repeat in my head.

"Did you thank Mason for taking care of you today?"

Is that what I did? Did I take care of Alec? No…I hung out with him. I'm not in any place to take care of anyone. I was just doing Mila a favor. We hung out and sparred…I wasn't taking care of anybody. My thoughts flip back to my mom and all of the times she tried and failed to take care of me, to me wishing for the day I could finally be in a place where I could take care of her, only to have her push me away once I was. She doesn't trust me enough to let me help take care of her. She chose to continue to prostitute herself out instead of letting me in. My chest feels like it's constricting, squeezing my heart and making it hard to breathe.

"Mason?" My eyes dart back to Mila, who is giving me a concerned look. "Are you okay?"

"Yeah." I breathe in deeply then struggle out an exhale. "Yeah, I'm fine."

"You sure? You look like you're having a hard time breathing."

I almost tell her the truth—what's going on in my head—but instead I play it off. "What can I say?" I lean in close to her so I can whisper into her ear. "Being in the presence of a gorgeous woman such as yourself…you take my breath away, and maybe, just maybe, I'm considering lifting my ban on moms."

Mila's breath hitches slightly. "Not happening, Mason." She backs away from me slightly and tries to appear annoyed, but her nipples poking out through her thin shirt indicates she's turned on.

"You say that"—I move closer to her again, this time cornering her between my body and the edge of the counter—"but your body says something else entirely." My eyes dart down to her tits, and her gaze follows. Her eyes widen, but before she can respond, I back away. "I'm going to grab my stuff and then I'll walk you guys to your car."

I turn away from her and run into the locker room. I throw my hoodie on and grab my flip-flops to quickly slide on, the entire time trying to get a grip on myself. I'm Mason, the guy who fights and fucks. The guy who goes fishing but never keeps what he catches. I'm not the guy who settles down and takes care of a kid.

I get back out to the main area and Alec and Mila are waiting for me by the door. "Ready?" I ask, and she and Alec nod. I walk them to their car, saying a quick goodbye to both of them, then jump into mine to head home.

When I get there, Tristan is sitting at the table on his laptop. "What's up?"

"Lexi asleep?" I ask, when I don't hear or see her.

"Yeah, Georgia is spending the night so Charlie can close the studio." He smiles warmly. "The girls are inseparable." The way Tristan and Charlie's worlds collided wasn't exactly conventional. Major shit went down with Charlie's husband, and had the two of them not been as strong as they are, it might've broken them. But they handled it together and came out even stronger and more in love, if that's possible. The moment they met each other's kids, they accepted them as if they were their own, and once they're married, they'll be adopting them, making the four of them a family, legally. I always viewed caring for someone as a negative quality. A weakness or a sacrifice. Making yourself vulnerable and setting yourself up for failure. But when I watch Tristan and Charlie together with their daughters, they don't ever seem like they're sacrificing anything, and they've proven that the two of them are stronger together than separate. It's almost as if they complete each other.

Tristan looks up from whatever it is he's doing and eyes me skeptically. "You okay?"

"Yeah…" I run my hands over my face. "My mom's out of jail, again."

Tristan nods, waiting for me to continue. I don't usually talk about my past, but Mila's words opened up old wounds I thought were healed, only to realize they were nothing more than deep lacerations tightly bandaged to appear like they were healed, but are still bleeding underneath.

"How did you know you could take care of Lexi?" I sit across the table from Tristan and his eyes widen, probably out of shock that I'm talking to him about this.

"Like be her dad?"

"Yeah."

"I didn't." He chuckles softly, shaking his head. "I couldn't even think of a damn name for her. I was in such shock, I almost named her after one of your conquests." We both laugh. "Shit, five years later and I still have no idea what I'm doing most of the time."

I scoff at Tristan's response. He's the best dad I've ever met. Growing up, when my dad was alive, he was there…yet he wasn't. He provided a home and the necessities, but he never took care of my mom and me like he was supposed to because he was too busy drinking and gambling. He never took us anywhere or did anything with us. I remember going to school every Monday and hearing the kids talk about their weekends: trips to the park, the aquarium, dinners out. I wished for any of that, something, but it never happened. Still, even without any of that, my mom was happy when my dad was alive. We lived in a nice home and she wasn't fucking guys for money. We didn't have much, but we had each other… until we didn't. Until she could no longer take care of herself, let alone me.

Tristan takes care of his daughter. He puts her first every day of his life. He thinks about her wants and needs. He loves her with every ounce of his being. My mom was given a shitty hand, and I know she did the best she could. What I don't understand is why, when I'm more than capable of helping her, taking care of her, she won't let me. Is it because I'm my father's son? Does she not trust me? Is she afraid I'll fail her the same way my dad did? Does she resent me for being the reason she had to prostitute herself out in the first place? Because I was too expensive. I had too many needs.

"Mason, what's going on?"

I stand, feeling confused. My head and heart are all over the place. Mila's fucking words are making me second guess everything I've ever believed and thought I knew.

"Nothing. I'm going to shower."

"Okay…Oh, by the way, the condo is under contract. We need to be out the first week of March."

"Nice. It sold quickly."

"Yeah, and they didn't even try to negotiate on the price. Are you coming to see the new house with us tomorrow?"

"Wouldn't miss it." Tristan picked out a house to surprise Charlie.

She fell in love with it, but it needed to have some renovations done, so she insisted everyone wait to see it until they were done. They'll be moving all of their stuff in next month before they get married.

"You know you're welcome to move with us."

"I know… but you guys need to do your own thing." I shrug. "I'll find a place before we need to be out."

After taking a shower, I lie in bed. I had made plans to meet up with a woman I met at the club the other night, but I'm just not feeling it. On my way home from the gym I texted her to cancel. After watching a couple crappy television shows, my eyes make their way to my phone. I click on the app store and type in Plenty of Fish. I deleted the app the other day to stop myself from messaging Mila back. My finger hovers over the install button for a good minute before I finally press it. I watch impatiently as the icon slowly loads. Once it's done, I click on it to log in, then I click on my inbox to retrieve my new messages. Shit! There must be a few hundred here. I bypass them all until I find the one I'm looking for.

Looking4Love: You must have fallen asleep… I guess I better get a couple hours as well. Good night/Good morning.

That's the last message she sent before I deleted the app. I see the green dot indicating she's on, so I shoot her a message, keeping it light.

GetHooked: How's the fishing going?

Looking4Love: I haven't caught anything LOL Well, maybe I have… but they weren't worth keeping. How about you?

GetHooked: I'm just chilling on the pier, beer in my hand, pole in the water, waiting for the right fish to come along and bite.

Looking4Love: Haha! Mind if I join you?

GetHooked: Sure! The more the merrier. Just don't try to steal my bait ;)

Looking4Love: I wouldn't dream of it. Plus, something tells me the fish you're trying to catch is nothing like the one I'm trying to catch.

And she has no idea how right she is about that…

FIVE

MILA

"WOW! CHARLIE, THIS PLACE IS HUGE!" I'M STANDING IN THE middle of her and Tristan's massive new kitchen, practically drooling. "Like, I could fit my entire townhome into your kitchen."

Tristan chuckles. "It's too bad Charlie doesn't cook."

"Hey! I can cook!" She pushes him against his chest, but he grabs her hand and pulls her close. "It's not my fault you can cook better," she says, pouting playfully.

The kids are running around, and you can hear their voices echoing off the bare walls. I can hear Alec counting and the girls giggling while they hide somewhere in the house.

"Tristan, Charlie, this is a beautiful home," Ashley gushes as she walks into the kitchen. "And I love that you will only be a couple streets over from us."

Kaden laughs. "You did good, son." He gives Tristan and Charlie a hug. "I know I've said it before but welcome to the family."

"Thank you." Tears spring from Charlie's eyes. "I never imagined I would go from my life before, to this. To having amazing people like you guys in my life…in my daughter's life."

"Aww…Charlie! I might just have to change my mind and move in here with you guys." Mason laughs and pulls Charlie into a hug.

"You know you're welcome to!"

"Yeah, yeah." He checks his phone. "I need to hit the gym." He slaps Tristan on the shoulder. "Great house, man. I look forward to moving all your shit in here in a few weeks." Everyone cracks up, and Mason says bye to everyone before heading out.

"Dad!" Lexi comes running down the hallway with Georgia and Alec running behind her. "I'm so hungry!" She sticks her belly out. "It's growling, and so is Georgia's, right?" She glances toward Georgia, who nods in agreement.

"All right. Let's go grab something to eat before my daughters shrivel up and die from starvation."

"Mom, where's Mason?" Alec looks around.

"He had to go work out at the gym."

Alec frowns. "Can we ask Dad when we see him about signing me up?"

"Sure, sweetie."

While we're waiting for a table, Charlie and I are sitting on the bench discussing everything she still needs to purchase for their new home when I let out a yawn, and Charlie gives me a look of concern. "Not sleeping well?"

I think back to my conversation with—well, jeez, I don't even know his name—*GetHooked*. We chatted for hours until I finally passed out at close to four in the morning. He's funny and silly and just so easy to talk to. He didn't send me any dick pics or ask what my favorite position is—refraining from doing that are automatic points in my book.

"I was messaging a guy on Plenty of Fish." I feel myself grin, and Charlie grins back.

"Go you! Are you going to meet him?"

"I'm not sure. I'm just enjoying talking to him."

It takes a little while for the restaurant to put a table together big enough to fit all of us, and when we're finally sitting down to eat, I get a text message from Gavin letting me know he's on his way to pick up Alec. I give him the name of the restaurant, and as we're all ordering, he shows up.

"Dad!" Alec jumps out of his seat and runs over to his father.

"Little dude!" Gavin pulls him into a hug.

"I'm ordering chicken fingers! Can we stay so I can eat, please?"

"Um…" He looks to me for help.

"Hey, man." Tristan stands and walks over to Gavin to shake his hand. "Why don't you join us? We're just ordering." Tristan and Charlie have met Gavin several times when he's come to get Alec from the house.

"You sure?" He glances toward me for the okay and I nod.

"All right, then." He waves to everyone else at the table. "I'm Gavin Sterling, this little dude's dad." He pulls a chair over and sits down between Alec and me.

Once everyone finishes placing their orders, introductions are made. The first time Tristan and Charlie met Gavin, they were shocked at how well we got along. He walked into my house and grabbed a bottle of water from the fridge without even asking. I explained to them later, that while we weren't meant to be together, that doesn't mean we can't parent Alec together. The funny thing is once we divorced, we actually began to get along a lot better. A friendship formed that we couldn't have while we were married. I'm glad we aren't putting Alec in the same position my parents put me in. Alec will never have to choose one parent over the other. We spend most holidays together, and luckily, the women Gavin have dated so far haven't been jealous or catty about it.

"What's up with your jersey?" Tristan asks Gavin. "Is that a local team?"

"Nah, I play for a men's softball league. We have our first game later today."

"Really? I've always wanted to do something like that."

"Well, there's room on our team. Are you any good?"

"Hell no! I just said I wanted to do it. I didn't say I would be any good at it."

Gavin laughs. "Then you'll fit right in. If you aren't doing anything after we eat, you're more than welcome to come down to the field and play. I've got some extra jerseys in my car. We practice a couple nights a week and play a game on Sundays."

Tristan glances toward Charlie, and she smiles. "I can't wait to see this!" She claps her hands together in pure excitement and everyone laughs.

"OH MY GOD! TRISTAN IN THAT JERSEY." CHARLIE WAGGLES HER eyebrows while she pretends to fan herself, and I crack up. We're at the softball field watching a bunch of grown men play a softball game that would more than likely be aired on America's Funniest Home Videos before ESPN. It's the ninth inning with only one strike left until the game is over, and Gavin's team is surprisingly winning. The batter strikes out, and the guys join in the center of the field to shake hands before parting ways.

Gavin, Tristan, and a couple other guys from Gavin's team come over to us. "You were amazing." Charlie wraps her arms around Tristan's neck, and he chuckles.

Gavin smiles warmly at me. "Thanks for coming. Alec hates having to stay cooped up in the dugout during the game." He points toward his friends. "These are a couple friends of mine." He points to a cute blond-haired guy with piercing green eyes. "This is Jack." Then he points to another guy who is just as cute but with a shaved head and amber eyes. "And this is Chris."

The guys both extend their hands out to shake mine. "This is my ex-wife, Mila."

"Nice to meet you," I say to them both. "You guys played a good game."

"Nah, the other team just played worse," Jack jokes, and his playfulness has me smiling.

We say our goodbyes and I take off, leaving Alec with his dad. Gavin asked if he could drop him off and pick him up from school tomorrow, which means I will have two days of *me* time, and I start my new job tomorrow.

When I get home, there's a text from an unknown number and one from Gavin.

Unknown: Hey, it's Jack. I hope it's not weird I'm texting you. Gavin gave me your number. I was hoping maybe I could take you out some time.

Gavin: Jack asked for your number...we're not really friends. Just play ball together and hang out occasionally afterward with the team.

That's Gavin's way of telling me he doesn't mind if I go out with Jack. I send Gavin a text back thanking him, then I send Jack one to let him know I would love to go out with him. If I never date, how will I ever find my forever?

SIX

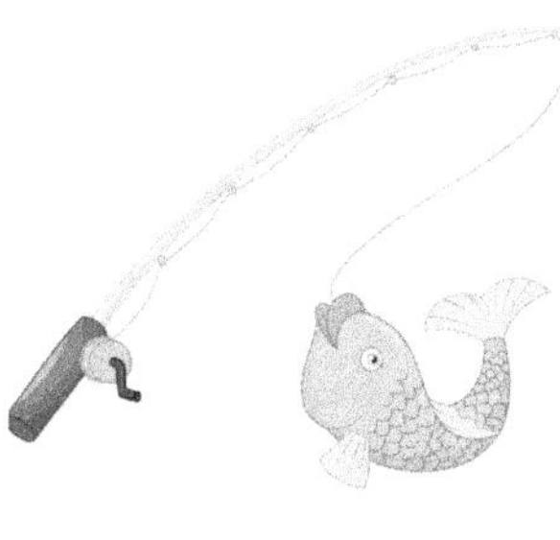

MASON

GetHooked: How's my favorite fisherman doing?

I'M HANGING OUT AT PLUSH WITH A FEW FRIENDS OF MINE FROM the gym. Plush is a members only club. It's actually where Tristan met Charlie when she used to work here. The bottom floor has a bar and dance floor, and there are half-naked women and men dancing in cages on the outskirts of the club. The second floor has a smaller bar and dance floor, but it also has several private rooms. The rooms can be rented by the hour or for the night along with the women or men. I've rented a room for the night. The liquor is flowing and Brent and Tommy, another fighter I'm friends with, have women giving them lap dances, their eyes glued to their tits and ass.

My eyes, on the other hand, are glued to my phone as I wait for Mila to respond. Earlier, when I told Tristan I was leaving to go out, he mentioned that he and Charlie were watching Alec for Mila. Apparently she has a date tonight and her ex-husband couldn't take Alec as planned.

Looking4Love: It's fisherWOMAN! And not good...

GetHooked: I'm sorry fisherWOMAN. What's wrong?

Looking4Love: I'm on a date and it's kind of sucking.

GetHooked: Ahh... so you finally reeled in a fish?

Looking4Love: More like an old, smelly boot! He seemed sweet when I first met him, but now he's just nasty. His attitude, his comments. Just

gross!

I chuckle, and the guys glance my way, reminding me where I am. One of the dancers comes over and gives me a flirtatious smile. She's got fake blonde hair, fat tits, and lips that are meant for giving head. She's the complete opposite of Mila in every way, and it scares the shit out of me when I look at her and she does absolutely nothing for me.

"Can I give you a lap dance?"

"Sure."

I set my phone down so she can straddle my lap and hopefully take my mind off Mila. Taking a pull of my Heineken, I try to focus on the woman in front of me: on her ass and tits and hips that are swaying seductively to the music. But for some reason, my mind keeps going back to the brown-haired, hazel-eyed woman stuck on a shitty date.

SEVEN

MILA

"HOW IS THE NEW JOB GOING?" CHARLIE ASKS AS SHE HANDS me a large bottle of red paint to pour into a smaller, squeezable bottle.

"It's going good. I'm loving the set schedule, and I still get to go to the hospital a couple days a week to assist in delivering the babies. Mostly, though, I see the pregnant patients, and I must admit, pregnant women are a lot nicer than the ones in labor."

Charlie giggles. "I bet!"

"Plus, I'm loving the fact that I get to be home with Alec every night."

"That's awesome. I'm so happy for you. Speaking of Alec, did he end up going with his dad tonight?" Charlie looks around, realizing my kid isn't in the studio complaining.

"No, he's next door with Mason." I roll my eyes, and she grins.

Before Alec and I could even make it to the front of the art studio, he saw Mason and asked if he could hang out with him. Mason said he didn't mind, so I let him go. Emma is finishing up a kids' class where they're all painting their version of Mickey's Fun Wheel from the Disneyland Resort, and once they're done we're going to go grab some dinner.

"I told him I'd go over to get him when the class is over, but Mason said he'd bring him over in a little while." We continue to fill more bottles while we talk about her upcoming wedding, her new house, and where we want to eat dinner. When we hear someone call out Charlie's name, we both look over at the cute guy walking our way. He has shaggy brown hair and brown eyes. He's dressed in a suit, complete with a dark navy blue tie.

"Hey, Evan. The class is almost done." Charlie points toward one of the little boys who waves our way.

"I don't think we've met." Evan turns his attention to me. "I'm Evan Gander." He puts his hand out to shake mine.

"I'm Mila Sterling." I shake his hand back, noticing he has a cute dimpled smile.

"It's nice to meet you. Do you have a child in class?"

"No, my child is next door, fighting." I laugh, and Evan keeps his smile, but now it looks forced. I could be wrong, but I don't think Evan is pro-fighting.

"Yes, I saw the gym next door."

We're both silent for a beat when I see Alec running toward me. "And speaking of which…" I open my arms so Alec can give me a hug when he gets over to me. "This is my son, Alec."

"Mom! We forgot to ask dad about me signing up. We need to remember. Where's your phone?" He puts his hand out and I hand it to him, stifling a laugh. Even at only eight years old, my kid knows me too well. If it's not in my calendar, I can't be held accountable for not remembering.

"Okay, Mom, I put it in and set the alarm." Alec hands me back my phone, and that's when I notice Mason is here with him. He's standing next to Evan and it's like day and night. Evan, in his business suit, and Mason, in his grey hoodie and sweats. Evan's clean shaven and Mason's sporting scruff that I want to rub my hands up and down. *What the hell? No, I don't! Mason is a player. I don't want to rub my hands anywhere on him.*

"Thanks for hanging out with him," I say.

"No problem."

The class ends and Lexi and Georgia come running over—Georgia, to show Charlie her pictures, and Lexi, to give Mason a hug.

Evan's son comes to the back as well to show his dad his picture. "Good job, son. Are you hungry?"

"Yes!" Brant yells before running off to play with the kids.

"We're all going to grab a burger at Burger Lounge. You're welcome to join us." Charlie smiles mischievously and it doesn't take a brain surgeon to realize she's trying to set me up.

Evan smiles at Charlie but directs his response to me. "Unfortunately, it's a school night, and Brant's bedtime is at eight o'clock so we're going to eat dinner at home, but maybe you and I could go out some time. If you're single that is." He flashes me a hundred mega-watt smile.

"Oh, um…sure. Yeah, I'm single." I can't believe I just said yes to another guy.

Evan pulls out his phone. "Great. What's your number?"

Just as I finish giving him my number, one of the kids starts crying. We stop and find the crying child. It's Brant, Evan's son. "Brant, what's wrong?" Evan bends to speak to him.

"Georgia knocked me on the ground," Brant whimpers, and Georgia frowns.

"I didn't mean to. We were playing tag. I was tagging him."

"It's okay," Evan says to Georgia, but his voice says it's anything but. Then to his son, he says, "We've talked about this. Games that include violence aren't okay."

"Really?" Mason scoffs. "It was tag."

Evan stands. "I choose to teach my son that placing his hands on anybody else is not okay, no matter what the reason."

"Okay, boys." Charlie stands between them. "It's time to close the place up, and I'm starving. Georgia, say sorry to Brant."

"I'm sorry."

"Does he need any ice or a Band-Aid?" I ask.

Evan says no, then adds, "I'll call you."

And for some reason, his words come out as more like a threat than a promise.

EIGHT

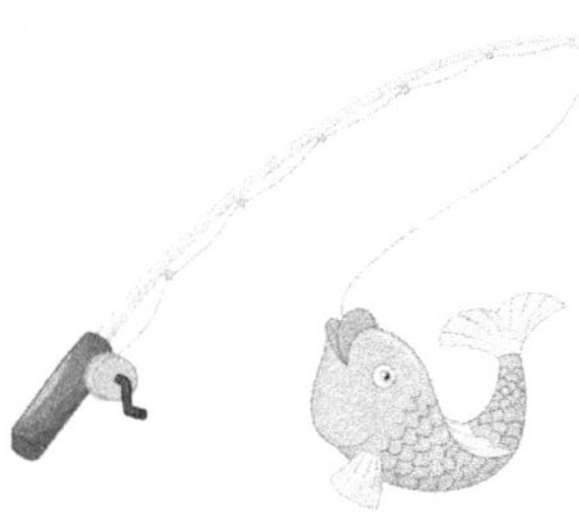

MASON

"OH! HEY MASON! WHAT ARE YOU DOING HERE?" I'M STANDING in the doorway to Mila's townhome. Her usually curly hair is straightened, and her face is makeup free. My gaze continues south. She's wearing a short, tight black dress. The straps are thin, and her breasts are full, spilling out of the top just enough to make it sexy and classy and not trashy.

"Mason." She snaps her fingers and my eyes shoot back up without finishing my perusal of her sexy as fuck MILF body. "What are you doing here?"

She lets me in and turns to head back down the hallway, calling out, "I'm running late for my date!" I watch as her perfect round ass sways in that dress. The material is thin enough that I'm able to see the outline of her thong. Her fuck-me heels click-clack against the tile and all I can picture is her under me with those heels still on.

"You should take a picture, it'll last longer." I swing my head toward the voice to find Charlie sitting on the couch. "If you like her, why don't you just ask her out?"

"You know my rule. I don't do moms, and that mom"—I point down the now-empty hallway—"she doesn't *do* anyone."

Charlie rolls her eyes. "Georgia is in our room watching a movie, and Tristan should be here soon with Lexi. Thank you for watching the girls. Ashley had offered, but then Kaden surprised her with a night away to the beach, and I didn't want her to feel guilty for not being able to watch them."

"No worries." I lean against the wall. "It's Valentine's Day, which means I'm staying in."

Mila walks back into the living room, putting an earring into her ear. "Poor Mason, are you afraid all the lonely women will be pouring their hearts out and require romance before letting you between their legs?"

Her face is now filled with makeup. Not overdone like some women do, but enough to know she's going out. My eyes wander down her face, taking in her plump shiny lips. They're light pink and kissable. I imagine the lip-gloss is sweet, just like her.

"Mason!" Mila screeches. "Stop staring at me like I'm a piece of meat!"

I smirk, imagining Mila splayed out in my bed, her legs spread wide open while I feast on her like she's my last meal.

"I wouldn't call you a piece of meat. More like a piece of mouthwatering fruit." I bridge the small gap between us. "Mmm… like a strawberry. I bet one bite into your sweet cunt and I would be addicted to your taste."

There's a knock on the door, and Mila moves away from me. "Well…" She gulps loudly. "It looks like you'll need to find yourself some other fruit to bite into because this strawberry has a date tonight." She swings the door open, and standing in the doorway is the anti-touch jackass from the other night at the art studio.

She says good night, and they're both out the door as quick as he came in.

"What a prick." I sit on the couch next to Charlie.

"He's okay." She shrugs. "He's a good dad and makes a good living. A little stuffy, maybe…"

"He told his son tag was too violent. He's a pussy."

"Hey! Don't be hating on pussies. They're tougher than you think. Just ask Betty White." I grab the remote and click on the television, giving her a side-eye. "You know…because they can take a pounding." She cracks up laughing at her joke and I shake my head.

The door opens and in walks Tristan. Charlie stands and meets him by the door, throwing her arms around him in a hug, still laughing.

"What's so funny?"

"You're fiancée thinks she's a comedian."

"Uncle Mason!" Lexi squeals when she sees me. "I brought so many movies to watch and stuff to color with. Where's Georgia?"

"She's in our room, sweet girl," Charlie says, grabbing her and giving her a hug hello before letting her go so she can run upstairs and find Georgia.

"Thanks for watching them, man," Tristan says.

"Yes, thank you. Mila said she should be home early, so once she gets back, you can take off," Charlie adds.

I give them a two-finger salute as they head upstairs to say bye to the girls. Once they're gone, I make three bowls of popcorn and the girls make a pillow and blanket bed on the ground to watch *Beauty and the Beast.*

We're about halfway through the movie when I pull up the Plenty of Fish app and message Mila. We chat every day. About our day, the weather, our favorite foods, colors, books, where we want to travel. I should feel bad that she has no clue it's me but it's not like I'm asking her out. It started off to see what was going on in her head but now I look forward to our conversations.

GetHooked: Happy Valentine's Day!

Looking4Love: Next year I'm going to put together an anti-Valentine's Day party.

Hmm… interesting. Guess her date with jackass isn't going well.

GetHooked: No date or bad date?

Looking4Love: Bad date. I should've known. He's not my type.

GetHooked: And what is your type?

This is the first time I've asked her anything dating related.

Looking4Love: Tall and muscular, so I feel protected. He has to be funny because I love to laugh. Sweet but not boring. Passionate. And NOT a vegan! I like meat!

I choke on my popcorn at her response. I know what she meant, but I have to fuck with her.

GetHooked: Small dick?

Looking4Love: OMG! No!

Looking4Love: He's a vegan! He doesn't LIKE meat.

Looking4Love: He took me to a restaurant that has no meat!

GetHooked: I have meat… and I'm willing to share ;)

Looking4Love: I haven't even seen your face. I don't even know your name. I don't think you sharing your meat with me is the next step.

GetHooked: I promise it's not vegan.

Looking4Love: I'm getting off now. He asked to take me to a movie, but I told him I'm not feeling well.

GetHooked: I wouldn't feel well either if I wanted a big juicy piece of meat and only got tofu.

Looking4Love: OMG! Good night!

NINE

MILA

I LOOK AT THE CLOCK ON THE DASHBOARD AND SEE I HAVEN'T even been gone for two hours. Evan drops me back off at home and doesn't bother to say he'll call me. We both know he won't be, and even if he did, I wouldn't be answering. The date was a disaster and will not be repeated. I unlock the door and step into the house to find Georgia and Lexi wrapped up in pillows and blankets, passed out on the floor. Mason is lounging on the couch, one of his arms over his head causing his shirt to drift up and show his delicious abs.

"You're home early." He sits up and pauses the movie before standing.

"Date sucked."

"That's too bad," Mason says, his tone indicating that he doesn't really think it's bad at all. I go to my room to change out of my dress and into a pair of cotton shorts and a shirt. When I come out, Mason is taking one girl at a time up to Georgia's room. Since my house is only three bedrooms, Charlie and Georgia are sharing the third bedroom upstairs. It has a connecting bathroom and a small sitting area. They'll be moving out in a couple of weeks, and I still need to find someone to rent the room to.

Once he's put both girls to bed, he comes back down to the living room and leans against the wall. When he notices my long face, he says, "That guy was a dick. I wouldn't let a bad date with him get you down."

"It's not him." I shake my head and take a deep breath.

"Then what is it?"

I almost consider telling Mason what's going on with me but then I remember who I'm talking to. The king of players. He would never understand. After all, everything I'm looking for in a relationship are all of the very same things Mason repels.

"It's nothing a pint of Ben and Jerry's chocolate fudge brownie won't cure." I grab the ice cream from the freezer then sit on the sofa, grabbing my throw blanket from the back. "You're more than welcome to go. I got the girls covered." I click off the Disney movie and search for something to watch.

When I stop on the movie *Valentine's Day*, Mason chuckles. "That movie's hilarious." He sits on the sofa next to me. I almost ask him what he's doing but then I wonder if maybe he's not leaving because he has nowhere to go. Tristan and Charlie are planning to spend the night at Tristan's condo, which is why Mason came over here to watch the girls.

Without thinking, I offer Mason a spoonful of my brownie covered ice cream and he grins, opening his mouth.

"That's some good shit." He snatches the spoon from me and takes another bite.

"Hell yes, it is. It's a staple in my house."

"I'd have to spend an extra two hours a day on the treadmill if Tristan kept this at our place."

"Oh!" I slap his chest playfully. "Now you're ruining it. I pretend like it's good for me, so I can eat it guilt-free."

Mason chuckles, sticking the spoon into the container and giving himself another bite.

"And how do you convince yourself this is healthy?"

"Simple." I shrug. "Chocolate comes from cocoa, which comes from a tree. That makes it a plant. I'm practically eating a salad. Everybody knows that." I giggle, and Mason laughs, taking another bite.

"Hey! You stole my spoon and you're not even sharing." I elbow him in the ribs.

"Here." He spoons up another bite then brings it up to my lips. I take the ice cream without looking at it and it's a huge bite! It barely fits in my mouth, and I have to stop myself from laughing. Mason's eyes zero in on my lips and my cheeks heat up. I swallow the ice cream down as Mason leans into me. His soft, cold lips press against mine and I sigh into the kiss as I part my lips, his tongue pushing into my mouth and swirling around.

Too quickly he pulls back, his face a mixture of remorse and pain. "I'm sorry. Shit, that shouldn't have happened."

Ignoring the swarm of butterflies I feel in my belly for the first time in I don't know how long, I agree. "Let's chalk it up to being drunk on chocolate."

"You mean salad?" He grins.

"Yes." I laugh, grabbing the spoon back from Mason and taking another bite. He backs up slightly but doesn't leave, and we watch the movie while sharing my ice cream in silence.

At some point we both must've fallen asleep because the next thing I know I'm being woken up by two very awake little girls, who are singing a song about kissing in a tree. I open my eyes, my neck stiff from sleeping on the arm of the couch, and see Mason sleeping with his head on my belly and his legs dangling off the sofa.

There's a knock on the door, and I move him carefully so I can answer it. His head falls onto the pillow but he doesn't wake up.

"C'mon, girls," I whisper. "Let's answer the door and let Uncle Mason sleep." When I open the door, it's Gavin and Alec.

"Morning!" Gavin announces, walking in like he always does before I can stop him. When he gets into the foyer, which is so small you can see the living room, he notices a sleeping Mason on my couch. "Um… did you know you have a guy sleeping on your couch… and he looks to be twice the size of it?" Gavin jokes.

"Mason's here!" Alec screams excitedly, and Mason jolts awake.

"Oh, damn! Mason Street is here?" Gavin asks, and I roll my eyes. Of course my ex-husband is a UFC fan just like my son. Mason sits up, and it takes him a second to remember where he is.

"Hey man! My name is Gavin. I'm Alec's dad." Mason darts his eyes from Gavin, to Alec, to me. "I didn't know Mila was dating you. It's great to meet you." Mason raises a brow, confusion marring his face.

"Oh, no!" I say before Mason can respond. "We're not dating. Remember, I told you a while back that he's Tristan's best friend and roommate."

"Ahh…gotcha. Sorry."

Mason stands and shakes Gavin's hand. "Nice to meet you."

"Dad! I want to take classes at the gym Mason goes to. Can I? Please!"

"I don't see why not. I'll have your mom send me a schedule and we'll take a look." Gavin smiles warmly at our son.

"Alec, Georgia, Lexi, why don't you guys go play in Alec's room?"

"Okay!" the three kids shout, and I wait until they're down the hall before I glare at Gavin.

"Why would you say yes without speaking to me first? It's expensive, and you know I have to pay half. Charlie is moving out in a couple weeks and I still have to find a roommate."

"Mila, breathe." Gavin puts his hands on my shoulders. "We'll handle it like we always do, and if need be, I'll pay for it and you can pay me back when you can." He turns toward Mason, who I forgot was in the room. "It was nice meeting you."

Mason's gaze darts from me to Gavin. "You too."

Gavin leans down and kisses my cheek. "See ya, Mila… and remember… breathe."

When he leaves, Mason is the first to speak. "That's your… ex-husband?"

"Yeah, he drives me insane. He knows I don't like to owe him money." I let out a sigh.

"The guy just kissed you."

"We're still friends." I shrug. "He's a good guy, just not the guy for me."

My phone buzzes, and it's a text from Charlie asking me to meet her and Tristan at the gym-slash-art studio.

"Kids," I yell down the hall. "We're going to the gym and art studio. Get ready to go."

"I better go as well," Mason says. "I need to go home and change and head to the gym to train." I take a second to check him out. He's wearing his same clothes from last night, but his hair is tousled from sleep, giving it that just fucked look. His eyes are a bit hooded over from just waking up and his lips are glossy from him licking them. Mason in the morning is hot.

"But it's Sunday," I say, trying my best to focus on something else besides his body.

"I like to train on Sundays because it's quieter," he points out.

"Okay, well maybe I'll see you over there."

"Yeah."

Mason leaves, and I get dressed, refusing to think about the kiss we shared last night and how it was the first time in years my body felt something. I thought when I finally felt those butterflies it would mean I met my forever. Damn my traitorous body. Doesn't it know I'm looking for a forever, not a for-now? Apparently, it doesn't care.

TEN

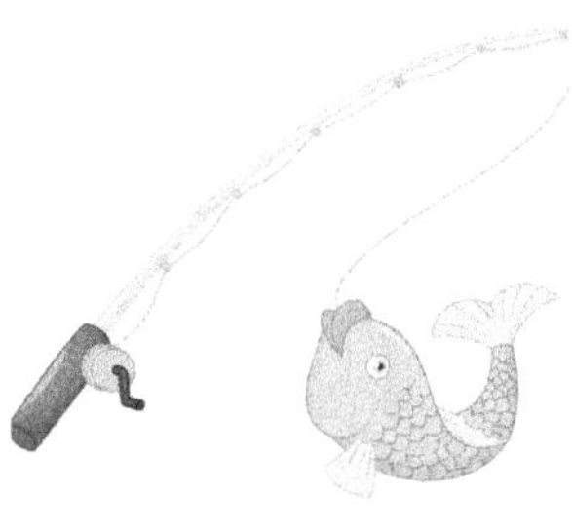

MASON

MY FISTS ARE SWINGING AND CONNECTING PERFECTLY. MY FEET are shuffling like they're supposed to. My body is ducking and weaving like I've been trained to do. But it's all robotic, instinctual and routine. My mind isn't on my training. I'm not visualizing Tristan like he's my opponent. My moves are completely mechanical and unemotional. Because every time I try to get my head in the game, my brain goes back to last night with Mila. My lips brushing against hers. The way she softly moaned into my mouth. It was only for a brief moment, but it was like nothing I've ever felt. When I kiss it's to connect sexually with a woman. Kissing and fucking come together in one sexually charged package. But last night when I kissed Mila—when my tongue dove into her sweet mouth—it was more than sexual and it scared the ever-loving shit out of me.

Then this morning, I overheard her ex-husband and her talking about Alec signing up for MMA classes. Her ex is nice. I've never met two people who are divorced and actually get along. He told her it would be okay and that he would lend her the money if she needed him to. He reminds me a lot of Tristan. But what got me wasn't their conversation, but his actions—or more importantly, my reaction to his actions. When I saw his lips graze her cheek, everything in me wanted to tell him to back the fuck off. He had his chance to make her happy and he obviously failed. The only thing that kept me from saying a word was the realization that if I was given the chance, I would fail her as well.

Tristan and I continue fighting: he punches, I block. I punch, he blocks. Then, in my peripheral vision I see Mila. Only she isn't alone. She's talking to Isaac, another fighter whose ass I kicked a couple months back when his dumbass got pissed over a woman he liked who I ended up hooking up with. Isaac is speaking all animatedly, waving his hands in the air and Mila's laughing, and then…his fuck-ass lays his hand on her shoulder. She smiles up at him and nods, and I consider breaking his hand so he's incapable of touching her again.

I don't even see it coming because my head is all fucked up—Mila has me all fucked up—Tristan bends down, grabs the backs of my knees, and throws me to the ground. He's on me before I can even make my move, straddling my waist and pulling my arm back into an arm bar. I'm tapping the fuck out before I can even comprehend what just happened.

"Where the hell are you?" He stands up and glares at me. "You have a fight in a few months and I'm taking you down?"

"Let me have a go at him!" Isaac laughs and walks toward me. Mother fucker wants to show off… sounds good to me. I'll whoop his ass for a second time.

"Nope! Not happening." Tristan steps between us. "I can see the look on your face," he says to me. "Go, walk it off."

"I'm good. I need the practice and Isaac is offering." I shrug, but Tristan is shaking his head. Asshole knows me too damn well.

"That's a negative. Isaac, go run or something." Tristan waves him off. Isaac puts his palms up in surrender, but when he turns to walk away, he doesn't leave. Instead, he heads back toward Mila.

As I head toward the two of them, Tristan steps in my way. "Don't even think about it."

"The guy is a player! Mila deserves better than him." I point at Isaac, and Tristan chuckles.

"And who does she deserve, exactly? You?" Tristan raises a brow, and I know he's got me there.

"Whatever…When she gets her heart broken by him, I won't say I told you so." I stalk off the main floor and over to the treadmill. I turn the speed up until I'm jogging, and stick my ear buds in my ears, focusing my attention on the hanging televisions and not on the two people to the right of me still talking and flirting. I mean, what the fuck! This is a gym, not a social club.

Alec comes over and joins me, so I take my earbud out of one ear. "Hey Bruiser, what's up?"

"My mom is signing me up for classes."

"Nice!" I fist bump him. "Evan teaches your class, and he's awesome."

"Yeah." Alec shrugs. "But can I still train with you sometimes?"

"Of course!"

"Alec," Mila calls. "We need to go! I have someone coming by to look at the house."

"Coming!" he yells to his mom before he says to me, "I hope the guy that moves in likes to play video games. Georgia likes to play with dolls." He scrunches his nose up in disgust. "Bye, Mason!" he calls out, running toward his mom.

I watch them both leave before I yell for Tristan to come over here. "Mila's having a guy move into her house?"

"I'm not sure. I know she put an ad online, but I don't know the specifics. Charlie feels bad because Mila can't afford the house on her own and live comfortably. I'm hoping she finds someone soon, otherwise Charlie might not move out because she doesn't want to leave her friend hanging."

"Hmm…" I think about this for a moment, considering the fact that I need to find a place to live, but quickly disregard that idea. Mila and I living together would be the equivalent of two semis coming at each other full speed with broken brakes. Inevitable destruction for everybody involved.

Jake walks in and gives me a head nod, and that's when I remember about the upcoming fight some of the fighters from this gym, including Jake, are in. "Oh! Hey, I was thinking of asking Mila if I can bring Alec to the UFC fight that's happening next month since it's only a couple hours away in San Diego. Do we have extra tickets?"

Tristan smiles. "Sure. I'll be away on my honeymoon with my girls, so there will be extra tickets. We're all going to have dinner at Mila's tomorrow night. Why don't you join and ask her then?"

"All right."

"DAMN, MILA! YOU CAN COOK." TRISTAN SITS BACK IN HIS CHAIR and pats his non-existent stomach dramatically.

"Thanks! I love cooking; I just never had the time to before. Now that I'm working a normal schedule I feel like I've added hours to my day. Plus, having weekends off. It's amazing."

"Can we go play?" Georgia asks, and Charlie nods.

"Go ahead, but only for an hour and then it's time for a bath and bed. Lexi and Alec have school tomorrow."

"Can I go to school too?" Georgia asks excitedly.

"We'll see. I would miss you like crazy." Charlie grabs her daughter and pulls her in for a quick hug before Georgia wriggles outs and runs away giggling, following the other two kids down the hall.

"I'm going to have to sign her up for preschool soon." Charlie frowns. "I know I can't keep her with me forever, but I feel like I just got her back."

"Sign her up once we get back from our honeymoon," Tristan

suggests. "That will give you some more time with her." He leans over and kisses his fiancée, and when I look at Mila, I can practically see the hearts shooting out of her eyes from watching their interaction.

Not able to watch the lovefest another minute, I stand to clear the table, but Mila stands as well and tries to stop me. "You don't need to do that." She reaches to take the dirty dishes from my hands. "You're a guest."

"You cook, I clean," I insist.

"Okay, thanks. So, while you're all here, we should discuss the bachelor-slash-bachelorette party." Mila follows me into the kitchen, Tristan and Charlie following behind.

"I don't want one," Tristan says.

"What? You have to have one," Charlie insists. "It's like a rite of passage or something." Tristan shakes his head as he pulls her into his arms. "I'm not going out with this fool"—he nods toward me—"to some strip club when I could be home with you. Not happening."

"What if we did a joint one?" Mila suggests. "We could do a spa day and then we all go out together."

"I like it!" Charlie grins.

"All right," Tristan concedes, grabbing the dishes from the counter to start washing them.

"Good! Mason and I can plan it." There's a knock on the door. "Oh! That must be Albert. He's here to see the place. Hopefully he's better than the guy yesterday." She scurries to the front door, and I follow her like a moth to a flame. When she swings open the door, standing there is what looks like a flashback to the '70s. The guy is wearing an AC/DC shirt that looks like it was literally made over forty years ago when the band was first formed. He's sporting some thick black-rimmed glasses and is wearing corduroy pants. The guy looks like the poster boy for *That '70s Show*, and I'm not talking Ashton Kutcher here.

"Hi! My name is Mila. You must be Albert." She puts her hand out, and he reluctantly takes it while kind of glaring at her.

"I am." He nods and glances my way.

"Come in." She ushers him inside and makes introductions. She starts explaining to him about the place, the neighborhood, how many bedrooms and bathrooms the home has, and then she says, "I'm a single mom, so it's just me and my son living here."

"I don't babysit."

"What?" She looks at him, shocked.

"I don't babysit kids. Don't ever ask me to watch him."

"Oh, no. I would never ask that." She guides him up the stairs, and I trail behind, keeping my distance. "This would be your room." The townhome is designed with the master bedroom—and attached bathroom—on the first floor along with a second bedroom, which is Alec's. There's a guest bathroom Alec and anyone visiting uses. Upstairs is the third bathroom and bedroom.

"Can I put a deadbolt on it…to ensure nobody comes in?"

"Um…sure. I don't see why not." I can't see Mila's face, but I can hear the tightness in her voice. They come back down and she shows him the rest of the house. When they get back out to the living room, she says, "What do you think?"

"I think this place could work." He nods absently, looking around.

"You know what? We actually have someone else coming to take a look at the place," I jump in. Mila glares at me, but I ignore her. "We'll get back to you." I practically push him out the door before closing and locking it. Then I turn toward Mila. "Are you insane? Where did you find that guy?"

"Craigslist. I can't believe you just kicked him out. Do you know how hard it is to find a roommate?" She stalks toward me, and I throw my hands up in the air.

"Have you never heard of the Craigslist killer? They made the movie for a reason."

"Oh my God, Mason! You can't be serious," she yells, right in my face. She's so close, if I leaned down I could place my lips right on hers…Fuck! Focus Mason!

"That guy was fucking weird!"

"Don't curse! There are kids around here," she fires back.

"Cursing will be the least of your concerns when he kills you in your sleep!" I bark. "Or worse, when you lose your house because he's using his deadbolt locked room to make and sell drugs!"

"You've been watching too many movies! This is LA, not Mexico!"

"You are so naïve, just like my mother! Put your damn son first!" I shout, and when Mila's mouth closes, I realize what I said. "Whatever," I say, trying to backtrack. "It's not my business."

"Are you saying I'm not putting my son first?" Mila glares at me but it's tampered down by the glossiness in her eyes—the glossiness from the tears building.

"No, I'm just saying…" I take a deep breath. "I'm just saying, you shouldn't move some stranger in here with only you and Alec living here." I notice Charlie and Tristan, who must've been standing in the dining room, join us in the living room. I hate talking about my past, but if I don't explain where I'm coming from, she's not going to understand why I'm acting this way. "My mom allowed a man to run a meth lab in our basement when I was growing up," I admit. "It's one of the reasons she went to jail, and I went into foster care. I just don't want to see that happen to you…to Alec."

"Okay," Mila says, her voice lower than before but now filled with desperation, "but I need a roommate. In order to put Alec first, I have to keep paying my mortgage."

"I'll move in with you." Mila's eyes widen. "I can afford the rent, and I'm looking for a place to live. I've put it off and I only have a couple weeks to find a place."

"There's no way you think that would be a good idea," she scoffs.

"Why not? I don't touch moms, and you're a mom. Alec likes me, and I'm almost never home. I'm always training."

"And how would that work? Bringing women over?" Mila flinches when she says the word *women*.

"I wouldn't. I haven't brought a woman to Tristan's and my place in months." I turn to Tristan for him to back me up.

"That's true," he admits. "Once Lexi caught one of the women the morning after and drew her a pretty picture of a fish, he stopped."

"Not helping," I say under my breath, and Tristan laughs.

"I, for one, think this is a great idea!" Charlie claps her hands together. "And you should totally charge him double! He can afford it." She giggles, and I shake my head.

Mila's face contorts into a look of confusion. "I don't think this is a good idea… but I do need a roommate. Okay, how about we do it temporarily, just until I find a female roommate?"

"Whatever you want." I shrug.

"Yay!" Charlie screeches. "Tristan! Our two best friends are going to be living together!" She jumps up and down like a crazy person before she hugs us both, appearing to be the most excited for this out of all of us. And then it hits me…I just offered to live with Mila Sterling. I was just supposed to invite her and her son to UFC Fight Night, not invite myself to move in. And then I remember I didn't even get around to inviting them. Well, I guess I'll have plenty of time to bring it up since I'll be living here soon. *Fuck.*

"BRO, THE BILL AT THE STEAKHOUSE WAS A BUCK TWENTY, BUT I'm telling you, it was well worth it. Staring at those fucking tits and dick-sucking lips all night. Fuuuuck!" Isaac groans dramatically, and I roll my eyes at having to listen to this fucker brag about another woman he's after. I step out of the shower and get dressed.

"Did you even get laid?" Simon, another fighter and Isaac's friend, asks.

"Not yet. She's playing hard to get, but we have a date for this weekend. Her ex is taking the kid to a movie or some shit."

"You know she's friends with Tristan's fiancée, right?" Simon says, and the pieces all come together. This fucker is talking about Mila. I haven't seen her in the last couple weeks. I've been busy as hell between training and packing. Tristan and Charlie have been busy with the gym and paint studio, and on top of that, planning their wedding. None of us have hung out since I offered to move in with Mila. I've seen her in passing when she drops Alec off at class, but we haven't really spoken.

I have, however, spoken to her through messenger on Plenty of Fish… that is until the other night when she said she had another date. Usually, she will message me during them, but now that I'm thinking about it, she didn't message me this time.

"She's a grown woman. Whoever she chooses to fuck… or suck is her business." Isaac laughs, and I hear the locker slam shut.

Pulling my sweats on, I stalk out of the shower area and into the locker room, making myself known. "She might be a grown woman," I say, shoving Isaac against the locker, "but if you fuck with her, I will fuck you up."

Isaac looks shocked at first but quickly composes himself. "What I do with Mila is my business."

"That's where you're wrong." I shove him harder against the locker. "In less than a week, I'll be living with her, which makes her and her son my business. So watch your fucking mouth and watch yourself." I slam him one last time for good measure before I let him go. Grabbing my shit, I stalk out of the gym to find Mila. When I get to the paint studio next door, Charlie is teaching a painting class to a bunch of little kids, but I don't spot Mila. I look at my phone and see it's a few minutes after four. She just got off work.

I go to shoot her a text but realize I don't know her number. Pulling up the dating app, I send her a message.

GetHooked: How did your date go? No messages during it…is that a good sign?

She responds right away.

Looking4Love: It went good! He took me to dinner and was a complete gentleman. Sorry I haven't messaged you. My best friend/roommate is moving out this weekend and I have another date with the guy. Plus, I got a new job, better hours, but I'm still learning the ropes. Any luck for you meeting anyone?

What the hell…so, either Isaac is playing her or he's bragging to his friend to make himself sound cool. Either way he's in the wrong, but can I say something to her without looking like a jealous asshole? No, I need to keep my mouth shut and keep an eye on the situation. Maybe I can mention it to Tristan and he can tell her.

ELEVEN

MILA

"IF YOU NEED ANYTHING, PLEASE LET ME KNOW." I CAME HOME from work to find all of Charlie and Georgia's stuff moved out, and Mason's stuff moved in. I felt bad that I couldn't help them move, but with my job being so new and the fact that I'm already taking off a couple days for the wedding next week, I couldn't take off today as well. Plus, Fridays are always crazy busy.

Alec was ecstatic when he learned Mason would be living with us. When I dropped him off at Gavin's place after work, he was pouting and begging to stay home, but it's his father's weekend. Plus, I have a date tonight with Isaac from the gym and tomorrow night is the bachelor-slash-bachelorette party, so Alec needs to stay with his dad. He'll have plenty of time to hang out with Mason once he comes home.

"Thanks, Mila," Mason says as I turn to head back downstairs.

Before I make it out of his doorway, I stop and turn around. "I'm going out tonight. We don't have to tell each other, right?"

"No, we don't have to tell each other." Mason chuckles. He's lounging on his bed, on his phone. His legs are bent and his feet are planted on the mattress. He's sporting a white Henley and navy blue sweatpants, and I have no clue how I'm going to live with this sexy as sin man. I need to start looking for a female roommate as soon as possible.

"Okay, cool. Well…I have a date tonight, so I better go get ready. He should be here soon." I scamper out of his room and down the stairs to mine to jump in the shower. Once I'm out, I blow-dry my hair straight, apply some makeup, and get dressed in a cute teal maxi dress.

Just as I'm putting on my heels, there's a knock on the door, and before I can get my other heel on, I hear Mason yell, "I got it."

"It's my date," I yell back, thinking he's upstairs. I grab my cell phone and purse and head down the hall toward the door, but once I make it out to the living room, Mason already has the door open. He must've been downstairs.

His muscular arms are up high, his hands latching onto the top of the door frame. His body blocking the doorway, so I can't see who's there.

"Mason, who is it?" I walk toward the front door and he moves a tad to the left. Isaac is standing outside on the front porch, his hands in his jean pockets. He's smirking with one brow raised. "Oh! Hey, Isaac." I push past Mason and step outside.

"Mila." Isaac curls his arm around my waist and pulls me into his side, planting a kiss on my lips. I pull back in shock, and that's when I see the smirk he's sporting is aimed at Mason. I turn around, and if looks could kill, Isaac would be a dead man. I have no idea what's going on with these two, but it's getting awkward.

"Ready?" I squeak out, and Isaac nods in agreement.

"Mila, wait." Mason approaches me. "Can I talk to you for a second?"

"We're late," Isaac answers for me, ushering me away.

"Can we talk when I get home?"

Mason's jaw ticks, and his hands fist at his side. It's obvious these two don't get along. "Yep."

"Okay." I give him a small smile before heading down the sidewalk with Isaac.

WE'VE FINISHED DINNER AND ARE WAITING FOR THE CHECK, and I'm ready to go home. Maybe it's the way Mason glared at Isaac, or the way Isaac smirked almost cockily at Mason, but it tainted the entire evening. Every comment Isaac makes, I wonder what he's thinking, what his motives are. Mason doesn't get mad, like ever. Even when he's fighting, he views it as one big game. He laughs and smiles, and it pisses his opponent off. So, for him to be mad at Isaac, something is up.

My phone buzzes in my purse, and I pull it out to check it. It's *GetHooked*. I feel myself grin. I've considered asking him for his name, but I kind of like the anonymity of us keeping our names out of it. He's sweet and funny, and he's become like a friend to me. I've thought about asking him out or hinting for him to ask me out, but I figure if he wanted to go out with me, he would ask.

GetHooked: How are you?

Just as I'm about to message him back, my phone vibrates with a text message.

Unknown: You're going to be pissed but I don't care. I got your number from Charlie. This is Mason. Please let me know you're okay. Isaac is an asshole and only wants to have sex with you.

All the blood rushes downward, and I immediately feel lightheaded. My heart begins to pound so forcefully, it vibrates throughout my body. I glance up at Isaac who is paying the bill and can feel my hands getting clammy. There's no way Mason would text me this without having reason to believe what he's saying is true.

"You ready to go?" Isaac asks, standing up.

"Yes." I type out a quick message to Mason to let him know I'm fine, then shove my phone back into my purse.

When we're in Isaac's car and he's driving, I say, "I'm not feeling well. I know it's early, but would it be okay to call it a night?" I've taken my phone out of my purse and have it in my lap. I'm not sure why but something doesn't feel right.

Isaac glances toward me then pulls over on the side of the empty road. I glance around and notice we aren't in the city. There are no street lights or cars. I have no clue where we are. I'm thinking somewhere near South LA, but I've never been in this area before. I should've paid attention.

"Are you really not feeling well, or are you messaging with Mason?"

My jaw drops in shock. "I'm not feeling well. And even if I were messaging with Mason, what does it matter?"

Isaac puts the car in park and turns toward me. "The guy has a problem with me for no reason." He places his hand on my thigh, rubbing his palm up and down my flesh, sending chills up my spine, and not in a good way.

"I don't know what's going on with you and Mason, but can you please take me home?"

He leans in to kiss me, his fingers now digging into my skin. I back up and move his hand off me. "Please take me home."

My phone vibrates, and Isaac glares down at it. I go to grab it, but he snatches it out of my lap first. "Are you fucking serious?" he booms and I jump. "He's texting you and filling your head with bullshit!"

"No." I shake my head emphatically.

"Don't fucking lie to me, Mila! I can read! He wants to know if you're still okay!" He throws the phone back at me. "Why the fuck are you texting with him while you're on a date with me? Are you fucking him too?"

"Too?" I blurt out before I can stop myself. "I'm not having sex with you."

"You would've been if that fucker wouldn't have filled your head with whatever shit he's spewing."

"Isaac," I say his name slowly and carefully, "can you please take me home? I'm not looking to have sex with you or anyone."

"How about you get the fuck out of my car and text fuckboy to take you home? I should've known better. All that playing hard to get… you're just a fucking cock-tease." He reaches over me and pulls the handle on the door, swinging it open.

"Are you serious?" My eyes dart from the open door to Isaac. "You're going to leave me here? By myself?"

"I've gone two weekends without getting laid thinking you would put out. Fuck this shit. Go call your fuckboy." His brows raise and I'm not sure if I should demand for him to bring me home or if I should get out. My decision is made when he adds, "Or you can come back to my place to fuck?"

I stumble out of the car, and before I'm barely all the way out, he yanks the door closed and takes off, peeling out and leaving me alone. Not wanting to look like a hooker on a street corner, I pull my google maps app up to see where I am so I can start walking in a direction while I call for a Lyft. Google maps says I'm only ten miles from my house. I see a corner store up ahead so I walk there, get their address, and put in a request for a car. It says it will be an hour! Of course.

My phone vibrates, and it's Mason again. Instead of texting him back, I call him and he answers on the first ring. "What's wrong?"

"Long story short, Isaac left me on the side of the road when he saw your text to me. I'm at a quickie mart, and the Lyft will take an hour to get me."

"Send me your current location, and I'll be right there."

"Thank you."

"Do it while we're on the phone. We're not getting off the phone until I pick you up, and wait inside the store. It's safer than outside."

I let out a sigh of relief. "Thank you," I say again.

About five minutes later, Mason's BMW comes into view. He pulls into the parking lot, and I jet out of the store and into his car. The ride back home is silent, but Mason's body—stiff and rigid—speaks volumes. He's pissed. When we get home and inside, I stop him as he reaches the first stair. "I should've listened to you."

"I didn't say anything."

"You tried to…before we left for dinner."

Mason cuts across the room until he's less than a foot away from me. "I should've stopped the date. He was talking shit in the locker room, and I warned him. I'm sorry, Mila." His beautiful lips are turned down. He moves a wayward hair out of my face, and I think maybe he's going to kiss me. My stomach tightens, those crazy butterflies making an appearance just from his touch alone. "I'll make sure he regrets what he did tonight." He turns his back on me and stalks up the stairs, leaving me speechless and confused.

When I get to my room, I consider going upstairs to talk to Mason, but decide to give him his space. Instead I message *GetHooked*.

Looking4Love: Hey

A minute later, the circle lights up and he responds.

GetHooked: Hey

Looking4Love: I've had the worst night. Tell me something funny.

A few minutes later, I see him typing.

GetHooked: When people go underwater in movies, I like to hold my breath and see if I would've survived that situation. I almost died in Finding Nemo.

I let out a snort and then giggle as I imagine him holding his breath, only it's hard to do because I don't know what he looks like.

Looking4Love: Ha ha.

GetHooked: Knock Knock

Looking4Love: Who's there?

GetHooked: Ivana

Looking4Love: Ivana who?

GetHooked: Ivana do nasty things to you.

Looking4Love: You are so cheesy! Those aren't even funny!

GetHooked: Did you laugh?

Looking4Love: Yes

GetHooked: Then it worked.

And he's right. With only a couple cheesy jokes, he turned my mood completely around.

GetHooked: What's wrong?

I tell him everything, just like I always do these days, about my date and how he called me a cock-tease. I tell him about Mason trying to warn me and then coming to get me. He, of course, tells me it's not my fault. Eventually our conversation steers away from my horrible date and into easy waters. And like most nights, I fall asleep while messaging him, wishing for the courage to one day ask him if he wants to meet. Hoping one day he'll ask me to meet him. Wondering if maybe it's for the best we never meet. The way my life is going, we would meet and whatever this is between us would be ruined, and that would just suck.

TWELVE

MASON

I SHOULD'VE STOPPED HER FROM GOING OUT WITH THAT motherfucker. I should've insisted she not go. I should've told her what he said. But I didn't do any of the above. Just another example of why I'm not in a place to be with someone. I could've saved her from ever being in that shitty situation, but I dropped the ball. A better man would've prevented it from happening. He would've taken care of her before anything happened. She could've been raped or killed.

And then, instead of hanging out with her and making sure she was okay, I ran upstairs. I was so pissed at Isaac, at myself, at Mila. Fuck! This is why I stick to no-strings-attached sex. I'm not capable of taking care of someone else. This is exactly why my mom wants nothing to do with me. She knows I'm no better than my dad. I would only fail at taking care of her just like he did.

Of course I wasn't even upstairs for five minutes before Mila was messaging *GetHooked*. She asked me to make her laugh, so I found some cheesy as fuck dad jokes online. They got her laughing, and in return got me laughing. She has no idea how amped up I was, and with just her message, she had me calmed down and enjoying our easy banter. I wonder if she looks forward to our nightly messages half as much as I do.

I push the door to the gym open, my gaze darting around for Isaac. I saw Tristan's truck in the parking lot, which means I have about two minutes to pound the fucker into the ground before Tristan stops me. I zero in on Isaac going to town on the punching bag. *Got you, motherfucker.*

I stalk toward him, and because I'm not a fucking pussy, I make my presence known. "I warned you, fucker!" I shout. His eyes dart to me, and before he can argue, I cock my fist back and swing, my fist connecting with his jaw. His face jerks to the side, and then he's coming at me, but he doesn't stand a fucking chance against me.

I lay into him, punch after punch to his face without giving him a chance to block or retaliate. His back hits the ground and I pounce on him, straddling his waist and bringing my hand around his throat to hold him still. His face is bloody so I don't bother punching him again. "I warned you, and you didn't listen!"

"Mason!" Tristan shouts as everyone surrounds Isaac and me. "Get off him!" I ignore him, my hand squeezing hard around his trachea, cutting off his airflow.

"You ever go near Mila again. Look in her direction. Hell, breathe the same air as her. I. Will. Kill. You." I let go of Isaac's throat, and stepping over him, make it a point to kick his ribs.

"What the fuck happened?" Tristan demands.

"What happened is"—I point my finger at Isaac, who is now standing, blood still covering his face—"that asshole took Mila out on a date, and when she refused to fuck him, he left her on the side of the road."

Tristan's brows crease in anger as he looks around me at Isaac, and without even asking him for confirmation, because he knows damn well I wouldn't make that shit up, he says, "You're gone."

"What the fuck!" Isaac shouts. "You can't kick me out without reason! And what I do in my personal life isn't reason! I'll sue you."

Tristan steps toward Isaac. "That's where you're wrong. When you sign with my gym, my training camp, you sign a morality clause. It states if you do anything that goes against the morals of the gym, I have the right to remove you, and as the owner of this gym, I'm removing you. Get your shit, and get out."

Isaac punches the wall, the drywall breaking and crumbling. "Fuck this!" he shouts, and storms off toward the locker room.

"I'm going to make sure he leaves without issue," Tristan says. "Go hang out in my office until he's gone."

"MASON! LOOK WHAT I FOUND!" LEXI SCREAMS FROM downstairs as I button my pants. Tonight is the joint bachelor-slash-bachelorette party, and Tristan's supposed to be dropping the girls off at his parents' place, so I'm not sure why Lexi is currently here, screaming my name at the top of her lungs.

"Mason!" Lexi yells again.

"I'm coming!" I shout back down. Grabbing my phone and wallet,

I shove them into my pockets as I run down the stairs. "What do you have Lexi Girl?"

"This!" She waves my boxset of Harry Potter movies at me. "Didn't want you to be sad without your favorite wizards!" She giggles, clearly making fun of me. "Poor Uncle Mason can't live without Harry Potter and Hermione Granger," Lexi says in her best British accent. I snatch her up—the movies hitting the floor—and flipping her upside down, tickle her sides.

"Stop! I'm going to pee!" she squeals like she always does when I tickle her, knowing I'll put her down because I'm not about to risk the chance of her peeing all over me.

"Then don't make fun of the best movies, ever!" I tickle her once more.

"Best movies ever, huh?" Mila questions through her laughter.

"Damn ri—" I stop in my tracks, my words cut off, as I turn around and see Mila leaning against the wall. She's in a strapless skin tight gold shimmering mini-dress with black fuck-me heels, looking every bit like the wet-dream every guy jacks off to in his bedroom at one point in his life. Only she isn't a dream. She's real…so fucking real.

My eyes stay glued to the striking woman in front of me. Her hair is down in waves, and her makeup is barely there—just a little bit of lip gloss that has me wanting to lick her lips to feel how silky smooth they are. It's only when Lexi squeals out, "Uncle Mason! Put me down," I remember my goddaughter is still hanging upside down in my arms. Flipping her right-side up, I place her back on her feet.

"Uncle Mason looooves Harry Potter," Lexi taunts, picking the movies up from the floor.

"Give me those." I grab them from her hands, and she giggles.

"So, you're a closet Harry Potter fan?" Mila laughs. "Didn't see that coming."

"Where's your father?" I ask Lexi, ignoring Mila's jokes.

"Outside. I told him I would tell Mila we're here, so I could give you your movies." Lexi giggles some more.

"You're getting a ride from Tristan?" I ask Mila. "What's wrong with your car?"

"It died this morning." She frowns. "I need to buy a new one." Shit, I'm surprised that piece-of-junk car has lasted as long as it has. It's got to be close to twenty years old.

"I could've taken you," I point out.

"Yeah, I know, but I figured if you were bringing someone with you or wanted to go home with someone…"

"Don't be ridiculous; I can take you. Lexi, go tell your dad that Mila and I will meet them at the club."

Lexi agrees and runs out the front door. I watch her run down the sidewalk and wait until she's safely in Tristan's truck before I close the door.

"You look stunning," I tell Mila once we're alone.

"Thank you," she says shyly, that beautiful shade of pink heating her cheeks like it always does when I compliment her. "Ready to go?"

"Let's do this."

I'M SITTING AT THE UPSTAIRS BAR OF PLUSH NURSING MY Heineken. Since Charlie and Tristan met while she was bartending at Plush, Mila thought it would be fun to have their party here. After speaking with the owner, who is the brother of one of Charlie's good friends, we reserved the top floor of the club for the night. Mila offered to help pay for it, having no clue what it costs to rent out the entire upper level of a club and have an open bar, but I wasn't letting that happen. I told her to plan and I would pay, and she reluctantly agreed.

My back is toward the dance floor where all of our friends and Tristan's sisters are hanging out and dancing. I know Mila is out on the dance floor, but I can't look at her. I drove us to the club in silence, my mind—and cock—stuck on the vision of her in that sexy dress and heels. The second we got to the club, I made some lame excuse and bolted away from her, needing some space.

I down the last of my beer and set it down. "Would you like another one?" a busty blonde waitress asks, bending unnecessarily over to push her cleavage out while flashing me a flirtatious grin.

"Sure."

Her grin widens as she grabs the bottle, pops the top, and hands it to me. "Anything else I can get you?" She tilts her head, her seductive smile never faltering. On a normal night, I would take her up on her not so subtle offer for a lap dance—or more—but tonight, the only female on my mind is Mila. Shit, maybe that's reason enough to take this woman up on her offer.

"I'll let you know."

"So, your knuckles…" The feminine voice has me looking to the left of me, and leaning against the bar is Mila. She glances down to my knuckles then to my face. "What happened?"

I shake my head and take a long pull of my new beer. "Nothing."

"The day after Isaac left me on the side of the road, you come home with bloody knuckles and spend the entire afternoon avoiding me like the plague." She lifts up to sit on the bar stool and my eyes go to that tiny dress as it rises up her thighs. "Please tell me he's still alive."

My head jerks up. "Who the fuck cares if he's still alive?"

"I do," she admits, "because I don't want anything to happen to you. Alec is excited to see you fight in a few months…and so am I." She shrugs, and I calm myself.

"He's alive."

"And how long are you going to avoid me?"

"I'm not avoiding you."

"So, you always spend the entire day in your room?" The bartender comes back over, and Mila orders a cranberry vodka. Then she turns to me, her fingers grazing the tops of my knuckles, her eyes staring down at them. "I don't know what I did." She lifts her beautiful hazel eyes and smiles softly. "You're my roommate and I don't want it to be awkward."

"You didn't do anything," I assure her. "I'm pissed that I should've told you—stopped you from going with Isaac."

"You tried."

"Not hard enough." My memory goes back to the night my mom was arrested. I know I was young, but too often I think about what I could've done to save her from going to jail.

"Come here." Mila stands and extends her hand out for me to take. Putting my hand in hers, I let her guide me away from the bar. We get to one of the private rooms where the door is open, letting people know it's available, and she walks us into the room, closing the door behind her. She sits us down on the couch, her hand still in mine.

"It was really loud. Now talk to me." My eyes stay glued to our entwined fingers as I consider telling her about my mom. She already knows about the meth lab and her going to jail…

"I was thirteen when my mom went to jail."

"Because of the drugs?" Mila clarifies.

"And because she was prostituting herself out. I don't really know all of the details to be honest. I was upstairs in my room and didn't go downstairs to help her. I heard arguing and knew shit was going down but then it got quiet, and I just sat there…waiting for her to come and get me. I didn't do anything. She was arrested for the first time that night, and it was the last time I saw her."

"Is she still in jail?"

"No." I shake my head. "She got out when I was seventeen but said she couldn't take care of me. A few years later she was back in jail again. She's been in and out several times over the years. She actually got out recently."

"I'm so sorry, Mason." The hand that isn't linked with mine, rubs my arm soothingly, and it doesn't go over my head that both times I've willingly spoken about my mom has been with Mila. "I can't even imagine. But you were thirteen years old. You can't beat yourself up over not helping your mom. She was the adult. You were the child. It was her job to protect you, not the other way around."

"True, but my dad, who was an adult, didn't take care of her either.

Anyway, my point was that when I got the call from you that Isaac left you on the side of the road, it hit me that once again I didn't take care of someone who needed me."

"Mas—" She begins to say my name, probably to make some bullshit excuse for me, but I cut her off before she can.

"And this time, I'm an adult." I pull my hand back slightly, our fingers unlinking and our contact breaking. "This is a perfect example of why I don't do relationships. You can't let people down when they don't depend on you."

"While I don't agree with your logic or reasoning, I'm starting to think maybe you're right in regard to the whole no-relationship thing." She shrugs, her eyes lingering where our hands were. I appreciate the fact she's taking the spotlight off me, not asking me questions about my parents.

"What happened? Aside from Isaac the asshole that is." I already know what's happened, but I can't say that. I should tell her who I am— that I'm *GetHooked*—admit that I'm the man she's been messaging for weeks. But I don't tell her. It will mean giving up our late night conversations, and selfishly, I'm not ready or willing to give them up, yet. They mean too much to me.

"I've been out with three guys in the last month or so and all of them have been horrible."

"From that dating app?"

"No, but maybe I should really give it a shot. At this rate, I'm going to plow through everyone's friends." She groans. "My ex-husband's teammate, the dad from the painting studio, Isaac, from the gym." Her face falls into her hands and she lets out another groan before she looks up at me. "I haven't had sex in almost five years."

I do my best to school the look of shock I'm sure I'm sporting. I knew she was looking for a relationship and not into one-night stands, but I didn't know it's been that long. "Because you don't do one-night stands?"

"Because my marriage sucked. We were young when I got pregnant. I wanted to do the right thing, so we got married. We worked okay together but the sex and the marriage was a bust and I wasn't happy. My mom told me life was too short to settle right before she died from cancer. So, after she passed away, I got divorced and set out to find the one. I had it in my head I would find my soulmate and we would live happily ever after."

"So, what happened?"

"Life." Mila laughs softly. "I didn't want my life to turn into a string of one-night stands, so I told myself if a guy was serious, he would wait to have sex with me until we're married. I heard once on the radio that if a woman wants to be marriage material, she can't give her goods away for free." She scrunches her nose up adorably and blushes a beautiful shade of pink.

"Huh?" I know what she means, but it's fun watching her squirm as she explains it.

"You know…" She giggles. "Why would a man buy the cow, if he can get the milk for free?"

I chuckle at her analogy. "So, what you're saying is, you won't let a man milk you, so he'll have to buy you?" I shoot her a wink, and she laughs.

"Yes…no…you know what I mean." She pushes my shoulder playfully, and our conversation reminds me of the ones we have on the dating app. "Only I got busy. Between raising Alec and going to school, then working full time. One year turned into five, and suddenly I'm a twenty-seven-year-old single mom who hasn't had sex in almost five years and I still haven't found the one."

"Don't do it." And as the words roll off my tongue even I'm shocked at myself for saying them. "You deserve the real deal… to be bought, not just milked." She giggles and I chuckle. "Trust me, one day the right guy will come along and buy the whole damn farm for you." *He would be a fool not to,* I want to add but don't.

Mila stops laughing. "Thank you, Mason."

"No problem." And then she leans forward and wraps her arms around me in a hug, and I have to force myself to remember I'm not that guy, the one to buy her the farm.

We get home from the party, but for some reason I don't want our night to end. "Want to watch a movie?" I ask as she peels her heels off her feet, dangling them by her fingertips.

"Sure, I'm going to go change. Pick something." She starts to walk toward her room but stops in place and turns around, a mischievous grin splaying across her face. "Just not Harry Potter. Maybe something for adults." She turns back around, laughing out loud as she continues back down the hallway.

"Don't hate!" I yell after her. "You're never too old for the Wizarding World of Harry Potter." Her only reply is her laughter getting louder.

I run upstairs to change as well, throwing on a pair of basketball shorts and a UFC shirt. I go through her DVDs and pick out 21 Jump Street, shocked she actually owns this movie. It's too inappropriate for Alec and Mila seems like more of a chick flick type of woman. I put it in and fast forward through the previews. A few minutes later Mila comes walking down the hall. She's wearing tiny grey cotton shorts, a long sleeve shirt with a few buttons going down the front—undone—and on her feet are colorful socks that go up almost to her knees. She looks adorably sexy and I'm completely fucked.

"What are those?" I point to her feet as she falls onto the couch, her head hitting the armrest and her feet landing near me.

"Reading socks." She waggles her eyebrows playfully. "Feel them."

She lifts her feet up toward me and wiggles her toes, laughing. "Seriously, feel them." I touch the tip of her toe, but she thrusts her foot closer. "No, *really* feel them." I chuckle at her tenaciousness but do as she says, rubbing my hand up the top of her foot. The socks are thick and fluffy, and I find myself wishing I was rubbing up her bare leg.

"Why are they called reading socks?"

"I don't know." She shrugs. "Because they're soft and fluffy and comfy, and women wear them while reading so their feet don't get cold." She turns her head to see which movie I picked.

"Ugh! 21 Jump Street. Of course you find the one movie Tristan left over here. I'd almost rather watch Harry Potter!" That has me laughing.

"I can make that happen."

"No way! At least Channing Tatum is hot. Press play."

We watch the movie mostly in silence, aside from the funny scenes when we both crack up at Channing Tatum and Jonah Hill acting like fools. Mila's feet remain on my lap the entire time, and occasionally I look down, shocked at how much I love her feet on me. I've never spent much time with women aside from having sex with them, but this is the second time I've watched a movie with her and I'm enjoying myself immensely. Being around Mila is comfortable. She's completely down to earth, and the more I'm around her, the more I want to be around her.

Taking her left foot in my hands, I massage circles into the arch of her foot. She moans softly, but her eyes never leave the screen. A few minutes later, I switch to her other foot and she sighs. When the scene begins where Channing learns that Jonah is fucking Ice Cube's daughter, and Channing is laughing and dancing like a five-year-old announcing it to the entire department, I glance over to Mila wondering why she isn't laughing. I mean, it's without a doubt the funniest part of the movie. Her eyes are closed, and she's snoring softly. Her chest is rising and falling slowly. She looks peaceful and content and so fucking beautiful. I turn the movie off, and picking Mila up, I bring her to her room and put her to bed.

"Good night, Mason," she says groggily.

"Good night, Mila."

THIRTEEN

MILA

"UP AND AT 'EM!" MASON'S VOICE BOOMS, AND I ROLL OVER TO my side, ignoring him. "C'mon! It's Sunday, and it's beautiful out! The perfect day to buy you a car."

At his words, I roll back over to face him. "What are you talking about?" I groan.

"Your car. You said you need to buy a new one because yours is out of commission." Mason sits on the bed beside me and the mattress dips at his weight, rolling me closer to him.

"Yes, but not right this second. I'm going to need to save first." Maybe in Mason's world, needing a new car means going out to buy one, but in mine, not so much. It's going to take time to save up for a down payment.

"So, what are you going to do until then?" Mason asks.

"Ride the bus or get a Lyft," I say, and Mason frowns. "You didn't seriously think I could afford to go out and buy a new car, did you? If I could afford a new car, I wouldn't need a roommate." I sit up and wipe the sleep from my eyes.

"You can't take the bus or a Lyft. How will you get Alec from school? You go back to work tomorrow."

"I'll handle it." I push the sheets off myself and notice I still have my reading socks on. I never go to sleep with my socks on. Then I remember last night after the party Mason and I watched a movie, and he massaged my feet. I must've fallen asleep because the last thing I remember is him pulling the covers over me before saying good night.

"Okay," he says slowly and I'm surprised he's letting this go so easily. "So, how about we go buy some groceries so you won't have to this week? Alec comes home today, right?"

"Yeah, this morning. Gavin has an appointment this afternoon with a client."

After showering and getting dressed, Mason and I head to the grocery store. Of course, while I'm trying to budget and make sure I have all the ingredients for dinners, Mason is throwing items into the cart without a care in the world.

"I hope you're planning to pay for that crap yourself," I point out, and Mason just laughs.

When we get to the checkout counter, I put my stuff onto the conveyer belt first. "Shoot, I forgot a bag of ice. Can you go grab it?" Mason asks.

"Sure." I run over to the front and grab a ten pound bag of ice, and when I return, the cashier hands me my receipt, thanking me for shopping with them.

"Here." Mason takes the ice from me. "I'll add it to my stuff."

"Wait! You did not seriously just pay for my groceries!"

"I did, but with good reason."

"And what's that?"

"Well, based on that delicious lasagna we ate a couple weeks ago, I know you're a good cook. So I figured if I buy, you'll cook." He winks and goes about paying the lady for his groceries.

"I don't think that's how it works," I say as we walk back to his car, Mason pushing the shopping cart. "Actually, now that I think about it, we do need to discuss the bills."

Mason waves me off as he pops his trunk open and starts putting the shopping bags in. "Just give me your account information and let me know how much my half is, and I'll make a deposit every month."

We get home, and Mason and I go about putting the groceries away when we hear the door swing open and in runs Alec. He completely bypasses me and goes straight for Mason. "You're really living here?"

"Well hello to you too," I mutter.

"I am," Mason says with a grin. "How was your time at your dad's?"

"Good. We hung out with my grandma. She's leaving to visit her sister in Florida," Alec says as Gavin enters the kitchen.

"Hey, man." Gavin shakes Mason's hand. "I've heard all weekend about the new roommate. This one kept begging to come home." Gavin points to Alec.

"Your mom is going to Florida?" I ask. His mom has talked about moving there for years, but she hated to leave Alec, especially since so many nights she helped watch him while I worked my shifts at the hospital.

"Yeah, she's finally sold her house, so she's going to stay with my aunt for a little while."

"That's good."

"All right, I'm off. I have an appointment and then my game later in the afternoon. You guys coming to watch?"

"No, my car has reached its end."

"Damn, okay. If you need me to get Alec from school, let me know."

"I will, thanks. Oh! Don't forget that Charlie and Tristan's wedding is next weekend. I'm leaving Thursday and won't be back until Sunday sometime, so you're taking Alec."

"Sure thing." Gavin says goodbye and sees himself out.

"Mom, I'm hungry. Can you make pancakes?" Alec asks.

"Do you have any homework you need to do before school tomorrow?"

Alec groans, which means he does.

"How about you go do your homework while I make pancakes?" I bargain.

"I hate homework," Alec complains.

"Come on, Bruiser," Mason says. "I'll help you, and if you finish quick enough, maybe we can play a game on the PlayStation?"

"Yes!" Alec pumps his fist into the air as he runs to his room to get his homework.

"Thank you," I mouth to Mason who simply smiles.

"HOW IS IT THAT CHARLIE SAID WHEN YOU LIVED WITH TRISTAN you used to leave for the gym every day before the sun came up, yet since you moved in with me, you don't have to be there until nine?" I ask. It's Wednesday, and Mason just dropped Alec off at school for the third day in a row and now he's dropping me off at work on his way to the gym. I hate that he's doing this, but at the same time I'm not going to argue because to take the bus or a Lyft would be a damn pain, especially to get Alec to school. He could take the bus, but he's never done it, and I'm terrified to let him.

"I make my own schedule," Mason says. "That's a perk to being a fighter. I can train whenever I want." He smiles my way, and my stomach tightens.

"I think you're lying, but thank you. Since we're leaving tomorrow to Vegas, Gavin is picking Alec up from school today. I can take a Lyft home."

Mason gives me a look that says it's not happening, then says, "When we get back from Vegas, we're going to figure out your car situation." The way he says *we* has my belly doing flip-flops even though I know he doesn't mean it the way it sounds.

"You've done enough. I promise I'll get it figured out when we get back."

Mason pulls up to the front of the doctor's office I work at. "I'll see you at four."

I don't bother arguing because I know he's going to be here at four regardless of what I say, so instead I thank him again before I get out. As I make my way onto the elevator to the third floor I think about how different things have been since Mason moved in. For the last several years, it's just been Alec and me. I do the cooking, the cleaning, the laundry. I help Alec with his homework. I watch TV or read a book after he's in bed. But the last few days, I haven't been doing it alone. While I cook, Mason helps Alec with his homework. While I do the laundry, Mason does the dishes from dinner. Afterward, we spend time with Alec, and once he's in bed, Mason and I watch crappy television together. I know I should put a stop to all of this, but it feels good to not be doing it all alone, and not just that…something about Mason, it just feels right. When I'm hanging out with him it's easy. It's too bad I can't find a guy just like him, but one who actually wants to get married and have a family.

I step off the elevator, and my phone dings. It's *GetHooked*. We still message every day, but with Mason around, it's not as much. I find myself wanting to give Mason my attention. I know in the end I'm going to end up hurt, but I can't help it. I'm drawn to him like a magnet, and I can't pull back no matter how hard I try to resist.

Gethooked: Have a good day at work.

Looking4Love: You too. :)

Before I clock in, I send a text message to Mason.

Me: Movie tonight with take out?

Mason: Sure, we can pick up the food on our way home.

FOURTEEN

MASON

FOR THE FIFTH NIGHT IN A ROW, MILA HAS FALLEN ASLEEP ON the couch. The woman is like supermom. She starts her day at the crack of dawn—making breakfasts and lunches and getting Alec ready for school, as well as herself ready for work—and she doesn't stop going until her head hits the couch for us to watch a movie. She's everything a mother should be and more. She's everything my mom didn't know how to be. Her car broke down, and if I wouldn't have forced her to let me take her and Alec to work and school, she would've dealt with it. She doesn't bitch or complain, she just handles it. Her ex-husband texted her last minute, letting her know he was going to be late picking up Alec and she left work early to grab a damn Lyft instead of texting me. And the only reason I knew that was because I pulled up early and caught her running out the door.

Gavin finally showed up close to nine o'clock and picked up Alec. Since we're leaving for Vegas tomorrow, it was easier for him to take him tonight even if it was after his bedtime. Mila was already passed out, so Gavin grabbed Alec and his backpack without waking her up.

My phone pings with an incoming text, and when I look at it, I see it's from Bianca—a friend of Charlie's. I've hooked up with her on a couple occasions since Charlie introduced us while working at Plush.

Bianca: Your friends were at the club tonight but I didn't see you there.

Me: I've been busy…

Bianca: Are you busy now?

Me: Leaving for Vegas tomorrow for Charlie and Tristan's wedding.

Bianca: That's tomorrow...come over tonight.

I look over at a sleeping Mila and debate whether or not I should go to Bianca. I haven't hooked up with anyone since I moved in here. While I used to spend my days fighting and my nights fucking, lately I've opted to come straight home. Sure, I can say it's because Mila's car isn't working, and I've been dropping them off and picking them up, but the truth is, if I wanted to, I could drop them off and then take off to go out—but I haven't. I've chosen to come home with them every night and hang out here. We've created a comfortable routine of alternating between who cooks, who cleans, and who helps Alec with his homework, and when all the chores are done we hang out with Alec until it's his bedtime.

The thought that this routine isn't boring but something I look forward to has me freaking the fuck out. This isn't who I am. I'm not the guy who Netflix's without the chilling part. Hell, I'm the guy who jumps straight to the chilling part. What am I doing here? I moved in so Mila wouldn't have some stranger trying to perv on her. So her situation wouldn't turn into one similar to my mom's. Where she wouldn't feel the need to hook-up with a guy because she can't take care of her son, or where men become a revolving door, coming in and out of her and her son's life. I didn't move in here to play house with Mila and Alec. That's not who I am. That's exactly what I don't ever want to be. Yet somehow it's exactly what my life is becoming.

I send a text to Bianca letting her know I'll be over in twenty minutes, and moving Mila's feet off me, I slide off the couch, careful not to wake her. That foot massage I gave her the night of the party has turned into a nightly ritual. I run upstairs and throw on a pair of jeans and a shirt and grab my car keys. I get back down to the living room and make it a point not to look at Mila, knowing if I do, I might not leave.

I lock the door behind me and drive over to Bianca's condo development. I buzz the intercom, and she presses the button to allow me up. While I'm waiting for the elevator to take me to her floor, I watch the numbers tick as I pass each floor. My thoughts go to Mila, but I force myself to push them away. Just as the elevator dings, my phone vibrates and I check it.

Mila: I woke up and you were gone... I hope everything is okay. Sorry for falling asleep... again lol But it's not my fault. It's those foot massages you give me. If fighting doesn't work out you could be a masseuse ;)

My feet still right along with my heart. I hear the door open and when I look up, Bianca is standing in her doorway. She's wearing a white negligee that leaves nothing to the imagination. Its purpose is to seduce, but for some reason, it isn't doing anything for me.

I glance down at my phone and think about Mila in her cotton pajamas and those freaking reading socks she wears every night—I swear the woman must own fifty pairs of them. Her outfits are the exact opposite of what should turn me on, but as my dick twitches at the thought of her, I know I'm fucked. I'm not supposed to want the woman who is looking for her fucking forever. I'm supposed to want the woman who wants the right now. The woman who's standing in the doorway and is willing to let me fuck her, no strings attached.

"Mason." Bianca calls my name as my phone dings with another text from Mila.

Mila: Good night. See you in the morning.

My eyes dart from Bianca to my phone. If I choose Mila, I will only hurt her. She will have expectations and needs, and I will fail at every corner. Bianca is the right choice. Her only expectation is for me to give her an earth-shattering orgasm. Why am I even debating this? Of course, Bianca is the right choice. She's the safe choice.

So then why am I not putting my phone into my pocket and walking toward her? Why am I stuck here in place?

"Mason," Bianca says again.

"I made a mistake," I admit. "I'm sorry. I gotta go." I step back into the elevator and hit the button to the lobby. This is probably the stupidest decision I've ever made, but what if it's the best?

FIFTEEN

MILA

THE WEDDING WAS BEAUTIFUL. MORE THAN BEAUTIFUL. IT WAS romantic and sweet and intimate—everything Charlie and Tristan deserve. They said their 'I do's' out on the veranda at the Bellagio surrounded by their close family and friends. I stood next to Charlie as her maid-of-honor and Mason stood next to Tristan as his best man. The girls were called up to say their 'I do's' as well since they will be legally adopted by both of them.

The dinner was held at the Picasso where Tristan proposed, and once everyone was done eating, toasts were made and cake was served. Shortly after, Tristan's parents took the girls for the night, and Tristan and Charlie excused themselves up to their honeymoon suite. They'll be leaving as a family to Disney in the morning, but tonight they're celebrating as newlyweds, just the two of them.

While I'm so freaking happy for Charlie and Tristan, it was hard not to get emotional. I am a twenty-seven year old divorcee with an eight-year-old son. I haven't experienced any type of romance or being close to someone in way too damn long. I want what Charlie and Tristan have. I want a lover, a friend, a partner. I want a man I can depend on, one I can share my life with. I want to laugh and have fun and be silly. I'm tired of being alone, but more importantly, I'm tired of feeling alone.

I think Mason sensed my hurricane of emotions as we walked up to our rooms to change out of our wedding attire because he told me to put on something sexy and meet him downstairs. When I tried to argue, telling him the bed, pay-per-view, and mini fridge full of liquor, were all calling my name, he wouldn't take no for an answer. I'm actually shocked he invited me out, especially since he's been extremely distant toward me the last few days. When I woke up Thursday morning, Mason was back at home. I have no idea where he went, but the morning after is when I noticed a difference in him. As soon as the rental car was delivered, we took off to Vegas. The entire drive he kept to himself, and since we've arrived he's been spending most of his time with Tristan and his family as well as friends he knows here. I would almost think he's purposely avoiding me, but I'm not sure why. And if I'm honest with myself, I miss him. The last two days have been busy with everyone getting ready for the wedding, but at night, in my hotel room, I've missed having someone to watch movies with. I've missed his foot massages and his playful commentary. I miss falling asleep on the couch and him carrying me to bed. I just miss him, period.

After going through every outfit in my luggage, I decided on the plunging V-neckline open back halter romper. It's black and lacy, and with the completely open back, it doesn't allow for a bra—the perfect mix of sexy and classy. I finished the outfit with a cute pair of three-inch black heels. I touched up my makeup, grabbed my phone, license, and room key, then met Mason downstairs. He introduced me to several of his friends I saw at the wedding but hadn't formally met, and then we took off down the strip to go clubbing. Since most of them have lived here for years, they knew which clubs to go to. Apparently Mason is a bigger celebrity than I thought. I knew he was popular in the UFC world, but I didn't know he was big enough to have people following and taking pictures. That was until I saw paparazzi outside a couple of the clubs snapping photos. Mason didn't seem fazed by it in the slightest, though. He even stopped to sign stuff for a couple of fans. When we reached the front entrance of each club, every bouncer knew him and we were immediately granted access. Once we were inside, we were escorted to the VIP section where nobody could bother anyone in our party.

It's now after two in the morning and we've hopped from club to club, losing people along the way—some going home alone and others finding someone to go home with. We're now at Club Reckless, sitting at the VIP bar, and Mason has ordered us another round of drinks.

While I watch him say goodbye to the last of his friends, my thoughts go back to the other night. To waking up and finding Mason gone. It shouldn't have hurt me but it did. I haven't wanted to admit it to myself but the fact is there's only one reason why a guy leaves at night and it's for a booty call. I'm not stupid enough to think he doesn't have sex. He was a manwhore when I met him all those years ago, and he was the same man when we came back into contact years later. I guess, for a minute I forgot who Mason really is. Since he moved in, he's either at the gym training or at home. He's just the guy who lounges on my couch and watches movies with me while eating a bowl of popcorn and helps my son with his homework.

He's sweet and caring and selfless. He's amazing with the kids, and he doesn't complain about helping around the house. He's funny and playful and he turns me on without doing anything more than smiling. And I've been slowly falling for that man. But the other night when he left, it hit me that he's still Mason. He's still the playboy who doesn't want to settle down. He's a complete contradiction and I'm an idiot to want him. I might as well rip my heart out of my chest, place it on the floor, and stomp on it myself. That way I don't have to watch and wait for him to do it.

While we're waiting for the drinks to arrive—and since I'm filled with liquid courage—I pull my phone out of my back pocket and pull up the Plenty of Fish app, shooting a message to *GetHooked*. I need to get my mind off Mason, and the only guy that has a shot of doing that is *him*.

> **Looking4Love: I know it sounds crazy but after having been on three horrible dates and watching my friends get married, it made me realize I don't want to wait for Mr. Right. Want to go out with me when I get back?**

I hit send then read what I wrote. Oh no! That came across completely wrong.

> **Looking4Love: I didn't mean you aren't Mr. Right...I just meant I'm done waiting for him. I'm ready to take action. Find him myself.**

Oh, great. Now I'm referring to him in the third person.

> **Looking4Love: What I mean is, you are sweet and funny and I enjoy talking to you, and I think we could have fun together.**

I send the third message, groaning to myself, and swear the next time I've been drinking I won't attempt to message anyone—and then I mentally blame Mason for this.

Mason finishes saying bye to his friends and turns to face me, pulling his phone and card out of his back pocket. He sets the phone down on the bar top and grabs the card to hand to the bartender, who sets our drinks in front of us. She takes the card and smiles then walks away to ring up the drinks. Mason's phone vibrates, and being nosy, I glance over at it thinking if I see proof of the other women I will stop falling for him. And when I look, I do see notifications from a woman, only the woman is ME! Snatching his phone before he can grab it, I press the circle home screen button to light up the notifications again. It takes a second for it to all click, but when it does, I feel so stupid.

"It's you," I say dumbly, and Mason gives me a confused look. Lighting up the screen again and pointing to the notification, I repeat my words. "It's you."

His eyes go wide, and he's speechless for a few seconds before he finally answers. "It's me."

"Great!" I yell over the music. "Of course, it's you! The one guy I talk to about everything. The one guy who's sweet and charming and funny, and who I enjoy and look forward to talking to everyday. It's you."

Then it hits me. His image doesn't have his face showing but mine does. "Oh my God!" I throw the phone at him and he catches it. "You knew it was me!"

I stand and down my drink, the alcohol burning my throat as it rushes down. "You knew!" I shove his chest in anger and embarrassment, ready to find my way back to the hotel alone.

But before I can pull my hand back, Mason grabs it and pulls me into him. "Come here." He downs his drink just as quickly as I did and snatches his card off the counter where the bartender left it. He quickly writes a tip and signs his name before he pulls me away from the bar toward a quieter area of the club.

His hands run down my sides landing on my hips as he turns me around to face him, pushing me against the wall of a hallway that looks like it leads to an emergency exit. Then he leans down, and his lips brush against my ear. "You looked so damn gorgeous at the wedding, Mila." His words send shivers up my spine. "And now, fuck, you're the sexiest woman in this club."

"Don't try to distract me with your damn charm! It's you."

"It's me." He nods and smiles softly.

"Why would you do that?" Hot traitor tears form, but I refuse to let them fall.

"At first, I was curious. I wanted to know what made you tick. What you were looking for in a man."

"You should've told me. I feel so stupid."

"Why? Because you didn't know it was me? Does it change anything you've said to me? Does it change our conversations? I've never lied to you, Mila. Have you lied to me?"

"No, but why didn't you tell me?"

"I started falling for you, and it scared the shit out of me."

He was falling for me? "Bullshit! Just a couple nights ago you left me to get laid." I don't know this for sure, but when he flinches, my assumptions are confirmed.

Mason quickly composes himself. "No, I didn't."

"Then where did you go?" I challenge.

"Yes, I left to get laid," he admits, "but I couldn't do it. I got there, and all I could think of was you in those cotton fucking pajamas you always wear and those reading socks, and I couldn't do it."

He couldn't do it?

"What did your message say?" He encircles his arms around my waist as my hands come around his neck, my fingers running through his sweaty hair.

"I messaged you to ask you out," I admit. "I'm done waiting for Mr. Right. I love talking to *GetHooked* and I didn't want to keep *just* talking when I could meet him and see where it leads." And it all clicks. How could I not have realized it was Mason? The guy is known for referring to women as fish! I chalked it up to a guy making a witty play on the name of the site.

"And I enjoy talking to you." His fingers hold my chin in place as he looks into my eyes, refusing to let me hide. "I look forward to those conversations more than you know."

A myriad of emotions, I'm not sure what to do with or what to make of, hit me all at once. What does this mean for us? He never did say he would go out with me. He never asked me out. Does that mean he enjoys talking to me but doesn't want more? I have so many thoughts and questions, but instead of allowing myself to overthink any of this, I do what my gut tells me to do.

I pull Mason's face down to meet mine. My lips collide with his, and our tongues delve into each other's mouths. Mason's hands find my butt, and he picks me up—my legs wrapping around his waist as he pushes me back against the wall for support. We kiss passionately and my body grows warm with desire. My heart feeling completely full. And when his mouth leaves mine, I let out a groan of displeasure, not wanting our connection to end yet.

But quickly, his lips are back on my body. Starting at my collarbone, he places soft open-mouthed kisses up my neck until he gets to my earlobe. "Fuck, Mila, we shouldn't be doing this. Tell me to stop."

Like hell I'm going to stop this! Neither of us are *that* drunk. "I want you," I moan out. "Take me back to the Bellagio and make love to me, please."

His body stiffens, his kisses coming to a halt, and I immediately know my mistake. I used the word love. He tries to put me down, but I tighten my legs around him, my ankles locking in place. "You know what I mean. I don't want to wait anymore. Take me back to the hotel and have sex with me, please."

"You're drunk."

"You know I'm not."

He stares into my eyes, looking for what, I'm not sure, but when he finally speaks, he says, "No."

"No?"

"I'm not renting you or milking you or doing whatever the hell it was that you said you don't want guys to do. I told you, you deserve more." Taking my hand in his, he pulls me out of the club using a side exit, so we're able to leave undetected by the paparazzi.

"Where are we going?" I ask.

"Back to the hotel. We've both had enough to drink and if we stay and drink any more, I might give in, and we both know that's not what you really want. Don't forget I've been the person on the other side of those messages. I know what you really want, Mila, and it's not a guy like me." We're walking fast, and my feet are groaning in pain from wearing heels all evening. Mason notices me slowing down and stops.

"Get on." He bends down slightly, and I jump up onto his back, my hands linking around his throat. "Don't choke me to death!" he yells through his laughter, and I giggle.

"Gitty up!" I squeeze his sides with my thighs, and Mason shakes his head, chuckling. As he carries me down the sidewalk, I start to recognize our surroundings. Mason is quiet, and I'm trying to think of a way to change his mind. He's only saying no because he thinks I still want to wait until marriage, and while that would be ideal, I'm done waiting. Especially now that I know Mason is *GetHooked*.

We're only a couple blocks away from our hotel when I spot The Chapel of Love. "Look!" I point to the church and giggle. "It's a church! We can get married and then you can own the cow! And then I can finally have sex!" Okay…maybe I'm a *little* drunk.

Mason stops and glances toward the Chapel, dropping me to my feet and turning around to face me. "I would make the worst husband ever."

I let go of his hand and bring my hands up to his neck. "You would make an incredible husband. Like you said, don't forget I've been the person on the other side of those messages. I now know both sides of Mason Street." I pull his head down and kiss him. "Marry me. Marry me and then fuck me. I know this sounds crazy, but we could be amazing together." I kiss him again and he groans into my mouth.

"Please," I plead. "Marry me."

SIXTEEN

MASON

WE'RE NOT DRUNK…TIPSY, MAYBE. BUT DRUNK? NAH. THAT'S what I tell myself as my wife pulls me into her hotel suite. We had a few drinks, a couple of shots. We're not drunk, though. That's what I try to convince myself of as Mila undresses in the center of the room.

I watch as she reaches her hands back and undoes the knot of her top. Because she's not wearing a bra, her heavy tits fall slightly as they're freed. Her pert nipples are hard and begging to be licked and sucked. I don't suck or lick them, though.

I just watch as she pushes her sexy as fuck outfit past her hips. It falls the rest of the way on its own, pooling at her feet and leaving her in nothing but a black thong. She steps out of the material and I notice she's still in her fuck-me heels. I want nothing more than to lay her on the bed and explore every inch of her body. I don't touch her, though.

I continue to watch as her fingers hook in the sides of her thong and she pushes it down then steps out of it. Her almost bare cunt is on display, begging to be fingered and fucked. I don't do either, though.

Instead, I stay right where I am, watching as she steps out of her heels, and as she bends down to move them to the side, her tits fall like perfect rain drops. My tongue darts out to wet my lips as I imagine taking each of her nipples into my mouth and sucking on them.

When she finally approaches me, she takes my left hand in hers—the matching silver bands glinting in the light—and walks us over to the edge of the bed. She unbuttons my shirt and removes it from my body. Then she undoes my belt and pants, pushing them down and leaving me as naked as she is.

"Your body is perfect. It's almost too perfect," she murmurs, giving me a shy smile before her eyes scan down her own body.

"Don't do that. Your body is beautiful." I expect her to argue, to mention her stretchmarks or to cover herself up, but she doesn't and that turns me the hell on.

"Thank you." She stands on her tiptoes and I think she's going to kiss me, but instead she whispers into my ear, "I know what I'm doing. I'm not completely drunk and I promise I will remember everything tomorrow. Fuck me, please, and don't hold back."

Her words melt away the last bit of resolve I have, and lifting her up, I toss her onto the bed, her hair falling against the pillow in waves. She smiles brightly as I hover above her, and my only thought is that she is without a doubt the most gorgeous woman I've ever seen, and she's all mine. "Are you sure, Mila?" I ask.

"Yes. Please, Mason."

My body is so close to hers, my cock pushing against her entrance, and that reminds me I don't have any condoms in here. "I need to go next door to my room to grab a condom."

She pouts but agrees. "Okay, hurry up."

"Where's your card so I can get back in?"

"On the table."

Still hovering above her, I dip my head down and give her a hard kiss on her soft lips. "I'll be right back."

Throwing on my pants, I run next door barefoot and unlock the door with my swipe key. I grab a couple of condoms then run back to Mila's room. I can't be gone more than two minutes tops. When I open her door, she's still lying in the same place I left her. Only she's snoring.

Chuckling to myself, I throw the condoms on the nightstand and pull her blankets up all the way to cover her naked body. *Not drunk, my ass.* Then I get into bed next to her and watch her sleep soundly, her eyelids fluttering softly like she's already dreaming. I wonder if tomorrow she'll remember any of this. Will she regret marrying me? I don't even know what I was thinking when I agreed to marry her. Actually, I do. I was thinking about how she found out I was *GetHooked.* She told me she wanted to meet *him,* and I thought if I married her maybe I could keep her. I could have her in every way possible instead of being hidden behind a phone and a dating app.

She was standing there in front of the church, begging me to marry her. If given the opportunity, who wouldn't marry this woman? But what I did was wrong. We both have been drinking. Both of us drunk to a certain extent. I should've said no. I should've taken care of her while she was drunk, not gone along with her crazy idea. It's not like it will ever work out. I'm not the marrying type. My longest *relationship* has been over a dating app. I think a part of me wanted what Tristan has, even if it was only for a few hours. To be somebody's husband without enough time to fuck it all up. All she wanted from me was for me to make love to her. I laugh softly at that. I didn't even get that shit right. She passed out without even getting laid like she wanted.

Her chest slowly rises and falls and I wonder, what if maybe this marriage could work? We already live together. What if I could give her everything she wants? What if I could take care of her and Alec? I'm not my parents. I make a good living, and I have money put away in the bank. I could spend my days training and my nights making love to Mila just like she wants. The chemistry is there. I feel it every time we're around each other. It's like nothing I've ever felt before. When she smiles, my stomach knots. When she frowns, I want to make it right. I want to make her happy. I couldn't make my mom happy. I was a burden to her. I was too young to take care of her. But now I'm in a place where I can take care of Mila and Alec.

Who the fuck am I kidding? Tomorrow, in the light of day, when Mila wakes up and freaks out over marrying me while drunk—even though she'll swear she wasn't—she'll insist we file for an annulment and we'll both move forward. Because we both know I'm not the one she's looking for.

SEVENTEEN

MILA

part my lips, but my tongue sticks to the roof of my mouth. *Yuck!* I
bet my breath is nasty. It tastes nasty. I open one eye slightly, trying to
remember last night.

The wedding.

The dinner.

The cake.

Clubbing with Mason's friends.

Drinking.

Drinking some more.

Finding out Mason is *GetHooked.*

Begging Mason to have sex with me.

Ughhhh! I begged Mason to have sex with me! Real classy, Mila.

Begging Mason to marry me.

Marrying Mason.

Whoa! Back up! Did I just say I remember marrying Mason? I
open both eyes and peek down to my left hand, and sure enough there's
a thin silver wedding band on my left ring finger.

What else happened? I remember coming back to the room,
stripping down for him, and then stripping him down. *Damn, that
body!* Then he told me he needed to grab condoms, and since I'm not
on birth control, I agreed.

What happened next? *Fuck! Think Mila!* Did I finally have sex and
not remember it? I squeeze my thighs together to see if I'm sore. Surely
after not having sex in five years, I would be a little sore after being with
Mason. I don't feel sore, though. Maybe it sucked? I mean, just because
his dick is thick and long and looks like it could please a woman doesn't

mean he knows what to do with it...

"Good morning." Mason's deep voice has me jumping slightly. When I glance over at him, he's lying next to me, his muscular arm propped up with his hand holding his head up. The blanket is only covering him up to his waist, leaving his tight pecs and deliciously ripped abs on display.

"Good morning," I croak out. "I need to get some water." When I pull the blankets off me, I immediately pull them back up because I'm naked. Like completely naked.

"I didn't want to dress you and risk waking you up. You looked too peaceful sleeping."

I whip my head to the side to look at him. "I passed out after we had sex?"

Mason chuckles a bit too loudly and my head pulsates. "You remember having sex with me?"

I consider lying but instead go with the truth. "Well, no..." I sigh. "I'm sorry. I swear I didn't think I drank that much. I remember everything else. From the wedding, to the wedding. I mean...you know. I remember from Tristan and Charlie's wedding, all the way to our wedding. I even remember us about to have sex and you going to your room to grab a condom. But I don't remember the actual act." I sit up against the headboard, pulling the blanket up with me as I go, suddenly pissed off. "Which really sucks. I mean the entire reason why we got married was so I could finally have sex, and I don't even remember it."

Mason swings his legs over the edge of the bed and stands, his hands resting on his hips, not even caring that he's completely naked. It takes every ounce of restraint to keep my eyes on his face and not veer down to his...*shit!* I did it anyway. And his dick is just how I remembered it: thick and long and veiny. I dart my eyes back up to his face.

"Well, you can rest assured," he says, unaware I was just ogling his goods. "You didn't *not* remember having sex with me, because we didn't have sex. You passed out. And trust me, sweetheart, if we had had sex, you would've remembered it for the rest of your damn life." *Oh, thank God!* It's good to know I wasn't so drunk I couldn't remember the sex.

"Sorry that you wasted your marriage on me, but I didn't think fucking you while you were passed out and snoring was the best idea. But hey, we're both awake now." He shrugs. "We don't have to check out for a few hours. I can fuck you every which way so our marriage won't be a complete waste."

I flinch at his words and stand, taking the blanket with me to cover my body. "Wow! So what you're saying is you only married me to have sex with me?"

Mason's jaw drops then he picks it back up and shakes his head. "Are you still drunk?" he asks slowly, and I shoot him a murderous glare. "In case you still are, let me remind you, you said you married me to get in *my* pants."

"Yes! But I didn't call our marriage a waste!" I yell, my head feeling like it's about to explode. "Just because you didn't get your dick wet doesn't mean the marriage was a waste." I remember our vows and how real they felt—at least for me.

Mason throws his arms up in the air. "You're fucking crazy!" He points at me. "You asked me to marry you and I said okay. You asked me to fuck you and I said okay. You passed out, and now you're going to accuse me of marrying you to get laid?" He scrubs his hands up and down his face and lets out a loud growl.

I'm so confused with this conversation. Maybe I am still drunk. I definitely need some water and a pain reliever. I thought he meant the vows he said, but then he called our marriage a waste. Maybe I got it all wrong. "Is that why you married me? So I would finally be underneath you like you said I would be all those years ago?"

Mason stares at me for a long second. "Yeah, that's why I married you," he says dryly. "So, are we having sex before we go file for the annulment or not?"

"Not!" I yell. Forgetting I'm naked, I let go of the blanket and run to the bathroom, slamming the door behind me. The tears begin to fall as I sit on the toilet, remembering our vows.

"Would you guys like the standard vows or would you like to say your own?"

"I would like to say my own," Mason said. He turned to face me, and taking my hands in his, smiled warmly at me. "I know you've been married before and it didn't work out. You told me you didn't want to settle and that you want to have an amazing sex life." We both laughed softly. "I promise you that every day you're married to me I'll make sure you never feel like you're settling. The sex will be out of this world." I giggled at his words. "But not just the sex. I'll make sure you and Alec are taken care of. I will do everything in my power to make you happy, to make you smile. I don't really know what I'm doing, but you seem to know what you want, so I was thinking I can vow to follow your lead. You tell me what you need and I'll make it happen. I promise."

Suddenly, the marriage didn't seem so fake. It seemed real, like even after tonight Mason would continue to be my husband, and the idea of Mason and me spending our life together didn't feel scary or crazy. It felt good. It felt right.

"Mila, it's your turn."

"I promise to tell you what I need every step of the way. I promise to always talk to you and never to go to bed angry. I promise to have sex with you every day so you never regret being tied down to one woman." I giggled, but Mason just shook his head.

"I could never regret being tied down to only you."

A tear formed, but I wouldn't let it fall. "I promise to take care of you back. I know you think it's your job to take care of me, but it's also my job to take care of you. So, the talking goes both ways."

The marriage officiant handed us the rings to place on each other's fingers, announced us husband and wife, and said, "You may now kiss the bride."

I know the wedding was quick. I know we weren't dating. I know people think love at first sight is crazy. But in that moment, I meant and felt every word we both said, and now in the light of the day, I still feel them. I don't want to get an annulment. I want to be Mason's wife, but if he didn't mean it, if he only went along with my crazy proposal to have sex with me, then it doesn't matter what I want.

I take a quick shower, brush my teeth and hair, then wrap a towel around myself since my suitcase of clothes is in my room. When I get to the living room area, Mason is sitting on the couch, no longer naked but in his dress pants from the wedding. He's typing on his phone, but when he hears me walk in, he looks up.

"I have good news and bad news. Which do you want first?"

"The bad news."

"Well, the bad news is, while Las Vegas allows people to get married on a whim, they don't allow annulments on a whim. In order to get a marriage annulled, we have to either be blood related, admit that one of us didn't consent to the marriage, or prove that one of us is crazy." My heart sinks. He was looking up how to get an annulment while I was remembering our vows.

"Okay…what's the good news?"

"The good news is I'm pretty sure you're fucking crazy, so maybe we can have you committed and use that as an excuse for the annulment." He smiles wide and chuckles. *Asshole!*

"Real nice!" I shoot daggers his way before I turn my back on him and head to the bedroom.

"Hey! Wait!" He follows me into my room. "I was just kidding… sort of. Don't worry, I already emailed my attorney with our information and he's going to get the documents together to file for divorce."

"You already emailed him?"

"Yeah…" Jeez, he's fast. I guess he really does want our marriage to be over, but that doesn't mean I can't enjoy him while we're still married.

I close the gap between us and make my move. "I know this is going to sound crazy." I pause and wait for him to laugh—which he does while I roll my eyes. "What if since we can't get an annulment, we just… I don't know… enjoy the perks of being married." I want to lower my eyes in fear of being rejected, but I keep them trained on Mason's.

"Like until we file for divorce?" he asks.

I shrug as a couple of traitor tears leak out of my eyelids. I want to tell him that I don't want to divorce. I want to stay married to him. But that's totally crazy, right? "I know we weren't even a couple before last night, but when I'm around you, I feel something awaken deep inside of me. Something that's been dormant for a long time. I want to see where this goes. I want the out-of-this-world sex and the connection. I want us to take care of each other. I know we drank a lot last night but I meant my vows."

Mason swallows thickly. "I'm going to mess up over and over again. You know that, right?" He nods emphatically at his own question. "And as long as we're married I'm going to hold you to the vow of never going to bed angry and having sex with me every day. Not so I don't regret being tied down to one woman, but hopefully because the sex will be so out of this world amazing, it will outweigh how crappy I am at the other parts of the marriage, like talking and communicating."

My lips tip upward into a huge grin over the fact that he remembered every part of our vows just like I did. "Well, we've been married for close to eight hours and so far all we've done is talk, and you've convinced me to want to stay married to you, so you can't be that bad at it."

"Remember those words when I fuck this all up," he warns.

"Can we consummate our marriage now?" I ask.

Mason throws his head back with a laugh before he sobers completely.

"Come here." He jerks his chin down slightly indicating for me to go to him. "Are you sure this is what you want, Mila?"

"Yes, I want you. I want us."

"And what happens once we do divorce? We go back to being roommates?"

I don't want to think about that. I just want to focus on right now. Call me ignorant or naïve or even delusional. Tell me I'm deep in denial and pretending will only hurt me in the long run. I don't care. I just want to live in this blissful bubble with Mason for as long as he'll let me.

"We'll figure it out." I drop my towel to the floor, hoping to end this conversation. And I know it works when Mason smiles softly, only one corner of his mouth lifting, as he scoops me up and carries me over to the bed, laying me down on the middle of the mattress. Kneeling over my thighs, he leans over me and takes my nipple into his mouth, sucking on it. I watch as his lips wrap around the hardened peak, his tongue licking and swirling around the tip. I release a moan, my head going back in pleasure. It's been way too long and my body is thrumming at his touch.

With Mason's mouth never leaving my nipple, his hand begins to massage my other breast. His middle and forefinger pinching my nipple, sending waves of ecstasy to my core before anything has even happened. And then his mouth and hand are no longer on me. But before I can look back down, his mouth is on my neck. Kiss after kiss, he worships my body. Over my collarbone, my breasts, back up my neck and then over to my cheek, finally settling on my lips.

My hands find their way to his hair while Mason fucks my mouth with his. If this man fucks like he kisses… holy shit! He backs up slightly and scoots down until his face is parallel with the apex of my thighs. He locks eyes with me for a split second as he spreads my legs open, settling between them. Then he lowers his eyes and plants a soft kiss right onto my pussy. Spreading my lips, he runs his tongue straight up my center, landing on my clit. I can feel him and licking and sucking, and I about come on the spot. My body jerking and shaking with want.

"Oh God… Mason!" My lower half rises as he fucks my pussy with his mouth. My hand comes down to his head without meaning to and I push his face closer, needing more. I'm drunk on his touch and can't be held accountable for anything I do or say from this point on. I feel the vibration of Mason's chuckles against my clit and I moan loudly, pushing his mouth to my pussy harder before I let go. My orgasm shoots straight through my body like a bolt of electricity.

He lifts his face, his mouth glistening wet, and his tongue darts out to lick my juices off his perfect lips. "You taste as sweet as I thought you would." I should be embarrassed, mortified, but I'm not.

Keeping his eyes trained on me, he pushes a finger into me. "Sit up and watch," he commands, and I do as he says, leaning up on my elbows. He pushes his middle finger in and out of me a couple of times before he adds another and then another. His three fingers drive in and out of my pussy as his mouth goes back down. He massages the inside of me with his fingers while his tongue massages my clit, and a few seconds later, I'm coming all over his tongue and fingers. This feeling, this craving, this raw desire. It's all new to me. Everything with Mason feels harder, deeper, more mind blowing, all consuming. I never knew it could feel this way. My body is shaking and my heart is thumping against my chest. I feel like I've just had an out-of-body experience.

Without missing a beat, Mason crawls up the bed, his fingers still fucking me, his thumb taking over for his tongue. My orgasm is still going strong as his mouth lands on mine. I can taste myself on him as his tongue pushes past my lips. My hand finds his dick, and using the bit of precum on his tip, I swirl it around his head and stroke his shaft up and down. It's rock hard and ready, but I need to taste him first. Pushing him down, I lower myself until I'm over him, his thick cock bobbing up and hitting his belly button.

Starting at the top of his scrotum, I lick my way up the underside of his shaft. Mason lets out a groan that vibrates down his entire body, and his fingers thread through my hair. I expect him to push my mouth onto his dick like I did to him, but he doesn't. Instead, his fingertips massage my scalp gently. My lips part and I take his entire length into my mouth. I suck and lick, my head bobbing up and down. I can taste the saltiness of his precum on my tongue, indicating he must be close.

"Fuck," he growls before he pulls my head up. "I need to be in you when I come." He reaches for a condom then grabs me by my hips and flips us over. He rolls the latex onto his hardened length and enters me. His hands are planted on the mattress on either side of me and mine are holding onto his strong forearms. He kisses me with abandon as he thrusts in and out of me. My legs are spread wide and he hits somewhere deep inside of me. The top of his shaft rubs my clit, as he fucks my mouth and pussy simultaneously.

"Mason," I moan as another builds. I've never come so many times this close together. My clit is sensitive, and my body is trembling.

"I got you," he murmurs against my lips, and I believe him. The man thinks he sucks at taking care of people but he doesn't see himself the way I see him, the way Tristan and Lexi see him. The way he is with my son. He doesn't see the way he defended my honor by beating up Isaac. The way he paid attention to my wants and needs when he said his vows.

"Mila, baby. Let go." Tears spring from my eyes at his words. I was married for years and never felt as close to him as I feel to Mason right now. He length gets harder, his thrusts quicken. My orgasm dangles over the precipice. Something deep inside of me tightening

"Let go," he says again, and this time I do. My body relaxes, and my climax hits me full force, pushing me over the edge. It's stronger than the others. My vaginal walls contract as Mason pushes himself deeper into me. His cock thickens inside me, and then he's coming. He stills, his lips never leaving mine. I can feel his shaft softening inside me as we both come down from our orgasmic bliss.

When his lips leave mine, he looks into my eyes. "I'm going to do everything in my power not to fuck this all up, but I don't know if that's possible. What I need you to know is that what happened last night and just now...it has nothing to do with what I said all those years ago and everything to do with the fact that you make me feel something I've never felt before. You make me want to be better than my father, better than my mother. You make me want to try."

EIGHTEEN

MASON

WE GET HOME FROM VEGAS, AND MILA STOPS IN FRONT OF THE stairs. "Okay, I guess I'll see you later?"

I think it's a statement, but it comes across as more of a question.

"Okay…I'm going to go put my clothes away."

I start to head up the stairs but stop when I hear her speak. "Put them away in your room?"

"Um…yeah, I think so…maybe?" I'm not sure why, but I feel like there's no right answer here.

"You're not sure?" she asks, her brows furrowed in confusion.

"Is there somewhere else I should put them?" I question. *Why is she acting so strange?*

She sighs. "Never mind."

"Wait! Never mind, what? Should I throw them in the washer?" She's never cared before when I do my laundry…

"Never mind," she repeats. "I need to go put my clothes away as well…in my room." She drags her luggage down the hallway, ending the conversation and leaving me wondering what the hell just happened as I bring my luggage upstairs to my room.

The entire four-hour drive, we didn't have a single moment of awkwardness. We talked and laughed the entire way back. We stopped for lunch at a small Mexican restaurant and split fajitas. I learned we both love shrimp and steak and hate chicken. We talked about an upcoming UFC Fight Night, which is taking place two weeks from now, and decided to make a weekend out of it with Alec. So, I'm not sure why the moment we stepped through the door, everything got weird.

As I'm unloading my clothes into the hamper, I hear the doorbell ring. When I hear Alec's voice, I run downstairs to join Mila. It's been four days since I've seen the kid, and I have to admit I'm missing him.

"Mason!" Alec yells from the living room, already lounged out on the couch, ready to watch some television.

He jumps up and high-fives me. "What's up, Bruiser!" I ruffle his hair.

"Nothing. Want to play the PlayStation with me?"

"Well, that's great!" I hear Mila say, sounding upset. *Shit! Did I already fuck up?* I knew I should've thrown my clothes in the washer.

"Sure," I answer Alec. "Just let me check on your mom first."

I walk into the foyer to find she's not talking to herself, but to her ex-husband. Before I can back away and leave them to continue their conversation, Gavin spots me over Mila's shoulder.

"Hey, Mason. How's it going?"

Not wanting to be rude, I shake his hand. "Pretty good, man. Sorry, I didn't mean to interrupt. I thought Mila was annoyed with something I did."

Gavin chuckles. "Nah, she's annoyed with me." He shrugs. "But the great thing about her being annoyed with me now that we're divorced is that I get to go home instead of being stuck sleeping on the couch." He laughs at his joke, and Mila growls. Like, legit growls at him, and that has me laughing. She's such a feisty little thing.

"Um…*she* is standing right here." She waves her hand in the air to get our attention and that's when Gavin zeroes in on her wedding band.

"Oh shit! Did you get married?" Mila lowers her hand and begins to fidget. "I didn't even know you were dating anyone. Who's the guy I should congratulate?"

"That would be me." I wave my hand in the air to show off my matching ring.

"You were dating him?" Gavin asks.

"No…" she says slowly.

"I'm confused." He looks from me to Mila, puzzled.

"It's not really your business now, is it?" Mila barks.

"Well, it kind of is. I mean, Alec does live with you guys. I thought Mason was living here until you found a female roommate."

"Well, you don't have to worry about it because nothing is changing. Mason's still sleeping in his room, and I'm sleeping in mine." *Oh damn.* Now the clothes conversation makes sense. Fuck! I'm already sucking at this, but she should have just told me. I just thought she was pissed I wasn't washing my dirty laundry right away.

"And we're not staying married. Right, Mason?" She keeps talking without waiting for my answer. "And if I'm honest, you're partially to blame."

Gavin's eyes bug out, and he looks like he's ready to bolt. "I'm to blame? How?" His eyes dart to mine, almost like he's begging me to help. *Oh, hell no, buddy. I'm new to this shit.*

"You set me up with Jack!"

"I'm pretty sure you married Mason, not Jack," Gavin points out.

'Why are you arguing with her?' I want to yell at him, but I keep my mouth shut.

"I know! But I had gone five damn years without dating, and then you just had to go and give Jack my number. It's what got the ball rolling. The first domino being knocked over! And then all the rest tumbled down after. It led me to go on a date with that uptight jerk, Evan, which led me to go on a date with Isaac!"

"Who the hell are Evan and Isaac?" Gavin throws his hands up in the air.

"Evan is an uptight single dad and Isaac the fighter who left me on the side of the road because I wouldn't have sex with him! And you know why I wouldn't have sex with him?" She points her cute little finger at Gavin. "Because I told myself I wasn't going to settle! The next man I was going to be with was going to be in love with me and want me." *Oh shit... 'Please don't respond,'* I silently beg Gavin… but he doesn't listen.

"I did love you and want you!" *Oh boy.*

"No, you didn't! You loved your job and your stupid video games, and you loved yourself! You didn't love me. You didn't want me!"

"We were young. I loved you but we weren't in love. You know that. You said it yourself, we're better as friends."

"It's still your fault! Everything is your fault!" I hear her voice waver and something tells me she's not really blaming Gavin but taking it out on him because she's too afraid to talk to me.

"Mila…" Gavin says her name slowly like he's approaching a lioness.

"No! Don't you 'Mila' me. I was just fine." She swipes the tears from her eyes. "I was working and raising our son, and I was totally okay with not having sex for the last five years, and then you just had to go and introduce me to Jack! So, it's all your fault. But don't worry because it was a drunken mistake and we'll be divorced before anybody even notices. Right, Mason?"

Gavin looks stunned and scared and I totally feel him. When Mila doesn't continue talking, I realize she's waiting for me to answer her this time. *Fabulous…*

"I tried to convince her to play crazy to get the annulment but she wasn't having it; however, after that speech, I might be able to give it a try."

Gavin chokes on his laughter, his fist coming up to fake a cough and Mila glares daggers my way. "You're such an asshole. Good thing you're sleeping in your own room."

She stomps away and a few seconds later, her door slams shut. "I don't think that was the right answer."

Gavin chuckles. "Good luck, man." He pats me on my shoulder. "I think she's upset because I was supposed to keep Alec this week but now I can't. I have a huge client, and he needs me to travel up to San Francisco with him to look at a bunch of properties."

"So, what's the issue? She usually has him during the week."

"It's spring break, so he has no school. She asked me to help pay for his camp, and instead I offered to take him all week. Now it's too late to get him into camp. My mom would normally watch him in an emergency, but she's out of town."

"I can watch him."

"Really?"

"If that's okay with you…I train during the week, but Alec can come hang out with me while I do. One of my friends is fighting in UFC Fight Night in two weeks, so I'll be mostly working with him. It's all good."

"Thank you." Gavin pats my arm. "And I'm sorry about all that." He nods toward Mila's room. I should tell him it was most likely not about him, but more about the fact that I went to my room instead of Mila's, but I don't. It's not his business, and I'm going to fix it anyway.

"No worries."

Gavin says bye to Alec and takes off.

"Hey Mason! Wanna play?" I debate whether to go speak to Mila now, but decide to give her some time. Yeah, yeah…I'm a total wuss.

"Sure, Bruiser."

We play the PlayStation for a little over an hour before Alec complains that he's hungry. "Why don't you go jump in the shower and I'll go talk to your mom?"

He groans, so I add, "You're coming to the gym with me tomorrow. That means you need to be up at six in the morning ready to go."

"Really? I'm spending the day with you?"

"Not just the day; the entire week. Now go get in the shower." He jumps up and runs down the hall to the bathroom and I follow him, stopping at Mila's door.

I knock once and hear her say, "Come in."

She's lying on her bed, reading a book on her kindle. She puts it down, but when she sees it's me, she rolls her eyes and puts the kindle back up to block her view.

"Can we talk?" I lay across her bed, taking the kindle from her hand.

"I guess." She shrugs.

"Remember the part where I said I was going to fuck this up, and I asked you to take the lead?"

She nods, biting down on her lip, and I can't help but bring my lips to hers, pulling the flesh away from her teeth. Then I kiss her softly before I pull away. "That means telling me what you need."

"We agreed to never go to bed angry."

"Yes, but that didn't mean going to bed in the same room."

"I want you in the same room as me."

"Then I'll be in the same room as you." I kiss her forehead.

"I don't want to divorce."

"Then we don't divorce." I kiss her nose.

"Really?" she asks, her voice sounding adorably hopeful. "Because I don't want to tell Alec we're together if you don't want to stay together."

"I would never agree if I wasn't serious. I would never do that to Alec. I was raised in a home where my mom had strange men in and out of our house, so I know kids need stability."

"So, we're going to do this whole marriage thing for real?"

"Yeah." I kiss her soft lips because I can't get enough of this woman. "But you have to talk to me."

"I'm done!" Alec yells, running into the room and jumping onto the bed with us.

"Done with what?" Mila asks him.

"Showering! Mason said I had to shower now because we're leaving too early tomorrow."

Mila turns her head toward me. "Where are we going?"

"You're going to work. Alec is hanging out with me all week."

Mila's shoulders slump in relief. "You're going to watch him all week?"

"Yeah, we have a fight to help Jake get ready for. With Tristan gone, we can use the help." I give her a wink, and she grins.

"Thank you. And you know, I can take the bus or a Lyft to work so you don't have to drive me around."

"Not happening. I'm borrowing Tristan's truck while he's out of town, and you're using mine until we get you a new vehicle. Problem solved. Now, what's for dinner?"

"Pizza!" Alec yells.

"No way, Bruiser. Do you want to be a fighter or not?"

"Yeah."

"Well, fighters have to eat healthy, otherwise we'll lose our fights."

"Does that mean I have to eat my vegetables?" He groans, and Mila covers her mouth to hide her giggle.

"Yep! Now let's go see what we can order."

"Fine."

NINETEEN

MILA

I give Alec a kiss good night, and Mason ruffles his hair before we close the door behind us. While we ate dinner from a local deli Mason orders from frequently, we told Alec about us being married. Of course, he was completely okay with it, and that probably has to do with the fact that Mason is practically his idol. We explained that Mason would be sleeping in the same room as me, and when Mason excused himself to shower, I made sure Alec was okay with all of this. For the last few years, it's been the two of us here, and my son will always come first.

Mason follows me into my room, and as I'm standing in front of the dresser unbuttoning my shirt to change into my pajamas, he comes up behind me. My shirt drops to the floor, and his fingertips run up and down my arms. I look in the mirror and see his body pressed up against mine. "I was thinking tomorrow I could move my stuff in here." He moves my hair to the side before he rests his hands against the edge of the dresser, caging me in, his face nuzzling into my neck.

"Okay." His teeth nip at my flesh and I giggle, moving my head to push him away. "Stop, that tickles." He stops nipping and starts suckling, and the feeling goes from ticklish to turning me on. He kisses his way down my neck and once he gets to where the top of my bra strap is, he moves it out of the way and places several kisses on my shoulder. My heart picks up and the butterflies in my belly flutter. The way I feel right now with Mason touching me, loving on me, I want to feel like this forever. Now that I know what it feels like to be wanted and desired, I never want to lose that feeling.

My backside rubs against his crotch, and he lets out a groan. "Have I ever told you how much I love your ass?" He grinds against my butt some more, and I can feel his hard bulge between our clothes.

"You've mentioned it…"

His lips work their way up and once they reach my ear, he murmurs, "Any chance of you letting me in the backdoor?"

It takes me a second, but once I figure out what he means, I crack up laughing. "How romantic," I joke.

"I never claimed to be romantic." He presses a kiss to my neck. "Is that a no?" He kisses my neck again, this time sucking on my skin.

"That's a 'I've never done it before.'" I let out a groan as he continues to lay kiss after kiss on me.

"How many guys have you been with?"

"Two… including you."

He stills his kisses momentarily. "And you two never…"

"Did it in the backdoor? No. He never asked."

"And what would you say if I asked?" He places a soft kiss to the sensitive flesh just under my ear.

"I…would say…you better not hurt me."

His gaze meets mine in the mirror. "Hurting you is the last thing I would ever want to do."

"So…tonight?"

Mason chuckles. "No, not tonight. We have to get you ready first. Tonight, I just want to make love to my wife."

"That sounds romantic." I smirk, and he chuckles.

"Don't worry, I'm planning to fuck you from behind so I can at least stare at your sexy ass. See? Unromantic." I shake my head and giggle at his words as he finishes undressing me, and then he does exactly what he said he was going to do…several times, and believe it or not, even from behind, with Mason, it's still romantic.

I'M AT WORK, CLOCKING BACK IN FROM MY LUNCH BREAK AND staring down at the pictures on my phone I received from Mason a few minutes ago. There's a selfie of him and Alec. One of Alec fighting in the octagon. Another one of Alec hitting the punching bag. And the last one is of Mason's abs. It looks a lot like the default picture on his Plenty of Fish account, which has me wondering if he still has an active account.

I pull the app up and click on his profile. It's still active, but it says he hasn't been on in a few days. Just to mess with him, I click on our message thread and send him a message.

Looking4Love: Hey there… I haven't heard from you in a while. Are you still single?

"Hey, Mila!" I look up, and Meghan, another nurse who works here, is waving to me. I close out the app and put my phone away as she approaches.

"How was your weekend in Vegas? Did you do any gambling or get drunken married?"

I choke on the water I'm taking a sip of, and she pats my back. "Whew! Jeez, it went down the wrong pipe."

"You okay?" We walk together down the hall toward the back office where all the files are kept.

"Yeah, I'm okay. Actually, I did get married while I was there." She stops us in our place.

"What? To who?"

"To my roommate." I giggle at the absurdity.

"Wow! Any pictures?"

"Not from the wedding. We were kind of drunk... but I have a couple he sent me today." I pull my phone back out and there's a new message from Mason on Plenty of Fish.

GetHooked: Actually, I'm not. This whole time I was fishing I didn't realize that I wasn't catching anything because I was waiting to be caught. Then this hot AF MILF came into my life and reeled me in and now I'm hooked. Sorry, but I won't be able to message you anymore. You see, my wife...she's keeping me real busy at night between her legs. It was nice getting to know you, though. Good luck on finding your one ;)

Smiling to myself, I swipe out of his message and pull up one of the photos he sent me earlier.

"This is Mason." I turn the phone around so she can see. She takes a closer look then frowns.

"Wait a second. Is that Mason Street...the UFC fighter?"

Oh, shit! I didn't even think about the fact that most people know who Mason is. He's probably not uber-famous like an actor or a football player, but I'm sure he has a following. I mean there were paparazzi photographing him outside of the clubs. Damn it! I hope I didn't mess up by telling Meghan. Mason never said I couldn't tell anyone.

Meghan types something on her phone and turns it around to face me. "This Mason Street?" I smile at the sexy fighter grinning in his Instagram photo. His eyes are twinkling like someone just said something he thought was funny. Then I notice the number of followers he has. 26.3 million. Holy hell!

"Yeah," I choke out. "That Mason."

"He's like a UFC god! Every woman wants him and every guy wants to be him." She clicks on the first photo on his account and I recognize it immediately. It's the one he sent me of him and Alec. Meghan hands me her phone and I read the caption underneath:

Hanging out with my man Bruiser during spring break.

#nextgenerationchampion #UFCfighter #Manny
I click to view all the comments and there are already 5,400! It was only posted an hour ago.

Amber_brinne: You're so sexy! He's adorable.

Alexissurferchick: I can babysit for you.

LydiajadelovesMason: Ohh! So cute! I can't wait to see your next fight!

MrsMasonStreet712: I can be your nanny!

The comments go on and on, and I'm pretty sure I've been stunned into silence as I hand Meghan back her phone.

"You look kind of pale. You did know who Mason was when you married him, right?"

"Yeah." I nod slowly. "I just didn't know so many other people knew who he was."

Meghan grabs my hand and assesses my wedding band. "What I want to know is why you're wearing this silver band? The guy is worth close to seventy million dollars, and I'm not talking monopoly money here."

I let out a strained cough. I knew Mason was wealthy. He drives around in a newer-looking BMW. Hell, this morning after we picked up Tristan's truck, I got to drive the BMW, and let me tell you, that thing drives like heaven on wheels. Plus, he and Tristan lived in that expensive condo in Downtown LA. But I had no idea he was worth *that* much. He was always just the fighter my son looked up to. I had no clue UFC fighters could even make that much money.

"It was a last minute thing." I shrug, suddenly afraid to say anything else. Meghan and I get along and we've chatted a few times, but I don't know her well enough to know if she'll tell anyone.

"Well, if I married a man like him, last minute or not, you better believe I would require a rock. Like five carats minimum." I smile and laugh along with her, but my mind is still back at his twenty-six million followers and net worth of seventy million dollars. Not because I care how many people are following Mason or how much money he makes. No, I'm wondering why the hell he would marry me when he has millions of women falling at his feet. And why would he move in with me? The guy could buy my entire neighborhood without blinking an eye. Oh my God! No wonder he emailed his attorney so quickly. We got married without even signing a prenuptial agreement. But when I said I didn't want to divorce, he agreed. Is he afraid I'm going to take his money? Is he trying to play nice until the divorce papers come through?

Not wanting to discuss any of this with Meghan, I excuse myself by saying I need to call the next patient back. As I'm walking down the hall toward the room, I send Mason a text thanking him for the pictures and for watching Alec.

TWENTY

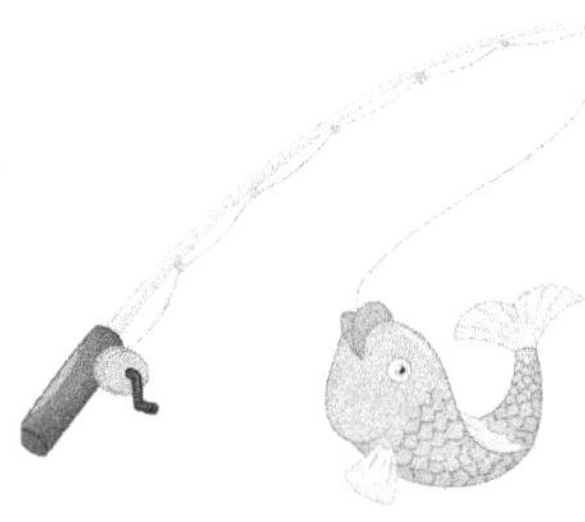

MASON

ALEC AND I HAVE JUST FINISHED SOME SPARRING AND CARDIO when I spot Jake coming out of the locker room. "Hey Jake!" I call him over. Once he spots me, he jogs my way.

"Hey, man!" We fist bump and then he fist bumps Alec. "What's up, kid?"

"We just finished working out, and we're about to pick up dinner so Mila doesn't have to cook when she gets home."

"Oh, shi—" He looks at Alec and changes shit to shoot at the last second.

I chuckle and shake my head when Alec says, "I've heard worse."

Jake laughs. "I saw the post on Twitter about you being married, but I thought it was a rumor."

My body stills. When we went to Vegas for Tristan's wedding, we managed to keep the partying under wraps for the most part. There were a few paparazzi around, but they didn't bug us for the most part. We stuck to all the clubs we knew would give us VIP treatment, and when Mila and I left, I took her out a side door. I didn't remember anyone following us when we went into the chapel, but just because I didn't see them, doesn't mean they didn't see me.

I pull my phone out and click on Twitter, and sure enough there are thousands of comments on a tweet I'm tagged in.

@MeghanLovesLA: Congratulations to my friend @MomtoAlec and @MasonStreetUFC on your marriage! Ladies, time to find a new #UFCfighter to hunk on.

Jesus! I knew it would come out eventually but not like that. As I'm scrolling down the comments, my phone rings in my hand. Shit! It's

Kenny, my publicist.

"Hey," I answer.

"Don't you 'Hey' me. Up until this moment I felt like I was ripping you off with how much you pay me. You never do anything wrong. You stay out of the spotlight, go to charity functions without arguing, you keep your sleeping around discreet for the most part. Did you decide I finally needed to earn my money?"

Kenny aka Kenneth Norton III has been my publicist ever since I moved to LA. My former publicist couldn't make the move from Las Vegas, so my PR company found me Kenny. Up until today, he's right, I've been paying him to schedule my events, run my social media when necessary, and handle anything else related to the UFC. Over the last several years, Kenny has played the publicist-slash-assistant roll. I'm low maintenance and don't require a lot. My life for the past ten years has consisted of fighting and the occasional fucking. It didn't even cross my mind I would need to let anybody know I got married. I contacted the attorney when Mila said she didn't want to stay married, but other than that, I don't have anyone to tell. Tristan is my closest friend, and I figured I would tell him when he returns from his honeymoon.

"Well, you know me, Kenny. Go big or go home." I chuckle and Kenny sighs.

"So it's true? You really did get married."

"That I did."

"We've received several requests for interviews and photo shoots. Everybody is shocked and has no clue who this woman is. Her social media platforms are all set to private and all they know is she's a mom based on her username. My advice would be to do an exclusive first interview and shoot with OK! or People magazine. Daniel West has already emailed asking, since you have a cover shoot coming out next month before your title fight, that you meet with the interviewer to add to the spread of the UFC magazine."

My head is spinning with all of this. Daniel West is the CEO of the UFC and he's all about using his fighters to gain attention to the UFC. I didn't think about any of this before I married Mila. She had no clue what she was getting herself into, and I didn't even prepare her for any of it. When I'm in her townhouse and we're hanging out, it's just the two of us and I forget about the outside world. The paparazzi rarely follow me because there's nothing to see.

Two years ago when I was named Los Angeles' Most Eligible Bachelor, I had gotten some attention. Women followed me for a while and the paparazzi would take pictures when I would leave the clubs and restaurants. But once they realized training and hanging out with Tristan and his daughter were the highlight of my life, they gave up. My guess is now that I've married a woman they didn't even know I was dating, they'll be all over me until they get answers.

"Okay, let me go home and talk to Mila. I need to see what she wants to do."

"Call me tonight, Mason. We need to make some type of announcement on social media, tonight."

We hang up, and I notice I have several texts from Mila.

Mila: I just got home and there are cameras everywhere. I'm afraid to get out.

Mila: I just left. I don't know where to go.

Mila: I'm so sorry! I saw twitter. I told my co-worker we got married. I didn't think she would post it.

Mila: Are you ignoring me? This is your fault! I didn't know you had millions of people following you. I have like thirty people following me.

Mila: I am going to Jumpin' Java to get coffee until I hear back from you.

Mila: I hope you're okay. You better be! You have my son with you.

"I'm guessing it wasn't just a rumor," Jake jokes. "Looks like you'll be canceling your membership to *Plush*."

"Yeah." I chuckle. The way he says it makes it sound like a bad thing, but the truth is since the day I moved in with Mila I haven't thought once about going to the club, and now that I have complete access to all things Mila, I have no desire to be around any other woman besides her.

"Hey, listen, can you do me a favor and go out back with Alec, and then I'll drive around and get him. I don't want him to be stuck in the mob that I'm sure is already forming outside."

"Yeah, sure."

"Thanks. So, about next weekend. You still driving up with Troy?"

"Yeah."

"Cool. I'm driving up with Alec and Mila."

"Wait a second! You married Mila? Charlie's best friend? The hot nurse."

I shoot him a glare. "Yes, and do me a favor and keep your opinions of her to yourself. I have a feeling these next couple weeks just got busier than I planned. Make sure you're training with Troy and getting ready for your fight. Call or text me if you need anything."

"Thanks, man. I will."

"C'mon, Bruiser," I call out to Alec. "Change of plans. We're meeting your mom at Jumpin' Java."

After having Jake go out back with Alec, I head through the front door of the gym and, sure enough, there's an entire slew of photographers standing outside waiting for me.

They yell out a bunch of questions but I don't say a word. After I pull around back, Alec gets in, and once we're driving away, I click on my Bluetooth and have it call Mila.

She picks up on the first ring. "Mason." She sounds nervous, and I immediately feel like shit. It's supposed to be my job to protect her and take care of her. We've been married for less than forty-eight hours and I'm already failing.

"I'm sorry. I was on the phone with my publicist when you were texting. Alec and I are on our way to you."

"No, I'm sorry! I shouldn't have told anyone we were married. I didn't know. I swear."

"You have nothing to be sorry about and don't ever apologize for telling someone we're married. It will all die down. They're just being nosy. I went from LA's Most Eligible Bachelor to being married, and they haven't even seen me date anyone."

"Well, aren't you a little full of yourself?" she smarts, and I laugh.

"Not when that's what I was titled two years ago in the Los Angeles magazine." She doesn't say anything, and I wonder if she hung up on me. "Mila? You there?"

"Yeah. Wow. Where are you?"

"We're on our way to you."

"Okay, I'll see you soon."

I press end, and Alec asks, "So does this mean you're whipped too?"

"Huh?" My eyes dart to the backseat.

"You said Tristan was stuck at the paint studio because he was whipped because he married Charlie. Are you whipped too?"

I bark out a laugh, remembering our conversation about never falling in love. "Yeah, Bruiser, I guess I am."

"Ugh! Not you too." He groans. "I hope it's not contagious like the cooties."

After settling into a corner booth with coffees—and pastries for Alec—I go over the different options Kenny gave me.

"I would imagine Ok! and People will pay the same amount no matter which one we go with. After the interview and photo shoot, they'll transfer the money over. I'll give Kenny your banking information, so that it'll go through without issue, and the fans and media will calm down."

Mila is staring at me like I have two heads, and I go back through everything I explained to her wondering if maybe I didn't explain it correctly. "Do you have any questions?"

"No." She shakes her head. "Not unless you know how to turn notifications off on my phone. I've received thousands of friend requests on every social media platform imaginable."

She holds up her phone, the screen illuminating with request after request. I take it from her and turn the notifications off in her settings. "There you go."

She sighs. "Thank you."

Taking her hands in mine from across the table, I spot her silver band, and it gives me an idea. "C'mon. I have an errand to run. We can leave my car here, and we'll come back and get it later."

I jump up from my seat and pull her behind me, Alec trailing behind. If we don't do this now, it won't get done without people watching. We pull up to the same jeweler I went to with Tristan when he picked out Charlie's ring, which reminds me I need to call him tonight.

"Mason, we don't have to do this." Mila stares at the jewelry store. "The band I have is fine. It's actually similar to the one I used to have years ago."

"No, it's not fine." I shake my head. "It was something cheap the chapel sold." And knowing it looks anything like what she wore from her previous marriage only has me wanting to buy her a new ring that much more. Plus, maybe if I buy her a nice enough ring, she'll forgive me for fucking this all up already.

"Okay, fine, but I want you to pick it out and nothing too expensive." She smiles softly at me and my heart squeezes. She's the complete opposite of the women I usually go out with. When Tristan met Charlie I thought she was a rare gem in a sea with stones, but it seems I've found my own gem, and I'm going to do everything I can to keep her.

Mila's eyes dart down to my hand, a frown marring her features. "I don't have the money to buy you a new ring." Even if she had the money, there's no way I would let her buy me a new ring. I don't want her spending a dime on me.

"I'm a guy. My band is fine." I turn around to Alec. "I need your help, Bruiser."

"With fighting?" He perks up.

"Nah, with picking out a ring." His nose scrunches up the same way his mom's does all the time.

"I don't know anything about that stuff."

"Me either, kid."

TWENTY-ONE

MILA

MASON INSISTED I GO INTO THE STORE WITH THEM. I THINK HE was afraid to leave me alone in fear the photographers would find us. We were greeted by a salesman and Mason told me to go away, then he followed the salesman over to the corner. I couldn't hear what he was saying but the salesman went around the counter and pulled out several trays to show him various rings. Not wanting to hover, I walked over to the men's rings. The woman was sweet and showed me a bunch of rings even after I told her I couldn't afford anything.

Looking at them reminded me of when Gavin and I got married. We were young and couldn't afford anything more than two simple bands. They weren't really pretty, but they symbolized our vows—to be partners and the best parents we could be to Alec. The day I took my ring off, I swore the next one would be purchased out of love, not out of obligation. But here I stand, and while the situation is different, the ring Mason is purchasing isn't any more out of love than the rings Gavin and I purchased. I feel my stomach knot and my throat close up enough that it's hard to breathe. I glance over at Mason and know I need to put a stop to all of this.

"Mason, can we talk for a minute?"

"Sure." He hands the card to the salesman. "I'll be right back."

"Wait, can you hold off on that for a minute?" Mason's brows dip in confusion along with the salesman's but he nods.

Taking Mason by the hand, I pull him into the corner of the store so nobody can hear. "I don't want a new ring."

Mason frowns. "Why not? What happened?"

I could lie but instead I go for the truth. I spent too many years lying to myself when I was married the first time, and I'm not going to make that mistake again. I vowed to talk to Mason, and I'm going to make sure I hold up my end. "The last time I got married it was because I was pregnant with Alec. Gavin and I had dated for a little while but we weren't in love. If I'm honest, we were on the verge of breaking up when I found out I was pregnant. We, of course, did the right thing and got married, but we were never really in love with each other. I told myself the next ring I wore, the next time I got married, would be with a man who loves me…a man who's in love with me, and you're not. We're not. I know I said I didn't want a divorce, but I was wrong."

A single tear trickles down my cheek and lands on my collarbone. "I'm sorry." I'm afraid to make eye contact with Mason, but after a few beats of him not saying anything, I do. He's staring at me, his features pained and confused. He grabs my hands and entwines our fingers, bringing our hands up to his lips and giving my knuckles a kiss.

"I'm sorry, Mila." He sighs, and I hold my breath, ready for him to agree that he wants a divorce. Instead he shocks me when he says, "But I don't want a divorce. I'll hold off on giving you the ring if that's what you want, and if you don't want to wear the wedding band, I understand. But we're not getting a divorce. We were sober when we said we meant our vows. I want to stay married to you. I know I'm messing this all up, but can you maybe give me a little more time? I'll get the paparazzi under control. Please."

"Mason, it's not that. Yeah, I was a bit shocked by the number of people hanging around my house, but that's not the issue. We can mean our vows, but we don't love each other." I choke on the last few words, knowing half of my statement is a lie…at least the part about how I feel. I've fallen in love with him, and I'm surprised at how quickly it happened.

"Can we please give it some time? We're already married and living together. Everybody knows we're married including Alec. Maybe over time you could love me. I've never done this before, but can you give me a chance to try, please?"

His pleading look causes a storm of butterflies to attack my belly. I want to tell him I already love him. I fell for him through every message on Plenty of Fish while falling for him every day since he's moved in with me, but instead I nod and agree. Maybe over time he'll love me back.

"Okay, but no ring."

"Fine. Let me go let the guy know. Head out to the car and I'll be right out." He hands me the keys, and as I go to grab them, he pulls the keys and my hand toward him, his lips crashing into mine. "Don't give up on me, Mila. I promise you, you won't regret it," he whispers into my mouth before backing up.

I get out to the car, and glancing down at the silver band on my ring finger, I pull it loose and put it into the side pocket of my purse. There's already a dent forming where the band has been resting on my finger. I swallow thickly, remembering when I took my ring off after I got divorced. It took nearly a year for the area to become tanned again and for the dent to disappear. It was like a constant reminder of my failed marriage.

We get home, and the paparazzi are camped out on the sidewalk of my house. Mason asks them to please give us some space and promises he'll be issuing a statement soon and then we head inside. Alec doesn't seem bothered by them in the slightest, in fact, he's more concerned that I'm making him shower before he can play his PlayStation.

We picked up dinner on the way home, so we don't have to cook. We eat and Mason plays a few rounds of UFC on the PlayStation with Alec while I throw a load of laundry into the washer, wipe down the counters, and pay a couple of bills. When nine o'clock rolls around, I let Alec know it's time for bed. He argues but Mason reminds him they have to get up early tomorrow so he stops and agrees.

After kissing him good night, I plop down on my bed and close my eyes for a second—debating whether to shower or just sleep like this, in my clothes. I'm spent—emotionally and physically—and the thought that it's only Monday has me wanting to go to sleep and wake up next week. I feel Mason's body shift onto the bed, his hands grabbing my shoe clad feet. He removes my shoes and I hear them hit the ground as he begins to massage the arch of my foot.

"What can I do to make this better?" Mason asks, insecurity in his voice. He told me I need to lead and right now he needs assurance.

"I can't compete with all those women," I admit. "I don't even know why you married me. All those hot young women, and instead you tied yourself down to me. I'm a divorced single mom."

Releasing my feet, he grabs the curves of my hips and pulls me into his lap. "You're right, there is no competition, because those women aren't even in the same league as you." He places a kiss to my lips. "You're a professional fighter, the sexy-weight champion. You're holding the belt, and they're not even in the Ultimate Fighter." I can't help but giggle. Only Mason would find a way to bring the UFC into this.

"Once we announce we're married, the women will go away. I'm not an actor in a bunch of movies. I'm just a fighter. Once they know I'm no longer available, they'll move onto the next single guy." Mason nuzzles his face into my hair, placing open-mouthed kisses along my neck. "Now, if I remember correctly, one of my vows was to make sure the sex is out of this world." He waggles his eyebrows. "And if nothing else, I'm a man of my word."

He flips me over onto my back and hovers above me. His lips meet mine and he kisses me deep and hard. "There's no competition, Mila," he whispers against my lips. "You're everything I want and need."

He doesn't let me respond, bringing his lips back down to mine and distracting me with, just as he vowed, out of this world sex.

I'M AT WORK, MAKING MY WAY FROM ONE PATIENT'S ROOM TO another, when my phone buzzes in my pocket. I quickly glance at it in case it's an emergency since Mason has Alec this week.

Mason: What time is your lunch break?

Me: Noon

Mason: We'll see you then.

I can't help the grin that pulls at my lips. The last few days we've fallen into a new sort of routine that I look forward to. Mason and Alec get up early and go to the gym. I shower and get dressed, grab a coffee on my way to work, and once I'm off, we meet for dinner or I come home to dinner ready. Yesterday when I got home, Mason was showing Alec how to grill on the new barbeque he purchased. We still spend our evening with Alec, usually watching television, playing a board game, or playing a video game. But once Alec is in bed, instead of us hanging out in the living room and watching movies like we did before, now the evenings are spent with my husband inside of me.

The morning flies by quickly. I meet with several new patients who are here to confirm their pregnancies. One is a teenager who's scared of what her future holds. I empathize with her completely. Looking back, when I found out I was pregnant with Alec, I was a baby about to raise a baby. I wouldn't trade my decision to have him for anything in the world, but I can now see why the odds were stacked against Gavin and me. He was right when he said we were young and completely different people. We had no clue what we were doing. Hell, eight years later and I'm still praying I'm not completely screwing up my child as I find my own way in this world.

After I hand the current patient a pamphlet on the facts and side effects of the birth control she has chosen, I notice I only have about ten minutes before lunch, so I seek out Dr. Burrows and find her in her office.

"Hey Dr. Burrows, do you have a second?"

"Sure." She smiles up at me warmly. I've only been working with her for a short time but I'm completely comfortable with her, which is important when you work so closely with someone all day, every day.

"I was wondering if you could write me a prescription for birth control."

"Absolutely."

I tell her which pill I'd like to be on and she types it up and sends it over to my pharmacist.

"Thank you. I'm off to lunch. I'll see you in an hour."

I walk outside to find Mason and Alec waiting for me in Tristan's truck.

"Hey!" I get into the passenger seat and give Mason a quick kiss. "What's for lunch?"

"You'll see."

A few minutes later we pull up to Grand Park. Once Mason parks the truck, Alec jumps down, pulling a picnic basket out with him.

"You packed us a picnic?"

"We did." Mason grins. "Let's go. We only have you for an hour." He lays out a giant blanket I didn't realize he was carrying, and Alec sets the basket down on top of it. They go about handing out our sandwiches, snacks, and drinks. We eat while chatting about our day, and when we're done, Mason says we still have a few minutes, so we go for a walk over to the fountains. It's a beautiful day. There are a few puffs of white clouds covering the sun, just enough to keep it from being too hot.

After Mason gives Alec some change to throw into the fountain, he pulls me into him. He smells slightly of sweat from working out, mixed with his body wash and deodorant from this morning. His arms wrap around my torso as I lean against his hard body, the back of my head resting against his chest. My arms and hands are covering his, and as I look down, I laugh at how large his body is compared to mine.

"What?" he asks, his lips brushing against my cheek.

"Your hands are so big." I take his hand and spread his fingers open, then place my hand against his. The tip of my middle finger only reaches his middle knuckle. His hands are rough and callused from years of fighting. He spreads his fingers wider and my fingers fall between, his hand clasping mine and swallowing it whole. Then he takes my other hand in his and does the same thing.

"Your hands. Your body. Your cunt," he whispers into my ear, and despite the warm weather, I shiver. "They were made just for me."

I'm beginning to think so, too, Mason. I'm beginning to think so, too...

TWENTY-TWO 

MASON

I CHUCKLE AT HIS TEXT AND PRESS THE CALL BUTTON TO CALL him back. I had my phone on silent while I was working out, so I didn't see his fifteen missed calls. I'm honestly surprised it took him this long to call me. While the phone rings, I grab a towel to wipe the sweat off my face and neck and turn around to keep an eye on Alec who is punching and kicking the bag like I showed him.

"I'm not even gone a week and you get married," he says when he answers the phone.

"Hello to you, too."

"Don't fucking 'Hello' me! You got married!"

"Awww…I'm sorry honey," I joke through my laughter. "Are you upset you weren't there to be my best man?"

"Mason! You. Got. Married. I'm your best fucking friend and I wasn't even there."

"Hey, in my defense, no one was there but me, Mila, and the old guy who married us. Oh! And his wife who was the witness."

Tristan sighs, and I think he might really be upset. I've never had to think about anyone else, so it never crossed my mind he would be hurt that he wasn't there. "Look, I'm sorry. It all happened so fast. We were out drinking after your wedding, and one drink turned into two and the next thing I knew we were getting hitched. I wasn't about to call you up and interrupt your wedding night with your new wife, so you could come to my wedding."

"Great, so a drunken marriage."

"No...Okay, maybe a little. More like tipsy."

Tristan sighs again. "You have Charlie freaking out that she's going to lose her friend because of this crazy stunt. She wants to come home to comfort Mila and I had to take her phone from her so she couldn't call her until after I talked to you."

"Why would she have to comfort Mila?" I ask, confused. I know the women are posting all over social media, but Mila has been good about it, staying off and ignoring the messages and requests.

"Um...I know you spend most of your days focusing on the sexual parts of a woman, but surely you know that they contain other parts as well, one vital organ being a heart, and when a guy marries her, even while drunk, and then divorces her, it will more than likely break that heart." He groans in annoyance. "And since you messed up your living arrangements, your ass is going to help me find Mila a new roommate."

"Who the hell said I'm going to break her heart or that I'm moving out?"

There's a moment of silence before Tristan answers. "You did file for divorce...didn't you?"

"No, I didn't, and I'm not going to."

"What do you mean you're not going to?"

"I mean I meant my vows to Mila, and I'm not getting a divorce. I'm staying married to her for however long she'll keep me."

"So...no divorce?" Tristan asks again, shock evident in his voice.

"It will probably be the biggest mistake she's ever made, but no, we aren't divorcing."

ALEC AND I GET HOME FROM THE GYM AROUND TWO IN THE afternoon and Mila's already home. There's some paparazzi standing outside but they don't bother us. The number of them go down each day, so it's only a matter of time until they move on and stop caring about my new relationship status. When we walk inside, the house is quiet, and I'm worried. It's Friday and she shouldn't be home for a couple more hours. I tell Alec to put his stuff away from the gym and to jump in the shower while I go in search of his mom. When I step into our room, Mila's lying in bed in the dark. The little bit of light filters through the blinds and I can see her eyes are wet with tears. She's wrapped up in her thick blanket in a fetal position.

"Mila, what's the matter?" I come over and sit on the bed next to her.

"Ugh!" She groans. "I started my period and it's always bad. I took a couple of pain relievers, but it got to be too much, so Dr. Burrows sent me home." I've never really been around a woman on her period. I usually make it a point not to be. To each their own, but getting my red wings isn't my thing, and up until Mila, there was only one reason I was around a woman.

"Where's Alec?" she asks, sitting up.

"He's taking a shower. Lie back down and I'll order dinner. What do you want?"

"Can I just get some soup from the deli down the street?" She asks, lying back down.

"Sure." I lean over and give her a kiss on her forehead. "I'll order the food and take Alec with me to pick it up."

Mila thanks me and closes her eyes, but before I'm out the door she says, "Oh! Can you pick me up a box of tampons, please? Playtex. I was in so much pain, I completely forgot."

"Sure."

Before heading to the deli to pick up the food, I swing by the drug store. Alec and I find the feminine hygiene aisle and about halfway down it, I spot the women's stuff. Ironically it's also on the same aisle as pregnancy tests and condoms. I locate the tampon section and find the Playtex brand, but as I go to grab a box, I notice next to it is the same brand, only a different colored box, and next to that one is another colored box.

"Yo, Bruiser. Do you know which one of these your mom uses?"

Alec looks up and down the aisle. "I don't know what these are, but this one says *sport* and my mom doesn't like sports." He shakes his head then points to the bright pink box that reads *Playtex Radiant.* "That's so pink and girly! What does she want this for?" He scrunches up his nose. "This one is blue!" He points to the box that reads *Playtex Pearl.* "Blue is my favorite color!"

Not wanting to bug Mila, I pull my phone out to call Charlie but remember she's on her honeymoon. So, instead I call Ashley, Tristan's mom.

"Mason," she coos. "How are you?"

"I'm good. How are you?"

"On my way to Morgan's doctor's appointment with her. I'm so happy to hear from you. Is it true? Did you get married to Charlie's sweet friend?"

"It's true. She's actually why I'm calling." I explain to her about Mila's period and cramps and ask her if she has any idea which tampons I should get.

"Oh!" She laughs. "I never imagined in a million years that you would call me to ask which tampons to buy for your wife. You're so sweet. I would pick out a box that has different absorbency levels. One that reads light, regular, and super."

"Mason," Alec cuts in. "This box says it smells fresh! Mom always buys laundry soap that smells fresh!"

Ashley hears him through the phone and laughs. "I would go with the non-scented to be on the safe side." I grab a non-scented box of multi-flow tampons and head to the front. On our way up, I remember once when Ashley was on her period, Kaden had brought her home chocolate and ice cream. I find the candy aisle and grab her some different types of chocolate.

"Pick something out, Bruiser." I point to the candy and he lights up. While he's picking out the candy he wants, I do a quick google search to see if there's anything else I should buy. I find several sites of women complaining about their periods, and then I find one that mentions items to buy to make a period more tolerable. It mentions Midol, bubble bath for a warm bath, and red raspberry leaf tea. After Alec has picked out what he wants, I find these items—with the help of the nice pharmacy employee—check out, and head to the deli to pick up the food.

"Mom! We're home!" Alec calls out when we walk in the door.

"Shh, buddy. Your mom isn't feeling well."

"I'm up," she says from the living room couch. She has her blanket over her shoulders and is watching television.

"Look! Mason got me candy." Alec shows her his Twix candy bar.

"After dinner," I remind him, setting the food out on the table. Mila comes over and rummages through the bag from the pharmacy. "That other stuff in there is for you."

She pulls the items out one by one and then looks up at me, tears shining in her eyes. My stomach clenches as I try to go through in my head what I could've done to upset her.

"You—you got all this for me?" She holds up the bottle of bubble bath and Midol.

"Um…yes?" I answer slowly. Before I can ask what I did wrong, she throws her arms around me and pulls me into her for a kiss.

"Does that mean you're not upset with me?" I ask once the kiss ends.

"Upset with you?"

"You have tears in your eyes." I wipe away a stray one that's resting on her cheek.

"I'm not upset with you. I'm happy. These are tears of happiness." Her fingers clasp together and tighten around my neck. "Every day, you do something that has me shocked and amazed and falling for you even harder. You keep this up and I'm never going to let you go."

A month ago, had a woman *threatened* to never let me go, I would've been running for the hills. But when Mila says those words, they have me thinking about the future. Like maybe I can do this after all. Maybe I can take care of her and make her happy. Make her smile. Maybe, just maybe, I won't fuck this all up.

TWENTY-THREE

MILA

FRIDAY NIGHT WAS THE FIRST NIGHT SINCE MASON AND I GOT married that we went to bed without having sex. Mason did, however, prove that just because sex was off the table, it didn't mean we couldn't do other stuff. And by other stuff, I'm referring to the amazing full-body massage he gave me. Who knew a man that made his living being violent could be so gentle. After Alec was in bed for the night, Mason had me strip down to nothing but my panties. He worked his strong hands over my shoulders and back and then moved down to my legs and feet.

When he told me to turn over, I was slightly nervous and a tad insecure. He always jokes I'm a MILF, but let's be real here. My body never completely bounced back after having Alec and I've seen the women Mason has been with. I wouldn't be human if I wasn't a little worried about him focusing so closely on my naked body. But I was stupid to feel any of the above because while Mason massaged my arms, worked his way up to my shoulders, and then focused on my collarbone, he told me no less than five times how beautiful I was. Of course he did cop a feel of my breasts. He wouldn't be Mason if he didn't.

While he massaged me, I relaxed—to the point where I just about fell asleep. For so many years I thought it was sex Gavin and I were missing, but I was wrong because it wasn't the sex. It was the chemistry. The want. The need. The desire to want to please another person. It was the closeness you can't force. It has to come naturally. And as Mason sat up against the headboard, with my head in his lap while we watched TV, and massaged my scalp, I knew that what I was looking for all these years wasn't simply good sex. Not settling doesn't mean finding someone to give me a good orgasm. It doesn't mean him choosing to pay attention to me instead of playing a computer game. It's finding the person who makes you feel alive. Who makes your heart beat a little faster. Who makes your body tingle without even touching you. It's your heart feeling full at the little things they do like massaging your body when they know you're hurting. I fell asleep in Mason's arms Friday night and felt closer to him than sex could ever provide.

Saturday we spent the day at home relaxing. Mason and Alec brought me breakfast in bed and we lounged around watching a Harry Potter marathon. When Mason found out Alec and I had never seen them, he parked us on the couch and refused to let us off until all eight movies were watched (We only made it through six of them with the promise to watch the last two this week). He was so freaking adorable the entire time as he explained how the movies are different from the books and insisted Alec read the books soon. We ordered dinner in, and once Alec was in bed, Mason moved all his stuff down to my room. He organized the drawers, and we talked while he put all his stuff away. The guy must own a hundred sets of workout clothes.

Now it's Sunday morning, and Mason has insisted we get dressed and head out. Apparently we have errands to run, which must be done today or the world will come to an end.

"Drive my car and follow me to Tristan's house."

He throws me the keys, and I do as he says. When we get there, Mason runs into the house quickly and comes back out, jumping into the passenger seat.

"Tristan will be back next week and will need his truck back," Mason says as way of explanation. He pulls up an address on his phone and tells me to go there. I follow the directions and we end up at a BMW dealership. I figure he must need to get work done to his car, so I'm shocked when he turns to me in the middle of the dealership and asks, "Sedan or SUV?"

"Excuse me?"

"Do you prefer a sedan like mine or do you want something bigger like an SUV?"

He can't really think I can afford a BMW and surely he doesn't think I'm going to let him buy me one.

"Okay, time to go." I start walking back to his car, but he stops me in my tracks.

"OK! or People magazine?" *Can you say whiplash?*

"I'm not sure yet. When do we need to decide?"

"Kenny would like to schedule it for next week if possible."

"I haven't had a chance to look into them. You can pick if you want."

"Nope, it's you who is being burdened by this, so you're picking." Mason flinches when he says the word burdened.

"It's not a burden." I bridge the gap between us. "You are never a burden. This is your job and I'll gladly do any interview you need me to do." Mason visibly relaxes.

"The amount they'll pay will cover whatever car you want from here. I'll pay for it today and you can pay me back once you get paid." Wow! When he said I would make some money from doing the interview I didn't know it was enough to pay for a new car.

"Why a BMW?" I ask and Mason scoffs.

"Because they're the best."

"Tristan and Charlie both drive Fords," I point out, knowing full well this is an ongoing battle between Tristan and Mason. Charlie told me about their Ford versus BMW feud one night when we saw a BMW commercial and Tristan growled at the screen like a man-child.

"Mila!" Mason mock-yells. "You're my wife! Don't you ever mention the F word again. We're a family of BMWs."

I laugh at the seriousness in his voice and feel the need to poke at him some more. "I heard BMW stands for 'break my wallet'."

Mason's eyes go wide. "You can't put a price on perfection! Who are you?"

"Mila Alexandria Sterling."

Mason glares at me. "Bull shit. You're Mila Alexandria *Street*."

"I haven't gotten anything changed yet."

"We will definitely be handling that this week. You're Mila Street. Now let's go get you a damn car." I laugh the entire way back toward the salesman while Mason mumbles under his breath something about his wife being the death of him.

I pick out the SUV I want, and once we're done, since Alec has been on his best behavior the entire time, Mason suggests we get some ice cream and go to the park.

TWENTY-FOUR

MILA

IT'S TUESDAY NIGHT, AND SINCE GAVIN IS BACK FROM SAN Francisco he picked up Alec from school today. I'm home from work and Mason texted me not to make dinner, that he'll handle it. So, I'm taking advantage of the quiet house and enjoying a much needed relaxing bath with the bubble bath stuff Mason bought for me last week. I have a vanilla candle lit and I'm reading a dirty and sexy romance novel on my iPad. My phone dings to signal an incoming text and I put my iPad down to check it.

Charlie: Oh my God! You and Mason are married!?! I leave for my honeymoon and miss everything!

Me: You weren't even gone when it happened...

Charlie: I KNOW! Tristan told me! He wouldn't let me text you! YOU should've told me!

Me: I didn't want to bug you on your honeymoon.

Charlie: Oh shut up! I can't believe you married MASON!

Me: He's nothing like I thought...He's different.

Charlie: What I want to know is how you tamed the untamable.

Me: Oh, trust me. He's not tamed. He's a beast...in bed ;)

Charlie: Gah!!! My eyes are bleeding! Haha! JK

Charlie: I'm so happy for you! We're totally going on a double date when we get back.

Me: Thank you! How's Disney?

Charlie: Magical.

Me: Magical is good! :)

I type up a follow up reply and then I delete it. I type it up again and hover over the send button. I've only known Charlie for a few months, but she's quickly become my go-to person.

Me: I'm in love with him.

I read my text over and over again, trying to see if maybe I'll read the words and call myself a liar. But I don't because I know they're true. I have fallen deeply and madly in love with Mason, and if I wasn't the one involved, I would call bullshit on whoever was telling me their story because it happened so fast, it's almost unbelievable.

Charlie: I hate that I'm so far away on a cruise and I can't hug you right now because I know you're freaking out.

Me: I'm okay. I just needed to tell someone. I can't tell Mason... he'd probably bolt.

Charlie: Be patient, Mila. Mason is one of the best guys I know... he just doesn't know he is.

"Mila! I'm home and I've brought dinner," Mason shouts from outside the bathroom.

Me: Mason is home with dinner. Enjoy the last few days of your cruise and I'll see you when you get back.

Charlie: Okay! Dinner. All of us. Tuesday night.

Me: Sounds good. See ya then!

I release the plug at the bottom of the tub so the water drains and grab my towel. After drying off and getting dressed, I head out of the room and into the kitchen. The lights are off, but it's not dark in the house because there are several tea lights twinkling throughout the living room and kitchen. When I get to the dining area, Mason has dinner set up with several more candles littering the table and counters.

"What's all this for?" I point to the candles, stunned.

"You don't like it?" Mason frowns.

"No, of course I do. I was just wondering why." Mason pulls my chair out for me to sit, and I thank him.

"Um...there's no reason why." Mason sits across from me.

"So, you didn't do something you think I'll be upset or mad about?" I question, and Mason looks perplexed.

"No. You said you wanted romance... you know... on your profile on Plenty of Fish. You said you wanted"—Mason sticks his index finger out—"to be married before having sex." He adds his middle finger. "You love fondue." His ring finger pops out to join the party. "Hanging out with your son." Now his pinky. "And that you're looking for romance." His thumb comes out. "You also mentioned the beach, so I was thinking we can go one weekend after we go to the UFC Fight." Mason shrugs nonchalantly and takes a bite of his grilled salmon. Either he's playing it off or he really doesn't understand the significance of what he just did.

He listened. He read what I wrote and then he acted on it to make me happy. How the hell does this guy not see how amazing he is?

Suddenly feeling hungrier for Mason than for dinner, I get up from my chair and come around the table, pushing Mason's food back and situating myself on his lap. He pushes his chair back slightly so I'm not squished against the table.

"You're not hungr—" he begins to say, but I cut him off.

"I want you. The only thing I'm hungry for right now is you." With my legs straddling his lap, I feel his hardness between my legs, and I writhe against him, the friction eliciting a moan out of the both of us. Our eyes lock and Mason's stare is heated, full of raw unadulterated emotion. I think he's going to pounce but instead he raises his hand up and cups the side of my face. Instinctually, I lean into his touch, and turning my face slightly, bring my lips to the inside of his palm and give it a soft kiss.

The second my lips touch his flesh, he loses all resolve. His fingers grip the bottom of my thin tank top and he pulls it over my head as I do the same with his shirt. Now skin to skin, my heavy breasts press against his hard muscular chest. Mason backs up slightly, and taking both of my breasts into his hands, brings them together and wraps his lips around my taut nipples, giving them his undivided attention until they're deliciously sensitive. Every touch from his mouth sends sparks of desire straight to my core.

He picks me up and stands, and my legs tighten around his waist. Then he walks us to our bedroom, lays me down on the bed, and tugs my pajama shorts down along with my panties. His fingers run down my neck and shivers run up my spine. His lips follow behind where his fingers just were. He presses his lips to my collarbone, his tongue darting out to lick my heated flesh. His fingers glide down to touch where his lips and tongue just were. His eyes never leave my body. I lie still, watching his fingers and mouth and eyes worship my body. I've never felt this wanted, desired, sexy, beautiful... as I do when I'm with Mason.

He pushes his shorts and boxers off, and after rolling on a condom, he parts my legs then slides into me. And as he makes love to me, it hits me that this man, in such a short time, has become everything to me.

I'm not settling.

I'm living.

I'm loving.

And it's all because of Mason Street.

TWENTY-FIVE

MILA

IT'S FRIDAY AFTERNOON, AND WE'RE ON OUR WAY TO SAN DIEGO for the weekend. Alec is busy watching a movie on his iPad and I'm reading a book while Mason alternates between listening to music and talking to a bunch of UFC people since Tristan is out of town until Monday.

I glance over at Mason, who is driving, and he darts his eyes to me quickly before looking back at the road. He looks kind of nervous for some reason, but I don't call him out on it.

"Have you decided on OK! or People magazine?" he asks.

"People." I did my research on both magazines…you know… while standing in line at the grocery store. It won't matter which one I choose. Nobody knows who I am. They're only nosy about Mason and whether he's really off the market. So, how did I pick which one? It was tough. Ok! had Brad Paisley on the cover and People had Luke Bryan on their cover. While it was close, I had to go with Luke.

"I'll let Kenny know." Mason moves his hand from the steering wheel and squeezes the top of my thigh. "Once we arrive at the hotel, it's going to be crazy. Kenny set up for security to meet us and escort us inside. The paparazzi and fans can't go into the hotel, though." Hmm… maybe this is why he's acting all weird. He's nervous about me coming face-to-face with the media. The last couple weeks we've managed to stay out of the public eye. Sure, there are still a few paparazzo lingering around my house, but for the most part it's been quiet.

"How do they know you'll be there? You're not even fighting."

"Daniel West, the CEO of the UFC, is a money-hungry asshole. When Marco and Bella were going through their shit, he twisted Marco's arm into having them both fight on the same night just to draw in attention. He doesn't give a shit about anyone's privacy." Marco and Bella are friends of Tristan and Mason. Marco is a retired UFC fighter and runs a UFC gym in Las Vegas where Mason used to train at, and Bella is still a fighter in the UFC. They're married and have an adorable six year old little girl named Micaela and a newborn named Liza.

"Is Bella fighting?"

"No way. It will be at least a year or so before she's in another fight. But she'll be at the fight with Marco since their training camp has a couple guys here fighting."

"I think it's cool how badass she is. Like, she could kick most guys' butts."

Mason chuckles. "Your seats are with hers since Tristan always sits with them." I met Bella and Marco last year at Mason's fight in Vegas, and then again at Charlie and Tristan's wedding. They're a sweet couple and I'm glad I'll be sitting with her, especially since Charlie never goes to the fights, and even if she did, she and Tristan won't be back before the fight.

We arrive at the hotel, and just as Mason warned me, the area is swarming with people. There are, of course, paparazzi with cameras, but there are also a lot of fans—men, women, and kids. Instead of driving under the overhang where the Valet is waiting, Mason stops the car and puts it in park. Then he turns toward me, pulling a black box out of the center console. "I know you said the next time you wear a ring like this you would be in love. But here's the thing. I'm falling in love with you, Mila, and I believe you will fall in love with me, too. So, it would mean a lot to me if you would wear this ring."

He opens the box, and nestled inside is the most exquisite ring I've ever seen. The band is white gold or maybe platinum, and the diamond looks like a beautiful snowflake.

"I picked that out!" Alec announces, taking his headphones off.

"You did?"

"Yeah! Remember when we watched that Christmas movie, and you said the snow was pretty and it made you feel happy?"

"I do."

"Mason said he wanted a ring to make you happy." I glance over to Mason whose cheeks are tinted pink.

"Are you blushing?" I joke, and he shakes his head.

"No," he deadpans. "But Alec is right. I bought this ring because I vowed to take care of you and make you happy, and…" Mason swallows loudly. "I know this isn't the most romantic place to admit this—sitting in a car in front of a hotel. But Mila, I love you." He shakes his head. "I've never been in love before, but I know without a doubt I'm in love with you. It's crazy. I've seen my friends go through it and I didn't get it until you. With every message and every day we've spent together, I've fallen even more in love with you. I want you to wear this ring because you're my wife and I love you, and this ring, it was bought out of love." Mason's eyes never leave mine. "I want us to get out of this car, and I want the world to know you're my wife. I want them to see you wearing this ring. Not because it's expensive but because it's the ring you deserve. "

"Mason." I say his name like a prayer, and in a way it is. I prayed for this so many times. To meet a man who would love and cherish me, and here he is, sitting across from me telling me he loves me. "You love me?" I ask dumbly and he chuckles.

"Yes, I love you, and it's okay if you don't feel the same way yet. I just need you to know—"

"I do." I nod. "I do feel the same way. When we were at the jewelers I already knew I loved you. And then the last couple weeks, the way you handled my… shark week." Mason laughs. "The dinners and romance and the way you treat my son. I am in love with you. I just assumed it was one-sided."

Mason sets the jewelry box down and frames my face with his hands. "It's definitely not one-sided. I love you and Alec, and even though I live every day scared I'm going to mess this all up, I've never wanted to get something right so bad in my life." Mason leans over the center console and kisses me. It's soft and sweet and ends way too soon.

"Okay, I'll wear the ring."

Mason grins, taking the ring out of the box and sliding it onto my finger.

"It's beautiful. Thank you."

TWENTY-SIX

MASON

I PULL UP AND THE VALET OPENS OUR DOORS. I POP THE TRUNK and hand them our luggage so they can bring it up before I tuck Mila into my side, her arm coming around my back and her hand landing in my back pocket. She squeezes my ass cheek and giggles. Alec comes around my other side to hold my hand, and I feel like the luckiest damn bastard alive. The fans and press start shouting questions at me, and Mila tenses. Leaning down, I give her a soft kiss, hoping it will calm her nerves. I know it works when I feel her relax into my side.

"Mason, is it true you guys got married in Las Vegas?"

"Mason, is she pregnant?"

"Mason, how does it feel to be officially off the market?"

"Mason, do you think you'll be able to defend your title against Jax Wilkens?"

The questions keep getting fired while we walk over to the front entrance. I make it a point to lift Mila's hand up to my lips to give her knuckles a kiss, and the cameras go off, each one trying to get a picture of her ring. I don't bother answering any of the questions. I do, however, sign autograph after autograph. Mila even offers to play photographer while I take some pictures with my fans. Alec hands me shirts and hats to sign, and when I'm done I thank them all for coming and promise them I will be winning my next fight. They cheer and shout and too many women beg me to fuck them.

Taking Mila's and Alec's hands in mine, we walk into the lobby to check in, the noise immediately fading as the doors close behind us. When we approach the front desk, the woman is ready with our keys, so we're able to head straight up to our room to get situated.

"Alec, want to go to the pool?" Mila asks.

"Yes!" he shouts excitedly. She throws him his swimsuit and excuses herself to get changed.

"Hey!" I grab her arm and pull her toward me. "Am I invited?"

"Of course, I just figured you would have other stuff to do with the fight tomorrow."

"And miss seeing you in a bikini? Not a chance." I shoot her a flirtatious wink, and she groans, rolling her eyes before she heads to the room.

"Mason, that was so cool!" Alec yells, jumping onto the couch. "Those people were crazy! When I get older I'm going to be a fighter just like you."

"That's awesome, Bruiser." I sit on the couch next to him. "But what if you can't be a fighter, what would you do then?"

Alec looks at me like I've grown two heads. "I can't be a fighter?" He pouts.

"Of course you can. You can do anything you want to do. But what else do you want to do?"

"What do you want to do?" he asks, answering my question with the same question.

"Before I knew I was going to be a fighter, I wanted to be a paramedic. You know the people that drive the ambulance." That dream began the day I found out my dad was hit by a car and the paramedics told my mom they did everything they could to save my dad. It didn't work, but it made me want to become one so I could work every day to try and save people. That same dream died the day my mom told me my father failed at taking caring of us and she wasn't sure how she would be able to take care of me. Without any money, there was no way I was going to school.

"That's a cool job, too!"

"What do you want to be?"

Alec thinks for a second. "I want to be a fireman!"

I chuckle, ruffling his hair. "That's a good job to have."

"Yes, it is," Mila adds. I turn to see her coming out of our room in a sexy two-piece burnt orange bikini. The material covers all the important parts, yet leaves nothing to the imagination. My wife has a MILF body I fully plan to enjoy. Her hips are curvy and her thighs are thick, and her tanned skin looks even darker against the dark orange material. She's in the middle of throwing a white cover up over her when I jump off the couch and grab it from her.

"We don't really need this, do we?" I toss it to the ground. "Alec, go get your swimsuit on, buddy." I waggle my brows at Mila who giggles uncontrollably as I push her into our room.

"Okay," I hear him say as I close the door behind us, pushing her up against the wall. My hands run along the thin orange strings leading to the triangles that cover her pert tits. Mila shivers, tiny goose bumps appearing along her skin. Pulling one triangle to the side, I wrap my lips around her nipple, sucking on it hard.

"Mason." Mila lets out a breathy moan. "Not now," she whispers, pushing my head back.

"Please, baby." I drop to my knees, her pussy directly in front of my face. I give the triangle covering her tight cunt an open-mouthed kiss, and she moans again.

"I'm ready!" Alec yells. I groan in frustration as Mila pushes my face away again.

"Tonight." She slides to the side and opens the door, leaving me and my hard dick alone in the room.

"I'm holding you to it!" I shout.

We get down to the pool, and after finding some lounge chairs, I order us drinks and dinner since it's already after seven o'clock. Jake and Troy spot us while they're walking by, both dressed in workout clothes.

"You ready for your fight?" I ask as they sit down on the chairs next to me. My eyes scan the area for Mila and Alec who are playing a game in the water. They're both laughing and splashing each other with water.

"Hell yeah."

"You turning in early? We need to be up at five to get you conditioned and ready for the press conferences and early weigh-in."

"Yeah, we're heading to our room now."

"And you're good with your weight? You saw what happened with Sheffield at the last fight." Sheffield came in weighing just over two pounds too much to meet the one-eighty-five mark. He had two hours to lose the weight and couldn't do it. He relinquished his right to fight.

"Yep. My weigh-in tonight was perfect and it will stay that way." Tristan wasn't thrilled about not being able to be here for Jake's fight, but I assured him I would fill in as if I were Tristan myself. He's been there for me and it's the least I can do while he's enjoying the last couple days of his honeymoon with his new wife and daughters.

"Nice. All right, then I'll see you bright and early tomorrow morning." We bump fists then the guys take off back to their room. I locate Mila and Alec near the deep end of the pool, and pulling my shirt over my head, I head over to join them.

TWENTY-SEVEN

MILA

MASON COMES WALKING OVER, AND I HAVE TO FORCE MY JAW to close and the drool to stop flowing down my chin like a broken faucet. I don't think I'll ever get used to seeing Mason without his shirt on. The man is ripped beyond belief, but not in a bulky way. He's simply toned everywhere—from his strong neck and shoulders all the way down to his calf muscles. He's got a perfect six-pack and his skin is flawless. His swim shorts hang low on his hips as he saunters over to join Alec and me in the pool. I was worried the fans—specifically the women—would be hovering everywhere we went, but the hotel has the area under lock and key and only registered guests are getting in.

Mason walks over to the edge of the pool and gives me a mischievous smirk that tells me he's about to do something bad. But before I can figure out what it is, he's cannonballing into the pool and soaking me completely. He disappears under the water, and a few seconds later he's tugging on my foot. I think he's going to pull me under the water, but instead his hands glide up front of my legs and stop at the apex of my thighs. My eyes stay trained on my son, who is playing water basketball with a couple kids, the ache between my legs growing by the second from Mason's touch.

He comes up for air and circles around me until his back is against the side of the pool and my back is against his front. His dick is pressed up against my ass, and his finger runs down my front. It's dark outside and nobody can see anything he's doing to me, but I can feel it. I can feel him separating my folds and then his fingers entering me. He pumps in and out of me, his thumb massaging my clit. His other hand brushes my nipple through my swimsuit and my eyes dart around, wondering if anybody knows what's happening.

"Fuck, woman. You're cunt is always so tight. Even in the water, it sucks my fingers in." And it may be partially because my husband just whispered the word cunt in my ear, or because I'm scared of getting caught, or it may be because he knows exactly what to do to get me off, but I come instantly. My body shakes as he brushes my hair to the side and kisses the pulse point on my neck as I ride out my orgasm.

Just as my body calms down, his hands grab my ass. "Tonight, baby, I'm claiming this ass." Then he lays a wet kiss to my cheek playfully as if he didn't just finger me and make me come thirty seconds ago in a public pool.

"Hey Alec! Want to go down the waterslides before the food comes?" Mason shouts to my son who is still playing with the other kids.

"Yes!"

"Be back, baby." Mason gives me another kiss before swimming away from me and toward Alec. And as I watch them head toward the water slides my mind goes to my mom, and I know if she's in heaven looking down on us, she's smiling because I've finally found my one.

❤❤❤❤❤

"WANT TO SHOWER WITH ME?" MASON ASKS. HE PUSHES HIS swimsuit down and his dick springs free. Alec is asleep in the other room and we're in ours. Want to wear a child out? Take him swimming for a few hours. After he showered and was in pajamas, we put a movie on for him, and not even five minutes in, he was sound asleep.

"Sure." I pull the strings to my top and let them fall, the material covering my breasts falling at the same time. I unknot the side strings and my bottoms hit the floor. I'm fully aware I'm putting a show on for Mason, but I can't help it. The way he looks at me… it's as if I'm everything he could ever want or need. I went so long without having a man look at me this way, and now that I have it, I want it all the time.

As we shower the chlorine off our bodies, Mason plants kisses along my shoulders and neck, but he doesn't make any moves on me otherwise, and I make a note to initiate shower sex before we leave. This shower is like twice the size of mine. Once we're out and dried off, I remember what he mentioned in the pool regarding my ass, and butterflies start to take flight in my belly. It's as if Mason senses my nervousness because he wraps his arms around my waist as his lips seal over mine. He guides us over to the bed, his mouth only leaving mine long enough to lay me down under him. Needing to touch him, my hands come up so my fingers can run through his hair.

Mason breaks the kiss and whispers into my ear, "Turn over,

baby. On your knees." He backs up slightly so I can do as he says. I'm completely naked and vulnerable with my butt in the air, and I love it. I love every new thing we try together. I love that no matter where we are or what we're doing, Mason makes me feel loved and cherished.

With my head against the pillows, I peek around in time to see Mason lick his lips before he spreads my legs and his face disappears. His warm, wet tongue hits my clit and licks up my seam all the way to my puckered hole. I let out a moan that would be embarrassing if I wasn't so comfortable around Mason. He continues to lick me from one hole to the other with purposeful, languorous strokes. Every time his tongue reaches my clit, he stops and sucks on the sensitive nub, eliciting a needy groan out of me.

"This is going to feel cool for a second and then it'll feel warm." I can't see what he's talking about, but a short beat later cold liquid drips down my crack. Mason spreads my cheeks, and with his fingers, rubs the warming lube over and around my puckered hole. I feel him blow, and the lube warms up even more.

"I'm going to put this in you, baby. Just relax, okay?" He shows me a silver raindrop looking toy that has a pink jewel on the end. I'm assuming it's a butt plug because a few seconds later I feel the cold silver against my hole. He pushes it in slowly, and at first I'm scared it's going to hurt, but as he continues to push the toy into me inch by inch, I'm surprised when it doesn't.

"It's in all the way," Mason says. "How does it feel?"

I wiggle my butt for a second. "Full."

"Oh, you will be… soon." I feel his lips on my shoulder blades and then down my spine as he trails kisses downward, ending at the dip directly above my butt. I try to see what he's doing but it's hard in this position, so instead I close my eyes and relish in his touch.

I feel his fingers at my breasts, tweaking and pinching my nipples from underneath, and then I feel them at my pussy, entering me. He pumps his fingers in and out of me, and I feel myself getting wetter, more turned on with every pump. I can hear the slickness of my juices against his fingers as he fingers me good and deep. My body rubs against the mattress as he works me over.

"Mason." I let out a heady moan. I'm so close to letting go.

"Come for me, baby," he murmurs, his fingers never stopping. He must insert another finger into me because my pussy is suddenly even more full. Between the butt plug and his fingers, I feel deliciously filled and my body must agree because a few pumps later and I'm coming all over Mason's fingers.

He pulls his fingers out of me and I instantly miss his touch. Then I feel his dick enter me from behind. His hands grip the curves of my hips and his dick thrusts into me until I'm filled to the max. If I thought I was full with his fingers, I was wrong. He begins to fuck me from behind, and I'm meeting him thrust for thrust. I don't know what he's doing, but I can feel the butt plug moving in my ass against Mason's dick, and it's hitting something in me I didn't know exists.

Needing more, I start to beg Mason for something I never imagined I would beg a man for. "Mason, fuck my ass…please." I let out a whimper. He pulls out, and I hear the crinkling of a condom that has me remembering…"I'm on birth control. I started the pills the day of my period." I peek around at him, and he's grinning wickedly.

"Thank god… I'm going to fuck this perfect cunt raw the next chance I get. But the condom is for your ass." He bends over and places a kiss on my butt check. "Wouldn't be very gentlemanly of me to come in your ass the first time." He shoots me a wink, and I turn my face around, not wanting him to see me blushing. Only Mason can be sweet and crass at the same damn time.

More warming lube drips along my ass crack, and then he pulls the butt plug out, and I swear I almost come from that action alone. "I'm going to go slow. Tell me if it hurts and I'll stop."

"Just do it," I demand. I'm too turned on. My body is craving him too much. I need him in me now.

He pushes the tip into the tight ringed hole, and at first it hurts, but as he continues to push himself into me slowly, the pain turns into pleasure. "Oh. My. God," I groan, sticking my face into the pillow so my son won't hear me from the other room. I've never felt anything like this before. While it's a bit uncomfortable, it also feels good.

"I'm all the way in, baby. You okay?" Mason's hand glides down the center of my spine, and I shiver at his touch.

"Yes," I breath. "Please move," I beg.

Gripping my hip with one hand, he slowly pulls out and then pushes back in until he bottoms out. His other hand comes around and circles my clit. The friction feels so good that my body starts to rock against him, meeting him thrust for thrust. Another orgasm builds, different from anything I've ever experienced. It has me grinding against Mason's body as my hands find their way to my tits, my fingers pinching and pulling my nipples. The sensation I'm feeling almost has me scared—I've never felt this worked up before—and when my body can't handle it anymore, I let go. My ass tightens and my pussy contracts, and then I feel myself gush as I come all over Mason and the sheets. My eyes close, everything going black as my orgasm rolls through me.

"Holy shit," Mason groans, and I can feel when he's coming, his dick swelling in me, and even with a condom on, I feel his warm cum inside me. We both still, and before I have time to be embarrassed over what my body just did, Mason says, "That was the hottest fucking thing I've ever felt in my life." He slowly pulls out of me and I roll over onto my back and away from the now soaked sheets.

"Let's jump in the shower and then I'll call for new sheets." Mason winks, and I groan, covering my eyes with the back of my hand. "Don't hide." His voice is close, and when I peek out from under my hand, he's leaning down to kiss me. "That was amazing, Mila. You're amazing."

TWENTY-EIGHT

MASON

IT'S MONDAY MORNING, AND WHILE I SHOULD BE TRAINING with my fight coming up, I can't focus. This past weekend was one of the best weekends of my life. Fight Night went perfectly—Jake won his fight and Alec and Mila had a blast. Bella invited us to join them the following day at Sea World, and since Alec and Mila have never been, we accepted. Alec wasn't too thrilled with having to hang out with Bella's daughter, Micaela, so he stuck to my side most of the time. We went on all the rides he was tall enough for and watched all the shows. We got back late last night, and after he was in bed I spent the rest of the evening inside my wife.

"Aren't you going to welcome me home, fucker?" There's a smack to my head and when I turn around, Tristan is standing there, grinning from ear to ear.

"Hey, man!" I give him bro hug and welcome him back. "I'd ask about your trip but Mila said we're coming over for dinner tomorrow night, so I'll just wait to hear all about your Disney adventures then," I joke.

"Funny." He slaps my shoulder. "And that's fine because I'd rather talk about you." He cackles and I groan.

"What about me? How I need to train for this upcoming fight?"

Tristan looks at me like I've got two heads. "No, I want to discuss how the hell my best friend came to my wedding as a best man and went home as a husband." We go into his office and I tell him everything. From Mila and I conversing over the Plenty of Fish app to us getting married. I tell him about how I ended up watching Alec during spring break, then I confide in him about Mila and I connecting on a level I never thought was possible. And when I'm done, Tristan is shaking his head.

"Well, goddamn. I always knew this day would come, but I didn't think it would be so soon, and not with a woman who swore she would never touch you. I'm happy for you, man."

"Thanks." I let out a sigh. "Now I just have to make sure I don't fuck it all up."

Tristan gives me a long look before he says, "You need to give yourself a break. You're going to mess up. It's a given. But the key is to learn from your mistakes."

"Mila's already had one failed marriage. I need to make sure I don't make it two."

"Mason, you can't predict the future. You can do everything right and it still not work out. You can't live your life waiting for the other ball to drop." He's right, but it's hard to push the possibility of failure out of my head. Every time I think about me failing, I think about my mom, and how my dad's failures led her to prostitute herself out. She used to tell me I was like my dad. At the time I thought she meant it in a good way, but the fact she refuses to let me help her tells another story. She'd rather fuck strangers and sell drugs than trust me to take care of her. My dad drank and gambled. He put his addictions above his family. He died and left my mom to fend for herself. He's the reason she couldn't take care of me. Why she went to jail, and I lost the only parent I had left at thirteen years old. I refuse to believe I'm anything like my dad, and I know if given the chance I would do everything in my power to take care of my mom, but until she lets me in, there's nothing I can do.

And don't get me wrong. I know Mila isn't my mom. She has a degree and takes care of her son. She was doing a damn good job of handling shit before I came along, but that doesn't stop me from wondering what would happen if I failed her, if I broke her heart. My mom was doing okay until my dad started drinking and gambling. His addictions broke my mom's heart and she was never the same. I don't want Mila's heart to ever break, especially because of me. I might not be able to predict the future, but I can do everything in my power to make sure Mila's heart is handled with care.

Tristan's phone beeps at the same time mine does.

Mila: Change of plans. Dinner tonight with the Scotts at Burger Heaven. I'll meet you there at 5:30 after I pick up Alec from school.

"I guess we're having dinner tonight," I say after texting Mila back and letting her know I'll see her then.

Tristan and I spend the next several hours training, and when five o'clock rolls around, we shower and head downtown to meet everyone for dinner. I spot Mila, Charlie, and the kids at a table, and with them is… Gavin?

"What's her ex doing here?" I ask Tristan.

"Oh shit, I had invited him since we're hitting the field right afterward for practice."

I stop in my tracks and glance at Tristan. "Hitting the field for what?"

"Softball." He shrugs. "I joined Gavin's team since he was in need of another player. Didn't I tell you?"

"No." I shake my head. "You most certainly didn't tell me you play softball with my wife's ex-husband."

"Well, in my defense, she wasn't your wife when I agreed to play."

"How the fuck did I not know you're playing softball? Can you even play?"

Tristan laughs. "I don't know…you were busy, I guess. I think you were out with the guys or maybe at the gym, and I've only played a few games before I left for my honeymoon."

"Isn't softball for pussies who can't play baseball?" I say to fuck with him.

Tristan eyes me for a second before he laughs again. "Are you jealous?" His laughter gets louder.

"No, I'm not jealous!" Okay, maybe I'm a little jealous. But c'mon! My best friend is having a fucking bromance with Mila's ex-husband? *What the hell!*

"It's just softball, honey," Tristan says sweetly. "Don't worry… I'm still saving myself for you." He bats his eyelashes, and I smack him in the chest, knocking him back a step before I walk away, leaving him bent over and holding his stomach.

"Not cool, Mason. Don't make me break up with you!" he shouts, laughter filtering through his every word.

I get to the table before him and sit in the empty chair next to Mila, giving her a kiss on her cheek. "Hey, baby. How was your day?"

She turns toward me smiling. "Busy but good. I heard from the woman with People magazine. We're scheduled to do the interview Wednesday night."

"Sounds good." I give her another kiss, this time on her lips. Then I pull away and find Alec on the other side of her, sitting in between her and Gavin. "Hey, Bruiser, how was school?" I reach over Mila to knock fists with him.

Alec grimaces. "Boring. I wish it was spring break again. I'd rather be at the gym with you."

"Eww! No way!" Lexi screeches. "The gym is yucky and stinky and gross. Right, Georgia?"

Georgia nods in agreement, her nose scrunching up. "Yes! Yucky!"

I glance over at Alec, and he rolls his eyes. "Girls suck," he whines before his forehead hits the table.

"Don't say suck," Mila scolds, and I force myself not to laugh.

"You won't be saying that for much longer," I tell Alec, and with his forehead still resting on the table, he shakes his head back and forth, mumbling something about it never happening.

"Gavin." I turn my attention to Mila's ex-husband. "It's good to see you."

"You too. Thanks again for watching Alec last week."

"No problem. He's a great kid." I turn my attention away from Gavin to Tristan, who's now sitting next to Charlie and staring at me, his eyes dancing with laughter. *Fucker.*

The waitress comes over and takes everyone's orders. Once she's gone, the kids beg for money then take off to play the video games.

"How was the cruise?" Mila asks Charlie, animatedly.

"So much fun! The Disney parks were a blast but the cruise was amazing. The girls had Club Disney every day which meant adult time for us." Charlie glances up at Tristan, who's nodding slowly.

"Hell yes. I would have paid triple for that club."

"Alec hates Disney." Mila pouts. "I need a little girl or a cruise that has Club Fighter."

I chuckle at the club part, but then my mind goes to her pregnant with my baby, and my heart starts to race, my chest feeling like it's going to collapse. No way! It's one thing to help her with Alec occasionally—he's not mine. He has his own dad and mom. It's another thing to be responsible for my own child. What happens if I get injured and can't fight? Sure, I save most of my money in case something happens, but if something happened and I couldn't support our baby—

"You okay?" Tristan asks me. His look of concern has me wondering if I look as freaked out on the outside as I feel on the inside.

"Yeah," I choke out, grabbing my glass of water and downing it. "Just tired from training. I need to eat."

Mila glances over at me, and I can tell by the hurt look on her face, she isn't buying it.

"So, Tristan said you guys play softball?" I ask Gavin, hoping to change the subject.

"Yeah, we're actually winning this year. Made it to the playoffs. But then our third baseman got hurt at work, threw out his back. I need to find someone before the playoffs next weekend. Any chance you play?" Gavin questions, making it hard to hate him.

Anyone else, I would say no to, but the guy has already recruited Tristan, so of course I'm going to say yes. Tristan chuckles under his breath, and I shoot him a glare. "Mason wouldn't be interested in playing a puss—"

"Yeah, I'll play," I say, cutting off Tristan, who barks out a laugh. The women look from Tristan to me confused, but neither of them ask what's going on.

"Cool. We have practice tonight. Can you make it?"

"Sure." And then I remember it's not just me anymore, so I add,

"As long as it's okay with Mila." I move my hand to her thigh, but she pushes it off and rolls her eyes.

"I don't care. I need to use the restroom." She stands and Charlie stands as well. Fucking women don't even need to speak to communicate. Once they're gone, Tristan chuckles.

"That was real subtle."

"What?" I throw my hands up in the air.

"She mentioned having a baby and you about passed out on the spot."

I glance over at Gavin then glare at Tristan, not wanting to have this conversation in front of Mila's ex-husband. He catches my drift, but it's too late because Gavin says, "Just let it go. She'll get over it…" He shrugs, then adds, "Or actually, maybe you shouldn't. I let it all go, and it ended with us divorced." He shakes his head. "Anything I say, you should probably do the opposite."

Tristan laughs, and I wonder how the hell this is my life. I glance over at Mila walking back over to the table. She's still dressed in her aqua blue scrubs with yellow ducks all over them, but it doesn't stop her from looking sexy as hell. Her hair is up in a high ponytail, exposing her neck that I could spend hours kissing. Her lips are a tad bit shiny, and I would bet my left nut if I kissed her right now she would taste of raspberry from her favorite lip gloss she puts on every time she washes her hands.

She stops by the video game Alec is playing, and he must say something funny because she throws her head back with a laugh. And in that moment, I know how this became my life. That woman. I'm completely in love with her, and if she wants fifty goddamned kids I would give them to her, and then I would work my ass off to make sure they're all taken care of.

Not able to be away from her for another second, I get up and cut across the room to her. She spots me coming over and smiles softly, but it's not the smile she was just sporting. It's a fake, cheapened version, and I don't like it one bit. When I'm close enough to her that I can touch her, I place my hands on her hips and push her against the side of the video game out of view from Alec.

"Mason," she says, shocked. My hands go around her body until they're resting on her perfect ass. My lips pressing kisses along her jaw and down her neck. Mila lets out a soft sigh, and I love how my touch can relax her so quickly.

"I'll give you twenty little girls if that's what you want," I murmur into her ear so only she can hear me. Her arms come around my neck and she pushes me back slightly.

"What?" Her brows furrow.

"I'll give you twenty little girls," I repeat. "Although, Alec may kill us," I joke. "But if that's what you want, I'm down."

"You just about hyperventilated at the mention of one, and I was only joking." She arches a brow. "Plus, you can't determine the sex. We could end up with twenty boys."

I kiss her lips—and smile to myself when I taste the raspberry. "But you do want a baby?" She shrugs. "Remember the part of our vows about leading?"

"Okay! Yes, one day I would like another baby, and sure, I would love a little girl, but I wouldn't care if it's a boy. But not any time soon, I swear."

"Promise me when you're ready, you'll come talk to me." I kiss her lips again.

"I promise."

"Good, and until then…" I waggle my eyebrows. "I'll look up the positions that are best for making girls."

Mila laughs. "It doesn't work like that! It's not like, 'Oh, let's do it doggy-style' and you'll shoot out only girl sperm."

"We'll see," I say, already pulling my phone out to google it.

TWENTY-NINE

MILA

the journalist for People Magazine shakes Mason's hand and then mine one more time. We both thank her for having us before we head out of the office. I'm still in shock over all this. When we arrived at two o'clock, I figured we would answer a couple questions, take a picture, and then be home for dinner by five. Luckily, tonight is Gavin's night, and he picked up Alec from school, because I never would've made it to pick him up on time. It's already close to seven o'clock and we're finally leaving.

After answering questions for what felt like hours, we were whisked into wardrobe, hair, and makeup. And yes, I said *we*, because Mason is totally wearing freaking makeup. He didn't even seem fazed by it, which makes sense since he's done a million professional photo shoots. I just never realized he was wearing makeup in any of them. They took several photos of Mason and me and then several of Mason alone.

When we get outside, Mason's assistant-slash-publicist comes around the corner, throwing his cigarette onto the ground. "You all done?"

"Yep." Mason bumps his fist against Kenny's. "Thanks again for making sure no questions were asked about my mom."

"Of course, man, this isn't our first rodeo. Dawn said she'll have the article and photos for you to proof by the end of the week, and the money will be transferred once you approve it all."

"Thanks."

"Don't forget I'm going to need to transfer the money for my new car back over to you," I remind Mason, and he grins.

"We'll handle it."

"How much was it?" I ask. The floor model didn't have a price, but Mason assured me I would be okay, and I trusted him not to let me spend more than I'll make from going to this interview.

"Um…I can't remember off the top of my head."

"The BMW you purchased?" Kenny asks.

"Yeah, he lent me the money."

"I think it was a hundred—"

Mason cuts him off. "Kenny, don't you need to get home to your boyfriend?"

"A hundred what?" I ask Kenny, ignoring Mason. Surely, the SUV wasn't a hundred thousand dollars.

"Um… yeah, I do." He gives Mason an apologetic look.

"Mason…"

Mason slides his arm around the back of my shoulders and pulls me into his side. "Well, have a good night. Since we're in the area, I'm taking my wife out to dinner to her favorite restaurant." I look up at Mason, silently asking him to clarify. "Fondue, of course."

"How did you know I love—" And then I remember he was *GetHooked* and it was mentioned on my profile.

"The place that sells way-too-expensive cheese?" Kenny asks.

"Yep!" Mason laughs.

"Well, I guess you can afford it now." Kenny winks, and Mason laughs harder.

"Yeah, yeah." Mason fist bumps Kenny once more. "See-ya."

"Bye." I wave to Kenny. "It was nice to meet you."

"You as well. Keep this guy in line for me, will ya?"

"Of course." I lift up on my tiptoes and give Mason a chaste kiss on his cheek. Once we part ways with Kenny, I ask again. "How much was the SUV?"

"It doesn't matter. Do you like it?"

"You know I do. I love it."

"Then consider it my wedding gift to you." Hearing the frustration in Mason's voice, I let it go for now, but the minute I get the money I'll be paying him back. And if he won't let me pay for the SUV, I'll find another way to pay him back.

We arrive at The Melting Pot in Thousand Oaks and I'm surprised to learn Mason made a reservation. The hostess sits us at a booth, and when Mason goes to sit next to me, I stop him. "Oh no. I need all this room." I spread my hands across the table.

Mason chuckles. "Jesus, woman. It's just cheese."

"Uh-uh." I shake my head. "It's fondue. Sit over there." I point to the booth across from me. We both silently peruse the menu, and a few minutes later a waitress greets us.

"I'm Michelle, and I'll be your waitress this evening. Have you ever dined with us?"

"I have," I say.

"I'm a cheese virgin," Mason replies, and the waitress blushes.

"Do you know what you would like to order, or can I help you go through the menu?"

Before Mason can answer, I say, "I know what we're ordering."

THIRTY

MASON

I'M SITTING ACROSS FROM MILA INSTEAD OF NEXT TO HER AT The Melting Pot—some ridiculously-priced restaurant that serves hot cheese—because apparently, she needs room to get her cheese on. The waitress asks about the menu, and before I can even blink, Mila is ordering without even looking at the menu.

"We would like the Classic Fondue for two. Extra shrimp instead of pork. Two house salads with the sweet and tangy dressing, cheddar cheese with beer, and for the dinner, we would like bourguignonne." She stops speaking—I think to breathe—and then adds, "And we would like extra mushrooms." She hands the waitress the menus. "Oh! And for dessert, we'll have the s'mores. Thanks."

The waitress finishes writing and looks up. "I guess you have been here before."

"Yeah." Mila smiles but then she frowns.

The waitress asks what we'd like to drink, and after we both tell her water, she says she'll be back out with the first course and our waters in a few minutes.

"What made you frown?" I ask once the waitress walks away.

"I used to come here with Gavin. Well, not this one. The one in Los Angeles before it shut down."

"And that has you frowning?"

"I didn't even think about the fact that we used to come here. I'm not sure if you're supposed to bring your new husband to the same place your ex-husband used to take you."

"It's just a restaurant, Mila." I play it off, secretly reminding myself to look up where else I can find another cheese place.

"Yeah, but it's the only place Gavin would bring me to. He hated it here, but he agreed to come once a year for our anniversary…when we could afford it." She frowns again. "Maybe this was a bad idea."

I push myself out of the booth and slide in next to her, turning to face her. Taking her hands in mine, I pull them up to my lips and kiss her knuckles "I'm playing on the same softball team with the guy. We had dinner with him just last night…Hell, he was giving me advice on what not to do when it comes to you." Mila groans, and I chuckle. "I think it's okay we're eating at a restaurant you guys ate at."

"I'm sorry. You're right. Okay, back over to your side! I need room to cook my food."

"Not happening. Now that I'm near you, you aren't getting rid of me." I give her a kiss and she pouts but lets me stay.

The waitress comes over, sets down our waters, and places a small pot on a burner. She starts naming off the ingredients as she pours each one into the pot and stirs. I look over at Mila who's grinning like a fool at the food. It's definitely cheddar cheese, but it looks like there's only enough for a damn mouse.

"Is this all you can eat?" I ask.

"Excuse me?" The waitress tilts her head to the side as she sets down a small bowl of cut-up bread and some diced apples.

"Will you bring us more when we run out?"

Mila giggles. "No, there are three other courses."

"Babe." I look at Mila. "I'm a growing boy. The next course better be triple this size."

"Oh, hush!" She laughs. Then to the waitress she says, "Thank you."

I stay seated next to Mila as she shows me what to do—shove a piece of bread or apple onto the two-pronged fork and dip it into the melted cheese. She alternates between eating her pieces and feeding me, and while the food isn't filling in the slightest, I'm enjoying her company. When we're done with the cheese, we get our salads, and after those, the meat is brought out. Now, when I read the menu it listed several types of meats and vegetables. So, here I am thinking I'm about to get a nice-sized meal. Imagine my shock when Michelle sets down a ceramic plate that is no more than ten inches long and four inches wide, and on the plate are bite size pieces of each meat. Next, she places a tiny bowl of vegetables on the table, and then she places an additional bowl of mushrooms in front of Mila.

And you ready for the kicker? It's all fucking raw!

"Okay, I know you've done it before, but just as a reminder, chicken is four minutes, shrimp is three minutes, and steak is anywhere from two to four minutes depending on how you like it. Potatoes are four minutes, and stuffed mushrooms are three minutes."

"Thank you!" Mila gushes.

"I'm sorry." I glance from the uncooked food to the waitress. "Are we supposed to cook this ourselves?"

The waitress frowns. "Um… yeah?"

"Let me get this straight." I look from the waitress to Mila. "We pay hundreds of dollars for food that even a mouse would still be hungry after eating, and to top it off, we have to cook our own food?"

"Um…yeah?" the waitress says again.

"It's not about the quantity, Mason," Mila chides. "It's about the experience."

The waitress's lips turn into a tight smile. "Let me know if you need anything."

"Babe." I turn back toward Mila. "I'm going to need to *experience* a whole lot more food than this."

"You'll be full once we're done. Trust me. It doesn't look like a lot but it's filling. Plus we have dessert coming too." She plants a wet kiss on my cheek and then stabs the raw shrimp with her fork, dips it into some orange batter looking shit, and puts it into the hot oil to cook.

We get done eating and I pay the bill. As we walk out to my car, Mila hugs my waist and says, "That was so good! And I'm so full. Thank you for bringing me here! Did you like it?"

"Yeah, it was good," I say honestly, because it was good. Aside from having to cook my own damn food, the meat was flavorful, the stuffed mushrooms were delicious, and I fully enjoyed feeding her chocolate covered strawberries. "But next time"—I wrap my arm around her and give her a quick kiss to her temple—"we're going by the steakhouse on the way."

Mila snorts. "It's about the experience!" she whines, and I laugh.

"And I totally get that. But next time I'm going to need to experience a twenty-four ounce sirloin strip before we come here."

"I give up!" She sighs. "I love it, so more for me."

Once we're home, Mila excuses herself to take a shower. While she's in there, I undress out of my clothes and throw on a pair of sweatpants. I go through the mail I finally picked up from my post office box and find a couple envelopes from my attorney. I stick them into my drawer to deal with later. It's probably contract stuff since I'm due to renew my UFC contract soon. Grabbing my laptop from the kitchen, I get comfortable on the bed and start going through emails. I pay a couple bills and make a transfer to Mila's account for my portion of our bills.

I hear the shower turn off, and a few minutes later, she appears. She's got her plush cream-colored robe wrapped around her body and a fluffy towel wrapped around her head. She's free from all that makeup they made her wear for the photoshoot, and she looks fucking beautiful.

"Whatcha doing?" She comes over and sits on the edge of the bed, her robe parting down the middle slightly, revealing the swell of her breasts. Pushing the laptop to the side, I lift her up so she's straddling my lap. Her body is still damp from the shower, and I can feel her hot, bare pussy against my crotch. She wraps her arms around my neck, and her fingers run through my hair, massaging my scalp. I've had sex with so many damn women the last several years and not a single one of those sexual experiences compare to simply having this woman sitting on my lap.

My hands move across her hips and belly, and when I get to her middle, I undo the tie holding the material together, separating her robe the rest of the way until she's completely naked in front of me. My eyes lock on her luscious tits and pert nipples before I glance up to her face. She's staring at me, her fingers still massaging my scalp.

"I was paying some bills. I transferred money to you for my half of the bills," I say, answering her question. "Now, I'm admiring my wife's naked body."

I bring my hand around to her nape and pull her face toward me for a kiss. The second our lips touch, my gut tightens. I feel it every time we kiss. It's as if my body needs her to flourish. Her touch, her kiss, our connection, it breathes air into my lungs and allows me to keep living. It's as if, until the day I allowed myself to need her, I wasn't really living, just merely surviving. I never imagined ever depending on someone else for anything. I swore I never would. The hardest thing I ever did was live with Tristan's family when I was eighteen. But even then, I made sure to never eat any of their food, to buy all my own toiletries, and contribute in any way I could.

But this need... it's different. It's inside of me. Mila doesn't ask for anything materialistic. I've seen her bank account and she's broke. She literally lives paycheck to paycheck just like my mom did. But she doesn't bitch about it or blame anybody. She doesn't make Alec feel like he's a burden or point fingers at her ex-husband, who, let's be real, can afford to give her more since his real estate company is doing damn good. She's the strongest woman I know and I wish my mom could've had half her strength.

"What's going on in that head of yours?" Mila tilts my chin up, so our eyes meet. "You look like you're a million miles away."

"Just thinking about us," I admit honestly. My fingers come up and tweak her pink nipples. Her body squirms and her pussy rubs my now hard dick.

"What about us?" Mila leans in and gives me a kiss.

"I know we've only been married for a short time, but I've never felt this content. Like everything I need is right under this roof. You, Alec..." I look her in the eye and tell her the truth of what I'm feeling. "I'm so fucking scared, Mila." Her beautiful, plump lips twist into a frown, but she doesn't say a word. "The only people I've ever needed were my mom and dad, and my needs proved to be nothing more than a weight they couldn't carry. I know I'm not a child anymore, but the concept is still the same. My mom and I needed my dad and he couldn't handle it. He drank and gambled his life away until he died. I needed my mom, and she couldn't handle it.

"I see you with Alec, and your situation is so similar. You live paycheck to paycheck to make ends meet. Gavin is a nice guy, but he still pays you what he was making years ago when he couldn't afford to pay you much. Yet, I watch you and see how strong you are. Alec needs you, and you take care of him. I don't want to be a weight holding you down, Mila. If I'm ever too much. If I want too much sex, or too much of your time... If I ever prevent you from putting Alec first, promise me you'll tell me."

THIRTY-ONE

MILA

I'M SITTING ON MASON'S LAP, NAKED, YET IT FEELS LIKE HE'S IS the one completely baring himself to me. He looks at me with unshed tears brimming his lids, and I want nothing more than to hug him tight and never let him go. My heart hurts so badly for the man sitting under me. He's almost thirty years old, but he sounds like a child as he confides his deepest fears to me. His father and mother made him feel like such a burden that he's terrified to depend on anyone, or for anyone to depend on him. He's petrified he'll let us down, and equally petrified we'll either let him down or we'll resent him when we try to meet his needs.

"You will never feel like a burden to me, Mason." I frame the sides of his face with my hands and bring my lips to his, hoping every ounce of love I feel for him will transfer to him through our kiss.

I feel him pulling back, but I'm done discussing this. Nothing I say is going to change how he feels. My actions, over time, is what will show him and prove to him his love isn't a burden. His parents were so damn wrong for what they did to him. And once his dad died, instead of taking responsibility and pulling her shit together, his mom tried to take the easy way out. She put her own needs above her son's. As a mother, your child's needs come first, always. You do everything in your power to make your child feel loved and wanted and cherished. You could be an inch away from living on the damn street and your child shouldn't have a fucking clue. What Mason's parents did, no parent should ever do to their child, and I'm going to spend the rest of my life showing him what real love feels like.

My lips meet his once again, our tongues swirling around each other. With one hand using Mason's shoulder to hold me up, I rise up enough so I can use my other hand to pull his dick out of his pants while he pulls the wrapped towel off my head and throws it to the floor. Gripping his shaft, I lower myself onto him, his hard, thick, length stretching me wide until I'm fully seated. Our kiss becomes harder, rougher, Mason's teeth nip at my lips as I move up and down. His fingers entwine around the strands of my wet hair, holding me close to him. Our tongues and mouths and bodies are connected in every way as we make love to each other. All too soon, I'm moaning out my orgasm, and soon after Mason is finding his own release.

"It's okay to be scared," I whisper against Mason's mouth. "Just know, when you feel like you're alone in the dark, I will be here. I will always be your light."

THIRTY-TWO

MASON

"SURPRISE!" EVERYONE SHOUTS WHEN I STEP INTO TRISTAN'S house. When Mila texted me to meet her here, I thought it was for a simple barbeque. I had no clue I was walking into a surprise birthday party for me. I glance around the living room and it looks like Harry Potter threw up everywhere. I'm talking balloons, streamers, posters. If it was created for a birthday party and has Harry Potter on it, it's in this house. Mila comes running over and hugs me.

"Happy Birthday! I know it's tomorrow, but I was afraid if I did it for tomorrow you would get suspicious." She gives me a kiss on my cheek and steps back so everyone else can wish me a Happy Birthday. I greet everyone, giving hugs to the women and handshakes to the guys, but the entire time I'm in shock. I've never in my thirty years been given a birthday party, let alone one as cool as Harry freaking Potter. Sure, Tristan would take me out for a drink or the guys would buy me a lap dance at a club, but men don't do parties. This entire ordeal is all Mila, and she has no idea how much it means to me.

"Mason! Look at the cake!" Alec grabs my hand and pulls me toward the kitchen. "Mom let me pick it out!" Sitting on the counter is a huge multi-layer cake. When I get closer, I see each layer is a different Harry Potter book, and the topper is none other than the sorting hat!

"You did a great job picking it out, Bruiser," I say, trying not to get choked up. "It's the best cake I've ever had." I don't bother to tell him it's the only cake I've ever had.

"I'm glad you like it," Mila says, joining Alec and me.

I pull her toward me. "Thank you," I whisper against her lips.

"Eww!" Alec yells. "I'm going swimming!" He runs out of the kitchen.

TRISTAN IS MANNING THE BARBEQUE WITH HIS DAD, KADEN, while the rest of the adults are all chatting and mingling near the pool, watching the kids swim. I'm sitting on a patio chair watching Alec and Mila. Alec is swimming away from Lexi who is yelling something about having the cheese touch and needing to get rid of it, and Mila is sitting along the edge of the pool, her feet dipped into the water, next to Charlie, laughing. Every now and then she locks eyes with me and shoots me a smile or a wink.

"So, the big three-oh, huh?" Ashley sits next to me and pats my leg, smiling at me. She's the closest thing to a mother I've had since my mom went to prison, and I'm glad she and Kaden have moved to California.

"Yeah, yeah. I'm getting old." I roll my eyes. When she doesn't say anything I look over at her and she's grinning like a freaking Cheshire cat.

"What?"

"Happy looks good on you."

"And what does happy look like?" I joke, but she answers seriously.

"When I saw you sitting outside of Cooper's gym, looking more like a lost little boy than like the eighteen-year-old man you were, as a mother my heart broke for you. But you wouldn't let anybody pity you. From the moment you stood up and shook my hand and told me you were there to train at the best gym because you needed to become a UFC fighter"—she laughs but it's watery from the emotion embedded in every word she speaks—"I knew you would conquer the world. And you did. You busted your butt and became the champion.

"But through it all. Every win, every laugh, every smile, every smart-ass joke there was something missing. Until now. Until *her*." She smiles at me warmly. "I can see it in your smile—it's bigger, brighter. I can see it in the way you watch her and her son—protective and loving. It's the way Kaden used to watch me and Tristan and our girls—the way he still does."

She sighs. "I'm not going to lie…I was starting to get worried this day wouldn't come. Not because you aren't capable of loving someone. We all know you are. You were such a godsend when Tristan went through everything. You stood by his side and helped him raise Lexi. But even after everything you did for my son and granddaughter, you still didn't believe you were capable of love, deserving of it. I watched you hide behind your one-night stands and your jokes and I prayed for this day. I'm so happy for you, Mason. I'm so happy you let love in."

I smile at her and nod in agreement, but I don't tell her what I'm thinking. It's not that I let love in. It's that I let Mila in. There's no love or happiness without Mila and her son. They are the definition of it.

"Mason!" Alec yells, and I turn my head toward him so he knows I'm listening. "Come play with me! It's all girls."

I turn back around to Ashley, unsure of what to say, but like the amazing person she is, she gives me an out. "You don't have to say anything," She smiles. "I'm just so happy you're happy." We both stand and she pulls me into a hug. "I love you, sweetie." This isn't the first time she's told me she loves me, but over the years I never said it back. Not only did I not understand what the word truly meant, but what I did understand, I didn't believe in. But now…those words…they mean everything.

"I love you too."

I hear her gasp softly at my words, but she doesn't say anything. She never has. She's always loved me as if I was her own son…from the first day she took me in.

THIRTY-THREE

MASON

"DON'T FORGET WE HAVE PRACTICE TONIGHT." I'M SITTING IN Tristan's kitchen at the breakfast bar while he makes us both a protein shake. We finished a hardcore workout, and since Charlie needs to be at the art studio late for an adult party Emma couldn't do, Tristan had to run to pick the girls up from preschool and bring them home.

"Are you bringing the girls?"

"Yeah, they just hang out in the dugout." He hands me my shake as Georgia and Lexi run down the hall and into the kitchen. Lexi swings the fridge door open and huffs not even a second later.

"Daddy, I can't find anything to eat. When will Mommy be home?" My eyes shift toward the fridge and see it's filled to the brim. If that's empty, I can't imagine what full looks like.

"Lex, grab some fruit. I'll make dinner in a little bit."

"But Mommy makes us snacks after school, and my belly is so hungry now."

"We can make them," Georgia whispers, her eyes flitting from Tristan to Lexi. She's come a long way from the shit her biological father put her through, but there are still times when she gets nervous about asking to do certain things. Tristan, the damn good dad he is, picks up on it immediately and stops what he's doing to kneel down at her level.

"You absolutely can," he says warmly to Georgia, and she grins softly.

"Yay!" Lexi squeals. "Let's play Mommy!" Then she turns toward Tristan. "Can we make you guys a snack?" She tries her best to sound like Charlie and I chuckle at her cute imitation.

"Sure," Tristan says, sitting on the stool next to me and taking a sip of his shake. The girls squeal and start pulling different packages from the fridge, laying it all out on the floor since the counter is too high for them. I catch Tristan watching them, a wide grin across his face, and I pat him on his shoulder.

"You look happy." Well shit, now I sound like Ashley.

He lets out a low chuckle. "I am. I really am. I have Charlie and our girls. My parents are living down the street." He gives me a pointed look. "And I don't have to worry anymore about your ass dying alone."

I let out a snort and take a sip of my shake. "I've only been married for a month. I still have plenty of time to mess it all up."

"What's that supposed to mean?" He turns toward me, and I tell him the truth, exactly what I'm thinking.

"Every morning I wake up and wonder why she's with me. I go through my day waiting for her to realize she fu—screwed up. When we go to bed, I wait for her to tell me she made the wrong decision."

Tristan's about to say something, when Lexi and Georgia come over to us, their cute little behinds carrying napkins full of food. "Here you go, Daddy." Lexi hands Tristan his afterschool snack.

"Thank you, Lex."

"Here, Uncle Mason." Georgia hands me mine.

"Oh, thank God!" I sigh dramatically. "I'm starving." Georgia giggles.

"Can we eat our snack at the drawing table?" Lexi asks Tristan. Lexi, Georgia, and Charlie all love to color and paint, so when they made their renovations to the house, Tristan added a nook type of area off the kitchen where the girls could do arts and crafts and not destroy the good table.

"Go ahead," he tells them. "I'm going to make dinner in a few minutes and then we're going to the baseball field." The girls groan but don't argue, taking their food to the table.

"Now, back to your insecurity issues. Why would you think Mila's going to regret marrying you? I've only seen you two together a handful of times, but she's always happy."

"That's just it!" I throw my arms up. "She's always happy. There's no way it's this easy. I read her profile on the dating site. She wants the fairy tale. I haven't done anything to take care of her. She pays her half of the bills. Takes care of Alec. She works every day. We switch off cooking. She does all the laundry, and I play video games with Alec. I haven't read many Disney stories, but I doubt that's the fairy tale."

"Did she actually say she wants a fairy tale?"

"No, but it's implied."

Tristan scoffs. "The fairy tale is make believe. Women aren't looking for a guy to find her glass slipper or save her from the bad guy. They just want to be loved and heard and appreciated." He shrugs. "Oh, and for their husbands to remember the important dates like Valentine's Day, your anniversary, and their birthday."

My mind runs through the dates. Valentine's Day has already passed, we just got married…shit, when's her birthday? She threw me a Harry Potter birthday party and I don't even know when hers is.

Pulling my phone out of my pocket, I shoot her a text.

Me: When's your birthday?

She replies immediately.

Mila: May 3rd

"Shit! Her birthday is in two weeks."

Tristan chuckles. "You need to chill out. You're going to give yourself an ulcer."

"This is exactly why I didn't want to be with anyone," I point out. "The odds are stacked against us. I can do everything in my to make her happy, but what happens when I can't? What happens when I forget a holiday? Or worse, what happens if I lose my job? What if she gets sick and needs a goddamned kidney and I can't give her one?"

I sigh and scrub my hands up and down my face. "I realize I'm freaking out, but I can't help it. The expectations are always present. Every day I have to think about someone else, their wants and needs. I have to make sure she's taken care of."

"And you don't want to do that?" Tristan questions, his tone completely free of any judgement.

"I do. That's not the problem. I want to take care of her. I want to make her happy. I thought I would hate it, resent her for it, but I don't. Knowing she's happy does some shit to me I can't even explain. But what happens when she's not happy? Because let's be real… it's a possibility. She's already been through one divorce. And look at my mom. My dad couldn't make her happy… I couldn't make her happy. And over twenty years later, my mom still isn't happy. So what happens when I can't make Mila happy? What happens when I can't take care of her?"

Even to my own ears, I sound fucking crazy, but I can't stop the words from vomiting out. "You know where it's going to leave me? Dying alone. Only, I will have known what it's like to be loved by Mila and I'll be fucked."

Tristan stands and walks around to the other side of the counter and looks me dead in the eye. "You're right." He nods, and I flinch at his words, not expecting him to agree with me. "You're absolutely right. You can do everything in your power to take care of Mila and her son. You could move heaven and earth to make her happy, and in the end, she can still leave you. I've told you this before. Nothing in life is guaranteed. But you can't live your life with that mindset—waiting to fuck up. Waiting for her to leave you. All you can do is wake up each day and love the fuck out of your wife. You make the best choices you can, and if it's meant to be, it will be. Stop focusing on the negative and focus on the positive."

Fuck, I know he's right, but it's so goddamned hard. Since the day I turned eighteen, everything I've ever done has been in my control—from moving to Las Vegas, to training at Cooper's gym, to choosing to move to California. Every woman I slept with and kept at arm's length were my choice. Every person I choose to hang out with. Every decision I make only affects me…until now. I swore to myself I would never be vulnerable again. The day my mom was arrested, and for the years following, nothing was in my control. Where I lived, who I lived with. I was a burden to my mom, to the state, to my foster parents. I learned to only depend on myself and to never put myself in a situation where I'm responsible for someone else's happiness. But here I am, and I know no matter how hard it is, no matter how scared I am, I can't walk away from Mila.

"Just know when you feel like you're alone in the dark, I will be here. I will always be your light."

Needing her light, I grab my phone and excuse myself to call Mila. She picks up on the first ring. "Mason." Her voice is cold and harsh, and my stomach drops.

"Mila, what's wrong?"

"I looked at my bank account when paying the bills today. Why is there two hundred and fifty thousand dollars in there?"

I let out a sigh of relief. "Jesus, woman, you scared me. I thought I did something wrong."

"Why is there two hundred and fifty thousand dollars in there, Mason?" she asks again.

"That's from the interview. Kenny told you they would be transferring the money over."

There's a moment of silence and then Mila says, "I—I didn't know it was that much. I'm not taking all that. I'm not even the famous one. I'm just the woman who got drunk and convinced you to marry me."

Now it's my turn to be silent. I know she didn't mean it as a dig, but it still hurt. "Can we talk about this tonight? I was calling to see if you're going to practice."

"I can't. I need to make Alec dinner and get some laundry done. I'll see you at home."

"Okay." I go to hang up but before I do, I add, "I love you, Mila." It's the first time I've said the words to her since I admitted to her the weekend of the fight I'd fallen in love with her, and I'm not sure why I pick now to say them again. Maybe it's knowing she's upset with me, and I can't show her how I feel. Maybe it's because I feel her pulling away. I don't know.

"I love you, too, Mason. I'll see you when you get home."

We hang up and my phone immediately rings. Assuming and hoping, it's Mila calling back, I hit the green circle, accepting the call. "Mila?"

"No, who's Mila?" The voice is low and raspy, definitely a woman's voice, and even after not hearing it for several years, I know right away whose voice is on the other end of the line.

"Mom."

"I was given your number from your attorney…" She sounds scared, and flashbacks of my past surface.

"I told him he could give it to you. Is everything okay?"

"I…um…never mind. This was a mistake. I shouldn't have called. I'm sorry."

The line goes silent and I pull up my recent calls list and click on the number she called from to call her back. It rings several times and then a man answers.

"Hello? My mom called from this number?"

"Sorry, this is a public phone." *Shit, they still have those?*

"Is there a woman in the area?"

"Nope. There's no woman around here."

"Okay, thank you." I hang up, and take several calming breaths to stop myself from punching something. I know my mom is hurting. I could hear it in her voice. I imagine she's too old now to have sex with guys for money, but then again, the guys she was with would probably screw anything with a hole. I have no idea where she's living or how she's surviving, and instead of letting me in, trusting me to help her, she would rather suffer. She resents me so damn much, she would rather live in and out of jail than allow me to take care of her.

I WALK THROUGH THE DOOR, DIRTY AND SMELLING OF CLAY from the baseball field. The house is dark and silent. I drop my bag to the ground by the door and make my way down the hall. I stop by Alec's room and peek in to find him fast asleep. When I get to our bedroom, Mila is already in bed. Her breathing is even, but I know she's not asleep because she's not snoring. Adorable fucking woman swears she doesn't snore but she does, and I love it. It reminds me she's sleeping next to me every night.

I jump in the shower and when I come out, I find her in the same position she was in when I first walked in—and still not snoring. I plug my phone in to charge and lie down on my side of the bed. I wait a few seconds just to make sure she's definitely not snoring, and when I don't hear anything, I bring my arm around her waist and pull her into me, rolling her over in the process so she's forced to face me.

"Mason! What're you doing?" Mila shrieks. "I was sleeping!"

"No, you weren't."

"Yes, I was." She glares.

"Nope, and even if you were, I still would've woken you up," I point out, and Mila huffs. "We agreed. No going to bed angry."

"Whatever," she murmurs, and I pull her closer.

"Talk to me."

"I don't want anything from you, especially your money." Her words are watery and I can tell she's doing her best to keep her emotions in check. "I already went to the bank and transferred it all to you." Tears spill over and flow down her face. She rolls away from me and off the bed, hightailing it to the bathroom and closing the door before I can even get a word in.

I follow after her and knock on the door. "Mila, come out please. I don't know what's going on, but we're still married and our vows said we don't go to bed angry, so I'm not going to bed until we discuss this." When she doesn't respond, I slide down the door, the back of my head hitting the wood.

"Mila, you promised to lead. I need you to talk to me, please," I beg, needing some guidance here. I have no clue what happened, and my emotions are already all over the damn place from hearing from my mom. I'm not sure I can handle letting down two women in one day.

As I sit on the other side of the door, I hear her soft sobs and they remind me of my mom. All the times our electric would get shut off and she wouldn't have the money to pay it. She didn't know I could hear her crying, but I did. Or after she would get home from work and I would hear her in the shower crying for God knows how long. Sometimes all it would take was me doing or saying the wrong thing. She would bawl her eyes out until she passed out in bed. Like the naïve child I was, I would constantly ask her what she needed, what I could do to make it better, and she would tell me there was nothing I could do. I always felt so helpless. I was hoping so fucking badly when I heard her voice today she was going to let me help her. Of course she didn't.

"Mila, please, baby," I plead. "Talk to me." The lock on the door clicks and it opens, the hard wood leaving my back. I get up off the ground and she's standing there, looking sad with her puffy eyes and tear-stained cheeks.

"I was paying the bills and saw way too many digits in my bank account."

"That's the payment from People Magazine."

"Two hundred and fifty thousand dollars for each of us?"

"No, two hundred and fifty total. I'm not that popular." I chuckle. "I don't need that money. I had them give it all to you."

"Mason." She sighs. "I don't want—" I cover her lips with my fingers before she can finish her sentence.

"That's all you were upset about? Having too much money in your account?"

"That's a lot of money, Mason! I thought maybe you were paying me off..."

"Paying you off?" I ask, confused as fuck.

"You know…like you were going to divorce me."

I pull her over to the edge of the bed and into my lap, then I kiss her hard. "That's not happening. That money is from the interview, and tomorrow morning it will be back in your account."

"Minus the money for the car."

"The car was your wedding gift."

"Ugh! I would argue but I know you aren't going to let me win," she says, giving in.

"Damn right." I pull her face down to kiss her again. "And now that we've gotten the not going to bed angry vow covered, let's move on to our other vows…" I waggle my eyebrows. "Like the out of this world sex."

THIRTY-FOUR

MILA

"RUN! RUN! RUN!" ALEC IS SCREAMING NEXT TO ME AT MASON as he rounds second base then third. "Go home!" he screams, jumping up and down as Mason runs toward home plate. Their team made it to the playoffs and then to the championship, and if Mason gets this homerun, they will be the champions. The player in the outfield throws the ball to the catcher, and as Mason slides into home, hands first, his helmet flies off his head as the catcher leans down to tag him. Their heads collide—the catcher's hard helmet to Mason's helmetless head—and the crowd gasps at the loud cracking sound they make.

"Oh, shit!" Alec yells. I should probably scold him for cursing, but I'm too busy running toward the field to see if Mason is okay. He's lying on his back, his eyes closed.

"Call 911!" someone shouts. Tristan and several of the guys are kneeling around Mason's unconscious body. I drop to the ground beside him and fall into nurse mode, my fingers checking for his pulse. Then I open his mouth to make sure his airway is open and he's breathing.

"Should we try to sit him up?" Gavin asks.

"No, he could be injured." My fingers glide down the side of Mason's face. "Mason, please wake up," I beg. His eyelids flutter slightly. "Mason," I say again. "Wake up."

The sound of the ambulance fills the air, and a minute later, two EMTs are running over to us with a stretcher. I explain to them what happened, then they carefully put a neck brace on Mason and turn him over enough to get a sheet under him. Once they have him ready, they transfer him onto the stretcher. As they're locking him in, Mason's eyes groggily open. He tries to sit up, but the EMT tells him what happened and to remain still. He could have a neck injury. A spinal injury. He could have a concussion. Brain damage. He could be paralyzed. My mind ticks down every possibility as I follow them to the ambulance.

Once they have him loaded, they let us know which hospital they're taking him to. Charlie offers to take the kids home, but Alec throws a fit. "I'm not going home! I need to go to Mason. Mom, please."

"I'll bring Alec," Gavin offers, "that way if he needs to wait in the waiting room, I can sit with him."

"Thank you." I'm already heading to my vehicle when Tristan grabs my hand.

"Leave your car here and I'll drive you. You're shaking." He lifts my hand up and sure enough, I'm trembling like crazy.

"Okay," I agree.

We arrive at the hospital and go straight to the front desk to get any information available. "I'm Mila Street, Mason's wife."

The woman at the front desk types something in on the computer. "It shows here you are Mason Street's emergency contact and next of kin. Can you come with me to fill out a couple forms while he's being checked out?"

I answer as many questions about Mason as I can, and what I can't, I call Tristan over to see if he knows. Once she thanks us and lets us know as soon as he's allowed to have visitors, she'll call us, we join Gavin and Alec in the waiting room.

"Do you know when Mason added me to his forms?" I ask Tristan.

"Probably this week. He had to update everything for the upcoming fight." This information has me stunned. So many times I've questioned if he really is all in, especially when that money ended up in my bank account, but him adding me as his emergency contact and next of kin tells me that he really is in this for the long haul.

What feels like ten hours later—but is really only an hour—we're taken back to Mason's room. Gavin stays in the waiting room, but Alec comes with Tristan and me. Mason's lying in a hospital bed, wires hooked up to him, and his eyes are closed. There's a nurse standing next to his bed, writing his numbers down.

"Mason," I cry out. He opens his eyes and looks at me, and I breathe a small sigh of relief. "What did the doctor say?"

"They brought me back for a CT scan and did a concussion examination. The doctor also checked me for any spinal injuries. I'm fine. Probably have a concussion, so I'm stuck here for a few hours. My head is pounding and hurts like a bitch," he complains. When he looks over and sees Alec standing there, he says, "I mean it hurts really freaking bad."

"Do you need more pain medication?" the nurse asks him.

"Yes," he whines, "I feel like death." I cover my mouth to stop myself from laughing because an injured Mason is such a baby.

Relieved he's okay, I take a play from his book. "You should be used to the pain…you're a fighter. Don't you get hurt all the time?"

Mason scoffs. "No, that would be the other guy. I always win." Tristan cackles and Alec fist bumps him.

"Yeah, Mom, Mason doesn't get hurt," Alec adds agreeing with Mason. "He's too tough."

"I'm glad you're okay, man," Tristan says. "I'm going to head outside to call Charlie. You know how she is about hospitals. She went home with the girls to wait and see if she should come up."

After hanging out with Mason for a little bit, I insist Alec goes home with his dad. He's not thrilled, but we aren't sure how long it will be before they release Mason. Tristan hangs around since he's the only one out of the three of us with a vehicle. A few hours later, the doctor prescribes some pain meds for Mason and has the nurse print out his discharge papers. With instructions to get some rest and to return if he experiences any symptoms such as dizziness, fatigue, vomiting, nausea, or ringing in his ears, we leave the hospital. Tristan drops us off at my vehicle and we agree to pick up Mason's car tomorrow. When we get home, he holds me close and I thank God he's okay and healthy. I've already lost both my parents. I don't know what I would do if I lost Mason too.

THIRTY-FIVE

MILA

 desk and gestures toward the chair on the other side. "I'm sure you've heard that Dr. Banks has decided to take an early retirement. Because we aren't in a position to hire anyone new, unfortunately we don't have a choice but to let you go."

I knew when I was hired there was a ninety day trial period, but I didn't actually think I would be let go. Doing the math in my head, I figure out I'm only a couple days away from the ninety-day mark. "Did I do something wrong?"

"Oh no. You are a wonderful nurse, and if it were up to me, I would keep you on. The problem is that the other nurses have been here longer and you're still in your ninety days. I'm so sorry." She hands me a sheet of paper. "I wrote a letter of reference for you, and please, if you need to use me when filling out any applications, do so."

She stands and sticks her hand out to shake mine. I shake hers as well, silently cursing her and this practice, but on the outside smiling because I will need to use her as a reference when I apply for other jobs.

Since Alec is with his dad for the night, I head straight to the hospital to speak to the Human Resource department hoping they'll have something open. Becky, the HR manager, tells me they've already found my replacement but has me fill out a new application to keep on file in case there's an opening in the future.

Feeling defeated, I head home. I'll have to hit the pavement tomorrow in search of a new job. I have the money from the magazine shoot, but I used the majority of it to finally pay off my student loans, credit cards, and my mortgage. I was hoping to put some away for Alec's college. Dammit, I knew I shouldn't have used that money to try to get ahead. Now I'm debt free but without an income.

When I step into the house, I hear Mason talking to someone. His voice is angry and feral, the opposite of his usual patient and easy going voice. I've never heard him speak like this, and it kind of scares me.

THIRTY-SIX 

MASON

MY MOM NEVER DID CALL BACK THAT DAY, OR THE DAY AFTER, or the day after that. But you know who finally did call me? My attorney, to let me know my mother had contacted him and asked if he could get her pimp out of jail. Apparently he was arrested for possession with intent to sell and is currently sitting in a holding cell trying to find representation. And instead of calling me so I could help her get away, she called my fucking attorney.

"She said she hates to ask but you're her last resort," my attorney said, repeating her words back to me.

I'm her last resort… She wants me to use my money, not to help *her*, but to help the man who cooked his crack in our basement and finds guys for her to fuck. She won't talk to me, won't let me help her or take care of her, but she wants me to help *him*.

I hang up with my attorney after telling him I need to think about this. I consider calling Mila, but then remember she's at work. So instead I call Tristan. As the phone rings, I realize my hands are shaking. I'm so fucking pissed…so fucking hurt. I've spent years wishing my mom would come to me and when she finally does, it's to help *him*.

Tristan answers the phone, and for the first time in my life, I lose it. I tell him about my dad and my mom and her pimp. I yell and scream and curse the goddamned world to hell. My words aren't directed at him and he knows this. He just listens quietly while I let it all out. I yell about her not wanting my help, about her not trusting me. I scream and curse, and when I stop talking, Tristan asks, "So what are you going to do?"

"I'm not giving her a goddamned dime of my hard-earned money. Fuck this, and fuck her. She's not getting shit."

"Mason?" I spin around and see Mila standing in the doorway looking nervous. This is exactly why I called Tristan. I don't want to bother Mila with my bullshit. Take my anger out on her.

"Hey Tristan, Mila just got home. Let me call you back." Tristan tells me to call him any time before we say goodbye.

"Where's Alec?" I ask once I've hung up the phone, ignoring her silent question.

"With his dad for the weekend. Is everything okay?" She tries to steer the conversation back to me, but I'm not ready to discuss this rationally. It all feels too raw.

"Can you do me a favor and put the conversation about the phone call you overheard on hold? It was regarding my mom and I just...I need to calm down before I discuss it. Why don't we go away? You and me. Two nights on the beach. Your birthday is next week. We can celebrate early."

She smiles softly. "That sounds nice." I sigh in relief that she let me get away with not discussing my mom, and grabbing my laptop from the end table, find us a hotel and book it.

"Let's pack and head out. We can check in as soon as we get there."

THIRTY-SEVEN

MILA

MASON ASKED ME TO GIVE HIM SOME TIME BEFORE WE DISCUSS what happened with his mom, and I agreed. Mostly because I was in shock over the one-sided conversation I heard. He was so upset about her asking for money I was frozen in fear over telling him I lost my job. Not that it's the same thing, but I didn't want to add to his frustration. The last thing he needed in that moment was me telling him I'm no longer employed, and him feeling like he needs to take care of me, which isn't the case. Instead, I'm hoping after our weekend away, I'll find a new job, and we can celebrate instead of stressing over me losing this one.

A couple hours later, we pull up to Hotel Casa Del Mar. It was once an exquisite private beach club designed to reflect on the Italian Renaissance in the early 1920s. It's since then been restored and turned into a luxury hotel. I've seen it many times when visiting Santa Monica beach, but I've never stayed here.

After checking in, we head up to our suite, which is beyond gorgeous. The first room I check out is our bedroom. A huge handcrafted king-size bed takes over the room. My hand runs along the comforter and you can tell it's of the highest thread count. I step into the bathroom and notice striking marble covering the spacious area. There's a large spa tub and a separate shower. I walk out of the bathroom, back through our bedroom, and into the living room. On the far side is a large window giving us the most amazing view of the Pacific ocean. It almost looks like a picture, it's so perfect. When I press my forehead against the window and strain my neck to the right, I can see the Santa Monica pier and the multi-colored Ferris wheel.

"Do you like it?" Mason asks, coming up behind me. I turn around, my back pressing up against the warm glass, and look around him. The living room isn't like a traditional hotel room, instead it reflects its original European style. All the dark wood furniture appears to be hand crafted just like our bed. The sofas and loveseats are plush with floral patterns accented with gold tones.

"It's like nothing I've ever seen. I would've been happy with the Marriott." Mason chuckles, and the sound reverberates down my body, straight to my core.

"I know, but I want this weekend to be special. We have reservations for dinner." He presses a kiss to my forehead. "And then I was thinking we could go for a walk on the beach."

"Could we…maybe…get room service and eat up here?" All I can think about is having Mason inside of me on that plush king-sized bed. My legs squeeze together, and Mason smirks.

"You totally want to stay up here and have sex."

My cheeks heat up. "No!"

"Yes, you do. I bring you to a luxurious hotel, and you want to spend the weekend in bed."

"That's not what I said."

"You don't have to say it." His hand pushes between my legs and his fingers find their way up the side of my shorts and into my panties. "You're soaking fucking wet." His fingers run over my slit, and my entire body shudders when he lands on my oversensitive clit. "Jesus, Mila. Fuck going to dinner. I'm about to make you my meal."

He pulls his hand back out of my shorts and lifts me up, my back hitting the window with a thud. He carries me to the bed where he deposits me in the center then positions himself over me, one muscular thigh on each side of me. Pulling my shirt over my head, he reaches around behind me to undo my bra. Then he sucks on my nipples for a few seconds before he makes his way down my body. After pulling my shorts and panties off me, he proceeds to show me just how hungry he is as he feasts on my pussy until we're both completely sated.

"I COMPLETED ALL THE ITEMS ON YOUR PROFILE." WE'RE SITTING on the blanket Mason bought us in a shop on the Santa Monica pier. He wanted to rent us a Cabana in the Terrazza Lounge at the hotel, but they're indoors, and this woman needs to feel the sand between her toes. I'm lying on my belly, my upper half propped up on my forearms, reading a book on my iPad. Mason is lying next to me except he's on his side facing me with his head resting on a balled up towel as he runs a finger up and down my back. I've noticed Mason loves to touch me.

Whether it's holding my hand, putting his arm around my shoulder, or simply running his finger along my body. He seems to need to touch me in some way. The thought makes me smile.

"Huh?" I click my iPad off to give Mason my attention.

"Your list…the one on the dating site. Going to the beach to read was the last one." I think about this for a moment, trying to remember my profile, and now that I'm thinking about it, he's right. The fondue, the picnic, the movies. He's used my list to make sure I'm happy. I know Mason has insecurities about being in a relationship. He's constantly afraid of failing, so I know when he says this, he's referring to the fact he's accomplished everything I asked for. He's not bragging, but instead seeking validation.

"You did."

Mason's quiet for a beat before he says, "I want a new list."

I turn over to my side to face him. "A list of things I enjoy?"

"A list of things you want to do that will make you happy. Like your other list." *Oh, my heart.*

"That list was just examples of what I like to do. I wrote it to keep the creeps who just wanted to have sex away."

"But it's everything you do love, and every time I complete something from that list you're happy. You never ask for anything. How do I know what will make you happy?"

I scoot closer to Mason, and his hand rests on my butt. "You make me happy. Just you."

"But you were married to Gavin, and he didn't make you happy. I must be doing something different, right? I thought it was the list."

I think for several seconds how to word my answer. "When Gavin and I got married it was because I was pregnant. We were so young. We were dating but we never would've lasted. What kept us together was Alec. Our life turned into a routine, which is okay to a certain extent. Life is a routine. We have to work and go to school and be adults. But I found myself feeling lonely. Gavin loved video games and I wanted attention. He was starting his real estate firm but never wanted to talk about it. We weren't partners. We were just two people living together, raising our son. I wanted him to see me as more than Alec's mom, but when he would give me attention, I was left feeling unsatisfied. I was craving intimacy, companionship. It was when I met you in the hospital everything changed."

"Me? I told you I wanted to fuck you." Mason laughs.

"It wasn't what you said. It was the way you looked at me. Like you wanted to devour me."

"Oh, trust me. I did."

I giggle and slap his chest. "You made me realize I was settling, and when I got home, my mom and I talked about it. I told her about you. How I wanted a man to look at me and want to devour me like you did. I wanted the spark, the intimacy, the connection. She told me it took her finding my stepdad to learn how incredible and fulfilling a relationship can be, and then she told me life was too short to settle. A few days later she died."

"Jesus, Mila. I'm so sorry." Mason squeezes my arm.

"A few months after she died, I told Gavin I wanted a divorce and he agreed. I thought finding someone would be easy, but it wasn't. Life with a toddler was hectic. I was working fulltime and I guess I gave up. Until you. It's not about what we do that keeps me happy. It's that I'm doing it all with you. You're my best friend, my partner, my lover."

"I still want that list." His face is serious, and like always when he gives me that look, I don't bother arguing.

"Fine. I'll write up a list of my wants and needs just for you. First item on my list"—I run my fingers down his tanned muscular torso, and once I get to his swim shorts, I squeeze his dick softly—"afternoon sex with Mason in our massive tub." I wink and he grins.

"Your wish is my desire." He stands and scoops me up into his arms. "But first I need to make sure you're very, very wet." He throws me over his shoulder, smacking my butt.

"I am wet!" I squeak.

"Nope! Not wet enough, Mrs. Street." And before I can say anything else, he's running us into the ocean and throwing me into the water.

THIRTY-EIGHT

MASON

"MASON!" I HEAR SOMEONE CALLING MY NAME. AM I DREAMING? "Mason! Do you know where my mom is?" I roll over to find Mila's side of the bed empty. I roll the other way and find Alec standing over me.

"Mason, do you know where my mom is?"

I sit up and rub my eyes with the heels of my palms to wake up. "I'm not sure, Bruiser. What's going on?" I stand and, remembering I'm only in my boxers, throw on my sweats and a T-shirt.

"My dad's here to drop me off."

I follow him out to the living room and see Gavin standing by the front door. "Hey man, what's happening?"

"I have a meeting with a big client in San Francisco and Alec has no school today. It's a teacher work day and Mila had assured me she would take the day off to watch him since my mom is out of town."

I don't remember Mila mentioning anything about taking the day off when we were eating dinner last night. "She probably forgot." Then I remember today is her birthday. "What do you say we pick up lunch and a cake and surprise her for her birthday?"

"Yeah!" Alex yells.

"Thanks, man."

"No worries."

A few hours later, and Alec and I are pulling up to the doctor's office Mila works at. I leave the car running with the food and cake in the car, and we run in to surprise her. It's five 'til noon so she's due for her lunch.

"Excuse me," I say to the woman sitting at the desk. "I was wondering if you could help me?"

She looks up and I can see it in her face when she recognizes me. "Oh, wow! You're Mason Street!"

"Yes, I am. Nice to meet you. I'm looking for Mila Street, my *wife*."

The woman frowns then leans in to whisper, "She doesn't work here anymore."

"Are you sure?"

"Yeah…she was let go last Friday."

"Okay, thanks." Last Friday? We spent the weekend together, and she never once mentioned she lost her job. And that would mean she hasn't been working all week, yet every morning she gets up and gets ready as if she's going to work.

"Where's mom?" Alec asks as we're walking back to my car.

"I'm not sure." Pulling my phone out, I hit Mila's name to call her. When she doesn't pick up, I try again. No answer. I have no clue what the fuck is going on, but I'm going to get to the bottom of it. I call Charlie, and she picks up.

"Mason, to what do I owe this pleasure?"

"Have you talked to Mila?" I put the car in reverse and start driving…to where? I have no idea.

"Not today…what's up?"

"Today's her birthday."

"Really? Damn her! She didn't tell me that!"

"Are the girls off school today?"

"Yeah, want to go to dinner for her birthday?"

"Actually, I need a favor. Can I drop Alec off to you?"

"Is everything okay?"

"I'm not sure."

"Of course you can drop him off. I'll see you soon."

I drop Alec off, leaving the food and cake for them to eat, and head home to see if Mila is there. When I don't see her car, I go inside the house. I call her a couple more times but she still doesn't pick up. When my phone rings, I see it's a Nevada area code. Not able to deal with my mom right now, I send her to voicemail.

As I sit on the couch, I think about the last week since we returned from the beach. She's usually full of stories about her pregnant patients, and not once this week has she mentioned any of them. Why wouldn't she tell me she lost her job? And if she found a new job, why wouldn't she mention it? None of this makes any sense. Just as I'm about to dial her number again, my phone rings. Same area code as before.

"Mom, I can't do this right now."

"I'm sorry. Is this Mason Street?"

"Yeah."

"This is Nevada General Hospital. Your mother, Denise Street, was brought here. She was found in critical condition and you're her emergency contact." My heart sinks.

"Is she going to make it?"

"All I can say over the phone is she's in the ICU. She was severely beaten. She was taken into surgery and the doctor was able to stop the internal bleeding. She has a couple of broken ribs and one of them punctured her lung."

"I'm on my way," I say. "I need to catch a flight, but I should be there in a few hours." I stand and see Mila standing a few feet away from me. I didn't even hear her come in. She's dressed in her scrubs like she always is when she comes home from work.

I hang up, and we both go to speak at the same time. "You go first," she says. "Are you going somewhere?"

"My mom is at Nevada General Hospital. She was beaten badly."

"Oh no!" Her hands go up to her mouth.

"Did you just come from work?" I ask.

"Um…" Her eyes dart around the room. At least she doesn't lie to me. "I forgot Alec has no school today. Gavin said he was with you." She looks around for her son.

"He's with Charlie."

"Oh, okay. I can go with you to see your mom. Let me see if she can watch him." She pulls her cell phone out of her pocket.

"Mila, did you just come from work?" She doesn't look up. "Mila, look at me." Her eyes slowly raise to meet mine. "Did you just come from work?"

She shakes her head.

"So where were you?"

"Looking for a job."

"In your scrubs?"

"No, I have a change of clothes in my car."

"Why didn't you tell me you lost your job?"

Mila flinches at the harshness of my tone. "I didn't want to bother you with my problems. Your mom had just called and you were upset," she says, her words rushing out like a dam that broke and is flooding the area. "I spent all the money from the photo shoot on paying off my debts. I didn't think I would lose my job. I was hoping to find one before—"

"You mean you didn't trust me to take care of you?" I cut her off.

"What? No!" She shakes her head side to side emphatically.

"Then why would you pretend like you were getting up and going to work for the last several days? Why did we spend forty-eight hours together at a hotel and not once did you mention it? You laid there on the damn beach and said the reason we work and you and Gavin didn't is because we're partners. Yet you couldn't even tell me you were let go from your job?"

She starts to open her mouth to speak, but I don't want to hear whatever lie or excuse she's going to try to feed me. "I need to go to

Vegas to see my mom." I turn my back on Mila and stalk toward our bedroom, grabbing my luggage and filling it with clothes.

"I can go with you," she offers.

"No, I think I need to do this alone. Plus, I have a bunch of promo shit I need to do for the upcoming fight." I go into the bathroom and pluck my toothbrush from the holder, grab my deodorant and other shit I'm going to need, and throw it all into the luggage.

"When will you be back?" Mila asks, her voice shaky.

"I don't know," I say, slamming the luggage shut and zippering it closed. "Fuck! You lost your job, Mila! And instead of coming to me, you hid it. You didn't trust me enough to tell me. I'm supposed to be your best friend, the person you turn to, yet you hid something important from me."

"No, Mason." But she doesn't say anything else because we both know it's the truth. I drop my luggage to the ground and pop the handle up.

"I gotta go. I'll call you." When I get to the front door, I stop and look at my wife one last time. Tears of pain are rushing down her cheeks and all I want to do is go to her and comfort her. But I can't do it. She didn't trust me. It's like my mom all over again. "By the way, there's a birthday cake at Charlie's. Alec and I went to your work to surprise you. Happy Birthday." I open the door and walk out.

AFTER TAKING THE NEXT FLIGHT OUT AND PICKING UP A RENTAL car, I finally make it to Nevada General Hospital at almost midnight. My mom is still in the ICU, so I'm told I can only visit for a few minutes since visiting hours are over. I walk into my mom's room and don't even recognize her. Aside from the fact her face is completely black and blue, both her eyes are swollen, and her lip is covered in stitches, she doesn't look anything like the woman who gave birth to me. Her hair is bleached blond, whereas growing up it was a natural brown, and she's skinnier than she used to be. Time hasn't been good to her.

"I was told you just arrived." An older gentleman walks in. He's wearing a suit and over it is a white lab coat. He's probably in his early fifties. He must be the doctor.

"I took the first flight out of LAX. My name is Mason Street."

The doctor puts his hand out to shake mine. "I'm Dr. Collins."

"Nice to meet you."

"And Denise Street is your mother?" he asks to confirm.

"Yes, but I haven't seen her in years."

"When she was brought in, we did a blood and alcohol test on her. She's free of any drugs or alcohol which is good. Often times, we see women in your mom's condition have been doing drugs. We performed surgery on her ribs and punctured lung. I'm fairly certain she will make a full recovery."

"Does it say how she ended up in here? How she got beat up?"

"The police were called and an investigation was requested because of how badly she was beaten. It was a drug deal gone bad. The police report also mentions prostitution." Dr. Collins hands me several papers.

"She's going to be here for a few days. I would suggest you get some sleep and come by tomorrow once she's awake."

"Okay. Thank you, Dr. Collins." We shake hands once again before we walk out of my mom's room.

I'm walking out of the hospital to find a hotel when my phone rings. It's Bella calling. My heart sinks it's not Mila, but it's probably for the best right now. Bella and I don't talk often anymore, our lives have gone in two different directions, but there was a time when we were good friends. Bella, Tristan, and I even spent our spring break their senior year of high school exploring New York together. It was the first gift I'd ever been given and it was given by Tristan's parents. From the beginning they treated me like one of their kids.

"Hey, everything okay?"

"Tristan called and told me about your mom. You know he's on his way, right? But I wanted to offer you a place to stay. It's late, and I don't want you to be alone."

"I don't know if that's a good idea, Bella. I'm not good company."

"Great! So, you haven't changed a bit. Get your ass over here, Street."

Not able to say no to her, I agree and head over to her and Marco's home. When I pull up, the automatic gate lets me in, and Bella is waiting for me on the front porch. While Marco is a decent guy, he and I don't really know each other. When I moved to Vegas, he was already living in California. Some shit went down between Marco, Bella, and Tristan, and since Tristan and I are best friends, I had his back. Marco and Bella moved back to Vegas, and Tristan and I moved to Los Angeles. Shit has been dealt with and forgiveness has been given, but now that I'm here, I'm wondering if this is the best idea.

I get out of my rental, leaving my luggage in the trunk, and walk up to meet Bella. She's sitting on the porch swing with her baby girl in her arms.

"Damn, woman. She's adorable." I sit down next to her. "Too bad she doesn't look anything like you."

She elbows me. "She looks like her daddy." She lifts her up and kisses her forehead. "Want to hold her?" she offers.

"Sure." I take her from Bella and she looks up at me with tired eyes.

The last baby I held like this was Lexi. "Can't sleep little cutie? Now's the easy part. You get to get spoiled by your parents." She coos at me and I laugh softly. I think about what Mila had said about wanting a little girl, and I picture a tiny baby: half Mila and half me.

"So, your mom?" Bella questions.

"She was beaten. I don't know all the details."

"When's the last time you saw her?"

"Saw her? When I was thirteen."

We're silent for a couple minutes before she says, "Your wife is freaking out. The way Tristan was talking when he called, it sounded like you guys are having some issues." When I don't respond, she adds, "We don't have to talk about it. But I'm here."

"Thanks, Bella." We continue to swing in silence, my arms holding the precious little girl who will hopefully never know heartache. I watch as her tiny lids eventually flutter closed. I never imagined wanting a baby of my own until Mila, now I have to wonder if it's too late. I don't want to think it is, but right now I'm fucking hurting.

"She's asleep." I hand her back over to her.

"For now." She giggles. "She's a night owl."

Bright lights from a car pull up and the gates open. A few seconds later, Tristan and Mila are getting out of Tristan's truck. They must've driven here.

"I'm going to lay Liza down," Bella says before excusing herself.

"Are you serious?" Tristan yells. "Let me see my goddaughter."

Bella lets out a dramatic huff and hands her over to Tristan. "Come with me to put her to bed? Marco's inside."

"Sure." Tristan looks from Mila to me. "I'll be back out in a second. I got us a hotel room near the hospital."

Once they're gone it's only Mila and me, neither of us knowing what to say to each other. Finally she comes forward and reaches out to take my hands. I pull back slightly, and her face falls.

"I'm sorry, Mason. I'm so sorry I didn't tell you." I can hear it in her voice, that she really is sorry, but it doesn't change the fact she didn't tell me. She didn't trust me to help her, to take care of her. She didn't even give me a chance. My head fills with the image of my broken mom laying in the hospital room.

"I need time, Mila. I know it isn't what you want to hear, but it's all I got. It's all I can give you right now." Her bottom lip begins to quiver and tears fall down the sides of her cheeks, so I pull her into my arms. "Thank you for coming out here with Tristan. Just give me some time. Please." She nods into my chest, and I can feel her hot tears soaking the front of my shirt.

We go inside and find Marco, Tristan, and Bella conversing. "Hey man." I greet Marco. "You ready to go to the hotel?" I ask Tristan.

"Yeah."

"Thanks for letting us make this our pit stop," I joke, pulling Bella into my arms for a hug. "Will you be at the fight?"

"Yep! We have two guys from our camp fighting. Are you staying here until the fight?"

"Yeah, I think so. I have some endorsement and promo shit I'm scheduled to do anyway. Mind if I crash your gym?"

"You're always welcome, man. You know that," Marco says.

"Thanks."

We say our goodbyes and head out. Mila rides in the car with me, but we don't say a word the entire way. When we get to the hotel, we check into the two bedroom suite. Tristan takes one room, and Mila and I take the other.

"I can sleep on the couch," she offers once we're alone. "I'm sorry for coming. I don't know what I was thinking."

"It's okay. We can share a bed. It's only for one night. You're going home tomorrow, right?"

"Yeah," she whispers. "I guess I am."

We change out of our clothes and lie down at the same time. We're in the same bed, yet she feels like a million miles away. Several times I want to close the space between us, but I don't. I can't. My head and heart are so completely fucked up right now. It didn't matter that I'd given our marriage my all. At the end of the day, my wife didn't trust me. Just like my mom didn't.

And as we both fall asleep, I can't help but think about the fact that in less than twenty-four hours we broke pretty much every one of our wedding vows we made to each other.

THIRTY-NINE

MILA

I WOKE UP BEFORE MASON DID. I TOOK A SHOWER AND LEFT A note telling him I love him and I'd wait to hear from him. Then I grabbed a cab and headed to the hospital. I checked in with the front desk and received my visitor's pass. I took the elevator up to the recovery level since his mom had been moved out of the ICU. But when I got to her room, she was sleeping. I went down to the cafeteria and got a coffee and a little while later went back up. Mason was in the room with his mom, but I couldn't hear anything that was being said, so I left without him knowing I came by.

I wanted to go to him, but I promised I would give him his space, and I didn't want to upset him more. So I called Gavin and told him I needed a few days. I didn't want to leave if there was a chance Mason might need me. I checked into the same hotel he's staying in, and I've gone to the hospital every day, hoping something will change but it hasn't, and now it's the fourth day since I arrived and I have a flight scheduled to return home this afternoon. As much as I want to stay, I have a little boy who needs me at home.

As I approach the room, I hear arguing. I look around and put my ear up to the door. Mason's mom, Denise, is yelling at him, telling him to go away and she doesn't want his help. Mason responds by begging her to let him help her. She keeps saying she can't, but he keeps begging. He sounds like a little boy begging his mother to love him, and my heart breaks. Finally he gives up and says he'll be back later. I slide around the corner out of sight and watch him leave. When he gets to the elevator, he slams his fist into the wall and then steps inside.

Once I know he's gone, I step into Denise's room. She's lying in her bed still covered in bruises and stitches, but they are already beginning to turn yellow. She's propped up slightly so she's not lying flat on her back and she's bawling her eyes out. She doesn't look like a mother who hates her son, who resents him and thinks he's a burden. No, she looks like a mother who has the entire world resting on her shoulders. And then it hits me. What if she isn't pushing him away because she doesn't want his help, but because she is afraid she doesn't deserve it?

I clear my throat, and she looks up, her eyes shining with fresh tears. "Can I help you?" she croaks out. I could go for the jugular. Yell and scream and beg her to let Mason in, but I've learned in my years as a nurse, you catch more flies with honey than with vinegar. So, instead, I sit in the chair next to her.

"My name is Mila Street." I wait for my words to sink in before I continue. "I'm your son's wife."

She nods slowly. "Did he send you here?"

"No. He doesn't even know I'm here. I wasn't going to come in here, but I heard your argument." I give her a pointed look and she doesn't argue. "You went from considering him to be a burden to not letting him take care of you. Something doesn't add up. My guess is you feel guilty, and your guilt is eating away at you. It's not that you don't want his help, but you don't think you deserve it."

When she doesn't argue, I continue. "I made a grave error and didn't trust him, and now I'm not sure if we're going to make it. But it's not too late to save your relationship with him. He loves you and wants to help you, to take care of you. Please let him. Mason is the most selfless, caring man I've ever met. He loves with his entire heart, and despite it being broken by you over and over again, he still continues to love with that same broken heart, even if he won't admit it." Denise closes her eyes for a moment and I can see new tears leaking out.

"The next time he comes to visit you, please let him in. Let him get you away from here. I know you're pushing him away. Mother's guilt. You couldn't take care of him, so you don't think you deserve for him to take care of you. Am I right?"

Denise nods. "The only reason I came to him for help regarding Al, my pimp, was because he threatened me. He found out Mason was my son and said if I didn't get Mason to help get him out, he would take away all my clients. I never wanted to ask Mason for anything. I don't deserve it." She begins to cry. "I failed him. I was his mother, and it was my job to take care of him and I didn't, and they took him away."

Grabbing a chair, I pull it next to her bed and take her hand in mine. As a mother I can understand where she's coming from. "Maybe so, but I lost both my parents and would give anything to have them back. You and Mason still have each other. All he ever wanted to do was take care of you. All you have to do is let him. Love him and let him love you back. You can't change the past, but you can put your pride and guilt aside and let him in now.

"Mason's going to come in here expecting you to push him away once again. Just like you've been doing since he was old enough to help you. For once, put your son first. As a mother, you're right. You failed your son. But you're getting a chance to make it right. Please, make it right."

I stand back up and walk to the door and Denise calls my name. "Are you going to make it right?"

"I sure as hell hope so. Maybe I'll see you in LA."

I leave and go to the cafeteria like I always do. I have a few hours before my car arrives to take me to the airport. Just as I'm finishing my second coffee and about to head downstairs, Tristan sits down across from me.

"I've seen you here every day." He raises his eyebrows, daring me to deny it.

"Has Mason?"

"I'm not sure. He's been all over the place. I was worried if he didn't get his mom to leave this city he wouldn't be able to focus on his upcoming fight. But funny thing…I saw you coming out of his mom's room this morning and then while he was at the gym working out, he got a call from his mom asking him to come back. First time she's called him willingly since she's been here."

"And?"

"And she agreed to let him help her."

"She's going to California?"

"Yep, he's going to rent her a place once she's cleared to leave. I'll be bringing her myself since Mason needs to stay here."

"That's good. I'm glad she's giving him a chance to help her."

"Mason might not know you spoke to her, but thank you. Whatever you said worked. How much longer are you staying?"

"I'm actually about to leave."

"Can I drive you to the airport?"

"I'm okay, but thank you. Take care of Mason."

"Always."

FORTY

MILA

 asked where Mason was and I used the excuse that he's in Vegas preparing for his upcoming fight, which is the truth. He hasn't called or texted me once. Mother's day was last weekend and I did receive a beautiful bouquet of flowers from him with a note saying I'm a wonderful mom. I cried for a good thirty minutes.

I hate that we're at a standstill, but I know he needs to get ready for his fight. It's his job and he doesn't need any distractions. While doing the laundry yesterday, I came across some papers pretty much confirming what I have suspected in regards to Mason and me. I wanted to call him and confront him, but decided it'll be better to wait until we're in person. His stuff is still at my house, so I'm assuming once he's done with his fight, he'll be back.

To stay busy, I've been applying everywhere for jobs and I'm crossing my fingers I find one soon. I've also helped Mason's mom get situated in her new place. Mason found a furnished condo for her to rent only a few minutes from where we live. Tristan has been by daily to check on her, bring her food, and see if she needs anything. He knows I've been coming by to hang out with her, but I've asked him not to mention it to Mason. I don't know where we stand and I don't want to upset him. His mom is filled with guilt, and we talk a lot about what she's been through, as well as what Mason went through. I mentioned that it might be a good idea for her to see a therapist and surprisingly she agreed. When I'm not looking for a job or visiting Denise, I've been hanging out with Charlie at the art studio, helping out. Her sister-in-law, Morgan, is due in two weeks, so she's at home resting.

But today I'm at Alec's school for a special event. He wrote an essay for a writing contest at school and the parents were invited to hear their children read their essay. Gavin and I are sitting together in the auditorium along with several other parents, while Alec and his fellow classmates, who chose to enter the writing contest, are sitting on the stage. I'm so proud of him. I haven't heard the essay yet, so I'm excited to hear who or what he wrote about.

The principal speaks for a few minutes about the essay contest and tells everyone the topic was to write about the person you want to be like when you get older.

Several kids are called up to read their essays, and they're so adorable. Finally it's Alec's turn. He comes up to the microphone and says, "My name is Alec Sterling, and I wrote my essay about three people: my mom, my dad, and my stepdad, Mason Street."

FORTY-ONE

MASON
TWENTY-FOUR HOURS AGO

MY PHONE RINGS AND ITS GAVIN. "HEY MAN, IS EVERYTHING okay?"

"It's Alec." My heart squeezes when I hear his voice, reminding me how much I miss him and his mother. I'm at the gym, where I've been every waking moment—when I'm not doing promo shit—since my mom left with Tristan back to California after she finally agreed to let me help her, starting with getting her the hell out of Vegas.

"Hey Bruiser, is everything okay?"

"Yeah" He sighs. "I guess."

"What's wrong?"

"My mom is sad you're gone. She said we couldn't go with you because I have school. Can we go to the fight, though?" Of course she spared him from knowing what's really going on because that's the type of mom she is.

"I'm not sure. I'll talk to Tristan and your mom and see if someone can bring you, okay?"

"Okay."

"How's school?"

"Oh! That's why I'm calling. I wrote an essay for a contest, and I'm reading it in front of everyone. Can you come see me tomorrow at my school? Please! It will only be a minute. Then you can go back to practicing." I chuckle at the mind of an eight year old. He has no idea I'm several hours away. He's just a kid who wants me there.

"That's awesome. What time?"

"Um… hold on." I hear papers shuffling then his dad says something before Alec comes back on the phone. "Ten o'clock in the auditorium."

"Okay, I'll be there."

"Yes! See you then. Bye!" Alec hangs up, and my phone rings again. This time it's my mom and she's Facetiming me.

"Mom?" I say when I answer and her healing face pops up on the screen. We've spoken a few times this past week, but it's been quick conversations to make sure she's settling in.

"Yes, I'm trying out this video chat. The phone arrived today. Thank you." She smiles into the screen.

"You're welcome. How are you doing?"

"I'm okay. Tristan and his wife have been so sweet, and Mila has…" She stops speaking for a moment and then says, "I mean…"

"Mila has what?" I press.

My mom looks guilty. "Um…"

"Mom?"

"I don't think you were supposed to know. I know you guys are going through something, but she's been here every day, bringing me food and coffee and hanging out with me. She even helped me find a therapist, someone I can talk to." When I don't say anything she continues, "I'm guessing you don't know this either, but it was actually Mila who spoke to me in the hospital and convinced me to stop taking my guilt out on you."

"She did what?" I ask confused. "When?"

"When I was in the hospital. She convinced me to stop taking my misplaced anger out on you and let you help me. I was so set on not letting you take care of me because I did such a shitty job of taking care of you when you were little, but she reminded me that while I can't change the past, I'm in charge of the future. Here you are asking me to let you help me, even after I was a horrible mom to you, and instead of pushing you away, I can let you in."

I look into the matching blue eyes of the woman who gave birth to me, the woman I prayed every day would simply love me—her words hitting me like a semi smashing straight into me at a hundred miles per hour.

"You didn't want my help because you were a bad mom?"

My mom's eyes turn down in what looks like shame. "It was my job as your parent to take care of you. A child isn't supposed to take care of his mom. I hate what I put you through, that you saw all of those men come in and out of our home. I was so angry with your father. Angry he died. Angry he didn't pay the life insurance policy and left us with nothing. I was heartbroken and sad, but none of that is an excuse for what I put you through."

I drop to the wall, my back resting against the mirrored wall in the gym. "I thought you hated me, that you thought I was a burden."

My mom shakes her head emphatically. "No, Mason! Never! I hated myself! I hated that I couldn't give you food or clothes. I hated when you would hear me cry and ask what you could do to help when I was supposed to be protecting and loving and taking care of you. I failed, Mason." Tears spring from her eyes. "I'm so sorry for failing you. I never wanted to touch a dime of your money. You worked so hard to earn that money. I watched you over the years. Every fight I could watch. Or I would go to the library to read about them. I'm so proud of you. I failed you and left you without any parents and you still succeeded."

My eyes sting as tears build up. All these years…I didn't know how she really felt. "Mason, do you think maybe we could have another chance? I know you're thirty and no longer a little boy, but could we see the therapist together? I don't want you to take care of me. I just want my son back."

There's a lump lodged in my throat preventing me from speaking, so I nod.

"Thank you. I love you, Mason. I'll see you when you get back from your fight."

I clear my throat. "I'm coming to California tomorrow."

"For Alec's essay reading?" she questions.

"You know about that?"

"Yes, I told you Mila and I talk."

"Yeah, I'm coming in for the reading. Do you…want to have lunch with me afterward?"

"I would love that."

We hang up, and I head over to the MGM Grand. I have a couple endorsements shoots I need to do for an energy drink as well as a clothing ad. Both are being shot at the MGM Grand: one in the arena and the other near the pool. I spend the next several hours with the photographers then book my flight to LAX. I arrive late at night and stay with Tristan and Charlie. She glares at me the entire time but doesn't bring up Mila.

I head over to Alec's school and get there a few minutes after ten. I sit in the back and spot Mila and Gavin sitting together toward the front. The principal drones on about some shit, and finally, after several kids read their essays, Alec is called up. He stands up on the stage, his tiny self barely reaching the microphone. Looking out into the crowd, I can tell when he finds his mom and dad, and then he finds me. His face brightens up, and I know I made the right decision by coming here.

"My name is Alec Sterling, and I wrote my essay about three people: my mom, my dad, and my stepdad, Mason Street. I know I was supposed to pick one person, but I picked three." He shrugs. "I want to be like my dad, my mom, and Mason when I get older. The first person I want to be like is my dad because he plays video games with me. He's really nice and plays with me when I ask him to. And when I go with him, he always lets me get French fries instead of vegetables.

He also lets me stay up past my bedtime when my mom doesn't." The parents chuckle.

"I want to be like my mom because my mom is a really good mom. She read all of the Diary of a Wimpy Kid books to me when I was too little to read. She plays games with me and takes me to the beach. She takes me to MMA classes too. She's also the best mom because she married the best fighter in the world. I want to be like Mason when I get older because he's the strongest person in the whole world. He's a fighter and he always wins. Except one time he lost." The parents all chuckle softly, but the boulder of emotion lodged in my throat prevents me from laughing. This is just an essay from an eight-year-old kid, and to some people it wouldn't be a big deal, but to me, it's fucking everything. He and his mother have become my everything.

"I want to be like Mason because I want to be a fighter like him. He's strong and fights hard. But he is also really nice. He helps other guys fight too and he helps me fight. When I go to the gym with him he is always nice. Even though when he fights he's mean. And he's nice to my mom. He makes her laugh a lot. The only bad thing about Mason is he makes me eat my vegetables but that's because he has to eat healthy to fight. I want to be like my dad, my mom, and Mason when I get older. The end."

Everybody claps and Alec sits back down. After the rest of the kids go, I consider leaving, but I can't do it. I can't leave without telling Alec how good his essay was. Once everyone is done, the principal thanks everyone for coming and says there are drinks and food in the back and encourages the parents to stay and congratulate their children on a job well done.

Alec jumps off the stage, and I hang back figuring I'll speak to him once he's spoken to his parents, but instead of stopping at them, he runs right past them to me. I can see the shocked look on Mila's face when she's learns I'm here.

"Mason! You came!"

"Of course I did, Bruiser. You wrote a good essay."

"Thank you! Are you going back for the fight now?" Before I can answer, Mila and Gavin join us. Gavin shakes my hand and tells Alec he loved his essay. Mila doesn't say a word to me, but goes straight for Alec and hugs him.

"Your essay was amazing, sweetie. Hold it up so I can take a picture." Alec holds up his essay and Mila takes a bunch of pictures using her phone. "Can we hang it up?"

"I want Mason to have it for good luck." He hands me his essay. "If I can't go to the fight, now it's like I'm there with my essay." *Damn this kid.*

"All right, well after the fight, we're hanging it up. You better head back to class. I love you." Mila hugs Alec again, and Gavin does the same. When he's done hugging his dad, he throws his arms around me.

"I love you. I really hope I can watch your fight," he whispers. "Bye." He runs up the walkway and out the door with the other kids and teachers, having no clue he just ran out the door with half of my fucking heart—his mom holding the other half.

"I better get going. Good luck at your fight this weekend." Gavin clasps his hand on my shoulder and walks out the door.

"I better go, too," Mila says, not giving me a chance to say anything. I follow her out the door and watch her get in her car and drive away. The plan was to go have lunch with my mom and then head back to Vegas, but the only place I want to be is wherever Mila is. I shoot a text to my mom to let her know I need to see Mila as I jump in my car and head to her house, hoping she's gone straight home. When I pull up I see that her car is parked, so I know she's inside.

Not wanting to risk the chance of her not letting me in, I use my key to unlock the door instead of knocking and find her sitting at the kitchen table. She's staring at some papers and tears are streaming down her face. She looks up startled and tries to swipe at the tears, but they keep coming. When I get closer, I see the papers she's looking at: **Petition for Dissolution of Marriage.**

My heart feels like it's being squeezed by a barbwire fence as I read the words over and over again. "You're filing for divorce." It's not a question because the papers are right there in front of her. She doesn't say anything, though. Instead, she shakes her head as the tears fall faster than lightning down her face. Pulling her chair back, I pick her up and bring us over to the couch, settling her on my lap.

"Baby, please don't do this," I beg her. Her tear-stained hair is stuck to her face and I brush it out of the way with my fingers so I can see her. Her cries get harder, her tiny body shaking with sobs. "I'm sorry, Mila. I just needed a few days. I won't leave again. I promise."

She tries to calm down, her cries turning into hiccups, and once she's calm enough to speak, she says, "I didn't file for divorce. Those aren't my papers. They're yours." *What the fuck!*

"What are you talking about?"

"I-I found the papers in your bottom drawer. I was doing the laundry and I saw the envelope. I was upset from you leaving and was being nosy. I opened it and found them." *The papers in my bottom drawer…shit!*

"Mila." I frame her face with my hands. Her cheeks are pink and splotchy and her eyes are red and puffy from crying, but she's still the most beautiful woman in the world. "The morning after we got married I sent an email to my attorney to draw up divorce papers. I told you I emailed him, remember?" She nods. "Later, I told him to hold off, but he must've sent them. I got some papers in the mail and threw them in my drawer to deal with later and completely forgot. I assumed they were for the UFC because my contract is due to renew. I swear to you, I didn't plan to file for divorce. I love you, and the only thing I want to do is spend the rest of my life with you."

FORTY-TWO

MILA

MY HEART CALMS DOWN SLIGHTLY AT MASON'S WORDS. WHEN I found the papers, I freaked out. And then when he stayed away for the last week, my heart and mind started to work itself up into a frenzy until I was so sure my marriage was going to end in divorce. And the thought of us divorcing only validated every emotion I feel for this man. I'm completely and utterly in love with Mason Street. Call our marriage whatever you want, but it's real. So goddamned real. The day I filed for divorce I never once felt the pain the way the thought of Mason and I divorcing about crippled me. Even when I was broke and lonely and tired, I never once regretted my divorce.

But the moment I thought I was going to lose Mason, I realized the difference between loving someone and *being* in love with someone. With Gavin, I loved him because I needed him. I was young and immature and lost and scared, and I needed him to face life's craziness with me.

With Mason, it's different. I need him because I'm in love with him. Because I can't imagine going a day without being with him. I don't need him to face life with me. I want him to face life with me. I want him by my side. I crave his touch and his words. I crave his laughter and his heart.

"I love you too, so much. I know how we started was unconventional, but you mean everything to me and I never want to be without you." My mouth crashes against his. We kiss for several minutes or maybe it's hours. I don't know. Like with everything between Mason and me, our kiss is all consuming. I get lost in it, and I don't want to be found. Eventually, he picks me up and carries me to the bed, tossing me onto the mattress and trapping me in the circle of his strong arms. His lips meet mine once again and he kisses me passionately, affectionately, with such abandon that every emotion is conveyed without even a single word being spoken.

We break our kiss just long enough to strip ourselves of our clothes, and once we're both naked, skin to skin, Mason parts my legs and guides himself into me. My legs wrap around his waist like he's my lifeline. "I love you, Mila," he murmurs, kissing the shell of my ear. "I need you." He kisses the sensitive flesh behind my ear. "All of you." He trails kisses downward and across my chest. "You're mine." He kisses each of my nipples and then his mouth is back on mine. "And I'm yours, forever," he says, his lips brushing mine before he deepens the kiss. Our bodies are flush against one another as Mason slowly makes love to me until we're both panting and sweating and shaking from our orgasms.

And when he stills and gives me one last soft kiss, I bring my hands to the sides of his face to hold him close to me, repeating the words he said to me. " I love you. I need you. All of you. You're mine, and I'm yours, forever."

FORTY-THREE

MILA
UFC FIGHT NIGHT

MASON HAD TO GO BACK TO LAS VEGAS TO GET READY FOR HIS fight and I didn't want to be without him. So, Gavin agreed to keep Alec for a couple nights and bring him over Friday after school for the weekend. When he got here, Mason made sure to include Alec in everything he did. From the press conferences to the weigh-ins, Alec was with Mason's team every step of the way. Charlie, Bella, and I hung out by the pool with the kids for most of the day on Friday. Saturday—because Charlie doesn't do UFC fights—she stayed at the hotel with the little girls while the rest of us went to the UFC fight.

The arena momentarily goes black, and the music begins. The announcer announces it's the main card event of the night. Mason is brought out first with *Hate Me Now* by Nas blaring through the arena, and then his opponent Jax Wilkens is called out. The crowd is definitely favoring Mason, but there is still plenty of love for Jax. Tristan's parents, along with Bella, Marco, Gavin, Alec, and I, are sitting as close as you can get, screaming for Mason even though there's no way he can hear us. Tristan is standing right outside the octagon in Mason's corner.

The rules are read and the referee gives them the option to touch gloves. Mason smirks and puts his hand out, but Jax walks away to his corner. The crowd boos, and Mason laughs. The fight begins and right away Mason opens with a few leg kicks. Jax tries to back up, but Mason hits him with a brutal combination that connects right to Jax's face causing him to stumble back and fall onto his butt. Mason smirks, and the crowd goes crazy. The women are screaming things I only pray my son doesn't understand. The men yelling expletives I'm going to have to make sure Alec knows aren't acceptable.

Jax kicks his feet out and then stands, and Mason lifts his arms up in a *come get it* gesture, his cocky smirk never falling. There was a time when I thought that smirk meant he didn't care. That was until I learned who the real Mason is. I learned that with every joke he tells and every time he smirks or laughs, looks can be deceiving. The man hiding behind the smirk, behind the false bravado, is a man who loves with everything he has and cares deeper than anyone I've ever met. Jax comes after Mason, throwing punch after punch, which Mason blocks. The blow horn indicates the end of the first round.

The next round begins, and Mason gets Jax into a corner. He swings a left hook and knocks Jax onto the ground. Jax gets back up and comes after Mason. He's throwing punches, but they're not connecting.

"Come on, Mason," Alec shouts. "End it now."

Mason couldn't possibly have heard him, but it's in that moment he goes after Jax. Punch after punch, he gets Jax into a corner. His elbow connects to the side of Jax's temple, sending Jax stumbling backward. He immediately bounces back and tries to bring Mason down, but Mason turns it around and takes Jax down to the ground. He throws punch after punch to Jax's face until the referee forces him away and declares the fight over—announcing Mason, the defending champion.

"He won!" Alec screams. "Let's go see him!" Bella and Marco move so we can make our way up there to congratulate Mason. We flash security our passes and they let us through. Mason's sponsor throws a hat onto his head as Tristan hands him a water bottle. Mason is answering questions when he spots Alec and me. Pulling us into his side, he gives my temple a kiss.

The man I now recognize as Daniel West says to Mason, "For a second, I think everyone thought Wilkens was going to be successful in his takedown. At one point he almost had you on the ground, but then you turned it around. What were you thinking when you decided to end the fight?"

Mason looks down at me and gives me his signature smirk. "I was thinking the only person who will ever successfully perform a takedown on me is my wife."

EPILOGUE

MASON
TWO YEARS LATER

I OPEN MY EYES AND ROLL OVER TO SPOON MY WIFE, ONLY SHE isn't there. I hear the shower running and my dick twitches in excitement. Throwing the covers to the side, I hop out of bed and head into the bathroom to join Mila. For a second I question where Alec is and then remember he's at his dad's and will be home later.

The bathroom door is unlocked and I push my boxers down and throw them to the side as I make my way to the shower. Before I open the door, though, I stop and watch my wife through the glass door. It's blurry from the steam, but I can still make out her silhouette. Her head is tilted back as she washes her hair. The water raining down on her perky tits and cascading over her belly and down toward her warm pussy. The pussy I need to be inside of.

I swing the door open, and she startles for a second before she grins. "I was hoping you would wake up and join me." She pulls me under the water with her and kisses me deeply. "I am so horny," she groans. I chuckle at how direct she is as her hand finds my dick and she begins to stroke it slowly, getting it hard for her.

My mouth goes to her nipples, and my lips wrap around each one, sucking gently. She lets out a moan, wordlessly telling me how good it feels. I move my way down, kissing each breast and stopping at her belly, where I place several kisses until she pulls me up. "You need to fuck me now," she demands, turning around and jutting her ass out.

I swat her ass playfully and she squeals. "You know better than to wiggle that ass in the air unless you're going to let me in the backdoor."

Mila looks over her shoulder and moans. "Yes, please." She slaps one hand against the shower wall and the other hand reaches for the bottle of baby oil. When she parts her legs, I notice a pink jewel shimmering between her ass cheeks.

"Did you put this in yourself?" I don't know why I even ask. Of course she did. The woman has been insatiable the last eight months.

"Yes, now pull it out and fuck me please." My fingers run along the curves of her ass and under her until I get to her sweet cunt. I stick a couple fingers in and find she's already wet. Circling her clit a few times, I damn near bring her to an orgasm. I pull the plug out and she groans in pleasure. Squirting some baby oil into my hand, I coat my fingers and then push them into her puckered hole. Mila lets out a sigh of pleasure as she pushes her ass against my fingers.

My wife is needy as fuck these days, but you won't find me complaining. Angling her ass just right, I push my dick into her slowly, and she once again pushes back. My hands grip her sides to hold her steady as I slowly pump in and out of her tight ass.

"Mason, please. Fuck me harder."

"Not in the shower. I'm not taking a chance of you falling."

"Mmmm," she moans as she tries to get me to fuck her harder, deeper. I continue my steady rhythm, working us both up into a frenzy.

"Baby, massage that clit," I demand.

"I already am." Her breathing becomes labored, and I know she's close. Her ass tightens, and she cries out in pleasure. I thrust several more times and then I'm coming as well. I pull out slowly, and she turns around, her face all smiles.

"Good morning," she murmurs, making me laugh.

"Good morning."

"I better get washed up before everyone gets here. Out you go."

"Jesus, woman, you use me and abuse me and then kick me out when you're done with me." I rinse off and step out of the shower, wrapping my towel around myself.

I can hear Mila laughing through the door as she yells out, "Don't be upset because I'm better at this game of catch and release than you." I tug the door open and pull her into a searing kiss.

"Baby, the day you hooked me and reeled my ass in, you knew there was no getting rid of me. Ever."

♥♥♥♥♥

"MASON! CAN YOU TIE THE BALLOONS ONTO THE FENCE, please?" Mila calls from the kitchen as I walk inside from lighting the barbeque in the backyard.

"Yes, ma'am." I grab the balloons and bring them outside, tying them around the wooden fence next to the gate.

"Well, well," Tristan says, coming up next to me. "The irony of this picture isn't lost on me."

"The irony of what picture?" I ask, double knotting the balloons so they don't fly away.

"When I met Charlie and freaked out. You talked me down and then said you couldn't ever imagine wanting the family or the kids or… how was it you worded it? The white picket fucking fence." Tristan laughs. "Now look at you…the family, the kids…" He points to the fence. "The white picket fucking fence."

I chuckle, remembering our conversation. "Yeah, I remember," I admit. "But at the time I was telling the truth. I couldn't picture it because Mila wasn't in my life yet. The family, the kids, the white picket fence. I wouldn't want any of it without her by my side."

"I completely understand," Tristan agrees. "Now, you ready to party?"

"Hell yeah."

♥♥♥♥♥

THE MUSIC IS PUMPING THROUGH THE SPEAKERS IN THE backyard. Everybody is talking and laughing and eating. The kids are playing in the bounce house and on the waterslides. I spot Tristan and go over to him.

"Quite a gathering."

"Hell yeah, it is. It should be. It's like six parties in one." Tristan ticks each celebration off with his fingers as he lists them. "Mila's baby shower, Charlie's baby shower, Mila's birthday, Mother's day, your housewarming party, a welcome to the neighborhood party."

"Speaking of Mother's Day, where's your mom?" Charlie comes to Tristan's side and asks, looking around for my mom, her hand rubbing up and down over her swollen belly.

A year and a half ago my mom found her passion: helping widowers and single moms get back on their feet after losing their spouse. When she asked what I thought, I told her it was a great idea, and so the charity, *Keeping Kids Off the Streets* was created. Since then, we've built a center for single parents and their children to go to. We offer services to help parents find income restricted housing and jobs, and we raise funds for kids who want to go to camp or participate in extracurricular activities their parents can't afford.

"She'll be here in a little while. She texted me that she's meeting a single mom who needs help finding a safe place to stay. She's getting them settled and then will be over." And just as I finish my sentence I see my mom and Mila walking out the back door and toward me. My wife is wearing a beautiful black sundress with bright pink and blue flowers all over it, and she's laughing at something my mom is saying as they approach us.

"How did it go?" I ask my mom as I pull Mila into my side.

"It went well. They're safe." She smiles softly and I think about how far we've come. Our relationship was strained at first, but with plenty of counseling, we worked through our issues. She's become the mom I always prayed for as well as an amazing grandma to Alec. When Mila and I decided to purchase a bigger home for our growing family, my mom took over Mila's townhouse.

"Mom! Can we have cake yet?" Lexi comes running over to ask Charlie.

"Not yet, sweet girl. We need to eat first."

"I can't wait to have cake!" Georgia yells. "Then we can finally know what the babies are."

Charlie and Mila both giggle. When they found out they were both pregnant, only a month apart, they were ecstatic. They decided it would be fun to make everyone, including all of us, wait until their baby showers to reveal the sex of the babies. They had the bakery bake two cakes, one for each of them and inside each cake is the color of the gender.

"Our baby is a girl," I insist, and Mila groans.

"Not this again."

"You'll see." And I know it's going to be a girl because after researching the topic, I found out having sex with the woman on top is the best way to ensure the baby is a girl.

"Three months of me riding you does not mean it'll be a girl," Mila whispers.

"Yes, it does, and once the cake shows pink, you'll see I was right."

MILA

"OKAY! CHARLIE, YOUR CAKE FIRST," BELLA SAYS, HANDING HER the knife. Charlie does as she says and cuts through the cake. She plops the first piece onto the plate, and the cake is bright blue.

"It's a boy!" Everyone yells.

"Oh no!" Lexi and Georgia groan at the same time. "But boys are gross!"

"No, we aren't!" Alec says, defending the male race.

We all give Tristan and Charlie hugs of congratulations, and then Charlie says, "All right, Mila, your turn." She hands me the knife she just used.

I slice down the cake and then lift the piece onto the plate, the pastel pink cake landing upright.

"I knew it!" Mason yells, fist bumping Tristan. "All those months you accused me of being lazy when I insisted you ride me. I told you!" Everyone cracks up laughing, and I hide my face in embarrassment.

"Ugh!" Alec groans. "I don't want a sister. She's going to be as annoying as them!" He points and glares toward Lexi, Georgia, Micaela, and Liza.

"Wait! I got it!" Lexi shouts excitedly. "We can take your girl, and we'll give you our boy!"

"Yeah!" Georgia agrees. "We can trade."

"Really?" Alec asks, sounding hopeful. "Mom, Mason, can we trade?"

"No!" Everyone yells through their laughter, and the kids all pout like trading siblings was seriously an option.

The End!

ABOUT THE AUTHOR

Reading is like breathing in, writing is like breathing out.— Pam Allyn

Nikki Ash resides in South Florida where she is an English teacher by day and a writer by night. When she's not writing, you can find her with a book in her hand. From the Boxcar Children, to Wuthering Heights, to the latest single parent romance, she has lived and breathed every type of book. While reading and writing are her passions, her two children are her entire world. You can probably find them at a Disney park before you would find them at home on the weekends!